I0577596

THE ELLIE GRAY CHRONICLES BOX SET

DRAIN ME & CHAIN ME

LANA SKY

DRAIN ME

Drain Me

Drain Me By Lana Sky

Copyright © 2014 by Lana Sky
All rights reserved.
No part of this publication may be reproduced, distributed, or transmitted in any form or by any means, including photocopying, recording, or other electronic or mechanical methods, without the prior written permission of the author.
This is a work of fiction. Names, characters, businesses, places, events and incidents are either the products of the author's imagination or used in a fictitious manner. Any resemblance to actual persons, living or dead, or actual events is purely coincidental.

Cover design by Sarah Hansen, Okay Creations
Edited by Gemma Fisk
Proofread by Mickey Reed
Proofread by Charity Chimni
Formatting by Charity Chimni

Dedicated to everyone who's encouraged me on this incredible journey.

ACKNOWLEDGMENTS

This story would be nothing without the tireless efforts of Jill P., who stayed up until two in the morning with me numerous times, hashing out chapters and listening to me whine. You coaxed Ellie out of her shell and convinced me to let Dublin play with knives—all while talking me down from numerous author temper tantrums. Jilly, this story is as much yours as it is mine. Thank you so much for helping me take these characters to the next level. You're right, you're not a writer—you're a miracle worker!

Thanks to Mel. You went over this story numerous times and gave me lovely, honest feedback.

Thank you, Paige, Keevs and Mira, my lovely beta bots. Mikhail says hi.

Thank you, Cherry B, Liz S., Ida and Ariel V. for volunteering to help me work with the first draft. You guys offered such amazing input.

Thanks to Eri for renewing my faith in Ellie's character.

Thank you, Brit/Imogen for the amazing cover and your tireless support. I know that I got on your nerves with my countless changes, but—like always—you stayed classy.

Thanks to my editor, Gemma Fisk, for cleaning up my messes and adding sparkles and shine to this draft.

Thank you, the many people who read the drafts online and encouraged me from the very first chapter. You guys have made everything up until this point a complete blast.

"The blood of the pure is the bitterest poison to a corrupted soul."

—A.R. Simone

MEMENTO MORI

I hated when people sugar-coated things. Straight and to the point was how I preferred it—and a rather infamous lack of bedside manner was the reason why I had elected to see Dr. Wallis in the first place. "I feel that it's best not to trivialize the more serious diagnoses," he warned, living up to his brutal reputation. "So I'll just come right out and say it: you're dying, Eleanor."

He sounded so formal. Hell, he could have offered me a handkerchief for all the emotion his voice held: *"Here, miss. It's clean."*

I felt tempted to laugh, but that pesky meaning couldn't be ignored.

Dying.

It took me only a second to process it.

Dead.

Dying.

Dead.

It took even less for the words to sink, like a stone, to the pit of my stomach and settle there, heavy and solid, but I wasn't surprised. Startled, perhaps—it was devastating news—though, in a sick way, I figured I'd always known that, rather than pass away peacefully in my bed of old age, I would die a horrible death. My own mortality had always fascinated me ever since I'd smuggled my first horror film from the servant's break room as a teenager and watched it while huddled beneath my blankets.

'*That will be me*,' some cynical voice had whispered inside my head, and I had known then, as surely as I knew my own name that I would die just like the unfortunate bimbo at the mercy of the knife-wielding psychopath. While I hadn't expected *said* death to come in the form of a terminal illness that would turn my own blood into the murder weapon, I had to admit that it was pretty violent in its own right.

"Hemohemorrahgia," the doctor began, reiterating the speech he'd given just minutes before. "It occurs in less than one percent of the world's population, but it is fatal in ninety percent of all reported cases. There is no cure, and—"

I stopped listening.

Hemohemorrahgia. Ironically, I had never even heard of the cause of my impending demise until a few months ago—

and the disease had been a guess, thrown out by a frustrated doctor as the potential cause of a bevy of symptoms.

Why was I so tired all the time?

Why did even breathing exhaust me?

Why had a paper cut required a blood transfusion, donated platelets, and stitches to stop the bleeding?

After months of tests, a team of medical professionals had all reached the same grim conclusion.

"The prognosis is rather bleak, Mrs. Gray," the doctor continued, "but I think it's better if we honestly discuss your options—"

"Miss," I corrected absently.

Dr. Wallis wrinkled his nose, causing the black frames of his glasses to twitch. "Pardon?"

"It's *Miss* Gray." I unlaced my fingers and held up my unadorned hand. "I'm not married."

"Oh."

From the way he swiftly glanced me over, I could tell that he had never looked up from my chart long enough to give me a good appraisal before—despite this being our tenth meeting. I could guess what registered now as his gaze took me in: dull brown hair, sallow skin, and enormous green eyes that took up too much of my small face.

"Oh," he repeated, and his tone revealed what even he was too polite to say, despite his reputation: *no wonder.* "Well,

Ms. Gray, I can arrange a consultation with social services or grief counseling. Whomever you need to help you through this very difficult time—"

"It's fine."

"Pardon?"

I cleared my throat, forcing my voice louder. "I said it's *fine*. I don't need anything, thank you." I shifted in my seat and fidgeted with the hem of my skirt as an uncomfortable thought took hold. "I guess this means I'll have to draw up a *will* though." I couldn't keep the petulant whine out of my tone.

I'd always dreaded the day I would have to draw up one of those legal documents to ensure that—after my unfortunate demise—the family fortune wasn't devoured by money-hungry lawyers.

At least the '*To whom I bequeath*' part would be easy; I would leave everything to Georgiana, the little sister I hadn't seen in three months. My, would she be ecstatic to finally get her hands on our parent's millions. True to stuffy, upper-class thinking, they had left control of the estate to me, the responsible one, rather than my "*willful harlot*" of a little sister, as Father had put it.

Despite everything, I felt myself smile thinking of her. Beautiful, blonde and unashamedly brash, Georgie was the type of person who everyone secretly wanted to be—myself included. She slept with billionaires for diamonds, and had jettisoned off to Paris rather than attend her final semester of university because, according to her, studying was, *"As boring as balls."*

One could only imagine what mischief she would get into with the family fortune at her disposal. Though, the prospect of being berated for eternity by the spirits of my parents did temper my curiosity a bit. In Mother's eyes, dying before the 'black sheep' would have been simply *unacceptable.*

"Ms. Gray, I do have to suggest some form of counseling," Dr. Wallis insisted. For once, he almost seemed concerned —at least until I realized that he would probably get a hefty referral fee from whomever he 'suggested' I see next. "A colleague of mine is one of the leading psychiatrists in the country. In fact, he's here right now for a seminar. I could—"

I shook my head. "No thank you."

I didn't need anyone to soften the blow of what I'd anticipated for half of my life. There wasn't much else that needed to be said anyway.

I was dying, the sky was blue.

I wondered if they were serving pasta in the cafeteria today …

"A-are you sure?" Dr. Wallis sputtered. "He has a rather extensive reputation—"

"Positive," I replied. "Can I go now? Please?" I attempted to stand without waiting for an answer, and the doctor rushed forward.

"Miss Gray!"

He caught me by the shoulder, and it was a good thing he did because, despite my bravado, it had been a struggle to even haul myself out of the chair. Deep down I knew that the doctor's firm grip was the only thing keeping me upright. He frowned as he steadied me, and reached across his desk to press the button on a small intercom with his free hand. Instantly, a sweet sound of acknowledgment came from the other end.

"Yes, Doctor Wallis? Should I send in—"

"Natalie," Dr. Wallis said over her, "have a nurse bring a wheelchair and escort Miss Gray to the inpatient wing."

"Yes, sir."

I waited until he took his finger off the button before wrenching my arm away, even though I had to cling to my vacated chair to keep my balance.

"No. No hospital," I hissed. The hell was I staying in this horrible place for another night. "No more tests. I can walk to the car quite fine on my *own.*"

"I can't let you do that." Dr. Wallis shook his balding head as if he thought I was a child who needed placating. "Ms. Gray, accept the wheelchair at least. The liability ..."

So nice to know that he only cared about me falling on hospital property out of fear that I might sue for it. Sighing, I dug into my purse with a shaking hand and withdrew my checkbook. After scribbling out a figure, I slapped the sliver of paper down onto his desk and gave it a little shove in his direction.

"Buy a new wing," I said, confident that the figure drying in ink was more than enough to do so. "On behalf of the Gray family. Dedicate it to—" I snickered. "*Bloodbath Five-Thousand.*"

"Pardon?" The doctor frowned.

"Nothing. Can I go now?"

I figured that I had my answer when he didn't prattle on about *counseling* or *liabilities,* especially when I heard the delicate crinkle of a check being stuffed into a pocket.

Wrestling my purse strap over one shoulder, I turned for the door. Near the threshold, I added without turning around, "I'll be sure to let Natalie know that you've changed your mind."

~

The very pleasant Natalie sent me on my way with a smile and an enthusiastic, "Have a good day, Miss!"

Oh, Natalie. If only.

I had barely gone two steps from the door that marked the entrance to Dr. Wallis' office suite before I found myself shaking. I had to lean against the wall and dig my heels into the carpet just to keep from sliding down to the floor.

In the end, I only managed to stagger three more steps before collapsing altogether.

My stomach heaved and, in a flurry of colorful liquid, I coughed up a breakfast of toast and jam right in front of a sign that proclaimed, *'Hand washing: the best defense against germs!'*

Lovely. You would think—considering how hefty my medical bill was—that the drugs they gave me during my stay would at least help combat my symptoms.

They didn't.

Gazing forlornly at my puke, I wondered if I should have donated a statue or something to go along with that new wing. Or at least tip the poor janitor unfortunate enough to have to clean up the mess, some grand, kind gesture to mark my final days. Instead, I allowed myself to wallow in self-pity for another minute before I finally found the strength to drag myself upright on unsteady limbs—mentally berating myself the entire time.

I should have let Harper walk me in like he'd insisted. He was the driver who'd served my family faithfully for over fifteen years—and I had threatened to fire him just to keep him from escorting me inside. I just couldn't shake the thought of what that would have looked like; the heiress, too needy to walk into a damn hospital without the company of a paid companion.

Never in a million years did I want to be *that* woman, the one with diamonds dripping from her neck who couldn't even catch a cold without the whole damn world holding its breath. Though, at least *that* woman never had to muck up her own vomit with a crumpled napkin fished from her purse and stagger down the hall before someone came by to notice the mess.

How many floors was it to the garage? *Three? Five?* I fished Dr. Wallis' business card from my coat pocket and scoped out the location of his office: the fourth floor.

Funny. It was a struggle to go even four *feet.*

The halls stretched for a hundred miles in either direction. My vision drifted in and out of focus, and with every step, I wobbled precariously on my heels. Damn those years of Cotillion where not wearing proper footwear in public had been seen as an even greater sin than forgetting white gloves at tea.

My thoughts were a blur, the only goal being to make it to the elevator without causing a scene. People were already staring at me: the woman in the burgundy Peacoat clinging to the wall for dear life.

Easy does it, girl, I chanted while urging my aching limbs forward. *Easy does it …*

I didn't even see him coming.

Wham!

I went sprawling. There was no scream, no gasp, just the sensation of everything suddenly jolting into motion like a tape slammed into fast forward. I hit the ground hard, hearing the sound before I really felt the pain.

"Are you all right?"

The voice came from a million different directions at once. I couldn't see—everything was white ...

But it was a full minute before I realized that the odd light came from someone who stood above me, so pale they practically glowed. I blinked frantically until the figure came into full focus.

He looked like a doctor, a beautiful, angelic doctor with hair the color of spun gold and skin paler than snow. He must have been foreign too, judging by that startlingly rich accent. English? As young as he was—mid-thirties at least— he definitely wasn't one of the old geezers consulting on my case.

He said something else that I couldn't discern, worried eyes scanning my body up and down. They were the oddest color. Gray?

I didn't realize I was still sprawled out on the floor until he offered a hand to haul me back to my feet. Dazed, I took it, and a jolt went through me as his fingers entwined with my own. He was cold—painfully so—but I held on.

"Are you all right?"

Rather than answer, I peeked through my hair, relieved to find that the hallway was empty of anyone else.

"I'm fine," I lied. My chest heaved with the effort to suck in oxygen. Pain danced down my spine while I clung to the man's hand a little longer than necessary in an effort to regain my balance. "Just a little dizzy, is all."

He gave me a funny look. It wasn't quite a smile, but the mocking tilt to that stern mouth seemed amused all the same. "Are you sure?"

A sudden rush of warmth coated my chin as I nodded my assurance that I was perfectly all right—within seconds, I found it near-impossible to breathe out of my nose.

"Damn it."

I recognized the sensation and what it entailed—but seeing as how I had used the last of my tissues to muck up my own vomit, I was forced to pinch the bridge of my nose with just my fingers. Desperate to staunch the blood flow, I tilted my head back, and that slight motion alone nearly knocked me off my feet. My body tensed, bracing for another impact. Only it never came.

The next second I found myself shoved onto a bench instead. Firm fingers batted my own away and replaced them with what felt to be a wad of cloth. I glanced down and recognized the shape of a white handkerchief with a monogrammed corner sporting the letters *D.H* in black thread.

His initials?

"Thank you," I mumbled around a drizzle of blood.

I figured I should have been alarmed, but I was more worried that Harper would notice the crimson stains on my coat. The old coot was sharp—he would figure out the truth no matter how much I lied. A third nosebleed in as many days might have been enough cause for him to *drag* me back into the hospital this time, whether I was willing or not.

"That's quite a lot of blood."

The casual observation brought my attention back to the stranger, and I felt my eyes widen as I observed him closely for the first time: blond hair, firm jawline, perfect, glowing skin.

Altogether, he was probably the most handsome man I had ever seen—but those piercing eyes honed in on the stream of blood issuing from my nose without a shred of real concern. He made no move to get help, and a bizarre emotion itched at the back of my mind.

Unease?

I didn't miss how that gallant smile never reached his eyes, and with every second that passed, the uneasy feeling became full-blown suspicion.

He wanted something. Years of dealing with people who coveted whatever my family name could garner had made it second nature to spot a hidden agenda. When he reached out—perhaps to merely adjust my sloppy grip on his handkerchief—I jerked back, spraying blood in a vicious arc.

"I'm *fine.*"

He retreated, but for the briefest moment, I caught something flashing across his gaze that I shouldn't have: *annoyance* —as if my reaction had not been a part of his plan.

Or months spent virtually alone had simply made me paranoid. I shook my head and pressed my nose more tightly into the handkerchief.

"I'll promise not to press charges against you for running into me if you go away," I mumbled into the cloth. Guilt pierced me at the rudeness; years of forced etiquette seemed to be draining from my body just as quickly as my blood.

Though, damn it, I was dying anyway.

"Really?"

I glanced up, only to find that the odd, mocking tilt to his mouth was back. Was he toying with me? "Seriously, I'm fine, so you can go now, please—"

"Pardon me for saying this, but you don't *look* very fine."

I wanted to take offense, but it was the truth. Designer clothes speckled with blood, skin so pale it was almost see-through, hands painted red. I must have looked horrible.

"In fact," the stranger continued, "I would go so far as to say that you are anything *but* fine, Eleanor Gray."

CHOICES

The fact that he knew my name didn't alarm me.

My family owned half the city, including a good portion of this very hospital. Considering that my sister's escapades were constant fodder for the tabloids, I would have been more insulted if he *didn't* know who I was.

But once again …it was that look in his eyes. It chilled me right down to the bone; *I know you, Eleanor Gray*, it said. *Way more than just a face from the Society Pages.*

Before I could choke out a reply, he smiled—for real this time—and my poor brain struggled to find the right words to describe it. *Dazzling. Magnificent …*

The flash of pearly white teeth nearly knocked me senseless. I lost my grip on the handkerchief for a split second, sparking the taste of copper over my tongue.

"Word travels fast around here," he said, voice traveling down my spine.

I felt my nose wrinkle as I frowned. Apparently, news of my terminal illness had spread before I'd even left the damn hospital. How long before my picture ended up splattered over the front of some tabloid beneath the headline, *Heiress given weeks to live?*

I didn't answer. Instead, I willed my nose to stop bleeding, though I had a feeling that I was quickly becoming in danger of needing transfusion number four.

I felt so dizzy all of a sudden. As if, at any moment, I could pass out. Faint.

"What do you see?"

"Huh?"

The question threw me off and had me turning to face him before I could help it. Wordlessly, he inclined his head and my eyes automatically followed.

The hall we were in opened onto a causeway, where patients and visitors alike wandered the pristine floor.

The sight reminded me of a hotel—albeit minus the IV poles some people sported instead of suitcases. The air was the same: that busy, *'places to go, people to see, get the hell out of my way'* vibe that made everyone seem closed off, further away.

Without meaning to, I found my gaze settling over a young girl who had her head wrapped in a polka dot headscarf. Beside her, a man I guessed to be her father pushed an IV pole that rattled over the floor.

She was almost as pale as I was, with dark, bruise-like circles underneath her eyes—but that wasn't what stood out to me the most.

She was smiling. Walking, talking and *...smiling.* Despite the obvious physical signs, if you went off that expression alone, you would have never guessed she was sick at all. My gaze remained glued to her, even as the mysterious doctor spoke up again.

"Mortality," he said grimly. "It's the most precious commodity in the world, don't you agree?"

I nodded. I may have not been that invested in my own life, but I could read the fervent desire on all the other faces— from the new mother carrying her infant in a car seat, to the elderly man clutching a newspaper to his chest.

The lust to live was always the same.

"There are some who would do anything for another chance at life, for more time."

He spoke so matter-of-factly that it wasn't until my mind processed what he was really saying that his morbid tone struck me like a blow.

"I-I don't know what you're talking about." I sounded like I was underwater. My nose was still dripping. Even the pressure of my hand wasn't enough to staunch the blood flow.

"You wouldn't," Mr. Gray Eyes said with a shrug. "Immortality doesn't interest you, does it, Eleanor?"

Alarm raced down my spine—no longer was I convinced that this was just a random chat with a stranger. It was all in his tone.

"I have to go." I clutched the now bloody handkerchief and tried to stand. My legs felt as flaccid as limp noodles. Sweat poured down the back of my neck, and the erratic beat of my heart quickened and then faltered. *Thump, thump, th-ump.*

"You're not afraid of death," the man—though I was now seriously doubting that he was a doctor—continued. "You welcome it, or so you tell yourself. But, I'm here to offer you a choice—"

"I think …I need a real doctor."

I was through humoring him. Without bothering to be polite, I attempted to stagger in the direction of the activity, grasping onto anything to steady me. My hands were slippery, and my once-burgundy Peacoat was now soaked scarlet.

Hemohemorrahgia kept haunting me in Doctor Wallis' curt tones. *90% fatality!*

"Mortality can be a hindrance of sorts."

The man was still talking, only I had no idea just what he was getting at. More importantly, why hadn't he gotten a doctor or flagged down a nurse? I clung to the wall and scanned the crowd of blurring faces, desperate to catch sight of another white lab coat.

"I think I …need …help."

It took all my strength just to get the words out. And he only ignored me.

"I'm here to offer you a choice, Eleanor: accept your impending death, or …something else."

What else? I struggled to ask but was only greeted with silence. It stretched on for a good five minutes before I realized that he had finally left. That strange vibe was gone at least, but so was any sensation or feeling in my limbs. Or sound. My vision was an inky shade of gray, nearly black, but …

When I finally gave into the darkness, I swore I could hear *him* whisper one last time, "It's your decision, but if you're smart, you will make the right one."

~

Beep, beep, beep played the horrible mechanical lullaby that lured me out of sleep.

Oh no.

I knew that smell. That icky metallic taste in my mouth that came from the solution they used to flush an IV. Heart sinking, I realized where I was even before I peeled my eyes open to a worried Harper and clinical white walls.

"It's been two days, Miss," he announced, frowning beneath his salt-and-pepper mustache. At least the man knew exactly what I wanted to hear: no sappy stuff, just the facts.

"Get the car ready," I rasped the moment I found my voice.

Ouch. It hurt to talk. I had to take a few sips of the water Harper poured from a pitcher just to erase the grittiness in my throat. I couldn't remember how I had gotten here or why. All that mattered was the fact that my trusty driver was already standing, ready to carry out my bidding.

"I'll have the car brought around in a minute, Miss."

I could tell from his expression that he wanted to say more —something other than the customary confirmation of orders.

That he was concerned, perhaps? Worried? That maybe this time I should *stay* inside this horrible place, strapped to a bunch of machines?

Whatever it was, at least he knew better than to mention it out loud. Without another word, he disappeared through the door of what I guessed to be a private room. *Oh, God.* I was definitely in a hospital—not even an emergency room bed, but an actual *inpatient wing* judging from the sounds of chaos coming from the hall.

What had Harper said? Two days?

I shivered at the thought. Forty-eight hours of blissful unconsciousness while these trigger-happy villains in white had been free to do whatever they wanted to me—all while gleefully charging my family's account.

I forced down a few deep breaths, and then tried to sit up.

It was a bad idea.

It hurt—everything hurt; my body, my skin, my head, even my hair. I felt tender and used and broken, which was probably why the IV snaking from my wrist wasn't clear with the usual maintenance fluid, but red.

For some reason, I wasn't alarmed by the sight of what had to be my fourth transfusion this month, merely annoyed. From experience, I knew that they wouldn't let me leave until the whole thing was finished running—no matter how many lawyers I threatened to call.

I sank back against a wall of pillows with a sigh. Everything that I had always put off loomed overhead, threatening to come crashing down if I didn't take care of it soon. That whole 'will' business would definitely need to be dealt with —and not only for the sake of the money. In fact, I was willing to put the welfare of my Siamese cat, Mr. Tinkles, above the entire Gray fortune.

Tinkles had been rescued from a shelter after an accident had left him blind in one eye and missing two hind legs. Like any true spinster in training, I had given him his own wing in the house and a personal cook. He was my special baby, and he absolutely hated me. I couldn't even look at the beast without him flexing his claws.

To be fair, he hated everyone, but if making sure he had fresh tuna every night was the price Georgie would pay for taking control of our inheritance, then so be it.

In fact, it seemed very important to ensure Mr. Tinkle's wellbeing. There were so many things Georgie needed to know: his nightly schedule, and how to rub his belly with the sole of her slippered foot so that it didn't hurt so much when he scratched, the importance of his favorite toy, Mr. Squeakers.

Oh, and the whole *your sister is dying* thing. That should probably be mentioned as well.

I glanced around the room and found my cell phone resting on the bedside stand, most likely courtesy of Harper. I attempted to reach for it, annoyed by just how badly my fingers shook. In the end, I settled for keeping it on the table and switching on the speakerphone. I tried six of the eleven numbers I had listed for Georgie before someone finally picked up on the third ring.

"'Lo?"

I sighed at the sound of a man's voice, and strained my own to carry. "Can I speak to Georgie or Georgiana or Peach or Sprinkles, whatever she's calling herself now—" She went by so many damn names these days, I could barely keep up.

There was a grunt from the other end. "Hey, sweetcheeks! Phone."

A second later, my sister's chirpy voice filled the room, laced with static. "Hello, helloooo?"

Wonderful. From the high-pitched giggle edging her words, I could tell she was already drunk.

"Georgie?"

"Ells!" Her shriek bounced off the walls, and I wished that I had the strength to slap my hands over my ears. Instead, they just twitched by my side, too heavy to lift. "Ellie-Bellie! What's going on?"

Her worried tone caught me off guard.

"What do you mean?"

Unease coiled in my stomach. Had Harper gotten to her first?

"You only call when something bad has happened," Georgie accused. "So what is it? Did the stock market crash? Are we desti …*destitute?*" Another tattered giggle.

"Destitute," I corrected offhandedly. "And no, we are not, by the way. Where are you? I'll send the car."

I rolled my eyes in anticipation of the answer; which seedy bar would Harper have to drag her out of now?

Her reply came on a bubbly bit of laughter. "Belize, darling!"

"B …B-what?"

"Buh-leeze," Georgie squealed, drawing out the word. "Paulo here has a Villa. We've had a whole beach all to ourselves!"

My guess was that 'Paulo' was the charming answerer of the telephone and with a hazy grasp of geography I assessed that Belize was somewhere in South America. Georgiana sure knew how to pick her men. Though, to be fair, she was in the tropics while I was stuck in a hospital bed. I shook my head to clear the rare bit of jealousy that thought stirred.

"When are you coming back?" I asked, though I guessed the real question was why I was so surprised that she had left the continent without even telling me?

That was typical Georgiana. I could only be grateful that, this time, she had remembered to bring along her cell phone.

"Not for three weeks," Georgie said. "Paulo has some business to take care of, and then we plan on going on a cruise—"

"Do you think ... Do you think you might be able to come home early?"

I hated how petulant I sounded. I might as well have added a *'pretty please'* to the end—though, from her tone one might think that I'd suggested my sister sprout wings and fly.

"Early? What on earth for?"

Was it really that much of a hassle to visit your only sister?

"I could send the family jet ..."

"Oh no. Something *is* wrong," Georgie whined. "What is it? The last time you sounded like this, Dad had his heart attack."

"Nothing," I lied. "I just ...*miss* you, is all."

"Miss me?"

I could picture her scrunching her nose up as she tried to puzzle out the meaning of those foreign words. My family never threw out terms like 'love' and 'missed.' We merely coexisted: a band of allies bound together by blood and money.

My parents never had a marriage—merely a business arrangement. Georgie and I weren't their children, but assets. I had only one other relative, apart from my sister: an eccentric uncle by the name of Orwell who hadn't been seen since Father's funeral.

"Well," Georgie said, "you'll see me when I get back. We'll get lunch or something, huh?"

"All right."

I didn't have the heart to mention that I wouldn't be alive in three weeks, according to Dr. Wallis' grim prognosis.

I was *dying*.

Only now did the realization hit me like a kick in the gut— and my irresponsible kid sister couldn't even come home on a private jet, just so that I could tell her in person.

I would be lying if I claimed to not feel *something*. Hurt? Though, maybe the ache in my chest was just *pity* at the thought of Mr. Tinkles going without his nightly belly rubs? What would he do without me …

"Ellie? Ells? You there?"

"Yes," I croaked, shaking my head to clear the troubling thoughts. "I'm here."

"I have to go. I don't get good service out here, so it's probably best if you don't call me for a while. At least until I get back. Also—" I sighed, guessing the turn of the conversation before the words, "Can you send me some money?" even left her mouth.

"How much?" I demanded, cutting her off mid-plea.

"About two hundred, give or take."

I wasn't naïve enough to assume that she meant the amount at face value.

"*Two hundred thousand?*" I clarified, just to drill the point home; she could jet off to Belize without a word, but it was nice to know that I, big sister Ellie, would always be her glorified ATM.

"Pretty please?"

I wanted to be annoyed, but she could have asked for two-hundred *million,* and it still wouldn't have made a difference.

"Fine," I said, forcing down a dry swallow. "It will be in your account by tomorrow."

"Thanks, Ells! You're the best! Smooches."

With a fake kiss, she hung up.

I didn't even get the chance to mention Mr. Tinkles and what should happen to him in the event of my unfortunate demise. For the longest time, I just sat there, staring at the plain walls of my hospital room while trying to ignore the commotion of doctors and nurses from beyond the doorway.

Several realizations hit me all at once.

For one, I was alone. I was dying, and I was *alone*.

I didn't even get the chance to tell my little sister that everything was all hers—apparently, beach-hopping with someone named Paulo was more important.

My kitty would go hungry.

"Miss Gray?"

I jumped as the door opened and someone entered the room. Assuming it was a nurse, I struggled to pull myself upright while pointing at the hated IV.

"I'm leaving as soon as you get that damn thing out of me …"

I trailed off once I realized that the small figure approaching me was a young girl. She was a pretty thing with charming blue eyes and a pink scarf wrapped around her head, turban style.

But it was nearly a full minute before I realized that I had seen her before; the girl from the other day.

From all appearances she looked to be the sickly girl I had seen on the causeway, but at the same time …

This girl wasn't pale. Her skin seemed fuller, and those eyes were less sunken in. The only thing on her arm was a tiny pink bracelet whereas two days ago, there had been an IV.

I'll take whatever she is having, I thought in awe of her transformation. Perhaps there was a trial for a new miracle drug being tested somewhere in the hospital?

"Hello," she greeted me. Her smile was beautifully crooked, revealing one missing front tooth and a dimple in her left cheek. In one hand, she held a single rose which she placed on my bedside stand. In the other was a folded slip of paper. "He told me to give you this," she said, offering the note.

He? "Who told you?" I asked, even as I raised my trembling hands in an effort to grab the ivory slip. *Harper? Dr. Wallis?* "Was it a man in a uniform? Was he wearing a hat?"

That smile widened as she shook her head. "Nope. *He* did."

I was confused. Even more so when she reached over to take my pathetically weak hand in her own. She was warm. Gently, she eased my fingers apart and slipped the paper into my palm.

"He said to read it and answer the question at the bottom."

Huh? I stared down at the white slip.

Was it some kind of hospital survey? A list of things I would have to 'pinkie promise' not to sue for if they let me out against medical advice?

I didn't care. I pulled the edges apart as the girl stood back, forcing my blurry vision to take in the words scrawled across the page.

Eleanor Gray, you have been chosen, the first line read in black ink. Certainly not the usual opening of a 'please do not sue us' letter. Intrigued, I read on:

Choose wisely. You will only be presented with this opportunity once.

Choices …that word triggered something—a memory. Blond hair, gray eyes: that strange doctor from the hallway.

Had he sent me this note?

By the time I reached the very bottom I was convinced this whole thing was a joke.

There were two neat lines of script, each in front of a box. A checkbox. It reminded me of one of those notes you received from a boy in grade school—or, like the ones I had received with strict instructions to pass on to Georgie. One of those, *Do you like me? If so, check yes!* Only, the options specified in this note differed slightly.

Well, Miss Gray, this mysterious 'he' had written. *Make your choice.*

Beside each box was a single word, and if I weren't so weak, I would have rubbed my eyes just to make sure they weren't playing tricks on me.

Live, read one option. The other was just as simple. *Die.*

Choose wisely, the writer reminded. *Either option, once selected, cannot be undone.*

"What is this?"

The note slipped through my shaking fingers to bounce onto my lap but, when I glanced up, I was shocked to find that the strange girl had vanished. All that wass left behind was that startlingly red rose on my bedside table. Next to it was a plain silver pen that I was quite sure hadn't been there before.

I blinked, shook my head and wearily rubbed my eyes again.

But all three items remained.

It's a joke, I told myself sternly. Obviously, that "doctor" in white had a thing for messing with the minds of the terminally ill.

Terminal.

For some reason, that word made my heart beat faster. I was *terminal.* Voice cracking around a laugh, I tested the word out loud.

"Eleanor Louise Gray is terminally ill."

Thinking of Mr. Tinkles and Georgie and my parents' two, cold plots on the family estate, the words died in the back of my throat. Impulsively, I found myself reaching for the pen. My fingers closed over the shaft, and I dragged it closer while spreading the note flat on the table's surface.

My choice?

Death, of course, I thought with a harsh bark of laughter. I wasn't afraid. I had stared down that dark abyss my entire life, as the girl who nobody really saw, but everyone wanted something from.

My parents had demanded perfection. Georgie, attention. Mr. Tinkles, tuna. Even Harper, as wonderful as he was, stuck around because of a hefty paycheck every month.

No one wanted *just* Ellie and, as I sat tucked in that hospital bed, I realized for the first time that I had never really lived my own life. The epitaph on my tombstone might as well read, *"Here lies Eleanor Gray; she lived to serve."*

Death was the one thing I had always had control over. From age thirteen I had gotten the grim gist that how, when, or where didn't really matter. It was something final. Something that—at that moment—would happen only to me.

No one else could take control.

Only now, I *needed* to take control. These days, the doctors and nurses called the shots. I was just the body strapped down, forced to suffer it all until …

I gulped and dragged the pen over to the box marked *Death*. I made a faint line—barely a mark on the ivory— before something made me move a little to the right.

Okay, Mr. Doctor, I thought as I formed a tiny check as neatly as I could. *Two can play at this game.*

He wanted to give choices, did he? Well, I choose *Life*. My own life, to live the way I wanted without being at the beck and call of someone else.

That vibrant, streak of black ink blazed from the page in triumph. I felt oddly proud of myself as the pen slipped from my fingers to roll across the floor.

When unconsciousness found me again, I could have sworn that I was smiling for the first time in months …

Even as a deep, accented voice chased me into the darkness, whispering, *"Choose wisely."*

MILLION DOLLAR MAN

Considering that the last thing I remembered was being strapped down to a stiff hospital bed, I couldn't imagine how on earth I had wound up in *mine*. The feather-soft mattress beneath me, outfitted with plush cotton sheets, was heavenly compared to the scratchy straw-like material that covered the beds in the medical ward.

Was I dead?

Or better yet, had Harper—aiming for a nice raise—broken me out of the hospital, with those bloodthirsty doctors clawing at his back?

The thought made me snort, but I had a feeling that that wasn't it.

No …the reason I was here probably had everything to do with the stranger standing in my room. I could sense them there. Not a servant, I deduced, not quiet and meek—this intruder's scent proclaimed their presence as loudly as if they had shouted.

It was spicy and dark, slightly musty as well—as if they spent most of their time in a place that lacked fresh air. It almost reminded me of how my father had smelled during those last days, when the dusty books of his study had impregnated him with their scent.

"Who are you?" I asked, too drained to even bother opening my eyes. "Is this about money?"

If they were a burglar, they could have every last penny as far as I was concerned. Hell, even a criminal probably had better intentions for it than Georgie did.

To feed a hungry family? I wondered. *World domination?*

Either way, at least those family millions would finally leave the vault.

Seconds passed, and I didn't receive an answer. Not even a threat.

Well, buddy, it's your lucky day, I thought without stopping to consider the reasons for the silence. I was simply too tired to play these games.

"The safe is down the hall to your right in a room marked 'staff only,'" I began. "Inside you'll find brooms, mops and a painting of fruit on the wall. Flick the switch underneath the frame, and it will open. The combination is—" I bit my lip trying to remember. "The combination is the founding of our first company, so 1794. Inside is all the cash we carry on the property; at least a few grand."

I had never bothered to count it.

"The accounts are a bit trickier. It would take days for me to transfer all the money wirelessly, but if you call Handson, our accountant, and tell him '*I have Ellie Gray hostage and I'll kill her if you don't blah, blah, blah,*' he'll probably be cooperative. He's a nervous little fellow so just promise him a percent or two, and he'll do all the work."

Silence *again*.

Here I was, panting with the effort getting all that out had cost me, and I didn't even receive so much as a *thank you* in response. Though, on second thought, there was no sound of eager footsteps rushing off to squander away the fortune either.

I sighed as another thought began to take hold. "If you have to kill me for whatever reason, just please—" I wearily tapped the bridge of my nose with a finger. "One shot, right between the eyes. Make it clean."

Still nothing. Not even the cocking of a gun.

That does it! I wrenched my eyes open, prepared to demand they do *something*—only to have the words die right in my throat.

Leaning against my bay window, fingers pressed against the glass, was a man almost as pale as the gray daylight that ghosted his skin. I noticed instantly that his clothes were too perfectly tailored for the average burglar, and while I couldn't conjure a name, his broad shape was eerily familiar.

Him, a part of me whispered in recognition. Even with his back to me, I somehow had no trouble picturing a face graced with the chiseled features and silver eyes of that strange doctor from the hospital—only today he wore a plain sweater and a pair of dark pants rather than a lab coat.

"Good evening, Miss Gray," he called over his shoulder, as cordially as if he were an old friend who'd just popped over for a chat.

I bolted upright, automatically clutching the top sheet to my chest—a glance down revealed why: I had been stripped naked. Parts of me were even still visible through the delicate sheets, and I hunched over, drawing my knees up to my chest.

Had *he* brought me here? Undressed me?

"Who are you?" I demanded, voice trembling. "How did you get in here? Where's Harper?"

"So nice to see that you're finally awake," was all he said.

Finally. I stiffened at his tone, threading my fingers together over my chest.

"W-What do you mean?"

"You've been out for three days."

Three days. The words spun around my brain, collided.

"What?"

The man shrugged. "Your reaction was stronger than most," he said. "Your body must have been in even worse shape than your doctors realized."

"Reaction? What are you talking about?"

"I read your chart, of course. It's customary for all potential cases."

"Potential …what?"

Was he there at Dr. Wallis' behest to convince me that I needed a therapy 'consultation'? Before I could fully consider the thought, something in his crisp, clinical tones triggered a memory that I supposed had been weighing in the back of my mind all along.

Life or Death.

"You!" I croaked, tightening my grip on my bed sheet. "You sent me that note."

The accusation didn't earn a single reaction. Not a frown, nor a flush of guilt. I might as well have said nothing at all. Apparently, gazing down at the estate's front lawn was a lot more interesting than placating me.

Too stunned to do anything else, I found myself following the line of his gaze through the window panes, surprised to find that it was already early in the evening. The sun was only a few hours from setting, and shadows loomed around the edges of my bedroom, threatening to swallow it whole. I barely recognized the plain layout with its simple, bare-bones furniture and lavender walls.

Days trapped inside the hospital might as well have been an eternity.

"What a very funny joke," I stammered, gathering the nerve to sit up further when nearly a minute passed without an explanation. "Tease the terminally ill heiress. I bet your friends got a kick out of that."

Still nothing.

"Well," I said weakly, "I'm sure you all will be *howling* once I call the police—"

"You've made your choice."

The man finally turned to face me, and just like the other day, his rare brand of handsome threw me off—a strong chin paired with a beautiful Roman nose. He smiled, and it should have been impossible for such a harmless expression to spark such a *dangerous* reaction inside my body. Suddenly there didn't seem to be enough air in the room. Lightheadedness alone probably would have dispelled my desire to reach for the panic button installed underneath the edge of my bedside stand.

As it was, my hand was already darting for it.

"I wouldn't do that if I were you."

My fingers stilled over the button. One little press and a hoard of private security guards would flood my room.

"Give me a good reason," I countered, hating the way my voice shook. The temperature in the room dropped within an instant. I couldn't stop shivering, and his eyes …

The intensity in them locked me in place, almost *daring* me to disobey.

"I'll give you *twelve*," he said coldly. "Twelve wives. Twelve lives. Twelve ...well, you get the gist. It's difficult to be both menacing and rhyme at the same time, so I truly suggest you take my word for it."

He smiled, fulfilling my unconscious wish, but the sight chilled me to the core of my being.

Twelve, I guessed, was the number of security guards under the estate's employ, and if my powers of deduction accounted for anything, then he had just threatened to kill them all.

Shadows cut over his gaze, making it seem fathomless, empty. A tense few seconds passed before a sudden cold sweat made my finger drift away from that button—for the moment. "Who are you?" I choked out. "Where is Harper?"

He frowned and raked a hand through his blond hair.

"Harper is out for a *stroll*—" I gulped; Harper wasn't the type for leisurely walks. Before I could argue that point, the stranger continued. "As for *who* I am? Well, that is a very general question, Eleanor. You probably just want a name, so I'll give you one: *Dublin*."

"Dublin?" I echoed. "Like the city in Ireland?"

"Dublin," he said. "Like the city in Ireland. What? Don't like it?" He scratched beneath his chin. "What about Helos? Dublin Helos. It's a rather fine name if I do say so myself."

I couldn't tell if he was serious. His accent made everything he said sound mocking. Though, at least the strange name would give the police something to call him in their trespassing report—but rather than reach for the panic button again, I found myself continuing the strange conversation despite every instinct warning me not to.

"Well, *Dublin*." I swallowed hard. "Why are you in my bedroom?"

He shrugged. "It seemed as good as any a place to conduct business."

That caught my interest. "Business?"

Was he a thief after all? Here to drain my family's accounts under the pretense of a medical house call?

I bit my lower lip, not liking the expression that crossed his face as he reached into the pocket of his pants and withdrew a neatly folded note.

"*This* business. You, my dear, have a contract to sign."

I waited for the punch line—obviously, this was another joke—but as the seconds passed, that stern expression never wavered.

He was serious.

My mouth fell open. No matter how hard I tried, I couldn't seem to form any meaningful words—but the shock didn't last long.

"Get out."

I clutched the sheet to my body as I stood, digging my toes into the plush carpet. The motion carried me away from the panic button, though hell, there had to be a servant—or someone—around to hear me scream. I sucked in air, only to have his laughter startle it back out again. The sound was electric, and Dublin was the definition of a devil-may-care attitude as he inclined his head.

"How strange," he murmured. "Just the other day, you could barely support your own weight, and now look at you …"

I glanced down before I could stop myself, and it wasn't long before I understood what he meant.

I was standing on my own. For the first time in months, I wasn't forced to hold onto something just to stay upright. Not only that, but my throat wasn't sore. I didn't feel dizzy. *Breathing* alone didn't exhaust me.

Alarmed, my gaze swung back up to his face. "What did you do to me?"

I was positive that *he* had done *something*, something dramatic enough to render me unconscious for three days.

An illegal drug?

An experimental treatment?

Rather than give me a definitive answer, Dublin merely flashed another disarming smile, but it was decisively colder than before.

"Have a seat, Eleanor Gray," he told me, gesturing to my bed with a wave of his hand. "We have much to discuss."

I remained standing—though, I *should* have screamed, run, darted for that panic button. He was unarmed, and a grin alone shouldn't have seemed more threatening than any weapon—but there was something in his tone that rooted me to the spot. I had to know ...

"About what?"

Dublin didn't respond right away. Instead, he offered something to me that I hadn't even realized was in his hand until right then.

At first glance, it could have been a leather binder, like the one a check might come in at a restaurant. However, when the surface caught the light, I noticed something sneering at me from the center of the cover: the golden emblem of a snake.

"Why don't you see for yourself?" he suggested, giving the object a shake.

It was a challenge. When I didn't move, he extended the book between us, a dangerous olive branch.

I knew then that I should have run despite his threat. Fingers shaking, I reached out and took the book instead. The moment I did, something cold raced down my spine like the caress of an invisible finger. I could have sworn I heard a voice whisper *'Don't'* in my ear as I settled the light object on one palm and flipped it open.

Trapped between the leather cover was a fancy-looking document that reminded me of my parent's will. For a brief moment, I wondered sarcastically if he had taken care of that dreaded chore for me. To bolster that hope, my name was written across the top in elegant black script. Only, below that, rather than *'To whom I bequeath'* was a line reading, *'Duties of the contractor, hereinafter referred to as the debtor, shall include:'*

A growing sense of dread coiled in my gut as my eyes swept over those scrawled words.

1. The debtor shall hereby fully submit to the will of the contract holder.

2. The debtor shall hereby perform any and all duties necessary to fulfill the contract.

3. The debtor shall hereby...

"What is this?" I wrenched my eyes back to Dublin's, unprepared for the emptiness I found in them.

"It's what you agreed to, Eleanor." He wiggled two of his fingers with that white slip of paper tucked between them. "Read the fine print next time—" His tone turned harsh. "Every choice comes with a *price*."

It wasn't until the waning light reflected off the paper in his hands that I remembered the note with those damn boxes.

Check for life.

Check for death.

Which one had I picked? Suddenly I couldn't remember.

"You're crazy." I slammed the binder shut and threw it at his feet for good measure. Once ...twice, it bounced over the carpet before rebounding off the polished toe of his shoe. "Now get out, before I—"

"Before you what?" In a burst of cool air, he was in front of me. His gaze locked onto my own as I stumbled back. Those grayish eyes were so dark they nearly touched on black. "Before you *what,* Eleanor Gray?"

I couldn't breathe. A chill wafted from him, as if he'd just come from outside, and my body reacted by tightening in places that made me wish my bed sheets weren't so damn thin. It didn't help any that, a split-second later, his expression shifted into another chilling smile.

"You're a smart woman," he declared in a tone so deceptively soft I would have preferred that he shouted. "You know the law of give and take. We made a bargain— and I've already upheld my end of it."

He gestured to my body with a wave of his hand. *Ta-da!*

"I gave you life."

"L-Life?" I sputtered incredulously. "I'm *terminal.*"

For a second, it didn't matter that he was a stranger nearly twice my size who had already threatened to kill a dozen people without batting an eyelash. I snorted; an act so unladylike that my mother would have dropped dead if she wasn't already tucked in her grave. "If you thought you could extort money from me, then sorry to break it to you, but—"

"Money?"

Dublin threw back his head and laughed. The odd reaction was so startling that I almost would have preferred that he'd punched me in the stomach.

"You poor, sweet girl," he murmured, shaking his head as the chuckle died off. "You think this is about your *money?*"

I didn't like the way he said that. *I* was used to being the only person who could act blasé about wealth—the Gray fortune was the only reason anyone ever took an interest in me, after all.

"Then what?" I demanded hoarsely. "What else could you want from me?"

Suddenly, his thumb shot out to trace my bottom lip. Beneath his touch, my teeth chattered. The bed sheet started to slip through my trembling fingers. Right before I lost my composure completely, his hand fell back to his side.

"A return on my investment," he said. "You owe me four days, Eleanor, whether you've changed your mind or not. Though be relieved; others have paid far more for even *less* of a taste."

"A t-taste of what?"

Dublin just smiled. "Hungry?"

Ironically, I didn't smell it until then—a faint scent that tainted the air. I turned, scanning my room more closely, and it wasn't long before I discovered the source.

I don't know how I had missed it before. Someone had set up a small table near the foot of my bed—as well as raided my mother's china cabinet, apparently. The best selection was on display: the priceless silver and imported porcelain. Mother's prized crystal vase was even full to bursting with roses that I guessed had been cut right from the garden. The flowers cast a crisp, calming scent that contrasted with the fear racing through me.

"Well, Eleanor?" From the corner of my eye, I saw Dublin incline his head in acknowledgment. "Ready to negotiate?"

I suppose I could have gone for the panic button or threatened to scream. I wound up doing neither—perhaps because a part of me wanted to believe that I was still sleeping. Even in this bizarre dream, I wouldn't let him think he had the upper hand.

"Of c-course," I croaked and took a step forward.

The room swayed alarmingly. It was a struggle just to clutch my bed sheet in place, though I tried not to show it. Instead, I tossed my hair casually over my shoulder and pointed to my wardrobe with what I hoped passed for an impassive expression.

"Can you grab me that robe?"

If my lack of threatening to go to the authorities impressed him, he didn't let on. That mouth just cracked into an amused smile, but he quietly did as I asked and returned to my side a moment later with a velvet dressing gown slung over his arm.

"Thank you," I stammered, unnerved by how close he was.

The memory of his touch lingered over my skin as he watched me drop my sheet and wrestle my arms into the sleeves of the robe. Once fully covered I didn't feel any less naked than I had before. From the way his gaze smoldered, I had a feeling that Dublin knew it—and relished in my discomfort.

"Have a seat, Eleanor."

At his prompting, I returned my gaze to the table, craning my neck to get a better look. The source of the enticing smell appeared to be bacon and eggs—but only one side of the table was set. Maybe he was watching his figure? Or perhaps bacon and eggs wouldn't be the only thing on the menu…

I attempted to take another step toward it and nearly lost my balance. Already that unusual burst of energy seemed to be fading. Realizing this, Dublin reluctantly thrust one hand out in front of me.

"Here—"

"No thank you."

Ignoring his hand, I staggered the rest of the way to the table. Somehow I managed to collapse into the chair before my legs gave out.

"Well, Ms. Gray…"

Dublin was across from me in the blink of an eye, already seated. His eyes gleamed, as if daring me to question how he had managed to move so quickly.

I didn't, and after a moment's pause, he continued. "Shall we begin?"

"Begin what?" I attempted to hold his gaze and had to bite my lip just to keep the questions inside. I was bursting with them: *why was he here? How had he gotten in—again?*

Without bothering to explain himself, he reached across the table and lifted a knife. The dull edge gleamed as he casually swiped through a chunk of butter, heedless of the way I flinched.

"Toast, Eleanor?"

When I didn't answer, he dragged the substance onto a slice anyway and placed it on the plate before me: a challenge.

The greasy smell of food was tempting—I couldn't lie—but starving seemed a better option any day than losing what little dignity I had left by giving in to him. So, I politely pushed the toast aside with the tips of my fingers while my stomach grumbled in defiance.

"Where's Harper?"

It was past the usual time when Harper would bring me the newspaper and ask if I wanted to go for a drive. I spared a half-hearted glance around my room, un-surprised when I didn't find a familiar, wizened figure lurking in the corners.

Dublin sighed and waved two fingers dramatically through the air. "Harper. He's here. He's there—" Suddenly his gaze honed in on mine and all trace of humor was gone. "He's *alive* if that's what you mean."

I shifted to hide my relief. He could have been lying, but the man seemed too…oh, I don't know. Maybe another one of mother's words would fit.

Posh.

Dublin Helos with those damn good looks and irritating manners was what my darling mother would describe as *posh*—sneering as she did so.

Posh were those gallant types who snuck into galas to chat up wealthy, little old ladies and charm the money right out of their ears. They were usually the bastard children of some obscure baron or business tycoon, but rather than the average 'cad' as mother put it, the 'posh' were honorable to a fault.

"How did you get in here?"

This question earned me an amused laugh. "I came in through the front door, Eleanor, *really*—"

"Don't call me that," I spat before I could help it. "I'm Ellie. Just *Ellie.*"

"Oh?" His mouth formed the basis of a smile, but the expression never reached his eyes. "That's where you're wrong, *Eleanor.*" He wagged a finger from left to right.

"Now is as good enough a time as any for a first lesson; nicknames are unprofessional."

I felt my eyebrow arch into the air.

"You sound like my mother."

Margaret Anna Louise Gray—who would rather be stoned to death than be called *Maggie*—had been a stickler for decorum. She never called me Ellie. Not once, even during a fleeting moment of affection.

It was always *Eleanor.*

"I'm Ellie," I insisted, though I stared at the violet wallpaper behind his head rather than meet his gaze. "I won't answer to anything else."

I couldn't see his reaction, but when he spoke again, his tone was level.

"I think now would be the best time for us to negotiate our terms."

"Terms for what?" The words distracted me enough that I turned to face him, and instantly regretted it when he placed something on my side of the table.

A familiar golden snake hissed at me from a rectangle of black leather, and I wanted nothing more than to push it— and the entire table, for good measure—away from me.

Fingers shaking, I choked down the fear and delicately flicked the book open with the end of my thumb instead.

"What is this?" I asked, even though I knew damn well what it was: the contract with all those strange terms. *The debtor shall do this. The debtor shall do that.*

Only, I had no idea on earth just what I was in debt *for.*

Rather than throw the book at him—along with a polite insistence to go to hell—I bit my tongue. My father had been a master businessman, and if there was one piece of advice he had sorely repeated, it was *never cut and run.*

Never let them see that you're in over your head, sweet pea, he'd recite around bites of ham. *You might as well hand them the company.*

Dublin Helos would never get my …company. So, biting my lip so hard I tasted copper, I started to read with what I hope passed for a casual expression. The more I read, the further my mask slipped. By the final line, my eyes were threatening to pop right out of my head.

"You can't be serious."

It was a slave agreement; that was the general consensus all the duties of the 'debtor' added up to. The signer of the contract, in this case, me, basically agreed to submit themselves entirely to the *'will'* of the contract holder.

I had an ominous hunch as to just who that was.

"You're insane."

"Oh I am," Dublin agreed without clarifying whether he was referring to the serious or the insane—or both. "But, maybe I'm getting ahead of myself here."

He pushed back from the table and settled his chin in the palm of his hand, elbow resting on his knee.

"What do you remember from the other day?"

I felt my nose wrinkle as I tried to recall my time in the hospital. My mind was all fuzzy, but like a jar being shaken, a few lucid thoughts popped out after a moment.

Blood, a girl, a rose, and a stupid check-box.

"The little girl," I heard myself croak. "You sent her?"

Though, who else would? I knew that he had watched me that day, watched *me* watch *her*.

However, if I was expecting guilt, I was sorely disappointed. Dublin's expression resembled a cat's as it waited for a mouse to figure out that it was hopelessly trapped.

"You sent her."

It wasn't a question this time. Dublin had been the mysterious 'he' she had referred to. Not only that, but I suspected that he had been responsible for her drastic change in health as well. I pictured how her skin had glowed with health and the way her eyes had sparkled. The same way, I knew in my gut, *mine* did now.

"You *changed* her—"

"We made a bargain," he corrected, voice deceptively soft. "The same one I made with you."

"You had her sign that?" I jerked back in horror, nearly knocking the chair backward. "A child?"

A revolting image popped into my head of the girl scribbling away her rights in crayon while Dublin sported that sinister, wolfish grin.

"Of course not, Eleanor." For once, he actually sounded insulted. "My, you do have a flair for the dramatic…"

"You said you made a bargain—"

"I did. With her *father*. His terms are the same as yours." He gestured to the contract book.

"And what will you have him do?" My voice shook. It took everything I had just to keep from bolting for the door. Though, I wasn't sure if the force keeping me in my seat was bravery or shock, as I envisioned some poor man in a suit and tie scrubbing the stone floors of Dublin's lair—because someone like him most definitely had a *lair*.

Fortunately, the reality seemed far less morbid.

"He's a businessman," Dublin grunted, almost reluctantly, as if he didn't like discussing this with me. "One who just so happens to be in touch with several rather sought after accounts. He will keep *me* in touch with those accounts. Our transaction is simply a business one, you see."

"So this *is* about money," I argued, annoyed that he had beaten around the bush. "I've already given you the location of the safe—"

"This isn't about money, Eleanor." His tone was too hard, too serious, and I knew in the pit of my soul that he wasn't lying. "Money is *paper*. Cheap. I deal in something a little more …sacrosanct."

"Like what?"

I was curious despite my better judgment. How *couldn't* I be, when I had grown up being told that money was everything?

As my father liked to boast, *"Money is God; the only thing worshiped by all."* In the world my parents had raised me in, Dublin might as well have just committed sacrilege by claiming that he didn't want it.

"What could be more valuable than money?"

Ivory teeth flashed as Dublin replied.

"Your soul—not *literally*," he added as I flinched back. "Figuratively, Eleanor; someone's will, mind, and body. Control those and essentially …" He held his hand out flat and curled his fingers one by one as if trapping something invisible within them. "You have their soul."

I stared for what had to be a good few minutes before I finally found my voice again. "So you want my s-soul?"

"Your *money* would be just a stack of paper to me," he said, "but *you* … You are invaluable."

Despite everything, I had to smother a snort.

Me, valuable?

It was the first time in my life that anyone had ever separated my worth from the Gray inheritance. Ironically, that same person wanted me to sell it to him. But for what purpose?

I blurted out another question, rather than pondering it. "Tell me what you gave me and that girl. Was it medicine?"

I wasn't completely naïve—he had to have done *something*. I was convinced that whatever it was must have been a drug or some type of treatment unavailable on the market.

I waited, but he never pulled out a vial or pills or a syringe. Without a word of explanation, Dublin merely extended his arm across the table instead. The finger of his free hand tapped a blue vein snaking through his wrist.

"Life," he said, eyes boring into mine, willing me to understand what he didn't put into words. "That is my commodity, Eleanor."

I stared, watching the indigo lines running beneath his skin and couldn't help visualizing the liquid pumping through them—the same liquid that ran through my own veins, slowly killing me instead of sustaining.

Then it all clicked.

"Blood." *Dear God.* "You gave me your *blood?*" I pushed back farther from the table, trembling with horror at the thought of him injecting me with a contaminated syringe. For all I knew, he could have been more terminal than I was. "You are insane," I croaked. "You're *psychotic.*"

"But, my dear—" Dublin withdrew something from his pocket and unceremoniously tossed whatever it was onto my lap. "You've already made your choice."

I glanced down to find a folded square of paper resting on my knee. I unfolded it nearly in a daze and was unsurprised to find that damn note with the check boxes.

Live had been my choice after all.

"This isn't a legal document," I said, balling the whole thing in my fist. "It was just some silly game."

"Oh, but you *don't* play games, Eleanor Gray," Dublin insisted, so damn matter-of-factly that I couldn't help but wonder if he had been following me my whole life, watching from the shadows as I chose a good book over a game of hopscotch at recess. "You're much too serious for that, and you knew damn well what you were doing when you marked that paper."

He sounded so sure, so confident. *You are this. You know that.* With just one damn look he could have me second-guessing myself and everything I'd grown up believing; around him, the sky wasn't blue anymore; the grass wasn't green; Ellie wasn't brave.

He leaned closer before I could even find the sense of mind to dive for the panic button. His gaze pierced mine, swirling with a range of emotions I couldn't decipher.

"What am I?" he asked suddenly, catching me off guard.

"P-Pardon me?"

"You heard me. What am I, Eleanor?"

Irritated, I spouted off a list of adjectives. "Loud, brash, rude, boorish, malevolent—"

"No." A laugh edged his words, but there wasn't a trace of amusement in it. "Let me try again; *what* am I? I know you feel it; there is something ...different about me isn't there?"

My throat jerked around a gulp. I didn't like him being so close. His eyes were midnight, daring me to voice out loud what was *really* running through my mind: *evil, dark, something dangerous.*

"Human," I settled on sarcastically, "and a rather annoying one at that."

"No."

Without warning, his hand struck the table with enough force to send the crystal vase jumping two inches into the air. It landed with a heavy thud, spraying water and blood-red petals all over the tablecloth.

"You out of everyone ...*you* know the truth," Dublin declared, eyes flashing. "It's lurking somewhere at the back of your skull, Eleanor. I could sense it in your eyes that first day when you didn't fall for my gallant knight routine. *You flinched back.* Why?"

"You were a stranger," I stammered. "I-I—"

"Wrong again." His voice took on a guttural edge. Nearly a ...growl. "You *sensed* something. What? Think, Eleanor, what did you feel? What did your gut tell you?"

It felt like he was shouting though he never raised his voice. White points flashed below the hood of his mouth. Sharp, triangular …

Fangs, my mind supplied. No, teeth. They had to be plain normal teeth.

"Instinct whispered a warning to you, Eleanor, as I am sure it is warning you now. I want to hear you say it. *What am I?*"

He was right. A single word slipped from my throat before I could stop it. "M-Monster."

Seemingly satisfied with my answer, Dublin sat back and propped a hand beneath his chin.

"I prefer the term, *'shrewd,'* Eleanor, but for now *'monster'* will suffice."

I was shaking. Wrapped in my thick robe, in my nicely heated room, I couldn't stop. My teeth chattered, but I clamped my jaw shut rather than give him the satisfaction of knowing just how badly he affected me.

"So, you gave me your blood," I rasped. "That means *nothing* other than the fact that you have a very sick sense of humor—"

"Does it?" he wondered.

I was unnerved by how calm he seemed, how collected. One might think that *I* had been the one to barge onto *his* private property and that he was merely humoring me.

"Is it magic or something?" I demanded next.

Seriously, this whole conversation was so strange. I had to curl my hands into fists just to keep from making 'spooky fingers' in the air for emphasis.

Dublin, however, did not seem to be in on the joke.

"You tell me." His eyes were a flat, horrible shade of gray that sucked all life from the room. "How do you feel?"

Like I'm dying, I wanted to say, taking the brave, sarcastic route. The truth slipped out regardless.

"Better ..."

I didn't feel as weak as I had for months now, nor as lightheaded. I hated to admit it. It made me feel so very pathetic ... But with him sitting across from me, I couldn't deny the truth.

"And do you know why that is?" he wondered.

"I guess because ..." I swallowed hard. "You gave me your b-blood."

Or at least some new form of medical treatment—I was determined to believe that *'my blood'* was a code word for something, though I had no idea what.

"Correction." He held up four slender fingers. "I gave you *four days'* worth of my blood."

"Why? What's in it for you?"

At this point, that seemed to be the only reasonable question to ask, apart from inquiring as to which mental hospital he'd escaped from.

"Why?" Dublin shrugged, raking his fingers through his hair. "With your resources? You have the makings of a valuable asset."

The word choice didn't upset me as much as I thought it would. After all, I was used to being seen that way: *Ellie Gray, not much by way of personality but at least she's loaded.*

"For what? What do you want from me?"

Those gray eyes clouded over and suddenly he was harder to read than a hunk of stone.

"Whatever I see fit."

"So, if I want more …of your *blood*—" I grimaced. "I have to sign that damn contract without even knowing what it is that you want?"

"You already owe me for four days, Eleanor."

My eyes darted back to the contract book, and I recoiled, physically repelled by the sight of it.

"You're insane. I don't believe any of this—"

"Shall I give you a demonstration?" Dublin leaned forward in a fluid motion, hands braced flat against the table. "I'm sure there are plenty of ways we could test out your newfound energy …"

I paled, the nails of my free hand piercing the armrest of my chair.

"W-What on earth would make you think that I would even *want* your 'help' in the first place?"

Oblivious to my unease, Dublin politely cleared his throat and pointed to the paper still balled up within my fist.

"You've already made your choice. Why else would I be here?"

"What, this?" I glanced down at the questionnaire, haunted by that damn question. *Live or die, Eleanor?* "It was a *joke!*"

I threw the stupid note, unconcerned as it landed in a steaming bowl of oatmeal. Then I stood and staggered over to the window, barely managing to catch myself against the glass.

My body was on fire, heart pounding so fiercely that my body trembled with the force of my pulse. I felt charged, like I could just punch something or maybe *someone*. I felt … *exhilarated*, I realized in horror.

It was a strange emotion considering that, these days, mine typically ranged from bored to exhausted.

I had never felt like this; excited, terrified, petrified and wholly *alive.*

I couldn't resist sneaking a glance at Dublin from the corner of my eye. He was watching me, eyes glinting as if he knew my every thought and then some.

Live or Die?

Choose wisely.

He didn't intimidate me—or so I tried to tell myself—and if he wanted to play this twisted game, then I would too. Without a word, I turned and headed toward my nightstand.

"What are you doing?"

He was beside me in an instant, hand on my shoulder, chilling me even through the thick velvet of my robe. I attempted to shrug him off, and when that didn't work, I put all my energy into reaching for the knob of a small drawer.

"I'm getting a *pen,*" I snarled back at him. "So that I can sign your damn contract."

Besides, I told myself, trying to ignore the way my fingers were shaking, *the lawyers would rip that baseless piece of paper to shreds anyway.* Any judge in the world would take my side, and Dublin Helos would be left without even a penny to smirk over.

I had nothing to lose.

Those gray eyes widening ever so slightly were the only sign of surprise. The next instant, Dublin was yanking me back toward the table.

"I have one," he told me, before shoving me down into my seat.

A second later a silver pen dangled from his fingers, as innocuous as a dagger. I took it and stared down at the contract book while Dublin flipped it open. My hand trembled as I pressed the tip of the pen to the parchment … only to hesitate at the last second.

The dotted line taunted me. *What are you doing?* It sneered. *The bored little heiress so afraid to die you'd play into some sick little fantasy?*

Fear was almost enough to make me back away, like every ounce of common sense *warned* me to.

But then I pictured Georgie and Mr. Tinkles.

It was easy to tell myself that the thought of dying without even being able to say goodbye was what finally made my fingers clench around the pen.

"Hold it like this," Dublin instructed.

A cool finger nudged my thumb until it struck a tiny golden emblem on the side of the shaft—a twisted serpent matching the one on the book.

I thought it might have been some strange form of decoration. At least until I attempted to sign my name; the moment I pressed down, a sharp pain shot through the pad of my finger, drawing a gasp even as my hand scribbled out a single letter E. The ink was bright red, suspiciously like …

Don't think about it, Ellie. Ignoring the color, I forced myself to continue forming the letters of my name. E-L-E-A …

By the time I signed the very last Y, it was too late to have any second thoughts.

My entire body trembled as I set the pen aside and watched it roll into a bowl of fruit. My thumb throbbed, and I knew deep in my soul that I would never be able to forget the sight of my own blood smeared across that golden snake.

But there was no going back. I felt as though I'd fallen off some giant precipice, only I had yet to hit the bottom.

"Finally."

Dublin snatched the contract book from the table. With some sleight of hand, it disappeared, most likely into his pocket. Then, he reclaimed the chair opposite from me, mouth split into another disarming grin.

"Now, we can begin."

A DEAL WITH THE DEVIL

I felt like I had made a deal with a devil, though that analogy didn't quite explain why my stomach was curled into a million little knots. It was a sensation similar to what you felt right before diving into water so deep that you couldn't even see the bottom.

Terrifying, but not exactly a *bad* feeling after all was said and done.

"B-Begin what?"

"You need to repay me for four days," Dublin explained. He formed a steeple with his fingers over his placemat and watched me from overtop it. "You have options, of course."

"Options?" I found myself leaning forward to meet his gaze, despite how every instinct in my body urged me to run in the opposite direction. I was curious as to what kinds of 'payment' could be more valuable than cold, hard cash. *Blood? Bodily fluids? My actual soul?*

"What are they?"

"Your family name does carry a lot of weight," Dublin grudgingly admitted. "I could use that to my advantage."

In other words, business arrangements and corporate intimidation. The socialite in me sniffed.

"And the second?"

He shrugged. "Unlimited access to your family's accounts—"

"I thought you said this wasn't about money."

"It's *not*," Dublin insisted. "I'm sure your charming smile could open more doors than a stack of Gray millions, but they certainly wouldn't hurt."

"And that's it?" I felt my lips curve into a frown. Was I, dare I say it …*disappointed?*

How anti-climactic. Here I was, prepared to sell my soul, and the proverbial Devil just wanted the same old thing I'd been giving to everyone for free: dutiful little Ellie and the Gray family name.

"No. That's not *it.*" Before I could react, Dublin reached across the table and lifted my chin with the pad of his thumb. Goosebumps erupted over my skin at the contact. He was one of the few people in years to touch me without wearing clinical rubber gloves, and my body didn't know how to register the sensation.

"I must admit, Eleanor," he began while his gaze searched mine. "I've brokered hundreds of contracts, but this is the first time someone hasn't taken the easiest of choices."

Easiest. I batted his hand away. "So there's more?"

I wondered what. *Not business*, something told me. His scoff all but proved it.

"Nothing *you'd* be interested in. I make contracts with people from all walks of life, Eleanor, and trust me—" That icy gaze raked me over once. "You're not the type."

"The type to what?"

His jaw clenched, and I was able to guess what even he had enough tact not to say out loud; the type to *matter.* So much for that 'valuable' nonsense. When it came right down to it, he saw me the same way everyone else did—as a body stuffed with dollar bills.

I tried rephrasing the question. "How *else* could I fulfill this contract—"

"Tell me, Eleanor," Dublin said cutting over me. "Would you steal? Cheat? Kill? Fuck strangers for no reason other than being *told* to do so?"

My mouth fell open. I didn't think anyone had ever spoken to me so crudely, ever. I was insulted, revolted, intrigued.

"Is that—" I had to clear my throat just to find my voice again. "Is that how you have some people *fulfill* their contracts?"

"Yes." Dublin's gaze was fathomless. "Those who have 'natural' talents to bargain with, rather than money."

"Like …"

He rattled off a list. "Intelligence, cunning, beauty."

I flinched at his insinuation of the opposite, though I should have been used to it by now. All my life I'd been the 'Gray girl,' or 'Sexy Georgie's sister.' Never—not once—had I ever been called beautiful. After facing the truth in the mirror for twenty-six years, it didn't hurt so much to admit it now.

I wasn't beautiful, or smart, *or* cunning—but that didn't mean that I liked having the fact rubbed in my face by someone who looked like a perfect, blond *Adonis.*

"You said I had a *choice,*" I parroted, throwing that word right back at him.

His reply was curt, irritated. "I did—"

"Then why should my appearance matter?"

A better question was *why was I pushing this?*

I had no damn idea. Perhaps because something in me railed against the thought of always being written off so easily? 'Gray' and 'money' might as well have been my definition. I waited for Dublin to come clean and admit as much. But when those gray eyes narrowed, I knew that I had made a mistake.

"Get up."

His tone was so harsh that I lurched automatically to my feet. Instinct urged me to *run*. Run fast, run hard and far, far away from him—screaming if possible. But all I did was just stand there, toes digging into the carpet.

With a predatory grace, Dublin stood as well. His gaze honed in on mine. Then, he issued a command that made my blood run cold.

"Take off your robe."

"W-what?"

"Your robe." In a matter of seconds, he skirted the table to stand in front of me, unconcerned as I stumbled back. "Take it off."

I shook my head, too terrified to speak. Suddenly, this game wasn't so thrilling anymore. The tables had turned, and we had come full circle right back to the obvious scenario; he was a dangerous male stranger, and I was …alone.

"Do you even understand what your choice *is*?" Relentlessly, he advanced, forcing me into a corner. My gaze darted for the panic button. I could feel my legs twitch, ready to spring for it. "Thought so." Suddenly, Dublin withdrew, leaving just enough space between us to keep me from panicking even more. "Now, which will it be?" he wondered. "Business or money?"

In an instant, I realized that he had been bluffing—dangling my own threat before me, like a belt before a misbehaving child.

That fact shouldn't have made me feel so foolish. *Who would want to ravish you?* A part of me scoffed. *Silly cow!*

"I suggest the first choice," Dublin continued as if we'd never left the table. "I have a few arrangements that could use the Gray family name to get underway. More than sufficient to cover four days—"

I stopped listening. Almost numb, I trailed a single finger down to my waist, following the sash of velvet cinching my robe until I reached the knot holding it all together.

Business or money, Eleanor? I wondered.

Then, I pulled.

"This is your only feasible option—"

Dublin froze mid-sentence, as the heavy fabric slid down my arms and pooled at my feet.

Baring myself before a stranger was nothing new. I had been bathed and dressed with the aid of servants my whole life, and months in the hospital had all but obliterated any sense of modesty I may have had left.

Still, I felt a strange sense of triumph as I stood there, shivering and utterly naked. I didn't know what kind of reaction I was searching for when I finally scanned Dublin's face. Guilt? Shock? Some damn common decency to turn away?

Instead, he caught my hands before they could creep up to cover my exposed chest and yanked them back down. Then, as composed as ever, he stood back and crooked a finger; *come.*

I couldn't explain just what made me take the tiniest of steps in his direction. Bravery? Sheer stupidity? An inexplicable urge to throw him off-balance the same way he seemed determined to unnerve me?

Whatever it was, I was left bared to his mercy, and I didn't feel brave in the slightest.

"Turn around." He made a twirling motion with his finger, and I found myself obeying the command, aware of his gaze inspecting every inch of me.

My arms, legs …

He eyed me the way a predator might a wounded, damaged bit of prey, wondering if anything useful could be salvaged.

"You're pale at least," I heard him mutter once I completed my circle. "Easier to see the veins."

What an odd thing to notice.

"For what?" I glanced at him from over my shoulder, but he didn't bother responding.

The minutes ticked by, and a tiny sliver of modesty had my hands inching back up to cover my exposed breasts before he could appraise them as well. The novelty of being bold and daring had worn off, considering that I didn't have much to validate it.

My body wasn't toned and curvy like Georgiana's. When it came to the opposite sex, I could be summed up in one word: *unappealing.*

"Pedigreed blood. That could be a plus," Dublin said under his breath. I jumped as cool fingers grazed the line of my throat, skimming my pulse. "You've suffered no major trauma?"

"N-No." I ducked out of his reach.

"Illicit drug use?"

"Of course not!"

He nodded just once, reminding me of a doctor performing a routine physical. *Now, open wide and say 'ah.'* His next question, however—while spoken in the same crisp, clinical tones—pertained to another orifice. "Are you a virgin, Eleanor?"

"P-pardon me?"

"A virgin." He enunciated the word in two sharp syllables: *vir-gin.* "Have you ever fucked a man? Woman? Anyone?"

My answer was a breathless squeak. "Of c-course *not.*"

Dublin frowned, annoyed by the response, though I couldn't fathom why.

My virginity had never really been a sticking point for me. Unlike the heroines in the romance novels I was sometimes bored enough to read. I didn't resent it, and I wasn't inclined to go on some dramatic adventure to lose it.

Georgie, rumored to have been deflowered by a cabana boy at age sixteen, was the romantic one. I, on the other hand, agreed with my mother on this point; sex was ...necessary. Like eating or breathing, it should be done only when there was a purpose for it.

Mother had been quite open about the fact that she and my father had only 'done the deed' roughly three times during their entire marriage. Twice, give or take, to create Georgie and me, and once more on my father's birthday when they had both drunk too much wine. There wasn't a point otherwise, or so I had been told.

Therefore, I had absolutely no idea why Dublin was *looking* at me like that: as if I had some sort of debilitating disease apart from the one I was dying from.

"That will need to be rectified," I thought I heard him mutter before turning away. "Get dressed."

Too dazed to argue, I stooped and eagerly slipped into my robe.

Now what? I wondered as I warily followed him back to our impromptu 'negotiation' table, arms crossed tightly over my chest. Dublin took his customary seat without a word, and I just stood there. When nearly a minute passed in silence, I found the courage to noisily clear my throat.

"So ..."

"*So,*" Dublin said, swiftly cutting over me, "you will have four days to repay your current debt, and we'll go from there." He leaned back, eyes seeking out mine. "Is *this* how you choose to fulfill your contract, *sans* your fortune?"

He didn't elaborate, though…maybe he should have?

All of a sudden, I felt woefully in over my head. Here was a stranger who'd claimed to have sold me his blood and I had just signed the legal document he shoved onto my lap. Not only that …

He saw you naked, a tiny, indignant part of me huffed. *Eleanor Louise Gray, what the hell has gotten into you?*

I dug my toes into the carpet rather than give him the satisfaction of watching me dart back to my bed in hopes of waking up from the nightmare.

"So, to repay this 'debt,' I would have to lie, cheat, steal or…" So much for being brave—I couldn't even get the word out, *fuck. Vulgar!* My mother scolded from the grave. Instead, I made a little sound at the back of my throat. "*Mmhm* …with strangers?"

Dublin seemed mildly amused. The corner of his mouth twitched, and he leaned back even further, lacing his fingers together behind his head. "There are people out there whose names aren't as weighty as yours," he began in a lofty tone. "Whose money isn't a weapon they can use to evade whatever irritates them. Yet …they have other 'assets' that are just as valuable."

His words pierced me right through the chest: in other words, apart from the Gray name, I wasn't important. The knowledge made me feel …well, certainly not worth a fortune. More, resigned. Dublin might have been insane, but he—better than anyone else—had illustrated perfectly just how the world saw me.

And I was sick of it. I was *sick* of being seen only as Eleanor *Gray*—sick of being tied to my parent's name. If Dublin, the insane doctor with the 'magic' blood, wanted me, then he would get *me:* the great, dull calamity that was *Ellie.*

Nothing else.

"Yes," I blurted suddenly.

"Yes, what?"

"Yes." I sucked in a breath and released it in a rush of words, "that is how I want to fulfill my contract."

"No." Dublin sat bolt upright. Those golden eyebrows arched, and his mouth deflated into a hard, flat line. He almost looked …surprised, before a cold expression wiped any trace of emotion away.

"N-no?"

"No." In a blur of shadow and ivory, he stood, drilling into me with eyes so dark they bordered on ebony. "Your *name* or your *money.* Pick one."

I staggered back, catching myself on the end of my chair. "B-But …why?"

His excuses were quick and succinct. "This isn't a game. You're inexperienced and untested. I would have to train you *myself*—" Which, judging from his tone, was the most unacceptable condition of all.

"You said I could choose," I pointed out, raising my voice as his deepened. "You said that other people have done *that* to fulfill their contracts."

"Other people," he snapped. "Not you."

I stomped my foot—*actually* slammed my heel into the carpet like a petulant child. "But you said!" My voice ricocheted off the walls, echoing back to me. "You *said* that you wanted my soul. Me! If you want the money and the Gray family name, then you can go dig up my parents. This is *me*, and this is all I have to offer you."

My lungs screamed for air. I couldn't seem to catch my breath. All the while I was left to wonder what in the hell had gotten into me—Ellie Gray didn't argue—especially not with dangerous, male strangers about her 'self-worth.' I had to resist the urge to curl up in a ball in the face of Dublin's expression. His jaw tightened, and for once, he openly displayed a real emotion—*anger.*

"There will be a car waiting at six o'clock," he hissed after a moment of unbearable silence. "Don't be late by even a *second,* or you will pay dearly."

My mind spun as I realized what I had done. What I had negotiated *for.*

"For what?" I rasped as he turned and headed for the door.

"You got your wish," Dublin called back. "Your name and money are now off the table. All you have is *yourself*." A gruff laugh told me how valuable he thought that was. "You should have just played the role of an heiress. It suits you better."

Yourself.

Suddenly drained, I sank into my chair, but when I spoke again, my voice was surprisingly steady. "You'll ...*train* me?" It was funny how that was the only thing that really stuck out from his venom-laced tirade. "To do what?"

"Whatever a client demands," Dublin replied from the threshold of my bedroom. "You didn't just sell me your body, Eleanor; you sold me your will, your dignity, and mind. *That* is what the desperate bargain with when they aren't lucky enough to have been born with a silver spoon engraved with the name *Gray* shoved down their throat. When I'm through with you, there won't be a single thing that you can stick that pert little nose up at."

I stiffened. What kinds of things *did* girls like me 'stick their pert little noses up at' anyway?

I was oddly curious.

"The amount I gave you should be enough to last you through the rest of the day," Dublin went on, returning to the apparent root of our problem; my life and his blood. "I'll replenish your dose tonight. Do you understand?"

I nodded weakly. *Tonight. Dose …*

"Six o'clock."

The reminder was the last thing he said before the door slammed behind him, and I was left alone to contemplate my fate, now that I had stubbornly gotten my way.

RUIN

So, what did one wear to one's potential ruin?

I had only a few hours to find out.

I spent the first huddled in the bathtub, until the water turned ice cold and my skin pruned—but despite how long I lingered, I still didn't feel any cleaner.

Funny. No one had ever told me that *shame* couldn't be erased with soap.

In the end, I gave up and stood, sopping wet, to grab a clean robe from the cupboard. I tied the sash around my waist as I wandered into the hallway, too restless to stay in one place.

The dark walls of the old house enclosed me, speckled with portraits of obscure ancestors: there was James, the first Gray to set foot in the Americas, hanging beside William, his perpetually disapproving elder brother. Near my bedroom hung the visage of Great Aunt Agnes who looked as pleased to have been painted as Dublin had when we'd struck our bargain.

Apparently, smiling was a foreign concept in this family.

As I tiptoed farther down the hall, I tried to remember what it had been like growing up in the cold, oddly formal lap of luxury.

Lonely. Oppressive. Dull.

Was it sad that Dublin was the first person in years to wander these halls who hadn't been paid to do so?

With that thought in mind, I drifted through the corridors without a true goal. I didn't even realize which section of the house I was in until I finally slipped into the drawing room where a pair of bay windows spilled waning daylight at my feet.

It looked to be an hour or so until dusk. The sun had already begun its descent below a horizon obscured by violet clouds. I didn't know how long I stood there, dripping water onto the wooden floor—but when I finally turned away, the sky had darkened and I had less than an hour remaining until my deadline.

Six o'clock.

Heart pounding, I returned to my room and threw open the doors to my wardrobe.

The shadows were a captive audience, watching as I tugged at cotton, pinched wool, and tossed designer garments onto the floor one after the other.

Blouse, skirt, blouse, skirt. Black, gray, brown—I was sensing a rather depressing pattern. In fact, the most fashionable thing I owned was the robe I wore now which Georgie had bought me. The rest were all dour outfits hand-chosen by my mother.

Modest, was the word she had used to describe the color scheme. To her, anything brighter than maroon was gaudy —hence why Georgie had made it her mission since the age of fifteen to stock her closet with as many pastels as she could. I was almost tempted to creep into the other wing and raid my sister's closet …

But in the end, I lost the nerve and settled on a burgundy blouse and a brown tweed skirt.

Perhaps it was time to look at this whole situation another way? *Business*, Dublin had insisted again and again.

I didn't think he even got the irony.

So, he considered my torment 'business,' did he? Well, I would certainly dress the part. With a grim sense of determination, I pulled on the clothes and shuffled before the mirror.

The results weren't very astounding: the dark color scheme sucked all life from my skin, and my hair was an afterthought of messy curls. All in all, the only detail I had any confidence in were my plain black heels—the one item I cared enough to buy for myself.

I looked like a crypt-keeper, ready to commune with the dead. Minutes from consorting with a deranged stranger convinced he had magic blood, I certainly felt desperate enough to have sought out even a ghost for company. Someone to tell my strange story to—*Well you see, this infuriating man broke into my bedroom and I kind of sold him my soul—long story short, he wants to whore me out.*

And you agreed to this, darling? My spiritual visitor would inquire, eyes wide.

Why yes. In fact, I insisted on it.

Darkness had fallen fully by the time I made my way into the foyer. Only a few lamps were lit, leaving swathes of shadow that loomed overhead. Once again, the house was empty—most of the staff went home after five anyway—though I still found it odd that no one had come to check on me in two days.

Because of him, a part of me suspected. Already, Dublin Helos seemed to have some eerie hold over the entire manor. I could sense a darker aura settling there within the corners, and even the curtains seemed to whisper warnings against the floor as I walked past. *Stupid girl!*

Finally, I approached the door, where a peek through a window revealed that the driveway was empty.

This all could have just been a dream, Ellie, I thought hopefully, tapping my foot against the floor. Perhaps my illness had progressed to the final stages already? *Brain hemorrhages could cause hallucinations …*

The sound of tires crunching over stone evaporated that theory. Seconds later, a dark car wandered up the path stretching from the main gates. Elegant, but not one of ours.

Dublin. I shivered as his voice echoed in my thoughts. *Don't be late by even a second …*

It was all bravado, of course—it had to be. He wouldn't dare hurt me. Not if he didn't want to be sued dearly for a single scratch. Confident of this fact, I was tempted to call his bluff and push my luck by dawdling until six o' *one* …

But I already had the door open before any thought of rebellion could really take hold.

It was the middle of January and freezing out. I half expected snow to come pelting down as I staggered across the stoop in my heels. My bare legs trembled, kissed by the chill while my gaze honed in on the strange car.

It definitely wasn't the usual Rolls Royce that Harper drove, but a newer, foreign model built solely for speed. My faithful driver wasn't the one to emerge from the front seat and circle around the car, either. Instead, an unfamiliar man wearing a black suit held open the door and faced me with an unreadable expression.

"Good evening, Miss Gray."

I couldn't seem to voice a greeting in return, even as I took a hesitant step forward, then another. The short walk down the front path might as well have lasted an eternity. By the time I finally settled onto the leather backseat of the car, I couldn't smother the tremors that rippled down my spine. Once the door closed behind me—trapping me inside—it took every last ounce of control I had to keep from panicking.

Easy does it, Ellie, I coached myself as the driver returned to the front seat and took the wheel. *Just breathe.*

That alone seemed laughable when it came to Dublin. I should have called the police rather than humor him. I shouldn't have given in to his sick little game. I should have found Harper.

What had I done instead?

Bargain. Contract. Soul.

It all had the makings of a sordid nightmare that I desperately wanted to wake up from.

Or perhaps I didn't.

As the car slipped through the gates, I was struck by the realization that this was the first time in years I'd left the house for a destination other than the hospital, or a boarding school, or a stuffy gala. Some sick, curious part of me was intrigued as to where this car might take me.

A secluded penthouse in the business district?

A parceled-off manor on a hill?

My mind spun, wild with imagination, but in all my little fantasies, a chic, brick building in the heart of downtown would have been the least likely of Dublin's potential lairs.

For all intents and purposes, it looked like a regular club— albeit the exclusive kind that you could enter only if your name were on a list. I couldn't make out much through the darkness, just sleek lines and a few windows cut like long, rectangular slits into the building's side. Above a set of glass doors hung a sign displaying the venue's name in blood-red script. *Anemia.*

Going off Dublin's apparent affinity for blood, I figured that he thought the name was a clever joke.

But, that's not it, a part of me argued. *You know the real reason …*

A light rap on my window was the only warning before the door was opened from the outside. The driver stood there, offering a hand and I took it, allowing him to help me out onto the curb.

This early in the evening, there was no crowd clamoring to enter the club, and the streets ran sluggishly with rush-hour traffic. Minus the oblivious drivers in their cars, there was no one there to witness me approach the sleek glass doors of *Anemia.*

Surprisingly, they were locked. I tugged on the handles until my shoulder ached and eventually, the driver spoke up from behind me.

"Perhaps try the back way, Miss?"

I glanced in the direction he indicated. Apparently 'the back way' was through a narrow alley that separated this building from another. In the waning light, it seemed about as appealing as traipsing into the mouth of a giant monster.

But, Dublin's threat kept echoing through my mind. *Six o'clock.*

I held my breath as I took a few hesitant steps forward and was instantly plunged into shadow. For an alley, it seemed clean, at least. Not one speck of litter dotted the ground, and I got the sense that it was traveled often. Perhaps an indirect route used only by those in the know?

It wasn't long before I came to a metal door at the very back of the building. Curling a fist, I sucked in a deep breath and knocked once. A second later the door opened, and ruby light spilled from the inside, casting my skin in a bloody glow.

"Eleanor Gray?"

Shadow obscured the speaker's face, but in a dance of beckoning fingers, he invited me inside.

Run! A voice screamed from the back of my mind. Alarm and danger warred with the parts of me too stubborn to move.

If they found my body on tomorrow's evening news—stuffed underneath some underpass—I would deserve it. Twenty-six years of obscurity warned me to just go back, tuck myself in my warm bed and hire twenty more bodyguards to thwart Dublin.

"Miss Gray?" Dark eyes watched me curiously from over the edge of the door. "It's cold out."

The polite display of concern startled me so much that I staggered inside.

"Th-thank you."

The door closed behind me, plunging me into darkness. Someone reached for my coat, and their fingers brushed my wrist by accident. I gasped—whoever the doorman was, he seemed just as abnormally cold as Dublin. Glacial.

"He's upstairs," that crisp tone informed me as I stood there, trembling and coat-less in the dark. "This way. The stairs are on your left."

Another door opened, pulled by an unseen hand, and orange light flooded in.

I stumbled over the threshold. However, when I turned to get a good look at the mysterious door-opener, they had already shifted deeper into the shadows. I only managed to catch a fleeting glimpse of pale skin before the door closed in my face.

I glanced around, taking stock of my surroundings. I seemed to be in a narrow hallway with gray walls and dark, tiled floors. There were no windows and, other than the door I had come from, the only way out seemed to be a metal staircase leading to an upper level.

Wobbling in my heels, I took a step forward …and then another when nothing seemed liable to rush from the corners to attack me.

I couldn't hear so much as a murmur of conversation drifting from above. Or anything for that matter—just the sound of my own shallow breathing playing an ominous lullaby; *in and out, in and out, in and out.*

I felt seconds away from snapping. The silence here was more oppressive than the hush in Gray Manor—but at least my home was fully heated. The air in here seemed more frigid than outside. I swore my breath painted the air in tiny clouds of white.

No wonder Dublin seemed so cold if this was where he spent most of his time.

I clutched my purse tighter at the thought of him, nails digging into the leather. Then, with another glance at the closed door, I continued my slow trek toward those metal stairs. It seemed to take an eternity before my heel finally connected with the bottom step.

You can do this, I urged, forcing myself to climb another.

It's just a game.

Another step.

Nothing he said can be legally enforced anyway.

Two steps.

The lawyers …

I managed to brace one unsteady heel against the top step just as a familiar voice lashed out like a whip.

"Get out."

My foot slipped, sending me down hard to one knee, and I barely managed to hook my hand around the guardrail—preventing me from plunging down the stairs altogether. I gaped through the shadows, expecting to find a certain blond male glaring down from the top step.

Instead, I only saw the mouth of a hallway hidden in shadow.

"Oh, don't be so cruel, Dublin." The second voice was a woman's low, playful purr—but I couldn't see who it belonged to. Both she and Dublin sounded muffled, as if they were in another room. "I only asked one teensy little question. After all, it's not just *anyone* that could have Mr. *'I'm the cold, emotionless contractor'* even more brooding than usual. Do tell; is she pretty at least?"

"No—" Dublin's reply was so cold that I wiggled my toes just to make sure they weren't frostbitten by the chill. "And *you* won't be very appealing either, if you don't get out of my sight."

"Oh, touché!" The woman giggled. "But I must admit that I am most intrigued by this new morsel. One simple contract and you're glowering like the Devil. Are you going to tell her?"

"Tell her what?"

"Oh let's not beat around the *bush*." The word was punctuated by another husky laugh. "The truth, of course! That she's just a pawn. This poor, pathetic—"

"Eleanor Gray."

After glancing around in hopes that another woman—coincidentally named 'Eleanor'—had crept up the stairs after me, I realized that there was only one unlucky fool the speaker could be referring to.

"You can come out," Dublin added, still unseen from my position in the stairwell.

Clutching my purse to my chest like a shield, I stood and gracelessly staggered up the remaining step.

The staircase opened onto a corridor that branched off into two directions. One led into a wide open room with black paneled walls and numerous closed doors. The other into what seemed to be a lounge, complete with sleek, black furniture. There, Dublin glowered from a leather chaise, dressed impeccably in a tailored suit.

I gulped and just stood there, mesmerized by those silver eyes. They seemed to pierce through me even from several feet away. It was a good minute before I even noticed the beautiful woman standing beside him.

"Saskia," Dublin said, waving a hand dismissively in her direction. "You may leave."

Saskia was a vision of red in an elegant cocktail dress. Her thick hair, in a matching shade of scarlet, had been scraped back into a ponytail so long it reached the small of her back. Blazing, amber eyes stared from a beautiful face that was almost as angular as a fox's. She lingered for a second in a way that I suspected was deliberate, rebellious. Then with a slow, ripe smile, she turned on her heel.

"Oh, Dublin," I thought I heard her murmur before she disappeared down another hallway. "She's *perfect.*"

The way she drew the word out—*puuuuurfect*—gave me the feeling that she didn't mean the term as a compliment. Either way, Dublin's expression certainly reinforced the fact that I was *anything* but perfection. He stood and took in my rumpled appearance with one sweep of his gaze.

"God, Eleanor. You look like you're on your way to a funeral."

I fidgeted, annoyed that he had picked up my own rather grim analogy. My blouse had some *color*—however dull—so I couldn't look that dreadful, could I?

Apparently so. Dublin surged forward before I could cringe out of reach. Like a disapproving parent, he tugged on my collar and fingered a wayward curl. When he finally took a step back, his frown had deepened.

"Should I take your outfit choice as proof that you've decided to rethink your agreement?"

He sounded like a stern father offering a naughty child a reprieve. *You've been a bad girl, but I don't have to punish you if you apologize.*

I felt my mouth open, but no words came out.

Tell him yes, a part of me hissed. *Write him a check for whatever he wants and go home.*

"I—"

"Is this her?" The voice drifted from the back of the lounge.

Where there had been no one a second before, a man now leaned against the wall, the picture of poise. His eyes were an odd shade of brown that glittered like gold—hawk-like. Coifed, ebony hair was cropped close to his scalp, and he too wore a perfectly tailored suit. In fact, he could have been a darker-haired clone of Dublin, if it wasn't for the simple piece of jewelry hanging around his neck.

The chain itself almost seemed feminine, formed of small, interlocking links of silver—however, the pendant dangling from the center of it was anything but delicate: it was the image of a falcon in mid-flight, talons drawn to seize prey.

"Mikhail," Dublin acknowledged without even turning around.

"Rumor has it that you've taken on a new contract," Mikhail murmured. A subtle accent toyed with his pronunciation. *English?* "Though, I'm surprised you've brought her *here.* Our client's tastes have changed some since the last time you 'visited.' Pity. Had she looked more like the other one, I might have offered to take her off your hands ..."

Dublin stiffened, and from where I was standing, I had no trouble seeing his expression: icy gaze and chilling frown. "Unfortunately," he intoned. "But unless the laws have changed in the last fifty years, then they state that only she can decide on the terms of her repayment. This is *her* choice."

My choice. Dublin's tone explained everything without him having to spell it out: I was the imbecile foolish enough to insist on my own 'self-worth.'

"Did she now? Interesting, the pawn actually set *itself* into play." I couldn't resist the urge to take a step back as Mikhail withdrew from the wall. He impassively eyed the way my curls threatened to burst from their bun before turning his attention to the rest of my dour ensemble. "You better pray that Yulia can do something with her," he advised. "Otherwise …"

At the unspoken threat, Dublin's gaze shifted to a color unlike any I had ever seen; a hot, molten silver. Without allowing Mikhail to leave first, he reached back and grabbed for my wrist.

"Come on."

I had no choice but to follow him down a narrow hall illuminated by a silver sconce in the form of a serpent. The walls were black paired with an industrial tile floor, and the whole layout seemed clean and crisply modern.

After a few feet, Dublin stopped before a seemingly random doorway and shoved me inside. The room was large with scarlet walls and black carpeting. It almost reminded me of my mother's dressing room. There wasn't much furniture other than a long table, a mirror, and a metal wardrobe in the opposite corner.

My heels sank into the flooring, threatening to trip me as Dublin forced me in farther, hands on my shoulders.

"Fix this," he snarled to someone I couldn't see.

It wasn't until the figure moved that I realized why. The woman's dress was the exact same shade as the wall. Her long, dark hair didn't help differentiate her from the background any.

"So Saskia *wasn't* lying," she murmured, eyes glinting through the shadows. They were green and unusually slanted, like a cat's.

"Just *fix* this," Dublin repeated. His tone reminded me of a dissatisfied customer forced to make the best of a faulty purchase. *At least cover up the broken bits!*

He let me go, and footsteps marched in the opposite direction. A second later, a door slammed shut.

"Well, you've gotten him worked up." The woman stood a few paces back, watching me. Her green eyes glowed with amusement.

"So I keep hearing," I choked out in response.

The fact that I replied at all made her smile widen.

"Who can blame him?" she wondered. "After all, it's not every day that one signs herself up for this life."

She didn't elaborate—but she didn't have to. By now, I was well aware of the extent of my own stupidity.

"Let's see what we have to work with. Come."

Before I could wallow in shame, the woman beckoned me with a crooked finger, and I forced myself to take a step forward, submitting myself to her inspection. Her expression was unreadable as her eyes darted from one plain feature to the next, though at least she wasn't frowning.

"You have good skin," she said, at last, eyeing the buttoned-up collar guarding my throat. "And your hair …"

With the same uncanny grace as Dublin, she suddenly appeared in front of me and undid the knot of my bun.

"It's beautiful," she murmured as the thick curls tumbled down my shoulders. She curled one around her finger before letting her hand fall. "A little long, but still far too lovely to be tied back."

"T-Thank you," I stammered politely.

Obviously, the light was too dim in the room, because I had never heard my hair described as anything other than unruly, stubborn and wild. It was the only part of me unwilling to stay neatly pinned in place.

"You're not the usual type," the woman went on, fingers propped beneath her chin. "Dublin usually brings the …" She paused, seeming to think of a fitting word. I waited, curious despite myself as to what kind of women Dublin found 'valuable' without money or some stuffy old ancestry. "Typical ones," she said finally.

"Ah."

Going off the way her eyes flickered over my mousy hair and shapeless body, I could guess just what she meant.

Busty. Lusty. Blonde.

It wasn't that hard to picture a smirking Dublin with some statuesque beauty on his arm, leading the way to a dastardly contract. *Here, now sign away your soul to me—and do be dramatic about it. I am the Devil, you know.*

"You're not a bad change," she added, "but you won't fit the clothes."

She gestured to a wardrobe in the corner, and I couldn't resist the strange impulse that had me creeping toward it, fearful of what could be inside. It was a sleek affair, formed of black metal and adorned with golden handles in the shape of two twisting serpents—the emblem *de jour*.

"I doubt we have anything in your size," the woman warned, almost apologetically, before I slowly eased the doors apart.

'Doubt' was an understatement. *Nothing* hanging neatly from the silver hangers seemed to "fit" me—both literally and figuratively.

Every article of clothing was made of the same silky material, cut into teeny strips more likely to cover Mr.

Tinkles than any human. I shuddered, unable to keep a finger from tracing the hem of what looked to be a black, lacy bustier with blood red trim. If nothing else had made it sink in—not Dublin's grim insistence, or the mysterious atmosphere of the club—then the sight of the clothing *did*; this was not the place for me.

"Are you all right?"

The woman frowned as I swayed, searching for anything to keep me upright. Spotting a chair in the corner, I rushed over to it.

Breathe, Ellie, I scolded myself as I collapsed onto the cushion. *Breathe!*

With Dublin's words in my ears, I couldn't even remember which muscles made my lungs expand with air—let alone how to *use* them. From the corner of my eye, I saw the strange woman drift closer.

"You are not the usual type," she repeated, gently.

I could only nod.

Then, "Did Dublin force you into this?"

Heart sputtering with dread, I thought it over. Had he, at any time during that venom-laced tirade about why I should just be a *'good girl'* and fall back to my fortune, insist that I do the opposite?

The answer horrified me. *No.*

I had done it. For some silly, intangible reason I would never fully understand, I had signed myself up for this.

As if her voice came from miles away, I heard the woman add, "If you were forced into this, he broke the rules, you know. Only the signer of the contract can determine the nature of the task necessary to fulfill the terms. You have a choice."

"A ...choice?"

She nodded.

No wonder Dublin had been so insistent on money. Apparently, I would have to foist my checkbook over *myself* —he couldn't just take it. Suddenly, my vision cleared. I could breathe again. Everything seemed sharper, and with a sense of grim determination, I stood.

"Are you all right?"

Cool fingers fell over my shoulder, but I politely shrugged the woman off and made my way toward that intimidating wardrobe once again. I tried to be detached and clinical as I eyed a teeny strip of black fabric that was apparently meant to be worn ...somewhere.

You're back in the hospital, I told myself, *and this is just some degrading gown.*

Fingers shaking, I grabbed a hanger at random and observed my selection in the dim lighting. It didn't seem so bad ...

If I squinted, I could almost pretend that the garment was a scarf—though I had no idea how this 'scarf' was supposed to cover my 'vital' parts.

Holding the garment to my chest, I crept before the mirror and watched my wide-eyed reflection play over the surface. Dublin's words echoed through my mind; *intelligence, cunning, beauty.* Only this time my subconscious added what even *he* had been too tactful to say out loud: *none of which you possess.*

For the first time in her life, little Ellie Gray was outside of the comfort and seclusion of luxury. I had never really thought as to what that might feel like—but this ...strange sense of *calm* wouldn't have been it.

I cleared my throat, addressing the woman. "Should I ... change now?"

She laughed. I got the sense that she found me wonderfully amusing but, unlike Dublin's, her reaction didn't make me feel ashamed.

"Yes," she said while gingerly prying the hanger from my hands. "But not into *that.*"

She stood back and observed me once again, only this time her emerald gaze cut me right to the bone.

"You are very different," she said finally. "Still beautiful ... just not in an obvious way."

I stared, enthralled, despite the logical part of me that wanted to scoff. *Ellie, beautiful? Ha!* Something in her tone made me suspect that she wasn't trying to be funny.

"Then, how?"

"Innocence," she said simply. "It shines from you—very subtle, yes—but no less enrapturing than physical beauty ...*more* so even." For a moment she drifted off, eyes staring into the distance. "Innocence is irresistible to those who have lost their own. Even a moth is drawn to the light, and we creatures of the dark are no different."

Creatures of the dark. The words affected me deeply, conjuring the memory of a dangerous question. *What am I, Eleanor?*

It was nearly a minute before the woman spoke again.

"Many of the girls who come here are one and the same," she went on. "For any of them, that clothing would be suitable, but for you? For *you* ...I will do something different."

I stared as she fingered the hem of her red dress. Then, all at once, she pulled it over her head and turned the garment inside-out.

"I'm Yulia, by the way," she explained, while running a hand along the dress' cream lining.

With a violent motion, she began to tear the two fabrics apart.

"I am the *stylist*."

In one hand she held a lone piece of silk that had made up the lining. The red remains of the actual dress, she merely allowed to fall to the floor. It didn't seem to bother her that she was left wearing only a plain black bra and underwear in front of a complete stranger. Unconcerned, she just hurried past me to spread the silky material out over a long table.

The light reflected off her eyes as she pulled open a drawer and withdrew a small case—a sewing kit, I saw, once she flipped it open. Her nimble fingers danced over spools of thread before settling over a neat line of glittering needles. Seemingly at random, she withdrew one and tested its sharpness over the pad of her thumb.

"Whether you are here by Dublin's will or *yours*—" As her eyes sought out mine from over her shoulder, I suspected that she knew damn well why I was here. "I will make the best of it. You will be just as tempting as any lovely face to those lurkers of the shadows, Eleanor," she promised. "You can bet on that."

Lurkers of the shadows …

"What is this place?" I croaked as Yulia set to work on the fabric. "W-What … What will happen tonight?"

She shrugged, though I couldn't help thinking that the motion seemed more ominous than even Dublin's warnings.

"You'll find out soon enough."

"Almost," Yulia insisted, as she tugged on a crooked hem one last time before finally stepping back. "Okay, you can look now."

I couldn't help the mournful sweep my eyes took over the thick, brown curls clumped on the floor as I prepared to face my reflection. *"This is necessary,"* Yulia had sworn before snipping a lock of my hair with a pair of scissors seemingly pulled from thin air. *"It is too long. Now you have nothing to hide those eyes behind."*

That was an understatement. When I finally confronted myself in the mirror, I was horrified to find that—after Yulia's impromptu haircut—I was left with a length that barely reached my chin.

Scandalous! Mother would shriek. In her opinion, only harlots and dreaded feminists kept their hair so short. Though, I had to admit that the cut did make my eyes seem larger—soul-sucking. If Yulia's goal was to make me resemble a freakish monster with enormous eyes, she certainly had succeeded.

It didn't help in any way that all I wore was the pale lining of her dress, hastily sewn into a simple, sleeveless shift. The garment had taken her mere minutes to complete, and yet could have hung in the stuffy boutiques my mother had frequented. The only obvious flaw was the fact that it was so short it barely covered my cotton underwear. Considering the white bottoms were *all* Yulia let me wear underneath it …

Well, *underdressed* wouldn't have been a strong enough word.

"I don't … I don't think that …"

"You look *perfect*," Yulia insisted while I blushed at the rosy bits of my body visible through the transparent fabric. "But don't take my word for it. As the broker of your contract, Dublin has the final say anyhow."

The thought of Dublin having any 'say' over me wasn't comforting in the least.

"Here."

Yulia turned her attention to the table and seized a tube of lipstick from the scattered objects. She swiped the waxy substance along my bottom lip, and then traced a careful line along both of my upper lashes with a stick of kohl.

The results weren't terribly dramatic; the red added a slight bit of color to my complexion, and my lashes looked a little thicker. I could barely meet my own gaze in the mirror, it seemed endless.

"One more thing," Yulia murmured, still not satisfied.

She headed to the wardrobe, pulled a small box from the top shelf and withdrew a silver hair comb. I stood still as she tucked it into my hair, securing back one lone curl. When she appraised me the second time, she nodded to herself just once.

"*This* is the final touch. You look like an angel tricked into hell."

That I believed. Glancing at my reflection, I was perfectly willing to believe that the woman staring back at me was an angel: a stupid, naïve, *foolish* angel who had merrily skipped through the gates of Hades without a thought as to what might happen to her.

"My, my, my—" I jumped, and turned to find the red-headed woman from before leaning against the doorway. *Saskia.* Her gaze drifted over me dismissively before settling on Yulia. "Are you finished?"

"Why?" In an instant, Yulia's friendly demeanor dissipated, and she seemed almost as icy as Dublin. "What do you want?"

"I have another for you—" Saskia snapped her fingers, and someone else staggered through the doorway. "One of *mine.*"

The stranger's gaze met mine just once before nervously flicking away again. She looked no older than I was, but she was pretty with big blue eyes and sun-kissed skin. Blonde hair hung down her shoulders, the length mine had been a few minutes before.

"Make her look presentable," Saskia ordered. "She starts tonight as well."

"Fine," Yulia snapped, but Saskia had already turned on her heel without a parting word.

Ice lingered in the air between them. Obviously, there was no love lost there.

"Pick something from the closet," Yulia told the blonde, flicking her fingers at the wardrobe. "I'll be with you in a moment. *You*—" Her piercing gaze returned to me. "Tell Dublin that I have finished with you. You can go."

She shooed me off, and I found myself unceremoniously ushered back into the hall on bare feet. Yulia had confiscated my heels, along with my clothes, muttering something about *should be burned* as she did so.

I tried to tell myself that the sheer shift was no less degrading than a hospital gown, though I mourned the loss of my hair more than anything else. I felt naked without a cape of curls to hide behind as I wandered the corridor in search of Dublin.

There was no one else in sight, but the air seemed heavy—electric. A prickling sense of unease raced through my skin.

Something's about to happen, my instincts warned. *Something not good for Ellie …*

"Is she ready?"

"I don't know. I haven't seen her—"

The voices seemed to come from the distant end of the hall. I headed toward them—but I had only gone a step before a cold grip encircled my arm.

"There you are." I found myself wrenched around so violently that I nearly staggered into the figure holding me captive. "Finally." Dublin's voice reached my ears before I glanced up to see his face, as well as the scowl forming there. "Yulia better have given you the clothing of a damn queen for it to take—"

Abruptly, he broke off. His eyes narrowed even more, raking over me once, twice. "She was supposed to make you somewhat decent," he growled. "But this … This will have to do for now. Come on."

He grabbed for me, and I struggled to keep up as he manhandled me in the direction he'd come from. In a matter of seconds, we were back in that mysterious lounge.

Only, there were other people there now.

A group of men was perched on the leather chaise, all wearing suits every bit as crisp as Dublin's. A woman, draped in shadow, stood along the back wall. More silent figures lurked at random intervals, watching as I was hauled across the room.

With every step I took, another hair at the nape of my neck stood on end.

Alone with Dublin, unease constantly lurked at the back of my mind. Whereas here, surrounded by strangers, I felt like a foolish doe who'd wandered into a den of wolves—though at least these predators had a sense of style.

The interior of the lounge was chic and utilitarian. The floors were polished to gleam, and reflected the dark colors of the walls like a pool of shadow. The few bits of furniture were placed strategically near the edges of the room, and angled toward the center to form a makeshift stage.

Gathered there for all to see, stood at least ten women, all wearing various versions of skimpy, black silk from Yulia's closet. A brunette wore a tight corset, while a sultry red-head dazzled in a sheer, lace number that left little to the imagination as to what waited underneath.

No one else was wearing white—and, ironically enough, I seemed to be the most conservatively dressed one there.

Not that anyone was looking at *me*.

For the first time, I noticed that the 'club' didn't resemble the posh places brimming with excitement that I had glimpsed in television shows or heard of from Georgie's tales. There was no bar; no DJ; no dance floor.

In fact, despite the elegance, the setting was almost bare in appearance, minimalistic.

Whatever the purpose of this building was, the women were obviously the main draw. Something told me that they were tethered to contracts, but—unlike me, with my coveted family name—they all used so-called 'natural' assets to fulfill their debts instead.

Intelligence, cunning, beauty.

"What happens now?" I asked as loud as I dared. "D-Do ... Do I need to go out there?"

Dublin made no effort to respond to me. I half-expected him to shove me out onto the center of the floor anyway, but he never did.

Desperate to give him a reason not to, I struggled to make myself small and insignificant, invisible. So much for that; eyes found me anyway, curiously peering at the underdressed fool in ivory silk, cowering at the heels of her master. Before I could die of mortification, the sound of two hands being clapped drew all eyes to the doorway.

Saskia strolled in a second later, trailed by the blonde woman who now wore only a sheer black blouse and lace shorts—apparently, Yulia had classified her as the 'usual' type. Head down, the latter slowly made her way to the center of the floor, allowing Saskia to take control of the room with all the gusto of an auctioneer.

"Welcome!" She smiled, seeming to drink in the collective attention—though, with that blazing hair and ivory skin, even I couldn't deny that it was warranted. "Here at Anemia, we strive to offer the best selection no matter your tastes, be them exotic, or ..." Her gaze cut directly to me. "*Plain.*"

Something told me that she wasn't referring to food, or drink, or some other harmless commodity. No ...

When she gestured to the women, they split off, as if on cue, to mingle with the silent visitors in the crowd.

"What's happening?" I whispered.

There seemed to be no 'cheating' going on. Nor any thievery, which only left ...

Dublin's reply was cold, spoken directly into my ear. "Watch."

I could *only* watch, entranced, as Saskia's blonde was cornered by a man near the back of the lounge. Leisurely, he took her hand, eyes trailing the length of her arm, and I wasn't sure why the sight struck me as so odd.

Her arm, I insisted to myself—not her breasts, or eyes, or whatever else a normal man would be interested in, all of which was on full display. But even from this distance, I could tell that he was focused solely on another part of her anatomy, one so strange that I found myself voicing it out loud in disbelief. "The veins ..."

A prickling sensation snaked its way through me. *This isn't right,* it insisted. But my mind was desperate to cling to any plausible explanation.

Because she's pale, I told myself, despite the healthy glow to her skin. *There's no other reason.*

As if to prove me correct, the man bowed his head as though he only meant to deliver a gentlemanly kiss to the inside of her wrist.

But then his mouth opened.

His upper lip pulled back from abnormally long canines.

And, as I watched on in horror, his teeth sank into her flesh.

~

I don't know if I screamed or even gasped—but the next second Dublin's hand was over my mouth, trapping any sound I might've made.

"Quiet, Eleanor," he hissed while dragging me into an overlooked corner. "This is the game that you wanted to play ..." My own words haunted me, as I watched sharp teeth pierce flesh and a pale throat work to swallow. There was no escaping it: a *real* man was drinking from a *real* girl's wrist, and ...

This was not a game.

This wasn't the reality I had pictured waiting beyond Gray Manor.

This ...was something else entirely.

"No!" Dublin growled as I tried to turn away. He seized my chin, forcing me to watch as drops of scarlet struck the polished floor. "*Drink* it all in."

I thought I might vomit. Terror flooded my veins. My pulse hammered against my eardrums, drowning out everything else. Though, to be fair, the blonde in question certainly didn't seem to mind the violation. Her head tipped back, red lips forming a perfect O-shape, while the breath left her lungs in a single gasp. As the man withdrew, licking traces of red from his lips, she swayed on her feet, eyes wide and unfocused.

But then, at his gentle prompting, she followed him down another shadowy hallway ...

All around, I could see various other 'meetings' playing out in much the same way. Each woman was approached by a pale figure, and then led into the shadows. It was a chilling sight, nearly silent, save for a few scattered gasps of shock and pain.

Oh, God. Suddenly, the massive room seemed miniscule, and I was drowning amid a sea of white faces. My heart quivered uselessly in my chest, too stunned to beat properly.

Red. Teeth. Red.

What the hell had I gotten myself into?

"Welcome to the darkness, Eleanor Gray," Dublin greeted against my ear. "A world where those of us without your precious family name dwell in shadow; this is the little game you wanted to play, was it not? So *play.*"

Only now, I wanted to pack up all my toys and go home. Fear guided my actions as I struggled against his grip. "No! Let go of me—"

"Oh, Dublin!"

Saskia's sensual purr made him freeze, nails nearly piercing my flesh as his grip on my arm tightened. Silence fell instantly, and I could tell from Saskia's satisfied smirk that that was just the way she liked it; all the better to capture the attention for herself.

"Isn't your new girl going to join us?" She gestured to me from across the room with a wave of her red-tipped fingers. "We have a client waiting."

Sure enough, the number of girls seemed to correlate with the number of 'visitors' present—all of whom had already found their own scantily-clad girl …minus one. A man partially hidden in shadow was the only one without someone to chow on and lead to a private room. I recognized those glittering eyes. *Mikhail.*

"She's not ready." Dublin's tone was iron, daring anyone to challenge him—though before they could, he turned and dragged me from the room, down the same corridor he had taken me to see Yulia.

Only now, he kept going, past the red dressing room and farther down, farther, farther. Without warning I found myself shoved into a windowless room with bare walls and a large bed dominating the center. Ominously silent, Dublin followed me inside.

The door closed, a lock clicked, and I was trapped. Any relief I may have felt after being rescued from the nightmare of the lounge dissipated as soon as Dublin uttered his next four words.

"Take off your clothes."

It wasn't a cutesy joke or a mocking taunt this time. I could read it in his voice.

He meant every terrifying word.

"*Now*, Eleanor."

I swayed, feeling in danger of doing something that my mother—with her aristocratic sensibilities—definitely wouldn't approve of—*faint*.

Only the desire to preserve what little dignity I had left forced me to stagger over to the bed. Once there, my knees buckled, depositing me onto the mattress with barely a *thump* to my name.

"*This* is how you wanted to repay your debt," Dublin reminded as he stalked forward with all the grace of a hunting wolf. "You seemed to have known exactly what this entailed when you so eagerly *stripped* for me before."

In a matter of seconds, he had swallowed the distance between us. Before I had the chance to react—run—cool hands pushed on my shoulders, hard. I fell back onto the mattress like a stone, sprawled out with him hovering above.

Right then it sank in: *intelligence …cunning …beauty.* There was only one way that women with 'natural' talents fulfilled their bargains.

I panicked.

When Dublin reached for me, I sucked in air, strained my lungs, and screamed louder than I ever have before. I kicked, scratched, bit the hand he tried to wrestle over my mouth to silence me—only, it wasn't until I heard the words echo back that I realized just what I had been shouting.

Monster! Freak! Devil!

I sounded like a bimbo in a horror movie. Shock and shame made me fall silent, and Dublin stood back, prepared to grab me if I decided to run.

"I *am* a monster, Eleanor," he declared.

His expression was fearsome. Two points of white flashed from beneath his upper lip, almost daring me to believe that for a second I was merely hallucinating.

"I am a monster, bound for hell …but if you recall, *you* were the one who hopped right into my mouth and prodded my teeth."

I flinched, resisting the urge to clamp my hands over my ears and chant until I couldn't hear him anymore.

But he was right; I had all but asked for this.

"If I am not up to your usual 'speed' of self-destruction, Eleanor, then I would be more than happy to go back into the showroom and find someone else willing to do the job for me," he suggested. "I hear that Mikhail has quite the reputation for being *rough* …"

I cringed at the thought of those hawkish eyes.

"You owe a debt," Dublin added, just to drill the point home. "A debt that must be repaid. You would have died without my blood."

It was the first time he had revealed that little snippet of information, but the sad part was that deep down I had already known it.

"I didn't ask for you to save me—"

Dublin whirled on me. With one hand, he seized my shoulder. The other went to my throat, fingers thrumming the pulse until my protests sputtered and died. All the while, his eyes bore mercilessly into my own.

"Oh, *yes* you did."

He seemed to wait for a shout or another scream, but when I remained silent, he finally withdrew and posed a challenge that made me shiver.

"So what will it be? *Me* ...or one of those men out there willing to take both your blood *and* your innocence?"

"You ...are ...the Devil," I rasped once I found my voice again.

No other insult fit. He *was* the Devil, frighteningly detached, even while he offered what he claimed to be a reprieve.

"I am," he agreed, cold eyes staring me down. "Though even the Devil can show mercy; accept my first offer, Eleanor, and this nightmare ends here. This is your *last* chance."

Within his tirade lingered a truth I didn't want to face; I could have given in and merrily fallen back on my checkbook. I *should* have, but …

Some childish impulse wouldn't let me, the same one that had driven me to accept his contract in the first place.

I am more than just Eleanor Gray …

"Fine," Dublin snarled when I remained frozen beneath him.

Aggravation leaked from his every pore as he looked over my trembling form in disgust. Then, with one firm yank on the hem, he tore Yulia's shift from my body and tossed it to the floor.

"Trust me," he insisted with a scowl as every muscle in my body tensed. "This disgusts no one more than it does *me*."

The seconds passed, painfully slow, as cold air assaulted my bare skin.

When I didn't try to run, Dublin glowered as if being here was one step above being burned alive at the stake. Then, with a resigned sigh, his eyes met mine.

"Touch yourself."

Those two words sucked all the air from the room.

I wasn't so naïve as to think he meant 'touch' as in the innocent *Simon Says* version of eyes, nose, head, and ears.

No, he meant …

Somehow, I still managed to find just enough breath to choke out, "W-why?"

His response was scathing. "You claim to be a virgin, correct? Well, if you don't want the *deflowering*," he said, actually making air quotes, "to hurt unnecessarily, then I suggest you take the standard *precautions*."

My cheeks flamed. In the end, I could only croak, "I-I don't know how."

"Drop the cowering prude act," Dublin snapped. "This isn't the place for modesty, and considering your nonexistent relationships with men, I'm sure you've *mastered* the art form."

He waited, but my expression must have revealed that I was *not* stalling for modesty's sake.

Only strictly professional physicians had ever touched me *there*, with prodding instruments and rubber gloves.

Hell, I didn't even look at myself when I put on underwear. Sex, according to Mother, was purely a means for producing heirs to the family fortune—a duty falling solely on Georgie's shoulders, now that I was dying.

Besides, who was I kidding?

Spinsterhood would've been my destination anyway.

"You can't be serious." From Dublin's expression, one might think I'd declared I was the Queen of England and that I liked to run naked through the halls of Buckingham Palace. "Oh, for the love of—"

He sighed, and the mattress creaked beneath his weight as he moved.

"Don't make this any more *difficult* than it needs to be," he warned as his hand slid between my legs, ruthlessly forcing them apart.

I couldn't resist the impulse to lock my knees together, even though I knew it was futile. Taking a thigh in each hand, Dublin easily spread them wider and muscled his way in between.

He was so large. Harper, who towered over me, had never made me feel so small and insignificant. I didn't think I had ever been so close to another living being—not to mention so exposed.

I shivered beneath him, though I suspected that the reaction had less to do with the chill emanating from his body and more to do with *him*. Our pelvises nearly connected as he drew back on his knees, taking me in with one, dismissive sweep of his gaze.

Without warning, he reached down to finger the elastic band of my panties, and every cell in my body tightened.

"W-wait!"

It was the first time someone had touched me without the excuse of a strict medical curiosity. *Ever.*

At my reaction, Dublin simply rolled his eyes and reached for my wrist.

I shook my head, but he peeled back the elastic of my panties with two fingers and forced my own hand beneath the cotton.

Stop, stop, stop, I chanted to myself, heart in my throat, as he pressed my fingers against the mound that I had never been brave enough to explore on my own. I cringed at the feel of coarse curls, skin …*dampness.*

I had no idea what to expect, but warmth, paired with the expert precision of Dublin's fingers steering my own was not it. He guided my touch into a clumsy, awkward rhythm against that intimidating mound, over and over. It shouldn't have been enough to coax a reaction from me—fear alone should have overridden everything else. But …

With every hesitant caress, a tiny knot inside me began to tighten. Nerve endings I didn't even know existed sleepily stirred to life. I couldn't deny it; those humiliating gynecological exams had felt nothing like this.

This is disgusting, I insisted mournfully to myself.

It certainly felt disgusting …much the same way that sneaking down to the kitchen and eating a chocolate cake out of the fridge at midnight felt *disgusting.* That stuffing yourself with honey-glazed donuts kind of disgusting—the aching, guilty sort of pleasure that made you hate yourself.

Lying beneath Dublin, mind a whirl, I absolutely hated myself for the way my legs fell further apart.

He was relentless in his ministrations—just light teasing, circles over and over and *over.* If I hesitated, he simply increased the pace, deepening the contact until my traitorous body flooded with the conflicting sensations.

Ice collided with fire in a chaotic whirlwind of *left, right, up, down, round and round* until my mind seemed to scream silent commands I could never voice out loud: *deeper, harder, more, more, more ...*

I was dizzy by the time he finally released my wrist and batted my fingers aside. One cold hand seized my waist, pinning me down, while the other began to tug my underwear down my legs.

I whimpered out a protest, too lightheaded to find real words. He was too heavy to resist and broad legs as hard as stone kept me from being able to fully close mine.

"*Really,* Eleanor," he spat, yanking at my panties until they cleanly tore away. "This doesn't have to be a case of the 'big bad monster brutally taking the innocent virgin.' You have the power to end this debacle now; all you need to do is say the word, and I'll allow you to fetch your checkbook and spare us both the trouble."

He sounded unbelievably annoyed. As if I should have been *thanking* him for allowing me the easy way out.

Again, when I made no move to leave, he hissed an irritated sigh, "Fine ...then lie still."

Biting my lip until I saw stars, I made myself stiff. Frozen. Dead.

No! The prude in me wailed, *this isn't happening ...*

But squeezing my eyes shut didn't make Dublin disappear. My Devil lingered, determined to carry out his strange mission to corrupt me—and for some insane, crazy reason, I couldn't find the voice to tell him to stop.

He was so cold without the warmth of my hand as a buffer. I flinched away from his touch instinctively, but then his forefinger came in a light, swift motion before the chill became too much.

Sparks shot up and down my spine. As if from far away, I heard myself gasp, but I couldn't slap a hand over my mouth in time to smother it.

The sound seemed to be all the encouragement Dublin needed, because his hand stilled. Then, one long finger curved, slipping through the heavy folds …

My entire body stiffened at the intrusion. I shouted, hands flying up to rain down blows over his shoulders, as I cursed him to hell and back.

Nothing fazed him. He was painfully solid, as if carved from granite, right down to the fingernails.

Ignoring my protests, he began to move, thrusting that single digit in, out, and around …harder each time until heat blossomed and swelled.

I tried to twist out of reach, but he was too strong, anchoring me in place, and I had no choice but to suffer every jolting sensation.

"Your clients won't take the time to do this beforehand," I heard him mutter, while that finger twisted, to rub against the inner parts of me. "So I suggest you take *notes* …"

Oh. My body went rigid, nails clutching the bed sheets. I gasped again.

This was horrifying, debasing, violating and …incredible.

Muscles I didn't even know I *had* sprung to life as they were stretched to the brink. Nerve endings flared and popped. Sizzled. Through it all, he kept moving; in and out—faster—until that odd heat continued to grow, surging through my skin.

Fire. Ice. Fire. Ice.

I was trapped in-between two polar opposites.

Suddenly Dublin pulled back. Was that a good thing? Or bad? I couldn't really remember …

I frowned in confusion at a ripping sound, before I realized just what it was; a zipper being undone.

His hand left my waist as he removed his pants one-handed, revealing muscled thighs that made me quiver at the thought of them pressed against me. Despite everything, I was struck by how beautiful he was up close—perfect—like a statue carved of ivory marble.

Who seemed to think that it was his grim 'chore' to 'deflower' me.

His eyes flashed in warning when I unwittingly flinched in anticipation of what was about to come. His hand was on my shoulder before I could even think to move, holding me down as his body settled over mine.

"It's like a Band-Aid, Eleanor," I heard him growl somewhere above me. "It's better if you don't draw it out."

I could feel something cold and firm nudge that little cleft between my legs—God, was his entire body made of steel? I didn't even get the chance to scream or even mourn my threatened virginity. With one single thrust, he entered me —hard. The pain was sharp, like the shock that came from accidentally cutting your thumb with a knife. Deep inside, tender flesh burned as my body struggled to accept him. I shrieked, but the sound was swallowed by the mattress squeaking beneath the sudden shift in weight.

Forget all those little romantic notions about fireworks and 'connection' and perfection—whatever nonsense romance novels proclaimed—this *hurt*.

He gave me no time to adjust before he moved in a series of hard, sharp jabs that pushed me deeper into the mattress.

Oh, God, oh God!

I squeezed my eyes shut and laid there, forcing down a scream with every thrust.

Like a Band-Aid, I told myself, *a painful, enormous, 'deflowering' Band-Aid*. Dublin was massive, and I was splitting apart at the seams.

I waited for it to be over but, as if reading my mind, he only quickened his pace, swiveling his hips, pounding deeper, harder, *faster, faster,* driving my body to its breaking point.

I could hear the sharp sounds of skin hitting skin; my own labored pants; the violent creaking of the bed. Pain loomed overhead, urging me to scream. Run. *Something!*

But beneath it all …was something else; this tiny ball of heat that coiled with every thrust. Tighter. Harder. My entire body seemed to focus on this one building sensation, distracting me—even from the fear—until …

Every single thought blurred. I couldn't speak. I couldn't breathe. My only conscious action was to grab hold of the bed frame and cling to it.

With each stroke, the knot in my belly tightened. Colors melded together. Senses sharpened.

Guilt or shame suddenly didn't matter anymore.

I was spiraling and I … I wanted more. *Don't,* I told myself even as my hips arched into him, body flexing against the mattress.

Above me, Dublin slowed his assault, eyes so dark they swallowed the shadows. Then he shifted, striking brutally in one long stroke.

A groan tore from my lips, and my back bowed, driving him even further.

He froze, gaze darkening into a color so black it seemed endless.

Eventually, he began to thrust again, violently, deep, deep, *deeper.* He was cruel, holding nothing back.

I was baking—burning alive—and he was dousing me with gasoline.

It was too much.

I couldn't … Something was … I needed …

Abruptly, he twisted, sparking a friction that had my head rolling back, eyes flickering beneath heavy eyelids.

Yes.

I broke apart.

My mouth flew open, but nothing came out. Every nerve prickled, sparked, exploded.

Ellie Gray was gone—everything was just a collage of colors.

I was flying, falling, tumbling out of control.

For a minute, I was afraid that I would never be myself again—just a mess of disjointed emotions and fragile thoughts.

Then …it was over.

I couldn't see as Dublin rolled from on top of me. I felt breathless and lazy and weak, but when my vision finally cleared, he was gone …

And I was alone.

BRACELETS

"**Y**ou have to forgive me; we're not used to serving breakfast."

I groaned as the voice pulled me from a heavy sleep. I peeled my eyes open, expecting to find the violet walls of my bedroom and a grumbling servant trying to rip the sheets out from under me.

Instead, I found a dark-haired woman holding a glass of wine beneath my nose. Or at least …I hoped it was wine. Suddenly, all red liquids seemed suspicious.

"I did the best with what I could find," she added, gesturing toward the tray someone had set on the bed. Her green eyes were familiar, and a name sprung to mind on a wave of dark memories. *Yulia.*

At her prompting, I glanced down at the tray. On it was a crisp package of crackers, a stick of celery and a piece of mint gum.

"The wine is unconventional, I know," Yulia admitted, swirling the liquid around with a tilt of her wrist. "But, we don't stock orange juice, and I thought you might appreciate this a little more, anyway."

She was right. Still groggy, I grabbed the glass and drained it while she watched. It was sweeter than even my father's old vintage, but I barely registered the taste.

I just wished it had been hard liquor instead.

I was sore in places I didn't even know *could* be sore. I was exhausted, drained beyond belief—but all of that could have been bearable if it wasn't for the underlying sense of satisfaction that was so heavy it felt surreal.

And shame, there was plenty of that too. *Both* made it impossible to ignore what I desperately wanted to. *Don't*, I told myself as I wrestled my body upright against a mound of pillows. *Don't go there.* Too late.

I, Eleanor Gray, was no longer a virgin. Even worse—the man who had done the deed of removing said virginity had done so under the duress of a silly contract.

Also, a part of me added, almost on a bored note, *he had fangs.*

I was pretty sure by now that he had fangs.

"Dublin told me that he gave you your dose last night?" Yulia inquired while scanning my arms as if looking for a bandage or a hint of an injection spot.

I flinched at the sound of *his* name before I even processed the meaning of her question. *Dose?* I shook my head.

"Hmph." Yulia shrugged. "It must have been while you were sleeping."

The thought was terrifying. *Almost* as terrifying as it was to look down and realize that I was neatly tucked beneath the blankets—not sprawled out on a pile of crumpled gray sheets. I didn't dare think that Dublin would take the care, meaning that someone else must have tucked the covers over my naked body.

"So ..." I glanced up to find Yulia watching me intently. "How do you feel?"

Going off her expression, I suspected that she wasn't asking out of politeness. God, did the whole world know? I had a vision of Dublin sulking around the lounge, complaining to anyone who would listen about the *'dreadful deflowering.'* Still, Yulia seemed genuinely concerned, so I bit my bottom lip and mentally assessed my throbbing limbs.

With every movement I winced, as an ache unfurled deep inside; the result of muscles being pushed beyond their limits. The sensation felt no more uncomfortable than I would have expected after a strenuous run or vigorous exercise. I could feel the beginnings of bruises taking shape over my waist, but I figured that had more to do with how hard Dublin had held me down, rather than any deliberate infliction of abuse on his part.

"Fine."

Aside from the physical pain, most of my suffering came purely from damaged pride, and my psyche was more than willing to nail that point home. *You stupid, spoiled cow! Idiot! Next time, just write the damn check!*

"Ah ..." Yulia nodded and her mouth opened as if she meant to say something. Then she seemed to think better of it, and the red lips closed again.

"Why are you here?" I wondered after a moment. "I-I mean ...you didn't have to help me."

I would have thought that Dublin would have wanted me to stew in my shame alone just to reinforce the fact that I should have accepted his first offer.

"Why not?" Yulia countered. Her tone seemed harmless enough, but I couldn't shake the feeling that she had evaded the question on purpose.

Though why did it matter either way? At least her company kept me from focusing too much on myself.

I turned my attention to her 'breakfast' and grabbed the celery stick at random, desperate to use the pretense of eating as an excuse to keep my mouth shut. I could sense Yulia watching as my eyes scanned the room.

It was plain. The only light came from a silver light fixture hanging from the ceiling—unsurprisingly it was in the shape of a serpent. There were no windows, so I couldn't tell if it was day or night. There wasn't any furniture other than the bed. Hell, it could have been a simple bedroom at Gray

Manor if the bed frame wasn't sleek metal instead of antique wood.

"Eleanor." Yulia's tone made me stiffen. "You can talk to me, about anything. Anything at all. I'm here."

I had a feeling that she wasn't referring to the typical girl talk.

"There is something," I began warily.

Several *somethings* to be exact—but one sordid little image in my mind was stuck on replay, and no matter how hard I tried, logic couldn't explain it away.

"What?"

"I saw …"

Goodness, how could I even say it? I cleared my throat and tried to find the words. "I saw someone b-bitten last night."

Not only that, but I was starting to suspect that pale skin and piercing eyes weren't just odd physical features that pretty much *everyone* in this building shared out of coincidence.

What am I, Eleanor? Dublin had asked. *I want to hear you say it.*

Rather than rush me to the insane asylum, Yulia simply rolled her eyes. "I knew that bastard wouldn't tell you himself," she scoffed. "He's much too fond of theatrics."

"T-theatrics?"

I had to disagree. Judging from the way he had acted as though my screams were poisonous acid dripped directly onto his eardrums, I was willing to go so far as to say that Dublin Helos was *definitely* not the 'theatrical' sort.

"He gets a kick out of watching people discover the truth on their own," Yulia explained with an exasperated sigh. "It makes him feel all *'mighty Devil, collector of souls.'* He can be quite an ass if you haven't guessed."

I choked on a bite of celery. While I sputtered, Yulia perched herself on the edge of the bed and gingerly patted my shoulder. Her warmth was a shock. I couldn't remember if I had even noticed it before, but in the wake of Dublin's icy chill, her heat hit me like a thousand degrees.

Nearly a full minute passed before I gathered the nerve to ask another question. "Are you a …"

What? Say it, Ellie, demanded Dublin's crisp tones. *Say it out loud—admit it!*

Yulia's laugh snapped me out of the waking nightmare. "No. I'm …different."

'Different,' other than fangs and blood? The look in her eyes warned me not to even ask. *You're not ready.*

I was too shocked to find the words anyway. Too many things swirled through my mind: fangs, pale skin, and a strange affinity for maniacal laughter …

It all added up to one horrible, impossible conclusion.

Say it, Ellie, my consciousness taunted. *Say it!*

"Saskia," I heard myself croak instead. "Is she?"

Yulia shook her head. "No. Most—" She seemed to pick on the way my entire body tensed—waiting for her to voice what I was too chicken to. In the end, she just allowed 'most' to linger on the air. "They don't tend to frequent the Den unless they need to feed. Mikhail is our overseer; however, Saskia manages most of the contracts. Dublin used to oversee our operations, but this is the first time in years that he's stayed longer than a few minutes."

Years? Interesting. Had I—with all my insistence on being 'just like everyone else'—pushed dear old Dublin out of a retirement of some sort? A part of me was almost gleeful at the prospect. At least until Yulia frowned.

"Speaking of Dublin …"

I stared as she moved to the foot of the bed. There, she reached down and lifted something from the floor. It was a slender box, I saw, as she placed it flat on the mattress and pulled off the lid.

Inside … At first, I wanted to believe that they were merely bracelets, two delicate, slender *bracelets* that just so happened to have been connected by a silver chain.

But one didn't need a key to unlock 'bracelets.'

"Dublin's orders," Yulia said, fingering a link of one cuff. "He wants you to get used to wearing them. Some of our clients have …certain fetishes."

I gulped, unwilling to even consider what type of person might request that someone else wear handcuffs—let alone pay for the privilege.

You got yourself into this, Ellie; you're the one who wanted to repay a debt based on your own 'merits.'

"Wear them?" My voice was a hoarse whisper. "How?"

Yulia's pointed glance at the headboard was all the explanation I needed.

"Oh God."

Suddenly, I felt pathetically small, huddled beneath the sheets while a woman beautiful enough to have stepped out of a fairytale told me that the monster in charge of my fate had requested that I wear chains- just to practice.

"It's customary for all of the girls," Yulia insisted, as if that made it any better. "Would you like to bathe first?" I nodded, wishing I still had a curtain of hair to hide the way I blushed once I realized that I was still naked. "I'll get you a robe."

Yulia left and returned a moment later with a garment made of black silk. I pulled it on only to realize that—despite reaching down to my ankles—it was no less revealing that my tiny white shift. Unwilling to ask for another one, I stood and silently followed Yulia down the hall and into a wide bathroom.

Like everything else in the building, the layout was sleek and impeccably modern. The floors were black marble, and the tub looked big enough to swim in. Yulia left me there with an apologetic frown and advice to use the violet-scented soap beneath the sink.

"It soothes the skin."

I didn't dawdle or waste time by soaking. Nor did I allow myself to enjoy the sensation of warm water rushing over my skin. Instead, I grabbed a clean rag from a cupboard along the wall and set about attacking my throbbing limbs with an almost clinical precision.

Bruised hips. Sore thighs. Oh, was that blood streaking the washcloth in a single rust-colored stain as I dragged it between my thighs?

No worrying, Ellie, old girl, I told myself. *Stiff upper lip. Don't think about it. Just focus on the task at hand.*

I finished up quickly and threw my robe back on without even bothering to dry off.

Yulia was in the bedroom, waiting for me. Without her even having to say a word, I moved toward the bed and sat down, close to the headboard, but still far enough away to …

God, what should I do? Lie down? Sit up? Funny, I had never had to contemplate my comfort while wearing handcuffs before.

I stiffened when Yulia approached, but she only grabbed the box and slid the chains from their perch of black velvet. Her fingers lifted my left wrist and seconds later I heard a *'clink!'*

I couldn't look. The weight of the metal was oppressive, but not as uncomfortable as I might have imagined. I still had room enough so that the cuff merely felt like a bracelet—at least until I tried moving my arm farther than a few inches from the headboard.

"He wants you to wear both until he returns," Yulia explained. I looked up to find her twirling a second set around her finger. "But I shall only attach one pair for now. *He* can place the other."

She promptly allowed the other set to fall back into the box.

It blew my mind how she seemed to respect Dublin's words and still thwart him at the same time, first, with my styling and now with the chains. The tiny acts of sabotage reminded me of a sister, humoring an older brother but still determined to keep him in his place.

"It's strange," she said. "You're the first girl Dublin's brought in years. Many of the ones already here belong to *Saskia*." Her tone made it clear what she thought about that. "I thought he was done with this part of the trade."

"The trade?" Apparently, collecting contracts based on the suffering of others was some kind of fulfilling career.

"Contracts," Yulia amended. "I assume that he's been negotiating other bargains, rather than the club recently."

Other bargains. I recalled the deal with the sick girl's father. Were simple business deals Dublin's preferred method of repayment after all?

"I'm surprised that he's brought you here," Yulia admitted, as if following the same train of thought.

I didn't have the heart to tell her that the only reason I was here was because I was a fool, too stubborn to let herself be used for her name and money like any proper heiress.

"He was furious with how I dressed you, by the way," she added, though she almost seemed amused by the thought. "He said that I made you look like a child, that you were unappealing, and that you are *never to wear white again.*" She frowned, mocking Dublin's crisp tones.

I felt my cheeks flame with mortification, though I doubted that I would have been any more 'appealing' in one of those tiny, black ensembles.

"I don't think I've ever seen him quite that furious," Yulia declared without a hint of regret. "So do you know what I did?"

She stood and moved to the door, but at the threshold, she glanced back over her shoulder, green eyes blazing.

"I bought yards of ivory silk. And *lace.*"

~

The next person to enter the room came what seemed like hours later and carried another tray, stocked with real food this time. The fare consisted only of a sandwich, a soda and another pack of crackers, but tucked beneath it all was a handwritten note: *He comes at midnight —Yul.*

Midnight.

The realization made my stomach churn, considering that I didn't even know how long I had to contemplate my fate.

There was no clock in the room, and the girl who'd brought the food had left without even a backward glance in my direction. I felt like a twisted Cinderella, doomed the moment the clock struck twelve.

Or, in a more morbid tone, a helpless Red Riding Hood tethered for the wolf's arrival.

Dublin. Even thinking of his *name* unwittingly conjured images of last night. I didn't want to think about them. I sure as hell didn't want to relive them—but they were still there, haunting me until I couldn't escape the memory of *it.*

Desperate, I attempted to distract myself with thoughts of hatred instead. It was easier to loathe him; despise him; curse him to hell.

Huddled against the headboard, I entertained myself with all kinds of lovely visions of revenge; Dublin, roasting on a fiery spit, prodded by eager demons armed with numerous pointy objects; Dublin, imprisoned by his own damn chains on the Gray property for my amusement.

Wait …

That last thought didn't seem quite as devious as I meant it to be. In fact, the image of Dublin, smirking even while manacled, didn't seem to affect his dream self nearly as much as it did *me*. My skin grew warm at the thought, though I had no idea why, or why something in me trembled at the prospect of ever holding that kind of power over him ...

Perhaps because, even while chained, he still would have been able to *speak*.

'Do you have it in you, Eleanor?' The fantasy Dublin wondered. *'Do you have what it takes to play games with the Devil?'*

Suddenly, the knob on the door twitched. A second later it opened, allowing in a gust of cool air that had me shivering beneath my thin robe. And then—at what I guessed was midnight on the dot—the source of my torment finally strolled in.

LESSONS

$\mathcal{H}$e stood there, my Devil dressed in black, and just watched me, waiting.

For the dramatics, I guessed, for me to shriek and scream, and curse him to hell.

I wanted to—o*h God*, how I wanted to—but like a true stoic Gray, I attempted to squash all emotion and face him head-on. '*Decorum,*' Mother used to sniff whenever my shoulders slouched even an inch out of perfect alignment.

Decorum.

"You're awake," Dublin remarked, chasing the ghostly admonition away. His tone radiated anger, but was oddly polite at the same time.

I wondered why. Perhaps the sight of me in chains put him in a good mood?

When I didn't answer, he took a step closer, and I ruined my brave façade by jerking back against the headboard.

"Did Yulia explain what is to be expected of you?"

"E-expected? There's more?"

Being chained and half-naked wasn't enough?

Dublin glowered for a long moment before launching into a speech with all the gusto of a stuffy professor: *Welcome to Sex Education 101, the bondage edition.*

"For the next two days, you will continue to learn how our 'employees' entertain their clients. The day after—" coincidentally, my fourth and last day indebted to him "—you will take a client of your own."

"Why?" I blurted stupidly. "I thought—"

"Must we go over this again?" His irises darkened around fathomless pupils. "You owe a *debt*, Eleanor. Unless you've changed your mind on how to *repay* it …" He paused, as if waiting for me to jump at the chance to do just that by lunging for my checkbook. When I didn't, his brow furrowed even more. "Then, these are the terms of your contract."

"But …why another client?" I asked after a dry swallow. "Wasn't last night payment enough—"

"I was not your client," he said harshly. "And last night was merely a convenience on *your* part, trust me on that."

Convenience. He made it sound as if my virginity had been something icky he'd disposed of and I should have been *thanking* him for it.

"Why?" I asked even though his expression warned me not to. "Why you?"

"You will take a real client in two days," he said, ignoring my question altogether. "While it's practically no time at all to prepare …you should still be somewhat ready."

Left with no choice—other than to resort to my fortune—I sat there, mulling it over as detachedly as I could.

Two days of instruction.

One day of application.

No mistakes …

I felt like a student back in University.

"And until then?" I couldn't even look in his direction, so I allowed myself to inspect the silver cuff encircling my wrist for the first time instead. There was no keyhole, just a seamless strip of metal.

How on earth would he take them off?

"Until then, you will continue your *training,*" Dublin said, snapping my attention back to him. "With me."

By some miracle, I managed to keep my expression blank. What kinds of 'training' could one learn in two days at the instruction of Dublin Helos? I had a sinking suspicion that chains were only the beginning.

"In what?"

Dublin shrugged, but there was nothing casual about the motion—tension leaked from him so thick that I could almost smell it; electric.

"Take a wild guess," he suggested. "After last night, I'm sure your mind is running rampant with possibilities."

That was an understatement. At the memory of blood and teeth, my heart sank through my body and flopped out through my toes.

I wanted to protest, to tell him to go to hell, that a true Gray didn't belong here, etcetera, etcetera.

But I knew that any display of fear on my part would cause him to revert back to that damn 'first' offer—and somehow the thought of being written off so easily seemed more unbearable than any horrors this club might hold. I had come this far. Three days should have been nothing compared to what fate had in store for me.

According to my diagnosis, I was already dead.

You're insane, Ellie, a part of me whispered as my nails dug into my palms, but it wasn't loud enough to make me demand he let me go. Yet. "So, would I have to ..."

"Tonight," Dublin began in a tone of steel without giving me the chance to finish, "I expect no less from you than I would from any other girl here."

His scowl proclaimed what he didn't bother saying out loud: *As much as anyone can expect from you.*

"And what would that be?" I rasped once I found the nerve to speak again.

"There are *standards* we follow here," he said, words raining down like blows. "We'll start simple. Your first lesson is *respect*. Do you understand?"

He deliberately paused.

"Yes," I croaked.

"Yes, what?"

I stiffened. What more could he possibly want me to say? *Oh yes, my Devil—beholder of my immortal soul?*

Then it clicked. Oh good Lord, he couldn't possibly mean … Resisting the urge to roll my eyes, I said it anyway, fingers clenching into fists.

"Yes …*Sir.*"

He didn't acknowledge the title. Instead, his gaze finally honed in on my unbound wrist, and his entire body went rigid.

"Yulia," he hissed, while marching to the foot of the bed where he snatched the spare set of cuffs from the box. Without another word, he grabbed my free arm, forcing me to lie down on my back or risk having the limb pulled right from its socket.

"Your second lesson," he growled while snapping the manacle in place, "will be obedience. We'll start simple; spread your legs, Eleanor."

My eyes widened. "B-But …you said—"

"You've failed already," Dublin announced, voice flat. "Let's hope your *bank account* is more reliable than its owner …"

He started to reach for the other cuff, but something made me speak out. "W-wait!"

He paused, hand outstretched, and I could feel my skin burn with shame as I slowly forced my legs apart.

The fabric of my borrowed robe was thinner than tissue paper, and Yulia hadn't left me with either a bra or underwear to wear underneath. I didn't want to guess how much of me he saw from his position.

Though, I might have felt more ashamed if he didn't look so *bored.*

"Good."

He sank onto the mattress and slid a hand beneath my calf. Every nerve stalled beneath his touch as he lifted the leg and forcefully flexed it at the knee.

"You do have smooth skin," he admitted as an icy finger traced the inside of my thigh, brushing tendons, veins … "At least that's *something.*"

My mind spun as he let me go and reached beyond my head to undo one cuff with a subtle *click.* Rather than command me to leave, he launched right into another 'lesson.'

"Let's review." As he spoke, he grabbed for my hand and dragged it down to my side. "Show me what you learned yesterday."

What I learned? My mind churned with images; *him, fingers, blinding heat.*

"W-why?"

"I told you once that this isn't the place for modesty," he warned, before pressing my hand to the apex of my thighs regardless of my protests.

I whimpered at the back of my throat, but was too breathless to fight him. Instead, I tried to look at it clinically.

This isn't your hand, I told myself as Dublin curled my fingers within his and pressed them to that intimidating mound of curls. *It's just a doctor's instrument ...one currently being shoved up your—*

I winced as Dublin forced a finger inside me. It didn't feel quite as painful as it had yesterday, more sore, but the sensation was unwelcome none-the-less.

Or so I tried to tell myself. I stiffened as once again he began to move that icy digit in and out ...

Out and in.

My cheeks burned with shame at my body's reaction. That odd heat returned, flooding through my belly, my veins ...

"I told you," Dublin grated against my ear, sounding miles away. "Your clients won't take the time to check whether you're ready or not and we don't stock *lubricant*—" He made it sound like a dirty word. "So, I suggest you take notes."

On *"notes"* he slid that probing finger in a deep, slow circle that made my eyes flutter.

Holy ...

Without warning, Dublin withdrew his hand and nudged my own fingers in its place.

"Show me," he commanded.

My eyes slid shut with a reluctant groan. I felt like a child again, forced into a horrendous confection of lace and velvet, and ordered to sing a warbling, off-key version of *'Silent Night'* for the stuffy investors at my parent's dinner parties. Dublin's expression was the same as theirs had been; cold, impassive, and indifferent.

But in all those horrible, pitchy memories, I couldn't remember ever feeling as mortified as I did now, with him sneering down at me while I ...

I squashed the thought and gave my head a firm shake. I could tell that he was only pushing the topic because he knew it embarrassed me.

He wanted me to give up.

Give in, and accept his first offer like a good, dutiful girl.

I refused to give him the satisfaction—it was *my* body, after all.

Right?

"No," I whispered, sounding stronger than I'd expected.

"No, what?" I could almost hear the triumph in his voice as he pictured me reaching for my checkbook in defeat.

I took a deep breath to steel my nerves and forced my eyes open to stare into his. It was a mistake; his gaze was endless, and I was drowning in it.

Miraculously, I managed to slide a trembling finger down that intimidating path of curls without collapsing into a puddle of shame.

I stiffened at the contact. It was nothing like when Dublin touched me, but it wasn't a *bad* feeling per se. That searing heat flared sleepily in response, and I pressed a little harder-while he watched.

His eyes were narrowed into slits, and I was reminded of a stern teacher, just waiting for the moment he would have to discipline a misbehaving student. However, when the seconds passed without him saying anything …I guessed that I was doing it right.

I bit my bottom lip and carefully applied a bit more pressure. I gasped. The sensation of warmth that surged in response caught me off guard.

It was pleasure, *I thought.* Deep inside my belly, I felt a familiar knot begin to tighten.

"It's not going to bite you, Eleanor," Dublin murmured, not satisfied. Bold and sure, his hand slid down to cup my own, forcing a deeper contact. "Shall I give you a quick lesson in anatomy? This …" His thumb slid up, striking a bundle of flesh that made every ounce of air leave my lungs. "Is your clitoris. I suggest you remember it. Trust me; no one wants to spend good money on a prude."

Good money. God, he made this whole thing sound like prostitution.

Duh, a part of me hissed. *What did you think this was?*

My heart faltered as Dublin's thumb drifted away from my clitoris and traveled lower. I wanted to run screaming from the room, butt naked and dripping with blood. No sooner had I thought about escape than I felt Dublin's fingers curve, replacing my own and suddenly I couldn't think of anything anymore.

A million conflicting sensations assaulted me all at once: *Heat. Hot. Hotter. Searing.*

God, I was burning alive. My hips arched, aching to feel the relief of his icy touch, but it was only when I heard him laugh that I realized what I'd done.

"At least you're not screaming," he said, and I doubted the real Devil himself could have sounded more menacing. "You learn quickly …but not quickly enough."

His hand returned to my thigh, creeping over my knee.

"Can you tell me what happens next, Eleanor?"

It was a dangerous question, made all the more ominous by his tone.

"Don't feign ignorance," he added. "I know Yulia told you some glimmer of the truth. Let's see how smart you are; put two and two together. What happens next?"

I shook my head, even though a grim idea was beginning to unfold in my mind anyway. *Nibble, nibble, Ellie. Those teeth aren't just for show.*

Yulia's words chose that second to run through my mind, seeming to reinforce what I was too terrified to comprehend: *Most only come to the Den to feed.*

"Take a wild guess," Dublin urged. One nail deliberately teased my skin. *Tap. Tap. Caress.* "I want to hear whatever dark, little fantasy is making your heart beat so quickly."

I squeezed my eyes shut, but a fearful guess slipped out anyway.

"Are … Are you going to b-bite me—"

"Are you going to bite me, *what?*"

His tone would haunt my nightmares for the remainder of my foolish days; so very smug, sinister. I could scarcely find the nerve to answer him.

"Are you going to b-bite me, *Sir?*"

I didn't dare open my eyes, but his finger never ceased tracing patterns over my skin. Just light, dangerous little circles, over and over …

"Again," he commanded in a voice so deep that it vibrated in my bones. "Say it again."

"Are you going to bite—*ah*!"

Pain jolted through my body, and I shrieked, eyes flying open.

My first thought was that he'd pinched me, finally sinking that nail into my skin, but no … Somewhere during the course of a few seconds, he had moved, and his *mouth* was affixed to the curve in my knee rather than his hand. His throat jerked to swallow, and blood dripped down to dot the bed. I tried to scream. I wanted to …

But just as my mouth opened, sensation flooded my body, and I couldn't do anything but *breathe.* It wasn't painful, like I would have imagined. Instead warmth seared through my veins, traveling right down to my bones; sharp, piercing. It felt …*indescribable.*

My eyelids fluttered. My vision blurred. Dublin, feeding from my leg, was miles and miles away and …

I was on cloud nine. Every single cell in my body came alive with a *pop.* I croaked for air. Tried to move—think, feel, anything.

Either Dublin was oblivious to my reaction, or he just didn't care. That tongue was ruthless, swirling, licking, tasting.

I wanted him to stop … Continue. Stop. Never, stop! *Drain* me of every last drop until …

"Eleanor."

Suddenly, the universe shifted, and I found myself back on the bed, staring up at the ceiling. Dublin's voice sounded louder than it had before, as if he were speaking inside my head, shouting.

"Eleanor!"

I blinked to find him hovering above me—but the expression on his face wasn't the usual infuriated scowl. Those gray eyes were wide, mouth stretched in a frown, and for the first time, I didn't get an overwhelming sense of hostility from him.

Could he be ...worried?

"Say something," he demanded, and my heart skipped a beat.

How many times had he made that request, I wondered? Would I be punished for not obeying quickly enough?

"Something ..." I said.

I felt dizzy. It was a struggle just to suck in air. Breathe ...

"Look at me."

My eyes scanned his face, settling over the fangs peeking from the hood of his mouth. Oddly enough, it wasn't hard to *finally* admit to myself what they actually were.

Not regular teeth or a figment of my imagination, but *fangs* ...

Honed to a point and dripping with blood.

"Can you move?"

Confused, I shook my head. Why on earth would I want to? I could just lay here forever, drowning in pain and pleasure …

I doubted Dublin could have looked any less shocked if I'd spat on him. His eyes scanned my thigh, narrowing over the scarlet stain spreading beneath my punctured knee.

"Must have bitten too deep," I thought I heard him murmur.

"Too deep?"

The words didn't fully register—I was too busy hating myself. Pain I could bear. Every tragic heroine needed to suffer in order to make her plight believable, but *that* …

That had been anything but painful.

Admitting as much made me feel like a dirty little traitor, but it had felt …*good*. My body was warmer than the effects of a glass of strong brandy. Even while chained, I was floating, flying, and I wanted more.

Suddenly, Dublin reached for my leg. Cold fingers curled beneath my knee and I waited, every cell alight as he observed the bleeding limb before lowering his mouth.

A sound I'd never heard myself make tore from my throat even before his lips finally made contact with my flesh. I couldn't remember being so on edge before in my life, so *electrified*.

But rather than bite, those two sharp points merely scraped the flesh, once …twice. Then his tongue came to lap away the blood. Liquid-quick it slipped back within the crevice behind my knee, caressing the bleeding wound.

"You taste …decent," he remarked after another careful lick, breath chilling my skin.

He sounded almost surprised at that. *Sweet, not bitter,* I could imagine him thinking. I expected him to take more.

I knew, deep in my bones, that I wouldn't have fought if he had, but he abruptly let me go instead and pulled back.

"Listen to me closely. It's time for your next lesson." His eyes sought out mine, reinforcing every stern syllable. "You must never allow yourself to be bitten more than three times in one night by a single client. Understood?"

I nodded, even though my brain struggled to process his words.

Three. Bite. Night.

"I mean it, Eleanor, no more than *three*. There are safeguards, of course—" He dragged the pad of his finger down to the center of my throat, and I could barely find the strength to focus on what he said next.

"But, if a single client ever tries to feed a fourth time, you fight—scream, claw, kick. You resist as if your very life depends on it. Understood?"

"Three times, no more," I managed to croak.

The funny thing was ...I wished *he* would do it a *second* time.

Instead, he stood and tugged his collar neatly into place. He would have been the picture of perfection if it wasn't for a single spot of blood that marred his chin. With little fanfare, he swiped it away with the pad of his thumb and launched into another 'educational' session.

"Lesson four," he began while pacing the length of the bed. "Your clients will combine various ...acts while feeding." He gestured to the chains. "Sex, bondage, sitting on their lap and calling them *Santa Claus*—whatever it is, you do it. No questions asked. No tantrums thrown."

This time he didn't even bother with a growled *'understood?'* The message within his gaze was crystal clear.

But I was still stuck on *Santa Claus.*

I had lost my virginity only yesterday. Now there was talk of bondage, fantasies and the drinking of bodily fluids—not to mention that I was currently in chains.

To say that I was overwhelmed would have been an understatement.

"I need to hear you agree, Eleanor." His tone was crisp, like a teacher waiting for affirmation from a naughty student; *I will not disrupt the class.*

"I ..."

"Repeat after me, Eleanor: *I understand, Sir.*" He mocked my high-pitched tones, but the fact just made him seem even more sinister.

"I ..."

Suddenly, he was crouched over the bed, and every cell in my body went on high alert. He ignored my fear, creeping toward me like a pale Devil with beautiful eyes.

"Perhaps things are moving too quickly?" he asked.

I nodded.

Too quickly.

"Too ...strangely," I said.

"Of course," Dublin agreed in a tone that was far too gentle. "You're inexperienced. You've probably never considered half the things I'm talking about in your dizziest little daydreams, but do not worry, Eleanor ..."

I flinched as an icy finger trailed the length of my throat once again, lingering where I knew my artery would be pulsing.

"When I'm done with you ...there won't be a single thing you'll be too haughty to try."

Before I could react, he was fully above me, bracing his weight on both hands. His chill hit me with all the force of a pile of iron chains, pinning me in place.

"We'll start slow," he promised in a tone that made my blood run cold. "Bare your throat."

Automatically, my head tilted back into the pillow, and his body lowered even further over mine.

I had to clench my teeth just to keep them from chattering. Ice wafted from him the way heat would from anyone else —but even that didn't terrify me as much as the way warmth flared through my skin wherever his chill touched.

Torturous seconds passed like eons while his icy breath fanned across my neck.

Then ...just when I thought the anticipation might drive me insane, he lunged, fangs piercing through flesh, and this time I didn't even try to smother my scream. It erupted for a second before he bit down harder, choking off the sound.

I was in agony. Searing, incredible *pain,* and then ...

I couldn't feel anything, nothing but a bubbly sense of calm that knocked me under. The sensation was unlike anything I'd ever felt.

It was sharp, almost unbearable, but underneath it all, was this tingly pleasure that had me gasping out. *"Oh."*

My mouth was open. My eyes were wide. I was suddenly reminded of how that blonde had looked while being bitten —only now could I begin to place the expression on her face. *Ecstasy ...*

"Eleanor!" Dublin's voice yanked me from my daze.

My vision cleared to reveal him kneeling beside me, but I could barely find the energy to focus on the gaze burning from beneath those golden lashes.

When had the earth stopped spinning?

"Maybe it's best to start you on one bite for now," he said slowly.

"Mhmm," I tried to speak—what, I didn't know—but it felt very important to say something.

To do something …

"Eleanor—"

Dublin sounded miles away, but everything had gone black once again. Were my eyes closed? Or had I finally given in to the silly little fool I was deep down and passed out?

Either way, a stern voice chased me into the darkness.

"Eleanor!"

VENOM

"**I** thought you might need something a little stronger than wine today."

The words seemed to come from a billion different directions all at once, all clashing inside my brain.

With a groan, I peeled my eyes open and attempted to focus. A pale blob hovered above me. After a moment of frantic blinking, the shape slowly converged into a frowning Yulia. In one hand she held a shot glass, which she promptly shoved beneath my nose.

The amber liquid smelled like mouthwash. I tried to refuse it with a shake of my head, but Yulia wouldn't budge.

"Drink up," she said sternly. "Think of it as medicine. Should I get you a spoon full of sugar?"

I cracked a tired smile and warily eyed the drink again. Brandy, I suspected. With a sigh, I opened my mouth, and

Yulia poured the contents in, watching as I choked it down.

"Good."

After setting the shot glass on the floor, she perched on the end of the bed. Today she wore a black sweater, paired with a set of black tights and leather boots that reached her knees. Her green eyes were guarded as they warily scanned my own.

"How do you feel today, Eleanor?"

I didn't like her tone. Neither did I like the realization that I was neatly tucked in bed with my upper body propped against a wall of pillows. Not to mention that I felt—as Georgie would put it—like *"shit scraped off someone's shoe."*

My body hurt. My brain hurt. My goddamn eyes *hurt*. It took everything I had in me just to suffer the burn of the alcohol traveling down my throat without vomiting.

"What happened?" I sounded like someone on their death bed. Considering that I had been in that exact situation a few days ago, it wasn't really an exaggeration.

I couldn't resist the frantic impulse that had me glancing around the room, searching for so much as a *hint* of an IV pole, or one of those damned beeping machines—or even, god forbid, a doctor. The fear turned out to be in vain once I recognized the same, windowless room I had awoken in yesterday.

"You've been out for a few hours," Yulia explained in response to my question. "Dublin thinks you must have had a bad reaction. It happens sometimes."

A reaction? "To what?"

She shrugged. "To the venom. It affects some more than others—"

"Venom?" The images of last night flooded back, one after the other: *teeth and blood...* I couldn't resist the almost childish impulse that had me wondering out loud, "So, is he a snake or a vampire?"

Vampire. I couldn't even begin to explain how strongly that word affected me. Goosebumps prickled all over my skin, which promptly brought up the realization that, once again, I had been stripped naked. At least the cuffs were gone, I saw, glancing down. The only sign of them was an angry red circle on the inside of each wrist.

"It's in their fangs," Yulia said finally. "It subdues the victims they feed on. Makes them docile and speeds up their heart rate for easier ..."

Bleeding.

She didn't say it, but I knew that was what she meant. My own heart in my throat, I brought a trembling finger up to my neck and wasn't really surprised when I felt the gauze of a bandage.

"He bit me."

It felt worse to say it out loud. Inside my head, the event could have been just some sick, twisted little fantasy—a nightmare. Out loud, the words hit the air with the finality of a death sentence.

There went my sanity.

"Dublin's furious," Yulia added. "Most people can handle at least five or six bites worth of venom. In his opinion, if you can't even handle *two*, then there really is no place for you here, is there?"

She made it sound like a challenge, and I could clearly picture Dublin grumbling. *All this time, wasted for nothing.*

"Where is he?" I didn't really process the motion of my hand flying out to swipe the blankets from my legs, but the next thing I knew Yulia was holding onto my shoulder as I swayed on my feet.

"Eleanor—"

"Where is he?"

Suddenly, it felt very important to see him, my Devil in the flesh. What little of Yulia's words I'd understood didn't sit right.

Venom. Reaction. No use …

If the bastard thought some teeny weensy fainting spell was enough cause to revert back to his *'name or money'* ultimatums he had another thing coming. I took a step, only to stumble as a sharp pain traveled up and down my leg. I gasped—it felt like I'd been stabbed, but a glance down revealed the true culprit.

There was another gauze bandage taped to the inside of my knee. *Oh.* I vaguely remembered that he'd bitten me there as well.

"Easy …"

With surprising strength, Yulia hauled me upright and steered me back to the bed. It was only when she politely draped a sheet over me that I remembered that I wasn't wearing anything at all.

"You should relax," she urged

I didn't want to relax. I wanted to see Dublin. I wanted to know why I currently sported *his* bite marks on my body.

You know why, idiot, a part of me hissed and I huddled beneath my sheet. *You just couldn't leave well enough alone, could you?*

"Dublin's not even here," Yulia insisted as I tried in vain to stand again. "He rarely comes before sundown."

Her words placated me somewhat.

At least I had the time to recompose myself. After all, it was hard to be intimidating when you looked like death warmed up. I observed the translucent flesh of my hand, watching the indigo veins snake and wind underneath. I was about four shades paler than usual. My hair felt like a bird's nest set on top of my shoulders. Only God knew what I looked like full-on from the front.

You had a bad reaction ... Glancing at Yulia from the corner of my eye, I wondered just how *'bad'* she meant.

"The first few bites are always the hardest on the body," she went on, glancing down at my bandaged knee. "It can overwhelm the system and cause dizziness or fatigue—"

"But?" I could sense a very big one hovering over the entire conversation.

Nervously, Yulia tucked a black lock of hair behind her ear. She wouldn't look at me. "*But* rarely do people faint. Even after more than one bite."

I was horrified. Being 'out for a few hours' was one thing, but 'fainted' just sounded so ...weak.

What would Mother say? *Tsk, tsk, Eleanor, a true Gray never loses control.*

"Just for a few hours," Yulia confirmed. "Dublin was worried—"

I didn't know why, but the thought of that stern face twisted in concern for *me* made something in my chest twitch.

"He hates leaving a contract unfinished," Yulia went on, dashing any suspicion that he might have actually cared for my welfare. "The whole thing is negated if the signing party is no longer able to fulfill their obligation."

Of course, that would be the reason for his concern; the man seemed to live only for his silly little contracts.

But you were foolish enough to sign it.

"So what does that mean?" I found myself asking of the wall while Yulia inspected the fingernails of her right hand.

"The terms have changed," she said after a moment. "If you can't be bitten, then that complicates the whole issue of you working in a *feeding* Den, doesn't it?"

That it did.

It was stupid—I *should* have felt relieved. If what she was saying was the truth then I was home free through no fault of my own. I could, for all intents and purposes, tell good old Dublin to shove his contract up his ass, along with that pen and still keep my stupid pride.

But I wasn't relieved. More like …disappointed, annoyed, and angry with myself, of all things.

Silly little Ellie, too damaged to even properly sell her soul.

"I do think he is overreacting, however," Yulia added softly. "It's rare, but if a client has exceeded the maximum number of bites per worker they sometimes resort to cutting. It gets the blood flowing, but without the injection of venom …"

Cutting? The thought of Dublin taking a *knife* to my skin was more terrifying than the fact that his *teeth* had already pierced through a vein.

I wasn't sure how long I sat there, staring at the floor, but it wasn't until I felt Yulia's hand on my shoulder that I glanced up again. While I was distracted, she must have left and come back, because now she offered me a black robe that I was sure she didn't have before.

"Let's get you cleaned up," she suggested. "I'm dying to get my hands on that hair."

~

*H*ours later, I was back in the red dressing room, sitting on a stool before the mirror while Yulia brushed out my shorn, damp curls.

It was a strange comparison, but I almost felt as if I was back in Gray Manor while a servant did the same—albeit Yulia was a lot gentler than the former.

"I was right," she declared while observing my chalky reflection in the mirror. "This haircut does wonders for you."

Wonders. I would have scoffed if I wasn't afraid that she might take offense. The only thing 'wondrous' about me was how damn *strange* I looked without a mane of curls to hide behind. My eyes were two emerald green saucers staring from the gaunt face of a ghost.

"I don't think I was meant for short hair," I said seriously.

"Nonsense!" Beaming, Yulia dragged the brush through my hair once again. "It gives you character."

I wrinkled my nose and observed my reflection, trying to see whatever she saw, this mysterious woman with *character.* After nearly five minutes I still hadn't found anything noteworthy, but Yulia suddenly pulled away and placed the brush on the table.

"I'll be back," she said. Without another word she turned and slipped from the door, leaving me alone.

I could hear her footsteps retreating down to the lounge. Voices came next, and then shouts, that quickly faded into murmurs.

When minutes passed, and Yulia didn't return, I stood and found myself creeping into the hallway after her. The angry voices came again, though from this distance I couldn't tell who they belonged to.

"So what now?" a woman was demanding. *Yulia?*

"Don't look at me. Ask your *Master*. He knows the code—"

"*There* you are."

My heart felt as if it stopped as someone spoke directly into my ear. I swear every ounce of blood in my body surged down to my toes. I recognized *that* voice, all right. Heart pounding, I turned around to face Dublin.

So much for him not visiting the club during the day.

He wore dark colors again: black pants and a deep indigo sweater that made those eyes gleam. They scanned my own coldly as if searching for any hint of emotion—to exploit, I guessed.

"Well, at least you're standing."

His voice gave nothing away, and I crossed my arms over my chest in an effort to hide just how badly they trembled. Yulia said that he had been furious, but looking at him I couldn't tell. He seemed like the same, arrogant bastard who had barged into my bedroom; ice cold.

"It's a good thing I ran into you," he went on, taking a step closer. With every step he took forward, I took two back. "It's better if we get this over with now."

His hand fell on the door, and I backed away until I was fully inside.

"Get what over with?"

"You're done—" He shoved something at me that I barely managed to catch; my plain, brown purse. "There's a car out front. It will take you back to—"

"B-But what about the contract?"

"Your contract?" His eyes widened and narrowed in quick succession. *Is she serious?* I couldn't tell if he was more surprised by the fact that I was asking about that stupid contract or that I had dared to interrupt him. "'But what about it, *sir?*'" he intoned nastily. "And we will revert to the terms that I first suggested."

Money and the family name.

"B-But …Yulia said that only *I* could set the terms of my repayment."

Dublin gaped at me. *Literally*, his mouth fell open, and he just stared—for so long that I risked a peek in the mirror just to make sure I hadn't grown six heads.

"Are you sure that illness was affecting your *blood* and not your *brain*?" He wondered finally.

I had to admit that he had a point. The way I was talking, there had to be something wrong with me mentally.

From inside my purse, my trusty checkbook seemed to weigh a thousand pounds. *Use me!* It pleaded. *You've been falling back on me all your life—what's so different now?*

Maybe it was the way he was sneering at me? Smug, haughty, as if he just *knew* that I would be a good girl and run back to my manor with my tail between my legs, eager to forget my naughty walk on the *'dark side.'* A part of me agreed with him; bravery was overrated. It was much simpler playing the role of the docile heiress who communicated only with dollar signs.

But at the thought of surrender, a larger part of me would scoff, and I would forget all about being afraid, if only for a second. Dublin was unlike anyone I had ever met, terrifying in so many ways. I should only want to run from him, but …

I had this insane urge to *pinch* him instead, if only to gauge his reaction. Jutting my chin defiantly into the air, I did the next best thing—I kept asking questions.

"Why did you bite me?"

I knew the only logical reason, of course; practice for the real thing. He'd said as much during his little lessons, but for some reason, I didn't buy that. He had noticed my reaction the first time. He had been worried …but then he'd bitten me again. *Deeper,* too—if the pain that flared whenever I moved my head accounted for anything.

I couldn't shake the way he had looked last night either—as if my reaction to his bites had proved some dark suspicion of his once and for all.

Silly, silly Ellie, a part of me scoffed. *Always so paranoid.*

"Why else?" The harshness in his tone made my nails clutch at the front of my robe. "Newsflash, Eleanor; it's not your *face* people would pay for."

My cheeks flamed as the insult hit its mark. "But …w-what about the contract?" I pressed, feeling like a child clinging to a ratty teddy bear as their only shred of comfort.

"*Forget* the damn contract," he snarled. "You can't be bitten. You can't work at the den. In fact—" he leaned closer until we were nearly nose to nose, throwing me precariously off balance. "I'm willing to go so far as to say you aren't of good use for *anything*. You should go now, while you have the chance."

He shooed me away: actually waggled his fingers in a way that told me to get the hell out.

I just stood there. Maybe I was stuck trying to think of a good comeback or perhaps I was just in shock? Either way, a silky voice took advantage of the silence before I ever got the chance to reply.

"It's too bad, Dublin." My head swiveled around to find Saskia leaning against the doorway. Ample cleavage strained against the v-cut of her ruby red gown. "Her contract isn't *yours* to dictate."

Quicker than I could comprehend, Dublin moved. My first thought was that he had only turned to face her—until I realized that I was way closer to him than I had been before. My chin bumped his elbow as he blocked me from view.

"What the hell are you talking about?"

Saskia giggled but, with Dublin in my way, the only part of her I could make out were long pale legs ending in blood-red high heels.

"Raphael owns her contract, remember?" she said sweetly. "And only *he* has the final say in how and when she fulfills it. It's all in the code, though I could understand your lapse in memory seeing as how you've been reclusive for so very long."

Raphael? The name didn't ring any bells for me, but Dublin stiffened, and the icy air wafting from him suddenly felt degrees colder. Almost without meaning to, he shifted, and I could see Saskia's face once again.

It was a few, tense seconds before he spoke again. "He's never had an issue with how I've managed them before."

"Well, he does *now*," Saskia replied, tucking a piece of loose red hair behind her ear. "He wants *her* on the floor. Tonight. Mikhail has already made the arrangements …"

If I would ever see Dublin Helos even remotely speechless, then this was probably it.

His mouth opened and closed—I could hear the *clink* of his teeth snapping together. Eventually, he managed to find only two words to spit out in Saskia's general direction. "Why now?"

Eyes glinting, Saskia pressed a pale hand delicately to her mouth as if to smother her laughter.

"Because I called him, of course. It doesn't matter why she's here, or *who* she is—" She sent a cold glance in my direction before returning to Dublin. "We must follow the rules, and they state that she *must* be up for auction like everyone else."

I guessed that the 'auction' was what took place in the lounge at night, when those pale figures selected their choice girl from the bunch.

"Though," Saskia added with a sniff, "whether someone *wants* her or not is another matter. Still! The rules must be followed—"

"She wasn't ready then," Dublin countered.

Saskia seized her bottom lip and made a noncommittal sound in the back of her throat; *So?*

"I don't make the rules, darling. Raphael does, and *he* wants her treated just like anyone else. In *every* way."

With a chilling giggle, Saskia turned on her heels and retreated down the hall. The *click-clack* of her shoes hitting the wooden floor echoed like parting gunshots. When she finally disappeared into silence, I gathered enough nerve to tiptoe away from Dublin and face him fully.

Confusing snippets of the conversation spun around my brain, making me dizzy.

Who was Raphael?

What had Saskia meant about my contract?

Eventually, the urge for answers outweighed any sense of self-preservation. "What was she talking about?"

"Are you happy?" Lightning-quick, Dublin seized my arm and yanked me closer, snarling the words into my face one by one. Anger blared through those silver eyes, threatening to scorch my skin from the intensity of it. "*You* wanted to play this game. You couldn't just take the easy way out. Well, it's too late to back out now."

He let me go so harshly that I stumbled back into the wall. My sore knee buckled, threatening to dump me onto the floor—but before I could so much as begin to sway, his hand was on my shoulder, holding me upright.

I didn't even want to put a name to the expression that crossed his face for only a second; rage? Anger? Pure, unfiltered hatred?

Fear?

"What's going on?" I croaked, "M-maybe if you would just talk to me, I could understand …"

Ha! Talk—the only thing Dublin liked to do was rant and rave and order. I waited for him to prove as much with another mocking reminder to call him 'Sir.' But he just stared me down for so long that for a moment all I could see was icy silver.

Beneath his scrutiny, my heart pounded, surging blood to every inch of my body. Could he hear it?

Abruptly, he turned his back on me.

"Get dressed. You want to talk? We'll talk." Near the threshold of the room, he glanced back over his shoulder and added, "I'm taking you to lunch."

TEA FOR TWO

*L**unch?* I berated myself for not asking whether or not *I* would be on the menu before Dublin disappeared through the doorway.

For a minute, I could only stare after him, until a bit of common sense finally managed to sink in. *Get dressed, stupid.*

I staggered to the wardrobe and appraised the teeny bits of black material with a sense of dread. Bustiers, leather skirts …

Not exactly casual wear. Yulia had to keep real clothes *somewhere,* and I determinedly pushed my way through hangers to reveal the very back of the closet.

As if conjured by my desperation, I found a garment bag hanging from a hook. I snatched for it, too distracted by Dublin's voice in my head—*hurry up!*—to worry about the implications of stealing. Swiftly, I undid the zipper and withdrew the two pieces of clothing stashed inside.

One was a white blouse, lighter than gossamer, with flowing sleeves and a delicate collar. Paired with it was a navy skirt way more fashionable than my mother's brown tweed monstrosity.

But that wasn't all. The bag still felt heavy, so I raced over to the table and dumped out the remaining contents. A tiny makeup case plopped out, along with a folded slip of paper. The case, once I gathered the nerve to open it, held a matching pair of black lace underwear and a bra, a tube of red lipstick and more of that mint gum. The note had been written in the same, elegant scrawl as the message from my dinner tray last night.

This is your chance, Yulia had scribbled in black ink. *Ask him anything you will, but remember*—the word was underscored by three heavy lines—*that quaint little saying about curiosity and that unfortunate cat! –Yul*

P.S., she'd added at the bottom of the page, *we don't keep toothpaste here (only mouthwash) so do the best you can with the gum. And, Belize is lovely this time of year, isn't it? I wonder if Dublin thinks the same.*

Huh? The gum thing I understood—and absently, I unwrapped the strip and began to chew it—but Belize?

Perhaps I was being too cynical, but Dublin didn't strike me as the type to serenely lounge on the beach, sipping Mimosas, let alone give a damn whether or not it was 'lovely' in the tropics this time of year. Rather than ponder the odd request, I shed my robe and dressed more quickly than I ever have in my life.

When I finally faced the mirror, I expected the usual 'Ellie the unfashionable' horror show. Instead …

The white of the blouse played over my skin, making it seem more porcelain than sallow. The blue countered the darkness of my eyes. I still looked creepy, of course—though more 'undead flight attendant' than childlike ghost.

Tucked in the corner near the door, I found my shoes and hastily pulled them on while shoving Yulia's note into my pocket.

"Are you ready yet?" Dublin snapped from the hall.

"Y-Yes."

I grabbed my purse and swung it over my shoulder before racing for the door. I hadn't gone more than a single step over the threshold before an icy hand seized my forearm.

"Keep your head down," Dublin hissed. I had to jog just to keep up as he sped through the hall, dragging me after him, down a flight of stairs.

I expected for us to go out the back way, the same way I had come in. Instead, Dublin turned through a door I had missed before, and I found myself in a brightly lit lobby where sunlight streamed in, inhibited, through sleek windows.

It was midday already. The sky was a glorious blue with no clouds in sight ...and I found myself glancing back at Dublin, heart in my throat.

Would he combust?

Burst into flames the moment a drop of sunlight touched his unholy skin?

As if my very thoughts were the trigger, he froze, and I waited for him to sizzle into ash right before my eyes. Instead, he eyed a potentially lethal puddle of light and frowned. "Damn. Forgot my sunglasses." Looking directly at me, he added, "The sun's *killer* today."

Had this been a movie or something that I was observing from the outside, I would have laughed—how funny, the vampire had jokes. As it was, I could only stare. What made it worse was that I knew that *he* knew I was gaping at him. Surely some nasty remark would come next? Maybe a quip about biting or blood?

As it was, he simply headed through the main glass doors, leaving me to catch up. By the time I finally stumbled outside after him, Dublin's only reaction was to raise a hand to shield his eyes in lieu of those missing sunglasses.

And he didn't even burn.

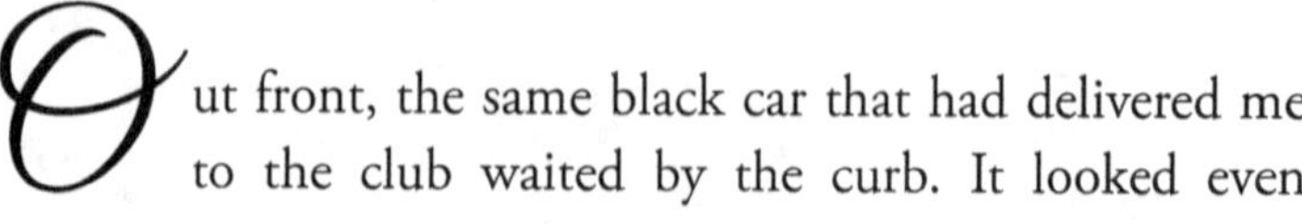

*O*ut front, the same black car that had delivered me to the club waited by the curb. It looked even more terrifying in broad daylight. The driver stood beside it, holding the door open and without pause, Dublin hauled me forward.

"Watch your head," he warned before shoving me inside.

I crawled across the backseat and sandwiched myself against the door—but it still didn't seem far enough away from him.

Dublin alone took up more than half of the backseat, and I had to do some fancy maneuvering with my legs just to keep any part of me from touching him. Regardless, I felt his chill without the need for any physical contact. His very scent seemed ingrained on my conscience; winter and spice.

"The *Café Claret*," he told the driver.

At his request, the car lurched into the mid-morning traffic. I didn't know how to react when Dublin leaned back against the leather headrest without acknowledging my presence. I watched him from the corner of my eye, unable to decipher a single emotion.

This is your chance! Yulia's voice urged in my head. *Ask him what you will.*

"So…" I cleared my throat. "You aren't burning to death in the sun."

Nice one, Ellie, I scoffed to myself. *Way to hit him with the tough questions.*

However, the remark didn't earn me the exasperated reaction I would have expected. Rather than roll his eyes, Dublin simply shrugged.

"I'm not." Then, with what I guessed was deliberate slowness, his finger struck the button that lowered the tinted window, allowing the sunlight to stream in uninhibited. "It's beautiful out," he remarked while gazing at the brilliant blue sky above. "Not too warm. The perfect day for a stroll."

Okay, so obviously the rules of *Dracula* did not apply in this instance—at least not to him. I squirmed, wondering just what that meant for *me*, but while we were on the topic of weather, I decided to take the rest of Yulia's advice.

"Belize," I blurted, gauging his reaction carefully; his jaw tightened, though it could have been just a response to me talking in general. "It's beautiful this time of year isn't it—"

A shrill tune cut over me; the beginning notes of *Beethoven's 5th symphony*, my ringtone for Georgie. How ironic, considering the location of her current impulsive getaway.

I fumbled inside my purse for my cell and brought it to my ear. As I did so, I happened to catch sight of the notice that flashed across the screen: *15 missed calls over two days*—all from the same three numbers.

Uh oh.

"Ellie?" Georgie demanded before I had the chance to even say hello. "Ellie, are you there?"

For once my chirpy, happy sister sounded strained and frantic.

"I'm here. What's wrong?"

"Did you send the money?"

Oh. Somewhere in the chaos of selling my body and soul to a vampire, I had forgotten all about Georgie and her two hundred grand.

"I'll have it to you by the end of the day," I promised, perhaps a little harsher than necessary, unable to shake a nagging sense of guilt that mingled with irritation. These days, I was lucky if she called me three times a year and I couldn't even remember to fulfill her usual monetary request.

What a horrible sister I was.

"Oh, Ellie ..." Georgie sighed. I could picture her readjusting the headset against her ear and nervously fiddling with a strand of blonde hair. "I didn't mean to sound so bratty. It's just that ...things with Paulo didn't work out at the villa—" Poor Georgiana. Had he run off on her? Found a new blonde to play with? God forbid that she would have to suffer the mess she created. "I just need a little something to tide me over."

"Just wait a few days, and you'll have more than enough," I snapped before I could help it—and I wasn't talking about the length of time it would take to process the transfer, either. Dublin, supposedly, would only give me enough of his magic blood to last another two days, counting this one.

After that …

Mortality was staring me in the face. I still hadn't gotten around to drawing up that will. Time was ticking.

My cat needed a guardian.

My sister needed to know some glimmer of the truth.

My wardrobe needed to be burned rather than plague the unfortunates at *Goodwill* with hideous fashion choices.

But what was I doing instead? Hopping into a car with a brooding man who claimed to want to take me to 'lunch' after all but damning me to hell.

"Don't talk like that," Georgie said. "I know that lately I've been playing the role of selfish little sister but I—" She broke off abruptly. "I love you, Ellie. I promise that I'll be home in a couple of weeks, but …I've got to go now."

Click! She hung up, and I was left to process her words; *I love you.*

The phone slipped through my fingers to land with a *thump* on the seat. I couldn't even remember if, outside of childhood, we had ever consciously uttered those words to each other. Not at Father's funeral. Definitely not at Mother's. Maybe, at Christmas one year, after too much wine?

Was it absolutely pathetic that I couldn't remember?

I could always blame the memory lapse on shock; it wasn't like Georgie to carry on a conversation longer than it took to say, *give me money, oh, Ellie, please? Ta-ta!* I couldn't shake the feeling that she had been trying to tell me something, something important ...

I'd be damned if I could even begin to guess what it was.

"We're here." Dublin's quiet declaration jolted me back to reality.

The car had come to a stop, and he already stood on the curb. I scrambled out after him and gaped up at the front of a chic hotel. It overlooked the bay and had a grand view of the harbor. The *Café Claret* was apparently housed inside of it.

"Come on." Without waiting for me, Dublin had already passed through the glass doors of the building. I hurried after him, clutching my purse to my chest.

Inside was an elegant affair of expensive wallpaper and antique furniture lined in gold—the kind of place my mother would have loved to hold court. A pretty young woman stood within the spacious lobby and smiled, as if she'd been waiting her whole life for the very moment that Dublin walked through the door.

"Mr. Helos!" she greeted warmly. "Your table is ready."

"Thank you, Abigail." I almost didn't recognize the man standing beside me from his warm tone. He even smiled with a charming grace that he never displayed toward me.

Abigail turned and led the way through a pair of French doors into a well-lit dining room. A row of bay windows revealed a stunning view of the waterfront. The soft yellow walls and polished wooden floors made the space seem charming, and I could picture people fighting to eat here.

Though, at least for now, it was entirely empty, save for us.

Odd. But it wasn't until Abigail came to a stop at a table facing a window that I realized why; it was the only table set.

"A private room, as requested," Abigail chirped, proving my suspicions to be true.

The table itself looked harmless enough. A cream tablecloth set off the gold filigree in the china plates, and a vase of daisies in the center added a splash of color.

No knives or goblets of blood in sight.

With a wary glance at Dublin I sat down, and he took the seat across from me.

"Thank you, Abigail," he said, flashing the woman a magnificent smile, and she skipped off, closing the doors of the dining room behind her. "All right, Eleanor." All at once, his voice changed. It deepened, taking on a hard edge, and something told me that it was a special tone he reserved only for me. "You wanted to talk? Let's talk."

He snapped his fingers, and a second later a man entered carrying a tray of food. One by one, he placed dishes of soup and salad and bread between us and then left again.

cold muscle. I squeaked out a sound that could have been a scream, only to find myself flipped over and shoved onto the table so hard that the wood buckled.

A vase of flowers fell to the floor.

Silverware clattered down.

It was all I could do just to throw my arms out on either side and grab hold of the table's edge for balance.

"Easy." Dublin hovered above me, hands on my waist. Those eyes were so dark that they were no longer gray but a fathomless black. "You make it way too *easy* …"

I shivered as the pad of his thumb came to trace my throat, brushing the bandage covering his bite. Through French doors leading to the lobby, I saw that Abigail had mysteriously disappeared from her post near the front desk.

"You make it way too easy to have your body coiled with fear, heart pumping so frantically that I could choreograph a waltz to your damn pulse." His nail tapped out a rapid rhythm against my carotid artery; *tap-tap, tap-tap, tap-tap!* "I only have to look at you for you to reek of fear, Eleanor. You must really think me the Devil."

I couldn't respond.

Right then, he *did* look like the Devil; undeniably handsome with fire in those eyes. My nails dug into the underside of the table, scraping wood as sweat trickled down the back of my blouse.

I waited for him to hurt me. Bite me? Kill?

Suddenly, he pulled back instead.

"You want to know the truth, Eleanor? I tried to give you an easy deal. Hell, I all but handed more time—more *life*—to you on a golden platter. But you couldn't just quit while you were ahead." He shrugged, but the motion was a violent display of tension. "Well now …it's too late."

"What-what do you mean?"

"I *mean* the terms of your contract are now set in *stone* Eleanor," he declared with all the warmth of a death sentence. "I don't make the rules anymore."

"Then, who does?"

He made a terrifying sound that could have been a chuckle. "I'm only the *salesman,* Eleanor and just like everyone else, I too have a boss."

A boss? So, he didn't go out collecting souls on his own sick whim—it was his *job*? I recalled what Saskia had said; *too bad, Dublin, you don't own her contract, Raphael does.*

"Then who? Who owns my contract?"

"Well, he's not the Devil," Dublin began, before the thought could even form in my mind. "Though, to be honest, he's not too far off."

～

A not-Devil who held my *virtual* Devil's chains. Interesting.

"So …" I cleared my throat and fought to keep my voice steady. *Stay in control, Ellie.* "You got my contract for him? Why?"

I was proud of myself—at least I sounded civilized. What I wanted to say, *'You're like a dog on a leash, how quaint,'* probably didn't have the same ring to it. Regardless, Dublin frowned as if reading my mind.

"All contracts belong to *him*," he insisted, apparently referring to this mysterious Raphael. "I am merely the broker."

'Merely the broker,' my ass. I could sense that there was more to it—so much more. Though, I figured that you could fill a book with everything Dublin *wasn't* saying.

Not that I was exactly in the position to demand any answers, considering that I was slung over the side of a table, holding onto the edges for dear life. I blushed at the realization that my skirt had ridden up dangerously high.

I clamped my knees together to salvage what little shred of dignity I had left, and slid forward until my heels hit the floor. Then I tugged my skirt back into place and ran a hand over my blouse. My eyes were on the floor when I gathered the courage to speak again. Two sets of silverware were scattered about, including my unfortunate salad fork.

"Do you pick your victims at random?" I wondered. "Or is there some kind of *Manifesto for the Dark-hearted'* which lists of all the sick and downtrodden souls ripe for the taking?"

No answer.

All righty then …

I had gotten my little dig in. I should have left well enough alone, but I just couldn't seem to help myself.

"Does this Raphael ever meet his 'contractors,' in person? Or," I added on a bitter note, "is he content with allowing *you* to perform the brutalizing and intimidation in peace—"

"This really isn't a conversation we should be having out in the open." Dublin sounded as if we were merely discussing the weather—but I wasn't fooled.

Not a bit.

His eyes were molten, threatening to burn if I stared at them long enough …

So I peered down at my heels instead.

"Why?" I prodded. "Is he like Lucifer, after all? Will saying his name out loud make him appear?"

I tried to sound mocking, but deep down I trembled at the thought of whoever could make Dublin so serious that he didn't even scold me for disobeying his little rules.

Someone, Ellie, my inner voice warned, *who you never ever want to meet.*

Still, I couldn't help the urge to twist the knife. My mouth opened, eyes narrowing. "Rapha—"

An ice-cold hand descended over my forearm, squeezing so tightly that I gasped out loud, but the sound had scarcely left my mouth before Dublin let me go again. I suspected that the contact had merely been a warning.

Watch your mouth.

Instead of saying as much out loud, he withdrew a wad of money from his pocket and tossed it onto the table. Then, he turned on his heel and headed for the lobby.

I was forced to run just to keep pace with him, and by the time I made it outside, the sleek black car was already pulling away from the curb and zipping into the thick of traffic ...

Though, Dublin stood on the sidewalk as well, watching it go.

I stiffened, as he glanced over and found me there, huffing and puffing. Rather than speak, he turned and began to stroll down the street, blond hair gleaming in the sun. The silent command to follow him was all in his posture; his shoulders set in a firm line that *dared* me to run.

Regardless, something held me back; an invisible hand on my collar, shaking me. *Use your brain, Ellie,* it told me, while I wavered there on the sidewalk. *You can run—go home—it's not like he can stop you in broad daylight.*

Though he certainly seemed to have no qualms about renting out an entire restaurant just to terrorize me in peace. I doubted that the police officer strolling into a doughnut shop across the street, or a bit of mid-morning traffic would ever deter Dublin from attacking me if the mood struck him. So, I swallowed, held my head high, and chased down my Big Bad Wolf in a pair of designer heels.

The bastard made me sprint after him for nearly a block, and it wasn't until a change in the traffic light forced him to stop at the curb that I finally managed to draw even with him. The moment I did, his hand shot out for my wrist before he turned down the other end of the street, pulling me along like a dog on a leash.

Despite everything, I found myself gazing around, embarrassingly wide-eyed. I had never seen the city like this. My family wasn't exactly the 'afternoon stroll' type, and I had only glimpsed most of the buildings and winding streets from the safety of a car.

This was so different.

So …real.

The cacophony of activity was overwhelming without a sheet of bulletproof glass to hide behind. A barrage of sounds assaulted me: honking horns, shouts, chatter. For a moment I could pretend that I was just an average pedestrian, hurrying through the chaos of mid-morning city life—but Dublin's icy grip was like an anchor tethering me to grim reality.

He steered me down a narrow street that opened onto a boulevard where a beautiful cathedral rose in the distance. It sat in the middle of a park amongst a strip of emerald grass littered with flowers, and was such an unexpected sight that I found myself staring.

"I never knew this was here."

Dublin didn't reply. He continued at a brusque pace down a path that cut through the green, heading straight for the church. It was an odd destination for a vampire. I had to bite down some nasty jab about crosses and holy water. With every step we took, the grandiose building loomed above, beautiful and imposing.

It had been built in the Gothic style, with tall spires aiming to pierce the sky. I think I even caught sight of a gargoyle or two scowling from the roof, cold and distant—but beneath the intimidating exterior, there was a faint softness that couldn't be denied.

Children played beneath the shadow of the bell tower. Couples strolled along the path, gazing up every now and again at the stained glass windows depicting biblical scenes in vibrant colors.

A sign near the entrance read, *The Cathedral of St. Jude the Apostle.*

"How fitting," I found myself murmuring. "The saint of lost causes and desperation ..."

St. Jude was definitely on my shortlist if I ever needed a patron; my entire life had been nothing if not a lost cause.

"You know the Saints?" Dublin glanced at me from over his shoulder, as we mounted the steps leading to the cathedral entrance.

I shrugged, trying to act nonchalant despite the way my insides twisted as his eyes met mine. He sounded so skeptical, as if he'd assumed that I didn't know *anything* outside of the inner workings of my family's accounts. Oh, and how to use my checkbook, of course.

"I went to boarding school," I admitted, fighting to keep the irritation from my tone. "To keep my sanity I used to read. At some point, I picked up a book listing all the Catholic Saints."

Not exactly the average light reading of a sixteen-year-old girl, but it had certainly passed the time.

"Hmph." Dublin made a sound in the back of his throat as he pulled on the handle of one of the building's main doors. "And here I thought that all you girls did at those schools was ride ponies and learn which doilies go best with which tea set."

"Oh, we did plenty of that too," I said, smiling at my quip.

Welstrom Academy had been the perfect hell of my mother's devising. There, the girls had been periodically stuffed into identical confections of starched white cotton, and forced to recite 'the duties of a proper lady' until our ears bled.

"But in between the tea parties and etiquette lessons I had to find some way of keeping my sanity."

Dublin didn't reply, but I was too distracted by my surroundings to really wonder why. Not counting the creature by my side, the interior of the cathedral was the most beautiful and intimidating sight I had ever seen in person.

The stone walls stretched at least ten stories high, leading to a vaulted ceiling that made every breath within its chambers echo. The pews were fashioned from solid wood, and yet everything seemed cared for down to the last piece of pristine glass hanging in the windows. There wasn't a single cobweb or item in disrepair.

Not a speck of dust.

I couldn't seem to think of a single thing to say—yet, at the same time, it didn't seem *right* to speak inside the cathedral anyway.

For once, Dublin appeared to be of the same frame of mind. He led me by the sleeve, past a seemingly endless aisle of pews, to a darkened corner. However, as we passed a crucifix of Christ nailed to the wall, he paused. With what I guessed was deliberate slowness, he reached out to trace the silhouette of the metal figure.

Not screaming in agony, I noticed when he pulled away. A little ways away from it was a basin of holy water that I assumed was used for blessings. Dublin dipped a finger into the liquid and allowed a crystalline drop to fall onto his tongue.

"Refreshing," he murmured, with a pointed look in my direction.

Once again, I cursed the vampire rules established by that esteemed Dracula—apparently, the whole bit about crosses and holy water was useless as well.

Had Dublin been merely a slave-of-the-night and allergic to all things holy, as the folklore claimed, I could at least *dream* of one day having the upper hand.

As it was, I was pretty much stuck in the same figurative situation that we were *literally* in now; him dragging me by the arm into the unfathomable shadow.

He didn't even have the decency to at least pretend that traipsing over sacred ground was painful. Without so much as a wince, he pulled me past the altar toward a confessional tucked into an alcove. Someone had placed a sign over the door the parishioner was meant to enter. *Out of order. Do not use.*

The sight struck me as odd, considering how everything else inside the church seemed so carefully maintained. I wondered why the object had just been left here, forgotten —at least, until Dublin pulled open the door, heedless of the warning.

Rather than a chair to sit and do the confessing, the cabinet opened to a set of stairs cut directly into the stone wall behind it. Something told me that the passage had been purposefully hidden.

But where would it lead?

"Ladies first," Dublin prompted, before I even had the chance to question.

I found myself gulping instead. How many people knew this was here? The few patrons spread out amongst the pews seemed too busy contemplating to notice us.

The staircase was pitch-black and narrow. The damp smell of decay tickled my nose, and despite my newfound bravery, I wasn't inclined to go skipping merrily into it.

Not that Dublin gave a damn whether I wanted to or not.

"Any day now, Eleanor," he growled against the nape of my neck.

Right. With a sigh, I squared my shoulders and took a step into the confessional. It was a tight squeeze. My shoulders threatened to brush the stone walls on either side, and I had to fight down the urge to scamper right back out. Only the thought of who waited behind me deterred me from doing just that.

It was dark. I could barely make out the next step before the door closed behind me with a solid *thud,* plunging me into further shadow.

"D-Dublin?"

No answer. I didn't dare risk turning to see if he followed, so I just continued to feel my way forward.

It was a long climb. I swore I counted at least *fifty* steps alone before I lost track.

And there only seemed to be countless more.

Sweat had glued my shirt to my skin by the time I finally came to a solid surface blocking my path. I reached out, feeling what felt like wood beneath the tips of my fingers. *A door?*

I searched blindly for a doorknob—but before I even found one, the door opened from the other end as if on cue.

"About time," Dublin harrumphed from within a puddle of bright light. He stood back, revealing a spacious room where a series of lattice windows overlooked the lawn below. I turned, even though I now had a pretty good idea that Dublin hadn't been behind me all along. In fact, he looked like he'd barely gone a *step*, let alone two flights of stairs to get here.

"How did you ... How—"

"Come." He jerked his head for me to follow and didn't bother to elaborate.

The room resembled a typical entryway. The layout was circular, with several archways leading into separate areas. The walls were covered in old wood paneling, but the style seemed different than the overall feel of the rest of the church—even simpler. A sleek chaise sat in a corner, paired with a silver light fixture that hung on the wall above it; this time, a candle, rather than a serpent-shaped sconce.

"I had you take the visitor's entrance," Dublin explained while closing the door I'd come in from. "Hope you don't mind."

His tone revealed that he didn't give a damn either way, but I was too busy pondering his words to really notice.

"The entrance to what?"

Rather than answer, he turned and headed through the closest archway. I assumed the room beyond was a study of sorts. Shelves covered almost every inch of the walls, lined with books that—at a glance—didn't seem to be the typical biblical volumes one might find in the average church. I don't think most parishioners were interested in reading *'War and Peace'* or *'The Complete Literary Volumes of Chaucer'* in between bible verses.

A desk sat in the room's center, before a large window that let in gleaming daylight. Without much fanfare, Dublin walked over to it and casually pulled open a drawer.

"I'll allow you to review the basics," he offered before tossing something onto the desk's surface. "I don't want to sound too melodramatic, but you did sign it in *blood*."

I gulped, knowing exactly what was beneath the cover of that leather contract book without even having to flip it open.

HOLIER THAN THOU

When I didn't move, Dublin snatched up the contract himself and lifted the cover.

"I, Eleanor Gray," he read, mimicking my voice, "hereby agree to *yadda, yadda, yadda,* body and soul." He closed the book with a *thud.* "I don't think it can get any clearer than that."

"I know what I signed," I said tightly.

Liar, my inner voice hissed. I had no damn clue—only I was just too stubborn to admit that I was in way over my head.

Dublin seemed to be of the same mindset. "Do you?" His tone posed an inescapable challenge.

Then prove it, Eleanor. Say it out loud: I'd like to be a good girl and consult my checkbook, please.

Rather than rise to it, I changed the subject.

"So, I start tonight, then?" I tried to ignore the part of me that cringed at the thought of being at the mercy of someone other than him. "Is ... Isn't that what Saskia said?"

Dublin just stared. As I watched, his gaze darkened into an unforgiving shade of gray that made me wish I'd never spoken at all.

"Were you dropped on your head as a child?" he wondered after a moment. "Deprived of love? Did mommy and daddy not give you enough attention to go along with your diamond-encrusted pacifiers? Is that why you throw yourself into danger at every turn? They offer *therapy* for that, Eleanor."

"My parents are dead," I countered, though I had a feeling that he already knew that. Either way, he didn't even have the decency to look guilty.

"I would prefer if you at least *shivered*," he spat. "Sobbed. I have a spare handkerchief, you know—" He dug through his pocket for a square of white cloth which he tossed at my feet. "At least then I would know that you somewhat comprehend the gravity of the situation."

Gravity? I chewed on my bottom lip. "What do you mean?"

"What I mean is: if you think that one night with *me* was so horrible, try spending it with someone who's paid for your 'services.' Someone," he went on, just to twist the knife, "who won't be as 'accommodating' as I was."

I don't think I realized just how terrifying the prospect was until right then. Within a day's time, I would have to take another client—someone *other* than him, and despite his cruelty, I wasn't inclined to meet anyone he considered to be worse.

"Let's hope you remember your 'lessons,'" he remarked as if reading my mind.

I turned so that I wouldn't have to see his face and found myself at eye-level with the spine of a leather-bound copy of *Hamlet*.

"Okay," I said, forcing out a shaky breath. "Let's say that I am sufficiently alarmed—hypothetically."

"Well, then maybe what I'm saying will finally sink in?" His boots struck the floor in tandem as he came up behind me. "This isn't some silly game you can just quit whenever the fancy strikes you. I won't have you making a fool of me."

Ice-cold fingers encased my forearm—though surprisingly, the grip didn't seem intended to hurt. He merely lingered, reinforcing every word he said.

"It's not like you haven't benefitted from our arrangement. After all, what's one night of debauchery for four whole days of life?"

"Days that I spent in bed," I pointed out. "*Unconscious.*"

"That's irrelevant," Dublin said, releasing my arm. "I gave you the time. How you *spend* said time is up to you." Which sounded like a cop-out, if there ever was one. "Besides," he added. "What else would someone like you do during your free time anyway? Crochet? Embroider napkins? Contemplate your impending spinsterhood?"

I hated the fact that he sounded genuinely curious.

"Technically," I groused, "I don't think you're considered a spinster until you pass menopause."

"Hmph." I glanced over my shoulder to find him taking in my appearance with a sniff. "All the better then."

He shoved my contract back in the desk drawer and locked it with a key seemingly pulled from his sleeve. With some sleight of hand, he made it disappear once again. Standing there before him, I tried to process my options. I felt more helpless then than I had felt chained to a bed.

"I thought you didn't 'own' my contract?" I attempted snark, but the words came out more hollow than anything else, tired.

"I *don't*," he insisted, glancing up to meet my gaze. "I merely keep the new ones until the initial agreement is fulfilled. Then it's sent for …filing."

It sounded so clinical. What, was there a library of countless contracts? At the thought, my throat went dry, and I couldn't even ask.

"I wish I had another day with you at least," Dublin admitted, almost to himself. His tone could have even been called *'sympathetic,'* if it wasn't so cold. "Let us hope that whoever buys you will be too desperate to care that you're …" His eyes raked me from head to toe and narrowed.

"Inexperienced," he settled on finally. "Though, I'll send Yulia over when you wake. Perhaps she can work some kind of *miracle*—"

"Wake?" I glanced at the window. It was broad daylight outside, but something told me that he didn't mean when I woke tomorrow morning.

He shrugged, mouth flattening into a grim line. "I'm giving you your dose early. Just part of it now, and the rest later. You'll need the strength."

"Oh," I croaked.

I had a sinking feeling at the thought of just what I would need the 'strength' for. *Sheets. Heat. Sweat.*

Dublin frowned as if reading my mind. "Oh do spare me the dramatics."

He came around the desk and snatched my arm. I flinched as he held it out flat, eyes on the fat blue vein rising from the crook of my elbow.

"Perhaps later, if we have the time, you can entertain me with full-blown hysterics once the extent of your stupidity sinks in," he suggested, sounding a little too eager at the prospect. "But for now, it's time to be a good girl and take your medicine."

On *'medicine'* he withdrew something from his pocket: a small cylinder with a metal casing, a syringe. I couldn't see the color of the liquid inside, but I could guess easily enough.

Scarlet.

Without so much as a *'by your leave'* Dublin pulled off the needle cap with his teeth and attempted to jab the bevel beneath my skin.

"Wait!" I jerked out of reach, clutching my arm to my chest. "W-what are you doing?"

"I'm sorry, do you know of any other way to get my blood into your system?" He made a sound of a mock surprise. "Oh wait, would you rather *drink* it instead?"

I cringed, shaking my head. "N-No!"

"Well, then …" He raised an eyebrow and gave the syringe a slight jiggle. "Shall we get this over with? I do have other appointments, you know."

I shuddered at a mental image of him, dolling out needles to the other poor souls tethered to him by a contract like candy. *"Now shoot up! It's good for you."*

"I d-don't want it." I staggered back into the corner, fighting the cliché urge to form a finger-cross and shout, *"Stay back!"*

"Funny—" He took a menacing step forward while I huddled against the wall. "I don't remember asking."

"This is a *church*," I squeaked out, as if he was the pious sort who might actually be against intimidation within the holy space.

"Technically," he said but, to my utter shock, he stopped and tucked the syringe back in his pocket.

I stared at him, wondering what he could have meant. Without explaining, he brushed past me and entered the main hall. "I don't have a guest room," he called over his shoulder. "So, you'll just have to make do with the couch."

"W-What?"

I tiptoed after him, nearly gasping out loud as the true meaning of his words sunk in. Suddenly it all made sense: the 'visitor's entrance,' and the strange study ...

"You *live* here?"

He turned to face me with a shrug. "I like the irony of it."

Which I guess was as much as a 'yes' as I was ever going to get.

I glanced around, trying to see everything in a different light. The furniture had the same, dark, muted feel to it as the lounges in the club—black leather. But there was a different aura here; that same sense of preservation as in the rest of the church, with everything neatly in its place.

Contrary, unusual and so very *Dublin*.

"You live in a cathedral?" I repeated, just to help it sink in. As he said, the 'irony' of it was mind-boggling; the damned vampire, dwelling in a house of worship like a beautiful reverse *Quasimodo*.

"I don't '*live*' anywhere," he said softly, stressing the word; a not so subtle reminder that he was supposedly undead.

I gulped, wringing my hands as he turned to stare from one of the windows. The seconds passed in heavy silence, while he gazed down impassively at the world below. The sound of chirping birds and muted children's laughter created a stark contrast to the grim interior of the suite. Finally, he spoke.

"I don't have time for this," he told me without turning around. "You need my blood to see you through tonight, and *I* have other matters to attend to. Don't tell me the silly, naïve Eleanor Gray has lost her bravery already?"

I bristled at the challenge in his tone. *So, he thinks me afraid, does he?* I didn't give myself time to think the action through before I stuck out my arm, baring the vein.

"Do it."

He turned, and surprise crossed his face for barely a second. Without a word, he withdrew the syringe again and crossed over to me as slowly as a predator approaching a bleeding doe. One good blow and it would be game over.

My eyes widened as I took in the sharpness of the needlepoint glinting in the sunlight. It looked so very long. Lethal.

"Grin and bear it, Eleanor," Dublin advised before sticking the needle in with one clean jab. The pain rose up as sharply as a bee sting but faded in mere seconds. "It will be over before you know it."

I blinked. The next second his words garbled together as darkness filled my vision and then, I was falling ...

"**G**ood evening, Eleanor."

I peeled my eyes open to find a grinning Yulia hovering above me.

My head throbbed. The room was spinning, and a glance down revealed that someone had unceremoniously dumped me onto a leather chaise. Surprise surprise, it didn't take me long to guess just who that might have been. *Dublin.*

If my memory accounted for anything, I was trapped in his evil lair, sleeping off the effects of …

I bolted upright, eyes darting to the inside of my arm. There, just along the crook of my elbow, was a tiny, red mark that stung with the slightest movement—courtesy of his so-called cure. Just like when I had woken up that first day, my entire body ached, though Yulia seemed to be aware of this fact because, once again, she was armed with booze.

"We have got to stop meeting like this," I rasped, while my free hand reached for the glass she shoved in my direction.

"Drink up," she commanded without explaining what was inside it.

I brought the glass to my lips as I scooted to the edge of the couch. After an apprehensive glance, I decided that the liquid looked and smelled like rubbing alcohol. Still, I managed to choke down two gulps as Yulia came to stand before me.

"We have to hurry," she said. "Dublin threatened to have my head on a pike if I don't get you to him on time." She imitated his frosty tones, hands on her hips.

Tonight her outfit of choice was a black dress that stopped above her knees, paired with emerald heels matching the color of her eyes.

I took another sip and glanced warily around the room as I swallowed. The windows were sheets of ebony, and the only light came from a lit candle, affixed to the wall above my head. The orange glow tossed shadows in random directions, making the room seem large and cavernous. Crypt-like.

"I brought you some clothes—" I turned as Yulia gestured to an open trunk at her feet. It was large and old-fashioned, like something a pioneer might have stored her things in during the long train ride out West. But rather than calico and straw hats, *this* bit of luggage brimmed with flimsy bits of white silk and lace—*clothes* only in the loosest definition of the word.

"You don't have many options," Yulia admitted. "I tried to bring some variety, however ..." She sank down on one knee and gingerly lifted three garments out, one by one. "You can wear white, *off*-white or *almost* white."

"Oh." I set my glass down at my feet and made a show of studying each one.

They were all shifts as light as gossamer, though they differed in the details. One had a delicate row of pearl beads along the collar while the second had straps so thin they looked incapable of even supporting tissue paper. The last one was the plainest of the bunch, with a simple shape and flimsy, see-through sleeves.

"This one won't win you any favors with Dublin," Yulia warned, most likely referring to the slightly longer hemline than the others.

To be fair, Dublin didn't seem to want me in white *at all*. But I was too busy focusing on the fact that, within a few hours I would be on display for a room of hungry vampires to give a damn about my fashion choices. The thought of being slightly more covered from prying, dissecting eyes was too tempting to resist. I could almost hear Dublin hissing *'tsk, tsk! Unacceptable, Eleanor,'* as I pointed to the sleeved one.

"I'll wear that."

Yulia flashed a mischievous grin. "I thought you might, but I'm not complaining. Come on—" She urged me upright with a wave of her hand. "Let's get you dressed."

I obediently rose to my feet and allowed her to tug my blouse over my head and undo my skirt. In one simple motion, she lifted the shift above me and brought it down, pulling my arms through the sleeves.

At her prompting, I spun in a circle, allowing her to observe the way the fabric hung over my lanky frame.

Even 'dressed' I didn't feel any more covered than I had in my underwear. The hem barely covered my buttocks, and the bold neckline plunged low between my breasts. I felt utterly ridiculous. Yulia seemed to reach the same conclusion, because she rummaged through her trunk for a tube of dark red lipstick and swiped it across my lower lip.

"Blend," she ordered, and I obediently rubbed my lips together. Still unsatisfied, she dug through her belongings once more for a single strip of white ribbon. "There," she breathed as she looped the length around the back of my neck and tied my curls back. "Perfect."

The next second, she was shoving everything back within that case, and then hefted it beneath one arm. "Come. Dublin's being even more of a brooding ass tonight than usual. He wants to make sure that you understand what is *expected* of you."

Her sharp gaze found mine from over her shoulder, and she paused expectantly.

Oh, I had a pretty good idea of what he expected. *Shrieks. Screams. Dramatics.* I would rather die than give him the satisfaction, so I gritted my teeth and jerked my head once.

"I understand."

"Good." For a long minute, her gaze seemed to search mine, peering deep, though I had no idea what she could be looking for. Finally, she continued, "I don't know what he's told you …but it's more than just sex. You are a commodity, of course—" Though at the moment, I felt about as valuable as a bottle of milk on a shelf in a supermarket.

"And yet, you still have the opportunity to wield some element of power."

Power? I waited for her to elaborate. How on earth could someone like *me* ever hope to have the upper hand over anyone—vampire or otherwise? Let alone in a stupid, gauzy dress?

Without explaining, Yulia turned and led the way down a corridor. I followed her and was surprised to find that Dublin's so-called "lair" was much larger than I had originally thought. The layout almost reminded me of a penthouse suite, and I could only guess what might lurk beyond the closed doors.

Torture chambers? Jail cells? A closet filled with a million priceless suits?

I didn't dare risk sneaking a peek behind one, as I traipsed past on bare feet.

"You wouldn't happen to have shoes in there would you?" I pitched hopefully with a nod at that trunk. I had left my heels on the floor of the main room and creeping back to get them wasn't appealing in the slightest.

Yulia shook her head. "You won't need them."

The words held an ominous edge; *you won't need shoes again. Ever.*

I didn't have long to contemplate her meaning before the hallway ended near–of all things–an elevator. Apparently,

Dublin saved the ordeal of the stairs only for his 'guests,' the bastard.

No wonder he hadn't had the decency to even seem out of breath, I groused as I followed Yulia inside.

The interior was made of dark wood with a single silver keypad featuring only three levels. Yulia confidently pressed the bottom one, and the doors slid shut before the cabin plummeted.

I bit my lip, desperate not to ruin my new shift already. As Dublin had suggested, I should save my dramatics—and the bastard was certainly due for a bit of nervous vomit on his shoe. Luckily, my stomach only managed to flip once before the descent slowed and the doors slid apart.

"It's dark," Yulia warned as she led the way. I only had the sound of her footsteps to guide me through the shadows, as a rank, damp smell tickled my nose. Were we in some kind of lower level, beneath the cathedral?

"I've asked Dublin to consider putting lights down here but, you know men." Yulia's laugh fluttered in the still air. "Anyway, here we are—"

There was a *click,* like that of a car door being opened, and then a wealth of light flooded the room. I blinked while my eyes adjusted and tried to make out as much as I could through the dark.

We stood in the middle of what seemed to be an underground garage, beside a red sports car that I assumed was Yulia's. The shrouded shapes of what seemed to be other vehicles were spread neatly in rows with the same care and precision that seemed to maintain the rest of the property.

"Hop in," Yulia urged, holding open the cheery-red passenger door. I slid onto the leather seat while she tossed her case in the trunk and circled to the driver's side. "I'm surprised he brought you here, you know," she admitted while starting the engine. "Even I haven't been invited in years …"

So Dublin *did* live here, then.

"How can he even *live* here?"

I pictured him lurking in the bell tower, unbeknownst to the pious parishioners down below. Wasn't there a commandment or something? *Thou shall not live in a house of worship whilst thou is a demon?*

From the corner of my eye I saw Yulia shrug. "You should ask him."

Her tone was polite, but I got the hint. While she seemed to love thwarting him, Dublin was strictly off limits. I shifted on my seat and preoccupied myself with gazing from the window.

Eventually, the long tunnel had opened up onto a gravel road. We were out in the country now, it seemed, surrounded by fields and wilderness. The entire drive must have taken only a few minutes, but a glance behind me revealed that the church had disappeared—along with the rest of the city entirely.

The tunnel itself had to stretch for miles, and I had a suspicion that the founding priests hadn't included it in their original floor plans.

"Is he Batman?" I blurted, which was the only comparison that came to mind according to my limited knowledge of popular culture. Did Dublin fancy himself as a vampire *Bruce Wayne*, with oodles of money to transform his domain as he pleased?

Yulia didn't reply. Nearly ten minutes more must have passed in silence before we finally turned onto a main road, heading toward some unknown destination. I had a feeling that none of the exits she took led back to the city, either.

As if reading my mind, she finally spoke. "Tonight's auction is not at the club."

Uh-oh. I sat straighter, instantly on guard. "What do you mean?"

"The venue has changed." Her tone was cautious. Hesitant. "Mikhail has decided that the newest crop of girls should be …put to the test, so to speak. Even I don't know what the hell he and Saskia have in store for tonight."

I definitely didn't like the sound of that. "T-test?" My voice raised an octave while my imagination conjured all sorts of unhealthy possibilities; *me, chains, spectators…*

"It's not what you think," Yulia assured me. "It's just something Saskia came up with to increase the appeal. Think of it as a marketing stunt. Dublin's not happy," she added, as if that lessened the blow. "But there isn't much that can be done about it now … You can't fault the venue, though."

As if her words were the cue, a monstrous shape appeared on the horizon, and I felt my apprehension only multiply.

While Dublin may have disappointed in all my comparisons to Dracula, this new 'venue' certainly didn't. The sight reminded me of some reclusive count's estate, massive enough to put even Gray Manor to shame. Even in the dark, it looked like an ideal haunt for any monster, and suddenly I felt uncomfortably similar to the heroine in that certain Bram Stoker novel.

"W-What is that?"

I waited for some grandiose title. Castle—*insert gothic-sounding name here.*

Yulia didn't humor me this time. "Just stay close to me once we're inside," was all she said.

Uneasy, I fidgeted in my seat, eyes glued to our mysterious destination. The path to the manor alone seemed to stretch at least a mile, lined by a row of naked trees whose branches tossed shadows that slithered over the landscape as if alive. When we finally approached an iron gate that barred the way to the front of the house, it opened, seemingly on its own.

I couldn't make out much of the manor house itself, but the stone seemed even darker than the night sky. The whole structure towered overhead, and I felt as insignificant as an ant in its shadow. Windows illuminated with orange light cast an eerie glow over the front terrace.

Yulia parked in the center of a stone courtyard and, in an instant, a pale figure appeared near her window with a hand outstretched.

"Don't scratch it," she warned the man—who was wearing a crisp suit topped by a blood-red tie—as she gracefully exited the car and dropped the keys into his palm.

Without a word, the man climbed into the driver's seat, took the wheel and drove off the second I scrambled out onto the pavement.

I couldn't see anyone else around, but something warned me that the house was full regardless. The whole property reeked of that same eerie vibe one might feel near the outskirts of the tiger's den at the zoo.

Predators be near …

"Let's get this over with." Yulia turned to the manor and craned her neck back to take it in entirely.

Impassively, her green eyes swept over the grand entryway where twin, marble staircases led to the grand, main doors. The longer she stared, the darker her expression became, before eventually, she surged forward with a sigh of defeat.

I scrambled after her, shivering as the cold ground met my bare feet. I felt horribly exposed as I hastened up those steps, naked. It certainly didn't help that the two ushers— both wearing suits identical to the mysterious driver's—

glanced me over once and then shared a look. I could almost guess what they didn't say out loud; *another one.*

However, they acknowledged Yulia with a monotone greeting spoken in unison, before pulling open the doors. "Evening."

She said nothing in return.

In fact, she seemed unusually distant, as she guided me into a breathtaking entryway, bathed in shadow.

An ornate chandelier hung from the ceiling. Dark paneled walls framed a large room where a winding staircase dominated the center—and none other than Saskia happened to be descending the bottom stair.

"Yulia," she greeted flatly. "What a ...surprise." Her tone was even colder than her expression, but despite the ice lurking in her gaze, she still looked regal. Her unbound hair blended with the vibrant scarlet of her dress and set off the ivory in her skin. "I would have thought that Dublin would deliver his own toys tonight."

"Not everyone can be like *you*, dear Saskia," Yulia replied. "Always free to do Mikhail's bidding."

Saskia's eyes narrowed, even as she flashed a poor imitation of a smile. "I hope you've explained what is to be expected of her—" She jerked her head in my direction. "We wouldn't want Dublin to be embarrassed in front of all the investors, now would we?"

Her sly tone revealed her true feelings on that matter.

"Expected?" A slight tremble in her voice was the only clue that Yulia might have been caught off guard. Of course, like any good predator, Saskia immediately picked up on it.

"Why yes," she purred, while approaching us on blood-red heels. "It's a showcase tonight, darling. I would have hoped Dublin had told her."

"Showcase?" Yulia's voice was harder than I'd ever heard it. "Is this a *circus* now, Saskia?"

The other woman shrugged off the apparent insult. Her smile reminded me of the way a tiger might observe fresh prey prance into its den, eager to deliver the killing blow. "I like to try new things," she said. "It keeps the mood interesting—we don't want our buyers getting bored with the same old routine, now do we? After all, if Raphael thought that we did not take our duties seriously …"

"He's here?" Yulia's voice caught, and her hand flew to her throat as if to trap more words inside it.

But it was too late.

"Well, of course, he's here," Saskia replied. "And you know just how *picky* he can be when it comes to these things—" She sent another pointed glance in my direction. "I wouldn't want dear old Dublin to present anything 'lacking' before him. Who knows what the consequences might be?"

With that, she breezed past us and disappeared down a darkened hallway. I gaped after her like an imbecile before I finally got the sense to turn to Yulia.

"What did she mean by *showcase?*"

The word had a horrible connotation from my boarding school days. Those wretched events where us girls were festooned with ribbons, thrust on stage, and expected to demonstrate 'all that we learned' to our board—and in my case intoxicated on the offered brandy—guardians. Call it a hunch, but I assumed that this version wouldn't be anywhere *near* as innocent.

"We need to find Dublin." Yulia took off through a nearby doorway, and I followed behind, fighting to keep from blurting more questions.

Mikhail had wanted the auction to be here, but why? And why this *showcase?* And why had Saskia seemed so smug?

My mind spun as I fought to keep pace with Yulia through the winding corridors. I was panting by the time we finally entered a room where a man stood before the only window, watching the moonlight seep in between the black curtains.

"It's about damn time," he grumbled without turning around—though, that voice needed no introduction.

"Saskia, the bitch," Yulia hissed, ignoring the hostility in his tone, "did you hear what she's planning?"

"Of course I have." With a shrug of his shoulders, Dublin turned. Tonight he too wore an impeccable suit, secured with a dark blue tie rather than a red one. Against the dark walls, the paleness of his skin stood out in stark contrast. "I've known for two days now. She is in control of the *public relations,* after all—" He put a mocking twist on the words. "There isn't a damn thing I can do about it."

"But—" Yulia glanced at me and then back at him. "You're just going to let Eleanor go out there with *nothing?*"

His gaze slithered in my direction and narrowed. "Surely, Eleanor, if you have some hidden talents capable of enticing potential buyers, then please speak up." He waited, tapping his foot impatiently.

I couldn't even come up with a snarky remark. My throat went dry, and every single breath rasped out, harsh and broken. Suddenly, it made sense why he'd been so angry at me before; *you have no idea what you've gotten yourself into.* Apparently, this "showcase" had been in the works for days, devised by Saskia in an attempt to catch him off guard. Humiliate.

I guess that, in his own way, the bastard had tried to warn me—but it was too late now.

"Well, that's settled." Dublin crossed his arms when I didn't speak, expression glacial. "There's no help for it."

"*He's* going to be there," Yulia said, stressing the word. "Raphael. Are you just going to let Saskia win this round and make a fool out of you?"

"It's not like I have a much of a choice," Dublin replied, but his voice was softer, resigned. "Those are the terms of her contract."

"Ugh!" With a growl of exasperation, Yulia whirled on me. "There must be something you can do?" she demanded. "Sing. Dance. Anything?"

I shook my head. The only talents I seemed to possess were warbling show tunes off-key and butchering the violin.

"Think!" Yulia urged. "There must be *something*?"

"I … I was a background dancer in the ballet recital during my senior year?" I pitched weakly. "I'm not even sure if I remember—"

"Well there you have it," Dublin interjected. "I'm sure some grade school ballet will have all the buyers drooling. Let's just pretend that she's ill, so we have an excuse not to put her in this sham."

"We *can't*." Yulia raked her hands through her hair. "Not with Raphael in attendance. He'll take it as a sign of weakness. Or worse, a taunt—which is *exactly* what that bitch wants—"

"Then what do you suggest we do?"

From the exhaustion in Dublin's tone, I sensed that this feud with Saskia was long-running. *Years,* my inner voice suggested.

Yulia bit her bottom lip. "I don't know. But I refuse to let her win. *And,*" she added in an undertone so softly that I got the sense that I wasn't meant to hear it, "what do you think will happen to Eleanor if she does?"

They both looked at me then, expressions guarded.

"We don't have the time for this." Abruptly, Dublin turned and headed for the door. "Get her ready as best as you can, but don't expect ..." He trailed off and sent me one last searching look, eyes settling over my face. Then, without another word he left.

"Damn it!" I flinched as Yulia formed a fist with one hand and smashed it into the palm of the other. Her eyes blazed as they honed in on mine through a fringe of black hair. "You said you danced?"

I shook my head, not sure where she was going with this. "J-Just ballet in school."

Horrible ballet, I might add. I had always been the clumsy sort who lacked the grace that everyone seemed to think should have come with the territory of being 'upper class.' But, like every girl at Welstrom Academy, I had been enrolled in that particular form of torture four days a week for five years.

"You have a dancer's body."

I followed Yulia's gaze, convinced that she couldn't possibly be observing the same lanky, stick-thin limbs that I was.

"I ...I'm not—"

"Let me see." She stood back and snapped her fingers. "Show me."

"B-but." I fidgeted, twisting my toes together. "I was just a cygnet, and that was years ago."

In our senior class production of *Swan Lake*, I hadn't even been cast as a "big" swan but a duckling—the only role suited to my skills. My part had more or less consisted of flitting around, flapping my wings while trying not to trip over my own feet.

Still, Yulia was insistent. "Try."

I sighed and weakly raised my hands over my head, attempting to recall that all-important first position. *Pretty hands!* Mistress Romata, my old instructor, used to shout in furious Russian, and I could sense the poor woman rolling in her grave as I did a clumsy imitation of the first few steps.

I waited for Yulia to cringe in disgust and admit defeat, but the tilt to her mouth reminded me of an artist wondering if anything worthwhile could be created from a shapeless lump of clay.

"Again," she ordered, only this time she came forward to guide my movements.

Expertly, she slowed down the motion, hands on my shoulders, as if her grace might seep into my skin. She corrected mistakes, added a few suggestions here and there. Then she made me run the dance, over and over and over again.

"This is a game, Eleanor," she told me when I finally came to a stop, panting and dripping sweat. "A game of the body and the mind. You must take control. Tease. Taunt—but never once let him forget that this game is yours, and *yours* alone."

I guessed that she was referring to my potential buyer, though—if my preparation for this showcase was any indication—I doubted I'd find anyone who would buy me at all.

"Now, again," Yulia demanded, before I could dwell on the fear, and I had no choice but to lurch into another pathetic spin and try not to fall.

"It's time."

I froze mid-step as Yulia broke off her instruction to observe a clock hanging on the wall.

"Damn it. If only ..." She shook her head, cutting off the thought, and reached for my hand. "You can't be late. Come."

Nearly weak with fear, I followed her out into the empty hall. Every step I took seemed to echo tenfold, resonating in my mind like shouts.

Shadows draped the dimly lit passage but weren't dark enough to obscure the odd, dangerous beauty of it. The walls were a deep shade of blood-red and the floors were polished wood. Unlike the sleek, ultra-modern *Anemia*, the dark colors cast an ancient aura that made it seem even more unwelcoming than Gray Manor.

I felt like a prisoner being led through a medieval castle on her way to the dungeons.

Right on cue, Yulia turned, bringing us before the threshold of a wide circular room that seemed no less terrifying than a torturer's pit. The archway was sheathed in gold, and the gilded doors were open, revealing what waited beyond. The layout resembled that of an old-fashioned theater: a circular stage, surrounded by elevated seats rising up to the high, domed ceiling.

My heart sped once I realized that every seat was full. There were so many people—no, so many *shadows*—watching from swaths of darkness. In eerie contrast, a single puddle of light illuminated the center of the floor, where a scantily clad woman danced before the crowd. With a grace I could only dream of possessing, she rolled her stomach in tune to an exotic beat playing from unseen speakers.

"Damn it," Yulia hissed from my shoulder, eyes on the performance. The woman's movements were sure and elegant—enticing.

If the amount of eyes fixed in the same direction was any indication, I knew that I could never compare.

"I can't do this." My voice broke. I felt five seconds from grabbing onto the end of Yulia's skirt like a child. "I can't … I can't—"

I took a step back, and a wall of ice met my back through the thin material of my shift.

"Get ready." The command accompanied the cold hand that descended over my shoulder, and I knew who stood behind me without even having to turn around. His scent had been ingrained within me by now—spice, ice, and all things forbidden.

"Get ready," Dublin repeated. "You're on next."

Oh, God. The elegant room swam in and out of focus. Dark wood and marble blurred into one indistinguishable cage. I couldn't breathe. His words had made it final; there was no way out. I felt like the pawn in a life-size game of chess, and Saskia already had me in an inevitable checkmate.

"I—"

"Look at me."

I couldn't resist his voice. Yulia had slipped into the shadows, muttering something about 'saving him a seat,' but the funny thing was …I barely even heard her.

For the split second that I turned and made eye contact with Dublin Helos, the world faded into the background. Those harsh shadows became muted gray, and the pulsing beat of music lowered to a hum. Nothing existed save for a pair of eyes dominated by fathomless irises.

"I can't do it," I croaked, hating the roughness in my voice. "I'll scream. Throw tantrums—whatever you want. Just don't make me *do* this."

"It's too late for that." Without warning, his thumb shot out to graze the bottom of my chin, unnervingly gentle and fearfully cold. "Look on the bright side," he suggested, moving that glacial touch up to my cheek. "We'll *both* suffer for your stubbornness."

I flinched, my entire body going stiff. He made it sound so deliberate—as if I had done all of this on purpose. Though, if he cared how his words affected me, his expression didn't show it.

"Every girl has at least three minutes," he continued, changing the subject to the task at hand. "The goal is to entice a potential buyer, though I'm sure that you could just *stand* there ..."

With that, he turned, disappearing through those open doors, and I was alone, seconds from having to 'perform.'

Terror filled me as the current act began to wind down. The woman had moved her arms above her head as she flexed her hips in a sensual, sure motion that I was certain had every man drooling.

My mind went blank. Everything vanished—that silly cygnet dance and Yulia's corrections. It was all gone. All that registered was that I was now the only one standing. Minutes must have passed without me even realizing it.

There was no clapping, or any fanfare to close the last act. The other dancer was simply gone and, in her place, Saskia held court with a mischievous grin.

"Well, then," she started as her eyes settled over me. "Our next selection is brought to us courtesy of none other than …*Dublin Helos.*"

Her voice took on a hard edge as she spoke his name—but it wasn't loud enough to drown out the scattered gasps of shock that erupted around the room.

Dublin had a reputation, it seemed. I turned like everyone else, hunting for that blond head among the crowd, but I couldn't distinguish him from the countless other pale faces.

Was it sad that I even *wanted* to see him? To take one last look at the face of my tormentor before I skipped into the lion's den?

I chalked the strange desire up to the fact he was pretty and just left it at that.

"Mm-hmph." Saskia cleared her throat, and I glanced over to find that her amber eyes were on me, pale arm outstretched.

Her fingers fluttered. *We're waiting.*

Blood surged beneath my skin, playing a haunting melody in the absence of any music. I wanted to crawl into the nearest corner and never come out. Or squeeze my eyes shut and hope that, by sheer force of will, I might wake up from this nightmare.

Maybe you could just stand there? Dublin's harsh suggestion echoed in my mind. Even Yulia had seemed doubtful that I could ever live up to whatever high standards this 'feeding den' seemed to set.

For once, we all were in agreement. I was doomed, doomed, doomed.

"Any day now, darling …"

At Saskia's insistence, I forced a dry swallow and took a step forward. Then another, painfully aware of the fact that at least a hundred sets of eyes were focused solely on *me*. As I approached the center, hushed murmurs of conversation swelled into a deafening hum. *Who is she? Dublin's?*

After three more steps, Saskia finally allowed her beckoning hand to fall.

"Bids will be placed after the show," she reminded the crowd. "Let's begin, then." After clapping her hands together twice she eased back into the shadows, abandoning me in that enormous puddle of light.

Think, Ellie! I told myself as I stood there, petrified. *Do something!*

But my body wouldn't obey my commands. Air stubbornly clung to the inside of my lungs. I couldn't move.

Helpless, I glanced up, hoping that, by some miracle, a reprieve might materialize from thin air—but the unsteady rasp of my breathing was the only sound in the entire room. A million body-less specters stared, waiting to gobble me up. And I could only stand there, in a pathetic white gown, with no clue of what to do.

I felt compelled to take Dublin's advice and curl into a ball. Wait it out. Hide. But then …

A flash of golden hair caught the light. My eyes latched onto the owner's features: ivory skin, eyes like silver, stern, inflexible jaw. He sat in the third row, in between Yulia and a man I didn't recognize. *Raphael?*

Regardless, Dublin was the only figure I could seem to focus on. Those infamous eyes honed in on my own with a spark of recognition. *Just get it over with.* I could imagine him growling—and he was right. I should have just stood there and suffered the confused looks of the audience, wondering why their sexy dance had been capped off by some fool in white.

There was no way in hell that I could ever prove them wrong. Just as he had insisted only a few days ago, my only redeeming attribute was my wallet. But at the thought, a confusing emotion flared before I could help it; that pathetic urge to prove him *wrong.* Pinch him, poke him— anything to push him off that high horse and get a reaction.

After all, this whole mess was his fault for ever pretending that I could have been 'valuable' in the first place.

My heel twitched against the floor. Suddenly, I could feel sensation in my limbs again.

This is your game, Yulia had insisted, as she made me run that dance a final time. *You are not a duckling but an angel with a broken wing—lost—and your dance is the only thing that can keep the monsters from gobbling you up, for a little while at least. You know that it's inevitable; they will get you eventually. But for now, you can keep them at bay with a dance …*

The words gave me the strength I needed to shakily enter the first step; my right foot struck the floor, as I rose up on one leg …

And I had to suppress a gasp at Dublin's reaction.

He lurched forward, eyes narrowing to slits. *What the hell is she doing?*

I should have left it off there. I had gotten a rise out of him, and it should have been enough …but, it wasn't. I found that once I started, it was much harder to stop.

My arm swung up into an arch, and I strived to make the movement slow and deliberate like Yulia had insisted. God, I felt utterly ridiculous. I wasn't graceful. The motion seemed more jerky and disjointed than anything else, but I staggered into the next step, heart pounding, without giving myself the chance to give up.

I could see Dublin curtly shake his head once. *No. Stop.*

Why? I wondered, as a prickle of irritation cut through a wave of fear. *Can the Devil not handle humiliation?*

Defiantly, I attempted to spin …and tripped as my foot caught on a slick patch of flooring.

I went down hard. One of my knees struck the floor, sending a burst of pain shooting up my spine. Both hands flew out to brace my trembling body over the marble—

polished to the point where I could clearly see my own reflection: wild curls, dark eyes and an expression that I rarely saw on my face these days.

Was that ...*determination?*

A hush fell over the crowd. There wasn't a single sound, not a laugh nor a gasp.

I glanced up warily and saw why; Dublin was standing.

He towered over the seated figures in the third row, eyes honed in on me with such ferocity that for a moment I couldn't breathe.

Those blazing, silver irises spoke for him. *Get up.*

Slowly, I crawled forward, almost to the edge of the stage, my eyes seeing only him. Fear kept me attuned to my body in a way I had never been before. I could feel each roll of my shoulders, every harsh intake of air, every sway of my hips as I came close enough to touch the faceless spectators in the first row.

Then, inch by painstaking inch, I rolled onto my knees, every cell pulsing in rhythm to the beat of my heart, in the absence of music.

My knee throbbed. Somewhere in the flurry of motion, one of my sleeves had fallen down my shoulder. Only God knew how much skin was revealed—how much of me that *he* could see. My fingers fluttered uselessly at my sides, aching to adjust it, but I didn't dare.

Instead, I met his gaze and waited.

Would he march down to me and haul me from the room? Command me to leave?

I waited.

And waited …

I couldn't put a name to the emotion that flooded my body as the seconds passed without a reaction from him. Shock? Foreboding? Smug satisfaction?

Soon the room blurred into impenetrable darkness, and I was alone in the spotlight, watched by a single pair of frightening silver eyes.

Nothing else.

No *one* else.

But it couldn't last forever. My time was ticking after all.

The next step required that I stand and turn, fluttering my arms like wings, and rise up on one leg again. Aware of Dublin tracking every motion, I stumbled through it, the rare moment of gracefulness gone. I couldn't stop myself from glancing back. A muscle in his jaw twitched, and I faltered again, foot wobbling in the air.

Every nuance in his body language urged me to stop and let him suffer his humiliation in peace. *Give up.* While the shadows shielded me from the reactions of the audience, only God knew what they were thinking …

But, driven by some impulse I couldn't understand, I kept going.

Two minutes felt like a lifetime. Ironically, I wanted it to last, extending the uncertainty of what would happen when I finally stopped. As long as I kept moving, being 'auctioned,' or sold, or whatever didn't matter.

I'm an angel, I chanted in my head as I struggled to follow Yulia's instructions: turning my body slightly left, rolling my hips right, fluttering my arms up as my belly slowly undulated.

Only one thought kept racing through my head; *keep going …don't stop. Don't stop.*

Until, at last, Yulia's instructions dwindled to one last motion.

I was panting by the time I completed the final step, head bowed, arm outstretched.

There was no clapping.

No booing or hissing.

Not even a sniff.

I had no idea what to expect as I lifted my head, eyes seeking out my captor one more time …

But he was gone. The chair between Yulia and the stranger was empty, and Dublin wasn't anywhere in sight.

"Hmph." I turned to find Saskia slowly making her way to the middle of the floor, eyes sparkling with amusement. The train of her red dress swished against the marble, reminding me of the hiss of an attacking serpent.

"That was …interesting," she sniffed. "And now, next will be another one of *my* selections …"

Taking her blunt change of the subject as my cue to leave, I backed away, blindly searching for a doorway, or a hall to disappear down. Everywhere I looked, I only saw the theater seats and pale faces. There was no way out …

"Eleanor—" I flinched, fighting down a shriek, as a hand clinched my forearm. The next instant, I found myself dragged through an unseen corridor and into the shadows. I turned and nearly collapsed with relief when I made out Yulia's emerald eyes through the dark. Before my knees could even begin to wobble, she wrapped her arms around me and squeezed.

"That was beautiful," she breathed against my ear.

A beautiful mess, I thought, still trembling with exertion. But it was over now. I was ready to curl up into a ball and accept my fate …though strangely, before I did, I found myself wishing for one last glimpse of those watchful gray eyes. I turned, eyes straining through the shadows, but the doors of the theater closed, sealing me off from that haunting crowd.

"What happens now?" My voice caught. I was shaking from head to toe. Yulia had to place her hand on my shoulder just to keep me steady.

"Now …" She glanced furtively over her shoulder and then steered me in the opposite direction. "Now, you wait. Bidding should start soon and then …"

My subconscious fears were more than able to fill in what she wouldn't say: *then we would see if my little flailing duckling act had attracted any hungry wolves.*

I felt sick and exhausted. Judging from the way my skin prickled, I guessed that I was beet-red with mortification as well. My head slumped on my shoulders, and I didn't look up from my bare, sore feet, as I followed Yulia into another room.

This one was furnished with only a chair placed before a window that overlooked a hillside kissed by moonlight.

"You'll stay here," Yulia said, forcing me inside with a gentle shove. "When it's your turn, you'll be called back into the theater and …"

"Sold off," I finished for her.

If anyone had bothered to buy me at all.

I shuffled forward, heart in my throat. I hardly noticed when Yulia left, and the door closed behind her.

All I could picture was silver eyes, watching me through shadow.

"Well, Ellie," I told myself as I stumbled over to the chair and collapsed onto it. "If years of safe, comfortable living have pushed you to be a thrill seeker in your final days, you've gotten your wish …"

*V*ampires apparently had no concept of time.

It felt like I waited for ages, stuck in that room alone. A morbid part of me wondered if this little bidding session could last an eternity—perhaps the spectators forgot that their 'commodities' had an expiration date?

Thinking of Dublin, and his disdain for all things pertaining to my welfare, the idea wasn't all that funny.

Calm down, I told myself. *Try not to panic.*

Of course, as the seconds ticked by, I failed miserably in that aspect.

I had to sit on my hands just to keep from wringing them together. When that didn't work, I stood. Paced. Tore at my hair and tried not to re-live what I'd just done.

My feet throbbed with the memory of that stupid dance. A thin layer of sweat glued my shift to my body, and my white hair ribbon had come loose—only when I tried to adjust it, the whole damn thing slid free to float to the floor.

How many girls were next? I wondered, too distracted to care that my curls fell into my eyes. How many half-naked beauties had already sashayed for the buyers, putting my poor, juvenile ballet to shame?

Though the even bigger question was; why the hell did I care in the first place?

Why hadn't I just done what Dublin had mockingly suggested and just stood there? Made myself invisible? *Hid.*

Why *try* at all? Because I did *try*.

I had done my best to perform in that sick sideshow of the damned.

Those three, pathetic minutes were some of the few in my whole life where I could say that I had actually *worked* at something—even a task as mundane as trying not to fall while flapping my wings.

And what good had it done me? For all I knew, the consequence of not being bought was getting your head chopped off. Even so, I still couldn't blame anyone for not wanting me.

"Eleanor—"

I flinched as the door finally opened, though I wasn't nearly as relieved to see Yulia standing there as I thought I would be. In fact, I wished more than anything else that my wait really *had* lasted an eternity.

"Eleanor," she repeated. "It's time."

"A-All right."

I felt like a certain French queen on her way to the guillotine. As I crept into the hall, I half-expected to find Dublin lurking in the shadows, ready to gloat over my humiliation—the icing on the mortification cake—but there was no one else around.

"Come." Yulia's face was drawn tight, revealing nothing. "You're the last one," she explained as she led me through the twisting corridors. "I know Saskia ensured that purposefully, the bitch. But the bidding's over now."

"D-did anyone …" I trailed off, unable to say it.

"I don't know." Yulia glanced at me from over her shoulder. "I wasn't allowed in," she admitted. "*Formalities* according to Saskia, but *if* anyone did buy you …" She trailed off as we approached the doorway of the theater. It seemed even more intimidating than before; a giant monster waiting to swallow me whole.

And I had no choice but to willingly enter it.

"If anyone bought you," Yulia repeated, "they will claim you here." The next second I found myself gently shoved forward. "Good luck."

Yulia's voice was the last comforting sound I heard before the door closed behind me, and I was trapped.

"Ah, finally." Saskia stood in the center of the floor, basking in the spotlight.

Her expression revealed nothing as to whether or not I had been bought. Instead, she merely cleared her throat like an auctioneer at a farm, readying to present the next prize cow.

"The last selection," she announced to the crowd, wiping her hands on the side of her dress. A slight slip in her fake smile was the only clue as to her true hostility toward me. "Would the buyer please come forward to claim your …*prize?*"

My breath caught as I scanned the rows of pale faces.

I waited …

But, no one stood up, or moved, or even coughed.

"Anytime, now," Saskia murmured, but her tone was smug. I got the sense that this whole show had been some sick joke on her part just to rub it in.

I hadn't been bought.

I don't know why the fact made me feel so small and insignificant. Or why a tell-tale burning sensation prickled behind my eyes.

Focus, Ellie, I insisted. My skin was on fire. It was a struggle just to breathe. *In and out …you can do it.*

I couldn't, and the seconds passed without a single attempt to claim me. It was only when I was afraid that I might actually wither and die beneath the shame, that I finally saw him.

He stood in the shadow of the doorway, mouth flat in a firm line. His hands were in the pockets of his suit, shoulders tensed. When he noticed me staring, all he did was incline his head once; *come.*

I had already taken two steps toward him without even realizing it. My heart pounded as I rushed the rest of the way, while the interior of the room twisted into shadow.

There was complete and total silence. Only the frantic sound of my own heartbeat ushered me out of that blinding puddle of light. The moment I came close enough, Dublin snatched my wrist and dragged me into the hall without a word. Not even a single, nasty insult. Still, I felt the need to say something—anything at all.

"I'm sorry …I'm sorry."

It was pathetic. If anyone should have been sorry, it was *him* for goading me into signing that all-important contract in the first place; for ruining my simple, sheltered life with his talk of blood and 'deals.'

I should have been *glad* to spoil his plans by not being bought. As it was, all I felt was this wrenching, churning guilt …

What the hell had gotten into me? I should have just laid there.

"I'm sorry—"

"For what?" He never looked back, but I had no trouble picturing his expression, anyway; stormy eyes and emotionless frown.

Was he trying to get me to say it? Admit it out loud?

I failed, now commence with the barrage of insults, please?

Instead, I could only manage a pathetic sentence spoken against the hard expanse of his back. "I didn't get a buyer."

My throat felt tight. Painful.

And it *shouldn't* have. I shouldn't have felt so damned ashamed.

"I'm sorry—"

"You did." My first thought was that my desperate brain had imagined the words to ease the shame. But, then he spoke again, clearly enough so that I could make no mistake. "You *did* secure a buyer."

He turned suddenly, shoving me into an empty room. Confused, I glanced around the unfamiliar interior, taking in the only furniture; a velvet chaise, a bed ...

But there was no one there holding a receipt for one *Eleanor Gray*. Even stranger was that Dublin had followed me inside. From behind me, the door closed and I heard the lock twist.

"W-who?" I asked, voice shaking as I eyed the bed's black, silk sheets. "Who bought me?"

I figured a part of me already knew the answer before he even said it out loud.

"I did."

SOLD

I waited for the punch line.

Some quip about how silly I was, maybe? How foolish?

The minutes ticked by, but he said nothing. Nor did he move, and I could only stand there as ice-cold breath caressed the back of my neck in a steady rhythm. Whether or not this was some twisted game, I had no choice but to play along.

"*You* b-bought me?" I hated how breathless I sounded, and struggled to keep my voice steady. "Is that allowed?"

"It's not unheard of."

I frowned. *What?* Did all men like him buy their own toys to keep them from getting lonely on the shelf?

"The rules say that you must be bought," he added, "but they do not specify by *whom*."

Ah. A loophole. It would have been nice to know that little detail before I'd made a fool of myself.

"So, why you?" I gathered enough nerve to turn and face him, shivering beneath the flimsy material of my shift. The room was massive, but with him blocking the door it might as well have been a closet. "Why me?"

He shrugged, expression unreadable. He didn't mention our tense standoff in the theater, though his body seemed free of anger-—for now. "I don't like to leave things unfinished," he said finally. "And I refuse to offer an 'unsuitable' commodity."

Unsuitable? I tried to hide the way I flinched by crossing my arms over my chest.

"So this is just another way for you to finish my training?" I wanted to make air quotes, but one look at those eyes and I squashed the urge. "To make me 'suitable'?"

"For what?" he wondered. "The timeline specified in your contract is almost up. You only needed to secure *one* buyer, and you *have*. You've fulfilled your bargain."

"Oh." I shifted on the tips of my toes. For some reason, it was harder to process those words than it should have been. *Fulfilled your bargain.* "So, was this just some way for you to save face?" I wondered. "Beat Saskia at her own game?"

"Possibly." His voice gave nothing away, and I felt lost, grasping at straws.

"But ..."

I shivered as his hand drifted to my cheek. I could only stare as he caught a stray curl between his thumb and forefinger and then tucked it in place behind my ear. Thinking of his crisp and clean suite above the cathedral I got the sense that he preferred for things to be nice and neat. Perfect.

"Don't make any mistake," he went on, returning that hand to his side. "I didn't buy you to 'save' you from the horrors of being auctioned. It was strictly a business transaction on my part, and I will expect no different from you tonight than I would from any other girl."

The words didn't affect me the way they *should* have. I didn't tremble with fear, like Little Red before her Big Bad Wolf. I didn't cower. Instead, I tilted my head back and observed him carefully.

I expect no different tonight …

"So you bought me for …" I cleared my throat, gathering up the nerve to utter that so very dangerous word. "Sex?"

I thought of all those busty beauties and laughed—I couldn't help it.

The idea of him wasting good money on *me*—to salvage his pride of course—while everyone else had probably beaten themselves bloody over one of Saskia's 'girls' was both pathetic and damaging to my pride. Laughter was the only way I could hide just how badly his utter lack of faith in me hurt.

"You must take your line of 'work' very seriously," I sneered. "How much was I worth to save your own skin, hmm? One dollar? Three? Five?"

"The cost is irrelevant—" His eyes slid shut and reopened a chilling shade of gray. "I never leave a 'project' unfinished."

His fingers encircled the ball of my chin and lifted it, forcing me to meet his gaze for so long that I swore I could taste silver—strange and metallic—on my tongue by the time he finally pulled away.

"Let's see how well you recall your lessons," he proposed suddenly.

Before I could react, he leaned in, lips grazing my jaw-line before settling near my ear. Then, he whispered something; a command so vulgar that I had to dig my own nails into my palms just to keep from gasping, horrified.

I figured that I should have slapped him, like any good socialite would, just turn dramatically on my heel and stomp away. *Why, I never!*

But I knew in the pit of my gut that was what he wanted me to do; to merely flash his fangs and have me run screaming from the room. I think he only knew how to play the role of evil villain and watch people react.

Well, not this time.

I pulled myself up to my full height and took a step forward. My gaze deliberately traveled from that cold, handsome face—avoiding those eyes however—and down to that blue tie, then lower ...and lower.

Look at it clinically, Ellie, I told myself, all the while reaching for his zipper. *It's only a duty.* The same way *he* liked to insist that everything leading up to this moment had been only 'business.'

You don't really believe that, my inner voice whispered. *Do you?*

I tried to ignore it.

Apprehension coursed through my body, as the pads of my fingers caught hold of the tiny bit of metal. Slowly, I dragged the zipper down, gulping as his words taunted me; a request so blunt that I couldn't even repeat it inside my own head.

He was watching me, expression blank as I undid the clasp holding his pants together while fighting to keep from accidentally brushing his skin.

Clinical, clinical, I chanted while I loosed my grip so that his pants could slide unhindered to the floor.

God, he was beautiful. I hated how my body noticed that—reacted to it—even though I should have been disgusted by him, by this.

But, the fact was that ...I was morbidly curious as to just how far I was willing to go. Innocent little Eleanor Gray.

He wore navy briefs underneath, and I never knew that such a simple piece of cotton could seem so menacing.

Come on, a part of me scoffed. *Be serious! You can't possibly mean to …*

But I only heard Yulia's voice as I stared down at the intimating appendage shaping the front of his boxers.

'Take control. Tease. Taunt—but never once let him forget that this game is yours.'

The advice was heartening, but Dublin didn't seem inclined to let me make the rules.

"Any day now." For once, there was no mocking edge or sarcastic pun in his voice. Just ice. "I'm sure that even *you* must have read a naughty romance novel, or two, in your spare time. They give a pretty good play-by-play of how it's done—"

He broke off, mid-sentence when I sank to my knees. I didn't say a word, even while I blindly reached for the waistband of his boxers.

I didn't look up …at first. I couldn't.

Instead, I took my time, winding the soft cotton around my fingers and slowly pulled the material down to his knees. Calves next. Ankles.

When the fabric finally hit the floor, only then did I look up.

My breath caught. His body was one of those sights that never failed to knock you senseless, no matter how many times you saw it—though once again I only saw half. His suit-coat and tie intimidated me too much to even think about taking them off.

So I settled for gaping at his lower body. Particularly *one* impressive aspect …

Crude drawings in sexual education textbooks could have never done him justice. His shaft was rigid, jutting from a thatch of golden hair and seemed every bit as menacing as the man himself.

"This doesn't work if you just stare at it," I heard Dublin comment from above, sarcastic once again.

Very well … I sucked in a breath and let it out slowly.

I guess I was supposed to touch it first? Was it utterly sick that I actually *wanted* to?

My hands shook. It seemed to take forever before they stopped trembling just long enough to make an attempt, and I couldn't breathe when I reached out and gently traced the tip with my finger.

Dublin's reaction was swift. His jaw snapped shut, teeth gritted while those eyes darkened into a color that bordered on ebony.

I had no clue what the hell I was doing, but he didn't bat my hand away, so that had to be a start, right?

Fighting down my unease, I reached out for him again, trailing a finger along his impressive length. The skin was surprisingly soft, almost like silk. I marveled at how damn cold he was—frozen. Hard too, like steel.

Focus, my inner voice hissed. *What had he mentioned? Romance novels?*

Sure enough, what few I had read did give me a vague idea of what was expected.

I curled my hand around him, forming a fist—or as much of one as I could. A prickle of apprehension flooded my belly when I realized that my fingers didn't quite meet.

He couldn't possibly think I could fit it all in, could he? I fretted. Still, I began to pump my hand up and down, watching the act with an almost student-like curiosity.

It didn't *look* erotic. In all honesty, it looked ...ungainly. Crouched as I was, I still had to strain upright just to find the right leverage. He was so cold it hurt to maintain the contact for too long.

Still, I could feel him stiffen and, God help me, lengthen even more beneath my touch—that was a good thing, right? I couldn't ignore the part of me that shivered, remembering that night in the club. The way he had felt inside me ...

The thought made my grip tighten involuntarily, and Dublin damn near jumped out of his skin.

"S-sorry!" I pulled back, afraid that I had hurt him—only to have a hand colder than ice descend over my shoulder, locking me in place.

He never moved.

I snuck a peek at him through my lashes and saw that he stood completely still. Frozen.

He could have been a beautiful Romanesque statue carved from marble, if it wasn't for the way that one part of him seemed painfully *alive*. Silken flesh strained against my fingertips, throbbing in a way that seemed to demand something that I had no real knowledge of how to deliver.

I was panting. My throat tightened, eyes drifting up and over the alabaster skin shielding muscles so hard they could have been chiseled from marble.

Run away, a part of me whispered, *this is your last chance.*

Then our eyes met—silver on green—and I stopped thinking altogether.

Keep going. He didn't say it out loud, but those eyes did the talking for him, black pupils dominating the pale irises. *Now!*

I could only weakly pump my fist up and down until I found a steady rhythm. A muscle in his jaw twitched, and as if I was suddenly psychic I knew exactly what he wanted next without him ever having to say it; those sordid little romance novels had covered *that* as well.

Heart pounding with anticipation, I lowered my head, using my hand to guide me, and closed my eyes.

Unacceptable! My mother hissed from the grave as my tongue slid out, brushing along the tip of him.

Would it be like licking a frozen pole in the middle of winter, a childish part of me wondered? Could I get stuck?

But my tongue glided over him easily, numb by his chill. God, he tasted like snow; delectable, glacial, *masculine* snow.

As if from miles away, I heard myself gasp—but I wasn't in my body anymore. Eleanor Gray was dead and gone, and some new creature was in her place. One who relished the tendrils of heat that prickled through her belly as her tongue hesitantly swirled, stroked, slid down his length from tip to base and back again. It was like some long buried part of me knew instinctively what to do.

And I guessed that I was doing it right.

A low sound teased the air. Like a good little heroine, I wanted to chalk it up as something other than what I knew in my soul it to be.

A rumble of thunder? I wondered innocently. *The roar of a distant jet plane?*

Certainly *not* a growl, primal and animalistic enough to match the ferocity of the fingers that came to fist in my hair.

"It's not a lollipop, Eleanor," I heard him croak after a moment. "They call it *'cocksucking'* for a reason."

That they did.

I wasn't insulted, oddly enough, or ashamed, or embarrassed.

I felt nothing at all but raw, sweltering heat as I shifted forward on my knees, parted my lips and took him slowly into my mouth. His hands coiled through my hair, goading me on, urging me to take more, more, *more.*

When I couldn't go any further, we both sucked in a breath; let it out in unison, drew in another. I don't know if he even *needed* to breathe—but the harsh sound played like a lullaby.

And there was no escape.

My inner prude taunted me; *slut, whore, skank. No heiress should ever debase herself so wantonly!*

But the barrage of insults couldn't smother the true emotion I tried so hard to deny—ignore.

It felt utterly *amazing* being wanton.

For the briefest of moments, I had control. Over him. Over myself. The simple act of my mouth on his shaft caused him pleasure, though he would never admit it out loud.

But neither could he hide it.

It was all in the way his body tightened. How he began to rock back in forth in tune with the slow rhythm he was urging on with that grip on my hair.

My tongue cradled the tip, which was the most of him I could fit in my mouth, brushing it as gently as I could. Once. Twice. Again.

And with a brashness I never knew I could possess, my lips closed around his shaft once more, urging him further into my mouth.

"Enough—"

I blinked, dumbstruck, as he shoved me back, though his expression was too dark to read. My mouth was open, lips wet. Moisture dribbled down my chin, and suddenly reality hit with a vengeance.

Oh, God ...

Shame and guilt flooded back, and in an instant, I felt worth even less than the five dollars I had accused him of spending on me.

Until those eyes flashed, a brilliant, hungry silver, and he moved.

"Get up." The order was more for show because he hauled me upright before I could even begin to stand on my own. A hand cinched my waist, lifting me easily from the floor as he staggered back the few steps necessary to reach the bed. Then he shoved me onto it.

I trembled as he mounted after me, wrenching my legs apart. I expected him to toss out another humiliating command, to force me to touch myself again.

But all he did was grab at my shift before tearing it right down the middle.

The next second his hands were sliding beneath my underwear, tugging them down. Eyes dark, he fisted the ivory lace into a ball before tossing it onto the floor.

And I had nothing left to hide behind.

Like a monster from a fairy tale, Dublin loomed above—still in that impeccable suit-coat and tie; the Big Bad Wolf with a weakness for Armani.

His pupils were dilated. Just a sliver of that infamous eye color remained, nearly lost amid a sea of black. The sight reminded me of displaced halos, circling the black demonic abyss their angelic possessor had fallen into. Two small bits of ivory glinted from beneath his bottom lip, and I knew in my soul what they were: *fangs*.

God, he looked terrifying ...

I could only lay there, half-naked and trying to catch my breath.

Every single nerve in my body prickled, warm and alive—conflicting with the goosebumps that rose to life in face of his chill. My throat ached in memory of what I had just done. What little of my shift remained felt more oppressive than the man on top of me.

And I still couldn't help the fact that my eyes kept darting down between us, to where that crisply tailored suit ended, and Dublin Helos began.

Oh God. Images swirled through my head, making my skin heat with shame. *Me. The floor. Him. My mouth. Him.* What in the hell had I done?

What was I still *doing*?

"Look at me—"

I was too breathless to admit that, technically, I had never stopped 'looking' in the first place. Instead, I forced myself to glance up, eyes passing over that mockingly bright tie, and met his gaze just as the last hint of those gray irises finally vanished.

Without warning, his right hand came to encircle my throat. The contact was light, though in my mind the embrace might as well have been a manacle chaining me down.

"Who am I?"

Huh? I blinked, confused by the question only to *tremble* as fear set in. That voice wasn't his. It sounded deeper, guttural.

"You're D-Dublin," I heard myself croak, only to have the words cut off entirely as his thumb slid down to my collarbone, caressing what I knew to be the path of a vein.

"Wrong answer—" My heart sank at his tone. "How quickly you forget your lessons already."

In disapproval, the icy tip of his nail grazed through the light fabric of my shift, slowly inching downward …

A strangled sound tore from my throat as the pad of his finger brushed the underside of my breast. He was so cold —my body's reaction was swift and unavoidable; a nipple tightened, rising sharply to graze his palm.

All the while, he posed that same question again, impatient.

"Who am I, Eleanor Gray?"

I choked in a breath. Held it in until my lungs screamed for air and tried to let it out without making a sound.

Good God. I never even knew that there were that many nerves in one spot…

"I want an answer," his voice came from miles away. "Who…am…I?"

"S-Sir?" I pitched halfheartedly, wondering if this was some not-so-subtle reminder to play by the silly rules he had set. "Dublin, *Sir*—"

His hand returned to my throat with slightly more pressure, cutting off the words.

"No. Come on, Eleanor," he goaded while caressing my windpipe with a thumb. "Use that witty little brain of yours. I want you to say the one thing I've been *waiting* to hear you utter since our first sordid little meeting."

There were so many possibilities. *You were right? I surrender to your magnificence, oh evil one?* Though, heart pounding, I had to admit that, this time, I knew exactly what he wanted to hear.

"V-Vampire."

His eyes narrowed in response, and my blood ran cold—though that might have had more to do with that icy touch creeping along my body more than anything else.

"I prefer the term *'Master,'* for tonight," he corrected, flashing teeth that seemed uncomfortably sharp. "After all …I did pay for the privilege."

"P-Privilege?" I gulped, distracted; *'Master'* seemed so much more demeaning to utter than *'sir.'* "The privilege of what?"

Having me butt naked and a slave to his every whim wasn't enough?

Dublin shrugged, as if the answer were so obvious that he didn't want to waste any time saying it. Instead, he slid his free hand beneath my waist, forcing my legs further apart, and settled into the space between them.

I held my breath, painfully aware of every ridge and curve of his palm on my hip. His body felt like solid ice against mine, and I knew in the pit of my soul that it would be so easy for him to crush me if he wanted, to utterly destroy me in an instant.

So why the hell did his nearness make my heart jump in a way that had nothing at all to do with fear?

"I thought I said that you were never to wear white?" His eyes were on the upper part of my shift, which was the only bit of it still intact.

"T-technically …I'm not wearing much of anything," I managed to croak.

The corner of his mouth twitched. Could that possibly be a smile? Or a *grimace*, as he eyed the way the fabric dipped dangerously low, baring more skin than I had realized.

I flushed, suddenly self-conscious, but as if reading my mind, Dublin moved before I could even attempt to cover myself. Very, very carefully he dragged a thumb along the pulse thrumming below my collarbone, following its invisible trail.

Down …down …all the way to my navel.

My entire body jerked, in tune to every feather-light motion. Anticipation turned to an almost uncomfortable level of neediness.

God. Just when I feared that this torture might last forever, he shifted, bracing a hand against the mattress, and lowered his head …

Alarm flared, blotting out everything else.

"W-What are you doing?" I tried to sit up.

Without speaking, his hand went to my thigh where he seized a bit of skin between his fingers and pinched. Hard. I gasped in shock, instinctively twisting to get away, but his knee fell over mine, locking me in place.

"Remember your manners," he warned, mouth hovering above my skin. Bursts of cool air assaulted me with each word. "*What are you doing …*"

He made an expectant sound in the back of his throat, and it took everything I had in me just to choke out, "Sir."

Satisfied, he released me, fingers cupping my leg instead, holding it tight against him.

"Do you know what happens next, Eleanor?" he asked in an undertone. Those eyes met mine again, unnervingly patient.

Oh no. Scenarios came to mind; *him, me, fangs …*

"N-No, Sir," I lied, until another sharp pinch forced me to rasp, *"Master!"* instead.

"Oh, I think you know …"

How in the world was he still capable of speech?

From the back of my mind, I was uncomfortably aware of the fact that the hard bulge pressing against my thigh was not a random metal bar. Going off the romance novels he liked to reference so much—paired with a basic grasp of biology—he should have been reduced to a rutting animal by now, humping anything he could reach and not … infuriatingly in control.

I was the one who felt barely tethered to reality. Who could barely process anything other than the sensations building inside her own body; a primal, almost animalistic need that demanded he touch me. Here …there … *Anywhere.*

"I think you *do* know, Eleanor." I could feel icy lips against the hollow of my throat when he spoke again. "Indulge me."

It was getting so hard to string together words, to think at all. I managed to gasp a strangled set of vowel sounds that I prayed he mistook for something intelligible.

Rather than reply, he seemed intent on just observing my skin, eyes narrowed.

It really shouldn't have been that much of a shock when his fangs prodded my flesh.

"Oh!" I jumped anyway, threatening to lurch off the bed—only to find both of my hands clasped by just one of his. His lower body fell across mine, and I was trapped.

And then, so slowly I couldn't stand it …

He prodded again.

Scraped.

At the back of my mind, I knew that those fangs merely grazed the surface, never sinking too deep—or drawing blood—but my body's reaction was just as violent as it had been that first night. I writhed. My toes curled helplessly in the black silk sheets.

My mind was dominated by a single thought: *More, more!* And when he finally allowed himself to go deeper, to bite … The world exploded.

Colors were sharper, more vibrant. Everything shifted and twisted and spun. I couldn't hear a sound above the roar of my own heartbeat.

With teasing scrape after teasing scrape, he taunted me. The cruel game seemed to last forever until finally, he pulled back.

Those eyes held me captive, once again dominated by black, as he adjusted his weight and mounted me fully. His free hand began to roam my thigh, and I tensed, heart in my throat, even before he forced a finger inside me.

I moaned at the intrusion. It hurt—though nowhere near as painful as that first night. On second thought, the sensation was more uncomfortable than anything else. Without giving me time to adjust he started to move, thrusting in and out. With every harsh slide, he returned a little easier than before—deeper—but it wasn't until he made a cruel accusation out loud that I realized why.

Like a teacher demonstrating the obvious to a naïve student, he held up a glistening finger for my observation.

"You're wet," he said before callously sliding the digit back in. And then another … "For me," he accused while I quaked, damn near senseless. "You want this."

The words bounced around the inside of my skull, unabashedly blunt. *Wet for him. I wanted this.*

God, I had no clue what he meant—something told me that I really didn't want to know.

With him inside me, I couldn't breathe. Couldn't think. His fingers alone were massive, splitting me apart, and worst of all …

Some greedy, terrifying part of me just wanted *more*. It craved the destruction only he could bring more than anything.

When I didn't reply to his taunts, Dublin fell into a brutal rhythm, twisting and curling those fingers, rubbing …until I was bucking greedily into his hand, gasping like a fish on dry land.

It felt good, I couldn't deny that. Wrong—but so very, *very* good.

I groaned in a mixture of shock and relief when those fingers finally slid free.

Maybe then I could think? Catch my breath?

The thoughts turned out to be nothing more than wishful thinking as the contact was replaced by something else.

"No more preliminary games," I heard Dublin insist on a barely restrained growl. I could feel his grip on my wrists quiver, as if every instinct he'd been fighting to control had chosen that moment to break free. Apparently, even a vampire could hold back only for so long.

"It's time for you to earn those so-called *five dollars*."

I flushed as he threw my own words back in my face—but I didn't have to suffer the shame for very long.

He entered me slowly this time, almost as if in punishment, forcing me to feel every single ridge and curve of the shaft I had explored so thoroughly only moments before with my mouth.

Inch by precious inch he filled me, dominating every cell; I barely found enough room in my lungs to suck in air, to breathe.

My teeth descended into my lower lip as he withdrew. Thrust again. Again. Again.

If there had even been any pain this time, it faded quickly, replaced by a heat that smoldered in my belly.

I didn't know if it was a lack of ability to draw in oxygen or sheer will that kept me from making a sound, or crying out. Only the creaking of the bed filled the silence—but somehow that was more shaming than anything else.

This was really happening. There was no escape.

I don't know when my eyes started to flutter shut, or when my vision blurred. I was only aware of a sudden clarity as he pinched me once on my hip, hard.

"Look at me."

I had no choice. My eyes drifted up to find that those swollen pupils had been reduced to mere pin-pricks amid a sea of gray.

His jaw was clenched, eyes glowing as he rocked his hips, filling me over and over until even a sharp pinch wasn't enough to keep me tethered to reality. Every action slowly pushed me toward some invisible threshold …and then over it.

I moaned. Shuddered. Trembled.

Fire filled me, building within my belly until I couldn't take it. Then, all at once, it boiled over into an inferno.

And I was consumed.

From light-years away I heard Dublin groan; the only sound he ever made during those twisted, silent minutes. Both of his hands had moved to my waist, holding me in place as he brutally pumped in a steady, unyielding rhythm. Newly freed, my fingers flew to his shoulders—the only solid thing within reach—pulling and grasping, heedless of the expensive fabric at risk of being torn in my clumsiness.

I couldn't help it.

Oh God, God, God, I chanted as my body rode some imaginary escalator *up, up, up,* driven by every thrust until …

I broke. Nonsense, meaningless words tore from my throat as Dublin drove deep, striking a part of me that made everything darken for the briefest second—and then shatter.

I wasn't in my body anymore. Ellie Gray was gone, and I was floating, flying, falling …

Until, gradually, I came back down.

One. Two. Three.

I counted every breath until my vision cleared sometime after *fifty*. I was lying face-up in the middle of a crumpled pile of black sheets, panting as the last tendrils of fire faded away.

Oh, Ellie, I thought as my eyes traced my still-splayed legs and the sad remains of Yulia's white shift. *You whore.*

But the word didn't sting. I didn't feel as ashamed as I should have, and I figured that was the worst revelation of all.

Dublin had already moved and sat at the end of the bed, feet on the floor, back facing me. That crisp, clean jacket hung off one shoulder, revealing a dark undershirt and broad, pale shoulders.

I gulped. *Had I done that?* I stared down at my hands, wondering if they were capable of clawing at a thousand dollar suit. While I may not have been the most materialistic of women, even I could appreciate luxury when I saw it.

Tsk, tsk, Ellie, I scolded myself. *You should ask him for the bill.*

But before my mouth could even begin to open, he turned to face me.

Those eyes had returned to normal—that frighteningly cold, impassive gray. His hands were at his throat, adjusting something that must have slipped free. Whatever it was flashed silver in the light.

A necklace?

The chain was delicately slender. As he tucked it back beneath his shirt, I caught a glimpse of the talisman on the end of it; a small, silver cross. He had never struck me as the jewelry-wearing sort, and the sight conjured all kinds of nosy little thoughts before I could help it; *a token from some past lover? A relic from his human life?*

Regardless of the origin, I was depressed to find that yet another vampire myth had been proven false. The only lore I had left to cling to now was some rubbish about garlic.

Dublin didn't say anything—not that I really expected him to. Instead, he merely watched me, shrugging to adjust that black coat. It was a silent, chilling game, our staring contest, a game that no one won, in the end, because we both turned away at the same time, as if by some silent agreement.

"So …is this it then?" I sounded strangely impatient as I addressed the wall behind his head. *Is this it then? Can I die now, and gracefully end my suffering?*

He didn't answer.

I registered every rustle as he stood—to retrieve his pants I guessed. Retie his shoes. Fix that tricky collar so that his tie showed neatly in the middle. Perfect …

Minus the one drop of blood peeking at the corner of his mouth.

He had pierced my skin after all, I realized with a jolt. A tiny smear of red streaked across my chest, unnaturally vibrant. I glanced up to gauge his reaction, only he was already half-way across the room. I wasn't that surprised when, a second later, the door opened and closed.

He was gone—but it startled me just how much that simple fact *stung*, as I curled up in the middle of a strange bed, alone with my newest shame.

What now?

Should I stay? Go?

But the only thing I seemed to be capable of was squeezing my eyes shut, blocking out the sight of that room, and just …

Wait.

For sleep?

For Yulia?

For a random burst of lightning to put me out of my misery?

Only God knew what.

NEGOTIATIONS

"*G*et up—"

The cold voice jolted me awake, and my eyes flew open to an unfamiliar room enclosed by ebony walls.

Pain and shame greeted me like two old friends. A cold sweat basted my skin, and from the way my cheeks burned, I suspected I'd been blushing in my sleep. To top it all off, my entire body ached inside and out. When I finally gathered the nerve to glance up, I almost hoped to find Yulia standing there beside the bed with a much-needed dose of alcoholic medicine.

Instead, I found Dublin, glaring down with empty eyes.

"Get dressed," he commanded. "Now."

He tossed something onto the mattress: a black jacket, tailored to perfection. The same one, I realized with a gulp,

285

that *he* had worn last night. My entire body heated up at the memory, not that I had long to sit and reminisce.

"Unless you want to be around when an entire manor full of vampires bed down," Dublin called ominously from the doorway, "I suggest you do as I say."

His tone conjured plenty of frightening possibilities, and I grabbed the jacket and shoved my arm through one of the sleeves without delay.

The garment was large on me and hung down almost to my knees when I stood up. A strange scent lingered in the fabric, making my stomach clench—ice, spice, *him*. My fingers shook so badly that I barely managed to fasten the topmost button before Dublin marched across the room and grabbed my arm.

We entered the hallway in silence. It was empty—not that we stuck around long enough to greet anyone who might happen to walk by. Dublin was ruthless, dragging me through the corridors in record time. I barely noticed the entryway passing by in a blur before I found myself outside, stumbling down those front steps.

The sky was a faint, navy blue that marked the early morning hour before dawn. The sun hadn't even risen yet, and I could still make out the moon, pale and partially hidden beneath silver clouds.

I guessed it to be four or five in the morning, *at least.*

A car was waiting nearby and, without hesitation, Dublin wrenched open the passenger-side door and shoved me inside. I scrambled to adjust myself as he circled around to the driver's side and took the wheel. Without a word, we took off, turning down the driveway and through the main gates that opened, once again, seemingly on their own.

I tried not to ask where we were going but once the city, glowing and vibrant, appeared on the horizon I couldn't help myself.

"Are you taking me home?"

Why in the hell did I sound so breathless at the prospect?

One night in a spooky vampire mansion and I should have been *begging* to be taken to Gray Manor. But at the thought of traipsing through those empty halls and back to my own bed …

I shoved my hands into the pockets of his jacket and fidgeted on the leather seat.

Of course, Dublin didn't answer or even spare a glance in my direction. He seemed entirely too focused on maneuvering through the slumbering city streets. He gave me no clue as to where we were headed, but when the car finally came to an abrupt stop, I felt myself frown in confusion as I took in our surroundings.

Thinking of the posh *Cafe Claret* and that elegant cathedral residence, I was stunned to find us parked in a narrow, filthy alley. Shadowy figures lingered on the corners nearby, and an odd stench reached my nostrils even with the windows firmly rolled up.

Going off Dublin's polished persona, it looked like the sort of place he wouldn't even have his trash dumped in, let alone enter himself. But there he was, already out of the car and pulling open my door without hesitation.

"Come on."

I had no choice but to climb out onto the pavement after him, painfully aware of my bare feet—as well as the fact that I wore nothing at all beneath his jacket ...

No underwear. No bra. No lacy white nightgown.

My cheeks flamed as I grabbed onto the hem of the coat and tried to yank it down as far as it would go; barely to my knees. Oblivious to my discomfort, Dublin snatched for my wrist, and once again took off with me in tow.

We went down half a block before entering what appeared to be a small café. A sign on the window claimed *"24 hr service."*

It was relatively clean inside, with linoleum floors and blue walls illuminated by a flickering ceiling lamp.

Dublin brought us to a booth in the back corner and shoved me onto the seat before taking the one across from me. When a yawning waitress appeared, he ordered two cups of coffee—black—without asking for my preference, and we sat in silence until she returned and placed the steaming mugs down between us.

Warily, I grabbed one, desperate for something to keep me busy rather than twiddling my thumbs. I made a show of pouring in two creams and ripping open exactly three bags of sugar while Dublin watched, his own cup untouched.

With the hot mug in my hand, I finally found the strength to voice a question. "Why are we here?"

Something told me that he wasn't the type to go out for coffee at four o'clock in the morning for the hell of it. Rather than answer me directly, he withdrew something from his pocket—a folded slip of paper—which he carefully unfurled before placing on the table.

A pen appeared from nowhere to roll in my direction.

"Your time is up," he told me, eyes on the surprisingly blank sheet. "Usually, this would signal a need to …renegotiate."

I blinked in shock and took a hasty sip of scalding coffee to hide it. "R-Renegotiate?" I stammered after I swallowed. "F-For what?"

He raised a blond eyebrow. "Surely, even someone like *you* had planned on bargaining for more than four days?"

More days? Was it funny that I had almost forgotten our little 'arrangement?'

Though I was more surprised by the fact that he wasn't running away from me, cursing the day he ever gave me his blood. Instead, he sounded every bit the businessman, and I took another sip, genuinely curious.

What on earth would someone like me do with *more* time? Contemplate my impending spinsterhood as he had so rudely implied the other day? But then I thought of Georgie and flinched; in all the chaos of the last few days, I had nearly forgotten that I was *'technically'* dying.

"And what would I have to do?" I found myself asking. "Be put on auction again?"

I couldn't disguise my disgust at the mere thought of ever appearing on stage before Saskia.

"No," he said quietly.

My head jerked up. Eyes wide, I waited for him to continue.

"Rather than the club, this time your contract would solely belong to …me."

He made it sound so casual. So harmless.

As naïve as he seemed to think I was, even I saw right through the act; brown liquid sprayed in an arch as I choked.

"*You?* Doing what?" I sputtered, aware that all eyes were on us: the bleary-eyed waitress, the cook, and a yawning janitor in the corner—not that Dublin seemed to give a damn.

"Whatever we agree on," he replied. "That is the meaning of 'negotiations,' after all. What? Don't believe me?" Suddenly, he reached for the pen and scribbled something down onto the slip of paper. "I'll start, then; while not unlimited access to your accounts, I want full use of your name."

"Like how?" I asked, curious despite myself—even more so at his reply.

"Your endorsement."

I frowned at a mental image of me smiling while holding up a box of cookies, or whatever else a vampire could possibly hope to sell.

"Not in the way you're thinking," he added, as if reading my mind. "Your presence would come in handy during several business arrangements. Nothing less. Nothing more."

"Huh."

When I didn't start raving about my name and money Dublin seemed to take it as a sign that I might play along.

He held out the pen.

Negotiations, hm?

"And no more auctions?" I asked just to make sure. My eyes warily drifted over his neat writing: *Unlimited use of the Gray name.*

"Done," he said.

"And—" I swallowed. "What about …"

My hesitation alluded to what I couldn't put into words.

"Yes." His expression gave nothing away. "Sex will be a part of your bargain; a fair trade for more time—"

"Two weeks," I interjected, trying to not let my shock show. *A 'fair' trade?* "I …I want just two more weeks."

More than enough time for me to face Georgie and secure a guardian for Mr. Tinkles. I shuddered at the thought of my poor kitty; he had been neglected for nearly a week now.

Dublin nodded. *Fine.* "You will have seven days," he clarified. "And so will I."

A creeping sensation blossomed in my stomach as I considered it. Seven days for me, with a day spent paying off each one in return, adding up to exactly two weeks.

Talk about a hard bargain.

You should leave, the logical side of me insisted. *Just get up and go home. This isn't right.*

I squirmed uneasily and reached for my mug again, only to discover that it was empty.

"What about the club?" I thought of that dark interior with a shudder as I set the mug aside.

His reply was swift. "You will accompany me there should I happen to visit on the days you repay me, and even then you would only service *me.*"

In other words, I wouldn't be dressed up and sold off to the highest bidder.

"Oh," I said. Given the swirl of emotions circling my mind, the word had a million different connotations.

Oh, I'm relieved I won't be auctioned off like cattle.

Oh, but that means I'll be at your mercy.

Oh, I am contemplating stealing your coffee out of desperation.

I couldn't hide my sigh of relief.

The pen was still in front of me, and I cradled it carefully between my thumb and forefinger before pressing it to the page. It seemed to take an eternity before I gathered enough nerve to write out a single sentence before shoving the page in his direction. I felt like a high school student, passing notes.

He read the line with one pass of those gray eyes; *no cuffs.*

"Nonnegotiable," he said, without elaborating on why. He grabbed the pen and, in a smooth stroke, crossed out my words. "But while we're on the subject ..."

After adding three neat lines, he held the page out for me to read. Considering the nature of them, I assumed that all three 'conditions' applied solely to me.

No touching without strict permission.

No kicking.

No shrieking.

I flinched at the last part, remembering his 'damsel' insult from what felt like a million years ago. How funny that in reality it had only been a few days. I thought for a minute, mulling over the strange fact that we were negotiating sexual preferences, as part of a contract, in the middle of a half-empty café.

"No kissing," I added, thinking that the request was fitting enough and without a word, Dublin added it to the list: *No kissing, on the mouth.*

I wasn't brave enough to ask why he felt the need to make that distinction. Instead, I wracked my brain, trying to think of something more to add to our strange list of agreements. "What about …b-biting?"

"Another non-negotiable point," he said quietly. "When I need to feed, you will suffice."

His eyes met mine for merely a second from across the table, and it was like time stopped and then started again in slow motion.

"Do *I* get to specify anything?" I stammered, trying to regain my senses.

Dublin didn't play along. "Of course not. My blood, my rules."

Suddenly, he drew a sharp line across the bottom of the page.

"The terms are set; make your choice, Eleanor. It's not dotted," he told me, holding out the pen while I eyed that long, black line. "But I'm sure you know what to do all the same."

That I did.

Run, Ellie, my inner voice urged. *Is your soul really worth two weeks?*

After *four days* with Dublin, it already felt tainted.

But it wasn't until his cup of coffee had grown ice-cold and a bit of light began to brush the horizon—visible through the café's only window—that I finally found the strength to pick up the pen ...

And I warily signed my name.

My drying signature taunted me. That piece of paper may as well have been a stone with my fate engraved on it—and, like a fool, I could only sit there, stirring the cold dregs of my coffee with a teaspoon.

"So ...what next?" I tried to act nonchalant, while inside I was berating myself.

Silly, stupid, Ellie!

What the hell had gotten into me?

Did I *like* being threatened or mocked or ...pinched?

Had I become some kind of thrill seeker in the span of four days?

I *must* have; what else could explain it? *Something* out of this strange arrangement must have appealed to me— enough that I signed again, right on the 'not-dotted' line. This time with nearly twice as much at stake, and *twice* as much Dublin to suffer.

I peered at him from beneath my lashes when he didn't answer. Those gray eyes were on the menu, as if hash browns and scrambled eggs were more appetizing than gloating over me. However, I didn't miss how his hand moved to grab the contract from the table and casually slip it into his pocket.

"Why me?" I found myself blurting. Now that I thought about it, the fact that he had brought up the 're-negotiations' himself was strange, especially when one factored in the little detail that my very presence seemed to irritate the hell out of him.

Judging by the four a.m. coffee and lack of proper clothing —without his suit-coat, he only wore that black undershirt —I guessed that this wasn't the normal course of action for him either.

In fact, I got the sense from my few, clandestine dealings with Mr. Helos that he was more accustomed to having people *beg* for more time rather than bringing up the subject himself.

"Why you?" I added, fingering the rim of my mug. "Why not have my duties tied to the club, like before?"

A part of me wanted to believe that it had something to do with me; that I was special. Different. I had done my 'bargaining' well enough that he wanted more …

His reply, of course, was a little less than flattering.

"I wouldn't *dare* foist you off to someone else."

"So then why negotiate at all?" I tossed back. "I would have been more than satisfied with just *dying*, you know."

It didn't matter that the piece of paper in his pocket proved the exact opposite. So what? No matter the contract, I didn't need Dublin or his time—or so I told myself.

"I told you." Dublin's icy tone forced me to meet his gaze— or at least stare at the plastic, vinyl booth behind his head. "Your name and your image could be very useful to me."

I frowned, remembering his mention of 'endorsements.'

"So what about the …" I cleared my throat. "Other stuff?"

He raised a blond eyebrow. "Please, Eleanor, for the love of God, do not get any cute ideas—" I blinked, distracted by a single, idiotic thought; *were devils even allowed to utter God?* "This isn't about lust, or even attraction," he added, his voice cutting through my mind like a knife. "Whenever I have 'needs' that must be slacked, I would prefer to avoid the hassle of having to purchase a woman every single time."

He sounded so damn blunt about the fact: *You're just a body. One I don't even prefer, but when nature calls …*

I shouldn't have felt so insulted. To be fair, it wasn't exactly like he needed to pay a woman, or indebt one to servitude, for them to sleep with him. Though, even if he *did,* who was I to judge?

I was the one who'd lost my virginity as part of a business arrangement after all.

"Fair enough," I said tightly. "And of course this isn't about attraction; you're not even my type."

I had no idea why I was on the defensive. As if piercing eyes, handsome features, and a body to die for—though I had never seen it in entirety—*wasn't* my type.

Hell, as sheltered as my life had been ...did I even have a type?

I wracked my brain, filtering through the memories of my few childhood crushes for a pattern. Sadly, Dublin did not possess the pimples, freckles, or runny noses that seemed to dominate my past, one-sided relationships.

"This isn't about attraction," he reiterated impatiently, drawing me from school-age memories. "This isn't even about sex. The *only* thing that matters is our contract, and if I have to add up your *few positive* qualities to reach an agreement worth even *one* day ...then I will."

My teeth descended into my bottom lip—drawing blood— in an attempt to keep from making a sound. I refused to give him the satisfaction of ever letting him know just how much those words hurt.

"Here."

With a thump, something landed on my placemat; a napkin.

Oh. A shiver ran through me, once I realized that Dublin's gaze had honed in on my bitten lip. Aware of him watching, my tongue flicked out to wipe away the blood. I dabbed at my mouth with the napkin for good measure.

He didn't say a word as I finally set the crumpled tissue aside.

Taking advantage of the silence, I couldn't resist asking, "How much did you pay for me?"

My heart lurched at the thought of knowing. I had a feeling the amount was even less than the few dollars I had joked.

Pennies?

"Why?" His tone was hard.

I risked sneaking a peek at those eyes and immediately wished I hadn't. That gray had taken on a frosty crust in which I could clearly see my reflection: pale skin, massive eyes. An overall mess.

"I'm j-just curious," I stammered.

His gaze held mine for so long that I swore I could feel frostbite creeping up my toes. Then, all at once, he closed the menu with a *thwack*!

"You threw out some pretty good guesses last night," he said harshly. "Take your pick. Five dollars, you said? I'm pretty sure you were in the right ballpark."

I didn't quite process the motion of feeling along my seat—searching for something—until Dublin suddenly leaned forward.

"What are you doing?"

I froze. That slight shift of his body was dangerous; a tiger brushing the bars of its cage with the very tip of one claw, warning all within reach to be on guard.

"I …I'm looking for my checkbook," I croaked—though I guess the search had been more symbolic than anything else, considering that I didn't even know where my purse was.

"For what?"

His tone *dared* me to continue, and alarm prickled down my spine. *Danger! Danger! Mayday!* It was as if he knew what I was going to say, even before I stupidly uttered it. "So that I can write you a check for five dollars—"

"The hell you are."

His rage was visible only within those silver eyes, but obvious to me nonetheless. For a moment, I couldn't breathe.

"I don't like owing debts," I said, gazing down at the cheery menu blazing with bright colors and promises of *"home-cooked"* food. "You buying me wasn't a part of our bargain." Though, for all I knew that *could* have been his original plan all along, to save him the humiliation of ever trying to sell me off. "I will repay you the—"

"You will *repay* me as I see fit," his voice cut over mine. Abruptly he snatched the menu from the table and practically shoved it onto my lap. "Eat something."

"W-What?"

"Eat *something.*"

I stared down at the selection of breakfast foods and rattled off the first item on the list. "I'll have a …an, um, omelet."

Dublin snapped his fingers, and within seconds the waitress reappeared, looking markedly more alert than she had before. Her brown eyes met mine, and I could only wonder just how much of our conversation she had overheard.

Dublin reiterated my request,, and with a forced smile she pranced off into the kitchens.

We didn't speak. Not a word, until twenty minutes later, the waitress returned with a steaming plate of fried egg and two mugs of fresh coffee balanced on a tray.

When she set the food down in front of me, I grabbed a fork and stabbed into a piece of omelet—the moment I did Dublin spoke.

"You can have the rest of today to yourself."

I glanced up, hearing the fork clatter to the floor before my mind even registered letting it go.

"What?"

His eyes closed. Re-opened and narrowed. I could practically *taste* his annoyance, mingling with the dregs of old coffee on my tongue.

"Monday you will begin fulfilling your contract," he continued as if I had never spoken.

"M-Monday?"

Dublin mistook my shock—at the thought that a week of my life had slipped by already—for something else.

"Yes, Monday," he parroted, amused. "Consider our previous arrangement as a 'free trial' of sorts. From now on, any day you bargain for must be paid off in *advance*."

I gulped at the implications. "So for the next seven days, I'm …"

His smile was chilling. "Mine."

I nearly fell off the bench.

He *doesn't mean it that way,* a part of me frantically insisted. *He probably meant 'his' in the same way that car was 'his.'*

Still, I couldn't breathe.

Unconcerned, Dublin reached for the untouched silverware on his side of the table, grabbed a fork, and held it out to me.

"Eat."

Warily, I took it, stabbed again at that same piece of omelet and brought it to my mouth. I held it there, weighing my next words carefully in my mind.

"What will I do?"

"Whatever I request."

I tried to hide my disappointment as I chewed. The food was surprisingly good, and I found myself swallowing the last bite before I could help it.

It unnerved me to realize that, the entire time, Dublin had been watching me. The moment I set my fork down, he tossed a wad of money onto the table and stood, reaching for my wrist.

"Have a nice day!" The waitress called as he manhandled me out onto the street.

The car was waiting, untouched, when we reentered the alley.

Around us, the city was just beginning to awaken. There were more people on the streets, I saw, as Dublin navigated through them. He didn't seem to be heading for the cathedral, but I almost didn't recognize the imposing monstrosity that was my family home when it finally appeared at the crest of a hill.

How foreign the place seemed to me after only a few days away ...

Even after my stint in the hospital, I didn't remember feeling quite so *cold*, staring up at the gray stone—though I was sitting beside a vampire, for God's sakes.

And the monster in question drove to the front gates without a word. He slowed near the small guardhouse where a bored security guard slumped in the booth.

It was only then that reality sank in.

I had been 'technically' missing for nearly four days. Distracted by Dublin, I hadn't even thought to call. Or send word that I was relatively okay or *alive*.

Which one? I wondered as I eyed the front of the house through the gate. Had Harper sent the SWAT team or my family's own private brigade of security guards after me?

"Let me talk to him," I insisted, as the guard came around to the car. "They've probably been worried sick—"

Ignoring me, Dublin pushed the button that rolled down the window and leaned out of it.

"Morning, Lyle," he greeted, as if I didn't exist. "How are the kids?"

Lyle made a show of smothering a yawn beneath the back of his hand as he flipped the switch to open the gate. "Same old, same old, Mr. Helos," he called, waving the car forward. "Welcome back."

Back? The car lurched into motion, and I could only stare, lost somewhere in between *'Lyle'*—whose name I had never learned until now—and the fact that Dublin had inquired about his children.

Without sneers or sarcasm.

Before I could even begin to choke out a request for an explanation, he started to speak.

"I've kept an eye on the property while you were away," he explained while navigating the car along the paved driveway. "I've also reassured the staff that you would return today."

"H-How?" I didn't know if I should have been alarmed by how he parked the car in front of the main walkway as comfortably as if *he* was the one who lived there.

I was too distracted by the thought of him wandering the halls, speaking to my staff and dolling out orders in my absence.

"How else?" He turned to face me fully, eyes bright in the growing daylight. "I am your new doctor, after all."

"New …doctor?" My head was spinning.

"Speaking of which, I have your next dose of *medication*." As he spoke, he pulled a small object from his pocket; another silver syringe.

I cringed into my seat as the inside of my elbow stung in memory of my last 'dose.'

If Dublin noticed, or cared, he didn't show it. Instead, he merely tapped the side of the barrel with his nail, mixing the liquid within.

"This should last you for a few days," he said. "Though it is a heavier dose than you're used to. I'm hoping that your body has built up enough tolerance by now. You should only be unconscious for a few hours; twenty-four, at most."

Well, so much for having the day to myself.

I could only stare, about as excited to receive my medication as a five-year-old child. Prancing back onto Saskia's stage butt-naked seemed more appealing than being unconscious for—as he put it—a "few" hours.

But it wasn't like he asked for permission.

Instead, Dublin merely warned me to "sit still" as he pried my wrist from my body and jabbed the needle into a vein.

I hissed between my teeth as pain ran through me like an electric shock. Sharp. Burning. At the sound, Dublin frowned.

"Count to ten," he told me, in a tone that challenged me to question him.

I sighed. Hesitated.

"Now, Eleanor."

"One …two …three …"

My mouth was still open, reciting numbers, but a funny thing happened between three and five. The world shifted. My heart flipped over in my chest. The sun was brighter than gold on the horizon, distracting me from everything else. And then Dublin himself changed. That white skin became almost translucently pale, as his body elongated like a snake's. All the while, those gray eyes held me captive.

"Keep counting, Eleanor," he growled, even as his mouth opened and promptly swallowed me whole.

WHITE

For the first time in days, I awoke without being confronted with booze or a frown.

"Good morning, Miss," a smiling Harper greeted as I opened my eyes.

He sat on a chair beside the bed and seemed to be in the process of folding up a newspaper.

I had to blink a few times just to make sure I wasn't dreaming. After the past few days, his sweet, crooked grin was a godsend.

"Where have you been?" I croaked, rushing to sit up. "It's been *days*—"

"I've been here, Miss," he said calmly.

I almost believed him. Dublin Helos and his brazen intrusions into the manor could have been some wild nightmare. If it weren't for how the inside of my arm stung from the after-effects of an injection, I would have believed that. But, before I could question him any further Harper spoke over me.

"How do you feel?"

"I feel ..." Respect for the old man was the only thing that kept me from blurting out the truth; *like hell. Dead, disgusting hell, run over and then scraped from the road.* "Fine," I said, though I could tell from the way his mouth wrinkled that he didn't believe me for a second.

"The doctor said you would be sore when you awoke," he remarked rather than argue. "Shall I have a bath drawn?"

"A bath sounds heavenly." I sank back beneath my sheets, allowing my eyes to drift shut. Then—as the rest of his words sank in like a punch—they flew open again. "D-Doctor?"

I scrambled out of bed and hit the floor on my hands and knees.

"Yes, *doctor*," I heard Harper repeat as he helped me to my feet. "In fact, he wanted to be notified the moment you woke up—"

"He's still here?" I could taste bile at the back of my throat as I scanned the shadows of my bedroom, searching for that familiar mocking face.

"Yes, Miss. He is in the upstairs solar—"

I didn't think.

I didn't even take the time to notice that what I currently wore was way more comfortable than an Armani suit jacket.

Instead, I barreled into the hallway, stumbling like a drunk in the direction of the solar.

It felt as though I had traveled a mile by the time I finally reached that room in the corner of the east wing—though it could have only been a few feet. Then, with fear stabbing my chest, I pushed open the door.

*I*nside the solar, my two worst nightmares became a reality all at once.

The first was Dublin, crouched in the center of the room, wearing another deceptively white ensemble. The second, was the fact that he was stroking a cat, who maneuvered as well as he could—despite missing his hind legs—to get scratched in just the right spot.

My heart plummeted at the sight.

"No!" I threw myself forward without thinking. "Leave him alone!"

The cat hissed at my presence and tried to dart out of reach, but I snatched him up into my arms before he could. Claws dug into my chest. The wheels that he maneuvered on— instead of hind legs—spun uselessly in the air. Loud, angry meows blared through my eardrums, and all the while I glared at Dublin.

"Don't you *ever* touch him."

It didn't matter that Tinkles apparently didn't seem to think he needed saving. He was the one creature in the world who *couldn't* hop on a plane when the mood struck him, or disappear on me for days. He needed me, and I'd be damned if I'd let Dublin Helos taint him the same way he'd already tainted me.

"Ever," I spat, just to make myself clear.

Dublin stood back, watching me through narrowed eyes, but for once, there wasn't any hostility in them, just a faint amusement that caught me off guard.

"You're strangling him," he said, finally.

Sure enough, Mr. Tinkles' howling had taken on a decidedly desperate quality.

I winced as he delivered a particularly painful scratch to my chin, and let him go. The beast bolted from my arms—but rather than dart into the corner of the room that had been designated for his own personal use, he merely wheeled his way over to the feet of the enemy.

There, he glared at me while hissing: *how dare you.*

"I wasn't hurting him," Dublin insisted as *my* cat proceeded to rub its body against *his* legs.

It was a simple display of affection that he had never shown toward me. In fact, I don't think he ever let me touch him without attacking.

"Just leave him alone," I commanded weakly—not that Dublin seemed to be the one in need of hearing those words.

Impatient, my kitty had taken to batting an ivory pant leg with his paw, demanding attention until Dublin had no choice but to sink down on one knee and scratch behind his ears. I could only watch, oddly jealous. While the cat hated *my* guts, he certainly didn't seem to mind my tormentor all that much.

Go figure.

"How was he injured?" Dublin asked as he trailed a pale finger along the harness holding Tinkle's kitty-version of a wheelchair in place.

"A car accident."

Dublin accepted the information with a nod. "I must admit that I was surprised to find only *one* cat," he continued, eyes on Tinkle's gray backside. "I was sure that you would have had at least a dozen. Though, his name isn't too shocking; *Gabriel*," he read off the collar in disgust.

"His name is *Tinkles*," I corrected, a little more harshly than necessary. "He was rescued. Gabriel is the name his original owner gave him."

"Tinkles?" From his tone, I could guess what even Dublin had enough tact not to say out loud; *no wonder he hates you.*

"It's the sound he makes," I tried to explain, though I damn well shouldn't have felt the need to. "When his wheels roll across the ground ..."

Both man and feline shared a look that made me flush crimson. *Women!*

I had the strangest, childish urge to stomp my foot; it seemed to be the only course of action I could take without screaming.

"What are you doing here?" I demanded instead, fighting to keep my tone level. "We had an agreement. I thought I was to have this day to myself?"

Though, from what I could tell from the window, the 'day' had already passed. Darkness stretched across the sky, black and endless.

"We did, but I wanted to make sure you woke up on schedule. Your body seems to be acting irregularly to the 'cure.'"

God, he made me sound like a robot that needed fine tuning.

"Well, I'm awake now."

I stuck my arm out and wiggled my fingers for emphasis. Only then did I fully realize that, during my unconsciousness, someone had dressed me in one of my old nightgowns. This one was plain, with long-sleeves and frilly lace on the hems.

It was something my mother had bought; a garment too modest even for me, which had been politely shoved to the back of my closet, hidden from any maid's view. I doubted that either of them would have dressed me in it, and I had a sinking suspicion of just who had…

With the hideous white cotton hanging down to my ankles, I probably resembled something out of 19th century Victorian England. Though, I had to admit that the fabric did give me sufficient coverage for once.

I continued to assess the rest of my body, taking mental stock of every bruise and ache. I didn't feel much of anything, oddly enough—even the places where he had pinched me weren't sore. Neither were my hips or any other place that *should* have been hurting. Perhaps rapid healing was a benefit of his so-called 'cure?'

In fact, the only injuries I seemed to possess were the recent results of Tinkles' claws. I flinched as a cool hand brushed my shoulder, and the scratches decided to sting at full force.

"I'm fine," I choked out before I happened to glance up, and remembered that Dublin wasn't someone who might be concerned for my welfare.

"They're deep," he concluded just by looking at the jagged marks. As he spoke, he withdrew something from his pocket; another handkerchief. "I hope that one of his claws didn't break off in the wounds. That can be very traumatic for cats."

Traumatic for cats. I wanted to be annoyed that he seemed to be more concerned for an animal than for me, but I couldn't disguise a hitch of fear in my voice. "You don't think? Should I call a vet?"

He gave me an odd look. "He seems to be fine."

When he offered the handkerchief to me, I obediently pressed it to the side of my neck. By the time I lifted it again, I was surprised by just how much scarlet had seeped into the white cotton.

From beside me, I sensed Dublin stiffen. Rummaging through what little I knew about vampires—the movie versions anyway—I wondered if the sight of fresh blood affected him much like an alcoholic having the world's best brandy shoved right under his nose.

"Does this bother you?" I asked.

"No," he said, though when I peered into his eyes, they had taken on a dangerous, silver sheen. "But you smearing it all over the damn place won't help either of us."

He snatched the handkerchief from me, folded it and pressed it to the worst of the wounds. I wanted to be annoyed, but his chill smothered the pain for a brief moment, and I lost the urge. To his credit, Dublin dabbed at the blood with the precision of a surgeon, taking care to make sure that not even a drop touched his skin.

Perhaps he was taking his role as 'doctor' a little too seriously? I nearly asked, but one look at those eyes and I kept my mouth shut.

He could have been rough, but even I had to admit that his touch this time was oddly …gentle. When the bleeding stopped, Dublin withdrew the cloth, folded it again and turned his attention to the marks on my chin.

"Do you like experiencing pain?" he asked suddenly while mopping up a drizzle of blood. "Or do you just like surrounding yourself with beings that are inclined to *cause* it?"

We both turned to stare at Mr. Tinkles, who promptly hissed as if to prove that he wasn't the least bit sorry for hurting me.

"I like being in my house, *alone* with no one there to judge me," I replied, surprised by just how hollow the words sounded. I had meant for it to be some snarky quip and it came out more like the morose declaration of a future spinster.

Dublin chuckled low under his breath—the sound was chilling.

"Oh, I don't know about that." He dabbed at another bead of fresh blood with the cloth. "Your staff seem to judge you plenty."

"M-My staff?"

"'Eleanor Gray: *so quiet, so mousy, so sweet.*'" He frowned as if all of those adjectives were the dirtiest of insults. "'*She's so sheltered. So fragile.*' I think they've started a betting pool on when you'll hang yourself in the foyer."

It was such a harsh assessment that I had to force down a swallow as the back of my throat tightened.

"My father had a 'heart attack,'" I said, once I found my voice again. "Which is Gray code for he blew his brains out in the downstairs study. Mother had an 'aneurysm,' which meant that she really took sleeping pills, a bottle of valium and a glass of wine before bed. So you really can't blame them."

I certainly wouldn't fault anyone for betting when I might 'off myself,' for lack of a better term. Hell, Georgie seemed to be the only well-adjusted one in this family, and she was off beach-hopping in South America with a man she probably met in the airport parking lot.

I had always been considered the smart, 'responsible' one, yet I was going to die in the same house I'd been born in. My fate taunted me, and I could only stand there until the icy fingers at my chin finally withdrew.

"Doesn't it bother you how easily the world writes you off?" His tone wasn't mocking this time.

"I'm not sure what you mean."

"I would bet the terms of your contract that some tabloid editor somewhere already has the article with your suicide byline saved to his desktop."

He watched me, seeming to expect a more dramatic reaction. I merely shrugged.

"That wouldn't be a very fair bet. I mean *everyone* dies one day." I'd been contemplating my own mortality since age thirteen and hadn't batted an eyelash when presented with a fatal diagnosis.

"Do they now?" His tone was the only indication that I had crossed some invisible line—only I had no idea what it was.

"You look well enough," he said abruptly, taking me in with one sweep of those eyes. Something told me that he didn't mean the words as a compliment. "Your body seems to have finally adjusted to the doses."

I nodded, even though I didn't *feel* very adjusted. More ...naked. Unbearably vulnerable. I shivered and crossed my arms, once I realized that I wasn't exactly wearing anything *else* beneath my nightgown. He was too close, and my stupid, traitorous body knew it all too well.

"Tomorrow you will accompany me on a business arrangement. Understood?"

I blinked, startled by the sudden change in subject.

Was he asking for agreement? I wondered. Or did he just want me to nod my head like a good little puppet dutifully accepting her orders?

I settled for both. "I understand."

"And," he said, his gaze holding mine, as frigid as winter, "I will expect nothing less from you than I would from—"

"*'Any other girl.'* I know, I know," I blurted. "I am to be obedient and subservient to you, oh Master." Those eyes narrowed in warning, but he didn't correct my overly dramatic tirade, oddly enough. I gulped, more unnerved than relieved by that fact. "May I ask just what this 'arrangement' is for?"

What on earth could he want that his dark brand of charm and intimidation couldn't get for him?

"No," Dublin said. "However, I expect for you to be ready and waiting at ten o'clock. I want you dressed *appropriately*." He stressed the word. "I'll even have suitable clothing sent over, so there should be no excuse."

I cringed at the thought of the kind of clothing he might find 'suitable.' A leash and gag to drill home whatever controlling urge over me he seemed to have?

Sadly, with every second that passed, the prospect seemed less fantasy and more likely.

"I wish you hadn't let Yulia cut your hair."

I jumped as he reached out and caught a loose curl between his thumb and forefinger. His expression darkened as he tucked it neatly behind my ear.

"You were so much easier to overlook with it down to your waist, falling in your eyes ..."

The words were spoken so softly that I didn't think he meant for me to hear them—but I took offense anyway.

"Well, I liked you better in white," I countered—only to realize that, lo and behold, he happened to be wearing that particular color now.

God, Ellie. I shook my head and forced myself to walk to the opposite end of the solar, putting as much distance between us as physically possible. A burst of artificial heat rushed to replace his lingering chill, but I was still shivering. Those gray eyes were steel, pinning me in place, no matter how hard I tried to ignore them.

"*Before* I knew about your fetish for blood," I clarified.

"Fetish …" His tongue toyed with the word, and somehow that seemed worse than any insult. "I've never heard it put quite like that before."

Suddenly, it became impossible to maintain eye contact. I glanced down to find that Tinkles had returned to his side and was rubbing against his leg, in search of attention.

"Ten o'clock," he told me, before reaching down to give the cat another scratch behind the ears. "I would suggest that you not be late."

"I won't." I didn't like the warning in his tone; *don't be late, or else.* "Ten o' clock."

"Oh …I almost forgot." He paused near the doorway and nodded toward a chair in the corner. I recognized the shape of my purse resting on top of it. "You left that the other day."

At his 'lair,' I remembered. The fact that he had brought it over shouldn't have been so surprising—but coming from him? I was shocked.

Without another word, he was gone. Some minutes later I seemed to feel him finally leave the manor once and for all. It was as if a black cloud over my head had lifted, but instead of relieved I just felt ...*cold* in anticipation of the next storm.

Ten o'clock was tomorrow's deadline, and only God knew what he had in store for me then.

BUSINESS

At the sound of hissing, my eyes flew open to find a furious Mr. Tinkles glaring at me from a corner, canines bared.

Apparently, he was not at all pleased that I had spent the night in his personal solar. Too terrified to leave the room—even though I knew that Dublin had long gone—I'd fallen asleep with my back to the wall, chin balanced on my knees. My body ached as I unfurled my limbs, and I had to brace one hand against the wall just to haul myself upright. But once I saw the sunlight streaming through the window, fear instantly overrode any discomfort.

Oh no.

Dublin's warning rang through my mind; *ten o'clock.* If my powers of deduction accounted for anything, then it was already mid-morning.

"Damn!"

I leaped over Tinkles, who had begun to stalk toward me, claws drawn, and I raced into the hall.

"Morning, Miss!" a servant greeted as I rushed past. I barely managed to squeak out a halfhearted reply before staggering into my bedroom in search of something 'suitable' to wear.

The clock on the wall gave me less than an hour's time, and I had no idea where to begin. I eyed my closet, doubtful I had anything in there that might satisfy Dublin. It was only when I took a step toward it in defeat that I saw *them*.

Several black garment bags rested on my bed, each bearing a purple emblem reading Mystic. Fingers shaking, I grabbed one at random and gathered enough nerve to undo the zipper.

It was worse than I'd imagined.

While not exactly a leash or gag, the short black dress was just as intimidating. I couldn't shake the paranoid suspicion that Dublin had picked it out only to reinforce that I didn't belong.

Still, I had no choice but to pull the dress on over my head and creep to the mirror. On me, the posh, sophisticated garment was a shapeless sack. It was as if I was cursed with the ability to ruin the allure of anything fashionable simply by wearing it.

"Suitable, suitable," I muttered under my breath, as if just saying the word might magically transform me into someone who didn't look so damn awkward. I briefly considered the idea of using makeup to salvage some semblance of beauty.

In the end, I settled on simply dragging a brush through my hair in the hopes that a few neat curls might help distract from my overall appearance. Once finished, I re-entered the hall with only minutes to spare.

I rushed back to the solar for my purse before stumbling down the stairs and out of the door just as a black car sped up the driveway. It came to a stop a few feet away, and I fully expected that stern-faced driver to be the one to climb out and greet me.

A flawless Dublin Helos did instead.

The man gleamed in a pair of gray pants and a white shirt crowned by a crisply starched collar. I felt struck dumb watching him, breathless.

At least until he caught sight of me standing on the front step and frowned. "You look even *worse* in black."

I flinched and self-consciously ran a hand along the silky hem. "It's what you sent me."

Therefore, my apparent 'unsuitableness' was entirely not my fault.

"I know that. But, damn …" He came forward and cupped my chin in his palm. Those eyes were hidden behind the lenses of sunglasses, thank goodness. But all the same, I had no trouble picturing the glare he wore underneath. "You look like an undead schoolgirl playing dress-up on Halloween."

Considering which one of us was truly 'undead' in this situation, the insult stung twice as much.

"I did what you told me to," I said in my defense. "S-Sir."

We were playing his game again, I remembered, by *his* rules, and I wasn't inclined to give him the satisfaction of berating me already for not following them. With his eyes hidden, I couldn't tell if my use of the word surprised him or not. He merely held my gaze for a second longer before turning back to the car.

"That you did," he muttered while wrenching open the passenger-side door. "Get in."

I had no choice but to follow and shimmy onto the leather seat. He closed the door behind me, and I tried to remember how to breathe while he circled around the car.

In and out, Ellie. Easy does it.

He didn't explain where we were going, and I was much too pathetic to ask. I merely sat there, peeking out the window as we headed into the city. It was much like that impromptu trip to the *Cafe Claret*; with him, I saw the city differently. Everything didn't seem quite as distant as it had when glimpsed from the tinted windows of my family's car.

Light glinted off the windows of skyscrapers. The crisp lines of buildings and streets were sharper, bolder. The world had color. *Clarity.* It was a far cry from the gray, lifeless universe

I was used to having stare back at me—but I wasn't sure if I liked this new view much, either.

Suddenly, the car came to a stop.

Glancing out of the window, I expected to find the intimidating front of *Anemia* or some other club—maybe that mysterious manor? Anything other than a gleaming building complex with a statue of *Hippocrates* out front and a massive sign reading, *Helos Industries*.

I gulped, blinked, rubbed my eyes and looked again.

Was it possible that my devil had a day job?

"You … You own this?"

I wasn't that surprised when Dublin exited the car rather than answer me. In a matter of seconds, he was by my side, ushering me out onto the curb.

"You own this?" I repeated, staring up at the gleaming letters that spelled out his name.

The building sat in the center of a massive, sprawling compound, surrounded by a lush garden that reminded me of an oasis smack-dab in the middle of the city.

"'Own' is such a relative term, Eleanor," he drawled as we made our way down a paved path and through a pair of sleek glass doors.

But his name was definitely the only one plastered all over the white lobby in gleaming letters. The secretary sitting behind the counter nearly fell out of her chair when he approached.

"Mr. Helos! Sir—"

"Morning, Becky." He pulled off his sunglasses with one hand and faced her head-on. "Is the boardroom ready?"

"Yes, sir." Beneath that silver stare, Becky blinked repeatedly and seemed to struggle to find more words. "Mr. Haswell is already waiting—"

"Excellent."

Without looking back, Dublin reached for my wrist and pulled me along. I had to jog just to keep pace with him as he crossed the wide lobby and entered a set of elevators. Once inside, he let me go and pressed the button for the twelfth floor.

"Why are we here?" I asked, though the answer was pretty obvious; the devil had an office in which to conduct his nefarious business.

Go figure.

"To fulfill your bargain," he replied, proving my suspicions true. "There is a man who has an asset that I want. *You* are going to convince him to give it to me."

"Convince?" I squeaked. "M-Me? How?"

He rolled his eyes while folding his sunglasses. "With your charm and wit, of course."

Which gave me nothing to go on at all.

Noticing my frown, he scoffed in exasperation. "Use that brain of yours, Eleanor. I shouldn't have to explain *everything* in black and white."

My throat went dry at a sudden possibility. *Would I have to 'persuade' him in the same way that I …*

"Don't let your imagination get the best of you, either," Dublin warned just as the elevator doors slid apart, revealing a hallway lined with plush black carpet and gray walls. "If he were *that* sort of man I would have just borrowed a girl from Saskia."

I was unsure whether or not to be insulted. Either way, I hated myself for the pout that pulled on my lower lip. "You are so beneficial to my self-esteem," I grumbled under my breath, eyes on the floor.

It was only when he grabbed my chin, forcing me to meet his gaze that I realized he had heard me. Those gray eyes held mine for merely a second, blazing.

"You'll do fine," he said before letting me go.

I gaped at him, speechless. Was that—dare I say it —*encouragement?*

"Because if you *don't*," he added as he turned away, "that would be a violation of our agreement."

Before I could respond, he exited the elevator, pulling me after him, and I promptly lost the ability to speak at all.

I had rarely traveled the halls of my family's businesses. *"Man's work,"* Mother would sniff at the suggestion. In her opinion, *our* time was better spent suffering through dull teas with her equally emotionless, but well-connected, 'friends' while Father was busy trying to turn our millions into *billions*.

Even after their deaths, I could count the number of times I had visited the business headquarters on a single hand—and even they didn't look anything like this.

With steel gray walls and a sleek floor plan, the interior of 'Helos Industries' was the sort of place that I had no trouble imagining Dublin in; impressive, but with a dark air that instantly put your entire body on guard.

I tried not to gape as he led me into a wide boardroom where a window opened up onto the courtyard. A man sat at the head of a table in the center of the room, watching us enter with shrewd eyes.

"Well, Helos," he grunted as Dublin all but shoved me into the nearest seat before taking the one beside me. "I'm here. What the hell do you want now? Another permit for one of your shady dealings?"

The tone was hostile, but Dublin just smiled, the picture of an unfazed businessman.

"Not today, Eric," he said. "But my *friend* here would like to negotiate instead."

Suddenly, the attention turned to me, and it took every ounce of pride I had to keep from curling into a ball underneath my chair.

"Her?" The stranger's expression was downright caustic as he glanced me over from head to toe and sneered. "*She* wants a multi-million-dollar tract of land? For what—to ride ponies? Where the hell did you find her, Helos? Bible study?"

Unsurprisingly Dublin didn't try to defend me. Instead, he sat there, eyes on the wooden table and I got the sense that he was waiting. For something I was supposed to initiate, apparently. I recalled his words from the other day. *I want your endorsement.*

"I … I'm twenty-six," I stammered.

"You don't look a day over fifteen," the man replied, taking in my pale skin and lack of makeup. "Where did you grow up? A nunnery?"

"Boarding school," I countered. "Twelve years in England."

That seemed to interest him. He sat straighter. "England? Which school?"

Warily, I rattled off my *alma mater,* and his eyes widened with recognition. "Not just any girl could get into *that* playpen for high society."

His disgust matched mine perfectly, and with a smile, I stuck out my hand.

"Eleanor Gray, at your service."

"Gray?" He took my hand and gave it a firm shake while Dublin watched without venturing a word. "*The* Eleanor Gray?" I didn't know that I was important enough to have a *the* before my name, but I nodded all the same. "Your family owns the knife business, correct?"

"Cutlery," I corrected with a small smile.

Considering how sheltered my upbringing had been, it was almost ironic that my family's fortune had been built upon a company that manufactured some of the finest blades and cutlery in the world. *The Queen of England no doubt cuts filet mignon with Gray silverware,* Mother used to smugly remark.

"Please, you can call me Ellie."

"Haswell," the man blurted in response. "Eric Haswell."

I looked at him with new eyes. Now that he wasn't frowning, he didn't look quite so old—maybe forty—with just a hint of gray mingling with the strands of his dark hair. He had kind blue eyes, and judging from his attire I guessed that he was some sort of businessman, though one who didn't seem to operate in the same 'trade' as Dublin.

"It's nice to meet you as well, Eleanor," he said in a slightly deeper tone than before. He seemed to be seeing me differently, too—I didn't miss how those eyes darted to my purse. I swore that his eyes flashed dollar signs.

"Ellie," I insisted, shifting in my seat.

I wished that Dublin would tell me what the hell he wanted from me. Sitting there, I was clueless, while Eric Haswell eyed me like a shark sensing fresh blood.

"I didn't know that you were interested in the Lakewood property," he said finally. "And if I had, I would have preferred that you meet me *alone.* How the hell do you know this cad, anyway?" He jerked his head in Dublin's direction.

Oh, him? Well, he just owns my soul.

It wasn't until an elbow rammed into my side that I realized I had said the words out loud.

Oops. Dublin glared, while Haswell just looked confused.

"What?"

"D-Dublin is an old business acquaintance." I was surprised by how easily the lie rolled off my tongue. "When he mentioned the …property, I just had to express my interest. My father taught me the importance of investments, you see."

Thank God that my father had *actually* instilled within me a sense of navigating business deals; or, as he called it, *"Verbal Poker."* As a child, after Mother had drifted off to bed clutching her nightly brandy, I would stay up, tasked with charming his business buddies out of house and home. Whenever he had an important business deal to seal, he would always bring the prospective partner by the house, and it was my duty to loosen them up with pleasant small talk and shy smiles.

After all, no one suspected the sweet, innocent Gray girl of sneaking a peek at their cards while they weren't looking. Eric Haswell seemed no different, and I tried my hardest to seem as polite and meek as possible.

"Is it still available?" Only God knew what Dublin wanted with a piece of land—construction of his own personal dungeons? But that touch at my side became insistent; *go on.* "T-To purchase?"

Haswell's eyes narrowed and cut to Dublin. "Where the hell did you find her, Helos?" He wondered. "Maybe you really do own her 'soul' after all?"

I burst into a loud round of nervous laughter. *Ha! Ha! Ha! Really …*

Dublin didn't speak, and with a sigh, Haswell turned back to me.

"You want the land?" he began warily. "What for?"

"I …um … For?" I winced as cool fingers pinched my side. "Personal use!" I stammered.

Haswell stared me, one dark brow raised. "Personal use?"

I could only nod, hoping he believed me—though I wasn't quite sure why I suddenly cared whether or not I failed, Dublin's threat aside. As far as I was concerned, the man didn't need anything that might further his devious plans, whatever they may be.

Haswell watched me for the longest time. Then he sighed. "Damn it, Helos, you win. I have never been able to resist a young woman's charm."

I was still reeling over the fact that someone had called me 'charming'—even indirectly—when the two men suddenly reached across me to shake hands, and the conversation turned to talk of 'settlements' and 'deeds' and 'land value.'

What had to be only ten minutes later, they both stood, leaving me to scramble to my feet.

"I'll have the paperwork on your desk by tomorrow morning," Haswell promised, adjusting his tie. "And the next time we meet, please do bring the intriguing Miss Gray."

He reached for my hand and pressed his mouth to my skin. His warmth was a shock when compared with Dublin's chill.

"Goodbye, Ellie."

I attempted to choke out a reply only to find myself dragged down the hallway after Dublin before I could. We'd gone only a few feet before he pulled me into another room; an office this time.

"Not bad," he admitted, letting me go. "I've been working on getting that damn land from Haswell for nearly a year now, and you've managed it in a day."

Did I dare assume that *awe* colored his voice?

"What did you want it for, anyway?" I found myself asking while I rubbed at my chilled wrist.

After all of his mystery and suspense regarding the 'business arrangement,' I had to admit that a simple deed purchase did seem rather anti-climactic.

"For a reason that you do not need to concern yourself with."

I tried a different tact. "So, is he one of your contracts?"

I nervously scanned the room as I spoke. All in all, entire space could be summed up by a few keywords; simple, clean and utilitarian—definitely his. It was neat, with an oak desk in the center and a row of fully lined bookshelves. A large window overlooked the gardens down below.

"No. The bastard doesn't know what I am," Dublin said. "And while I would love to have the use of his assets, he is not desperate enough to bargain with. For now."

For now.

It all sounded so …calculated. Had he watched me the same way? Waited for that moment when I was apparently 'desperate' enough to take up his bargain?

The thought gave me chills, and I staggered over to the window, huddling beneath the warm rays of sunlight streaming in.

"You did well," Dublin said a moment later, and I was stunned by the fact that he seemed so surprised to admit it. *You did well. It wasn't a complete loss bringing you along after all. Quick! Look out of that window there and wave hello to the flying pigs.*

Still, considering his mood, I decided to risk asking another question—one I knew he would never normally tolerate.

"What makes you decide to offer someone a contract?"

In other words; *me.*

His answer came without hesitation. "They possess something of value, something worth more time."

Fair enough.

"So, what happens if someone wants out before their contract ends?" I turned to face him, watching the sun reflect off his pale skin. "Say they change their mind halfway through?"

"All debt must be repaid." A warning laced his tone: *so don't get any ideas.*

We stood there for a moment, just staring at each other. Then he sighed and ran a hand through that golden hair. "You've fulfilled part of your bargain," he admitted reluctantly. "Were you anyone else, I might even give you a *reward.*"

Uh-oh. Something told me that he wasn't the sort to dole out sweets and candy as thanks for being a good girl. His idea of a 'treat' was probably another's idea of cruel and unusual torture.

Still, curiosity had me in its grasp, and I couldn't escape it.

"Like what?" I blinked, and suddenly he was in front of me. Every muscle in my body tightened as his icy fingers skimmed along my jawline before he cupped my chin entirely in his palm.

"What would you want?" His tone threw me off; it was gruff and low but—for once—I couldn't sense any irritation or anger. Just …curiosity.

My mouth opened. "I …"

But my mind went blank.

"Hmm. I suppose that's a trick question," he said finally. His head was tilted to the side, thumb centered on the globe of my chin. "After all, what could the heiress, who's always had everything, possibly want?"

I winced at his tone. "I have not always had *everything*." Though, when I tried to consider what I had ever gone without, I couldn't come up with a single thing. "I've just never wanted anything," I added weakly.

To my defense, the so-called 'coveting' of luxury items had been deemed 'tacky' by my mother and therefore taboo. A pretty pathetic reason, but if such a thing as 'sheltered heiress syndrome' existed you would find my picture in the dictionary alongside a fitting definition: *Always needs someone to tell her what to do, think and/or feel in order to properly function as a human being.*

Dublin wasn't satisfied with the answer. "If you could have anything in the world, what would it be? Even for someone like *you*, there must be one thing."

I was surprised to find that, once again, he sounded genuinely curious. My mind spun as he released me and turned his attention to the window, watching the daylight filter down. But I wasn't fooled—he still wanted an answer.

"Anything?" I wracked my brain for an interesting reply, desperately trying to combat a voice—distinctly my mother's—that shot down every thought.

Diamonds? Gaudy!

New clothes? A waste!

A lion? Tiger? Bear?

Impractical! Useless! Selfish!

"A ring," I settled on finally, surprising myself. "One of those cheap, plastic rings that everyone just throws away because it turns your finger green."

I had never had one, of course, but at school, some of the braver girls would sometimes sneak into town and bring back their "treasures" from a few hours spent outside the lap of luxury: cheap jewelry, candy, and toys.

"A ring?" Dublin repeated. I jumped as his voice brushed my ear in a burst of cool air. He was closer than I had realized. "Of all the things in the world, you would choose a ring?"

His tone told me just what he thought of that, but I nodded, unashamed.

"The cheapest, tackiest thing I could find."

"Of all the … I would have thought that even someone like *you* might have a more interesting wish."

I turned to face him. "What is that supposed to mean? *Sir,*" I added hastily.

"It means …" He began to advance at a pace that had me instinctively backing up. For every step he took, I scrambled back two. "Eleanor Gray, the twenty-six-year-old virgin—until two days ago—wants nothing more in life than a plastic ring. I must say that I'm rather disappointed."

He took another step. Another. I knew I was trapped even before my hip hit the side of the desk.

"W-What else is there?"

I gulped as hands colder than ice caught me by the waist and lifted me on top of the desk before I could even blink. I tried not to react as his hands came down on either side, locking me in place. A shudder rippled down my spine as my eyes seemed to focus on his against my will.

He held my gaze for so long that I felt dizzy. Weightless.

"What else is there?" he repeated under his breath. "I can think of a few things."

My mind ran wild. *Vulgar, primal things. Ice-on-the-tongue, breathless and panting things …*

I struggled to breathe, hating myself for the weak little flutters that came to life inside my belly—especially when his hand disappeared between us to trail the length of my inner thigh.

FUEL TO THE FIRE

*H*e stroked me through the silky material, and I couldn't believe that my body was capable of feeling so many emotions at once: fear, shame, and something else that made it so much easier to ignore the first two.

Heat flared with every light caress—hot, hotter, *searing*—smothering my own half-hearted protests before I could even voice them; *this is indecent! Bad Ellie!*

All the air left my lungs. I couldn't breathe. *Think.*

Sitting there, on the edge of the desk, I was trapped, and Dublin's cold smile told me that he was well aware of the fact.

With a shift of his body, he leaned closer, placing his mouth directly against my ear.

"I believe that your body has different needs besides just a cheap, plastic ring," he informed me, unnervingly matter-of-fact. "Different *wants* ..."

A lump formed at the back of my throat—choking me—as his hand slid between my knees and nudged them apart. Before I could react, he seized the hem of my dress between two fingers and began to draw the fabric up, pausing before he could reveal more than just mid-thigh.

"Should I stop?"

I blinked and tried to remember English. *Stop? What's that?*

"Eleanor?" His tone was impatient, but the way his thumb toyed with the flesh of my inner thigh, made it impossible for me to form a coherent response. "Use your manners; is this a suitable reward?"

On *'this'* he brushed me through the lace of my panties, and I nearly came off of the desk. Instinctively, my hands flew out on either side to grip the edge of the wood for dear life.

Breathe! I was so lost in the sensations swirling through my body that I almost missed what he said next.

"I can't hear you. Should I stop?"

Say yes! But, before I could even open my mouth, the pad of his thumb began to ease beneath the rim of cotton ...

And I was lost.

Fire licked up and down my spine as he carefully began to pull back the material from the sensitive flesh. As if of their own accord, my legs sprung apart, freeing that touch to roam …and all the while, he spoke heatedly into my ear.

"Should I stop, Eleanor?"

My teeth descended into my bottom lip so fiercely that I tasted blood—all in an effort to hold back a reply. Pain rose up to combat the pleasure, but it was a losing battle; I had begun to arch into his touch, anyway.

"You want this," Dublin murmured as if reading my mind, voicing what I wouldn't say.

Oh, God. I did. I wanted it—this hazy pleasure he promised.

It was wrong. I had no idea why my body reacted this way only to him, but …

I couldn't pull away.

Without warning, he added a second finger alongside the first, twisting and teasing my senses into oblivion.

I felt nothing—and then I felt *everything.* Sensation exploded in dizzying degrees, and I could only fight to keep my eyes from rolling back into my head as Dublin steadily gave me my *'reward.'*

He was gentler than he'd ever been before, caressing my flesh with an intimate knowledge that made my skin flush with shame. In and out …

Around.

I couldn't deny the ache that had my hips arching into him despite myself, seeking *more, more, more!*

With every stroke, that inferno raged higher, pushing me closer to a terrifying promise that made my mouth water in anticipation. A desperate thought played like a song through my mind; *so close.* I could only cling to the desk for dear life as Dublin delivered one last stroke.

The last thing I was aware of was falling back against the desk. My mouth was open, but little sound came out. In fact, it seemed way more important to focus on just breathing as reality splintered into a million jagged pieces.

When clarity returned, it came in tiny snatches.

Piercing gray eyes burning through my blurred vision.

The fact that my dress had been shoved up over my waist.

That I was slung over the side of a desk like a cheap, tawdry office slut.

Oh, God.

I pulled myself upright, wincing as the last tendrils of heat flared and died. Dublin stood a few paces away from me, tugging at his collar, and I wondered in horror if I had clawed at his clothing again.

That crisp white shirt wasn't the only thing out of place.

One of my heels had fallen to the floor. A stack of papers had been knocked off the desk—disrupting the otherwise neat and clean office.

As I struggled to collect my senses, Dublin watched.

One hand toyed with a button at the hollow of his throat, while the other hung down by his side. My cheeks burned with shame as I observed those slightly curved fingers.

"Satisfied?" he asked, eyes burning bright.

I choked on my own voice. It took me a good five minutes before I could even remember how to form a proper sentence.

"I ... I—"

"It's polite to thank someone who has bestowed upon you a gift," he reminded in a casual tone, cutting over me.

My stomach flipped. *Gift?*

"T-Thank you."

Those eyes narrowed, expectant, and I hastily added a whispered, "Sir."

He stood there for a few seconds. Then his hand fell from his collar, and he turned. A single jerk of his head was my only indication to follow, as he crossed the office to stand beside a different door than the one we had entered through.

I slid off the table, sinking down to my knees, and grabbed my fallen shoe from the floor. Then I stood and crept after him, painfully aware of every single nerve in my body.

He pushed open the door to reveal a small bathroom and entered first, washing his own hands at the marble sink with a silent vigor.

I watched him, oddly entranced as the water glanced off that pale skin. Without shutting off the faucet, he dried his hands on a rag fished from underneath the counter and faced me, eyes silver.

"Come here."

My body jerked forward, tethered to the sound of his voice, unable to resist. The moment I was close enough, he grabbed me by the arm and steered me before the counter.

I stared at my reflection as I would a stranger.

My eyes were wide—enormous. I could make out every single shade of green swirling through the irises. I had this distant, far-off look, like the survivor of some traumatic, life-changing catastrophe.

Numb, I could only stand there as Dublin wet another fresh cloth and crouched down before me on one knee.

"N-No! You don't have to ..." I jerked back, shaking my head but his free hand latched onto my wrist. The pad of his thumb brushed the back of my hand in warning. *Stay still.*

I hissed out a sigh and tilted my head back to stare at the ceiling while those icy hands pulled the rest of my underwear down my legs.

"W-why?" I stammered when he tossed the black cotton into a nearby trash.

He didn't answer, and I could only grit my teeth as he brought that cloth down between my legs.

He swiped a few times with the washrag and then dried with a towel. The whole time I merely stood there and tried to reiterate to myself that his touch was just as detached as a real doctor's would be…

So why the hell couldn't I *breathe* even as the warmth of the water replaced his icy chill?

When he finished, Dublin stood up and yanked my hem back down. Then he switched off the water and maneuvered me back into the main office with a hand on my shoulder.

"I have another meeting in an hour," he said, closing the bathroom door behind us.

I gulped. *Another 'arrangement?'* Even more terrifying: *another chance to earn a 'reward'?*

"But you've done enough for today," he continued before the dark fantasies in my mind could truly take off. "I'm sending you home. Though, I'll have you stop for new clothes, first. Obviously, none of my selections are fitting, and I'd rather not have you looking like an underage convent escapee."

He turned back to the desk and settled himself into the plush chair behind it, while I just stood there, still with one shoe dangling from my fingers.

"Leave?" My voice was unusually high pitched. I felt like a child who wasn't sure if they had just received a spanking or a cookie—albeit a frozen, bitter, mind-altering cookie.

Dublin bent to retrieve the stack of papers I'd knocked off and shoved them into a drawer. Then he sat back and laced his hands together behind his head.

"Yes. Follow the hallway down to the elevators. Go to the first floor. Becky will show you out, and the car is waiting out front."

Everything sounded so neat, precise. Though, after glancing around his flawless office, I was pretty sure by now that he was a perfectionist.

In fact, the only thing remotely out of place in the entire building was *me*, standing there with my hair in my eyes and one sad heel on my foot.

"Most people would take this opportunity to leave now," Dublin said quietly, expression unreadable. "Unless you would like for me to find something else for you to do …"

I turned and staggered through the door before he could do just that. In the elevator, I managed to slip on my other shoe, but I was in a daze as I wandered past a smiling Becky, who chirped a pleasant goodbye I barely heard.

The sunlight was blinding as I made my way through the sleek glass doors and out into the courtyard. Sure enough, parked beside the road was that same black car, where the familiar driver stood beside the backseat.

Without a word, he held the door open for me, and I scrambled in onto the leather.

It seemed like once the door closed after me, my brain felt it was the time to swamp me beneath a barrage of images; *Dublin. Me. Ice.*

I was hyperventilating by the time the driver took the steering wheel and pulled away from the curb. Thinking of Dublin's last words, I expected that—ten minutes later— when the car finally came to a stop, it would be in front of Gray Manor.

Not a plain brick building without so much as a sign on the front. The driver exited the car and came around to my end without a word of explanation.

"Is this …the right place?" I asked, fearfully eyeing the battered front door. It wasn't my house, that was for damn sure.

"Yes, Miss." The driver nodded. "Mr. Helos mentioned something about clothing."

Oh. I shuffled forward, daintily placing my heels on the curb—though I had no idea what kind of clothing could possibly be bought in a place like this.

The driver didn't give me any hints or words of encouragement as I straightened my back, wobbling a little in my heels.

It felt very much like that first night at *Anemia* …

But I forced myself to wander toward that battered metal door, and hoped that nothing nasty waited inside.

KING ME

I lingered over the threshold while my eyes adjusted.

I couldn't make out much, just a high ceiling and cavernous space. The only light came from a naked light bulb dangling in the center of the room, and at first glance, the place appeared to be deserted.

At least until I noticed a flicker of motion to my right.

"This venue is by appointment only!" The voice came from behind what seemed to be a moving stack of clothing. It swayed unsteadily on pale legs supported by dangerously high heels. "If you would like to make an appointment then please call—Oh!"

The clothes fell to the floor, and an exhausted-looking Yulia stepped out from around the pile.

"Eleanor!" She wore another black dress, and her dark hair was twisted into a loose bun on top of her head. "Dublin did mention something about sending you over … Oh my—"

She broke off frowning as she took in my appearance, hands on her hips. "I warned him that those clothes would *not* suit you *at all*."

Before I could offer a word in my defense, she turned and beckoned me forward with a wave of her hand.

"Come. Let's see what we can find."

I hurried after her, gaping as I did so.

The place appeared to be a warehouse, enclosed by metal walls. Burgundy carpet and a pair of leather couches in the far corner added a touch of homeliness. But nearly every inch of the room was dominated by a maze of shelves, sporting countless fabrics: brightly colored silks, velvets, and delicate cotton.

It was a seamstress' dream.

As Yulia led me deeper into the chaos, I noticed a familiar emblem emblazed in the middle of the floor: a silver crescent moon with *Mystic* written in flowing script across the bottom. The clothing Dublin had sent me had come from here, apparently.

"Is this your…store?" I asked, glancing around—though I couldn't see a single salesperson, let alone a cash register.

Yulia paused to dig through a stack of fabric on a nearby shelf. "I suppose you could call it that—" She waved a bit of silver cloth triumphantly through the air before rummaging through another pile. "We all have our day jobs."

"Like Dublin," I grumbled, thinking of that gleaming office building.

"Yes." She glanced at me from over her shoulder. "Like him." Her mouth remained open, as if she meant to say something else. Then she seemed to think better of it and snatched up another random bit of cloth instead.

"Come," she commanded, moving toward the room's center. "Per Dublin, you are 'forbidden' from wearing white." Her scoff revealed what she thought about that. "And black just does *not* work."

I glanced down at Dublin's creation and wholeheartedly agreed with that assessment.

"I suppose we'll have to try *gray* next." I blinked as Yulia twirled around and draped a bit of gauzy fabric over my shoulders.

With a tug here, and a pinch there, she arranged the material to her liking. Every now and again she paused to pin everything in place with a needle seemingly pulled from nowhere, forming a makeshift dress over my black one.

"It's not as flattering as the white," she admitted as she placed another bit of gray fabric against my throat. "But it doesn't make you look quite as *helpless* as the black."

Nodding to herself, she began to unpin all the work she had just done and gathered the fabric in her arms.

"I should be able to whip up a few things tonight and have them sent over in the morning."

I could only stand there, stunned by the whirlwind fitting session. "So …you're a fashion designer?"

Now her role as 'stylist' at the club made perfect sense, though I guessed from her sly expression that it wasn't as simple as it sounded.

"Something like that," she said, while folding all the fabric over the crook of her arm. "We all have our own …talents."

"So," I blurted, desperate for answers, "does that mean that Dublin really is a doctor?"

An invisible curtain fell across her face, blocking off all emotion. "He should be the one to tell you that."

I swallowed back a protest, irritated by the mystery. How hard was it to just come out and say the truth, without riddles or double-talk?

"Oh, like how he 'told' me about the 'auction' or the 'bidding,'" I wondered before I could stop myself. "Or how much he even spent on me?"

"Eleanor …"

"Or," I added, suddenly furious though I had no clue why, "how he was able to weasel his way into my household? Or why he even offered me a contract in the first place? And who is this Raphael person anyway?"

I broke off panting, only to realize—as my voice echoed back at me—that I had been shouting.

"I know this is confusing for you," Yulia began softly. "I can't tell you much. I *can't*. But ...I can try to fill in the basics as much as possible."

I didn't miss how she stressed that word—*can't*. Perhaps her silence was more than just loyalty to Dublin? The thought sent a shiver down my spine.

"Here, sit down." She nodded to a leather chaise, and obediently I perched on the very end of it.

"Now, Eleanor, what you need to understand is —" Abruptly, she broke off, shook her head, and seemed to change tactic. Sitting down beside me, she raised both hands and formed a triangle by connecting her thumbs and forefingers. "The *business* that Dublin and I 'work' for, so to speak, is like this triangle," she said. "There is only one person at the top—"

"Raphael," I guessed, and she nodded.

"Yes. Directly below him are 'commanding officers,' of sorts." Something told me that Dublin and Mikhail fit in that category. "And then below that ..."

She paused expectantly and surprisingly I knew the answer.

"Peons." Or in this case, people like *me* tethered to a contract.

One of my father's business associates had spoken of his own business in the same way, after he'd had one too many glasses of wine.

Yulia nodded again. "Peons. Pawns—whatever you want to call them, they provide support for the …business."

Something in her tone told me that she wasn't just speaking about some kind of money-oriented pyramid scheme.

"You mean, like a society?"

Those green eyes flashed, but she didn't answer—at least not directly. Instead, she shifted, folding her hands neatly in her lap and turning to face me head-on.

"Hypothetically speaking, how would such a *society* be able to exist, parallel to yours?"

She waited until I finally answered, taking a stab in the dark. "By having friends in high places?"

It was something that my father had claimed to rely on. *'Charming, powerful friends,'* otherwise known as *blackmail.*

Yulia nodded once again. "Very high places, and very many friends who are bound to this hypothetical world by *favors.*"

A nice way of saying 'contracts,' I supposed, but the thought was alarming.

One Dublin was enough— but she made it seem like there was a whole network of *'contractors,'* with even more *contracts* spread between them.

In other words: a secret, shadowy world, complete with its own rules.

"Those 'favors' allow this society to exist in secret," she went on, "but everything comes with a *price*. A price that must be paid—by anyone wishing to partake in this hidden society —to one person." She connected two fingers together, forming part of a triangle once again.

"Like, to a king?" I supplied, playing along with the guessing game.

Yulia smiled, but there wasn't any warmth in it, just an ageless chill that made me shudder.

"Ah, but 'king' is such a mortal concept," she said. "After all, how can one be a 'king' without a set reign? Do you know of any rulers who've held power for centuries? Millennia?"

I gulped at the prospect. Frankly, I never wanted to meet a man who could amass that kind of power.

"So all contracts belong to this …not-king?"

Or, in other words, *Raphael.*

"All are owned by him, *usually*," Yulia corrected.

I frowned. "But I thought you said that—"

"*Usually*," Yulia insisted. "But in rare cases, the contracts of certain individuals have been known to change hands, for a price." I was lost, but those green eyes were insistent, unnerving. They peered deep into my soul, willing me to see whatever she seemed unable to say. "For a *price,* sometimes the contract of another can be bought," she repeated. "And a very *steep* one, at that."

Oh. Suddenly it clicked. 'Bought,' like mine had been apparently by Dublin.

"What kind of price?" I pressed when she didn't continue.

She lifted her shoulder in a shrug.

"You tell me; what is a soul worth?"

The words struck deep. There was something hidden within them; a message she seemed desperate for me to understand, though her cryptic tale ended on that note.

"It's getting late," she said, rising to her feet, though I was pretty sure that it wasn't even past noon. "I'll start on your wardrobe and have the first few items dropped off in the morning."

She showed me to the door before I could ask more about this 'hypothetical' world and the 'favors' that may or may not have been contracts. Seconds later, I found myself standing on the curb while Dublin's driver ushered me inside the car.

And then I could only sit there, staring into space as I tried to puzzle out what, through that whole convoluted tale, Yulia could have possibly been trying to tell me.

~

"Get up."

The harsh command gave a whole new meaning to the term 'rude awakening.'

Nightmare? I wondered groggily, but the icy chill clinging to my feet seemed to negate that hope—the result of a very *real* person yanking the blankets from over me. With a groan, I peeled my eyes open only to have a coffee mug shoved beneath my nose.

"No," I croaked, picturing Yulia and her customary serving of alcohol. My stomach pitched at the thought of another liquid breakfast. "No, thank you."

But when the hand didn't move, I had no choice but to sit up and take the mug in both hands.

I forced down a careful sip, only to discover that the amber liquid was *tea* rather than alcohol; sharp, incredibly bitter tea that kicked twice as much as the strongest shot of brandy ever could.

Or maybe it was just the sight of the man standing at the foot of my bed that sent my heart into overdrive?

"I don't have all year, Eleanor," Dublin snapped, infuriatingly impatient.

He tossed something down onto the mattress and then turned, tucking his hands into his pockets. I hated myself for the way I stiffened at the sight of him. Today, he was dressed from head to toe in elegant black—the only hint of color was that blazing yellow hair.

"I'll expect you to be downstairs within the hour," he called while marching for the door. *"Fully dressed."*

I stared after him, shivering, as his words finally sunk in. Was today the day I would finally have to put that 'endorsement' clause in our contract to use?

He didn't give me a clue before disappearing over the threshold, and I took a hasty sip of tea rather than ask. Only when I was sure that he was gone did I leap out of bed. My gaze automatically went to the item he'd left for me; another *Mystic* garment bag. This one, however, contained a simple, sleeveless dress in a soft shade of gray.

Unwilling to test my luck by keeping Dublin waiting, I barreled into my bathroom and dragged a brush through my hair. Then I pulled on the dress and paused only to grab a pair of heels from my wardrobe, before tip-toeing out into the hall.

I wasn't brave enough to look at my reflection this time. Instead, I focused on retaining my sanity as I made my way down the stairs, knowing just who waited for me at the bottom.

This is your house, Ellie, I told myself sternly. *Don't you dare let him intimidate you.*

That seemed easier said than done once I caught sight of Dublin standing in the foyer. At the sound of my approach, he turned, eyes narrowing as they took me in.

"Decent," he announced as I descended the final step.

I nearly tripped over my own feet in shock. Coming from him, the statement could have been either a veiled compliment, or just another one of his many insults. Still, I decided to give him the benefit of doubt; at least he wasn't scowling.

"Thank you," I replied, running a hand over the soft material of the dress. It was a modest length, reaching down past my knees. Dublin's eyes followed, tracing the hem. Then, surprisingly without a snide remark, he pulled another pair of sunglasses from his pocket and faced the door.

"I need to stop by the club today," he announced. "*You* will accompany me."

His words had the effect of a bucket of ice water being dumped over my head.

"The ...club?"

"It's just business."

Considering that his 'profession' dealt in the trade of souls, I wasn't at all comforted by the term.

"Are you going there now?"

He didn't answer. Instead, he inclined his head, placed his glasses over those sharp eyes and moved through the doors, leaving me to follow. I scrambled out after him, surprised by a dreary, cold rain that steadily fell outside. A mist of gray clouds covered the sky, but Dublin never removed those sunglasses, oddly enough.

The driver waited for us, holding open the door and I rushed inside, shivering on the leather seat. Beside Dublin, I may as well have been inside a freezer. Without a word, the driver headed toward the city while I tried my hardest not to stare at the man beside me.

When we finally reached *Anemia*, Dublin said nothing before stepping out onto the curb. He didn't even reach for my hand this time to drag me along. I had to race after him just to keep from having the main doors slammed in my face.

It was dark inside. There was no one at the front desk or in the entire lobby for that matter—though realistically, in a club for vampires, who *would* be at eleven in the morning? I was quite willing to classify Dublin as an abnormality in his ability to withstand sunlight and the like, but to believe that *all* vampires were like that? It would have been too strange.

I observed the abomination in question, who stood beside me, dripping wet. The rain didn't seem to bother him. He didn't even lift a finger to wipe a damp strand of hair that had glued to his forehead with the moisture. It was only when he turned to face me—with the lenses of his sunglasses gleaming like mirrors—that I saw my own reflection; eyes wide, mouth gaping open, cheeks red in a way that had absolutely nothing to do with the cold.

I turned away, gazing down at the floor instead.

"Wait here." Without another word, Dublin retreated down a hall that I guessed led to the upper level—but not without first issuing another command from over his shoulder. "Stay."

Very well then. I grounded out a sigh between clenched teeth and observed the lobby with a frown.

It was spacious and decorated in the same mode as the rest of the club; dark colors and bold lines. Cold. Foreboding.

Only now could I appreciate just how different Dublin's lair above the cathedral was in comparison. The dark wood had seemed softer, and yet there the silence had echoed endlessly. Yulia had mentioned that he didn't have visitors very often. Picturing his charming personality, it wasn't that hard to imagine why.

When the minutes passed without Dublin returning, I sat down on the very edge of a leather chaise and waited. *God, Ellie,* I scoffed at myself, disgusted by my own obedience. Maybe he should have gotten me a leash, after all, to go along with my new wardrobe? I was acting more and more like his pet every day ...

"Well, that's because you *are*, dear."

Alarmed, I bolted to my feet just as Saskia appeared from the shadows lining the hall. Red hair was piled elegantly on top of her head, amber eyes burning. Today her dress was a somber navy blue.

"Oopsies!" She giggled. "Was I not supposed to sense that? Look!" She made a show of slapping her hands over her ears and winked. "Can't hear a thing."

I couldn't move. The little voice at the back of my mind was whispering, *Impossible! There was no way in hell she could have heard me unless ...*

"D-Did you—"

"What?" Her sly grin turned playful. "Read your mind? Now, tell me, darling, how on earth *could* I have?" On razor-sharp heels, she came forward and circled me once; a hunting shark in a beautiful dress. "*Unless* Yulia told you all of our dirty little secrets," she added, frowning. "Though if she *did*, you sure as hell wouldn't be standing there now, would you? Hopefully, like a smart little girl, you would have already run far and fast in the opposite direction."

Running sounded like a good option now. I should have gone back to the car—and not taken the bait by asking the obvious question.

"Know what?"

Saskia tilted her head to the side like a cobra about to deliver a lethal bite. "The truth, of course, about *you* and our dear friend *Dublin*. What? You didn't think that he just picked you out of the crowd, did you? A plain, unassuming little thing like you?"

She threw her head back for a harsh bark of laughter. When her gaze met mine again, it was ice-cold. "Did it never cross your pathetic mortal brain that there might have been ...*a reason*?"

Oh, I could guess his 'reason' all right—and it had everything to do with gaining control of my family's fortune. But before the suspicion could fully form in my mind, Saskia shook her head.

"No," she said quietly. "An insubstantial thing such as 'money' is something only mortals feel the need to obsess over. Here, I'll let you in on a little secret—"

She sauntered closer, and it took everything in me not to react as she cupped my chin in her palm. Nails sharper than tapered steel scraped my jawline in a dangerous caress.

"Dublin probably has more money lining his trash bins than is in any bank you could think of. We have no need for it. No desire for *money*." She spat the word like a curse and let me go, turning on her heel. "Men like Dublin deal in the trade of *lives*—and they treat them with less reverence than you mortals do your precious money."

I vaguely remembered Dublin saying something along those same lines; *your name means more to me.* Once again, Saskia shook her head—though, I figured that she didn't even have to read my mind to guess my line of thought that time.

"There's more to it, my sweet," she purred, eyes gleaming. "So, much more. I would tell you, of course, but I'm not sure your little soul could stomach the answers."

Listen to her, Ellie. Walk away ...

But, once again, I couldn't help myself.

"Like what?"

I tried to remain still as she came toward me again. Saskia's movements were like those of a lioness circling its intended victim—fluid, graceful, deadly. Each pointed tip of a heel struck the marble floor in tandem.

"I'm sure he's fucked you already, hasn't he?"

"W-What?"

Calmly she reached up and snagged a piece of my hair between two pale fingers, twirling it around and around.

"He probably couldn't resist. Our Dublin has always had a soft spot for *innocence*." She sniffed as if the word were something utterly disgusting and released my curl. "How he loves to taint and destroy pretty, pure things. He sure as hell didn't want to share you, his sweet little *Eleanor*. One could only imagine what measures he's taken to secure your contract—to ensure that you had *no choice*."

"W-What do you mean?"

Her expression hardened. "While they tout their *code* ad nauseam, they rarely follow it, my dear. We are all but mere pawns in their grasp, meant to be manipulated as they please."

"We?"

Rather than respond, Saskia raised a scarlet eyebrow, as if daring me to put the pieces together on my own. She was alluding to something. Something about Dublin, and more importantly ...me.

Only, I was too stupid to figure it out—at least until an elementary grasp of grammar revealed the answer for me. *We.*

"You have a contract ..."

"We are *all* tethered to contracts," she interjected. "Even your precious Dublin has another's claws digging into his soul—so is the price of this life. You were damned the moment he laid eyes on you, and you poor pathetic thing, you probably didn't even notice. You still don't. There is *nothing* that a man like Dublin wouldn't stoop to in order to get his way. Nothing."

For a split-second, something crossed her expression: wrenching, tormented agony the likes of which I could only dream of.

"Nothing is sacred to them," she hissed. "There is no part of your life they wouldn't hesitate to destroy if only to meet their end goal. You would do best to always remember that. To him, you are a pawn, nothing more."

Her words were chilling, I couldn't deny that. Chilling and haunting—even more so, because they echoed everything that Dublin himself had said.

"How much did he pay for me?"

Saskia frowned at the interruption—in retrospect, I had no damn idea why I even spoke up in the first place. I would have almost preferred to cling to my indignant guess of five dollars ...but this instinctive pull in my gut goaded me; *there's more to it. You need to know.*

"Oh I'm sure Dublin told you *all* about that," Saskia hissed. "Did you gloat when he did? You probably felt so pleased to be his *favorite* little puppet—" She broke off abruptly, eyes widening as if she discovered something in my expression that she hadn't seen before. "Unless you really don't know …"

"Know what?"

"He didn't tell you," she went on in awe. "Oh, darling, this is *rich*." She laughed again, but it seemed more like a witch's cackle, full of malicious glee. I half-expected her to clap her hands together like a child given an unexpected treat.

"Know what? What didn't he tell me?" I was confused. Horribly confused—and *terrified*, because I knew deep in my soul that whatever could make her so smug was nothing good at all.

"Oh, Eleanor," she murmured, in a tone much softer than before. "Unlike Yulia, I am not bound to that bastard. I can tell you *everything*, but first, you must do something for me."

Run! My conscience warned.

If Dublin was the Devil, then Saskia was a creature far, far worse. I would be a fool to make any sort of deal with her. Still, that tiny voice I couldn't ignore spoke up once more; *you need to know.*

I swallowed hard. "What favor?"

"I want you to say something to Dublin," Saskia said innocently. "Just one little word, whispered right into his frigid ear. That's it."

It sounded so harmless, so innocent.

I wasn't fooled.

"Like what?"

Amid a cloud of cloying perfume, Saskia leaned forward, allowing her warm breath to graze my shoulder.

"Just one little word. You can't just blurt it out, of course," she warned. "You must wait for the right time. Oh, I know!" She grinned, eyes glowing. "The next time he takes you to his bed, while he's buried inside of you to the hilt. I want you to say it only *then*."

I grimaced at the imagery. "Say what?"

"This—" She leaned close enough to whisper a single word into my ear before pulling away.

"Cael?" I frowned, tasting the strange syllables over my tongue.

"Uh-huh!" Saskia wagged a pale finger. "Only at the right moment. God, I wish I could see the look on his face …"

"How will you know?" I asked around a dry swallow. "Once I've said it—*if* I say it—how will you know?"

Her answering chuckle sent a shiver down my spine. "Oh, I'll know. Trust me, he will make that moment very, *very* clear—"

"What the hell are you doing?"

My entire body went cold. Instinctively, my mind conjured up a fearsome silver stare to go along with that voice, even before I turned and saw Dublin standing there behind me.

"*D*ublin," Saskia greeted flatly. "Eleanor and I were just having a little chat—"

"Oh, I'm *sure* you were."

He approached us with all the grace of a hunting lion, and I couldn't help the childish part of me that noticed how his demeanor was even *colder* toward Saskia than to me. Unlike his customary frigid expression, he held her gaze with a glare that would have reduced anyone else to a quivering pile of fear.

To her credit, Saskia didn't even flinch.

"You called me here, yet you weren't even where you said to meet," Dublin continued in a tone laced with suspicion. "One might wonder why that is ..."

"Oh, don't be so dramatic, darling!" Saskia shooed him off with a wave of her hand. "I was just getting some fresh air."

But as she spoke, her eyes slithered over to mine in warning: *Careful, little girl. Hush.* Sensing her glance, Dublin reached for my arm, and I found myself unceremoniously shoved behind him and out of her line of sight.

"What did you want?"

"Don't shoot the messenger, darling," Saskia huffed. "I'm just the bearer of bad news; Raphael has requested that you take over one of my contracts."

I flinched as Dublin's grip tightened, nails indenting my skin.

"What? Why?"

"I don't know," Saskia chirped. "Maybe he thinks you've decided to take a more *active* role again, considering that you've come out of retirement?" Those amber eyes darted pointedly in my direction.

"For how long?"

Take over a contract? What on earth did that mean?

"I can't be bothered to remember the terms of every single contract." Saskia waved a hand absently through the air. "Mikhail is around here somewhere. Ask *him.*"

With that, she turned on her heel and headed for the door. However, near the threshold she paused, one foot poised in the air and a coy smile shaping her lips.

"Oh and, Dublin? I almost forgot …" Her tone was casual, as if the detail had simply slipped her mind, but the look in her eye was anything but innocent.

From the way Dublin tensed, I knew that he had sensed the ominous edge in her tone as well. I had a horrible suspicion that Saskia had been waiting for this moment all along, like a cat toying with a mouse right before delivering the killing blow.

"Raphael has *also* requested an audience with you tomorrow night," she began. "And he wants you to bring the lovely Eleanor along as well. Ta-ta!"

Smiling, she slipped through the doors with an elegant toss of her head, leaving me alone with a man who seemed inclined to break my wrist. I gasped as the delicate bones compacted beneath his grip.

"D-Dublin, you're—"

He whirled around, and the expression on his face struck me senseless. "What did she say to you?"

A shiver ran down my spine at his tone; I don't think I'd ever heard him sound so cold. His eyes were glacial, filled with such hatred …

It was a split-second before I realized that the emotion wasn't directed at *me.*

"N-Nothing—"

"Nothing?" A single raised eyebrow was my only clue as to the true extent of his rage. "Don't lie to me. Saskia isn't one for small talk. What did she *say*?"

"S-She just wanted to gloat over how little you paid for me," I lied, hoping that the small bit of truth might placate him enough to let the subject drop. But the words had the opposite effect.

He drew back violently. His mouth opened ...

Then closed again. I don't think I could have gotten that same reaction even if I'd slapped him.

For the longest time, he just stood there, staring at me until I was forced to consider the impossible; Dublin Helos was *speechless*.

"She was just being cruel," I rushed to add. "She only wanted to rub it in that I hadn't been bid on—"

His eyes narrowed as he processed my words. Then, after another tortured second, he became his arrogant, distant self once again. "Stay away from her."

Before I could even hope to respond, he turned and dragged me down the hall after him. With lightning speed, we mounted a set of stairs and entered the hallway that I recognized as leading to the lounge.

There, a voice greeted us from the shadows. "So the reclusive Dublin Helos shows his face once again ..."

A beautiful man—whom I recognized from my first visit to the club—appeared around a corner.

Mikhail.

Today, he only wore a pair of black pants, a smug expression and ...nothing else. I tried to ignore the way my eyes darted over his body once before settling on his face. His strange pendant caught my attention again, only now something about the design of it seemed familiar.

I had seen a chain like that before ...

"Mikhail," Dublin greeted in a voice of steel, dragging my attention back to him.

"Tired of her *already*, have you?" The man wondered, nodding to me. "Though she's lasted longer with you than I thought she would. If you're finished, I'm sure I could find some use for her *somewhere.*"

Dublin didn't rise to the bait. "You have a contract for me. Where?"

"It's somewhere around here," Mikhail said, his eyes glinting from beneath a fringe of dark hair. "Though it's nowhere near as *important* to Raphael as that of Eleanor Gray—"

"The contract, Mikhail," Dublin growled, so low that I could feel the vibrations resonate in my bones. "Now."

Unlike Saskia, Mikhail didn't simper in the face of Dublin's rage. Instead, he simply nodded to the lounge, the embodiment of indifference—but not without one last quip. "Careful, Dublin. Become any less of a recluse, and one might think you seek to return to the fold ..."

A threat laced the words more than any hint of a greeting.

Rather than respond, Dublin watched expressionlessly as Mikhail disappeared within the shadows of the corridor. Then, he shifted his attention to someone else. I turned along with him, and saw a woman sitting on one of the couches who I hadn't noticed before.

She faced away from me, but that peachy skin and wavy blonde hair seemed familiar. Somehow I knew—even before she finally looked over at us—that she was the same girl Saskia had brought along on my first night in the club.

Seeing Dublin, she stood, clutching a purse to her chest, and made her way toward us on a pair of black heels. Once she came close enough, she reached into the purse and withdrew a square, black object: a contract book.

Letting go of my wrist, Dublin took it and then casually lifted the cover.

"You are to remain here ...Katherine," he informed her while his eyes scanned the page nestled in between. I attempted to sneak a peek from over his shoulder, only to have him slam the leather case shut before I could read a single word.

"Only from now on, you will answer to *me*. I'll expect no less from you than would Mikhail."

"Yes, sir."

Katherine nodded, but from the way her eyes had widened while he'd spoken, one might think that Dublin had five heads, his fangs bared and had spit a few flames while he was at it. Her shoulders trembled as she hurried past

Mikhail—who lurked a few feet ahead—and vanished down the hall.

Confused, I watched her go; was she now indebted to Dublin as well?

More importantly …would he have her do the same things *I* had done in order to 'fulfill' her bargain?

It wasn't jealousy that stung through my chest like a hot poker at the thought.

It wasn't.

"Interesting," Mikhail murmured, brown eyes thoughtful as he watched the woman go. "Did you not have enough room on your arm for *two* pets?"

Dublin didn't dignify him with an answer.

Instead, he turned, pulling me after him so suddenly that I was afraid my shoulder might be ripped right from its socket. In a blur, we descended the stairs, barged through the lobby and reentered daylight just as the clouds above were beginning to break. Sunlight filtered down, bouncing off the black paint of the car.

I felt like someone who'd just re-entered reality after leaving the *Twilight Zone*. Saskia's bargain kept circling my brain. *Cael. Cael. Cael.*

Considering how Dublin had reacted to her and I merely being in the same general vicinity, there was no way in hell that I would ever risk saying that word out loud. For all I knew, it was some kind of magic spell meant to kill us both

—and no amount of information was worth the potential consequences …I supposed. I hadn't quite convinced myself of that when Dublin suddenly spoke while man-handling me onto the passenger's seat.

"Lunch?" he grumbled, expression unreadable.

I didn't get the chance to answer before I found the door slammed in my face. However, in a matter of seconds, he appeared in the driver's seat,, and the car slipped effortlessly into the mid-morning traffic.

I kept quiet as he navigated a series of twists and turns through the downtown—but rather than stopping in front of the *Cafe Claret* or even that smaller coffee shop, I was surprised to find the imposing façade of Gray Manor looming above.

No sooner had Dublin parked the car than servants burst through the front doors as if they had played out this scenario a thousand times. One took his jacket, while another assured him that everything was "ready, as requested."

He didn't take my arm again and instead left me to catch up while he marched through the front doors—as if he owned the damn place—and headed straight for the drawing room.

My mind was a blur of questions—about Saskia's pointed little 'hints' most of all—but when I passed through the doorway, I promptly forgot all about it. Someone had already set a small table for two, and shock couldn't even begin to describe the emotion that ran through me at the sight of steaming plates of food being carried in by a maid as if on cue.

Dublin sure knew how to run my staff like clockwork. He could have given Mother a run for her money in the art of slave-driving—I mean *management.* Without a word, he pulled out a chair for me, but I could only stand there, gaping, until he cleared his throat pointedly.

"Are you going to just look at the food or eat it?"

My jaw snapped shut, and I perched on the chair's very edge. Satisfied, Dublin took the seat across from me and observed the platters being placed between us like a diligent overseer: dish of soup, followed by a bowl of salad and a platter of fresh bread.

It was more than I was used to being served on a daily basis. However, a regular meal didn't have the usual connotation when it came to Dublin. I thought of his *breakfast* from all those days ago—coincidentally where he first presented me with his 'cure'—and shuddered. All of a sudden, the crisp, white tablecloth and priceless china took on an ominous aura.

At the clinking of silverware, I glanced up to find that, once again, Dublin had taken it upon himself to serve me. He cut two slices from the loaf and spread each one neatly with butter before placing them both on my plate. Then he ladled a serving of steaming clam chowder into a bowl and placed it on my side as well.

Sitting back in his chair, he raised a single eyebrow in a way that conveyed what he didn't say out loud; *eat something. Now.*

Rolling my eyes in exasperation, I scooted closer to the table.

"You never eat," I said and reached for a fork before he could even begin to snap at me. As I fixed myself a serving of salad, I added, "Is that a *vampire* thing—"

"It's a preference thing," he said, smoothly cutting over me.

Though, as if to prove me wrong, he ripped off a chunk of bread and took a bite. Entranced, I watched him chew, deliberately slow. The motion looked awkward—stiff—as if he were only mimicking the action and couldn't quite remember how to do it naturally.

Finally, he swallowed.

"Preference," he insisted, while dabbing at his lips with a napkin lifted from the table. "I'm sure that you wouldn't enjoy the things *I* prefer to feast upon."

Feast upon …

The word choice conjured up all sorts of unsightly images— namely *me,* trapped beneath him, while his fangs teased my knee. At the memory, my body jumped as if remembering the jolt of heat that had run through my skin.

My tongue dampened, my throat tightened. I couldn't breathe.

"Actually …that is something we need to discuss," I heard Dublin begin, snapping me back to reality.

Uh-oh. No doubt this 'something' was the real reason behind our little 'lunch.'

Warily my eyes met his. "W-What?"

"I need to feed."

It was such a blunt admission that I blinked and tried to right myself before I could slide off my chair in shock.

"F-Feed?"

"I need *blood,* Eleanor," he snapped. "I believe this was one of the conditions mentioned before you signed your new contract."

The scathing tone stung, but there was something hidden beneath it; a dark sense of desperation that had me reaching up for my throat before I could help it. Tentatively, my finger prodded a pulse, and I gulped at the thought of him leaping over the table for a bite.

"D-Do you just …"

As if reading my mind, he scoffed in disgust. "Not in *here.*"

I was confused. "Then, where—"

"Is there nothing you're afraid of?" I flinched at the change of subject. His tone was too soft, and those eyes flashed an alarming shade of gray. "You need to realize, Eleanor," he practically growled. "This isn't a game."

As he spoke, ivory glinted beneath his upper lip, sharp and undeniably terrifying.

"I could *kill* you."

I waited, though I had no idea for what.

Maybe the punch-line to this morbid joke?

But it never came.

He wasn't laughing.

"And this," he said next as if to prove my darkest fears, "is the part where you run."

I couldn't deny how tempting the suggestion was.

My heart pounded, aching to give into that very urge, to dash from the room screaming and waving my arms through the air like a true damsel in distress. Instead, my father's voice chose that moment to ring from the grave. *"A Gray always fulfills his debts ..."*

I couldn't quite remember the context in which he had first given me that advice—but it seemed more than fitting now. *Five dollars* or no, there was no way in hell that I would ever allow Dublin to have more of a hold over me than he already did.

He appeared shocked when I only crossed my legs politely at the knee. I couldn't quite face him yet, so I stared down at the table, fingering the edge of the white cloth with a trembling thumb. "I don't understand," I began in the strongest tone I could manage. "You've already fed from me before—"

"I *bit* you," he corrected harshly. "And trust me when I say that I was adequately *restrained*."

I glanced over to find that he had withdrawn something from the crisp collar of his shirt; the long, silver chain with that delicate cross dangling from the center. Had wearing the necklace somehow held him back from truly 'feeding' from me—sort of like a vampiric version of a leash. Or perhaps Dublin was the pious sort, and the cross represented something more significant.

I started to ask, but he spoke over me.

"It would take a lot more than a few drops to satisfy my hunger," he said without elaborating.

Oh. Surreptitiously, I cleared my throat enough to ask, "How much?"

"Enough that could be easily replenished by a dose of *my* blood."

It was a deceptive answer. Kind of like if I had asked him, *'How badly will jumping off this bridge injure me?'* And he had replied, *'Not badly enough that the world's best surgeons wouldn't be able to patch you up—maybe.'*

"Why me?" I found myself asking. "Why not just get a girl from Saskia?" As he had so rudely suggested the other day.

"Because I don't *want* a girl from Saskia." *Oh?* Before my mind could even consider the pathetic chance that he might have only wanted *me*, he continued. "A word of advice, Eleanor; never eat from the hand of your enemy."

Fair enough. Feeding from me would have just been convenient—still, the prospect gave me an idea, one that I couldn't resist, no matter how foolish. I shifted in my chair and tried to gather up enough nerve to meet his impassive stare.

"You *biting* me was a part of our agreement," I began. "Not being chained and drained."

"Just what are you saying?" There wasn't any sort of expression on his face. God, he looked terrifying.

"I'm *asking* …if you have to put a monetary value on this new 'condition' what would it be?"

"What?"

I sucked in a deep breath. *Here goes …*

"I wasn't kidding about repaying my debt. If you maintain that five dollars was how much you paid for me, then I remain determined to *repay* every cent."

I don't think he could have looked more shocked than if I had climbed onto the table and done the *Can-Can* over the salad bowl. "You can't be serious—"

"I am."

"Fine," he snapped. "If I had to put a 'price' on what your blood would be worth to me, then …twenty-five cents."

"Done," I blurted without even wasting the time to be insulted. "From now on, every time you feed from me, twenty-five cents will be deducted from my debt. Fair enough?"

"Are you insane?"

I frowned at his tone more so than the question. "Probably," I admitted. "But I told you; I don't like leaving debts unpaid."

He sat back in his chair, watching me with an expression that made me squirm. Taking advantage of the silence, I attempted another question. "What have you been, um … drinking up until now?"

"I have my methods," he said softly. "But nothing compares to feeding fresh from the vein."

It was such a blatant admission. I don't know if he had ever spoken so freely to me before.

"Ah," I croaked. "So do you have …regulars?"

"I don't pick up random damsels from the alleyway like it's a drive-thru restaurant, if that's what you mean." His tone was cold. "I may be a creature bound for hell, but I am *discrete*, Eleanor; feeding from you would merely be convenient."

He watched me for the longest time. I supposed he wanted a definitive answer.

"It … It's not like I have a choice," I said finally.

"No," he agreed. "But I like the drama when those in your position try to refuse," he said, which just strengthened my resolve to never give him the same satisfaction.

"What do you need me to do?" I demanded, fully prepared for him to sprout some cryptic riddles.

I have to pierce a vein?

Eviscerate you over an open spit?

"I'll have to tie you up."

"W-What?" *Tie* was the polite word. I knew what he'd really meant: *chain.* "Why?"

He shrugged and suddenly jabbed a finger toward my bowl. *Eat.* It was only when I attempted to swallow a spoonful of the scalding liquid that he explained, "For your own safety. This won't be like before, Eleanor."

As he spoke, my gaze trailed down to that silver cross. He held it between two fingers, unconsciously swinging the chain back and forth like a pendulum.

"W-When?" It was the only thing I could think to say.

"Tonight."

"Oh?" I tried to play nonchalant, while inside I was screaming. "At the club?"

"No." His eyes darkened, daring me to ask why. I kept my mouth shut, until he grudgingly added, "I'll have a car sent around midnight. I shouldn't have to tell you what will happen if you aren't out front at that time."

I shook my head even as Saskia's voice ran through my mind. *One little word.*

"Midnight," he repeated, rising to his feet.

As he did, I remembered something. "What do you want me to wear?"

It was a foolish question, but I was surprised to find that it was the only one I could think to ask.

He turned, glancing back at me from over his shoulder. "It won't matter."

I sat there, dazed as he disappeared down the hall in a flash of dove-gray, and wondered *why* that might have been.

RED

I hid in the drawing room for hours after he left.

I couldn't help it. Whenever I attempted to leave, I would picture *him* there, behind the door, waiting to jump from the shadows and shout, *"Boo! You think you're so brave, Eleanor? You're just a silly little fool; you can't hide from the devil."*

Gradually, darkness fell, and it was only when I saw the moon peeking from beyond the window's long curtains that I found the strength to finally stand. By the time I skulked back to my bedroom, midnight was approaching fast. After a frantic glance at the clock, I realized that I had barely an hour's time to get ready—*without* a set of ominous instructions.

Using Dublin's ambivalent answer—*"it won't matter"*—as my excuse, I decided to aim for comfort as I crept toward my closet, or as much 'comfort' as one could find in a wardrobe composed entirely by my mother. Pants, slacks or —God forbid—jeans had all been deemed unacceptable.

I found a tracksuit, surprisingly, hidden within a drawer; a holdout from the brief month when Yoga had been 'fashionable' enough for Mother to let me consider it, before all forms of sweating were deemed *unseemly* once again. The material was a soft lime-green and clung to my body like a second skin.

Wearing it, I felt like some deranged schoolgirl preparing for a field trip—though this was more like a one-way excursion to hell, no refunds.

Feeling helpless, I ran a brush through my hair and paced my bedroom until exactly eleven forty-five. Only then did I make my way downstairs where I managed to slip through the front doors just as a black car glided up the driveway. The driver ushered me inside, and I climbed aboard the dark chariot, ready to be delivered to my doom.

The ride didn't take long. It felt like I'd only had time to blink before I found myself gazing up at the ominous spires of the cathedral, eerily silhouetted against the light of the moon. I wasn't surprised that Dublin had chosen this place as his 'restaurant' of choice. *After all,* I thought in a weak attempt at humor, *everyone likes a good, home-cooked meal* …

"Miss," the driver prompted, and I realized that he'd been holding the door open for me.

Trembling, I climbed out onto the curb. The grounds were deserted. There was no one there to see me walk cautiously up the front path. *No one to hear my screams,* I thought with a nervous glance back at the retreating car. Though, while I couldn't see anyone, the standing hairs on the back of my neck warned that someone-or something- was watching my every step ...

My heart twitched in my chest when I finally approached those massive oak doors. They were unlocked, surprisingly, and I lingered on the threshold while my eyes struggled to adjust to the darkness.

You could still run, I thought while taking in the rows of empty pews and a desolate altar. *You could still—*

"You're late."

In a flicker of shadow, Dublin appeared from behind a column and escape was no longer a possibility. He wore black again tonight; a collared shirt, paired with dark pants. That blond hair hung uncharacteristically loose—as if he had impatiently been running his hands through it—instead of slicked back into that perfect coif. The longest strands nearly brushed his shoulders, longer even than mine.

"I-I'm not late!" I shifted, keeping my back along the stone wall as the door closed with a *thud,* trapping me inside. "I was waiting at twelve, just like you said."

He held up his wrist, revealing a small watch, and tapped the glass front with his finger; *liar.* "One minute past your expected time."

My heart raced as his words from earlier screamed through my mind; *if you are late by even a second, you will suffer for it.* His eyes glazed over and his nostrils flared as if he could smell my fear, but in an instant, his gaze returned to a neutral gray. Then he turned and jerked his head in the direction of a nearby corridor rather than recall his threat aloud.

"Come."

I crept after him, not surprised when we came before another *"out of order"* confessional at the hall's end—only this one revealed a hidden elevator when the false panel door was removed.

Without any explanation, Dublin slid inside and pressed the topmost button.

"Get in," he snapped when I didn't move.

I would have rather walked all those flights of stairs again than be alone with him in such an enclosed space. Still, I held my head high and shuffled closer.

A good foot separated me from his bulk, and yet I still felt the full brunt of his chill. A freezer would have been warmer. As we ascended, my heartbeat counted the seconds —*one, two, three,* and ironically I imagined that had the elevator been heading down I would have truly descended into hell with the devil looming next to me.

Nearly a whole minute passed before the elevator reopened and I could breathe again. I recognized the entryway to his lair as our destination. This time, only a few candles on the walls were lit, leaving the rest of the hall swathed in shadow.

"You've already agreed to this," Dublin reminded me as we headed down a random hall.

His voice was so low that I could feel the vibration of every single word in my bones. Any other day, I might have had the sense of mind to wonder why he felt the need to reiterate that. As it was, I couldn't focus on much of anything.

"*You* signed the contract," he reminded in the same, ominous tone. "So ...I will expect no tantrums or hysterics."

He turned, and I found myself inside a wide room, the contents of it made my mouth fall open. I vaguely remembered speculating once that he might have had a 'torture' chamber hidden somewhere within his lair. As it turned out, the thought wasn't so funny after all.

At first glance, the room seemed bare to a fault; plain, sterile even. The walls were a dull shade of black, and the floors were pristine, silver tile. It could have been something as innocent as an unused spare room if it weren't for the drain cover in the middle of the floor and the chains hanging from the ceiling. *Actual* chains—long and silver—dangled from hooks to pool in neat piles, ready for use.

Looking at them, I couldn't breathe.

The only other objects were a metal footlocker in the corner and a long, stainless steel slab, resembling one that might be found in a morgue—all within easy reach of those chains.

How ...convenient. I might have crumbled into a puddle on the floor if Dublin wasn't there beside me.

"What is this?" I heard myself croak instead.

My eyes darted around the room, too terrified to settle over one object for too long: sharp points, metal cuffs, convenient drain and all that silver raining down from the ceiling, waiting to ensnare me if I got too close. It looked like the lair of a serial killer.

"Restraints," he explained in the same tone most might proclaim *'the sky is blue.'* "I warned you. You will need to be—"

"Chained," I finished for him. My voice shook. I had to suck in air just to find the strength to ask, "But *why?*"

I flinched in anticipation of the answer; you taste better that way? Because it's standard vampire dining procedure? Because I said so?

He merely shrugged. With his back turned to me I couldn't see his face, which made the impact of his next words all the more terrifying.

"So that *when* you struggle, I don't hurt you."

I had to dig my nails into my wrists just to keep from hyperventilating. *'When' you struggle.*

"I can hear your heart racing," he announced on a mirthless laugh. I blinked, and he was in front of me, eyes burning. "What? Don't tell me ... Has the brave Eleanor Gray finally realized how foolish she really is?"

I staggered back, nearly tripping over my heels. "I n-never claimed to be brave."

Just foolish! A point that was proven when I just *stood* there meekly, while he reached for the zipper of my jacket and yanked, revealing the simple white top I was wearing underneath. He twisted the hem between his fingers and then pulled the jacket off with one hand, while the other wrenched the shirt up over my head.

"From now on, whenever you are with me, wear only the clothing Yulia supplies you with," he said while tossing both garments into the corner without a second glance.

I wasn't bold enough to mention that *he* had commanded I dress myself tonight. Instead, I nodded, relieved that he was speaking in terms of the future and not, *if you survive tonight ...*

Besides, I wasn't so attached to my wardrobe to mourn the loss of matronly skirts and dowdy blouses—though, I would have given my soul for either as Dublin began to tug my sweatpants down my legs.

"Wait," I croaked as his icy fingers brushed my bare hip. "I-I thought—"

"This isn't about sex," he spat as if insulted. "But if you don't mind, I'd rather not make a mess."

Mess. The word conjured all sorts of horrific imagery: blood splatter, gore, all circling down that drain in the floor.

God, what in the hell had I gotten myself into?

I could only eye the chains with a lump in my throat as Dublin crouched to undo my heels and wrenched them, one by one, from my feet. Then he stood and steered me around to face him.

"Don't look so terrified," he snapped. But the way his eyes honed in on the frantic pulse surging through my throat resembled a wolf about to feast on a helpless fawn and …for once, my fear irritated him.

"I could always render you unconscious first …"

Suspicions about just how he might do that aside, I shook my head.

"No! I want to be awake."

To be fair, whether I was or not didn't seem to matter to him either way.

Stupid, foolish, idiot. He didn't have to say the words out loud. My own conscience sufficiently berated me in his place. *Do you have a death wish, Ellie?*

Standing there in my underwear while a vampire prepared to strap me down, I had to consider that possibility.

"Having second thoughts?" Dublin asked, almost as if he was willing me to say yes. He watched me from beneath a fringe of blond hair that he hadn't even bothered to tuck back into place. The slight flaw was *not* a good sign. It made him seem feral. Wild ...

A Dublin *without* his obsessive need for perfection in all things was not a man I wanted to be at the mercy of. *Ever.*

My mouth opened, though I had no idea what I had meant to say; answer *yes* to his question? Maybe. Tell him that my clothes were much too expensive to leave lying around on the floor? Ha, a poor excuse for a stall tactic. Scream? It was the obvious choice, but it was already too late.

He caught me by the wrist and hauled me forward without waiting for a reply. I staggered, almost running right into his chest—however, before I could make contact, he shoved me sideways and onto the morgue-like table.

My head hit a pillow placed at one end of the slab while my feet were lifted from the floor and unceremoniously dumped on the opposite end, all within the blink of an eye. A second later, my right wrist was immobile, then my left. Ignoring the chains attached to the ceiling, Dublin had apparently withdrawn two sets of cuffs from his pockets and secured my arms to the headboard. Uselessly, I tugged on both, just to help the fact sink in.

I was pinned down, unable to so much as lift my head.

The only part of me that remained free was my legs. I couldn't resist flexing my toes against the cold, solid surface for leverage while Dublin stood back to observe his handiwork.

"I should immobilize you," he surmised, eyes on my flailing feet.

"W-Why?"

He shrugged, eyes an unreadable shade of steel. "Contrary to popular belief, Eleanor …I do not want to hurt you."

The sincerity of that statement knocked me senseless. For once, there was a real emotion hidden within that deep tenor as well—*unease.*

How funny that he seemed to speak more freely when I was tied up.

"Not only would I completely waste my investment in you," he added in an undertone, "but the mess …"

I grimaced at the thought of my blood splattering the walls.

"So nice to know you care," I croaked, but something in his words struck me once again; *the mess.* I thought of his 'not-biting' bites from that night in the club, that pain, that mind-numbing ache. The blood …

If those had been mere 'nibbles' according to him, then just what horrors awaited me tonight?

My teeth descended into my bottom lip at the possibilities.

Dublin caught the motion, and his eyes narrowed even more. He walked over to the door, casually closing it with a swing of his hand.

Trapped! The thought exploded through my mind, laced with fear as he came to stand before me. For the longest time, he just stood there, an intensity burning in his eyes, watching me carefully.

Was this how a steak dinner felt, at the mercy of a hungry diner trying to decide where to make the first bite?

I flinched when he moved, but it was only to reach for his collar and swiftly undo the buttons of his shirt.

In an instant, I forgot all about the potential 'feeding' or the fact that I was currently strapped down to a bed by my wrists.

God, he was beautiful. *Evil* and cold and unnervingly pale, yes—but breathtaking nonetheless, and as he slowly shed his shirt I had to admit that I was struck dumb. He was perfection in human form, shaped from ivory skin and chiseled muscles.

That silver chain hung from his throat, mingling with the golden thatch of hair covering his chest. Long, it almost reached his navel, where the cross dangled, glinting off his skin.

Does that necklace ever come off? I wondered, and in answer to my unspoken question, Dublin unclasped the chain and lifted it over his head—but just as the cross was ready to clear his shoulder, he hesitated, and for the first time I could make out the expression that I guessed had been lurking behind those eyes all along—*hunger.*

In a violent motion, he swung the chain up, gathering the entire necklace in a fist, and then tucked it into his pocket.

It was as if a spell over him had been lifted. His eyes seemed lit from within, fiery, calculating, demonic. No longer enslaved to perfect posture, he leaned forward on the balls of his feet, like a wolf ready to lunge for my throat at a moment's notice.

My gloating, infuriatingly emotionless Dublin was gone. The man standing above me was a predator, ravenous and untamed. In his eyes, Eleanor Gray had ceased to exist, and all that remained was prey.

Tendrils of terror coiled in my belly—especially when he opened his mouth, revealing fangs that glinted in the light: sharp, curved and the color of ivory.

An instinctive urge to survive flooded my veins and I struggled against my bonds as he crept closer.

Panicked thoughts raced through my mind: *Fight! Run! Scream!*

Ironically, the room remained so silent that I could hear my own breathing, loud and erratic as he crouched down near the foot of the slab. He seized my calf and lifted the left leg for inspection.

I imagined him scanning the skin, searching for a vein.

Was he like a bat with sonar in his ability to sense blood? Could he hear my pulse, even now rushing with every beat of my heart?

Or did technique not matter at all, as he lowered his head, spread those icy lips against the skin, and finally bit …

It was just like the first time he'd bitten me at the club.

I *wanted* to scream.

I tried to.

But I didn't even have the time to gasp for air before he clamped down—fangs piercing through flesh—and suddenly nothing else mattered.

Heat flooded my veins, smothering everything with a raging fervor. Loud and intense, it hammered against my eardrums.

Time slowed. The world stopped spinning.

I could only lay there, pinned, as Dublin consumed me.

I now realized that he hadn't been bluffing; this was nothing like before. He had merely been nibbling then, I suppose—tasting me like one might sample wine.

This time, he *drank*; unashamedly, uncontrollably. Not even my pathetic little whimpers were enough to hold him back.

He clutched my ankle so tightly I thought it might snap, keeping the limb immobile while he fed, unconcerned by the alarming amounts of warm liquid dribbling down my leg to pool on the cool steel underneath.

Drip.

Drip.

I could only stare, entranced, as his shoulders moved in sync, rippling with coiled muscle and I swore that I could hear every ravenous swallow, felt every savoring caress of his tongue …

Oh, God! He is out of control; he's draining you dry, Ellie, I thought hysterically. Gulp, sip … Soon there'd be nothing left.

A smart woman would have been afraid. But when *I* finally remembered how to make my body move … It was only to flex my calf, silently urging him to bite deeper, *harder*, swallow every last bit of me until there was nothing left at all …

Suddenly, my leg hit the slab with a *thump*. The icy chill withdrew, and I glanced down, dazed to find a scene from a horror movie.

Blood was everywhere. A bright, garish scarlet painted my leg. It flowed over the edge of the table, splashing the floor beneath … So much blood.

"Eleanor—" I shuddered as Dublin appeared above me. *How in the hell had he moved so quickly?* "Say something," he demanded.

I obeyed solely out of habit. "Something …"

My voice sounded foreign to my own ears—high-pitched. Though, maybe shock had something to do with it?

Dublin was covered in red. It coated his chin, his hands. Splotches of scarlet painted that flawless marble skin. There were even streaks of crimson tainting his golden hair. The blood on his lips was so thick that it almost resembled lipstick and I snickered—until I realized that he would have made a much lovelier woman than I did.

Damn. It just wasn't fair that someone could be so beautiful …

"Look at me." His tone was sharp, forcing me to focus.

Those eyes were a dangerous shade of gray, but hidden within them was what could have been *concern* in anyone else. *Worry.* Was it real …or just a figment conjured by delirium?

I was too dizzy to care.

"How do you feel?"

Feel? A million different sensations pulsed through my body, collided, exploded.

"Fine," I settled on finally.

Better than fine, my inner voice insisted. Amazing. Incredible. Weightless.

Dublin didn't seem convinced. His eyes narrowed, trailing down to my throat as if he thought that the truth lingered somewhere within my pulse.

"You're not in pain?"

I shook my head, too distracted by how close he was to wonder why he cared.

Even slathered with gore, the man took my breath away. Shamelessly, I allowed my eyes to greedily drink him in.

His fangs were bared, threatening to pierce his lower lip. At the sight of them, every single nerve in my body throbbed with longing, though I had no idea why.

Warnings echoed through my mind—*Ellie, what the hell are you doing? Stop!* But nothing could prevent me from tilting my head back into the pillow and baring my throat.

It was as if my mind and body were two completely separate entities; what mattered to one completely horrified the other.

Scream.

Moan.

Resist.

Accept.

I was torn in half as Dublin watched with a frown, twisting his mouth.

"Eleanor." He sounded different: colder. "Tell me what you feel."

Ha! A tattered giggle broke loose and scattered on the air. I couldn't help it. There was that 'feel' word again. I must have truly been in Hell if my Devil gave a damn about my 'feelings.'

"*Now*," he snapped when I didn't respond fast enough. "Answer me."

Gasping for air, I blurted the first word that came to mind.

"Drunk …I feel drunk."

Gloriously, amazingly *drunk*. Father's best brandy couldn't achieve such a bubbly, giggle-inducing high. I doubted that even the world's best champagne could either.

Dublin Helos was a drug unto himself …and I wanted *more*.

"Can you feel this?"

I frowned, annoyed that he wanted me to concentrate when my head was spinning, and I was flying somewhere above Cloud Nine, way too high to come back down …

"Eleanor." That deep tenor hardened, warning me not to disobey, and I forced myself to focus.

His hand was on my inner thigh, heavy and cold.

The sight should have been alarming I guessed, but it wasn't. I felt way too dizzy: *numb*. In this euphoric state, it just seemed …right.

So, I sighed instead while my head drifted somewhere above my body.

"Don't feel a thing," I heard myself reply.

For once, there was no shame—my emotion *du jour*—just this frightening sense of abandon, driven by a desire I had never felt before and one I couldn't shake: *more, more, more.* My body begged for release.

Dublin's eyes narrowed and widened in quick succession. If anything, my answer seemed to have annoyed him even more. Alarmed …

Perhaps, he wanted a more dramatic reaction? Should I cower like a damsel before Dracula? Beg to not be cast out into the flames of hell? Or, perhaps, scream like some horror movie blonde bimbo?

The thought was strangely amusing.

I pictured myself down on my knees, groveling at his feet: Oh, please, Dublin, the great and terrible. Oh please don't chain me up! Unless you really want to …

A golden eyebrow shot up into that fringe of hair. Had I said those words out loud? I didn't have the time to wonder, before his hand rode up, deliberately encroaching toward that intimate part of my body.

"Can you feel *this*?"

The sensation was the equivalent of someone yanking the needle off a record.

The happy daze shattered.

Suddenly, I was back inside my own body and clarity returned like a kick to the stomach; namely, *pain*—sharp and fierce—throbbing through my calf. How had I missed that before?

But the most alarming realization was how his icy touch felt against my heated skin. I could feel his fingers inching up my thigh, painting my flesh like a canvas with my blood.

They continued to roam, heedless of the way I shook my head.

"Can you feel this?"

I shivered as his touch crept higher, traveling uncomfortably close to the hem of my panties.

"Yes," I gasped.

Too terrified to kick him, I writhed instead, feeling my wrists strain against their bonds.

"I-I can feel it."

"Good." The word held absolutely no emotion. I worried Dublin was gone. The monster was back, and he watched my pathetic attempts to resist with no expression at all.

This is bad, Ellie.

As if to prove my worst fears, he tugged, sending the cotton down my legs in one fierce pull. I squealed in shock, yanking on the cuffs so harshly the metal bit into the flesh.

"W-What are you—"

"Hush," he growled, sliding that thumb boldly over my hip, and then down my inner thigh, raising goosebumps as he went.

Lower.

Lower still …

"Do you feel this?" he asked, almost innocently, as I struggled to breathe. "This?"

Nerve endings flared as his thumb teased the apex of my thighs, slick and wet …but from my own blood or my excitement? I had no clue. He lightened the pressure of his thumb—barely touching now—almost as if he was forcing me to move, to seek out what I needed …to respond.

Don't, I told myself in vain, as that familiar heat began to build in the pit of my stomach. *Don't you dare.*

But I had already begun arching into him anyway, forgetting all about my damn pride.

My mouth flew open, eyes wide as tiny sparks prickled all over my skin. I was no longer in a daze, but painfully aware of every single touch, every slight tilt of my hips as my traitorous body sought more.

Thunder rumbled in the distance—or perhaps from his chest? I wasn't sure of anything as he nudged my legs apart without warning and crouched down between them. Bracing one hand against the headboard, he lowered his head, hovering above my exposed throat.

At the same time, he repositioned his hand, allowing more contact. A brush. A slight nudge—deeper, harder than before. Every motion resonated tenfold all over my body until I was burning alive and it still wasn't enough.

"What about this?"

Too breathless to respond I could only shiver. I could feel him, all right. Everywhere …

"And this?"

A burst of cold air on my throat was my only warning before the sharp points of unseen teeth raked along my skin, teasing …taunting, driving me insane.

A moan tore from my throat when he applied the slightest bit of pressure, drawing forth a delicate bead of blood that he lapped away with an icy tongue, a cold, victorious smile spreading across his lips. Dizzy, I could only wonder why he was doing this, especially after his previous insistence that this was only about his need to feed, *'nothing more.'*

As if reading my mind, his voice vibrated against my eardrum, low and guttural. "Your heart is pounding faster …your blood tastes sweeter."

I tasted better.

How logical. With his hand down between my legs, and his mouth dangerously close to the pulse surging through my throat, Dublin had nothing on his mind but the discerning tastes of a blood connoisseur.

Even still, he was almost gentle as he coaxed me up that terrifying peak with every stroke of his hand. He drew it out, slowing down when my breaths turned to rasps and my vision blurred. Then—just as the sensation began to ebb— he would pick up the pace, rubbing harder, faster. It was a cruel mix of pleasure and denial of release, and I was helpless. I bit my bottom lip, fighting back the moan I could feel threatening to break loose.

I felt painfully aware of every inch of him—down to the delicate piece of bloody hair that had fallen across his forehead. He was so close …but not close enough.

His chill encased me from head to toe, and I only wanted *more.*

More fire mixed with ice. More soaring and falling. More pain mixed with intense pleasure … Oh God help me, I *needed* more.

"Don't move," he warned against my ear even as his frigid lips brushed the line of my pulse.

Over and over and over again. Then he sucked, lapping up the mess and my neck was coated in wetness.

He's drinking too much, a part of me whimpered. *Too fast …*

As if he was well aware of that fact a dangerously possessive sound resonated deep in his throat. Those fangs only slid deeper, and he added another finger beside that taunting thumb, sliding around …

He stroked a furious rhythm that was forcing me ever closer to the edge of sanity.

Mindless, I found myself gaping at the ceiling, forgetting all about his order to stay still as my body shuddered beneath his weight.

My head was detached again, floating somewhere against the ceiling. My legs writhed against that cold hard steel slab still slick with blood, feet slipping and sliding in a desperate quest for leverage.

Suddenly nothing else mattered. No matter how wanton or insane or desperate it made me seem—I wanted him to touch me.

I needed him to. *Take all of me*, but even as the thought crossed my mind, I heard him whisper something, nearly unintelligible against my skin. "Forgive me, father, for I have sinned ..."

"W-What was that?" I gasped, barely clinging to reality.

I hadn't been meant to hear it. He stiffened, mouth stilling against the line of my pulse. When he finally answered me, his voice had regained some of that infamous coldness.

"It is customary to give a prayer before one dines is it not, Eleanor?"

Prayer?

Before I even found the sense to muster a reply he surged, fangs piercing my flesh at the same time he filled me with the broadness of a thumb.

Just like that ...the rest of the world fell away, plunging me into hell.

Only this time, I relished every bit of my destruction.

MOONLIGHT

I awoke to the sound of music.

Beethoven's *Moonlight Sonata*, if I wasn't mistaken.

It was a careful, if somewhat halting, rendition. The pianist forgot a key series of notes midway, but the mistakes did nothing to detract from the overall beauty of the piece.

However, unless Harper had hauled my grandmother's Baby Grand upstairs, I couldn't fathom how I was hearing it so clearly when our only piano was on the opposite side of the house.

In fact, even my much-beloved bed was nowhere as soft as the mattress beneath me now. It felt decadently luxurious— not to mention that the silk sheets draped over my body would have never been found within the practical linen cupboards of Gray Manor.

"No," I croaked as my eyes opened to an unfamiliar ceiling. "Definitely not in Kansas, Ellie."

Neither, it would seem, was I in one of those strange rooms at the club. Or, I added on a hunch, that mysterious manor in the hills, leaving only *one* likely scenario ...

With a heavy sense of dread, I rolled over and forced myself to take in the interior of a room that I knew in my heart to be part of a certain vampire's lair.

The walls were gray. There were no windows. Only a single black rug served as décor in addition to the bed.

But no chains, either, I realized with a sense of relief that left me breathless. My arms moved freely, and I raised a hand to find that the skin of both wrists was pale and unblemished. The memories of last night lingered like a dark cloud on the edge of my consciousness, threatening to overwhelm my exhausted brain at any moment. *Blood, ice, warmth ...*

In a desperate attempt to distract myself, I sat upright and pushed back the blankets.

The bed I had been lying on was enormous, yet it didn't even take up half of the room, despite being the only piece of furniture here. Its sleek, ebony frame was in the modern style, with a square headboard that clashed with the ancient rafters supporting the ceiling above.

Trembling, I placed my feet flat on the floor and stood.

Someone had dressed me again while I had been unconscious—this time in a simple gray shift. The hem barely reached my knees, and I stared down in shock at my *unmarked* legs.

Somehow, I knew, even before I reached up to feel for myself, that my neck was also free of any injuries. No identical puncture wounds. No stray patches of dried blood.

And the questions only continued to build from there.

The door had been left open, allowing the music inside. I took a cautious step over the threshold and found myself following the notes, down the hallway and into a small lounge.

It was storming outside. Rain pounded against the panes of the sole window, adding a muted backdrop to the melody. *Go back, Ellie*, a voice inside my head urged as I crept closer. *Go back to that room and hide.*

I couldn't feign ignorance. I knew damn well that there could only be one person playing that tune. The same figure who starred in dark, hazy fantasies that I couldn't quite yet force myself to remember.

Regardless, the sight of Dublin, studiously peering over a row of piano keys still caught me off guard. For one, he didn't look like the proverbial Devil in charge of my fate— merely a man stuck inside on a dreary afternoon.

The room itself was painfully simple. In fact, the piano was the sole source of both furniture and decoration. There were no curtains lining the window. No paintings on the bare, white walls, but somehow the notes of music made it seem more lived-in than even his well-stocked study.

As I approached, the final, thudding note of *Moonlight* rang through the room, and he quickly moved into one of Chopin's nocturnes without missing a beat.

"You're awake." I jumped as his voice rose above the melancholic notes, and gray eyes found mine from over the raised ebony lid.

I shouldn't have been surprised that he had sensed I was there. He'd probably know the second I opened my eyes. I'd bet that he could even hear the way my heart raced at that very moment.

"I-I'm awake."

"I can see that."

His expression was wary, guarded. Almost as if he knew some dark, disturbing secret that he was waiting for me to puzzle out.

Unfortunately, I had no clue what it could be.

Perhaps that I probably wasn't the first woman he'd brought here and 'chained' down in order to feed? The setup of that room had been methodical, and while inside of it, Dublin had been …different. Terrifying questions lingered, but I was much too chicken to voice them. As the seconds passed in suffocating silence, I glanced downward at the piano instead.

It was a marvelous instrument, really. Sleek and black and probably worth a small fortune, which struck me as strange.

Considering the lack of adornment throughout the rest of his domain—aside from those books in his study—the piano seemed even more out of place.

I found myself tiptoeing closer, too distracted by the steady notes of music—which he still played despite my intrusion —to notice how his gaze never really left me for even a second.

During the decorum-laced hell that had been my school days, I hadn't really minded the forced piano lessons all too much. Of course, it was one of the many things I was subpar at, but playing hadn't seemed quite as torturous as everything else a proper 'lady' had to learn.

Practically holding my breath, I came up beside the bench.

My gaze strayed to Dublin before I could help it, greedily drinking him in. He was wearing black again. This time, a crisply tailored shirt of the finest quality, but the first few buttons had been left undone, and for once, that necklace hadn't been tucked beneath the collar of his shirt, but hung freely.

Entranced, I watched his fingers fly effortlessly over the keys.

This was one of my favorites, actually. I had always been a staunch worshipper of the Romantic era—but I couldn't help frowning as I noticed a faulty note here and there as the refrain was inching toward a crescendo.

And just like that …the music stopped.

"Can I help you?"

I flinched at the cold sarcasm in his tone. "Nothing. It's just that …"

I came as close to the bench as I dared, trying to ignore the way his shoulders tensed at my nearness. He didn't move—not even to turn and acknowledge me standing there. A part of me was torn between scurrying out of there with my tail between my legs, and staying to prevent one of my favorite musical pieces from being, if only slightly, butchered.

"You switched up that last bit a little." Holding my breath, I reached down to quickly tap a series of keys. "It's supposed to be like this—"

"Eleanor Gray," he began, cutting over me, "not only a *prima* ballerina, but a concert pianist as well?"

I flinched, stung by the apparent insult—until I saw his face. He had turned to look at me from over his shoulder, but the expression in his eyes wasn't cold or mocking. "Not a concert pianist," I blurted out of shock. "More like an amateur; trained out of fear of being rapped on the knuckles by Master Grudsky should I make a mistake."

He didn't reply.

"Were you trained?" I risked asking, just to fill the silence.

"No …" He glanced down at his fingers as if noticing for the first time that they even rested on piano keys. "Though," he continued, "it's not every day that one's playing talents are called into question by a woman who's probably never performed anything other than 'Twinkle Twinkle, Little Star' at a school recital."

Suddenly, he withdrew his hands and shifted over on the bench, leaving just enough space for someone my size to slip in next to him. "And I must admit that I am doubtful your memory could be better than *mine.*"

It was only then that I realized there wasn't a sheet of music in front of him.

I swallowed hard, unable to resist the challenge he posed, despite the risk. "Oh, really?"

Tossing what remained of my hair over my shoulder, I perched myself on the bench beside him, as close as I dared. Ice danced down my spine in an excited thrill that I couldn't bring myself to examine just yet. Instead, I settled my hands into position without bothering to realize that I hadn't played this particular piece in nearly ten years. Biting my lip, I tried my hardest to remember the dizzying array of notes that comprised just the first line of music.

Then, aware of Dublin's unwavering gaze, I began to play. My fingers seemed to flicker across the keys of their own accord, and I found myself pleased at how much I could recall—apparently all those torture sessions masquerading as lessons had paid off.

Nonetheless, I was still horribly out of practice. I could feel my cheeks flush as my fingers struck a stray note. Then another. I faltered ...wracking my brain to remember what came next, and missed yet another note before butchering the order of the next few. Years of inactivity were my enemy; I doubted I could have played Twinkle Twinkle flawlessly.

Finally, I stopped, unable to even look in Dublin's direction. "Well," I said with a weak laugh. "I guess I wasn't ..."

"Keep going." I didn't even realize that he had moved until I felt an icy chill ghost my hands. Without my noticing, he had gradually repositioned himself on the bench.

One muscular arm encircled my shoulders so that his hands rested on either side of me. His thumb nudged my index finger, forcing it to strike the next key, and the melody picked up again; slowly, haltingly. All the while, he continued to guide my motions with nothing more than simple, light nudges, no less impersonal than taps from Master Grudsky's infamous cane.

But, limited by the narrowness of the bench, he was close. Too close ...

His head dipped low over my shoulder. I could feel the slow glide of what felt to be his nose, back and forth across the skin at the nape of my neck. The sensation sent a current through my body, causing my fingers to falter yet again. I swore that I could hear him breathing ...*inhaling?*

Though, beneath his silent instruction, I didn't miss another note. He hadn't needed my 'expertise' after all, and I couldn't help thinking that something else must have caused him to stumble over the music before, but I was too distracted by his touch to wonder what.

After what felt like an eternity, I struck the final key at his prompting. The next second, Dublin withdrew and wordlessly slid back across the bench—but his chill lingered on my skin. When I finally gathered the nerve to glance in his direction, I found that his eyes were a wintry shade of gray. Frozen, and yet brimming with some unfathomable emotion I couldn't put my finger on.

Without warning, he reached out for a loose curl. Only, rather than tuck it back into place, he merely observed the lock from between two fingers, twisting it around and around before releasing it.

"Is there anything you wouldn't stubbornly attempt out of pride?"

Without thinking I turned to the window, watching as the rain came down. "Flying," I blurted. "Eleanor the bumbling Gray has never learned to fly ...and I've yet to gather the nerve to leap from a roof."

I was surprised by the wistful tone in my voice; I hadn't meant for the words to ring so true. Either way, Dublin didn't respond, and I never mustered the courage to say anything else. For the longest moment, we sat there in complete and utter silence.

Then, finally, I heard the bench creak as he stood.

"I gave you your dose last night," he said, explaining the lack of injuries. "That should be enough to get you through tonight—"

"Tonight?" I sucked in a breath at his morose tone.

Rather than explain, he reached over me to shut the piano's lid.

"I have some business to attend to," he said while heading for the door—when he didn't make some backhanded comment about favors and contracts, I assumed that I wasn't invited this time. "You can stay here until the rain stops," he added, proving that thought to be true. "I'll have a car sent around midnight."

"Midnight?" Suddenly, it all clicked. Saskia's pointed little reminder yesterday: we were to meet Raphael, it seemed. *Tonight.*

In all the chaos of last night, I had nearly forgotten. Considering the way Yulia, Saskia, and Dublin all seemed to refer to this man with that strange sort of uneasy reverence, I should have been terrified—but all I could bring myself to ask was, "What should I wear?"

He turned around to face me fully, and this time, his expression was nothing but condescending.

"You must be mad if you think I'd leave that up to *you.* Speaking of which—" He casually flicked the edge of his collar with a thumb. "I've had that horrible creation you wore last night burned."

I flinched at the mention of *'last night.'* Instead of reliving those memories, I focused on those gray eyes and the disgust in his words. Despite myself, I mourned my little tracksuit; it was the one clothing item I owned that had *not* been approved by Mother.

"Burned?"

"It was a mercy killing." He shrugged. "*Yulia* will help you get ready tonight."

I noticed the way he said that as if getting dressed tonight would, for the first time since I'd met him, entail more than just slipping on some flimsy shift and a hair ribbon. Before I could ask why that might be, he had already disappeared through the doorway. Stupidly, I found myself rushing after him.

"If you do decide to stay here," Dublin went on, as if he fully expected that I would, "I shouldn't have to warn you *not* to go snooping and poking about, do I?" I stiffened at the ominous tone and shook my head, despite the fact that his back was turned. With my eyes on the floor, I didn't notice the way he suddenly turned, reaching out to snag my chin. "I will anyway," he told me, eyes boring into mine. "Keep those pretty hands neatly folded, Eleanor. You go peering into something you shouldn't ...and I might just have to punish you."

I gulped so hard that my ears rang from the force of it. Without elaborating on what said *punishment* might be, Dublin dragged a thumb over my lower lip.

"Yulia should come after nightfall," he added, pulling away. "You'll be brought to meet me a little before midnight." He paused, his back to me. "I shouldn't have to tell you this, but I will say it again: Eleanor, this isn't a game. I won't be very forgiving should you choose to make a fool out of me."

His tone was ice, and I had no idea what he meant. But before I could ask him to elaborate, he was gone.

~

The rain just wouldn't stop.

It lasted the whole damn day, lashing at the windows of my Devil's lair with a vengeance. Like a whipped dog I found myself huddling within the piano room, too afraid to even touch the instrument, let alone attempt to play again.

I tried to keep Dublin's threat at the back of my mind: *keep those pretty hands to yourself.* Something told me he wasn't overstating his threat by a single bit, but still …

The temptation to wander was too great to resist. Besides, it was either sit in the corner and re-live every fuzzy bit of last night, or take my chances and roam.

So, I settled for the latter.

I'll just look, I told myself as I shuffled down the hallway. *One little peek …*

But even his lair turned out to be just as infuriatingly pristine as he was. There wasn't as much as a speck of dust on any surface. No lint on the floors. Every room was bare bones with hardly any furniture, paintings or even a throw rug. Just stark colors, neat lines and polished spaces.

Mother would have loved it. Dublin's abode was minimalistic without so much as a shred of anything that might have held some sentimental value. All in all, the place was as empty and cold as his soul. Or, so I believed, until I entered his study.

It was in the center of the maze of rooms, near the elevator entrance. At a second glance, the books on the shelves seemed to be more than just random volumes with the sole purpose of being decoration. There was Chaucer, and Shakespeare. Poe. Even the odd Brontë novel, oddly enough. Some were old and tattered to the point where I suspected they might have been first editions.

Did my Devil do a little light reading in between terrorizing? Intrigued, I tiptoed closer, peering over at the desk before I could help it.

There, right in plain sight, was a stack of papers, tempting, mysterious papers just begging to be read by one particularly curious mortal.

Don't even think about it, my conscience hissed at me, *who knows what he'd do if he catches you?*

But I was already moving forward despite common sense.

He said I couldn't touch, I thought to myself in an attempt to rationalize my snooping, *but he didn't specifically mention that I couldn't 'look.'*

Therefore, I didn't feel a shred of guilt as I merely 'glanced' over the papers scattered there. The topmost one was just a slender strip of paper that read *Receipt of Delivery.* The business in question had a fancy, foreign-sounding name that I assumed belonged to some kind of boutique. The delivered items were listed neatly on the next line: *one bed set, linens, headboard, mattress.*

The total amount for all the items was absolutely obscene, but that wasn't why I found myself frowning in confusion— growing even more perplexed when I realized that the date of delivery was … yesterday's.

Had Dublin had a sudden urge to purchase furniture? Perhaps he wanted to rest his weary head on something refined after gorging on my—*cringe*—blood?

But, then I remembered the bed. *My* bed to be exact; the one I had woken up on in that bare empty room.

No. I shook my head, despite the fact that it seemed to be the only rational explanation. To even consider it would mean having to take into account two impossible facts; one, that Dublin Helos had actually cared enough not to leave me in that terrifying room, strapped down to a metal cot. And two …

He had *bought* me a bed instead.

The possibility threatened to send my whole assessment of my Devil and his cold demeanor crashing down, so on an impulse, I did the only thing I could think of to distract myself. I reached out and yanked open the nearest desk drawer, ignoring the part of me that exclaimed in panic. *No!*

I half-expected for some kind of alarm to go off and for Dublin to appear glowering in the doorway. *Naughty, naughty, Eleanor.*

But the doorway remained empty, and I just couldn't resist my own curiosity any longer.

The first drawer held nothing of interest, only a pad of monogrammed paper and a set of silver pens. The second, however …

Nestled against a box of envelopes I found something a little more interesting. At first glance, I assumed that it was nothing much—just a crumbled tabloid. Though, to be fair, did vampires even partake in the consumption of mindless gossip?

In my mind, I pictured Dublin sitting at his desk reading the latest on the newest trashy celebrity and grumbling to himself about what kind of contract he could use them for. I snickered at the absurdity, but a teeny part of me couldn't help but wonder. Forcing myself to focus on the task at hand, I blindly flipped through the pages until I came across a section that had been dog-eared.

Georgie Gray: Back in The City After Italian Jaunt, read the blazing headline that presided over a spread of pictures. In one was my beautiful sister, looking like she'd stepped off a runway rather than through the doors of the airport.

Behind her, partially hidden in shadow, was me, bundled in a hideous sweater.

I frowned, remembering that day, nearly six months ago. It had been one of the few times that I'd gone to meet Georgie directly at the airport. As always, I was the last to find out about her little rendezvous until she showed up needing money, but that time had been different.

Georgie had almost seemed glad to see me, as if we were two ordinary sisters meeting after a long absence. That is, until she had disappeared once again, this time for Belize.

It was only then that I realized I had never sent her the money I promised. *Poor Georgiana.* Had Pablo, or Fabio— whatever the hell his name was—run off on her already? Knowing Georgie, she had probably moved on to the next without shedding a tear.

The fact that Dublin had called attention to her picture didn't surprise me. Even in the grainy, candid shot, she was still undeniably gorgeous. Though it did bring to mind something that Saskia had said: *You didn't think that he had just picked you out of a crowd? Did you?*

I frowned while replacing the magazine and pushed the drawer closed.

Georgie was on my mind as I stood and returned to the main room, watching the storm rage outside. Lightning flashed across the horizon—just as suddenly as the thought that raced across my consciousness. *Why me?*

Surely, if anyone had wanted to add a Gray to their collection of souls, they would choose my beautiful sister over me?

Maybe it was like Dublin had said; he only preyed on the desperate, those pathetic enough to bargain. In a nutshell, *me.*

But you're not exactly the one begging your older sister for money every damn month.

I don't know how long I stood there, leaning against a wall. The muscles in my legs had begun to ache when a sudden noise snapped me from my daze. I was surprised to find that the sky had already grown dark.

"Eleanor?" I started at the sound of Yulia's voice. A second later, light flooded the room, cast by a nearby sconce. "I thought you might be here," Yulia added as she crossed the room. Over her arm hung another black garment bag; no doubt the infamous outfit for tonight. "I went by your home, but you weren't there."

There was a question in her eyes, one that I wasn't quite ready to answer considering that I was standing in the middle of Dublin's secret lair wearing only a flimsy shift. Instead, I jumped slightly and glanced at the window, startled by a sudden rumble of thunder.

"Well," I turned to find that Yulia had set aside her garment bag. Her slim fingers flashed as she undid the zipper. "What do you think?"

I could only stare in shock as she withdrew a floor-length gown in a dark, deep shade of red comparable only to blood. It took a minute before I realized that she meant for *me* to wear it.

"Are you serious?" I shook my head. "I don't think …"

"Dublin's orders," she said, gazing at her handiwork with pride. Her expression was uncharacteristically gleeful, and I had a suspicion that once again she had taken her liberty with my wardrobe, Dublin be damned. "And that's not all."

With a mysterious smile, she reached into the garment bag and withdrew something small and black that seemed even more foreboding than the gown did. It was a mask. Elegantly formed, and decorated with shiny, ebony feathers, each half of it resembled a wing.

"Am I going to a masquerade?" I asked weakly, more intimidated by the prospect than I cared to admit.

Dublin and *balls* were two subjects that didn't seem inclined to mix—not without some morbid twist, which made me picture another dreaded auction. Or perhaps even a newer, more humiliating form of torture?

Yulia's expression didn't help relieve my suspicions at all. "Let's get you ready," she said, tossing her hair over her shoulder. "Dublin made it quite clear that you cannot be late—"

"T-To meet Raphael?" I couldn't explain how it felt to say that name outside of Dublin's presence; it was a bit like mumbling *Bloody Mary* before a darkened bathroom mirror. Shivers ran down my spine.

"Yes," Yulia said, but if I had been hoping for reassurance, I was sorely disappointed. Her expression was guarded—that stupid mask held more emotion. *You're doomed,* it whispered to me, staring through empty eye sockets. *Doomed ...*

But at least you'll be in a pretty dress. There was no denying that. After Yulia led me to an unexpectedly large bathroom, I showered and found myself draped in yards of red silk.

On me, the gown had no shape, despite how many last-minute alterations Yulia attempted with a needle and thread pulled from nowhere—but the cut was pretty, sophisticated. However, a long slit, reaching nearly to my hip, had me apprehensive as I took in my appearance.

Biting her lower lip, Yulia arranged my hair, smoothing the shorn curls as well as she could before she finally settled the mask over my eyes.

"There," she breathed from over my shoulder. "You look the part."

"Of what?" I wondered. A deranged Alice in Wonderland about to wander down one rabbit hole too many?

"Of ...a woman mysterious enough to be on Dublin Helos' arm."

"Mysterious? Me?"

The only thing remotely *mysterious* about me was how little I managed to fill out the gown in spite of how tightly it clung to my body.

"What should I expect?" I asked to change the subject. It was strange watching my mouth move from beneath the line of the mask. I hardly recognized myself. Who was this pale stranger with haunting green eyes? What secrets hid beneath the mask?

Yulia stood back, eyes shrouded in shadow. For the first time, I sensed the unease that I suppose she had been trying her hardest to hide all along. Dublin had seemed just as ominous, I remembered.

This *meeting* tonight might as well have been synonymous with *'your demise.'*

"What has he told you?" Yulia asked, reaching up to twirl a piece of black hair around her finger. "Anything at all?"

I shrugged, though I couldn't resist the urge to scoff. Dublin? Tell me things? Ha!

Not that you truly wanted answers, a part of me whispered. *If you did, you would have taken Saskia up on her offer, damn the risk.*

I cringed at the thought, and almost didn't notice that Yulia had started to speak again until she reached out to cup my jaw in her palm.

"Just stay close to Dublin," she said softly, eyes peering deep into my own. "Believe it or not, he won't let anyone harm you."

I blamed shock for the fact that I didn't snicker at the statement like I should have. *Dublin, protect me?*

Yulia's gaze was way too dark for her to have been joking. Though, the larger question was—from what would I need protection?

"Forgive me for the word choice, Eleanor," she added, a little cautiously. "But what was that saying, again? You will be the shiny new toy on the playground. Be careful."

I frowned. Strange word choice indeed. After all, even if I was a 'new toy,' who on earth would want to 'play' with me?

I wasn't exactly the ravishing sort—as proven by that disastrous auction. Perhaps that was why Dublin had been given another contract? Someone *worth* auctioning, like the beautiful blonde?

Once again, I was reminded of Georgie, and I couldn't help but picture her here, a vision in red.

"Don't worry," Yulia insisted, tucking a loose curl behind my ear. "Come, the car is out front."

Heart heavy, I turned away from my reflection.

Who knew? My Devil's Hell might have been safer than anything else that awaited me in this dark world.

What a terrifying thought.

"Oh!" Suddenly, Yulia paused, snapping her fingers in the air. "I forgot to remind Dublin to give you your dose tonight. I will—"

"He already did last night," I said, remembering his words from earlier that morning; *enough to get you through tonight.*

"Last night?"

"After he fed," I clarified.

"What?" Abruptly, Yulia whirled around to face me. She looked horrified, as if she had suddenly put two confusing puzzle pieces together and couldn't believe the outcome. "He ...*fed* from you?" Her tone implied something else entirely: *and you're not dead?* Without warning she reached out, batting the hair away from my neck to peer at the smooth, pale skin. Her frowned only deepened. "And you're ...okay?"

I didn't like the way she said that. *Okay?*—as if I had gone tap dancing through a field of lions and lived to tell the tale.

"Is something wrong?"

"No—" Yulia shook her head once. "No ... It's just that ..." She trailed off, biting her lower lip and I wondered if his feeding habits were one of the many things about Dublin she wasn't permitted to tell me. "It's just that ...he doesn't often feed from a live host."

My breath caught at her choice of words. *'Live'* host.

It was a statement far too dangerous to question, once I recalled the morgue-like setup of that feeding room. The metal slab in the center took on a new, morbid connotation and it was a painful few seconds before I could feel air start to trickle back into my lungs.

"I was surprised, that's all," Yulia added, though it was obvious that she was still shaken by what I'd told her. Her eyes never quite left my face, even as she turned back to the doorway. "Come," she said finally, ushering me forward. "You cannot be late."

Dublin's words whispered across my mind just then: *don't make a fool out of me.*

Dressed in the color of blood, moments from meeting a vampire who, apparently, would make all my worst nightmares seem like fairy tales …

What could possibly go wrong?

BELLY OF THE BEAST

I shouldn't have been so surprised when the driver pulled through a familiar pair of haunting black gates, after all, what better setting for a vampire's ball than a reclusive manor resembling Dracula's summer home?

Fear held me captive as I stared up at the imposing mansion and tried to talk myself out of sprinting back to the city in a pair of heels—the main reason being that I didn't know which direction the city even was.

"Miss?" the driver prompted.

He stood on the pavement, holding the door open, and I had no choice but to climb out. I was alone. Yulia had stayed behind, and for the first time, I didn't have an escort.

You're at the mouth of the beast, Ellie, my conscience warned as my gaze flickered over the impassive fortress of dark stone. *Enter, and you will be gobbled down whole ...*

Apprehension swelled within me as the wind tore at my hair and played with the skirt of my gown. I must have looked ridiculous, standing there like an imbecile while the car drove off.

In or out, Ellie? I wondered. The two footmen watched me from their positions near the doors, and their empty gazes revealed no hint of what awaited me within.

You could always run …

In the end, fate decided for me.

"What in the world are you doing out here, darling?" The sultry voice accompanied the arm that slipped through mine, forming a link. Alarm raced down my spine. I had an uncomfortable suspicion as to who my new companion was, even before I turned to take in the beautiful woman standing beside me.

In the dim glow of the light filtering through the manor windows, Saskia gleamed. Her hair streamed in the wind behind her, eyes sparkling mischievously from behind a scarlet facemask. A matching gown hugged her body tightly in all the right places, putting my elegant ensemble to shame.

"You'll catch your death out here!" she told me with mock-concern. "It's freezing out."

I didn't have the nerve to mention that technically, the creatures inside were colder.

She's a predator, Ellie, a part of me warned. *She can smell your fear.* As if to prove it, her nostrils flared as the wind picked up and those red lips parted into a malicious smile.

"Have you considered my offer yet?" she wondered. "Or, have you decided to go above my head and get your answers from someone else?"

Her tone was casual—as if she didn't give a damn—but I wasn't fooled. What she really meant was: *You could always go ask somebody else, but only I will tell you the truth, Eleanor.*

Gritting my teeth, I kept quiet until she gave up with a bored sigh.

"Very well then. Come along!"

Tossing that mane of hair over her shoulder, she surged forward, all but dragging me behind her. I struggled not to trip as I scrambled up the marble steps, ensnared by her iron grip.

The closer we came to the manor, the more my apprehension grew.

Music spilled from inside; a faint and haunting melody barely louder than a whisper. Through the doorway, I could make out that grand entryway with its blood-red walls and polished, ebony floors. Paired with Saskia's costume, I once again felt like *Alice* about to enter a terrifying, Gothic *Wonderland.* The comparison seemed even more fitting once I caught sight of a man standing beside the winding staircase, frowning down at his wristwatch.

"You're late," Dublin snarled, looking up. "Another *second* and I was going to drag you here by your —" He noticed my current escort and broke off. Within an instant, his already hard expression was replaced by one of pure ice.

"Saskia."

"I found your little pet off her leash," she told him, unhooking her arm from mine. "Don't worry. I didn't let her stray too far—"

"Eleanor."

I stiffened at his tone; hidden within it was a silent command. *Come here. Now.* I obeyed, heels scraping the floor in my haste to his side. When I came close enough, he shifted to block me from view, though he never took his eyes off Saskia for a second.

"Leave."

"Let's chat again sometime, Eleanor," Saskia purred, unconcerned by the hostility. "You just say the *word*." I jumped at her not-so-subtle insinuation. Luckily, Dublin didn't seem to notice the petty hint.

"Get out."

"Oh, don't be so *cruel*, Dublin." Saskia casually tossed her hair over her shoulder. "Luckily, for the sake of your manners, I have a previous engagement anyway ..."

She took her sweet time gliding past us while Dublin tracked her every movement with unwavering precision.

When she finally disappeared down a hallway, he waited, as if to make sure that she was really gone before he finally turned to me.

"I thought I told you to stay away from her?"

"She … I …" My voice faltered, and to my utter shame, not all of it had to do with fear.

His eyes smoldered, a frozen shade of gray that offset the paleness of his skin and two surprisingly pink lips. My gaze fell to them before I could help it, watching them move as he spoke again. "Perhaps I just haven't made myself *clear* enough?"

I shivered in anticipation as his fingers came to brush my collarbone, raising goosebumps in their wake. The brief contact seemed to trigger something; unwelcome images from last night flooded my brain one by one. *Blood, pain, scarlet …*

I couldn't stop myself from reaching up to brush the skin along my throat in his wake, as if remembering the feel of him there. However, the act only served to draw his attention downward. For the first time that night, he seemed to realize what I was wearing. In one, long sweep, his eyes skimmed the low v-neck, before honing in on the pale flesh bared through the high slit.

"I told her to bring you the gray," he said, no doubt referring to another gown Yulia had been meant to dress me in—but he didn't sound angry, more resigned.

At least he wasn't threatening to burn my clothes again. Before I could relish the indifference, he hooked his hand around the back of my head and swiftly undid the ties of the mask. I blinked as the black silk was withdrawn. Somehow, I felt more naked then than I had lying beneath him wearing nothing at all.

His eyes saw more than just my face, it seemed. They bore deep, past my fragile defenses, sensing the fear that I couldn't even begin to hide. It was too intense. Too searching …and I was frozen in place.

Don't look away. The thought was instinctual; the same impulse that warned you not to turn your back on a wild animal—that the moment you did, it would *attack*, hunt, make you its prey.

I could only try my hardest not to move an inch as Dublin stared me down. Though, in the end, I didn't know what in my expression caused him to abruptly turn away, with my mask still clenched in his fist.

He didn't order me to follow, not that he had to. I dutifully crept in his shadow, down another corridor, and into a wide, open room. Blood-red carpet covered the floor in eerie contrast to the dark paneled walls. A glittering chandelier cast sharp bits of light, bright enough to rival the moon revealed through a bay window. A single, closed-door ominously waited at one end.

There, Dublin faced me once again.

When he didn't speak right away, I allowed myself to observe him surreptitiously from head to toe. Tonight he wore another exquisitely tailored suit, without a mask shielding those gray eyes—surprise, surprise.

This devil needed no disguise. Though if he *had* worn one, I had no trouble picturing what it might have been: the snarling face of a demon.

"I don't know what Yulia's told you," he began in a grim tone that snapped me back to reality. "But make no mistake, Eleanor; you're playing with fire."

My breath caught. "Am I?"

I half-expected a scathing laugh in response. Or for him to make some taunt about how my presence really didn't matter. I was merely another lost soul tucked into his devilish pocket, after all. But tonight he seemed …distant. We might as well have been miles apart, though we stood side by side, shoulders nearly touching.

"You have no idea."

He turned to face me fully, gaze boring into my own.

"You don't know how *hard* I tried to convince him that you were *worthless*. A necessary evil. That we only needed your contract long enough to—" He broke off, and seemed to change tact. "I hope you've gotten your bit of fun out of this, Eleanor, because trust me when I say that it's all over."

"This hasn't exactly been *fun* for me," I stammered, shocked by the change in his mood. In a matter of seconds, he went from ice to smoldering fire. His eyes burned with an intense light that I couldn't recall ever seeing before—not even when he'd fed.

"Oh really?"

I gulped back a hasty reply. Did he assume that I got my kicks from throwing myself into dangerous situations?

Can you blame him? My inner voice objected. What kind of sane woman signs up for virtual slavery?

Unable to think of an answer, I took a page from his book and changed the subject. "So, what happens now?"

If it was even possible, those four words seemed to irritate him even more. The tension wafting from him flared in intensity, like gasoline dumped on a pile of sparking tinder.

"What *happens*," he began, taking a step in my direction, "is that you finally get to play out those dramatic little fantasies I'm sure you've been entertaining about *me*—" Before I could react, he seized a wayward curl and pulled. Rather than tuck it into place, he let it hang there, wild and disgruntled while his gaze held mine for what seemed like an eternity. I swayed on my feet when he finally turned away. "You're about to meet the *real* Big Bad Wolf, Eleanor Gray," he called over his shoulder. "How fitting; you're even wearing the right color."

That morbid comparison echoed in my brain—though I was sure that *Little Red Riding Hood* had never felt quite as helpless as I did right then.

"What is it?" Dublin demanded.

I jumped at the hostility edging his tone, but it was only when I turned toward the doorway that I realized that someone else stood there in the shadows, watching us. A pair of familiar, hawkish eyes flickered over mine and my stomach twisted.

"I'm just here to let you know that the 'party' has begun," the man said. His name ran across the edges of my consciousness in a whisper. *Mikhail.*

"How *kind* of you," Dublin remarked in a tone that was anything but grateful.

"It's the least I could do," Mikhail said, voice equally as cutting. "After all, we do have a *guest* in our midst tonight. Though, if that *is* the best Yulia could do with her—" He glanced at my dress and frowned. "Then, perhaps it's time to purchase the services of another *shiftspinner*, Dublin. Though, to be completely honest I didn't mind her in all that white."

"We'll be down."

Mikhail shrugged, though he had the sense to finally turn on his heel. "Oh," he called over his shoulder. "Before I forget my manners …welcome home. Though he may call himself by another name, the prodigal son has returned."

It sounded like a riddle. *Prodigal son? And another name?* A milieu of questions swelled in my mind, but for once, I knew better than to push my luck by even asking.

Dublin wasn't in the mood to humor me. He glared at Mikhail's retreating form until he disappeared down the hall. Once again, I was left alone to face my Devil's wrath.

"Put this on," he growled, shoving the mask into my hand. Without another word he turned and left the room.

My fingers shook as I clumsily tied the silk strings behind my head, all the while racing after him. He made no effort to slow down, and I was forced to sprint down the hallway with my vision obscured by the narrow eye-holes of my mask.

"Eleanor."

The sound of his voice was my only warning before he came to a sudden stop—luck seemed to be on my side, as by some miracle I was able to stop myself before completely plowing into him from behind.

We stood before a pair of closed doors. Once again, music drifted from beyond, so faint that I could only just make out a single, mystifying melody. *A harp?*

"Let's refresh," Dublin began with his back still turned to me. I flinched as his hand reached for mine, fingers clenching tight—but there wasn't any comfort in the gesture, just cold, cruel possession. "Once we pass through these doors, I am no longer '*Dublin*,' understood? If you need to address me at all—which you shouldn't—you are to call me only *Sir*, preferably *Master*."

There was no mockery in his tone this time, just a grim insistence that made my toes curl in my heels.

"I-I understand."

He didn't acknowledge the response. Not even to shoot me one of those infamous glares. I received no words of reassurance at all, before he finally pulled open the doors …

And we entered a whole new realm.

When I followed Dublin over the threshold, I felt like a trespasser in the middle of Dracula's Halloween ball.

Priceless tapestries hung from scarlet walls, depicting ancient scenes with a detail that made my heart seize in my chest. Shadows draped the polished, ebony floor like the finest Persian carpets. Paintings framed in gold illustrated haunting views of what seemed to be the Italian countryside and portraits of nameless figures dressed in Renaissance Era clothing.

Gray Manor might have seemed impressive to most, but this was *opulence*—the kind of atmosphere one would never find at my parent's stuffy business *soirées*.

Hell, even the dust bunnies in the corners probably wore crowns. The ceiling was miles away, obscured by countless gleaming chandeliers that seemed to cast more darkness than light.

Much like the people gliding across the floor beneath them.

Nearly every pale face sported a mask of some kind. Many were festooned with gleaming feathers, like mine, while others sported more animalistic features: fangs, wolfish eyes, snake scales and even the odd pair of horns.

Apparently, it was the Devil's masquerade.

Mother would have fainted. My sister, on the other hand, would have fit right in. Amongst it all, *I* felt as worthless as a mouse scurrying underfoot, which was a good thing, I supposed, because hidden within Dublin's shadow, I might as well have been invisible.

Keep your head down, Ellie, I told myself as I followed in his wake. Regardless, I couldn't resist sneaking little glimpses of the ballroom with every step. My own reflection greeted me from the surface of the gleaming marble floor, eyes wide from behind that mask.

I kept waiting for something to snap at us from the shadows, something threatening enough to bolster the tension I could sense coiled within Dublin's shoulders, but whenever anyone *did* open their mouths, it was only to utter the same reverent greeting.

"Dublin."

With my eyes on the floor, I only caught a partial glimpse of the various figures that came forward; a woman in a pair of red heels greeted him politely. Two black loafers addressed him coldly, and a figure in two silver stilettos sounded fearful.

The latter reaction appeared to be the norm.

Wherever we passed, those nearby seemed to pull back, withdraw. Dublin scared even the other monsters, it seemed, and I couldn't help recalling that phrase he loved to repeat: *I am a creature, bound for hell.*

What did that make everyone else?

He never returned a word anyone said to him, but with every step, his grip tightened. When we finally reached our apparent destination—a raised dais at the back of the room —he damn near broke my hand.

The surface of the dais was draped in blood-colored silk, reminiscent of a platform some Medieval King might hold court from. Only *this* ruler had opted for a sleek leather chaise rather than some stately throne. I knew instantly just who that was – who *else* but the mysterious Raphael could be the dark figure dominating the center of the platform?

I couldn't bring myself to really *look* at him just yet, so I stared down at the floor, counting the seconds that passed without any circulation to my right hand as Dublin's grip took on vice-like qualities.

"Dublin." The music died almost on cue, allowing the speaker's words to hit the air like their own distorted melody. "What a surprise."

I tried and failed to picture a face to go along with that voice. It was cold—the unnerving chill that resulted from an absolute lack of emotion: no hate, nor amusement, nor fear.

Nothing at all but *ice.*

"Raphael," Dublin replied, and a shiver ran down my spine at the restraint in his tone.

When I glanced at him from the corner of my eye, I saw that his head was bowed in the same way one might to acknowledge a king—but something faint scorched the air. *Hostility? Hatred?*

Whatever it was tainted the atmosphere despite the show of respect. I figured that *I* was the only one who could sense the tension coiled in his muscles—by now, my poor fingers had lost all feeling.

"Surprise?" he echoed, as he returned to his full height. "Saskia made your invitation seem like one I *couldn't* refuse …"

"Well, I suppose that next time I shouldn't send my message through *Saskia*," Raphael remarked in that unnervingly lifeless tone. "Perhaps, I should deliver it myself?"

Dublin's grip tightened, until I feared that the imprint of his fingers would be forever etched into my skin.

"Was there a reason that you requested an audience?" he asked without addressing what even I had enough sense to realize had been a threat.

"Does one *require* a reason to visit with an old friend?" Raphael wondered. He didn't seem to expect an answer. "Despite your years of …solitude, I would have never thought that I would have had to resort to requesting your presence, Dublin. However, if I am to be completely honest, I also desired to meet the *illustrious* Eleanor Gray in person."

I stiffened at the way his tongue seemed to linger over my name, drawing it out in one sensuous line. I could feel his gaze taking me in—peering right *through* me.

"Well, here she is, as per your request," Dublin said.

"I can see that. And I must say that I am pleased to finally make her acquaintance—" There was a sudden displacement of air as a pale hand appeared outstretched beneath my nose, only the fingers were far too slender to have belonged to Dublin. "Welcome to my humble abode, Eleanor. I must say, I was expecting ... Well, you look nothing like your sister."

I blinked. Georgie's reputation preceded her everywhere, it seemed; even the Devil's own soiree. I couldn't help but think that *she* would have known what to do in the midst of a manor full of vampires. I could picture her flashing a charming smile and fearlessly shaking Raphael's hand while they discussed her various exploits over wine.

I, on the other hand, could only stare.

His fingers hung in the air expectantly, daring me to take them. I wavered on what to do, but in the end, Dublin made the decision for me. His grip receded, and he nudged me forward: *take it!*

I did. My fingers interlaced with Raphael's and I had to resist the urge to snatch my hand back immediately. The man was *glacial.* So cold that Dublin's chill seemed like an inferno in comparison. His touch lingered, and I had no choice but to finally look up.

If someone had asked me a second ago to name the most handsome man I had ever seen, the answer would have been easy: Dublin. In a way, he still was, because Raphael was simply *beautiful.*

Gleaming black hair fell down his shoulders to frame a pale, angular face that was striking even without a mask. A simple black shirt and pants made him appear no less regal than the robes of a king. Like Mikhail and Dublin, he too wore a silver chain visible around his neck.

The chain itself was thicker than those of the other two, considerably so, and hanging from it was the curved body of a silver serpent with ruby-red eyes, and bared fangs. A shudder ran through me as I realized how similar it was to the creature that adorned the front of every contract book, not to mention the halls of the club.

Regardless, at first glance, Raphael himself could have been summed up with one word: *angelic.* He was every bit as ethereal as his biblical namesake. Only those eyes ruined the façade. They were ageless—empty. I had no idea as to what impression he had of me, if any at all, when he finally pulled back.

"Welcome, Eleanor." He gestured to the crowd with a wave of his hand—all of whom, I realized had turned to stare in our direction. "I trust that Dublin hasn't been too inhospitable?"

The words *seemed* like a question, but I knew—even before I felt that infamous grip return to my forearm in warning— not to answer him directly. I glanced at Dublin, who jerked his head once. *No.* The slight display of dominance did not go unnoticed by Raphael. His smile deepened as I struggled to choke out an answer.

"N-No."

The man continued to watch me, eyes fathomless. When he finally turned away, it was only to beckon to someone lurking in the corner. A second later, Mikhail appeared on the edge of the dais.

"My lord?" His eyes were now shielded by a wolfish mask, but I didn't miss the emotion that flickered through them as they darted over me: *curiosity.*

"Mikhail. Why don't you entertain Miss Gray? Dublin and I have much to discuss."

My heart sank to my toes. Mikhail seemed about as likely to 'entertain me' as a Doberman would a piece of steak. As if sensing my thoughts, the grip on my arm tightened even more.

"She could stay here." Dublin's voice was completely devoid of emotion, but he released my arm as if knowing the answer before Raphael even spoke.

"I don't think this topic would interest her," he replied. "It deals with some old ...friends of mine—you know the ones." He waited until Dublin nodded; the motion was laced with tension. "Well, it seems our 'message' was not very clear. They appear very determined to overstep—" His gaze cut to me. "Perhaps I need to be more firm in my *correspondence?*"

The words fell with all the subtlety of a nuclear bomb. Whispers exploded throughout the room, and the next thing I knew I was being shoved in Mikhail's direction.

"Go." The order in Dublin's tone was clear, but I couldn't resist one last look over my shoulder.

There was something in his eyes again …

Only this time, it was easy to name what it was: *fear.*

Before I could fathom the reason for it, he turned, and I was shut out. I could only follow behind Mikhail, and try not to trip over the skirt of my gown as he led me across the ballroom and through a wide set of doors.

I shuddered to find myself inside of what seemed to be a dimly lit drawing room. The walls were the same bloody red that adorned the rest of the manor, and spread throughout, several pale figures lounged on various pieces of furniture.

"A new toy, Mikhail?" a woman in burgundy asked from a velvet chaise. She lowered her violet mask to cast me an appraising glance. "She's a little scrawny for your taste, isn't she?"

Mikhail didn't even spare a glance in her direction.

Instead, he headed for a sleek sofa in the center of the room and threw himself on it. His eyes brushed over me once before settling on the wall behind my head, as if the antique wallpaper was far more interesting.

"Meet Eleanor Gray," he announced in a dry tone—though, I figured his nonchalance was more for dramatic effect than anything else.

A hush fell over the room, and I could only stand utterly still as what had to be ten pairs of eyes took me in.

"Eleanor Gray?" In a blur of black silk, another woman appeared before me, frowning from behind her ruby-red mask. "She looks nothing like I had imagined. For all the gossip one might think she looked like her sister. At least *that* one seems worthy of the hype—"

"Why would it matter?" someone else countered. "Raphael wanted her simply to prove a *point* to the Grayne. Maybe now they will learn their place."

"Enough." Mikhail raised his hand. "Let's not frighten our guest."

He sounded polite, but his tone conveyed another meaning: *Shut up before you say too much.* Regardless, my mind was already struggling to register the strange words. *Grayne. The other one—Georgie?*

"I wonder if all the rumors are true?" The woman in black mused with a thoughtful tilt of her head. "Regardless of her purpose, they say Dublin bought her contract specifically. He never buys anyone—"

"Except for that *shiftspinner* he's so fond of," another man interjected.

"Yes," the woman agreed, "but I doubt he *fucks* the *shiftspinner*."

My cheeks flamed at the coarse insinuation, but something else distracted me from the shame—there was that strange word again. *Shiftspinner*. Could they be referring to Yulia?

"He certainly went out of his way to purchase her at the auction," another voice added, snapping me from the thought. "Usually he doesn't even bother to show up. I heard he had to bargain for her from Raphael himself—"

"Now, now," Mikhail scolded, wagging a pale finger. "Let's not gossip, my friends. Engorge your blabbering mouths instead. Have some refreshments."

He said the word so distinctly that I supposed I really shouldn't have been surprised when, at a snap of his fingers, two women appeared in the doorway.

They were dressed in the same way Saskia's 'girls' had been back at the auction: dark silk, very little of it, cut to reveal as much skin as possible. But these women also sported another other 'accessory,' one so much more horrifying than anything else I had been presented with so far.

Inflamed, round puncture wounds dotted their bodies. Their arms, legs, and even the torso visible through their skimpy costumes had all been brutalized by the markings. It didn't take much thought to guess what they were: bite marks, hundreds of them.

Something that Dublin had said ran across my mind in a whisper; *never allow yourself to be bitten more than three times in one night.*

Apparently, no one here had gotten the memo.

As I watched, Mikhail beckoned a woman closer with a wave of his hand. The moment she approached, he snatched her arm and held it flat. He observed the flesh the same way one might a picked-over buffet, appraising the few remaining options. Then, his upper lip pulled back from his teeth, revealing fangs that glinted in the light of a chandelier. I could only remain there, frozen in the center of the room as he bit down, groaning in response to the flow of blood that flooded his mouth.

Red dripped down to splatter his collar, and all the while the woman stood there, swaying on her feet, eyes unnaturally empty, glazed, soulless.

The room blurred. I could sense the others shifting and more women entering, but nothing registered.

I jumped as a cold hand fell over my shoulder, accompanied by a deep voice that sent a shiver racing down my spine.

"Whose pet is this?"

"That one's *mine.*"

I turned, forgetting all about the creature behind me as my eyes fell on the one standing in the doorway.

Dublin's expression was as glacial as always, but this time there was a darkness in his eyes that seemed to make everyone in the room instinctively flinch back. Even I could sense what it was: *possession.*

"Eleanor." He raised an eyebrow, and that was the only warning I needed to rush over and follow him down the hall.

I held my breath with every step, unwilling to release it until he pulled me into an empty drawing room and closed the door behind us. A cream-colored chaise rested against a wall lined with elegant wallpaper and adorned by the portrait of a pale woman in a medieval gown.

"I trust you've been enjoying yourself," Dublin spoke from behind me. "Have you sampled the menu? I hear they have *delectable* options …"

I couldn't see his face. I didn't want to. Instead, I merely stood there, enduring his mocking tirade as my face heated with shame. Every time I blinked, I saw those women—their empty, haunted faces.

I didn't realize, until a cold hand fell over the small of my back, that I had been trembling. Goosebumps prickled as two of his fingers lingered there, imparting ice. The contact wasn't reassuring—more *acknowledging,* as if he had had to touch me just to make sure that my response was real.

How pleased he must have been. Finally, I was playing my part by living up to his flair for the dramatic. All that was missing now were the 'sobs and hysterics.' I waited for him to insinuate as much, but when he finally spoke, his tone caught me off guard.

"You can choose to believe me or not …but I did not want you to see that."

"Is that what you want me to be?" There was no need to elaborate on what I meant. *Broken. Dead. A zombie.*

"You signed the contract," he replied—but the next second his hands moved to my shoulders, turning me to face him. He cupped my chin, forcing me to meet his gaze. "However, I wouldn't get any pleasure from breaking you, if that's what you mean. You're much too stubborn."

The words seemed truthful, but I couldn't—or maybe *wouldn't?*—believe him.

Contract be damned. There was more to this than some slip of paper. I didn't *want* to think so. It was so much easier to just believe that I was some mousy waif he'd picked up on a whim—but even Saskia had alluded to the truth.

You didn't think he just picked you out of the crowd, did you?

"What do you want from me?"

Dublin raised a blond eyebrow and seemed to mull it over. "The truth?"

I nodded into his palm.

"I want *you.* You're smart, Eleanor," he clarified. "When put to the test, you manage to succeed, though, I have no idea how. Your loyalty could prove invaluable to me."

"My … My loyalty?"

My mind was stuck somewhere on *I want you.*

"Let me ask *you* something." He frowned and his hand fell down to his side. "Why did you accept my bargain?"

"It wasn't like I had much of a choice," I said, recalling his methods of persuasion, including that mid-morning intrusion into my bedroom.

"You're lying." His tone had hardened. The icy mask was back in place. My answer had irritated him—though, for once, I had no idea what I might have said wrong. "I want the *truth*, Eleanor. Why did you accept my bargain?"

"I-I don't understand." I wracked my brain for the memories of that first day when I had met him in the hospital. "I suppose it was because I needed to tell my sister in person. I want her to look after my cat when I—"

"Wrong again." He took a step toward me and then another, swiftly backing me into a corner. My back hit the surface of the cream wallpaper with its delicate golden filigree. The color reflected in Dublin's gaze, making his eyes smolder.

"You seem to be unwilling to admit the obvious," he observed while stalking close enough that his breath fanned the hollow of my throat. "So shall I say it for you? You, the pathetic, dreary heiress, were nothing more than *bored*."

Bored? The word ran through me on a current of shock. It was a long moment before I managed to gather enough of my senses to attempt to respond.

"P-Pardon me, Dublin, but I'd much rather read a Jane Austen novel during my downtime instead of *selling* my god-damned soul."

"And I'm sure you believe that wholeheartedly," he agreed with a nod. "I assume that, after twenty-six dull years of life, you've convinced yourself of a lot of things, Eleanor. I'm here to tell you that it's all *lies*. Deep down in your little soul, you know that you were suffocating …and that I offered you a way out."

A way out? Those three little words had the same effect on me as a vicious slap to the face. My head reeled back. Heat flooded my cheeks.

"Well, how gallant of you," I choked out turning on my heel. "You don't know *anything*."

This was too much. I was done with humoring Dracula and his cohorts. It was time to go home—back to the pampered life he seemed to think I wanted an escape from.

Eager to do just that, I meant to breeze past him, nose in the air like a good, snotty socialite—and the Dublin Helos I thought I knew and loathed would have gladly let me prance away.

Only *this* man caught me by the wrist and dragged me back so fiercely that I stumbled into a chest made of stone.

"I offered you life, Eleanor," he hissed into my ear. "And not in the poetic sense. You aren't afraid of death, oh no. You *welcome* it. You're not afraid of dying any more than you're afraid of me—though, I'm sure that you've convinced yourself of the opposite."

I struggled to pull away, but his grip tightened, holding me immobile. "Let me—"

"I may haunt your nightmares, Eleanor," he said over me, "but when you wake up from those nightmares, you know that it isn't *fear* making your heart pound like mad in your chest. It isn't *fear* surging through your veins. You almost had me fooled …but to you, this is all nothing more than a game."

He finally let me go, and I staggered away. His disgust pierced me, right down to the bone—but shame and hurt weren't why my body trembled like mad.

It was rage.

"A game?"

First, the man terrorized me and then wanted to claim that *he* was the victim? Mean, bored Ellie, how dare she play along with the Devil's game.

"Forgive me," he said, "'Game' suggests the participation of both parties. To you, this is simply *entertainment*. What do you fancy me as, Eleanor? A dancing bear? A caged tiger? Does your stomach flip excitedly whenever I bare my fangs?"

"I-I don't know what the hell you're talking about—"

"Stop lying to yourself. The sensible, meek woman you pretend to be would have never gotten into the car that first night. She would have called the police. She wouldn't still be here now."

"Oh really?" I croaked.

A part of me wanted to suffer the insults in silence, hold my chin up high and allow him to spew the tirade that, I supposed, had been building within him all this time. Any other day I most likely would have—even now, my mother's words berated me from the grave. *Decorum, Eleanor! Decorum!*

But she couldn't hold me back this time.

It took two steps to reach him. He stood iron-rod straight, and I had to crane my neck back just to see his face.

His eyes were cold, glacial. I don't think I'd ever seen him so visibly angry, not even when he dealt with Saskia.

"I find *nothing* 'entertaining' about being tormented by some ass who fancies himself the Devil," I said, mustering every ounce of strength I had to put into my voice. I had no idea where the ice in my tone came from, or the scorn. I was channeling Margaret Gray in all her pretentious glory, and I hated myself for sinking to his level. "Maybe I'm not afraid of you," I lied, "but why *would* I be, when all you do is berate me for taking the choice that *you* offered me in the first place?"

"Oh?"

I knew right then that I had just leaped over some invisible line and there was no going back.

"I haven't even begun to scratch the surface of what I could ...*would* do to you, Eleanor," Dublin began, taking a step forward to bolster the threat. "But if nothing scares you ..."

He lunged.

Cold hands seized my waist, ruthlessly cinching the thin fabric of my gown as he yanked me forward. I had no warning. No chance to react. His jaw nudged mine, forcing me to tilt my head back. His mouth hovered somewhere along my lower lip imparting tendrils of ice...

Then, he *bit*.

I gasped, the sound slipping between his lips, as the edge of one fang teased the rim of my mouth. A burst of metallic flavor coated my tongue: salty, hot, *blood*. Fear exploded through my veins, but before I could even begin to struggle, he pushed me away.

I barely managed to catch myself against the wall.

"You don't want me to be an active participant in your little game," Dublin warned, unconcerned as I swayed on my feet. "So, I highly suggest you drop this 'little girl lost' routine, because if you want a *real* monster, Eleanor, I would be more than happy to supply you with one."

With a casual motion, he swiped some scarlet liquid from his chin with his thumb. His fangs flashed in a flicker of ivory, streaked with red. My heart seized at the sight—but for once it wasn't because of fear.

I hated the way warmth welled against my bottom lip.

I hated the way it stung. How the pain made me realize that it was the closest I had ever come to being kissed.

I hated him.

I don't think I even mentally processed the motion when I staggered forward. My hand flew out, seemingly disconnected from my body.

And I slapped him—hard.

He was so solid that it felt more like ramming the flat of my hand into concrete. Bones that I didn't even know existed screamed with pain. But shock overrode the agony.

Thwack! The sound resonated around the room and it felt ...*empowering*, until the realization of what I had just done sank in only a second later.

My hand stung. I didn't recognize it. I barely recognized myself. And yet the man I'd just assaulted seemed unconcerned by the violence—*pleased*, even.

"There she is," he finally said. "The *real* Eleanor Gray. Not that rich little bitch you pretend to be for everyone else. *This* is the woman who could be of use to me."

"You're mad." Helplessly, I stumbled back, unwilling to turn my back on him for even a second. "Stay away from me ..."

"Funny," Dublin said, head tilted to the side. "I should be the one telling *you* those exact words. But I am done playing with you, Eleanor."

I nearly jumped out of my skin as he shifted his weight to the balls of his feet. The expression on his face reminded me of the snarl of a wolf right before it tore into the throat of a bleeding doe.

Merciless.

"You may have been able to convince yourself that this is just some horrible predicament that you found yourself in through no fault of your own. But you and I both know the truth: you *crave* danger, Eleanor. You surround yourself with creatures who only want to hurt you—" As if to emphasize that very point, his eyes darted over to my shoulder, where Tinkle's scratches had faded beneath the remarkable healing properties of his 'cure.' "You *desire* pain. Admit it, and I could give you all the danger you desire."

His voice was heavy with innuendo. More than sex, I sensed.

Violence.

Pain.

More.

It took everything I had in me just to shake my head.

"You're *sick*," I spat. Literally, specks of spit flew out to splatter the toe of his shoe, but he didn't even seem to notice.

"And yet, I'm not the one who's dying. But I'll tell you what … Consider this an offer that you *can't* refuse."

His gaze held me captive and …God help me, I couldn't turn away.

"You could leave *right* now," he told me. "Have your seven days. Spend them wasting away in your mansion, trying your hardest to convince yourself that everything I've said is nothing more than lies. I'll even send my car around to take you home. Or …"

I froze, afraid of what he might say next.

"Or, you and I make a new bargain. No more lies. No more pretending. I don't want *Ellie* Gray, dowdy heiress extraordinaire. I want the woman who stripped naked before a stranger because she was too damn stubborn to take the easy way out."

"You don't know anything about me," I whispered, finally desperate enough to make a break for the door.

Surprisingly, he let me go, and I knew even as I started running that he wouldn't follow. Still, his parting words chased me over the threshold on an icy gust of air.

"You have twenty-four hours …"

I ran.

Shadowy figures gazed on in amusement as I staggered from room to room like a lost child, but no one tried to stop me—not that they would dare. I was Dublin's 'pet,' after all.

My bitten lip throbbed.

The pain spurred me onward until I was running blindly through the corridors, heedless of anything but the need to escape. Somehow, I found myself outside and the icy air—as startling as a slap in the face—snapped some clarity back into me. I inhaled deeply, desperate to get my bearings.

Then I saw it.

As patiently as if this had been the plan all along, Dublin's black vehicle idled in the driveway. The driver climbed out to hold open the door, but I didn't waste any time contemplating the fact that *he* must have known all along what my answer to his little game would have been.

It didn't matter.

I was done being stubborn, through with being brave. For once, I was perfectly content to huddle in the backseat and face the fact that I was a foolish idiot who'd finally been put in her place. Those four little words taunted me during the entire ride; *this isn't a game.*

For once, Gray manor was a beacon of safety that I couldn't enter fast enough. I stumbled up the front step, nearly tripping over the hem of my dress. Heedless of any servants who might have lingered after hours, I wrenched the silk over my head and threw it onto the floor. Half-naked, I raced up the staircase clothed only in my underwear and heels. My room was a chilly, empty refuge that greeted me with darkness and dull furniture; safe, boring, mine.

This is where you belong, Ellie, I told myself as I wrenched off my heels one by one and tossed them into a corner. *This is who you are.*

I spotted my mother's hated nightgown resting over the edge of my bed and gratefully slipped it on over my head, fastening the buttons up to my chin.

On an impulse, I gathered up the other clothing scattered about as well—all those black garment bags from Mystic— and carried them down the hall. The first room I entered was my father's old study, complete with its very own fireplace, where I promptly tossed the lot of fabric.

He's wrong, you don't crave danger, I told myself as I scavenged a package of matches from the top of the mantel and struck one.

You don't like pain, I added as I allowed the match to fall over the topmost pale gray shift.

"I don't want *him,*" I said out loud as I watched the clothing burn.

I tried not to care as every handmade garment smoldered, but when that last bit of silk finally disintegrated to ash, I didn't feel any less unsteady than I had staring down Dublin. In fact, as I curled up in a corner, I could almost hear him laughing at my pathetic attempts to erase him.

~

The sound of the doorknob turning jolted me awake. As my eyes flew open, I half-expected to find a pair of mocking, gray ones peeking through the crack: *Did you think it would be so easy? Guess again, silly Eleanor—you can't escape the Devil.*

But rather than Dublin, another familiar face greeted me.

"Harper?" I yawned as I pulled myself upright. "Is something wrong?"

It wasn't like him to seek me out on his own without a specific reason; one that I figured had something to do with what he held in his hands.

"A call for you, Miss," he said as he offered a silver tray, on top of which rested a slim, portable phone.

Warily, I took it and pressed the receiver to my ear. "Hello?"

"Eleanor, God! *Finally!*"

I flinched at the bubbly, yet irritated tones. "Georgie?"

"Yes," my sister snapped. "Where the hell have you been? I've tried calling for at least *two* days!"

"I … I …"

As always, she didn't give me the chance to speak before launching into her real concern: herself. "Oh, it doesn't matter! I don't mean to sound like a brat, really, Ellie, I don't, but you did promise me that money *days* ago …"

The money.

Of course, she wouldn't be calling about *my* welfare or wondering as to the reasons behind my two-day absence. After all, I was dutiful, dowdy Ellie; what kind of life could I have possibly led outside the family's home?

"I'll have it sent today," I heard myself respond, cutting her off mid-sentence.

"Thank you." She sighed, and the sound was as heavy as a gust of wind—relieved. Could she, perhaps, be in more trouble than just lacking funds to buy the newest, pretty sundress? "I'll be back in town on Thursday. I'll see you then, okay?"

She hung up before I even had the chance to say goodbye. Numb, I set the phone back onto the tray while Harper watched.

"I can take care of that for you, Miss, if you would like."

By now, of course, he knew the drill as to what any one of my sister's rare phone calls meant.

"Thank you." Suddenly exhausted, I sank down into a nearby chair and cradled my head in my hands. Mentally I counted the days from now until next Thursday: *seven.*

The coincidence had me shivering so violently that my teeth chattered.

What had Dublin told me again? *Have your seven days …*

"Are you all right?" Harper sounded concerned, but I brushed him off with a shrug.

"Fine. Would you mind terribly if you handled the transfer?" I knew that Mother and Father had used him to send Georgie her hush money before—but it still felt wrong, somehow. Poor Harper had already been shoved in the thick of one Gray drama too many.

But the man was dutiful to a fault.

"Of course, miss."

Grateful, I told him the amount, but right when he turned, heading for the door, something made me call him back. "Wait! I've changed my mind." A sudden thought appeared before me like a stabbing dagger; sharp, dangerous, irresistibly shiny …

Years of being *'good, dependable Ellie,'* goaded me toward the rebellious plot like a moth to a flame.

I want you, Dublin had said.

Liar. He merely wanted my checkbook; they all did. As Georgie had just reinforced, money was my only purpose. That bastard wasn't any different, and I would prove just how true that assessment really was.

I knew the idea was stupid—even as it formed most deliciously in my mind—and that I'd most likely end up injured in the end, broken.

But it wasn't like I had much left to lose. Nothing but my pride, life, and blood, of course …

"I'll do it myself." My voice rang out, confidently clear as I tried to shake the doubts away. "In fact, I need to make a withdrawal."

~

I barged through the sleek glass doors of the office building, clutching a leather handbag to my chest and holding my head high.

For the first time in days, I wasn't wearing a flimsy shift or pretty fabrics. Instead, my outfit of choice would have done Mother proud: a brown tweed skirt and a sensible, emerald blouse. In other words, I looked like a nun on her day off, and I was damn proud of the fact—never again would I forget who or *what* I was: dependable, homely and *safe* Eleanor Gray.

Whether he claimed to be the Devil or not, Dublin Helos would *never* change me.

"Good morning," the blonde receptionist chirped as I marched past, but her cheerfulness soon turned to confusion when I headed straight for the elevator doors, rather than stop at the desk.

"Miss?"

Her voice followed me up four stories, but unfortunately, I remembered the way without any need for direction. Like the remnants of some sick, twisted nightmare, every inch of this place seemed ingrained on my sub-consciousness.

When I finally reached that infamous corner office, I wasn't surprised to find *him* already there, dressed in a gray suit, intently studying a stack of paperwork. My, he certainly was dedicated to that 'doctor' rouse of his.

I didn't think he even heard me come in until I slammed my bag down on his desk.

He glanced up and observed me with a pen still trapped between two fingers and a line of ink drying on a sheet of parchment. His eyes honed in on mine, a dark, stormy gray completely devoid of emotion. Contrary to how I had envisioned him while planning this little rendezvous in my head, he didn't look shocked.

Not even when I proceeded to pull stack after stack of money from the depths of my black bag and drop each one onto his desk.

"Five-hundred *thousand* dollars," I announced, laying down the final amount. "More than enough to settle our debt."

"Is that so?" Dublin sat back in his chair, lacing his hands behind his head, though he barely spared the money a passing glance. "I suppose it would be, if we were talking about some cheap piece of art or a limited edition copy of Pride and Prejudice."

There was no emotion his voice. Those eyes perfectly displayed what he felt; uninterested, bored, un-amused.

"Even *your* soul has a heftier price tag," he added, while my simple grasp on the world imploded for the umpteenth time.

"B-But—"

"If absolution could be so easily bought with *paper,* then where would that leave me? You've sold your soul to the *Devil,* Eleanor, and believe me …it is a long road to redemption from the pits of hell."

Something told me that he was no longer referring to our hand-written contract.

I opened my mouth to respond, but the words wouldn't come. In the end, I could only *stand* there, stunned, as he lifted each stack of bills, one by one and then proceeded to toss them all into the wastebasket. In the space of five seconds, a small fortune settled in amongst balls of crumpled paper.

"S-Stop!"

I knew that I was being ridiculous, even before I lurched forward to salvage the discarded bills. Silver eyes burned the back of my neck while I foolishly placed each one back onto the desk. When I finished, I stood, smoothing out the front of my skirt with shaking fingers.

"Why can't you just take the damn money?" I demanded in exasperation.

My own sister had no problem with using me as her personal ATM. What made him so damn different? My thoughts or feelings *never* mattered to anyone, just as long as I followed my usual routine.

Dependable Ellie.

Dutiful Ellie.

Stupid, predictable, Ellie.

Heaven forbid that I forget my place.

"All anyone ever wants from me is money," I insisted, painfully aware of how naïve I sounded.

Nevertheless, Dublin humored me with a shrug. "Not everyone," he said. "Though, why should it matter? You're still clinging to your role of a dowdy spinster, and as I recall, I've already sent you on your merry way. You're *free*."

Free.

Why was it so hard to breathe all of a sudden?

The word should have been my salvation—seven days was still enough time to draft a will and explain everything to Georgie. So why did it feel like my damnation instead? As I tried to imagine myself living out the rest of my days in Gray Manor, I only saw an endless, dark eternity.

"I have your contract," he added, as an afterthought before returning to his paperwork. "Though I won't bother enforcing it."

"E-Enforce?"

"In other words, *you* are no longer my concern." He made me sound like a naughty child who'd been spanked into submission.

And suddenly, everything was crystal clear—his so-called 'new bargain' had been a bluff; nothing more than a ploy to get me out of his hair once and for all. Apparently, even my money meant nothing to him in the long run.

"So why do any of this in the first place, if it doesn't even matter?" I demanded, furious though I had no clue as to why. "Why even offer *me* a contract at all and not someone like—" Somehow, I managed to stop myself before I could utter the name *Georgiana*.

Regardless, those gray eyes narrowed, fathomlessly dark and I had enough sense to read the warning flashing through them. *Watch yourself, Eleanor.*

"As I recall, I've told you what I wanted," he said in a tone that made me shiver. "*You,* without the charming, yet unattractive emotional baggage of a naïve, sheltered spinster. I want you to stop pretending, Eleanor. I want the woman who climaxes whenever I sink my fangs into her throat."

My cheeks flamed. I sputtered. "How dare you—"

"Let us drop the pretense, shall we?" He stood, hands slamming down hard onto the desk and leaned across it as if threatening to lunge for me right then and there. "Forget your Goddamned contract."

He reached into his pocket then, giving me the feeling that he had been prepared for this 'ambush' of mine all along. He withdrew the folded slip of paper, which I knew in my soul to be our 'renegotiated' agreement, an agreement that he promptly tore in half before tossing both slips of paper into the wastebasket.

"Do you understand now?" he all but growled, eyes burning in a way that made him resemble the infamous Lucifer more than ever. "I don't want the empty shell of Eleanor Gray that you show the world—I want *you,* willing and bound to me by something more than a damn piece of paper."

"Bound?" I heard myself croak. How pathetic that it was the only thing I could think to say. "Why?"

He glowered, his handsome face all but transformed into a snarl. "Shall I put it crassly so that you can understand? I want to be able to fuck you, and take your blood, and have you bend to my will, without you *once* being able to fall back on that damned contract as an excuse. I want you to submit to me, and only me, because you simply *want* to."

The world swam in and out of focus. *Submit. Bound. Contract.*

This wasn't about blood anymore, and I couldn't understand. Men like him didn't desire women like me—at least, outside of the realm of possible food choices.

"Don't mock me," I hissed, voice shaking, convinced that this was some elaborate joke at my expense. "You could have any woman you wanted—"

"Oh, but I don't want any other woman," he snapped. "I want *you*. I'd be damned if I knew why."

The grudging sincerity in his tone sliced into my core, forcing me to submit to the truth—but I wouldn't, *couldn't*, when this frantic little voice at the back of my mind was screaming, *he's lying! He's lying!*

"You're being ridiculous."

If only he didn't look so damn serious. His eyes were nearly pure black, without a shred of amusement glimmering within their depths.

"Am, I now?" Suddenly, he sat back in his chair and once again his demeanor was dismissive. He even lifted a hand to wave me off; *sayonara.*

"Then, I suppose we're done here. Go return to your Ms. Austen, Eleanor—"

He froze at the sound of a brass button snapping loose to bounce across the floor.

So did I.

But *my* hands were at the collar of my blouse, shaking as they slowly undid another button, and then another …

What the hell was I doing?

This time, real surprise crossed Dublin's face. A greedy, childish part of me relished the way his eyes traced the growing triangle of bare flesh, wide and unnerved for once.

The reaction goaded me on. Clumsily, I continued to unhook my blouse one button at a time, never taking my eyes off his face. My hands were somewhere over my navel when he stood, eyes so dark they swallowed all the light in the room like two black holes.

The temperature in the room plummeted as he surged forward like a true creature from hell. I jerked, and abruptly the two final buttons went flying. But Dublin only blew past me for the door, which he promptly slammed shut.

"Eleanor—" I had never heard him sound so rough, and I knew without even having to turn around that his eyes would be that dangerous shade of silver. Wolfish. "I'm only going to ask you this once: why are you *really* here? Say it."

Don't listen, Ellie, my conscience whispered. *You could still leave. The door's right there …*

Regardless I glared at his empty chair as if it were a good enough substitute for the man himself.

"Why am I here?" I spoke while yanking my arms from the sleeves of my blouse. "I'm here because I would rather string myself up by my toes for your amusement than *ever* let you think that you have some kind of power over me. I am not afraid of you."

Liar, my inner voice hissed. *You're shaking. You can barely stand up. Your heart is racing.*

But, a tiny part of me wondered if that had anything at all to do with *fear*.

"I know—" Suddenly, he was speaking directly into my ear, body pressed against mine from behind. As I stiffened in shock, he took my blouse from my shaking hands and tossed it to the floor. "Eleanor Gray, the woman who doesn't even fear death itself. What is a mere *vampire* in comparison?"

I couldn't tell if he was taunting me. Without warning, those ice cold hands shoved me toward the desk, and I had no choice but to grab onto the edge of it or risk falling altogether.

His palm thudded against the wood, as he came up behind me and reached across my shoulder to wrench open a drawer. From it, he withdrew what seemed to be a small black object with a golden dragon embossed on the casing. I gasped as he casually tapped the head of the dragon and a silver blade sprung free, gleaming in the sunlight. A *knife*? I tensed, watching as he drew a thumb over the knife's edge, smearing a drop of his own surprisingly bright blood on the metal.

"Bend over," he grated.

"W-What?" My voice came out sounding tiny, weak and pathetic, but there was an edge to it that even I couldn't deny no matter how much I may have wanted to …

Excitement.

"Don't question." With a hiss of irritation, he shoved me down himself, placing one hand on the small of my back. "Don't move."

His voice was low with warning, and I could only lay there, heart pounding as he brought the blade down, slicing through the side of my shoulder. I jerked in shock, but the pain wasn't as sharp as I would have expected. It stung briefly—a burning, fiery line—but before agony truly had the chance to flare, an icy chill smothered the heat, caressing …

His tongue.

I knew without even having to turn around and see him there for myself, tasting me.

He swirled his tongue almost reverently around the wound once, as if to seal it, before his icy lips returned to my ear, imparting three, guttural words that made me tremble. "You are *mine*."

He slammed the knife down in front of me, and I could only gape at my own blood streaking the silver.

"There is *no* contract, Eleanor Gray," Dublin growled, drawing my attention back to him. "Make no mistake: there are no more easy outs. No more games. You are *mine*, body, and soul."

*M*ine.

I wished I could have said that terrifying little speech was what finally made it sink in that Dublin Helos was a madman bound for hell.

But there was no way out, even if I had wanted one.

Dublin was inescapable. His shadow loomed over me as I clung to the edges of the desk and tried to remember how to breathe.

"You are *mine*, Eleanor," he insisted, stressing every single word.

I wasn't naïve enough to take them romantically. To him, I was nothing more than property—but that fact didn't make it any easier to take my eyes off that blood-stained knife. Nor could I ignore the liquid warmth dripping down my arm to form small puddles of crimson at my feet.

Uh, oh, I thought hysterically. *You've done it now, Ellie. You're playing with fire.*

Or *ice,* I corrected, as Dublin's fingers came to bat the curls away from my throat. A frigid thumb caressed my pulse, once, twice.

"Say it," he said impatiently against my earlobe. "I want to hear you say it."

"I …" When I didn't answer fast enough, his fingers fisted in my hair, tugging on a handful of curls.

"Answer me, Eleanor," he warned, sounding more feral with every syllable.

The snob somewhere inside me wanted to jab my nose into the air, and deny him. I was Eleanor Gray, and I belonged to no one. But that woman lived alone.

She had no friends, family who couldn't be bothered, and no life outside of her polished, pampered manor walls.

She was a ghost …and only now could I finally face the fact that I was *tired* of pretending to be her. Maybe Dublin was right. Maybe I really was just wearing the mask of who I thought everyone else wanted me to be.

But that doesn't give him the right to do this, I thought, biting my lower lip so hard I tasted blood—cut, push, taunt and demand things from me no one ever had before.

I hated him for it.

But, a tiny voice at the back of my mind countered, *you're not running away ...*

And I didn't. As the seconds passed, I merely stood there, stunned, leaning over the desk with fresh blood painting my skin. Dublin gave me a full minute before he pulled on another curl. "I'm only going to ask you this one more time; *who do you belong to?*"

Run! My conscience wailed. *You don't have to give in!*

But I was too tired to move. Too tired to push him off and crawl back to Gray Manor alone. *Besides,* that tiny, disembodied voice whispered, *you're dying anyway. It's not like you have long to suffer the consequences ...*

When those cool fingers began to seize another handful of my hair, I finally voiced the one word I would have never thought in a million years could sound so dangerous.

"You."

I was shocked when my voice came out steady, without a hint of hesitation. No fear. No shame. Just acceptance.

Slowly, the grip on my hair loosened, allowing me to turn so that I could finally see his face. His eyes burned with unholy fire, just *daring* me to run. Red coated his lips, vibrant against that ivory skin. He was the devil incarnate, dressed impeccably in Armani, and I had never seen a sight more terrifying.

"Me," he agreed in a growl, fangs glinting beneath the hood of his mouth, "and do you know what that means?"

Did I?

Without tearing his gaze from mine, his thumb teased the wound on my shoulder. The pain made my eyes water, but the tiny gasp that broke from my lips betrayed anything *but* fear.

I could have lied to myself—as, I supposed, I had been all along.

But when my eyes went directly to the glistening canines threatening to impale his lower lip, I couldn't deny it any longer: I *knew* what this meant all right.

The mere fact that I had come crawling back, tail in tow, proved that his assessment of me had been correct all along. That I *liked* this; I liked having him dole out pain as easily as he could pleasure.

I liked being at his mercy…

As if the thought alone was his cue, Dublin shifted, placing both hands flat on the desk, on either side of me—and there was no escape.

"Tell me what you want from me," he commanded against the nape of my neck. His tone was softer, but no less frightening than a growl. "And don't you dare spout that rubbish about some silly ring."

What I wanted?

Words sprung to my lips even as I shied away from voicing them: *you, destruction, more …all of it.*

"Should I remind you?" Dublin goaded, when I didn't respond.

My entire body stiffened as he lowered his head. I knew what he would do next, but I felt any protests die in my throat, as he teased the skin along my shoulder blade with the points of two deliciously sharp canines. Slowly, he scraped a path up to the side of my neck, hovering predatorily over the thrum of a pulse—but before he could pierce the flesh, both fangs drew back.

As if to tease me, he did it once more, applying just enough pressure to sting before withdrawing.

My eyelids fluttered. I was still bleeding, but all I could focus on was the sudden desire to have him take more. *Drain every last drop.*

Before I could stop, I found myself gasping out, "Just do it—"

He never even lifted his mouth. All I heard was a metallic *clink,* as he snatched the knife from the desk and brought the blade down in a single swipe.

The second cut was much deeper than the first.

It was a struggle to fight down the instinctive urge to run— fight—as pain and ice shattered through tendrils of pleasure.

Unconcerned, Dublin's mouth continued its lazy descent, tongue lapping up the fresh blood as he went, with the delicacy of a connoisseur sampling wine.

I could feel my heart picking up speed with every slow, deliberate pass of his tongue. My head tilted before I could help it, offering him better access to the veins … Soon the pain was just a bad memory, all but swept away beneath a wave of aching pleasure so heavy it hurt.

Bit by bit, I could feel my body relaxing—leaning into him rather than pulling away. His arms edged closer to my body, no longer restraining but supporting.

That unexplored, forsaken area between my legs began to throb, sharp and demanding. Mindlessly, I shifted, rubbing my thighs together just to relieve the ache. I had to consciously stop my hand from reaching down.

Without warning, Dublin withdrew from my skin, leaving a moist trail across my shoulder blades. At the same time, his cold fingers tugged at my bra, undoing the clasp and wrenching it down my arms before I could protest. The next second that same hand was beginning a slow ascent up my inner thigh …

Every cell in my body was held in thrall by those creeping fingers.

He maliciously toyed with the rim of my panties before peeling back the cotton and sliding a finger underneath. My teeth descended into my bottom lip to trap the sound that threatened to break free as he rubbed in a single, fiery circle, erupting sparks that traveled down my spine …

Just when I thought the teasing might drive me insane, he pressed harder, and a strangled cry broke free from my lips before I could smother it.

"Do you want me to stop?"

I could have lied to myself, told him yes …

But my answering groan seemed to give him all the encouragement he needed; in one fierce yank, my underwear slid down my legs, followed quickly by my skirt.

Both garments hit the floor, and not even a second later, I found my legs being wrenched apart.

Taking a knee in one hand, he forced it onto the rim of the desk as the other leg struggled to support my weight.

The position was awkward, and it terrified me to realize that Dublin was the only thing keeping me upright. As if aware of that fact, he muscled in closer from behind, until I couldn't tell where the hardwood of the table ended and he began.

Then, hands harder than steel palmed my waist, guiding my hips backward…

I knew what would happen next. Little Red Riding Hood wasn't so naïve anymore that she couldn't guess the intention in the wolf's eyes.

He gave me no warning this time. No more tortuous stroking of icy fingers to urge me closer to the brink. No blunt overview of what he planned to do and how he planned on doing it …

I had nothing but the sound of a zipper being undone before I felt the length of him slide against my inner thigh, hard and solid and frozen.

I shuddered as the blunt head of him rubbed against me, brusquely seeking my entrance. Fear began to sink in with the intensity of a thousand stabbing needles, as I waited for him to push in, hard and fast without a care. Maybe ...I even *wanted* him too ...

But he used his thumb to spread me apart, before advancing so slowly that I forgot how to breathe, to think.

My nails dug into the wood of the desk as my body struggled to adjust to the invasion. With a muffled groan, he entered another inch. Then another. And *another,* until he was finally buried to the hilt.

He waited, ominously patient, before pulling back and thrusting again—only deeper this time, lunging so hard that he forced me flat against the desk.

And again.

Again ...

God. My eyelids fluttered while my sweat-soaked fingers desperately sought purchase against the polished wood. Every sensation felt sinful. *Harder. Hotter. More explosive.* Frantic thoughts flooded my mind. *Too much. Too much. Not enough ...*

From this angle, he struck parts of me I hadn't even known existed. Fire swept through my abdomen, building through my skin until I could feel my toes curl within their heels.

He was right; this wasn't a game.

With every thrust, his tongue raked the torn skin of my shoulder, capturing each drop of blood. Whichever cut he didn't wickedly caress with his tongue, he toyed with instead, using the sharp points of his nails to mimic biting fangs.

My head flew back, baring my throat, silently urging him to take more as I forgot for the briefest of seconds that this wasn't just about pleasure. With every passing second that my blood flowed, common decency—or even sense—didn't matter.

I just wanted him to stop teasing and bite. Consume. Tear me apart.

Like some sick premonition, his earlier words taunted me. *I want the woman who climaxes whenever I sink my fangs into her throat.* And I *wanted* to be her and not just for him, but for me ...

"Please," I heard myself rasp, weak and broken. "Just ..."

"What?" His voice was steady with enviable control. "Say it, and do remember your manners."

"Dublin, please—"

He nipped, just once, as if to shut me up, and white-hot pleasure hit me like a physical blow.

Yes ...

My body quivered with anticipation, excitement racing through my veins; waiting, wanting, needing.

I strained on tiptoe as he forced himself deeper, trying to remember how to form words. He was moving too quickly ...not quickly enough. I needed more—less.

I needed all of him.

One cold hand gripped my waist while the other palmed the desk. Using the leverage to his advantage, he swiveled his hips, sparking a carnal friction that sent sparks exploding behind my eyelids.

My left shoulder was a wet, sticky mess, bathed in crimson. I waited for him to clamp down—to finally drink like he had that night in the cathedral—but he still held back.

"You know the rules, Eleanor ..." His tongue grazed my shoulder, no longer teasing, as he rammed into me so hard that I tried my best to muffle my moan with my own hands. "Please *what?*"

I gave up, broke, shattered—whatever it was called when you lost your one last shred of pride and just didn't give a damn. All I wanted was ...

"Tell me," he growled against the crook of my neck. His tone was different this time—it was damn near encouraging. *Obey me, and I'll end this ...*

"Please, *Sir*," I croaked. "I need to—" I gasped as his hand returned to my hair, using it as a handle to yank my head upright.

"You need to what, Eleanor?" That oddly gentle tone was back, and my aching body latched onto it.

This time I didn't hesitate. "I need to come."

Orgasm.

Climax—whatever the hell it was called. I was willing to say anything he wanted. Newly discovered nerves buried deep within my core throbbed in torment. With every thrust, I whimpered and groaned until my jaw clenched. Every vein in my body felt alive, aching to be pierced ...

I couldn't take any more of this.

As if to drill the point home, I felt him move against me, icy flesh against heated skin. In a slow, torturous circle his hips swiveled—hard—and I moaned in relief ...

But it still wasn't enough. It wasn't the sharp, quick rhythm that a part of me – or all of me – desperately craved. My entire body rippled in tune to the pulse of his shaft. But I needed more.

So close ...

"*Please*, Dublin!"

The brief break in character earned me a hard slap on the hip. *Thwack!* The pain was electrifying, and mingled with the pleasure that was encasing me from head to toe until ...

My back arched, hips thrusting back, forcing him deeper and even his grip on my waist wasn't enough to stop me. I groaned, shuddering somewhere on the precipice between fear and sweet agony as icy fingers fanned out along the back of my neck.

He was angry, furious at me for taking my own pleasure without permission. I could sense it in the way his grip tightened, applying subtle pressure—but he only used the hold for leverage as that massive body positioned fully over mine.

"Oh!" The sound tore from my lips as he lunged, striking in one, deep stroke.

This time, he didn't hold back. His hands were in my hair, grasping at the clumps of curls, pulling me into him, forcing my body to arch back and take him deeper. *Deeper,* still ...

I was incoherent. It was all I could do to scrape my nails against the wood and hold on as every thrust brought me closer to the brink.

God ...

Yes ...

One more ...

I jerked, straining against him, desperate and needy – and then I was falling, crashing, *breaking* into a million tiny pieces.

As if from miles away, I felt Dublin stiffen and the grip on my waist became a manacle, holding me in place as he thrust deep one final time and then held himself there before collapsing hard against my back.

I was lost.

It seemed to take eons before I finally returned to my body, dizzy and dazed. After that, the seconds passed in silence, and everything began to sink in.

One, I was lying beneath a man so heavy he could have crushed me beneath his pinky toe.

Two, I was naked save for my heels, slumped face down over a desk in the middle of a fully populated building.

And there was blood dribbling down my neck.

Three …I vaguely remembered promising the proverbial Devil my body and soul, in exchange for pain and pleasure.

So I remained there, naked and breathless, as I listened to every single drop of my blood splash against the floor and waited for the rude awakening I knew was coming.

～

*T*he desk creaked as Dublin pushed back with his hands and stood.

I could hear him moving behind me, grabbing the loose papers that had fallen to the floor. They ruffled as he smoothed them all into a neat stack and returned the pile to the drawer.

Then he stood, merely a few feet away, and I could feel his gaze searing the back of my neck.

"Get dressed."

I flinched. While outright banishment wasn't exactly a surprise, the words didn't sting any less. I felt like one of the cheap maids my father had his not-so-secret dalliances with; the fun was over, and now it was time to *get dressed. Get up. Get out.*

I tried to tell myself that I was more than happy to comply with all three commands—once I remembered how to *move* …

Everything from my hair down to the tips of my toes ached. I could only slump against the desk, wobbling on my heels, and squeeze my eyes shut. I hoped that wishful thinking might have been enough to erase everything that had just happened; all I had to do was click my heels three times, and I could be back at Gray Manor, normal, boring Eleanor Gray once again.

Though not if my Devil had anything to do with it.

"I have a meeting in an hour." The impatient tone was as bracing as a slap. I peeled my eyes open, but rather than being faced with a frowning Dublin pointing to the door, I blinked as something was tossed in my direction so quickly I didn't have time to catch it. "Here."

There was a muffled thump as the object landed on the desk; but instead of my emerald blouse, I found a man's shirt lying there. One that just so happened to be in a haunting shade of black.

Utterly confused, I couldn't resist running a hand down the silky material even as I expected for him to growl, *don't touch!*

"What is this?"

When Dublin didn't answer, I snuck a peek over my shoulder to find that he had moved to the other side of the room, and now stood in front of an open closet stocked with several crisp shirts. For some reason, I wasn't surprised. Something told me that being splattered with blood was enough of a typical occurrence for him, that he felt the need to always be prepared.

In the space of a few seconds, he had already changed. With a flick of his wrist, he straightened the fresh, ivory collar, and just like that, he looked shiny and new again, save for a tell-tale dot of scarlet on his lower lip.

I hated him.

"I don't have all day," he added, sensing my gaze. He sounded irritated, as if I was wasting his precious time just by being there, by breathing.

"I ...I need my clothes," I blurted, allowing his shirt to fall back to the desk.

He turned to face me with one blond eyebrow raised. *Are you an imbecile?* Without a word, he stooped to lift a bit of green fabric from the floor; my blouse. I held out my hand, but rather than offer it he promptly tore the garment in half.

The sound echoed violently in my ears. Then, as casually as though it had been just another scrap piece of paper, he wadded it in a fist and tossed it into the wastebasket.

"Get dressed," he commanded once again. Before I even had the chance to obey he came forward and snatched his own shirt from the desk. I could only stand there, as he grabbed my hand and forced it through a sleeve. He did the same to the other and then brusquely fastened the buttons one by one up to my chin.

"You have good timing," he told me, as he bent down for the underwear. Manually, he lifted my ankles, one by one from the floor to slide my panties back into place. "I was just about to leave."

Huh?

I didn't know whether to be confused or insulted at my supposed 'convenience,' as he proceeded to yank my skirt on as well.

I waited for him to shove me to the door, or storm out himself—leaving me there to my shame. Instead, he snatched my bag from the desk. Next, he reached for my arm, and I only had enough time to grab my money, before I found myself dragged after him and down the hall.

"Come on."

Don't panic, I tried to tell myself. Perhaps escorting me to the car himself was his strange, personal way of confounding my humiliation?

His face gave nothing away; even that usual scowl was absent.

If I hadn't known any better, I might have described his appearance as …well, *not* brooding and angry for once. Calm, even? It was a terrifying thought. I almost wished he would snarl and bare his fangs. *Growl* at least?

One might have thought that I had just met him for tea rather than barged into his office and thrown money in his face. Speaking of which …

The bills felt unbearably heavy. They weighed me down, causing me to stagger as Dublin man-handled me into the elevator and hit the button for the lobby.

When the elevator doors split apart, there was no place left to hide as the wide-eyed receptionist noticed me beside him. Cool and in control as always, Dublin inclined his head in greeting as though nothing was out of place—I was merely his dowdy accessory with tousled hair.

"Good morning, Becky."

"M-Morning … Mr. Helos."

Despite her frozen smile, poor Becky looked horribly confused. Even more so when I proceeded to drop a wad of cash on her desk as Dublin hauled me past.

"Morning, Becky," I croaked, before I found myself unceremoniously dragged out the door.

The daylight was blinding. I had to shield my eyes with my hand as Dublin took a hold of my sleeve and used it like a leash to pull me after him.

Don't panic …

I felt dizzy with relief when I noticed Harper, standing by the car where I'd left him last. I attempted to wriggle free from Dublin's grip, ready to duck within the dark safety of the Rolls Royce—but to my immense horror, his grip tightened like a vice.

Rather than the promise of a quick trip home to wallow in my shame, I found myself steered toward another, equally familiar black car and unceremoniously shoved into the backseat.

"Dublin?" I paled as he promptly slammed the door in my face.

Dark, sordid scenarios flooded my brain. I tugged frantically on the door handle, only to hear the *click* of the lock being engaged a second later.

"Sorry, Miss," the driver replied from the front seat—but I could tell that he didn't really give a damn; *just following orders.*

Horrified, I could only watch as Dublin approached Harper and said something that made the driver nod his head in response. *Yes, Sir.* Then, as cool as you please, Dublin proceeded to reach into his pocket for a wad of cash, which he casually counted before tucking into Harper's hand.

Just like that, my faithful servant climbed back into the car and left me behind.

Should I panic now? I wondered. I made one last-ditch attempt at the door—but when Dublin finally turned in my direction …

For an instant, I forgot to be afraid, as heat flooded my veins at the sight of him, hair gleaming in the sunlight.

He was so beautiful.

It was easy to overlook that fact in between all of his terrorizing. Now, safe behind inches of metal, I could finally admit that the sight of him struck me dumb. A part of me almost couldn't believe that only a moment earlier, he had been crushed against me, had been hungry for me, had wanted *me*.

However, when he saw me there, face practically pressed up against the glass, he frowned and the trance shattered.

I scrambled back as he wrenched open the door, even before he waved a dismissive hand for me to do so. *Move.*

His icy chill hit me like a slap as he sat down. I squeezed myself against the opposite door, but it wasn't nearly far enough away from him. The moment he closed the door, the car lurched into motion, and I was trapped.

It was only then that I realized I was still bleeding. Rivulets of warmth dripped down my back, pooling beneath the waistband of my skirt. As if my realization were his cue, I saw Dublin stiffen from the corner of my eye. The next second he was withdrawing something from his pocket and pressing it into my hand.

"Clean that up."

I frowned at the sight of another pristine handkerchief. It rested on my palm, almost as pale as I was. I hated the thought of accepting his help but, with a sigh, I loosened the topmost buttons of my shirt and eased the wad of cloth underneath.

I had to grit my teeth against a gasp as I applied the tiniest amount of pressure. *Ouch.* The cuts stung. To make matters worse, I could feel a pair of gray eyes on the back of my neck, watching like a hawk as blood seeped through the ivory cotton.

Gingerly I dabbed at the wounds, only to draw a hiss of disgust from Dublin. Apparently, I wasn't moving quickly enough for his liking.

"Turn around."

I gulped at his tone, though I had enough sense not to argue. I merely obeyed, while reaching up to swipe my hair out of the way. A part of me expected for him to just play the role of uncaring doctor, like he had that night in the solar—but he reached around me instead. Then, without warning, he unhooked the front of the shirt and wrenched it down my shoulders.

I froze. Images of what had happened in the office flooded my mind, one after the other. I waited, body so tense it felt like one good bump in the road might have been enough to make me shatter into pieces. Dublin took the handkerchief from my hand, but rather than trying to staunch the bleeding, he set the cloth aside, and his finger trailed the line of a cut instead.

Bit by bit it inched its way up my shoulder, ghosting the sore flesh.

"Does it hurt?" he asked after a tortuous few seconds.

I blinked. He sounded genuinely curious, but I shook my head as his icy touch trailed down to encircle my wrist.

"Really?" The dark note in his voice warned me not to lie.

"A little," I admitted. It was the first time I realized how deep the cuts really were. *Would I need stitches?*

Though, if anything, his touch felt worse; the brush of those fingers disrupted my breathing. Within seconds, I was suffocating.

I tried to tell myself that this was *Dublin*—who had certainly touched me in much more sensitive places than my damn shoulder—but this time, the contact felt different. I was keenly aware of him, so close. My body trembled. My teeth chattered. My heart sped up. Unbidden, those four dangerous words echoed in my mind; *you belong to me.*

"Good," he murmured in answer to my admission. "You'll remember how it felt."

Fear ran through me like a punch; something told me that he was no longer talking about the pain, but my *reaction* to it ...as well as to his touch.

Desperate to change the subject, I glanced out of the window to find the city passing by in a blur. I had no idea where on earth we were now, or where he could have been taking me. Too uneasy to care about the danger, I decided to risk his wrath by asking.

"Where are we going?"

I hated how pathetic I sounded. My voice shook. No matter how hard I tried, I couldn't seem to find enough air. Any moment I was afraid I might scream—either out of fear or shock; whichever one became more unbearable first.

"Why should it matter?"

His voice took on a slightly harder edge, and an icy finger strayed deliberately close to one of the cuts. I hissed at the sharp pain, eyes watering.

"Isn't this the part where you send me off in ruin and add another notch on your bedpost?" I asked through gritted teeth. "One more soul corrupted?"

I was surprised that the words came out sounding carefree, with all the 'ho-hum' attitude of a snob who didn't give a damn. I almost felt pleased with myself.

"You're not even *halfway* corrupted," Dublin scoffed as if insulted. He cupped my chin, forcing me to face him. "Why, look …" His gaze trailed down over my chest as if seeing something there that I couldn't. "You still have your soul. Turn around."

He yanked on my arm, forcing me to face the window. I waited for him to pull a needle full of his mysterious "cure" from his pocket—but, he merely settled the shirt back into place, leaving me to fasten the buttons on my own.

When I finally turned to face him, the bloody handkerchief was gone, and he was leaning back into the leather seats. No one could ever guess that not even ten minutes earlier, he had cut me twice before stripping me naked in the middle of his office, among other things …

The memory made my cheeks heat with shame, and I tried my best to gather the remaining shreds of my pride as I fiddled with my purse on my lap.

"So …what happens now?"

Unsurprisingly, Dublin didn't answer. When I finally had the nerve to sneak another glance at his face, I saw that his eyes were closed. Apparently, terrorizing young damsels was a tiring affair.

I just couldn't fathom him. Cold one minute. Intense the next …

"You didn't answer my question." I copied him by sinking back into the leather cushions with a sigh. My shoulder throbbed in protest, but it was easy to overlook the pain in comparison to everything else.

It blew my mind how, despite everything that had just occurred we were once again back to our usual dynamic; a frustrated me, needling him for answers. Apparently, verbally selling my soul meant *nothing*—I was still pathetic, and still at his mercy.

You could always give in to Saskia and just say the pesky word, I thought, crossing my arms over my chest. *It's not like you have anything left to lose.*

It was only when those glacial eyes turned to me that I realized I had said the last sentence out loud.

"I have another business arrangement; you will accompany me."

He made it sound so damn simple, harmless—but I felt like a mouse invited to accompany a cat on a hunt.

"Why?"

He raised a blond eyebrow. "Would *'because I said so'* sound too melodramatic? Really, Eleanor. You *did* willingly pledge your soul to me; use your imagination."

I stiffened at the reminder, but I had to admit that, once again, the words lacked the biting sting of an offensive remark. Had I had any sense of tact, I would have shut my mouth, realizing that even too tired to tear apart my pride, Dublin was not a man to be trifled with.

But I couldn't resist; I could always blame it on the blood loss.

"A vampire 'business arrangement?' Or ...a *normal* one?"

"Why should it matter?"

I bit my lip, weighing my next words carefully as the car darted over a bridge and Dublin's eyes flashed a warning shade of silver. *Careful, Ellie ...*

"I've lost quite a bit of a blood already," I said quietly. "I'm not fond of the prospect of losing any more—"

"It concerns the land you helped me purchase the other day," Dublin admitted, cutting over me. "I'm overseeing the development of it."

That was fast. I counted back the few days since I had helped him win over Haswell. What kinds of real estate might a vampire desire to build in such a hurry? *Another club? Another reclusive mansion in the hills?*

The thought sparked another question that I found myself blurting before I could help it. "What was that about, last night?"

Excluding my impromptu slap and his scathing assessment of me, of course. I was annoyed, but not surprised, to see that his face held no hint of a bruise to remember the broadside of my hand by, just flawless, pale skin.

"What do you mean?"

Watch yourself, Ellie girl ...

"I sensed some …hostility."

The sad part was that I didn't even have to specify whether I was referring to Raphael or the people at the strange ball in general. Dublin certainly seemed to lack for friends; it appeared as though Yulia was the only one who didn't hate nor loath him—at least not outright.

"Hmmm …" He reached up to rub his chin. "And here I was thinking that I had played my part of sycophant so well."

"You … You don't like him?"

He made a small sound of amusement in the back of his throat. "I 'like' very few things in this life, Eleanor. You would be wise to remember that."

Point taken. I backed off the topic, but was unable to resist posing another one. I knew better—though who could blame me? After all, *he* was the one who had accused me of liking danger in the first place.

"Last night …they said that you had bargained for my contract from him?"

"They?" Like a predator presented with fresh meat, Dublin bolted upright, expression cold as he turned to face me. "I had wondered what Mikhail and those other fools might have whispered in your ear."

I gulped, unable to miss how he deliberately ignored my question.

"What else did 'they' say?" he demanded.

"Nothing," I said a little too quickly. "Only that …you bought my contract from Raphael. As well as Yulia's."

Dublin didn't look convinced that was all there was. "It's been a long while since I reminded Mikhail the importance of minding one's business. Perhaps such a lesson is long overdue."

His tone conjured images of violence, and I cringed at the thought of what such a 'lesson' might entail. Desperate for another distraction, I blurted the first thing that came to mind.

"What's a shiftspinner?"

Dublin held my gaze for so long that I was convinced he wouldn't answer. Despite myself, I truly wished that he *would* explain; the damn word had been on my mind all night. I had pondered the meaning countless times, but I still had no clue.

"A shiftspinner is a witch," Dublin said finally. The fact that he had answered at all nearly made me fall off the seat in shock. "One whose power comes from the natural essence in fabrics, left behind by whatever plants or animals formed it. They have a skill to create clothing that, when worn, can bestow the wearer with different strengths: invisibility cloaks, impenetrable armor and the like …"

He sounded so matter-of-fact, the same way someone might have said *'a burger flipper? Well, they flip burgers, of course!'*

I, however, had to clench my jaw shut just to keep my mouth from falling open. First vampires, now witches?

"Yulia?" I asked, eyes wide, though I figured that a part of me already knew the answer even before he nodded.

'Something like that,' she had answered when I asked if she was a fashion designer. No wonder she worked for the club if her clothing was *literally* magical. *And no wonder I had looked so decent in it.*

"Can they read minds?" I asked, staring down at my pathetic tweed skirt, which looked so plain when paired with the exquisite fabric of his shirt. "Is Saskia one as well?"

"No." Dublin sounded amused. "Though, she has 'read' you, I assume? I was wondering when she'd pull one of her little tricks." He flashed a cold, mirthless smile that reminded me of a shark's yawn—nothing but teeth. "Saskia is a succubus. She cannot actually read minds—merely the subconscious fears and desires of those around her. A trick she loves to exploit to ensnare her contracts."

"Succubus." The word tasted strange on my tongue. "Can she read your mind?" I wondered, oddly entranced by the idea of someone being able to sneak past Dublin's defenses.

"Oh, I'm sure Saskia would love to play her games on me. However, I am always one step ahead of her." He adjusted his collar as he spoke and I caught a glimpse of silver; that strange cross.

Did the talisman possess some kind of magic ability? I opened my mouth to ask, but before I could, the car came to a stop, and my Devil's demeanor shifted once again.

"Time's up, Eleanor," he announced. "I have humored you long enough. Make yourself decent."

I automatically reached up to feel my hair. My curls were wild—some of them completely knotted by his pulling fingers, which served as a blunt reminder as to what had happened just a few moments earlier. My cheeks heated with shame as I clumsily adjusted my collar and tucked a wayward strand behind my ears.

Without bothering to wait for me, Dublin opened his door and climbed out. I scrambled after him, glancing around in confusion.

We had left the city. Now, nothing but trees loomed above in place of skyscrapers, lining a narrow road and a wide, open field of lush green grass.

It was a lovely place, quiet, secluded.

And, as Dublin came up behind me, I had to wonder why the hell he had brought me here.

BAUBLES

"We're early," Dublin announced, frowning down at his watch.

A moment before he had been surveying the landscape with the same critical expression he wore whenever he looked at me—as though searching for flaws.

Early, I thought, but something told me the truth was that whoever we were waiting for was simply *late.*

I wondered who would dare to keep the all-powerful Dublin Helos waiting, let alone who could possibly a have use for land brokered for by a vampire? A reclusive villain aiming to build a blood factory? Raphael? Another 'Dracula' in training? Unwilling to try my luck asking another question, I kept my mouth shut.

The seconds flew past, then minutes. All the while I had nothing to preoccupy myself but the dark thoughts circling my mind. *What kind of game was he playing at?*

I didn't have the nerve to ask what him 'owning' me entailed—besides the obvious physical aspects—but so far the arrangement seemed no different from our tense contract. Albeit, I had the marks on my shoulder to prove that *something* had changed.

And …I was here. While Dublin was certainly going out of his way to make it appear as though my presence was a burden, he *had* brought me along in the first place, and I was beginning to learn that men like him didn't act on mere whims.

Curiouser and curiouser, I thought sardonically. *Just be careful, Ellie …who knows where this rabbit hole may lead?*

The thought taunted me until the sound of an approaching vehicle caught my attention. I turned, witnessing the moment a battered station wagon crested the hill and sputtered down the road in our direction. I didn't know what type of figure I had expected to see emerge from it—but a haggard woman with graying hair wasn't it.

"Mr. Helos," she greeted, spotting Dublin. "Good afternoon. I hope you don't mind, but I've brought along a few relevant *investors* to help me make a decision."

She rapped on the roof of the decrepit vehicle and, like clockwork, several tiny figures scrambled out: three small children who rushed to form a neat line, each dressed in a dark blue uniform.

I blinked, convinced that shock was the only thing that kept me from reaching up to rub my eyes just to make sure that I wasn't hallucinating.

"Marvelous," Dublin said. He sounded as cool and distant as always—but I couldn't help noticing that his usually stern jaw was relaxed, and there was a softness to his gaze that hadn't been there before. "Shall we?"

He led the way toward the field, leaving the rest of us to catch up. After a moment, he grudgingly jerked his head in my direction. "Mrs. Brandston, this is my associate, Eleanor Gray …she is the one who secured the sale of this property."

"Ms. Gray." Mrs. Brandston turned to face me, brown eyes warm. "On behalf of the Leyfair Orphanage, I thank you."

My mind skidded to a thudding halt. *Orphanage …*

I damn near choked. My heels caught in a patch of grass, nearly causing me to tumble to my doom—not that the benevolent Mr. Helos would've given a damn. He was beside me in an instant, yanking me upright without so much as a grunt of concern. The next second I found myself shoved aside and he was paces ahead, as if he had never assisted me at all.

"Are you all right?"

I glanced down, into the kind blue eyes of a young girl, whose blonde curls were barely contained by her navy headband. "You should be careful when you walk in pointy shoes," she advised.

Like an imbecile, I could only nod while my mind raced with a million conflicting thoughts. *Dublin. Orphans. Land.*

Was he, perhaps, planning on opening a blood factory supplied by innocent orphans? Or perhaps he really had drawn too much of my *own blood,* and I was hallucinating?

But when the girl smiled at me, there was nothing insubstantial about it at all. "I'm Anna," she said, still grinning wide enough to reveal her missing front tooth. "What's your name?"

"Ellie," I croaked.

She nodded studiously as if expecting that very answer. "Do you think we'll get to have a soccer field with the new house?"

New house? I glanced around the wide, open expanse of land and only then did it finally sink in like a punch to the stomach. *New house. Orphanage. Dublin's special 'plans' for Haswell's land.*

"No bloody way …"

The children snickered. Both Dublin and Mrs. Brandston's heads whipped around in my direction—and a pair of familiar gray eyes found mine a second later, narrowed in warning.

"Shall we discuss a timeline, Mrs. Brandston?" Dublin suggested before leading the woman to another end of the field. Left behind, I found myself immediately swarmed by all three children.

Anna spearheaded the motley crew, flanked on either side by a boy, the youngest who appeared to be no more than eight years old.

"She's pretty," I heard him mutter into the sleeve of his blue sweatshirt.

The other, who seemed a bit older, glanced at him with a scoff. "No, she's not."

My cheeks flamed, though I couldn't blame the boy—whose name I guessed was "Rory!" as Anna exclaimed it in horror—for just saying what the whole world thought. Once again, I was resigned to my status as merely the "other Gray sister."

"Yes, she is!" The first boy shouted indignantly, surprising me. "She glows," he added, peeking at me from underneath his eyelashes. "Like an angel."

A wave of gratitude unlike anything I had ever felt crashed through me, and I found myself sinking down to one knee. "Why, thank you!"

"I guess," Rory grumbled, but before I could respond Anna launched into a rather dramatic retelling of a game of jacks and I was riveted.

For almost ten minutes, I allowed the children to regale me with stories. They were fascinating little creatures. I didn't think I had ever interacted with anyone younger than thirty outside of my own childhood, apart from Georgie and the younger servants. In my world, a 'child' had been more or less a mythical creature that could serve as a convenient prop for photo ops.

"See this?" Anna exclaimed, brandishing a cheap ring on her finger as though it sported the Hope Diamond. Its plastic band was painted silver and adorned with fake filigree resembling a flower. Glued to the center of it, rested a cracked blue bead—the kind of worthless bauble I would have killed for at her age.

"I love it, Anna," I gushed with genuine admiration.

"It's my most prized possession in the whole, wide world," she gloated.

"I have one too!"

"Me too!"

Not to be outdone, the two boys—Lucas and Rory respectively—both launched into declarations of their own worldly passions; a mud-encrusted baseball, a chewed, partially torn trading card.

I could only stare, oddly entranced, and wonder if this was all some kind of bizarre hallucination brought on by blood loss.

It had to be a joke, some sick prank on Dublin's part. I waited for the punch line, for the other proverbial shoe to drop. *This is a new home for orphans—though, some may use the term 'sweatshop.'* But not even five minutes later, he and Mrs. Brandston reappeared without a single sinister glance shared between them.

"Thank you, Mr. Helos," the older woman said, voice trembling with gratitude. "The land will do perfectly. Leyfair enjoys your continued patronage."

Continued?

"I'm glad the property satisfies you," Dublin said, sounding way too humble for my liking. "It's a donation, of course, though I would be more than willing to oversee the construction."

Mrs. Brandston continued to spill her thanks, and I could only gape at the exchange like some witless imbecile. Then, without much fanfare, the woman began to wrangle her charges and usher them back to the van.

Once again, my gaze drifted over to Dublin. His jaw had tightened as if he was aware of the thoughts unfolding in my head and wasn't at all pleased with the picture they presented.

"You can wait in the car, Eleanor," he said.

I swayed as those gray eyes found mine, cold and unfathomable. Obediently, I turned on my heel, too confused to object—but before I could even go a full step a sudden thought took hold, and I was shrugging my purse from my shoulders before I had even really processed the motion.

"Wait!" I turned to the station wagon and staggered toward it, all but shoving my bag—and the money stuffed within— into the hands of a startled Mrs. Brandston. "Take this," I insisted. "Please. Consider it an ...overdue donation from the Gray family."

I spun back around before I could see her reaction and all but ran to Dublin's car. My family had always made their token donations to charity, but the rush of a genuine act of goodwill affected me more strongly than I would have ever expected. I reached out, fingers scraping the handle of the car door, but before I could pull it open, a cool hand batted mine away.

Without warning, Dublin yanked me around by my wrist. I tensed, not knowing what to expect. Disapproval?

He had never looked at me this way—as if he was peering deeper beneath the same old 'Ellie' exterior. I felt stripped naked, exposed. The next second, he turned away, and I could only slump against the car and stare as he returned to Mrs. Brandston. They exchanged a few words, before the woman entered the vehicle smiling.

Moments later, the wagon drove off, and the sounds of the children squabbling about who should sit in the middle faded to silence. Once again, I was left alone with a man who barely seemed to acknowledge my existence.

Without a word, Dublin brushed past me and entered the car. I could only follow him, collapsing weakly on the seat.

"An orphanage?" I blurted as the car lurched into motion. "All for an orphanage?"

Ice crossed my vision as his gaze found mine and held it for so long that I felt frozen when he finally turned away.

"I have many investments," he remarked while tilting his head to gaze from the window. "*You* are one of them."

I flinched at the not-so-subtle reminder.

"Why an orphanage, though?" I pressed. "Why not a blood factory or a torture chamber, or another club?"

All evil, dark establishments that I could easily picture someone like him owning.

"I must say that I'm getting rather annoyed with all these questions."

My heart lurched at the threat in his tone—especially as two pale fingers came to lift up my chin, forcing me to meet his gaze. Instead of anger, the only thing I found there amongst the silver was an elusive emotion I couldn't put a name to—and I wasn't willing to try. It terrified me, that look. I could taste my own pulse even as he finally turned away.

"Here," he grumbled, tossing something unceremoniously onto my lap.

I glanced down, not knowing what to expect—but a tiny, silver piece of plastic was not it. Confused, I shifted to trap the object in my palm.

"What is ..."

I trailed off as a glimmer of sunlight caught the cheap, plastic stone that formed the centerpiece of a small, gaudy ring. My eyes widened, and my throat went dry. It was *Anna's* ring—apparently, her most 'prized' possession—and fear lanced my chest as I realized that she wouldn't have parted with it easily.

"How did you—"

"Relax …" Dublin's mouth twitched. If I didn't know any better, I'd say he was actually insulted. "I acquired it in a fair trade."

He deliberately tugged on the sleeve of his jacket, and I noticed that only *one* arm was sporting an expensive, silver cufflink. Its mate was missing.

"W-Why?" I stammered, as the magnitude of what he had done sank in. While he claimed he didn't give a damn about money, trading a priceless accessory for a worthless plastic ring was not something that even the most philanthropic rich bastard would do—not without a motive.

If I wanted to believe that it was because of some sort of a sentimental, caring reason, Dublin's frown promptly squashed that suspicion.

"I wanted you to see how foolish it was to ever desire such a thing in the first place," he said coldly, but the fact that he had remembered my trivial confession at all negated the impact of his words. "Now tell me, Eleanor; how does it feel to have everything you've ever wanted?"

He was mocking me—but I couldn't escape this sneaking little thought that there was something else hidden in his tone as well. Something hoarse that grew as I proudly slipped the ring onto my finger and brandished it like a hard-fought spoil of war.

"It feels wonderful," I declared with an impish grin. "It's not exactly from a gumball machine ... Regardless; I shall *never* take it off."

There was a dare in my tone that I couldn't deny. An eavesdropper might have suspected that the proclamation was made out of gratitude, but no—rather than *'I shall wear it and remember you always,'* I meant, *'I shall wear it stubbornly even if my finger turns gangrene and falls off.'*

Oddly enough, Dublin's eyes took on a satisfied tint.

"I will hold you to that. Let's just hope it doesn't turn your finger green. After all, the purity of your skin is one of your few *redeeming* qualities ..."

I let the barb slip by unchallenged.

"Perhaps my next life goal should be a necklace?" I wondered, eyeing his throat for a glimpse of that silver chain. "One like yours?"

"No."

Something in me tightened at his tone, but I didn't have long to ponder why before his face fell back into its usual blank mask.

"I have another meeting," he said, shrugging me off physically as well as verbally. "I'll have you dropped off at your house."

"So, I'm being dismissed then? Until ..." I prompted, suddenly uneasy as to the terms of our new 'arrangement.'

He shrugged again. "Until I have *use* for you, of course."

HELL BOUND

Some sort of feeling comes over you when you've completely lost a hold over everything that made you the person you thought you were—only I couldn't think of the right word for it.

Loss? Grief? Relief?

I felt drowned by the emotion, whatever it was, as I trudged up the staircase of Gray Manor after being dropped off at the doorstep like unwanted luggage. Once inside my bedroom, I undressed, leaving my skirt on a chair for a maid to retrieve, but Dublin's shirt I hung on a hanger and tucked at the very back of my closet.

I couldn't explain why.

Naked, I drew a bath as hot as I could stand it and climbed inside, sinking up to my neck. I sat there, unmoving, as water poured down and attempted to dissect a wave of emotions I couldn't decipher.

This isn't right, I thought, gazing mournfully up at the ceiling.

I should have felt …worse. So, so much worse—especially considering that my wounds stung beneath the water and I couldn't stop twirling that cheap, plastic ring around and around my finger.

I should have been about ready to duck my head underneath the water while spouting some morose poem about life and woe, prepared to follow in the footsteps of my parents.

I *shouldn't* have felt … Well, in all honesty, I didn't really know how to classify just *what* I was feeling. Shame wasn't it. Neither was regret, truth be told, which confused me to the point that I frowned into the cloud of steam.

No matter how hard I tried to ignore it, there was one little word that kept appearing in my mind, something so cliché that I rolled my eyes at the mere thought of considering it. But, just as the water began to encroach on my chin, I found myself whispering it—just once—out loud.

"Free …"

It didn't sound quite as pathetic in the open air as it had in my head, which unnerved me even more. I didn't even receive a frantic admonition from my dead mother along the lines of freedom *is an illusion, Eleanor. Money is freedom!*

Sighing, I curled my toes against the rim of the tub, trying not to relive every second with Dublin, though the memories played through my mind regardless.

He said that I had been "pretending" that night at the masquerade. If being polite and conservative was what he mistook for pretense, then I shivered at the thought of this …

Uninhibited Ellie. Lord have mercy.

I cringed and waited for a fitting interjection from my ghostly maternal unit, but all I received instead was silence once again.

Confused, I lingered within the water until it turned ice cold and the skin around the cuts on my shoulder was a bright, violent red. On pruned toes, I climbed out and slipped into a robe, tying the sash around my waist.

The house was silent around me—like a tomb, enclosing someone who had no idea that she was already dead. With that melancholic thought in my head, I dragged a brush through my hair while pondering my own reflection in the mirror.

My new ring sparkled on my finger—just about the only shiny part of me. I looked ghoulish from behind a cloud of steam. Impulsively I reached out to swipe through the condensation with the pad of my finger, leaving a streak across the mirror.

My eyes gleamed against the glass, along with an angry slash of red along my collarbone. A good, decent woman would have felt shame, I supposed. Perhaps she would have torn through her wardrobe in search of a scarf to obscure the sign of her impurity?

All I did was tilt my head further to the side and observe how the cuts had already begun to scab over. I wondered if I happened to touch one …would the skin around it still feel cold, impregnated with an icy chill? My fingers trembled with the thought, and I had to brace both hands against the mirror's surface just to keep from testing out that theory.

Instead, I traced meaningless patterns against the glass and eventually found myself forming a single sentence in clumsy, blocky letters. *Eleanor Gray is …*

What? I wondered.

Stupid?

Foolish?

A whore?

My index finger hovered inches from the glass hesitating for only a moment before I sighed and reluctantly added those three little words my Devil was so fond of tossing about as his mantra: *Bound for Hell.*

The words taunted me. Was the fiery pit what truly awaited this new Ellie?

Should I have been terrified?

Dublin certainly seemed to think that was his ultimate destination: the Devil, who would eventually dwell in Hell. It was a fitting comparison.

Dublin Helos is bound for hell …and seems determined to drag poor, naïve Ellie Gray right on down with him.

Moving to an untouched sheet of steam, I carefully sketched the letters: DUBLIN HELOS.

Even the sight of the name was intimidating—or maybe it was just thoughts of the man himself—but something about the eleven letters conjured an old memory of Georgiana and me as children.

We had often loved to challenge each other with word scrambles; puzzles formed of letters that, once unscrambled, revealed a single, coherent word. *Rayg* became *Gray*. *Rgoegie* for *Georgie*. *Lorenae* for *Eleanor*.

I had especially relished the challenge of tackling the most difficult, innocuous ones. What meaning might a pile of gibberish actually have buried underneath?

I tried to tell myself that I was being foolish now. After all, what mystery could possibly lurk within a name as seemingly random as *Dublin*? Regardless, I found myself dissecting it against the glass. *An H, two L's and an E …*

The tedium resurrected the old, methodical part of me that relished a riddle and eventually, three words emerged. Three words all formed from the letters of his name …and they chilled me right to the bone: *IS HELL BOUND.*

It was an eerie coincidence. *I am bound for hell, Eleanor,* he liked to insist time and time again. Was he so sure of his own damnation that he liked to remind himself of it, even in the spelling of his own name?

I didn't know. I didn't *want* to know.

The thought would have been too jarring; Devils simply weren't allowed to possess self-reflection.

I banished the words with a swipe of my hand and took a step back from the mirror. I was shivering as I finally turned away and settled my damp curls over my shoulders. The specter of Dublin haunted me as I padded into the bedroom, intending to slip beneath my bed covers and disappear into a world of nightmares, most likely starring one infamous vampire …

Only, in an instant, the prospect was shattered.

There was a man standing in my room, rummaging through my nightstand.

With his back turned to me, he rifled through the drawers and tossed knick knacks and loose bits of paper to the floor. Obviously, he was looking for something. Jewels? Money?

His filthy, mud-stained leather jacket made me highly suspect that he wasn't a servant or in my employ.

I figure I should have screamed or reacted like any normal, sensible woman would, but Dublin had obliterated all my sense of normality and all I could do was linger over the threshold, dripping water onto the floor.

"Can … Can I help you?"

He turned. Matted brown hair tumbled down his shoulders, matching an equally unkempt beard that hung from his chin. He looked like the dangerous, wild sort who might break into young ladies' bedrooms, intent on robbing and murdering, but before I could truly feel afraid, I saw his eyes—they were the same piercing green as mine.

I blinked as recognition hit me like a punch.

"Uncle Orwell?"

His was a face I hadn't seen in nearly ten years—not since my father last had him sent away under the pretense of him being *unwell,* which, of course, was just Gray code for 'flipping nuts.' I tilted my head, wondering if the day's blood loss was truly making me hallucinate this time.

He certainly didn't look as though those years in an asylum had done him any good. His eyes were wild, slightly crazed, though they narrowed when they landed on me.

"Eleanor. So you're still alive."

I flinched at the gruffness in his tone. *Alive?*

"Am … Am I not supposed to be?" I wondered if he had heard of my failing health.

He shrugged. "Bet you know that better than I do."

I blinked, stumbling closer before my mind chose to register the fact that—despite the blood connection—I knew nothing about this man. Nor, I might add, why the hell he had broken into my room.

"Why would I be hurt?" I asked, conveniently overlooking the facts that I knew proved the fallacy of that question: *Because I had sold my proverbial soul to a vampire; because I had a fatal blood condition; because I was a fool,* or more importantly, because of *Dublin.*

Rather than mutter some confused nonsense about bunnies —or whatever it was crazy people raved about these days— Orwell reached into his jacket and tossed something flat and square at my feet. It was a newspaper, I saw as I bent down; one of those trashy tabloids that Georgie tended to star in whenever she returned to the city.

Only now, another Gray's picture rested beneath a blazing headline: *Reclusive Heiress Steps Out With New Man.* The so-called 'new man' needed no introduction; I'd have recognized that gleaming blond hair anywhere, but it took a few more moments of blinking before I realized that the pale woman standing beside him was …

Me.

Someone had caught the moment a few days ago when he had dragged me to the *Cafe Claret.* I recognized Yulia's crisp outfit. Dublin's hand was on my arm, and to any ignorant observer, the assumption might have been that we were lovers.

The irony was so bitter that I found myself laughing out loud.

Good heavens! I wondered if Dublin would be upset at having been publicly linked to me. Absolutely gleeful at the prospect, I stooped for the paper. It was only when I had it tucked under my arm and stood that I realized Orwell most likely hadn't presented it out of shock.

He looked uneasy, for one, and disgusted. He eyed that silly magazine as though it was my head on a platter—only I was just too stupid to realize it.

"They got to you," he said in a tone that made my skin cold. "Where is your sister? Where is Georgiana?"

He pushed his way past me for the bedroom door and peered into the hallway as if expecting Georgie to come strolling down the hallway. "Georgiana?"

"She's not here," I said, puzzled as he whirled on me with a grim frown. "She won't be back until Thursday. Would you like me to give her a message?"

I politely refrained from voicing my doubts that the posh and sophisticated Georgie—who couldn't even take the private jet home to see her dying sister—would want to chat with our estranged uncle, freshly released from the mental hospital.

"She probably already knows," Orwell said with a crazed light shining in those green eyes. "I reckon they did this—" He jabbed a grimy finger at the tabloid still tucked underneath my arm. "Just for *her*."

I doubted that Georgie would care that I had been photographed with a man—other than the obvious shock that I had left the manor at all—but something in Orwell's voice …

It made the little hairs at the nape of my neck stand on end.

"Know what?" I found myself asking, though I was pretty sure that it wasn't exactly a good idea to feed into a madman's delusions. "Who's …'gotten' to me?"

He didn't answer. Instead, those green eyes darted to my shoulder and narrowed, as if sensing the blood that I could feel seeping, once again, from the cuts there.

"*They* have," he growled, stressing 'they' as if it were obvious who he meant.

I felt my heart sink to the pit of my stomach, despite the logical part of me trying to rationalize that he couldn't possibly mean who I thought …

"I'll call someone," I stammered, blindly stumbling for my nightstand. I didn't know who; *Harper? The police? The mental institution?*

I had barely gone halfway before a harsh grip yanked me back.

"No!"

Unprepared for the assault, I went flying, landing hard on a surface that I assumed was the wall—at least until I heard it splinter beneath my weight.

In a daze, I could only stare at the shards of glass littering the floor. Shock ran through me like a lance, even before I felt the pain.

Oh God. Fiery agony danced up and down my arm. In what seemed like a matter of seconds, the crisp, white sleeve of my robe was scarlet.

"I need to regroup," I heard Orwell mutter, oblivious to my injury. "I need to contact Georgiana. They would only retaliate if she'd gone too far …"

I barely registered the words. I was too busy trying to stay upright. Large blotches of crimson were seeping through the thick terrycloth of my robe. Frantic, I tried to count back the days since my last dose of Dublin's mystic cure, but I came up blank.

Oh dear.

A normal person, I supposed, might have gone to the hospital—something that was out of the question for me. After all, I assumed they would wonder why I was no longer dying, or question the cause for those two, nasty wounds on my shoulder.

I even considered phoning the private, family doctor that my mother had kept on a retainer all these years, but I couldn't remember his name or where Harper filed the important numbers. It was late, I saw, glancing at the clock on my wall. Even Harper needed to sleep and— hemorrhaging to death or not—I didn't want to bother him for something as silly as a few, little scrapes.

Deep, jagged, little scrapes I saw as I peeled off the terrycloth to get a better look.

I hissed at the sight of my forearm. Profuse amounts of red liquid seeped out of a lovely hodge-podge of cuts. If I looked close enough, I swore that I would find tiny bits of glass still glinting within them.

I tore my gaze away and focused on sucking in air.

Orwell was gone. I didn't know where, but his stench lingered in the air—a stale, bitter musk. I tried to tell myself that he wasn't dangerous, but his words kept running through my mind: *you're still alive. They got to you.*

I quickly tore through my options; there were none, at least none that wouldn't cause more trouble than they were worth.

Except …

I mulled it over as I hauled myself upright and staggered to my wardrobe.

With one hand, I managed to wrap myself partially in a black sweater and pull on a skirt. Blood stained both garments within seconds, but I tried to ignore the vibrant color dotting my floor as I yanked my coat from a hanger and stumbled out into the hall.

The short descent down the staircase felt like an eternity. Every step seemed to take more concentration than usual. My trembling fingers struggled to grip the banister.

You're being ridiculous! I tried to tell myself, gritting my teeth in disgust. *It's just a scratch …*

A 'scratch' that burned like hell as I stumbled over the bottom step and made my way to the door. It was only when I stood on the threshold, hand gripping the doorknob that I realized there would be no mysterious black vehicle awaiting me. No Harper with the Rolls Royce.

Call a cab? I wondered. But I wouldn't even know where to begin. My knowledge of any sort of public transportation came only from television—though I doubted that many taxi drivers wouldn't be curious as to why their customer was oozing an alarming amount of blood.

I don't quite know when I got the idea in my head to turn down the opposite end of the hall and drift in the direction of the servant headquarters; those offices near the back where I rarely ventured.

This time of night, there was no one there. Nothing but shadows and silence greeted me as I pushed open the door to the lounge where I knew the staff spent their breaks— and where I knew Harper kept the keys to the family vehicles.

Plenty of admonishments ran through my mind as I ruffled through the drawers and scanned the surface of a desk. I hadn't driven in nearly ten years—not since Harper had first taught me in secret on the house grounds. According to Mother's philosophy, women like me didn't need to know how to operate a car when we paid people to do it for us.

If Mother could see me now, fishing a pair of silver keys from a hook on the wall, she'd probably drop dead again.

It took me ages to stumble to the garage. By then my arm had grown numb, and every part of me tingled with an icy chill I couldn't escape. My teeth chattered, fingers shaking so badly that the keys jingled like bells.

When I finally found the Rolls Royce, parked in a shadowy corner, I could barely fit the key in the door. Suddenly, the black machine with its tinted windows seemed about as imposing as a snarling beast waiting to swallow me whole. How did one even start a car anyway? Was there some sort of button?

Idiot! A disembodied voice hissed—only this time, it didn't belong to my mother. It was Dublin. *Fool, he snarled. A man breaks into your bedroom, mortally wounds you, and your main concern is if the gas pedal is on the left or the right?*

My eyes narrowed at the thought of that happening, and somehow I managed to wrench open the door and climb into the driver's seat.

I didn't stop to consider that I had no idea how to leave the property let alone navigate the city, or that I was staining priceless leather with my blood. Driven by determination, I was able to get the key into the ignition and jerkily maneuver the car to the garage entrance.

Ten minutes later I was creeping down a side road at a pace more befitting a snail, thankful that the roads were mostly empty this time of night. My trembling hands could barely grip the steering wheel, and I strained to see over it in search of a certain, imposing steeple.

Call it luck—or fate—but after a random turn, I glanced up to find the shadowy silhouette of the church of St. Jude the Apostle, and I figured that I was the only person in the world *relieved* to have found the gate to their own personal hell.

BLEED

The door opened before I could even knock. I supposed he'd heard me clamoring up the stairs anyway, far too dizzy to aim for stealth.

Or, perhaps he'd merely smelled the blood.

I reeked of it. Puddles of crimson formed a morbid trail behind me, staining the ancient stone floors with every step. The sound beat against my eardrums as Dublin pulled the door open wider, blond hair gleaming, eyes narrowed in suspicion.

"Eleanor—"

I staggered forward before he had the chance to utter any intimidating remarks: *Have you come basted and tenderized for the slaughter?*

Instead, I shoved my arm in his face, spraying drops of scarlet all over the front of his gray shirt. "I need …help."

Pain stabbed down my spine, intense and all-consuming. I barely saw his expression darken, nostrils flaring with the scent of my blood.

"What in the hell—"

"I fell."

I tried taking a shaky step over the threshold, and the next thing I knew, I was lying flat on a solid surface with Dublin hovering above. His mouth was moving—but only snatches of what he said actually registered.

"Blood … Listen to me, what happened?"

I didn't even have the chance to respond before he was tugging my jacket off by the collar.

It hit the floor with a damp plop as he threw it aside and went to work on my blouse, icy fingers undoing the buttons too quickly for me to follow. All the while, the pain grew into an unbearable ache.

Don't think on it, I told myself as my gaze drifted up to the unfamiliar ceiling. *Focus on something else instead.*

I guessed that we were in one of those strange bedrooms. The walls were dark, and the surface beneath me felt way too soft to have been the floor. I tried to pull myself upright— get a better look—only to be shoved right back down.

"Don't move."

I shivered as he yanked at the sleeve of my blouse next. A whine broke loose from my lips before I could help it. Dublin frowned, and tore the sleeve at the seams instead.

Once my arm was fully bare, he recoiled, eyes so bright they almost glowed. "Damn."

I glanced down to observe the damage and immediately wished I hadn't. *So much red ...*

The cuts were deeper than I'd realized. Dublin's alarmed hiss just reinforced the severity. I swore I even saw the grotesque collage of wounds pulsing in rhythm to my heartbeat.

"Did you run into a wall of knives?" he demanded.

"Broken glass." My voice sounded so high-pitched and breathy that I barely recognized it. "Will I need stitches?"

He didn't answer.

I felt so light-headed. It was a struggle just to focus on the pale planes of his face. I wanted to sleep instead—sink into darkness and forget the pain and the blood and the fact that his frigid chill felt more comforting than any ounce of warmth ever had.

"Don't," he warned before my eyes could even begin to drift shut. His jaw was clenched, eyes darker than steel. "Fall unconscious and you'll suffer for it."

Without another word, he slid his arm beneath my shoulders, hauling me upright, and settled on the mattress beside me. The pain made my mind roil, but he was there, edging closer before I could collapse again.

I should have resisted. *Shouldn't* have felt grateful. He was evil, and I was ...

So tired.

Idiot, a part of me scolded as my head came to rest on his shoulder. He was so cold it felt as though I were leaning on a wall of ice. A funny realization crossed my mind just then; I didn't think I'd ever been so close to him while fully clothed.

"You *are* going to tell me what happened," Dublin promised. The stern tone left no room for argument—but rather than demand any answers now, he seemed more intent on fishing something from his pocket.

I watched, intrigued, as he withdrew a familiar black object. My stomach twisted into knots as his thumb glided over the distinct shape of a golden dragon and a strip of metal slid from a narrow opening with a metallic hiss. Once freed, the gleaming blade taunted me.

"Have I not lost enough blood already?" I heard myself croak.

Rather than answer me, Dublin brought the knife closer ...and then surprised me completely by placing the blade against his own throat. His hand jerked. There was a sound like that of metal being dragged through skin. The next second, he took hold of my shoulders and pulled me into his chest. Before I could question, one of his hands latched onto the back of my skull and guided me into the curve of his neck.

"Drink," he grunted.

The feel of his throat was like ice, so cold it burned, and I instinctively withdrew. Or at least, I *tried* to, considering I felt too weak to even keep my eyes open.

"What are you—"

"Shut up." His fingers curled into my hair, forcing my mouth against the crook of his shoulder. Deliberately, he pressed until my protests were muffled against his skin. "Drink!"

All at once, my exhausted brain finally connected the dots, and I knew what he wanted.

Apparently, the situation was dire enough to skip the injected dose altogether. He wanted me to take his blood in the same way he took mine; straight from the vein.

What would mother say, I wondered, *were she here to see me, mouth at the base of a vampire's throat?* Though, to be fair, I figured she would have passed out the moment I'd successfully parked the car.

"Drink," Dublin growled when I hesitated. His grip was iron, leaving no room to escape. I cringed as a cool liquid pooled against my bottom lip. My stomach churned, expecting the taste of death and decay, but when I hesitantly sought out a single drop with my tongue, words couldn't begin to describe it ...

My mind tried. Mustering all the words in my meager vocabulary, I struggled to name the sensation flooding my senses: *Yummy. Rich. Decadent.*

There were no salty or metallic undertones. No sickeningly sweet aftertaste. Where I figured human blood was akin to wine, his was the purest Belgian chocolate. My tongue darted out greedily, seeking more—and with every swallow, the pain faded away, bit by bit, into nothing.

It was a thought that I would regret, but I couldn't deny it. Dublin tasted …good. Better than good, exquisite even. I wanted more.

More.

His grip loosened now that I wasn't fighting. In fact, my own hands, as weak as they were, clutched his shoulders and I struggled to get even closer, parting my mouth against his marble skin.

The man was decadent sin. I was drowning in him—and I *wanted* to drown. I wanted to utterly lose myself in all that was Dublin Helos and never be merely 'Ellie Gray' ever again. I inhaled, pulling the taste of him deep within myself like a dark secret I never wanted to forget.

But he didn't bleed like I did. His was merely a slow, stingy trickle. I felt like a straggler, dying of dehydration in a desert, forced to drink the sweetest, coolest water through a narrow straw. Instinctively, my teeth caught his flesh, bearing down to make the blood flow faster.

As if from light years away, I could feel his hands tighten. When my tongue raked over the cut, ruthlessly seeking more, he stiffened.

"Eleanor ..."

Something in his tone made me pull back, tilting my head back to see his face, even as my tongue slid along my lower lip to capture every bead of scarlet.

"Am I hurting you?" I slurred like a drunken fool.

I didn't know why it mattered if I was, why the thought of causing him pain had me frowning even as a longing for *more* of him swept through my belly in a greedy wave. God, I wanted to swallow him whole.

"No ..." His jaw clenched, and his eyes flashed molten silver. I couldn't name the expression on his face—but whatever it was terrified me worse than his usual scowls. "You need more."

He didn't have to force me this time. I was back at his throat in an instant—unease forgotten—prodding the wound without an ounce of remorse. I wasn't aware of the blood on my skin—or my own body for that matter. The loss of fear made me feel as light as air, weightless. Then, I was drifting, losing myself in the sensation of him.

And nothing had felt more right than giving in.

"Give me some sign that you're alive."

The cold voice cut into my dreamless sleep like a knife. I groaned and rolled over in a futile attempt to escape it. However, the reaction seemed to placate my rude awakener.

"About damn time."

My eyes flew open. The owner of the voice needed no introduction. Like a gleaming angel of death, Dublin stood at the foot of what I assumed to be a massive bed. I was lying in the center of it, tucked beneath a crisp, white sheet—but I was naked underneath. And that wasn't all ...

I felt different; renewed, refreshed. It was as if someone had taken me apart, piece by piece, then sewn me back together with all new parts.

"What did you do to me?" I demanded, voice rough with sleep. Though, in all honesty, I wasn't exactly complaining. I had never felt so good—not even after one of his 'cures.' "I feel ..."

"Eat."

I blinked to find a breakfast tray unceremoniously dropped onto the mattress beside me. Without waiting for me to haul myself upright, Dublin snatched a piece of toast from it and promptly broke it in half.

"Eat," he commanded, shoving the slice underneath my nose.

I started to reach for it, but his impatient hiss gave me no choice but to take a bite right from his hand. My stomach fluttered, churning as I swallowed. His eyes bore into mine —though, he held my gaze for merely a second before turning his full attention to my shoulder.

"You've healed," he grunted, eyes raking down my skin. "Finally."

I glanced down as well. From the hazy memories of last night, I didn't know what to expect—but the flesh of my shoulder was pale and unblemished. The images in my mind could have just been one dizzying nightmare …

If it weren't for the dark, crimson blotches still staining the white sheets.

Slowly, I sat up, clutching the top sheet to my chest. I recognized the same, dark, windowless room I'd woken up in the day after he had fed from me. A single light fixture on the wall illuminated the sparse furniture as well as Dublin, standing beside the bed.

"Stand," he ordered with all the tact of a drill sergeant.

With a sigh, I bundled the thin sheet closer to my body and shuffled to the edge of the bed.

"Is this necessary?" I demanded, though, surprisingly, I felt no weakness as I braced both feet on the floor and stood. It was strange.

My muscles hummed, throbbed. I felt this desperate urge to move—run, which was strange, considering that my usual daily exercise consisted of climbing up and down the stairs.

Dublin watched me, eyes catching every flicker of motion I made. "How do you feel?"

"Fine." If I didn't know any better, I might have suspected that he cared. Bitterly I added, "Your investment is still intact."

He flinched—so imperceptibly that I nearly missed it—but a second later his expression was blank. Like ice, those eyes held me captive, and every part of me stiffened in anticipation beneath my bed sheet.

"What happened?" His voice was too controlled, too robotic. Something told me that he knew damn well what had taken place. He simply wanted to hear me say it.

"Do not lie to me."

"N-Nothing," I stammered, picturing Orwell. While insane, he was still my uncle—and obviously, something had upset him. *Correction,* I remembered on a shiver, seeing me with *Dublin* had upset him.

"Nothing?" the vampire in question echoed. The soft, dangerous tone had my heart galloping loudly in my chest. "Funny. Your bedroom was in shambles."

He made it sound so harmless; *the sun was shining.* But I wasn't fooled.

"I f-fell," I countered, shocked that he had gone to Gray Manor when I damn well shouldn't have been. "I tripped into my mirror—"

"And rifled through your drawers while you were at it?"

Damn. I had forgotten the mess Orwell had made of my bedroom. A million excuses raced through my mind, and I blurted one at random. "I was looking for something."

"What?"

"A ... Um ... I—"

"Was this before or *after* you picked the locks to your own home?"

"You ... Why should it matter what happened?" I settled on indignantly.

"Why should it matter?" I had no chance to react before he snagged both of my wrists in one grip and yanked them down to my belly. The motion tore the bed sheet from my grip. It fluttered to the ground, leaving me naked.

Sheer, fragile pride was the only thing that kept me from shying away from his sight. Instead, I held his gaze, even as I felt every inch of my skin flush crimson. The seconds passed like hours, and all the while Dublin watched me with an expression that I couldn't name.

"I'll tell you why it should 'matter,' Eleanor," he said finally. "You are *mine*." He took a step closer, invading my personal space without care. His hands tightened over my wrists like cuffs. "My property." Icy breath ghosted my shoulder, and I could feel every muscle in my body tense as his gaze swept along the slope of my throat the same way it had Haswell's land. "*My* investment."

"I don't belong to anyone," I countered.

"Oh?" His shoulder jerked, fingers clenching. He didn't touch me anymore to restrain my wrists—but for some reason, I felt as alarmed as if he'd just branded his name on my skin. "Guess again, Eleanor; how soon you forget your own bargain."

My shoulder burned in the same spot where I knew his cuts had been—his mark. *You are mine ...*

"Anyone who touches you, touches me," he went on in a tone of steel. "Anyone who harms *you,* harms *me.* Now, Eleanor, do I really have to drag the truth from you?"

"It was nothing." I crossed my arms to hide the way my body shuddered. "Just ..."

With a sigh, I admitted my 'sick' uncle's sudden reappearance.

"He's harmless," I added in a rush as his eyes narrowed into slits. "He just saw some silly tabloid and over-reacted. He was looking for my sister. I haven't even seen him in years. His name is—"

"Orwell."

I was shocked more by his harsh tone than the fact that he knew my uncle's name at all. "D-do you know him?"

His eyes narrowed even more, recovering some of their detached coldness, but I could sense that his veneer had slipped—if only for a second, I had caught him off guard.

"Despite your rather non-existent relationship with the media, Eleanor, your family is well known. You only have one uncle."

The explanation was plausible—but some part of me wasn't buying it. I couldn't forget the way he had said his name; *Orwell*, full of recognition. For a rare, brief moment I had glimpsed a real emotion on that face besides anger; hate.

"What did he say to you?" He sounded nonchalant, but the look in his eye was anything but.

"He just …asked for my sister."

"And that's all?"

"Yes. I know that he's not 'well,' but I don't think he's dangerous."

Abruptly, Dublin turned his back to me. "Eat." He gestured at the tray on the bed.

It was only then that I remembered I was naked.

With a gulp, I stooped for the bed sheet and draped it over my body like a cloak, holding it closed tightly over my front. Then I sat on the edge of the mattress and blindly lifted a fork from the tray. It was stacked with eggs and two crisp pieces of bacon.

I couldn't remember whether or not I had seen a kitchen somewhere within the maze of rooms—but the fact that he had bothered to get me something to eat at all left my head spinning.

As if aware of my thoughts, Dublin's shoulders tensed and I hastily stabbed at a piece of fried egg.

"What now?" I asked before popping the morsel onto my tongue.

He glanced over his shoulder, and there was a frosty gleam in his gaze that I didn't like.

"Now? Well, I suppose *now* we discuss the terms of repayment."

I choked, sputtering yellow egg across the satiny—and no doubt very expensive—bed sheets.

"R-Repayment?"

He raised a single eyebrow. "Yes. Repayment. My blood doesn't come cheaply."

I frowned, an argument poised on my lips. *Well, it wasn't exactly like I asked to drink it ...*

Directly from the vein, I might've added. At the memory, my heart quickened. Tiny, erratic sparks burst to life beneath my skin as I remembered the taste of him...so damn heady that I could feel my mouth water.

"You took triple your usual dose," Dublin added. "You've been out for two days—it's a miracle that you woke up at all."

Days? Horror washed over me for one completely vain reason. In the hospital, my stint of unconsciousness had been monitored by medical professionals honor-bound to preserve my dignity by taking care of any uncontrolled … bodily functions.

Dublin Helos offered me no such guarantee. But I felt clean, and there were no unsavory smells wafting from the bed sheets.

"Why did you keep me here?" I asked while surveying the room, rather than voice the dangerous question that my decent state presented. "You could have taken me home."

"I could have."

Warily, I kicked my feet against the floor, staring down at my bare toes. "Why do you live here, anyway?"

The question came out of nowhere, slipping out before common sense could reel it back.

"I mean—"

"Why *wouldn't* I live here?" he countered in a voice so low it could have been whispered inside my mind rather than out loud. "Would you prefer a cave? A castle?"

"No," I said, thinking of Raphael's imposing manor —*that* dwelling was close enough to the Dracula legends, thank you very much. In comparison, the Cathedral was almost a relief. Despite the ancient walls and stone façade, there was a sense of quiet serenity about the place.

And Dublin, with those haunting, chilling eyes, just didn't …fit.

"Were you a Christian in your past life?" I blurted. Perhaps all that blood loss had made me an even bigger idiot than I already was?

At least he hadn't ordered me to shut up or made an otherwise threatening reaction—yet.

"In my past life?" he murmured, reaching up to scratch his chin. "What makes you think that I'm not pious *now*? For all you know …I could all but *live* inside of a church."

The lack of a smile tempered the joke—but the echo of it was still there, lingering in the air between us.

"Is that a yes then?" I couldn't understand why I was so curious. Something in me seized the chance at sneaking even a glimmer of information about him—even if it was potentially damaging to my health.

"Would you dare to mistake *me* for a Holy man?" Two fangs glinted beneath the roof of his mouth as he spoke. "I'm genuinely curious."

An involuntary gulp contracted my throat.

"Well," I croaked, "you do seem to love wearing the color black."

Today was no exception. He wore another ebony shirt, collar crisp, paired with a dark pair of pants—but even clothed in the color of shadow, the man still glowed.

"Ah …but do I inspire hope in you, Eleanor? Serenity? Piety?" Suddenly, he was much closer than before, leaning down so that his breath caressed my neck in a swipe that raised goosebumps. "Do I possess a priestly aura that makes you want to confess your secrets, lest you be damned?"

I couldn't ignore the genuine note of curiosity in his tone— as if I, Eleanor the bumbling Gray, actually had secrets *worth* sharing; secrets that someone like Dublin Helos would actually be curious enough to learn.

I scoffed. "Sorry, Father, but I have not sinned."

In fact, my life had been so boring that no God in existence would bother 'damning' me to anything. At least …until I'd sold my soul.

"Fair enough." Dublin pulled back, returning to his full height. Silently, he observed me for almost a full minute— long enough to spark a nervous bead of sweat that dribbled down behind my ear. "But I don't believe that's entirely true. Even *you* must have done something to put a single strike against your name in the Book of Reckoning. What was it?" He tilted his head. "Have you stolen a cookie? Worn your skirt two inches shorter than school regulations?"

I shook my head. "Nothing. At least not until …"

"What?"

"Until I met you."

God, I could feel my ears prickling with shame. How many twenty-six-year-old women could truthfully admit that they had done nothing relatively 'naughty,' in the majority of their lives?

No sneaking from windows to meet unacceptable boyfriends.

No stolen kisses under the moonlight.

No sips of alcohol snuck from the liquor cabinet.

My life may well have been one blank page, whose only redeeming quality was the glaring coffee stain that was Dublin Helos. I flinched at the thought and wrapped my sheet tighter around myself.

"I corrupted you," he announced, but he almost sounded confused—as if this were an *'Ah-ha!'* moment and he had just now realized how pathetic I was without the threat of his cure hanging over my head.

"In a sense," I choked out. "How pleased you must be. What am I, the *millionth* soul you've corrupted?"

If I had expected any sense of guilt in response, I was sorely mistaken.

"Pleased? I'm disappointed," he said with a shake of his head. "You call this—" He gestured toward my body with a disapproving wave of his hand. "Corruption? Dear God, Eleanor …I haven't even *begun*."

Before I could react—before I could even begin to process his words—he was in front of me, eyes boring deep into my own, piercing parts of me I had never known existed until that very moment.

"I have decided how you may repay your newest debt," he began in a guttural tone that made my breath stop. "But, let's make this interesting …as well as give you the chance to earn your *true* corruption."

I waited a heartbeat and then cautiously voiced a single word. "What?"

"A bet, Eleanor," he said. "I'll make you an offer you cannot refuse."

"And what is that?"

Horror! A part of me that sounded suspiciously like my mother shrieked. *Something bad! Improper! Indecent! Run away!*

Dublin only smiled, revealing two fully elongated fangs, before turning to the door. "A taste of control, Eleanor," he murmured, "a mere taste of control …"

CONTROL

*D*ublin's last words—a *mere taste of control*—were still ringing in my ears by the time he finally returned. "For now, the sheet will do," he said from the doorway. "Come."

Reluctantly, I crept after him, wrapped tight in my sheet and increasingly aware of just how little space separated us.

Only a few lamps were lit throughout the rest of his lair, casting small pools of orange light. As we passed the entryway, a glance out of the windows revealed that the sky was still an inky shade of black.

It could have been late at night or just very early in the morning. Dublin turned down another hallway before I had the chance to ask. When he eventually came to a stop before an open doorway, I peeked inside and felt my heart sink to my toes.

"What … What is this?"

The room was large with marble floors and gleaming fixtures: a bathroom. I vaguely recognized it as the same one where Yulia had helped me dress for the masquerade ball. But now—with words like 'control' and 'corruption' floating around—the huge, claw-foot bathtub seemed to take on a more sinister purpose.

I shivered at a sudden image of Dublin using it as a giant goblet while he 'exacted' as much blood from me as I had taken from him as 'payment.'

"Don't be so dramatic," he scoffed as if reading my mind. "You are covered in blood. Stale, *dried* blood …"

Oh. From the way he sniffed, I figured the smell was about as appealing to him as rotting food was to me.

Obediently, I shuffled forward toward the sink and caught sight of my reflection in the mirror. Sure enough, streaks of scarlet painted my cheeks. My hands …

On top of it all, was a strange taste in my mouth that I hadn't noticed until then: *salty, metallic, rich.*

Trembling, I turned the faucet on full blast and viciously scrubbed at my hands. A burst of cold air tickled my flesh, and I turned to find Dublin standing at my shoulder, as silent as a shadow. In one hand he held a white cloth, which he quietly damped beneath the faucet.

Our gazes met in the mirror for a second—long enough to send a chill lancing through my body. Then, without asking for an invitation, he dragged the damp cloth along what little of my throat wasn't shrouded by my blanket. Nerves prickled to life as cool water sank through the sheet, gluing it to my skin. When he tried to move lower, my traitorous body reacted, tightening …heating …

"Let go," he said, eyes on the way my fingers clutched at the sheet.

When I didn't budge, he snagged a corner and tugged—but I held even tighter. I knew that resisting him was like giving a dog a bone, but I couldn't fight the instinctive urge that had me digging my nails in regardless. This was different. This time, there was no bed or chains or threat of fangs. Just silence and running water and his hands separated from my body by a thin sheet of cloth.

"Let go, *Eleanor*."

Something in his tone made my fingers finally loosen their grip. Silently, the sheet drifted down to the floor, and the wet cloth continued to travel unhindered, guided by ice-cold fingers …down around my shoulders, my arms. When finished, he stood back without granting me permission to cover myself, and I could practically feel those silver eyes raking over my body from head to toe.

The scrutiny was even more unbearable than physical touch. Seconds passed. The water was still running, and the sound of my racing heartbeat had grown into a deafening hum.

Then …

"You can leave."

"What?" I turned to face him, too shocked to care that my thin little covering was still pooled at my feet.

"I'll even have my car brought around so that you don't have to risk killing yourself behind the wheel of that Rolls Royce," he added. "Something tells me that driving lessons weren't a main priority at that boarding school of yours."

I shrugged, too ashamed to even take offense. It was a wonder I hadn't killed myself by crashing into a telephone pole.

"At least I got here in one piece—"

"You parked in a fire zone," he countered.

"Well, it was an emergency after all." I smirked, oddly proud of my joke, but rather than respond with more cutting banter, Dublin's expression hardened.

"Do you ever think through the consequences of your actions?"

I flinched at his tone. It was lethally soft, dangerous. "I …"

"Or better yet," he continued, cutting over me, "do you have any idea that coming to me was the *worst* mistake that you could have made?"

The cold, menacing edge to his voice made me shudder. He wasn't joking or teasing or trying to scare me just for the hell of it.

He was serious.

"Why?"

"There are rules," he said tightly, nothing else.

"Should I have gone to the hospital?" I managed to choke out.

Some dark emotion raced through those silver eyes, disappearing before I could name it.

"No." Without elaborating on why, he crossed over to me and picked up my sheet from the floor. I stood still as he draped the fabric over my shoulders, drawing it closed over my front. Then he turned and headed for the doorway, once again leaving me to catch up.

This time, he simply headed into the next room; a plain one adorned with only a black leather chaise and a large, imposing window that overlooked the back of the church. The moon hovered in the sky, lonely and pale.

"Sit," Dublin told me as he moved to stand before the window.

As still as a statue, he stared out into the night. When he turned back to face me, he looked the same—but something wasn't right.

For the first time, I noticed the little nuances in his posture that I had missed before. How his shoulders were set in a firm, stony line, the way his jaw had been clenched, the faint, ominous tilt to his mouth. All of it added up to one startling conclusion; he was *angry*—perhaps angrier than I had ever seen him.

Only I had no idea *why.*

"There is a reason why I've never had you drink from the vein," he began, "did you assume that the injections were merely out of convenience?"

To be honest, I had never questioned it. Only *now* did I realize that, up until two nights ago, I had never actually tasted his blood. Never before had I noticed the liquid in those vials.

"Why not?" I rasped, though I wasn't sure if I really wanted to know the answer.

"The substance running through your veins merely sustains life. My blood *is* life." As he spoke, his eyes bore into my own, daring me to look away, flinch. "Plenty of mortals would kill for the chance to consume even a drop."

"So I keep hearing …"

"So you keep hearing," Dublin repeated. In the blink of an eye, he was closer. I had to crane my neck just to maintain eye contact. "And yet, you *still* don't seem to understand. If you had any idea of what I've given you—"

He broke off, but I got the sense that I had witnessed another tiny crack in his façade; he had said too much.

"How long do you think that we've been doing this, Eleanor?" he asked, abruptly changing the topic. "My kind, dolling out blood to humans desperate to stay alive for even a *second* longer?"

I swallowed. Not for the first time I wondered just how many contracts he really owned. Hundreds? Thousands?

"I don't know—"

"Take a guess."

"A hundred years?" It sounded like a decent amount of time to me, but Dublin merely laughed.

"Longer than your country has existed," he declared, fangs flashing. "Longer, even, than your ancestors have lived on this land. Try again."

"Three hundred—"

"Five hundred. I've been gathering contracts for nearly *five hundred* years," he said in a flat, empty tone. "I couldn't tell you how many souls pledged their lives away for a single drop of the substance that you, yourself, seemed to so thoroughly enjoy."

I hated myself for the fact that my mouth watered at the mere mention of his blood. The taste of him was like some hazy fantasy too fantastical to have been real. Before I could help it, a single thought raced through my mind. *I want more …*

"This country was built on the blood of my kind," he added, snapping me from the longing. "Don't tell me that you *really* believed an army of farmers and aristocrats alone could have beaten what once was the most powerful empire in the world?"

"I don't remember the history books mentioning anything about George Washington consuming vampire blood in between battles," I replied, but my mind was reeling. *Colonial vampires? Ancient contracts?*

"They *wouldn't,* would they?" He took a step closer, and I could feel his chill in my bones. "Old George wouldn't want anyone to know the real price for his '*independence.*' Though, he wasn't one of *my* contracts specifically." He sounded so casual. It was as if we were merely discussing what he'd eaten for lunch rather than the fate of one of the most important men in American history. "He was given the same choice that you were—that every unfortunate soul to cross our path is given."

"B-But he died," I said. "If your cure is so wonderful, why didn't it last?"

Dublin didn't speak for the longest time. It felt as though the temperature in the room had descended into negative temperatures by the time he finally gave me an answer.

"Because mortals have the luxury of changing their minds …" He spoke so softly that I barely heard him. "When he realized the true price of immortality, even someone as grandiose as George Washington understood that more time wasn't worth the stain on your soul."

I remembered reading something about his death years ago in school. "He died after catching a cold."

But, no …

On second thought there was more to it. In a trembling whisper, I forced myself to say it. "He died from being bled by his physicians." Considering that a vampire stood before me, that morbid little fact seemed too chilling to be mere coincidence. "But bloodletting was a common practice of the time," I stammered, trying to rationalize it regardless. "Normal."

"Oh?" Dublin merely raised an eyebrow. "Old George stopped drinking the blood—but even that alone does not negate its effects entirely. So he tried to drain the 'tainted' blood from his body. The preceding illness was merely an invented detail to pacify historians. Really, Eleanor. How common do you think it was to live to the age of sixty-seven in the eighteenth century?"

George Washington had consumed vampire blood. A part of me wanted to accuse him of lying, but …

I couldn't help but wonder, with a frown, just how many of our admired historical figures might have tried to cheat death by signing a contract. Even more chilling; what exactly had they done in order to fulfill them?

"What was George Washington's price?"

I expected for Dublin to cross his arms and refuse to tell me, citing some mysterious vampire code. In fact, a part of me almost *wished* that he would.

Instead, he surprised me with a direct answer.

"For him, merely to continue forging ahead with his rebellion."

"Why?"

He shrugged. "The old world with its entrenched religion and filth had grown …unappealing. We wished for somewhere new to roam."

Apparently, when vampires got bored, they decided to form new countries. Good to know.

"Why did he change his mind?" I found myself asking, incredulously. "You gave him everything. He was the father of an entire nation. What made him—"

"The price," Dublin snapped. "You mortals, so compliant in your history, never thinking through the lasting implications of the decisions you make until it's too late. Use that brain of yours, Eleanor. Why would a *vampire* take an interest in a new country? An untamed land teeming with virtually ungoverned mortals ripe for …"

All at once, the answer hit me like a physical blow. "Feeding." Just saying the word out loud made me sick— but I knew even before I saw Dublin's grim expression that it was the truth. Without even trying, I had hit the nail right on its proverbial head. "George Washington allowed you to feed on colonists."

He nodded again.

"But wouldn't people …notice?" I could barely get the words out. This was a version of history not mentioned in any history book I could recall.

"There is a reason that slavery was implemented into the foundation of this country," Dublin said, arousing all kinds of dark suspicions that I could never bring myself to consider on my own. "The founding fathers believed that it would serve as an enticing buffer to protect the 'higher' members of society."

Suddenly not even my flimsy sheet seemed like a good enough buffer against the cold, hard truth, though I wrapped it tighter around myself regardless.

"Eventually Washington decided that he couldn't live with his choice," Dublin added.

I wasn't sure if I could either. I wished more than anything that the smiling figure on the dollar bill could have remained as such. Some things just weren't worth knowing.

"That's a rather grim outlook," I croaked. "I guess I should be relieved that all you seemed to have wanted from *me* was the use of my name—"

"No." That simple word shattered everything like a piano note played out of tune. "Things have changed, Eleanor. Should I tell you what it is that I desire from you *now*?"

My breath caught on that dangerous word. Desire.

"N-Nothing?"

"Perhaps 'desire' isn't the right word," he continued as if I'd never spoken. "Crave. Should I tell you what it is that I *crave* from you, Eleanor Gray?"

Suddenly he was in front of me. Icy fingers brushed my shoulder before skimming the cropped length of my hair, where he seized a curl and twisted around his thumb.

"Fear," he said simply before I had the chance to respond. "I want to know what terrifies you, and *when* I win our wager, you will tell me."

"W-Wager?"

"Do try to keep up, Eleanor," he scolded with a sharp, firm tug on my hair. "You owe me. Remember?"

"But it's obvious." I gulped. "*You* terrify me."

"No." His voice was flat, annoyed. "No, I do not. You may tell yourself that, but deep down … I merely amuse you." His words echoed in my ears, even as he let me go and turned away.

He amused *me?* It was the same accusation he had made that night at the ball. A part of me flinched from the memory, and I grasped for a change of subject.

"What do you mean by wager?" I wasn't sure that I truly wanted to know the answer; a sinister voice inside my head was whispering tons of possible suggestions.

"What do you think?" Deliberately—as if making sure that I couldn't help but notice—he reached into his pocket and withdrew something slender and black, like string.

Whatever it was, it hung down almost to the floor. A solid minute passed before I realized what it was; a length of black ribbon, only in his hand it might as well have been a metal chain.

"You claimed to be corrupted, but do you even know what true corruption is?" He wound the ribbon slowly between his fingers. "It's total submission. No questions. No resistance. You relinquish *everything* in exchange for nothing more than …an escape."

"But I've already given you everything—"

"No, you *haven't*." Every word was as cold and hard as his expression. "Not everything."

I didn't know what was more confusing, the thought that I hadn't already given him my body, blood, and soul? Or that he still wanted *more*?

"What else is there?"

"It is simple." His breath ghosted my shoulder. I hadn't even seen him move, but now he stood behind me. The moon taunted me through the window glass as his glacial chill ran down my spine.

He reached over my shoulder, and I could only stare as he threaded a ribbon over the delicate bones of my wrist, as innocently as a makeshift bracelet.

Or a shackle.

"Control, Eleanor," he said finally, lips brushing my earlobe. "I want you …to lose control."

My mind was spinning. Every molecule of air in my chest congealed as I watched ebony silk rasp over my skin. Once. Twice. Again.

"Deny me nothing."

He seized my other hand and looped a length of ribbon around it. Then he pulled, ensnaring both wrists together as effectively as those handcuffs had all those days ago.

"Give in to me."

The spare length of ribbon had pooled in my lap. Slowly, another hand reached down to trap it between a pale thumb and forefinger. He yanked and suddenly the ribbon was torn in two, with the second half dangling between his fingertips.

"Surrender yourself completely; all of you …"

He released my bound hands, and held the second ribbon taut before my eyes—perhaps so that I could guess what he was going to do next. I could only stare, oddly entranced as, in the space of a heartbeat, my eyes were covered, icy fingers brushing my ears as he tied the ends tight.

"Then," he breathed, "you will have given me everything."

And just like that, I was at his mercy.

"Can you hear me, Eleanor?"

I nodded.

I could hear him all right though I almost preferred to have heard my mother instead. *Eleanor Gray, you get out of there this instant! He's dangerous.*

But the only sound above the frantic hammering of my pulse was *his voice.*

Nothing else.

"Good."

I jumped as a tendril of ice brushed the nape of my neck. *His thumb?*

He traced the line of my shoulder before drifting down to graze my spine with a frigid nail.

"Stand up."

I lurched obediently to my feet. It was disorienting trying to maintain my balance while blind and bound. I swayed, fearful that I might trip over my own two feet.

"Why did you cover my eyes?"

Bad Ellie! I knew that I was breaking his little rules by not playing along. To my shock, he sounded eerily calm when he spoke again.

"Maybe I simply *like* seeing you this way."

Hogtied and helpless? Strangely, I wouldn't have been surprised if that were the case.

"Why?"

"I think I should have covered your *mouth* as well as your eyes." His tone was still level, but a stern warning laced every word. *Do not question, Eleanor. Just obey. Be a good damsel now and allow me to play my devious little mind games unchallenged.*

"Do you think that darkness scares me?"

"Does it?" He sounded even closer. I could imagine him standing over my shoulder, relishing my unease.

"I thought we already established that *you* scare me," I managed to croak.

A burst of cool air was my only warning before two cold hands caught my waist, yanking me backward. Gone was the detached, clinical care he'd used to clean me up. This was different.

His nails grazed my flesh, scraped.

"Do I really?"

"Yes ..."

"Then you, Eleanor Gray, have never been truly afraid. *True* terror," he added, cold breath fanning against my shoulder, "is nothing like the games we play."

My heart sputtered as he let me go. There was a horrible second of anticipation before I finally felt his fingers encircle my throat, leaving just enough space to allow me to breathe.

"Your heart is racing," he acknowledged. "But is your pulse surging so violently that you can almost taste your own blood, right *there* on the tip of your tongue?"

I wanted to run, just shove away from him, turn on my heel and bolt from the room. I could have. My hands were bound, but not so tightly that one good yank wouldn't be enough to break free. In fact …

I had a sinking suspicion that was exactly what he wanted me to do.

"I'm not hearing an answer, Eleanor," he taunted when I didn't respond.

"If being asked a million questions is what it means to be corrupted then I'd rather not, thank you."

I'd barely finished before he leaned closer. The only warning was a creeping, icy sensation over my flesh—but I could almost hear the slide of his fangs descending from beneath his upper lip, ready to pierce, to tear.

"Corruption is *pain,*" he explained while cresting my hip with the tip of a nail. "It's relishing in it, savoring the violence. It is feeling your own defenses shatter and knowing that you are helpless against the onslaught. Even worse, while deep down you know that you should run from the pain, fear it even, instead …you crave it."

I could only tremble, hands held out awkwardly as heavy footsteps circled where I stood. My teeth chattered—but why did I feel a suffocating wave of heat that only intensified the lower his finger drifted? After tracing a path down to my navel, he pulled away.

"Shall I continue your education on corruption and fear? Let's start with a simple question to gauge how well you've been paying attention: Why do you seem to throw yourself into danger at every single turn?"

I frowned. "I don't—"

"Careful now, Eleanor ..."

The pad of his finger slowly crept back up my torso, skirting the globe of one breast, before tracing the curve of my rib cage. I hated myself for the heat that flared to life despite his glacial chill—only his tone kept me from just giving in to the urge to arch into his hand and damn shame to hell.

"Do not lie," he warned. "Even when mortally wounded, you came to me. *Me.*" He made it sound synonymous with *'gouged out your own eyes.'* "Why?"

"There ... There was no one else."

"You could have gone anywhere," he countered.

I supposed I could have. Just like I *could* have stood on a street corner and loudly proclaimed the fact that I was dying and consorted with vampires.

"You and your silly rules made it so that I could only come to you," I explained once I found my voice again. "After all, do you know anyone else with magic blood?"

"Is that the *only* reason you came to me?" His tone had me frowning before I could help it. Gone was the mocking bravado of the Devil I knew.

Left behind was a cold, eerie curiosity that made me shiver.

I had a horrible suspicion that George Washington's secrets wouldn't be the only thing exposed tonight. A storm was brewing, and I felt trapped in the midst of the oncoming destruction.

"Why else would I come to you?" I wondered, just as confused as he seemed to be.

He didn't answer. I could sense him there, lurking just beyond reach as if waiting for me to put the pieces of some puzzle together on my own.

Tick, tock Ellie. Time's running out.

"It's not as if I come over regularly for titillating conversation," I added, only the words fell flat.

These past few days I had spent more time with him than I had anyone else. Two weeks of near constant contact surpassed the scattered handfuls of time I'd spent with my parents over a lifetime.

How utterly pathetic did that make me?

"I don't …enjoy being around you," I insisted stubbornly, mainly for my own benefit.

What sane woman would go out of her way to spend time with a man who brutalized and teased her and had an unhealthy propensity for drinking her blood?

But when have you ever been 'sane,' Eleanor Gray? A part of me whispered.

"I don't ..."

"I gave you every chance to walk away." His tone was scathing. "And yet here you are, ready for more. I think a change of course in this discussion is in order. I know. Let's start with Saskia."

My entire body stiffened at the mention of her as I wondered if she had told him of our little wager.

"Tell me, Eleanor, what do you think is the reason behind her contract?"

I blinked. "I don't. I ..."

"What do you think a woman such as Saskia would desire? Eternal youth or beauty? Power?" His tone had changed. No longer was it teasing, but as sharp as a freshly honed blade. Cutting. "Come now, Eleanor. I'm sure you've had your suspicions."

"I don't know."

Saskia might have been cruel, but I doubted that even she would have sold her soul for such superficial reasons. As if to echo that suspicion, her words chose that minute to creep beneath my skin. *'Nothing is sacred to them. There is no part of your life they wouldn't hesitate to destroy if only to meet their end goal. You would do best to remember that. To him, you are a pawn, nothing more.'*

"Love," Dublin said suddenly. "There is no limit to what a person would do for *love*. Would you like to hear the tale of how I used her emotions against her, Eleanor?"

His tone took on a sadistic edge that churned my stomach, and I imagined that his eyes were a cold, distant shade of silver. I felt like a child on the playground, having a bully stick a worm in her face, just to hear her scream.

"No," I croaked.

He forged ahead as if I'd never spoken. "Being a succubus, Saskia would have proven an invaluable asset. They are rare to come by, you know…Raphael suspected that her *'talents'* would be useful to us, and I was sent to secure her services with little more fanfare than when we obtained George Washington's soul—but she was different back then, Saskia. She claimed to be a good, 'God-fearing' woman despite selling her body for money on the filth-ridden streets of London. She knew of my kind, but she didn't want to forsake her soul …not for any price. Unfortunately for her, I am not one to take 'no' for an answer."

His tone dripped derision and scorn, but it was almost too much; an actor playing the role of the villain in an over-the-top play.

"You have declared me to be a monster on several occasions, and yet here you are, at my mercy. To you, I must seem no more menacing than someone like Mikhail, but if you only knew the real monster that dwells deep within ...What Mikhail does with his toys now is *nothing* compared to what I oversaw when I controlled the Den. Saskia would know better than most just what I am capable of ..."

I didn't want to hear any more. The picture he painted was of a man recklessly desperate to tell the world *I am the Devil bound for hell, hear me roar,* just like that unscrambled message in his name proclaimed.

I wanted to beg him to stop now—surrender for once—but I couldn't deny the part of me that needed to know.

"W-What did you do?"

He allowed the question to linger for merely a second.

"I made her an offer she couldn't refuse. I knew a man who, with the prompting of a few coins, sought her out under the guise of purchasing her usual 'wares.' Unbeknownst to her, he also possessed an illness which, at that time, was all but a death sentence."

My heart sped up with every word. I had a horrible, sinking suspicion that whatever he was about to say was something that I would never be able to erase from my mind.

"This man went to Saskia, but she turned him away. However, he decided to slake his lust with someone else—it was a whore house after all. How was he supposed to have known they wouldn't all be willing ..."

He trailed off, and somehow the chilling anticipation of where this tale would lead was even worse than the story itself.

"What happened?" I rasped. Every bone in my body was tense with dread. I couldn't escape the mental image of a pre-contract Saskia, desperately trying to keep her soul from the Devil's clutches.

Dublin seemed to hesitate, and for the first time his words came slowly, labored, reluctant. I could almost picture him wincing with every uttered syllable.

"Saskia had a child that she kept hidden away in her chambers ... The girl was fifteen."

Horror washed over me like a bucket of ice water being dumped over my head. I couldn't breathe. Think. He couldn't be implying that ...

"In the end, I still received my contract, and that is all that mattered to me, Eleanor. It's all that *still* matters—"

"You're lying."

I had no idea where the protest came from, but my heart was pounding with a sense of disgust I had never felt.

"Oh really?" Dublin countered. "Do tell; did I forget to include enough details to frighten even you? I'm sure she screamed—"

"Stop it!"

I felt sick to my stomach, but I couldn't decide if it was his actual words that sparked such a reaction or just the way he said them; cold, callous. As if that girl, or me or *nothing* mattered, but once again, he seemed too careless, *too* harsh.

"This is who I am, Eleanor," he insisted with all the intensity of a lion's roar. "I am the Devil, remember?"

"The Devil doesn't brag," I retorted. "He doesn't feel the need to run around stating 'I am the Devil' over and over again. Who are you trying to convince?" I wondered. "Me? Or yourself …"

Even my slap didn't earn the same reaction from him. The world went dead silent. With my vision obscured by the ribbon, it was almost too easy to imagine for a moment that I was dead: Dublin Helos had killed me quicker than it took for me to blink.

Then …

"I wouldn't have to repeat it," he began in a voice quieter than a whisper, "If only you would *see* it."

"What do you mean?"

I could sense him standing in front of me now, mere feet away.

"I walk into a room of vampires, and it doesn't take much to have even their cold, undead hearts pumping with fear. A glance. A word. Such is the power of a fearsome reputation, Eleanor." I briefly recalled the reactions of the vampires at that ball, and had no doubt he wasn't exaggerating. "But you … I look at you the same way, and I can almost sense you yawning, un-amused, unimpressed." He made it sound worse than an insult, worse than fear. "I can chain you, bite you, slice into your skin and yet you only come back for more."

"Well, aren't you the one who claimed that I *like* pain?"

The accusation was out before I could help it, and I wanted so badly to take it back. Fighting with him was like sticking my finger in an electrical socket just for kicks—I'd always wind up burned.

"I did." His tone warned me to shut up. Be a good little captive and cower—better yet, run away—but I couldn't. All of a sudden, I had an irrational urge to knock him off balance as badly as he seemed determined to unnerve me.

"Perhaps *you're* the one who likes being in pain?" I spat in his general direction. "Or maybe just feeling irritated? Why else would you keep me around?"

"Yes," he agreed. "Why else?"

The breath caught in my chest. If a voice alone could kill …

I would have been six feet under, in the family crypt, by now. Every instinct in my body warned me to pull back. Let him take control again.

The walls he'd crafted between us were falling, shattering into pieces and the carnage would swallow me up.

Shut up, Ellie. Shut up—

"Because," I went on stupidly, "despite all of your bravado you can't control me."

It was such a silly thing to say—especially considering that I was pretty much at his mercy now—but when he didn't laugh or scoff in response my stomach dropped right through the soles of my feet.

"Do continue," he said instead. I swore that I could hear the swish of his fangs, piercing the air as he spoke. "This is quite enlightening."

"You want to, but …"

"But *what?*"

Suddenly, he was too close. His body jarred mine, knocking me off balance until I was forced to take a step backward or fall.

"Go on," he goaded.

"I don't know—"

"I could kill you, Eleanor Gray." He might as well have casually stated what day it was. "It would be easy. Don't think I haven't considered it before."

But I *had.* Countless times, and that was the scary part.

"Then do it." I barely recognized the sound of my own voice. "Kill me. Hurt me. After all, agony is what I crave, right? If you truly are the devil you claim, then it should be as easy as taking candy from a—"

"Shut up."

My jaw snapped closed. His tone was too soft; I had pushed him too far.

"So now you *want* pain, Eleanor?" he questioned. "That can be arranged."

There was a sharp hiss, almost like the sound of metal scraping metal. A second later, the icy touch was back. Only it was a second before I realized that the point grazing my skin was way too sharp to have been a fingernail.

"Shall we forge a new wager?"

The point gently scraped along my flesh, teasing. I could picture the culprit; a weapon with a black hilt dominated by a roaring dragon, probably held expertly between two fingers—the same knife he'd used to draw his own blood. Unease crept down my spine as the blade tickled a path along the exposed skin of my hip.

Pull back, Ellie, a voice in my head urged. *You've gone too far, way too far …*

As if echoing the thought, Dublin wondered out loud, "How far will the innocent mortal push the vampire?"

He waited and the seconds ticked by like eons. Fear surged through my veins. Logic warned me to give in, that the creature standing before me was dangerous. I didn't recognize this Dublin. And yet, a part of me was more afraid to walk away.

"It seems that you aren't so foolish after all," Dublin remarked after nearly five minutes had passed. Before I had the chance to respond, he applied just enough pressure to sting, making me lurch on the balls of my feet. "Now display an ounce of common sense for once and *beg* me to stop."

I could only grit my teeth as the knife returned, cutting deep to form a short line and then another, nearly parallel to the first.

"When will you learn?" Dublin wondered coldly. "Not everything is a game."

Only he was wrong. This *was* a game, one of his, and I knew that the moment I pulled away—cried out—would be automatic surrender.

I refused to let him win, no matter the detriment to my own soul.

Another fierce jab sent agony shooting down my spine, and I couldn't smother the groan that broke free. Warm, wet drops of liquid dribbled down my thigh, chased by his next words. "You claim to fear me? Well, I can give you plenty to fear ..."

He sliced two more lines in quick succession, *nearly* superficial but deep enough to sting, bleed. I struggled to keep breathing, gulping at air.

"Tell me to stop, Eleanor. I *need* you to say it."

My silence earned me three more nicks, one right after the other.

God, it hurt. Involuntary tears sprang from my eyes, sinking into the black silk before they could fall.

It was nearly a full minute before the sharp tip of the knife returned, quivering against another strip of untouched skin —and it was only then that I realized every single mark had been deliberate. He was carving something into my skin. *Letters.*

My mind worked to assemble every aching slash as if it was some bizarre, twisted word scramble. The first four had been close together, connected. An *M?*

The second had been a single, solid upright line. *An L? Or maybe an I?*

The last four were trickier. Three of them felt connected, but the last line was farther away. *An N.*

I struggled to piece the letters together as Dublin's voice entered my ear, hitching over the three, final words. "Tell me to stop."

Before I could even speak, he sliced three more lines, completing four letters that felt as though they had been carved into my soul rather than my skin.

Mine.

Seconds passed in near silence as my own blood steadily dripped. The only other sound was a sharp, metallic *clink* of something falling to the floor. Whatever it was, it brushed my toe as it slid past and I shied back, feeling my heart pulse in my throat.

Run. The urge was too strong to ignore this time.

"Untie me." Trembling, I jerked my bound hands in his direction. "*Now!*"

He caught my wrists. One sharp tug and the ribbon came undone. Fingers shaking, I reached up and tore off the blindfold myself.

I didn't want to look at him—I *wouldn't*—but with a traitorous impulse, my eyes drifted over in his direction anyway.

He stood barely three feet away, as perfect and impeccable as always—except, there was something in his eyes that had never been so clear before now. *Fear.*

Blood dripped from his fingers, and they twitched as if it took every ounce of control he had just to keep from bringing his hand to his mouth.

"Eleanor—"

"Let me go." He hadn't even tried to touch me, but as if my words were his cue he reached for my arm.

My entire side throbbed with the pain of twelve little cuts as I jerked back out of reach. *Mine. Mine. MINE!* They screamed possession with each torturous ache, and I scanned the shadows, desperate for a way out.

"Eleanor—"

His hand cinched my forearm before I'd even taken a step toward the doorway. I tore away from him, lunging for the opposite side of the room.

My heel caught a warm, wet patch of blood and the next second I was barreling toward the window. In terrifying slow motion, I approached the sheet of glass, and I knew with a horrible sense of certainty that I would hit it, and go through.

I squeezed my eyes shut, waiting to feel the pain of a million shards of glass skewering my skin. Instead …

I only felt *ice* as something cinched my waist, yanking me backward into a solid surface.

Fear held me immobile as everything slowly lurched back into motion. My heart started to beat again. I could breathe. Finally, I gathered the nerve to open my eyes—but the sight of a pale arm wrapped tight around me was more frightening than the prospect of plunging twelve stories.

"Are you hurt?"

I couldn't speak.

No … Yes …

A million conflicting answers to his question darted around my mind.

"I don't know. But you should be thrilled, you've won your wager," I finally said, barely recognizing the sound of my own voice. "Then again, the Devil never really *loses,* does he?" I added before he could pull away. *Lose control,* he'd told me. An impossible request, considering that I had never had it. "Should I give you my answer now?"

He moved slowly, withdrawing just enough for me to crane my neck back and see his face. His eyes were dark, guarded, but I could easily see through the tiny cracks in the mask he had tried so desperately to hide behind.

Perhaps I had been as well.

Something was draining from me almost as quickly as my blood was—the truth. Those dangerous emotions I supposed I'd been trying to suppress ever since the first day he strolled into my bedroom and disrupted my neat, perfect life with blood and contracts.

I was so used to having people leave me once they had taken what they wanted—but *he* was always there, and I still had no clue what he sought to gain from me.

"*You* scare me," I admitted, nearly choking on the words, "but not because you're the Devil." His expression remained carefully blank. "If you really want the truth… I just don't know how I *should* feel around you."

No matter how hard I tried—no matter how every bone in my body *warned* me—I *couldn't* be afraid of him, even with my blood on his hands. His nearness made me feel dizzy, and off balance, and insane, because I felt no awkward need to pretend the same way I had to around anyone else.

And that was the pathetic part; I felt more comfortable in my own skin around a man inclined to *carve* into it, than I ever had.

"I know I should be afraid of you … Deep down, I probably am. But …"

"What?" His voice sounded deeper than ever before.

"I don't know," I whispered. "I just can't make myself believe I should be afraid …"

It was such an insane concept that I wanted more than anything for him to push me away—through the window maybe? Or laugh. Scoff.

Anything.

He just stood there for the longest time, face unreadable, eyes so dark they nearly touched on black. For once there was no harsh taunt designed to throw my own flaws back in my face. As crazy as it seemed, I had caught him off guard.

No, Eleanor! Stop! My mother's voice screamed through my head. But it wasn't enough to overtake the compulsion that darted down my spine. I was sick of being controlled, sick of pretending.

'I want the real Eleanor Gray,' he had told me once. Well, here she was in all of her insane, complicated glory.

It seemed to take years before I gathered the nerve to reach up, trailing my fingertips along his jaw. He felt cool to the touch and hard like stone—but when my thumb accidentally brushed the corner of his mouth, he jerked.

I expected him to push me away. Not …lean closer, icy breath ghosting my cheek. His eyes were a glazed, confused shade of silver, so bright that I could almost see my reflection in them: enormous green eyes and frizzy brown hair.

I shifted against him, rising up on the tip of my toes as his hands slid down to the small of my back in response. His grip was stiff. It felt like being in the embrace of a statue, and yet …

I was on fire.

The heat surged through my body. I could feel it racing through me from the top of my head to the tips of my toes. Pulsing …urging me on, daring me to let go.

Go Back, Eleanor, this is insanity, a frantic voice inside of me whispered as my hands firmly cupped his jaw. Only, I knew that there would be *no* going back, not if I followed through with the impulse that had me lurching forward on the balls of my feet, because I had no doubt in my mind that Dublin Helos would throw me from this window.

Regardless, I couldn't bring myself to stop until my lips finally met his.

GLASS

He didn't throw me from the window.

Cold fingers tangled in my hair instead, yanking me forward. Our lips met so fiercely it hurt as he lunged, pinning me against the glass with the weight of his body.

I should have bitten him, pulled back.

I *shouldn't* have slanted my mouth against his, allowing his tongue to slip inside.

Just like that, I knew instantly what true corruption felt like. It was *this*; surrender, Dublin Helos claiming me in a way that no one else had—more intimately than sex.

And this time I couldn't blame a contract.

His tongue dominated mine, clashing and demanding submission. Boldly, his hand slid between us, stroking a tortuous path to my inner thigh.

God.

He caressed, dragging his thumb up and down …around. My eyes fluttered, threatening to roll back into my skull as a million, hazy sensations rollicked through me all at once. Then, as if knowing instinctively what I needed, his thumb jerked upright, striking right *there*.

He felt good.

Rough and wrong, but so …damn …*good*.

I shifted, rubbing myself against him like a wanton whore —and I didn't care. My nails raked the skin beneath his shirt as I clutched fistfuls of it for stability.

He teased, brushing his fingers along the length of me, before striking that bundle of nerves that had my body jerking on the tips of my toes. I was breathless when he finally pulled away—but it was only to swiftly tug at the fastenings of his pants, still keeping a hold on my wrist.

Heat flared, washing any shred of hesitation away.

I watched, almost dazed as he undid the zipper one-handed with speedy precision. Within the blink of an eye, his pants were on the floor.

I swallowed hard as I took him in.

God, every inch of him was chiseled, perfect. I couldn't stop myself from reaching out to brush a finger along the length of his hip.

He wore nothing underneath. No boxers. No briefs.

I bit back a hysterical urge to laugh. Dublin Helos was an enigma that somehow managed to avoid answering that age-old question. *'Boxers or briefs?'*

His fingers seized mine, wrenching them up to pin my arm against the glass. His hips rocked into me, and I could feel the cold, hard length of him pressing against my inner thigh. My legs drifted apart before he could even begin to issue a command.

There was no slow teasing, no gentleness. He entered me so fiercely my vision exploded into shards of white.

As if from far away, I heard myself cry out as nerves deep within me came to life, exploded. Ice and fire swelled inside my body until I could have screamed from the intensity of it—but before the sound could even build in my throat, his mouth was on mine.

He devoured me, fangs nipping my lower lip, drawing beads of blood for his tongue to lap away. I tasted a metallic flavor, and for some reason, I wasn't disgusted. I relished the taste of my essence mixed with his.

The fingers in my hair became ruthless, tugging—pulling—forcing me to respond to him. Move. I lifted my hips, meeting him thrust for thrust, stroke for stroke, until I couldn't breathe, think.

The ominous sound of the window protesting against our weight barely registered above the thud of my own heartbeat. At some point, a part of me realized that he might send us both crashing through the glass.

And I didn't care.

Ecstasy began to build, coiling in my belly and crawling through the rest of my body. My hands broke free from his grasp and clutched his shoulders, nails digging into his skin, not caring if I hurt him. In fact …I almost *wanted* to draw blood—to mark him the same way he'd marked me.

Mine.

He lunged, thrusting so deeply I knew my hips would bruise. His mouth was at my throat, and a burst of cool air was the only warning before his fangs sank deep and pleasure exploded through my body, so intense I could taste it.

The world fell away.

And the last thing I was aware of was drowning in ice.

~

I woke up to silence.

It wasn't like the suffocating emptiness of Gray Manor, where the servants crept around like mice, trying to avoid notice on purpose. This was more …still. As if I were the only living soul left in the world.

With a sigh, I peeled my eyes open to a concave ceiling and attempted to get my bearings. For one, I was naked. My entire body ached—my hip in particular throbbed with every breath I took—but that wasn't all …

I was lying on a bed. Someone had draped me beneath a single, white sheet, and even before I rolled over to face the vacant sliver of mattress beside me, I knew that Dublin was gone …and I was alone.

In his place sat a neat pile of clothing, and a folded strip of paper.

It took me ages to gather up the nerve to open it. My fingers shook as they pried the pages apart to reveal the message written in elegant script.

The car is out front to take you home, read the first line. *Wait for me there.*

And then …scribbled hastily across the bottom of the page as if he had hesitated before adding them were four, simple words.

We need to talk.

Anxiety coiled in my stomach, mingling with the throbbing pain in my hip. *Talk?* The Dublin Helos I knew only communicated in commands and cryptic messages hidden within words or carved into skin.

Talking was blunt. Talking was …terrifying.

Nearly ten minutes had passed before I managed to gather up the nerve to crawl out of bed and into the bathroom. After finding a clean cloth, I washed myself robotically, trying to ignore the reddish liquid that circled the drain—and those four words echoing in my brain.

We need to talk.

I focused on running my fingers through my hair until I no longer resembled something my cat might have thrown up. The clothing he'd left for me was oddly simple: a plain white blouse and a brown, tweed skirt—but it wasn't until I was fully dressed, staring at my reflection, that I realized they were both *mine*, taken directly from my wardrobe.

The realization sent an ominous chill running down my spine. *We need to talk.* I tried to ignore it as I returned to the main hall.

My shoes and purse were there waiting for me. The only objects that seemed to be missing were the keys to the car. Go figure. Something told me that the trusty Rolls Royce was already safely returned to the garage.

I tried to tell myself that was a *good* thing as I descended the stairs to the main level of the church. The fact that Dublin had effortlessly tied up loose ends meant nothing. His *'talk'* was most likely another *re-negotiation* in disguise.

Right?

I wasn't fully convinced by the time I crept into the main Cathedral.

A few pious souls had already started to fill the pews, but they didn't even look up as I headed for the door.

Regardless, I felt like an outsider—an unholy soul who didn't deserve to set foot inside of such a sacred place. I could almost imagine the statues of Saints set in the walls glaring down at me as I scuttled out into the daylight. *Sinner! Sinner!*

Outside, bright sunlight filtered down through a smattering of clouds. It was overcast, but the weak sun still seemed blinding. I felt like a prisoner, seeing freedom for the first time after years of imprisonment.

But I almost wished the sky was an endless black instead. The thought haunted me as I wandered down the path that led from the church where, as promised, a familiar car was there waiting.

Now what? I wondered as I crept forward, feeling uneasy for reasons I couldn't explain. The last bit of Dublin's message still reverberated in my skull.

"Morning, Miss."

With a stern expression, the driver pulled open the car's door. He hardly looked in my direction as I settled into the leather seat—and my unease only grew. What did he know?

You're being paranoid, Ellie. I told myself as I wrung my fingers together over my lap. *You're not thinking rationally.*

Ironically, once the door closed behind me, and the tinted windows shut out most of the sunlight, I could finally seem to focus—namely on two rather important developments.

I had kissed Dublin Helos.

He had kissed me in return.

It felt unnatural thinking on those two statements, one right after the other. As insane as *'I died'* and *'I'm alive'* uttered at once—though, when dealing with vampires I supposed the normal rules no longer applied.

When the car finally came to a stop, I was prepared to begin the long journey up the winding stairs to my bedroom where I could panic in private. However, the building waiting beyond the car's window was not Gray Manor. In fact, it wasn't a 'house' at all. What seemed to be a restaurant sat on the corner of an innocuous city road. A line of red paint across the darkened window-front read, *Sanguis.*

It was a name that would have had little meaning to someone not inducted into the shadowy world of vampires —or, at least who hadn't been forced to suffer through two years of Latin instruction.

Sanguis was the word for blood, and I had a sinking suspicion that only one type of creature would think to name a restaurant so 'creatively.'

Alarmed, I turned to the front seat.

"Weren't you supposed to take me home?"

"This is the stop, Miss," the driver replied, staring dead ahead.

Perhaps Dublin had changed his mind and decided to spring for another intimidating lunch. Confused, I reached for the handle of the door, only to be distracted by the destination once again.

I didn't even recognize this part of the city. There was no one else on the street. As I warily climbed onto the curb, a voice in my head sounded a warning. *Run, Ellie! Something isn't right …*

"Are you sure?" I glanced over my shoulder. "Dublin told you to bring me *here*?"

In the rearview mirror, a pair of dark eyes finally met mine, but they were guarded, furtive.

"Yes," he said, but then after a second's hesitation he added, "I'm sorry—"

"Eleanor Gray." The familiar, husky voice came from behind me, and my entire body went rigid. "Right on time."

Before I had the chance to react, a warm hand snaked over my wrist, wrenching me around to face a grinning Saskia. She was dressed to *kill*—and something told me that, in her case, that wasn't just a figurative expression. Scarlet hair tumbled down her shoulders in thick, heavy ringlets, and the black dress she wore was undeniably elegant.

"Come along," she told me, flashing a crimson smile. Without another word, she reached across me to close the car door. Then she turned, pulling me after her.

Frantic questions tumbled out of me, one after the other. "Where are we? What are you doing here?"

My heart raced with every step closer I came to the intimidating front of *Sanguis*. It looked normal on the surface …

But underneath I could sense the same foreboding aura that had permeated the air of Raphael's Manor—that instinctive knowledge that predators lurked within. The feeling only intensified as Saskia grasped the handle of a blood red door and pulled it open.

It was dark inside.

The faint scent of food hit my nose, but there was a musky undertone as if nothing edible had been prepared within these walls in a long while. It was quiet, but as the tiny hairs on the back of my neck stood on end, I knew we weren't alone.

"This way," Saskia chirped before pulling me down an unseen hallway.

Faint light emanated from a doorway up ahead, a dining room.

It was large and sparsely furnished; only a few paintings, framed in gold, decorated the dark red walls. Regardless, I could tell in a single glance that it made even the most elegant room in Gray Manor look like a worn down shanty in comparison.

In the center of the room, at a table draped in a pristine, white tablecloth sat a man so pale his skin seemed to swallow the light of the chandelier that dangled overhead. Long, ebony hair framed an angular face, crowned by two black eyes that cut through me with more precision than any blade.

I had only seen him once before, but recognition struck me instantly.

"Eleanor Gray," Raphael greeted, his voice as chilling as ice. "So glad that you could join me."

SERPENT

I wanted to run, but Saskia's grip tightened until I had no choice but to stumble inside the room after her. She pulled me over to the elegantly set table and then stood back, leaving me alone in Raphael's line of sight.

He took me in slowly, starting with the top of my head before his obsidian gaze roved all the way down to my heels. His expression never changed, but I felt stripped bare, exposed.

Similar, I supposed, to how a gazelle might feel while a lion sized it up.

"Have a seat." He gestured to the empty chair across from him. "Can I get you anything? Water? Wine?"

"N-No." I shook my head as I perched on the very edge of the chair. Pure instinct kept me from turning on my heel and trying to bolt.

Keep your mouth shut, Dublin's voice hissed in my mind, rather than my mother's for once. *Say nothing.*

I glanced around, half expecting to find him brooding in one of the corners. Even though a part of me already knew the answer, I couldn't resist asking, "Is … Is Dublin here?"

From her position against the wall, Saskia scoffed, but Raphael's face remained expressionless.

"No," he said. "I thought that I should arrange a time for us to meet. Alone."

His words sent a shiver racing down my spine, and I knew instantly that the driver's little detour had come on *his* orders.

"Why …would you want to meet me?"

Raphael smiled, but there was no warmth in the expression. "Why wouldn't I? There seems to be no end to the gossip circling Dublin's newest 'friend.'"

His deliberate pause made me guess that he'd intended to say another word instead: *Pet.*

"I'm glad that we finally have the chance to speak. Bread?" I flinched as he gestured to a basket in the center of the table, full of steaming rolls.

"N-No thank you."

Raphael shrugged. "I've scoured the menu." He picked up a sliver of crisp, cream-colored paper from the table and held it out to me. "What would you like? A tazza with lamb or linguine?"

I vaguely recognized the dishes. *Italian?*

"N-No thank you."

"Well." The menu slid back to the table. "I suppose we could just make do with a little conversation."

He paused expectantly as if that was my cue to speak.

The seconds crawled past as I remained silent. Instead, I scanned the polished wooden floors, the rich red walls, the ceiling—anywhere but in the direction of those soulless eyes.

The restaurant was grand, more elegant than the *Café Claret.*

I felt underdressed. Saskia would have been a more fitting companion to dine with Raphael, who still managed to look regal in a black shirt and dark pants. Before I could help it, my eyes caught something glinting against his chest: that long, silver chain, so much like Dublin's.

The menacing serpent-shaped pendant dangling from the center of it enthralled me. Its ruby eyes seemed to glow almost with the intelligence of a living creature, and I found myself gazing at it longer than I meant to. I swore that I could almost hear its hiss inside my head quelling my urge to flee. *Stay ...*

"Remarkable, isn't it?" Raphael murmured, reaching up to brush a finger along the silver chain. "I have lived a long time, Eleanor, and yet the creativity of other beings still surprises even me."

The words were wistful even though his voice was still unnervingly flat and emotionless.

"It's lovely," I croaked. Inside I was morbidly curious as to why he, Dublin and Mikhail all sported similar pieces of jewelry. Were ancient necklaces passed out among their organization like friendship bracelets at a summer camp?

"As are you," Raphael said. The compliment caught me off guard, but there was no warmth in it. His tone was as dry as someone pointing out that the gum on the sole of their shoe was rather pink. "Though …I must say that you are not the type of woman Dublin usually surrounds himself with."

It was with those simple words that the false, elegant façade of this 'meeting' was ripped away. Suddenly the air in the room felt a million degrees colder. The back of my neck prickled. I couldn't seem to sit still, and my fingers fidgeted against the tablecloth.

"He's gone through beautiful women like a connoisseur through wine. *Exquisite* women," Raphael added, as if only to drill home the fact that I didn't fit the mold. "And yet his interest in them waxes and wanes—" He waved a hand dismissively. "Not to mention that he's been a bit of a recluse, these days. Rarely venturing out from the shadows … Tell me, Eleanor, what do you know of our world?"

The question seemed simple enough, but I wasn't fooled.

"Dublin doesn't tell me much of anything," I said as innocently as I could manage.

The corner of that ageless mouth quirked. *Liar.*

"It is a simple existence we have," he replied rather than prod me for more answers, "those of us in this shadow world. We keep to ourselves. Most mortals never know we exist."

Except those unlucky enough to forge a contract, of course. I thought of George Washington and shuddered.

"Do not believe the common rumors about my kind," Raphael warned as if reading my mind. "We are not all monsters or fiends. In fact, we've had a rather peaceful co-existence with mortals. Even your own family ..." He paused, watching my reaction. "What do you know about the history of the Grays, Eleanor?"

I shrugged. "Just that we have ties in this region that go back decades—"

"Centuries, even," Raphael said, cutting over me. His eyes glimmered. Was that amusement I saw in them? "Your family has ties in the foundation of this very country, Eleanor. I even knew your ancestor, James, personally ..."

I didn't know why the statement shocked me so much.

James Gray had lived nearly three hundred years ago, but Dublin claimed to have lived nearly five hundred. According to my father, our ancestor had been a nut who'd abandoned his comfortable home in England and journeyed to the new world out of some misplaced sense of adventure. Everyone knew that our money came from his brother William and his descendants who had wisely cultivated their fortune.

"You must have lived a very long life," I said, choosing the most non-threatening words I could think of.

"An unnaturally long life, yes," Raphael agreed, "but does that make me evil?"

It was a dangerous question, so I licked my lips rather than answer.

Raphael's mouth twitched into the shadow of something that could have been interpreted as a smile on a different person.

"Our world may seem complex to you—brutal even—but it is how we survive. Do you know why I had Dublin offer you a contract, Eleanor?"

If Dublin had asked me that question, a mocking quip would have sprung right to my lips. *Why for my family name, of course.*

But with Raphael, I didn't dare. The walls themselves seemed to warn me to be on guard.

"No."

He smiled again—but it was a terrifying imitation of the real thing.

"Not surprisingly," he murmured. "I suppose that he wouldn't. Especially not when he seems to have grown so very fond of you …"

"What do you mean?" I sat straighter, feeling every muscle in my body tense. 'Fond' and 'Dublin' were two words that should never be linked so closely in a sentence—especially one referring to me.

Some shadowy emotion flickered across those ageless eyes but was gone in the blink of an eye.

"That is not important," he said finally. "Do you know what he paid for you, Eleanor?"

"No." I shook my head, even as Yulia's words haunted me. *Money is meaningless among our kind.*

So much for my guess of five dollars—and something told me that I was much better off not knowing the real answer.

"I know that Saskia offered to enlighten you," Raphael stated in a tone as dangerously soft as a snake's hiss. "What did she want in exchange?"

My gaze darted to the succubus in question who leaned against the wall, admiring a pale hand topped by blood-red nails. She didn't look in my direction, but I knew that she listened to every single word.

"She wanted to me to say something," I managed to croak, turning back around. "To Dublin. A word."

Raphael shifted in his chair, and the motion reminded me of a lion impatiently batting its tail as it waited for the antelope to skip closer in range.

"What was it, if I may ask?"

I swallowed, and it took everything I had to keep from asking for a glass of water after all, if only to keep myself from having to speak any further.

"Cael."

Even without Dublin in sight, my stomach flipped. That name tingled on the tip of my tongue, forbidden. For the longest time, Raphael just watched me as if noticing every uneasy tremor that slipped down my spine.

"Cael was the name of a friend of mine," he said finally. From the corner of my eye, I saw that Saskia had gone rigid. "A very old friend …"

His tone slithered against my eardrums and I frowned. Why would Saskia want me to mention the name of Raphael's 'friend' around Dublin? Was there some kind of bad blood between them?

Saskia's face was turned away from me, and Raphael's was as blank as a sheet of ancient parchment.

"Why do you think we broker contracts, Eleanor?" he asked, catching me off guard.

"For favors?" I remembered Yulia's 'hypothetical' story that I now suspected had been more factual than anything else.

He laughed, but I'd heard the wind howl with more emotion. "We share our …gifts and require simple things in return. That is all."

He made it sound like a harmless transaction, but I could still remember those empty women Mikhail and his cohorts had dined from like an all-you-can-eat buffet.

There had been nothing simple about it.

"Dublin used to understand this," he added, only his tone wasn't quite so flat anymore. There was an edge to it that made me shudder as those black eyes scanned my face. "In a way, you could say that he designed this system we live by. But …rarely has he purchased a contract for his own—at least not without a clear reason. So, as you can see, I am rather curious as to why he bought yours."

"He had no choice," I blurted, cringing at the thought of that fateful auction and the fool I'd made of myself. "No one else wanted me—"

"Dear God!" A sharp bark of laughter had me turning to where Saskia clung to the wall as if for dear life. "Did he really tell you that?" Her eyes blazed as they found mine. "While you may be dowdy and dull and unattractive, Eleanor, make no mistake, Yulia is not a fool. She knew damn well what she was doing by having you prance around like a virginal little innocent. You," she snarled, "were the most requested morsel of the evening. What?" she added at my expression. "You don't believe me? Even your precious Dublin couldn't resist you. He all but begged

*—groveled—*for me to let him have you over anyone else. Personally, I was more inclined to let you go to Mikhail—"

"Saskia." With a word, Raphael had her silent. Her spine stiffened, eyes downcast.

"Milord."

With little more than a wave of his hand, Raphael sent her out of the room, leaving us alone.

A million thoughts raced through my mind, and I fought to keep my face from revealing them. *Dublin. The auction. Mikhail. Cael.*

Saskia was lying—she had to be.

Any other possible explanation was far too lethal to consider.

"I will make you a wager, Eleanor," Raphael began, cutting through the tumble of thoughts crashing through my mind. "I will tell you what Dublin bartered for you—in fact, I will *give* it to you. As long as you help me discover something that he might value more. I think that's a fairer transaction than your arrangement with Saskia."

No, Ellie! Say no! Run away!

"What would I have to do?" My palms were slick with sweat. I could barely get the words out. Those black eyes held me captive, boring deep to scrape my soul.

Suddenly, Raphael sat back.

"Nothing at all." I shivered as his hand reached across the table for mine, as quickly as a striking cobra. "I already have my suspicions."

He was so cold—shockingly, abnormally so. I could tolerate Dublin's glacial touch, but Raphael was a different matter entirely. It felt as if death itself had taken hold of me.

"All you would be required to do is help me prove it to be true or false. Then, I shall uphold my end of our bargain. Simple enough?"

A frigid thumb traced the back of my hand. Every instinct in my body warned me to pull away, to push back from the table and run. However, as if drawn by an invisible force, my eyes drifted back down to the serpent pendant. Its red gaze seemed to mesmerize me once again, and I could only sit there as Raphael continued to stroke my hand.

Then, almost casually, he brought it to his mouth as if he meant to kiss the back of it like some gallant, old-fashioned gentleman.

"A simple suspicion," he repeated in a burst of breath so cold that I half expected frost to crystallize right there on my skin.

Then he lowered his head, bared his fangs …

And before I even had the chance to scream, he bit.

A NEW WAGER

The initial sting was no worse than the jab of a needle, just a slight little pinch.

It was almost as if he was taking care to pierce only the first few layers of skin—steal a taste of my blood—and nothing more. A second later, he withdrew his fangs and released my wrist, allowing me to jerk my hand back.

"There," Raphael said, settling back into his seat. It was as if he'd shaken my hand rather than bitten me. "Let's see what course of action he takes now ..."

Who? I wanted to ask, but my lips felt numb. A strange icy chill had drifted up my entire body, sinking into my muscles. Shock?

Dazed, I could only gaze down at the two marks piercing the back of my hand.

Bite marks, I told myself sternly like a student trying to reinforce the use of a new vocabulary. Tiny beads of ruby blood had bubbled forth, oozing down my wrist.

For the first time in my life, I was oddly aware of every breath I took—every pull of air entering and leaving my chest. It was almost as if my body was waiting for me to realize something that my brain hadn't fully registered.

Then I felt it.

The *pain.* It was just a sharp jolt, stabbing through my wrist, my arm, my shoulder. With every second the pinch became a throbbing, then an aching. Burning. Within only a minute, my entire arm was engulfed in invisible flames. Unbearable pain seared up my wrist, consuming every cell, every pore.

I tried to speak, but the words stuck to the back of my throat.

Across from me Raphael merely stared—but his face was different. As I watched, those dark, Roman features morphed into the face of a snarling demon, laughing as I tried to stand. Almost in slow motion, my chair tipped backward, pitching me into oblivion. The ceiling loomed above, miles away, and I was floating ...

Falling.

The table disintegrated into ash. Pieces of silverware turned into blindingly bright stars that whizzed past my head as the world spun.

My mouth was open. I knew that I was screaming, but the only words I heard weren't spoken by me.

Let's see if he comes …

Comes.

Comes.

Comes.

The voices ricocheted while the interior of the dining room morphed into a torrent of blood that pooled at my feet. In seconds it was a churning river, sweeping me away. A pair of haunting, amber eyes chased me as the agony threatened to swallow me up.

"I've called him." The husky feminine purr seemed to come from a million directions all at once, splintering like broken glass. "He hasn't shown his face here in years, but something tells me he'll come now."

It was as if I was hearing everything from underwater, drowning beneath pain so heavy it crushed. My body was gone, consumed by the agony.

You're dying, Ellie, a part of me cried—but if it meant escaping the pain, I would have gladly given up.

I wanted to die.

"Eleanor—"

All at once, the fire turned to ice. The world stopped spinning, and clarity started to return in stingy snatches.

I was lying on the floor, curled on my side with my right hand clutched to my chest. Someone stood nearby, casting a shadow that fell over me like a blanket.

"I can't believe you actually came." I vaguely recognized Saskia's voice. She sounded light-years away and yet close enough to have been whispering in my ear at the same time. "After decades of pretending to be above it all, the great and terrible *Cael* comes dashing to the rescue—"

"Eleanor," a man said, cutting over her. Something cool brushed my cheek. *A finger?* "Can you hear me?"

I couldn't speak. My throat felt raw. Every breath ached. I wanted to sleep. Just sink into oblivion and be washed away

…

"Look at me." I knew that tone, that voice.

It was a long moment before I realized that my eyes were already open. My vision was a blurry mess, but somehow I managed to focus on a pale blob that hovered above.

Dublin.

"You know this is just what he wants," Saskia continued, though I couldn't see her. Nothing registered but Dublin's face as it slowly came into focus: a pale jaw, that crown of golden hair, and two gray eyes that were so wide they could have sucked me in whole.

"You just gave him the very thing he needs to get you right back under his thumb; a *weakness*. You were so close to your precious freedom—everyone knew you only had a few years left. And yet you just threw it all away—"

"Say something," Dublin growled, low enough only for me to hear.

I felt too weak to even suck air into my chest, but the command in his tone was inescapable.

"Hurts …"

Though, the pain had actually started to recede—I could think again at least. However, when I tried to take a breath something heavy weighed on my chest. A piece of silverware from the table?

I looked down, shocked to find a slender strip of metal disappearing beneath the collar of my blouse. *A necklace?*

"At least everything makes sense now," Saskia went on smugly. "Without that amulet around your neck to hide behind, I finally understand. Who would have guessed that after all this time …some pathetic mortal would be the one to finally bring the great Cael to his knees?"

The hand against my cheek stiffened. I could sense Saskia prowling nearby; a ruthless lioness ready to pounce.

"Tell me, how does it feel?" she wondered. "She suffers because of *your* sins. Raphael will use her to ensure that you can *never* escape …and there is *nothing* you can do to stop it."

Dublin didn't respond to her. Instead, his eyes bore into mine as everything but him slowly began to fade to black.

"If you die, Eleanor," he growled as his face drifted in and out of focus, "I will personally follow you to the gates of hell …and my resurrection services do not come cheaply."

~

*W*hen the world finally stopped spinning, I knew where I was—or mainly, *who* sat beside me, emanating a chill so potent that I could taste ice on my tongue.

"Say something," Dublin demanded as I started to shift.

He held my hand.

Somehow, I knew that even before I peeled my eyes open to find his fingers laced within my own.

I was lying on a bed, draped in ivory sheets and he sat on the end of the mattress with his back to me. The dark walls of the bedroom were familiar, but it was a solid minute before I realized that we were in his lair.

"He bit me," I croaked, still marveling at the fact that my fingers were actually entwined with his. I tried to sit upright only to wince as a sharp pain shot down the length of my arm. Still, the words kept tumbling out. "Oh God. Raphael. He *bit* me—"

Dublin's grip tightened.

"It's all right."

The fact that I could still feel pain was the only thing that convinced me I wasn't dreaming. Even a hint of comfort from him shocked me to the point that I laid back down, observing the way my pink hand contrasted with his icy one. It throbbed, but the pain was barely noticeable once a few minutes had passed, allowing me to focus on the rest of my body.

I was still fully dressed, wearing the clothes that he had left for me—but my skirt was crooked. Three buttons on my blouse had come undone, and tiny streaks of red smeared the front of it. Not to mention that something heavy had been draped around my neck, weighing on my chest like an iron manacle. Confused, I glanced down to find a long, coiled chain pooled on the mattress beside me. *Had he resorted to something a little stronger than ribbons this time?*

Whatever it was sparkled against the white sheets and formed one long, complete loop. Dangling from the end of it was a simple cross. Tentatively I reached out, brushing the line of it with the pad of my finger.

Only then did it sink in; *this was his.* I glanced up, shocked to find that the infamous silver chain he usually wore was gone. When I tried to grasp the charm hanging from my throat and observe it more closely, his free hand was there, dragging it further out of reach.

"Eleanor," he began without looking at me. "What did he say to you?"

Raphael's words still circled my mind. *Help prove my suspicion about what he might value more ...*

I tried to relay them but, in the end, all that came out instead was a tired croak. "What did you pay for me?"

He let go of my hand.

It was strange how I felt even colder without him there as he pulled away and stood. For a moment, he paced—but when he finally turned back to face me, his expression could have been chiseled from stone.

"Why don't you ask your good friend *Saskia*?"

I flinched. His tone was icy. Venom laced every word, and I wondered just what the hell had happened in *Sanguis*.

Raphael had bitten me, I remembered that much. But the rest was a hazy blur punctuated only by a few disconnected words.

Bargain.

Cael.

Contract.

"She offered to tell me," I admitted. "That day we met her at Anemia. As long as I played one of her little games …"

"And what was that?"

I swallowed. For some reason, I couldn't bring myself to meet his gaze directly, so I stared down at his oddly bare throat instead. "Who was Cael?"

He flinched. The motion was so imperceptible that I probably wouldn't have noticed had I not been watching him so carefully. My eyes darted up to see a pure, raw hatred flash through those silver eyes—only this time, it didn't fade.

It lingered, directed solely at *me.*

"Where did you hear that name?"

"Saskia. Who was he?"

An old friend, Raphael had said—but something told me that there was more to it than that.

"Cael?" Dublin's eyes narrowed into slits. "He was a fool who sold his soul for five hundred years for nothing more than power. Much like *you,* Eleanor, he had no qualms in staining his soul. He was a monster, a fool. He killed. He relished the destruction of lives. In fact," he added coldly, "you would have *loved* him."

"Why would she want me to say that name?" I managed to ask in a whisper. "Was he one of your contracts?"

No, Ellie, a part of me whispered. *Don't be so naïve.*

"I don't know," Dublin spat, but he wasn't looking at me. He glared at the wall above my head. If looks could kill, the centuries-old stone would have crumbled to dust. "What else has *Saskia* told you?"

I hesitated. "She told me about the auction. That …"

I couldn't even repeat the rest; apparently, I had been the most *'requested morsel of the evening.'*

It was a lie. It had to be.

I stared at Dublin, waiting for him to laugh and prove my suspicions wrong—but he didn't. Those eyes took on a frosty hue and any resemblance to the human he might have been was gone.

"Say it," the vampire hissed. "Use your words, Eleanor."

"You didn't have to buy me," I croaked. Mikhail had been a willing buyer, according to Saskia. "Right? I thought, I-I mean, isn't that what you *wanted*, to auction me off?"

"What I wanted …" His mouth curved into a terrible smile that sucked all of the air from the room. "Eleanor Gray, you don't know a damn thing about what I *want.*" He flung the words at me like the snap of a whip. "You should have been the easiest contract I've ever brokered, nothing more than some dowdy little heiress who should have jumped at the chance at more time. So *simple,* that I decided to handle it myself rather than turn the job over to Saskia. Simple …but nothing *ever* is with you, Eleanor. Is it?"

I couldn't speak. This wasn't Dublin. Gone was the mocking persona and the cutting insults. In its place, raw anger leaked from him in waves, searing my skin.

"You weren't offered a contract at random. Oh no, Eleanor," he said. "I was ordered to *ensure* that you made one. Do you remember the 'therapist' your doctor recommended to you that day in the hospital?"

As if his words were the trigger, I recalled the day Dr. Wallis had given me his diagnosis—my death sentence. *I at least suggest some form of counseling,* he had recommended. *A colleague of mine is one of the leading psychiatrists in the country …*

"Yes."

"That was me," Dublin said. "Dear old Doctor Wallis wasn't a very willing accomplice, but his job was simple. I was waiting in his office when he'd delivered his diagnosis. All you had to do—the woman who'd been given a death sentence—was sit there and cry like so many others have before. Accept me and my offer. But you …left. You refused." He took a step closer, feet pounding against the floor. "That was the *first* time you denied me. Even in the hallway, you knew instantly what I was, and you denied me again. Did you ever stop to think how odd it was that I had 'accidentally' bumped into you at just the right moment?"

I couldn't speak. I could still picture him, a virtual Angel of Death in that white coat. He had been waiting for me.

"Congratulations, Eleanor," he continued, "I've been gathering contracts for centuries, and yet *you* are the first person to react to their impending demise without even batting an eyelash."

"I don't know what you're talking about," I stammered. My head was spinning. *Dr. Wallis. Therapist. Him.*

"There is no illness by the name of *hemohemorrahgia*."

He might as well have punched me.

"W-What?"

"It was a clever ruse to explain away a medical condition that most mortals aren't even aware of." He reached down to snatch my hand from the mattress, gazing down at the two angry red marks that pierced the skin. His thumb swept over them in a burst of pain.

"Do you want to know why a single *bite* from Raphael nearly killed you? Don't you think there's a better question?" he added before I could answer, eyes so dark they touched on ebony. "Why you can tolerate *my* bites so very exquisitely? Why you don't even shiver when I touch you?"

He brushed a curl behind my ear as if to prove it.

"Use that clever brain of yours, Eleanor. Let's see if you can think back to our very first 'lessons.' What did I tell you about being bitten?"

The words marched across my mind as suddenly as if he'd whispered them in my ear.

"No more than three times a night by a single vampire," I said.

"And do you know why that is?"

I swallowed, painfully aware of just how close he was. His tone was mocking, loathing.

"No—"

"Mortals have adapted to my kind without even knowing it. Once a vampire's venom is introduced into the bloodstream, it changes it—more powerfully than any human drug. Too much venom from one particular vampire, and over time the blood grows to suit that particular brand of venom. The human subconsciously becomes addicted to it. Their body ceases to function without a daily dose, and the withdrawal effects can be …violent."

Withdrawal effects.

In Dr. Wallis' crisp tones, a list of symptoms marched across my brain. *Headaches, dizziness, uncontrollable bleeding.*

"You've been unknowingly consuming my venom for months, Eleanor," Dublin said. "I've had it slipped into your drinks, your meals."

He said it so calculatingly. As if it was completely irrelevant that he had poisoned me for months only to ensure that I would have no choice but to sign a contract.

"How?" I rasped.

Dublin raised an eyebrow. "How else? Do you really think that you're the only soul on Gray property to have a contract? Your friend Harper was particularly *useful.*"

The words had the effect of a knife stabbing deep into my chest. Harper—the only man I figured I'd ever really trusted. My throat contracted. I tried wrenching my hand from Dublin's, but he held tight, nails nearly piercing my skin.

"You were dying from two months of venom withdrawal, Eleanor," he repeated, as if to help it sink in. "That's why your body subconsciously craves even a drop of mine. Your blood is linked to me and *only* me. There is no cure. Without my blood in your system, you would have died."

Somehow, a mythical blood disorder had been easier to swallow.

It had been almost too easy to face Dr. Wallis and accept that I would die without shedding a single tear. But this was different—horrifying. The man standing before me had deliberately made sure that I had no choice …

And he didn't even seem to care.

"Tell me why you bought my contract at the auction," I croaked. Was it a game? A joke? A way for him to take my virginity and just inflict more pain? "Why? Why?"

His cold expression faltered, revealing a flash of real emotion underneath. I had caught him off guard, but I was too confused to even relish in the victory.

"Tell me," I said, not even recognizing the sound of my own voice; an old woman had to be speaking, not me.

Finally …his jaw unclenched, and the words came like blows.

"My methods were *too* effective, Eleanor. Your blood accepts only *my* venom. I knew it the first night I bit you. Had someone else fed from you, you would have died. Raphael knew this as well, but you were too stubborn to take the easy route. Once you were signed to the club, you *had* to be auctioned …and I was forced to save your life yet again."

Again.

"You said Raphael's bite nearly killed me." I sounded weak, faint; a ghost barely clinging to reality. "How did you save me? Did you give me your blood—"

"No." His eyes were a stormy gray, flashing with hints of silver but his tone was softer. "Even that wouldn't have been enough this time."

"Then how …"

Like a punch to the chest, the truth became clear. The necklace.

Without thinking, I reached down to clutch the chain with my fingers. It felt strange; cold and yet hot at the same time. *Alive.*

"It's enchanted," Dublin explained. "The magic inside it is the only thing keeping you alive."

I was too exhausted to question it. One day I needed his blood to live, and now his necklace apparently.

"And if I remove it?"

He didn't have to respond—a part of me already knew the answer before he did.

"You'll die."

Forget the weight of the contract; I would have almost preferred to have to drink his blood every day for an eternity than—literally—have my entire life hanging from a thread. The shape of the cross haunted me from the surface of the bed.

"Why did you even go into that damn restaurant?" Dublin demanded suddenly. "Do you have no ounce of self-preservation? I told you to *go home*. Nothing else should have convinced you otherwise. Nothing."

Something in his tone triggered a horrible thought.

"The driver …"

"He's dead," he said without a shred of remorse. "Technically Raphael owned his contract, but I killed him for betraying me none the less. Another body to add to your growing list of casualties."

The driver's stern face flashed through my mind. *Dead.*

"Why?"

He turned away from me again.

"And why would Raphael want to kill me if he ordered you to secure my contract in the first place? Why me?" My voice trembled as I finally voiced the questions I supposed I should have the moment he'd declared our 'contract' null and void.

His hands were clenched at his sides, shoulders set in rigid lines. Anger had settled into a cold, icy crust that encased him from head to toe.

"I've told you all along that you don't understand the game you've so stubbornly decided to play," he began in a tone so flat and emotionless that it resonated down my spine like a physical blow. "Well, now you're a pawn in it. Raphael sees you only as a tool to obtain whatever it is that he wants. The fact that you're still alive means he's succeeded."

"What does he want?" I forced a dry swallow. "Money?"

God, I didn't know why it hurt me so much just to say it out loud.

Rather than agree, Dublin …stood there.

"You and your damn money," he spat. For a moment, I feared he actually might strike me, tear me apart with his bare hands, just like he'd threatened the other night.

"Do you have *any* idea what some people would give for a *day* of freedom? A year? Ten? You may have no trouble with throwing your life away, Eleanor, but not all of us have that luxury."

He advanced, step by step until he stood by my side of the bed. He was too close, too loud—even though his voice was little more than a whisper.

"Maybe I should have just put you out of your misery the first day I saw·you?"

"You're scaring me." My voice was monotone, dead.

"Good," he countered, though he pulled back, "because you *scare me*. You dance on the edge of the proverbial cliff, ignoring everyone who screams at you to back away. Death welcomes you, and you welcome it. It's living that scares you, *Ellie*. Not me."

Without another word he turned, heading for the door.

"If this wasn't about money, then why?" I croaked after him. "Why get my contract in the first place?"

"Why else?" He paused to glare at me from over his shoulder, words echoing like the aftershocks of a slap. "To get to the only Gray that matters."

A second later, he was gone, and the sound of a slamming door cemented the ache I felt in the pit of my stomach.

My face was wet, and I reached up almost surprised to find warm beads of moisture sliding down my cheeks. Tears? Blood?

Whatever they were …they wouldn't stop falling.

THE OTHER GRAY

This time, Dublin hadn't bothered to take off my shoes. My purse was even waiting for me on the floor beside the bed. All I had to do was make it to the door, climb down those countless stairs and run.

Go home.

Go back.

Die.

I had tasted my little bit of freedom, and I had choked on it.

I shifted off the bed and took a step toward the door. But the next thing I knew, I was on my knees. I couldn't breathe —the air refused to enter my lungs. My vision blurred into one colorless mess as those damn tears continued to fall.

Pull yourself together! I scolded. I would have given anything to have heard my mother's voice just then, harsh and judgmental. *Grays do not cry, Eleanor!*

But all I heard was Dublin's growl on a loop.

The only Gray that matters …

With the grace of an old woman, I turned and felt along the floor for my purse. My phone was inside, fully charged though I didn't have the strength of mind to consider who would have taken the care to charge it.

What was I even doing? I had no idea, even as I robotically flipped through the notifications that flashed across the screen. There was one missed call, left only hours before the time listed on the phone.

I didn't recognize the number, but I played the message anyway, and my heart turned to stone as a familiar voice came from the receiver.

"Ellie Bellie! Sorry I couldn't make it into town tonight. My plane touched down only for a bit, and something came up. I promise to make it up to you! Smooches!"

Somehow, the sound of my sister's voice made the tears fall faster. I couldn't stop. My shoulders shook. I had to grasp the end of the bed just to keep from lying flat on the floor, utterly drained.

A mysterious horde of vampires had *poisoned* me in order to get to my sister, and she couldn't be bothered with me. Not even for a moment.

The irony had me laughing hysterically between sobs. The sound ricocheted off the walls in a distorted, morbid melody.

I was insane. Dublin Helos had shattered me into pieces …

His damn necklace was a lead ball around my throat. I reached up, prepared to rip it off—but a sudden sound made me freeze.

A creak.

It was a footstep. Several in fact, I realized as my sobbing trailed off. They were soft and deliberate, as if the figure in question were trying their hardest to go unnoticed.

Not Dublin, something warned me.

My cell phone was still clenched in my fist, and I stood, trying not to make a sound as I crept to the doorway and peered out.

Only a few lamps were lit, leaving swaths of shadow large enough for a trespasser to lurk in. There seemed to be no one in this part of the lair, but the intruder was close. The footsteps had receded, and I could imagine whoever they were, sneaking into Dublin's study. *Raphael? Saskia? Yulia?*

Cautiously, I slipped into the hallway and headed for the main entryway.

I supposed I should have felt some kind of fear, trepidation, anything.

But I only felt numb as I followed the wall until I reached the doorway of the study.

A horde of Dublins could have been standing there, waiting to snap my neck and I doubted it would have made a difference. *'It's living that scares you, Ellie. Not me.'* Those words haunted me, cutting deeper than I thought the sound of my own self-imposed nickname ever could. There was nothing left to harm. He had made sure of it.

But, rather than a murderous vampire, a woman stood at the desk, and I could tell from the tan hue of her skin that she was human.

Her back was turned to me. Long blonde hair spilled down to her waist, obscuring her simple, dark outfit: jeans, sturdy boots, and a long-sleeved shirt. Something was clenched in her fist, a long object with a triangular point; a *dagger?*

With a sigh, she jabbed the blade into the surface of the desk.

Then she turned, circling around to observe the books lining one of the bookshelves. Her finger traced the spine of Moby Dick before she drifted back behind the desk.

I tensed, waiting for her to see me there, lurking in the shadows, but she was too intent on searching through drawers and rustling papers. She was looking for something.

A contract? I wondered. Was she another woman from the club too impatient to bide her time?

I watched her—but as my gaze fell on her face something hit me like a punch, and I knew that I had to be dreaming. Dublin and his cruel tirade had traumatized me to the point of unconsciousness, insanity.

His voice echoed through my shattered mind once again, *'The only Gray that matters.'*

No.

The phone was still in my hand. In a daze, I reached down and redialed the last number that had called.

Impossible, some frantic part of me whispered.

It couldn't be.

I would have known those blue eyes anywhere, but it wasn't possible.

A vampire admits to poisoning you for months, and yet you still harbor doubts about anything, Ellie?

The phone rang, and the flat melody echoed, muted through the speaker.

Suddenly, a different sound pierced the silence—the default, monotone ringtone installed on most cell phones. The blonde woman frowned, reaching down to pull something from her pocket.

No ...

Every shred of sanity I had left was tied to the futile hope that this was some horrible coincidence. She would answer the cell phone she held in her hand—only mine would keep ringing, ignored by the sister who was most likely on another plane with some random lover. Not here, not now, right in the middle of my own living nightmare.

For what seemed like eons, she stared down at the screen while the phone in my hand still rang, so loudly that it was a wonder she didn't seem to hear it. Every note cracked like a gunshot.

One.

Two.

Three.

Then …

With a sigh, she brought the receiver to her ear.

"Ellie Bellie?"

Her voice blared from the speaker of my phone as it slipped from my grasp. I barely registered the sound of it smashing against the wood a second later.

I only saw Georgiana as she finally glanced up and noticed me there. Her face paled with recognition, and it was a long, cold minute before I could breathe again.

"Ellie …" Georgie's voice was barely a whisper. Her eyes took me in, settling on the blood that streaked my wrinkled blouse. "No. No. Not you … He got to you …"

She took a step forward, and I staggered back, hands held out in front of me as if that alone might have been able to make her disappear. The sight of her there made everything come crashing down. I didn't remember making a sound, but a wordless noise ricocheted off the walls that I instinctively knew had come from me.

Dublin was right. This was not a game—and yet, I was still the pawn.

"Eleanor!"

"No!"

It didn't matter why she was there, or how, or even why she'd lied to me.

I needed to get away. Run.

I turned on my heel and raced for the door to the stairs like a mad woman. In the darkness, I took them two at a time, nearly tripping over my own feet.

The church was empty. The sound of my frantic footsteps echoed as I headed for the door and raced out into the night.

Then I—the woman who had been chauffeured to and fro her entire life—ran all the way home.

It was eerie how quiet a mansion could seem when you've fired all the other inhabitants or how small and enclosed a room really was …once you locked the doors and barricaded the windows.

I hid inside my bedroom like a refugee in the midst of a war —one where the entire world was the enemy. From the corner, Tinkles hissed, hating being trapped with me almost as much as I hated myself.

Idiot, a voice in my head hissed, but for once, it wasn't my long-dead mother. *Did you really think I wanted you?* Dublin scoffed. *Please, Eleanor. You were just a means to an end.*

The words shouldn't have hurt me as badly as they did, but they *cut*, piercing through my chest, tearing.

The night I had run from his lair—and whatever dark truths it might have hidden—I had made sure to take off his necklace. It was somewhere in the foyer I thought, I couldn't be sure. The damn thing haunted my nightmares, twisting around my body and threatening to swallow me whole.

I knew that it had saved my life from Raphael's bite and, for whatever reason, Dublin hadn't taken it back. I tried not to think of him, *I tried*, but the man dominated my thoughts. My mind was a prison, with him as the jailer taunting me with the keys.

And there was no escape.

Raphael had ordered Dublin to procure my contract for some reason, and he had poisoned me to the brink of death to ensure that I couldn't refuse.

And? A part of me prompted when the thoughts became almost too painful to contemplate.

It had been all to ensnare Georgiana; the only Gray who mattered to anyone, even the Devil himself. Always Georgie.

And yet ...

He had bought my contract to keep me from being bitten by anyone else. He had come to the restaurant when I had been in danger—and something told me that I had been the bait to lure him there in the first place.

Raphael had set a trap for him, but why?

I almost wished that Dublin had stayed committed to his role as Dracula: an evil vampire who'd nearly killed me for reasons unknown.

I could understand that creature—but not the man who claimed to have saved my life, who kissed me so violently that my bottom lip still stung in places where his fangs had nipped …

I almost wanted him to come barging into my room, as boldly as always, with Georgiana in tow—if only to give me a reason.

Perhaps he loved her?

The thought pinched something inside of me, and I clutched the blankets so tightly my nails dug into the cotton.

Maybe Dublin was right after all? I *had* to enjoy pain, because the cruel thoughts kept coming.

Was he just another one of Georgie's scorned paramours? One he had loved so obsessively that he'd poisoned her dowdy sister just to get back at her?

Or was the truth behind everything more sinister?

My Uncle's words chose that moment to strike me like blows. *This is for her. They did this to get her.*

Whatever the reasons, I had only been a means to an end.

In his own way, I supposed Dublin had tried to warn me.

So, why in the hell did I feel so betrayed?

By *him* most of all …

~

It only took a day for me to die—or at least become so weak that my blankets felt like slabs of steel weighing me down to a concrete mattress.

It was as if all of the combined strength of Dublin's 'cures' had faded overnight. I felt drained. Breathing didn't seem worth the effort it took to suck air into my lungs. I may not have been a vampire, but a heavy, undeniable stench of demise clung to my skin like perfume.

And I was glad, impatient even.

Dublin had said that I welcomed death. Well, here I was with open arms. The only soul to witness my departure from the world of living would be my cat—not that Tinkles was shedding any tears.

The silence felt heavy, oppressive.

Other than the occasional plaintive meow from the corner, there was only the rushing sound of my own heartbeat. I supposed it should have hurt that no one had come after me.

Not Georgiana, the sister I had caught sneaking through a vampire's lair. Or even the vampire in question.

To be fair, I had left only one guard on the grounds with strict instructions to keep *everyone out.*

But still …I had no one. Not even Harper, who had all but killed me and yet I *still* missed his reassuring presence.

Shut up, Ellie I thought as my breath rattled in and out of my chest. *Just focus on dying.*

But even dying turned out to be much more boring than I had ever anticipated. I drifted, at the mercy of my own relentless thoughts—at least until I heard the voices.

"Hello, Eleanor." I vaguely recognized the lilting accent, and I stirred, struggling to lift my head from the pillow.

"Y-Yulia?" It hurt to speak. My lips were so chapped that when my tongue shot out to dampen them the dried skin scraped like glass.

"Yes." I had no idea if she was really there—an elegant dark blur perched on the end of my bed—or just a figment of my imagination. "I thought I should explain …"

There was a heavy note in her voice. *Explain.* There was only one thing—or person—she could have been referring to.

"I don't want to hear—"

"I used you, Eleanor," she said, ignoring the fact that I'd spoken at all. "I am not proud of that, but …you seemed to be the only one who could reach him."

Even the mere mention of *him* had the power to make my entire body recoil. A broken cough rattled from my chest.

"You made him see you," she went on before I had the chance to get a word in edgewise. "But I made sure that he couldn't *ignore* you. He can be stubborn, Dublin, but the moment he brought you into the club, I knew that you were different. I merely …helped things along."

As she spoke, several things seemed to click magically into place.

The different wardrobe.

The haircut.

The constant rebellion against Dublin's wishes; she had done it all for a reason.

"Why?" I rasped, straining to see her expression. Had she wanted to push his temper to the brink in the hopes that he'd kill me?

"Not for the reasons you might be thinking," she murmured, eyes on the wall. "We tend to do crazy things to protect the ones that we love, even from themselves. Sometimes all it takes is giving them something to live for."

"I don't understand."

"You wouldn't," she said softly. "You're a mortal. You can't possibly understand living through so many centuries that even a *day* passes like an eternity. You, humans, glamorize immortality, but it is a curse—especially if the time you live isn't even your own. Imagine being chained to a life you no longer wanted …"

I could barely follow her. The words buzzed around my brain, and it was too exhausting to try and make sense of them—not that Yulia seemed to mind. Something told me that she spoke more to soothe her own conscience than anything else.

Suddenly, she turned to face me.

"You should have seen him after the auction. After you danced, he nearly struck me. I thought he might kill me." She spoke without a shred of fear or anger. "*Why would you make her so appealing? Why? Does her life mean anything to you?* I don't think he believed me at first, when I told him the same thing I'm telling you now; dressing you, Eleanor, was a challenge for me because I did not use a *single* bit of my magic."

She paused, allowing the words to sink in.

"Every garment I made for you was no more powerful than the rest of the clothing in your closet. I want you to know that before he comes. I want you to know …he would have come anyway."

She stood, heading for the door. "He will always come."

"Wait!" I croaked, reaching out weakly as if to pull her back. "Wait …"

But she was already gone, and the silence swallowed me up again.

~

*H*ours passed it seemed, though it could have been minutes before someone else appeared at my bedside.

"Ellie? God, Ellie, can you hear me?"

My eyelids felt too heavy to lift them fully, so I took in the beautiful woman through slits.

Was she an Angel? Blonde curls formed a halo around her flawless face, gleaming so brightly my eyes watered.

Gently, she took my hand from where it clutched at my blanket, and I didn't have the strength to pull it back. Her warmth was a shock. I was freezing.

"Ellie, I don't have a lot of time," she said quickly, and something clicked like a light bulb switching on. I knew who she was.

Georgiana was wearing black again. The plain tank top showed off her tan arms—but it was subdued compared to the brilliant, pastel-clad image of her I had always had in my head.

"I just want you to know that I'm sorry," she continued in a rush. "I'm so *sorry,* Ellie. If I had known, I would have never —" She broke off, shaking her head. "I'm sorry. I know you don't understand everything—there's no way, really, that you can. Just …keep in mind that every family has their dark secrets. It just so happens that ours is darker than others."

She spoke almost too quickly for me to follow, but there was a desperation in her words that I couldn't ignore. For the first time in her life, my silly, flighty sister was …*serious.*

"I can't tell you everything," she repeated. "There isn't enough time. But, I screwed up. You should have never been a part of this, Ellie. I'm sorry ..."

She stood back, finally revealing the figure that stood behind her, someone so pale they shone even brighter than the pendant they held, dangling from two ivory fingers.

Yulia's words echoed in my mind as he came closer, haunting me as my vision faded to black.

I want you to know ... he would have come anyway ...

CROSS TO BEAR

When I finally regained consciousness, someone held my hand once again, but they were warm.

That realization had me frowning as I peeled my eyes open one by one.

Bright sunlight streamed in through the windows. I had to blink several times just to make out the person who sat on a chair at my bedside.

"Ellie …"

Georgiana looked so much *older*. There was a maturity shaping her beautiful features that I couldn't remember having been there before—though, to be fair, I hadn't seen her in nearly four months.

And who knew? Sneaking around a vampire's lair could have aged anyone a few years.

"Belize treated you well," I croaked, but my voice was too weak for the insult to come across.

"I know you're confused, angry even," she said, squeezing my fingers as if anticipating the moment I'd try and pull away. But I felt too drained.

Dublin had already shattered me to pieces. I supposed it was her turn as well to hammer home just how much of a fool I was.

"Ellie, I wasn't in Belize for fun." She paused, letting the words sink in. "I was there for business …a mission."

I raised an eyebrow. *Business?*

"Is this your way of telling me that you're involved in criminal activity?" I wondered. It was just so much easier if I just ignored the vampire aspect and focused on the typical Georgiana drama. "What is it? Drugs? How much money will you need this time—"

"Ellie, you have no idea," her tone caught me off guard. For the first time, I realized that she wasn't speaking in her usual high-pitched cadence. Her voice was low and level instead —a stranger's. "Every family has their dark secrets, remember?" She frowned, picking an invisible piece of lint off her jeans. Shocked, I realized that her nails were unpainted, and a few were even chipped. "I don't know how else to say this, so I just will …"

I waited as she sucked in a breath. I could sense her fingers trembling. Every muscle in her slender body seemed tense like a coil ready to spring.

"Our family is nuts, Ellie," she blurted on a shaky laugh. "Even more than you realize. Mother … Father… I don't think they even knew the full truth. But somehow I think even they understood that our family was cursed."

Something in her tone gave me the strength I needed to ask that one, burning question that seared at the back of my brain.

"Why were you in the church?"

"Research," she said tightly. It was a good minute before I realized that she wouldn't say any more than, "I was looking for something."

"You know who lives there?" I couldn't even say his name. Regardless, Georgie's expression hardened with recognition, and I don't know why I was so shocked by the fact. Georgiana knew *everyone*—she was the only Gray that mattered after all …

"Eleanor, of course, I know *him*." She raised a blonde eyebrow. "He's one of the most feared monsters in history, second only to one …"

A feral scowl shaped her mouth—an expression that would have never crossed the face of the carefree Georgie I thought I knew.

"Dublin."

"Huh?"

I swallowed. "He calls himself …Dublin." Though I had a feeling that his real name was something else entirely.

"Ellie," Georgie began before I even hoped to put the suspicions running through my head into a coherent sentence. "While we Grays have our fortune, there's another side to the estate that isn't exactly public knowledge."

"Like what?" My stomach churned as I considered the usual skeletons a rich family might have in their proverbial closet.

A secret family living in the attic?

A widespread criminal organization?

Actual skeletons?

But nothing could have prepared me for what Georgie said instead.

"We hunt vampires." She might as well have said *we vacation in Spain,* her tone was that casual—but her eyes told a different story. "From every generation, one Gray gets inducted ..."

"Into what?"

She wouldn't look at me. Her eyes swept the floor instead. "It's an old society that dates back to the colonial period, started by our ancestor—"

A name came to mind, and I blurted it before she had the chance. "James."

Raphael's ominous statement drifted through my mind; *I knew your ancestor ...*

"Yes." Georgie raised an eyebrow, but didn't question how I had settled on that particular long-dead Gray. "James. It was founded by him solely to track vampires and combat their hold on society. He called it *'The Grayne,'* and from every generation of Grays, a new member is chosen—*must* be chosen. Uncle Orwell was inducted from his and father's line, and me from ours."

"Inducted?" My head was spinning. Our family being a cold collection of individuals bound only by money I could understand—but this?

"Only one Gray from every generation is chosen ...usually at the discretion of a member from the last generation," she said. "Orwell pulled me into the fold when I was only fifteen. My 'boarding school' days were really spent in Rome training with the other inductees."

"But I don't understand ..." I thought back to the night Orwell had assaulted me—mainly his reaction to seeing me linked with Dublin.

No wonder he'd shoved me into a wall of glass.

"Did mother know?" I croaked. "Father?"

She shook her head. "No. It's forbidden to tell anyone outside of the Grayne—barring any 'extenuating' circumstances of course," she added softly.

Such as finding your older sister in a vampire's lair.

"This ... This doesn't make any sense—you're *Georgiana Gray.*" I said the name as if it were a title: *Duchess. Empress. Queen.*

"We all have different faces," she explained with a shrug. "The air-headed socialite act gave me an excuse to travel the world and throw off suspicion. After all, no one suspects the rich, blonde bimbo of packing an extendable stake in her back pocket."

I glanced down at her dark jeans, wondering if she had such a thing in her pocket now. The Georgie I thought I'd known couldn't even hold a butter knife properly. Though the fact that she wore pants at all was more than enough proof that her 'air-headed socialite' ruse had been real. My sister, a real-life Buffy.

Only why did it hurt so much to know that she had merely 'acted' around me for most of our lives?

The pretty, confident and somewhat morally scrupulous sister I'd known and tolerated was dead. Left in her place was someone I barely recognized.

"What about the phone calls?" I thought back to the past few weeks. I couldn't remember her mentioning anything about hunting creatures of the night.

"No one can know about The Grayne, Ellie," she said softly. Her eyes met mine warily. "Not even you."

"But what about Belize? What about the man you were with?"

"His name is Gregor," she said, "he's an associate of mine. Sometimes he comes in handy."

She cracked a faint smile that made something inside my chest ache.

"What about the money?"

"That …is complicated," she sighed. "My world isn't like it's portrayed on television. It's more *political.* Bargains and favors. Getting important information sometimes requires *very big* favors. One contact, in particular, is fond of Italian-made sports cars."

Hence the massive transfer. Everything that had happened over these past two weeks was slowly clicking into place, though I didn't like the picture the pieces made.

"So what were you doing there? Why couldn't you come back?"

She'd resisted coming home to the extent that made me positive that she was hiding more from me.

"I was doing …more *research*," she said finally. "I can't tell you everything—I *can't.* But there was something in Belize I needed to find. Answers."

"Answers? About what?"

Considering everything I'd already discovered in the past few days, I was sure that there was nothing she could possibly say that would surprise me anymore.

"It's more like …who. I was trying to gain background on a vampire called Raphael," she blurted, proving me wrong. "I have a feeling that you've already learned about the way contracts work."

I could only nod.

"They all belong to him. Everyone connected to that world has a contract either directly or indirectly owned by Raphael. *Everyone.* He controls it all—but even then there are still rules. If the holder of a contract dies, then ownership of it passes on to their killer."

She paused as if waiting for me to put the pieces of some puzzle together on my own. Then, she continued, "If you want to take out the entire world of the vampires and their cohorts, then you take out the man who holds them all by the leash."

I don't know what was more shocking? Hearing my sister— who, until two days ago I had believed knew nothing about the world outside of a magazine—talk casually about a secret world of vampires, or the fact that I understood almost every word she said?

"You wanted to kill Raphael." I pictured the haunting gaze of the man in question, and I had to suppress the urge to shiver.

"Yes," Georgie said without pause. "But I overstepped. While The Grayne make it our mission to destroy the contract system, there are still rules we have to follow, treaties we have to respect. By going into the heart of Raphael's territory …I provoked him."

Her voice was throaty. She wouldn't look at me.

"Ellie …if I had known that he would go after you … I never thought that—" She broke off, and I could see that her shoulders were shaking in the way that meant she was trying her hardest not to cry. Her teeth would be clenched, eyes a dark shade of navy.

Was it sad that I was relieved that not all of her had been a façade? At least some things remained the same.

"It's all right." I reached out with my free hand, brushing her shoulder.

It was then, as I shifted, that I finally noticed the feel of cool metal beneath the collar of my nightgown, and the weight of a distinctly shaped object resting ominously against my stomach.

"It was the only way," Georgie said softly. Her gaze drifted toward the amulet in question, tracing every contour of the silver chain.

A sudden thought occurred to me as a fuzzy image drifted on the edge of my consciousness; her and a shadowy figure standing at my bedside. Only one reason could explain it.

"You made a contract."

She didn't deny it. Her fingers clenched mine so tightly I could feel her pulse throbbing beneath her skin.

"He said it was the only way." It was as if every single word was being ripped from her throat against her will. "I had no choice, Ellie. I couldn't just let you die …"

"What did you bargain?" My blood ran cold at the thought of her making the same deal I had, and I glanced up, scouring her tan throat for bite marks.

"I only had to promise to drop the trail I'd been hunting in Belize and allow his 'business' to relocate without retaliation," she sounded as surprised by that fact as I was. "I thought it was some kind of sick joke, but when he put that necklace on you, it—"

"Who?" A part of me didn't even want to consider the possible answer lurking at the back of my mind.

Raphael? I wondered almost hopefully. It would have been easier to believe that my sister had made a deal with the Devil, rather than …

"Dublin," she said. "He said that it was the only way to save your life—he told me what he did to you, Ellie. He poisoned you."

She broke off, eyes narrowed with so much hatred that I almost didn't recognize her as my sister.

"You begged him to save me?"

How he must have enjoyed that, the pretty Georgie on her hands and knees begging for my life…

"No." She slowly shook her head. "He came to me."

"I don't understand …"

Georgie lifted her shoulders in a shrug. "I don't really care what his reasons were. You're alive, and that's all that matters to me."

Before I could blink, her hand was in mine again, holding so tightly that I could feel her warmth leech into my skin.

"We're family, Ellie."

I marveled over those words. *Family.*

It was a rare phrase to throw around the Gray household. After all, how could you love anyone who only revealed a sliver of who they really were?

I guess father hadn't been lying when he claimed that money was everything.

But …I doubted that father had ever come across someone like Dublin Helos, who could throw thousands of dollars into the trash without batting an eyelash and make someone like me feel …

I don't know, alive, even for a second.

I clenched Georgie's fingers just as tightly, staring down at the chain draped around my neck, as heavy as iron.

"Family."

DEBTS

ONE MONTH LATER...

*E*very family has their secrets, my mother used to say. Every woman has her mysteries.

I wondered if she had known of our family's little secret, or of the darkness that had nearly driven Orwell insane and forced Georgiana to live a double life. I wondered if she had known much of anything apart from the carefully crafted world she'd created for herself. To her credit, denial and secrecy seemed to be an inherited trait among us Grays.

Georgie, once shrouded in silly mystery had become an enigma. She still wouldn't tell me the whole truth; the only clues she had let slip free were snippets about Raphael and contracts and …

It all made my head hurt, which was a figurative pain, of course, because with Dublin's chain around my neck, I felt absolutely nothing. Things that would have normally tired me no longer did. It was as if the magic infused in it enhanced everything to an exquisite degree—but it was merely an illusion; a temporary fix.

The damage wrought by Dublin's venom couldn't be undone by any cure. The moment I took it off, my body would begin to deteriorate again.

I wondered if he was limited without it. If he couldn't go out in the sun or whatever it was the magic seemed to enable him to do? I tried not to care. I *tried* … But so many things had gotten out of my control lately that it was laughable to think that I could. Almost as laughable as the fact that I sat in a town car, staring up at the boarded-up building that only I knew had once been a club for vampires.

Under the guise of needing *"fresh air,"* I had taken off in a hired cab rather than risk driving the Rolls Royce by myself —we still hadn't found someone to replace Harper.

My instructions were clear, but when we had reached the skeleton of Anemia, I still had to double check the name on a nearby street sign.

Just to be sure.

Apparently, Dublin had wasted no time in putting Georgie's contractual promise of allowing him to 'relocate in peace' to the test. Yulia's shop had been emptied as well, and the warehouse door had been sealed with a rusty chain.

"Ma'am?" I blinked as the driver spoke from the front seat. "Sorry, but the meter's still running …"

I glanced up to find him watching me in the rearview mirror with a puzzled expression.

Nut, I could imagine him thinking in disgust.

"That's all right," I said softly, folding my hands in my lap.

I sighed, sparing one last glance at the remains of Anemia. What would the building become now? I wondered. *An office? A store?*

Would the new tenants ever have any clue about the creatures who had once wandered through the walls? Or the use of those mysterious rooms at the back?

"Miss?"

"We can go now."

I started to tear my gaze from the window, only to jump as a hand appeared to rap against the glass. A man stood on the curb. His expression was stern, but something in the way he was dressed—in a dark, crisp suit—made me warily hit the button to lower the glass.

"For you, Miss," he said, before slipping something through the gap so that it landed on my lap. My eyes fell to the object, and I barely noticed as the stranger stood back, disappearing as quickly as he'd appeared.

It was a small parcel. My name was written across the front in elegant, unfamiliar script; an unusual occurrence in more ways than one. I rarely received personal mail these days— not to mention that very few people would send a messenger to approach me on the street.

My fingers trembled as I tore off the brown wrappings to reveal the object inside—a small, flat leather-bound book. It was so old that the bindings had started to come apart. In the center of the dilapidated cover, ironically in near pristine condition, was the symbol of that familiar serpent with ruby-red eyes. As I let the binder fall onto my lap, a single, square sheet of paper slid out.

'*Thank you, Miss Gray, our arrangement has worked out quite well,* the first line read. *As promised, I have upheld my end of the bargain.*

-Raphael'

My throat jerked around a gulp. I had to pinch myself just once before I slowly peeled the book apart, unsurprised to discover that it was a contract, much like my own.

The lettering was barely visible—I could only discern a few words. *Five hundred years. Bound.*

Across the bottom, however, in a bright shade of ink, so fresh it could have been written days ago, someone had added: *With the addendum of ten more additional years in exchange for the contract of E.L.G.*

I knew what those initials stood for; my name.

I also knew of a man supposedly bound for five hundred years. A man who called himself something that I now knew was nothing but an unspoken mantra, intended to reinforce those words he repeated so often: is hell bound.

But knowledge didn't make the words written on the contract any easier to stomach.

On the line specifying the contractor was only one name. *Cael.*

And below that was the name of the beholder. *Eleanor Gray.*

The Story Continues in:
Chain Me

CHAIN ME

Chain Me

Chain Me By Lana Sky

Copyright © 2019 by Lana Sky
All rights reserved.
No part of this publication may be reproduced, distributed, or transmitted
in any form or by any means, including photocopying, recording, or other
electronic or mechanical methods, without the prior written permission of
the author.
This is a work of fiction. Names, characters, businesses, places, events and
incidents are either the products of the author's imagination or used in a
fictitious manner. Any resemblance to actual persons, living or dead, or
actual events is purely coincidental.

Cover design by Sarah Hansen, Okay Creations
Edited by Mickey Reed
Proofread by Charity Chimni
Formatting by Charity Chimni

To my very patient fans. Thank you so much for believing in this story and allowing me the time to write it.

"And at all at once, I was consumed; a darkness borne of blood and torment, laid bare at the feet of the Storm."

—A.R. Simone

D.H.

*J*may have been the heir to one of the richest families in the country, but alas, our vast fortune couldn't buy me *everything*.

Love was beyond the reach of my checkbook—though affection had never been synonymous with the Gray name anyway. Sanity was another elusive trophy, and the past year had served as a biting testament to how little I had left.

But my millions couldn't procure *answers*. Especially the ones pertaining to the brooding vampire who had destroyed my life on a whim and then disappeared.

What else did a bored heiress with too much time and money on her hands have to do with her days besides track him down?

Nothing—*apart* from blatantly lying to the doctor standing in my way, of course.

"Do you think you can help me?" I meekly asked the woman seated across from me. A polished oak desk separated us, the most eye-catching fixture of her rather plain office.

"Good news! I don't think you're dying, Eleanor," Dr. Goodfellow declared. A severe bun kept the graying brown hair back from her round face, enhancing her stern "trust me" expression. If I squinted, her concern almost seemed genuine. "However, I'm glad you dropped by, because I do have some mild concerns. I think another round of tests would help to put us both at ease."

"More tests? Are you sure? I think I'm feeling a lot better, actually—" A cough ripped from my throat, and I attempted to smother it within the sleeve of my sweater. "I feel fine."

"Th-That may be so, dear," Goodfellow stammered. Her gaze settled over my chest, her blue eyes suspiciously narrowed. "But I'm concerned. Your lab results have been… puzzling, to say the least. For instance, your hormone levels seem to be spiking, but since you wrote"—she shuffled a stack of documents before her and scanned the topmost page—"*never* in answer to *could you currently be pregnant?*, well… I must admit that I'm flummoxed. I've even consulted some outside experts for insight. I wish I could get my hands on your old records, but it seems there was a mishap because your file for last year appears to be incomplete…"

She paused as if waiting for me to clarify. Where oh where could a year of my medical history have gone? I knew the answer of course. Into a vampire's coat pocket.

It wasn't an explanation Goodfellow could comprehend, however. When I said nothing, she cleared her throat. "Well, it's only been a month since you were last cleared by your last provider, Dr. Wallis, hasn't it?"

I shrugged. The last time I'd seen Dr. Wallis had been a mere month after the vampire pulling his puppet strings disappeared. He had eyed me the way one might a ghost before promptly refunding my health insurance for every penny spent on the treatment for my supposed illness.

Then he too vanished.

"Is he still in Tahiti?" I wondered, parroting the reason his office secretary gave for his absence.

"Tahiti?" Dr. Goodfellow blinked and adjusted her wire-rimmed glasses. "I'm not sure, dear. But you can rest assured that, even with the gaps in your history, I can address your concerns—"

"I'm fine." I even flashed a charming grin for emphasis. "I don't think more tests are necessary."

"Oh? Over the phone, you said you've been feeling poorly for weeks. Isn't that why you made the appointment? Frankly, I wish you had been more specific, and I would have booked you an emergency consult." She wrinkled her delicate nose in distaste. "That sort of cough is no minor symptom, my dear—"

"It's nothing." I shrugged as my fingers toyed with the silver cross hanging from my throat. Little did the good doctor know that, as long as I wore it, I supposedly was the picture of health. Or so a deceitful vampire claimed. Batting the talisman aside, I tried to look as un-sickly as possible. Another unforced cough didn't help much in that regard. "Do you have a diagnosis yet?"

"It could be fatigue," she said. "But your case has puzzled me. Your symptoms don't seem to fit into any logical diagnostic criteria—"

"So you're saying I'm fatigued?" I sighed to hide my skepticism. Compared to my last life-shattering diagnosis, what a boring ailment.

Thankfully, Goodfellow was right; my health wasn't the real reason for this visit anyway.

"This is quite the premier establishment," I blurted out, eyeing the diploma framed in gold, hanging on the white wall behind her head. "I'm sure you have people of high esteem on the board?"

I knew firsthand that it *did*. Stationed right in the heart of downtown, St. Mary's was one of the leading medical facilities in the country, prestigious enough to attract backing from a variety of benefactors.

The undead kind in search of a power trip, for instance. The kind of man who liked to disappear without so much as a word or a *"Thanks for your virginity, Eleanor. Oh, and your blood, too. Have a nice life!"*

Such a creature would relish the influence this hospital could provide—it was the perfect place to hide in plain sight.

"Ms. Gray?" Dr. Goodfellow had an eyebrow raised, her tone delicate in that annoying way when someone tended to stare off into space for uncomfortable periods of time. A tone I had grown accustomed to.

"R-Right." I snapped out of my daze and cleared my throat. "As you well know, my family has a long history of providing donations to hospitals and charities alike. I would love to do my part to contribute, by any means necessary. Perhaps I could be introduced to the board?"

"Of course!" Dr. Goodfellow couldn't even disguise the greedy twitch of her lips. Suddenly, all concern for my welfare vanished. "We welcome any form of donation. I would be happy to connect you to our Community Outreach Department—"

"Actually, I've already done my research. Here." I fished a brochure from my purse. Its dog-eared pages betrayed how many times I'd peered through them in anticipation of this meeting. One in particular sported a tear right down the middle, suspiciously close to a mysterious name.

"I found a roster of your most recent benefactors, and I'd love to ask them some further questions before I invest. I'm familiar with most, but this person..." I pointed a trembling finger to one entry in particular. Initials, really.

Squinting, Dr. Goodfellow read them out loud. "D.H.?" She seemed oblivious to the shudder that racked my spine. I had to clench my hands into fists to keep them from shaking, crumpling the brochure further. "I'm not familiar with that person, to be honest, Eleanor. But we really should discuss your treatment options. I'll be blunter: Going off your recent results, I found some of your labs a tad alarming. We should schedule an immediate follow-up."

"I don't think that's necessary." Another cough rattled from my chest as I pushed the brochure into my purse. Disappointment was surprisingly hard to swallow down.

My gagging prompted Dr. Goodfellow to shove a napkin into my hands. This time, my coughing fit succeeded in bringing up liquid, which I spit into a nearby wastebasket. Snot, perhaps.

Red, vibrant snot.

"Eleanor..." The doctor's gaze was fixated on whatever substance clung to the tissue. "I really do think we should run a few more tests—"

"So, you don't know that name?" I pressed, impatiently wringing my hands. "What a shame. I thought he might provide a unique perspective on the establishment."

"He?" Goodfellow cocked her head. "Do you know this person? I was under the impression that you didn't."

"Um..." I blinked and coughed again. "I'm sorry, what?"

"You said *he* might provide a unique perspective—"

"Did I? Um, anyway, as you were saying… My symptoms. Are you sure you'll be able to find a diagnosis soon?"

"Of course." She nodded emphatically. "As you yourself mentioned, we are a state-of-the-art facility, Ms. Gray. You can rest easy under our care. I'm glad that you came in when you did."

For all the good it had done. The poor woman didn't even have enough sense to transfer my case to a psychiatrist. Or perhaps a priest would have been more fitting in this instance?

Someone used to dealing with the damned and hopeless.

Still, I attempted to return her smile with a thin grin of my own. "Let's hope it's nothing serious."

"Oh, let's not jump to the worst just yet. However…" She snatched up my hand without warning, lifting it to display the quivering fingertips. "This tremor. It's more pronounced than when you first entered my office, and I see from your preliminaries that you've lost more weight. That cough is concerning as well, considering the color the sputum—"

"Color?" I echoed innocently.

"It looked like blood, Eleanor." Her gentle smile slipped, revealing something far more unnerving underneath. Alarm. "I'm beginning to think that Dr. Wallis may have been a bit hasty in clearing you so soon. It's only been a month since your diagnosis was reversed, after all. I would like to order another blood test—"

"More?" I eyed my forearm where the sleeve of my sweater was rolled up to reveal a bandage—my souvenir from the last round of tests done earlier that morning. "I feel fine, honestly. I would hate to waste your time." I gingerly untangled my hand from hers and started to rise from the leather armchair facing her desk. "Thank you."

"Of course, my dear. We can use your sample from this morning for the new tests. I'll make sure to call you with the results." She folded her hands together. "Now, you should go home and get some rest. I'm sure we'll have an answer for you by the end of the week. In the meantime, keep your chin up."

Her smile widened.

But I merely stooped for my bag and scrambled from her office before she could suggest another battery of tests to suffer through.

My disappointment loomed, inescapable. Even the sky visible beyond the windows of the corridor seemed to reflect it: dark, churning clouds and a smattering of raindrops.

What a fuss for nothing. Though the poking and prodding should have been a small price to pay if my hunch turned out to be correct. *Small,* I insisted as my hands shook over the handle of my bag. Though Goodfellow didn't need to try so hard to feign concern. Apart from my brain, nothing else was wrong with me.

Physically, at least.

For the first time in years, I theoretically had a clean bill of health.

No life-threatening illness to worry about.

No vampire lurking in the corridor to smuggle me his magic blood.

No crippling, fearful uncertainty, no siree...

I was *fine*.

"Are you all right, hun?" someone asked as I made my way to the nearest elevator. A woman, her gaze on my shaking fingertips. A tiny figure clung to her hip, clutching a ratty doll that had seen better days. Paces away a man eyed a wristwatch and sighed impatiently, but as his gaze shifted to the woman before me, all traces of impatience faded from his expression.

"Do you need to sit down?" the woman asked.

For someone so nosy, she should have been older. A gnarled biddy with nothing better to do than butt her nose into other's affairs. But she was young—my age, if I wanted to be generous. A healthy woman who didn't sport blood dripping down her chin and wasn't trembling on her feet. Someone who possessed a family, and security, and all of those pesky things my money couldn't afford.

Someone who seemed conjured by the universe as if to spite me with an eternal truth: *you're alone, Eleanor. You're probably dying, Eleanor. Stop pining over him, Eleanor.*

"I'm fine," I replied with a smile, though the small family didn't seem convinced. The child stuck her head out from around her mother to gape at me, her tiny eyebrow raised.

Who cared? I was past letting strangers comment on my health.

Once I had made it to the front of the hospital and climbed into the back seat of my family's Rolls-Royce, I closed my eyes—only to be thwarted again in my quest for peace.

"How did it go, miss?" my driver inquired.

I peeled one eye open, observing him with a frown. He was a new hire who had come highly recommended. To most, he probably ticked all of the right boxes—overly friendly, sufficiently charming. He was even pretty for a man, with dark, curly hair and eyes the color of chocolate.

I only *slightly* hated him—he wasn't Harper, my long-time confidant and friend. But Harper was probably dead, so this man would have to do.

"It went fine," I replied, closing my eyes again. "I'd like to rest, if that's all right."

As requested, the rest of the journey to the house passed in silence, broken only by the crunch of gravel as the vehicle turned onto the driveway. I startled to awareness, taking in the desolate landscape awaiting me beyond the window with a strange sense of guilt.

I had some damn nerve peddling my money and my resources to hospitals rather than spending it on the only thing my parents had ever deemed important: our supposed legacy. After months of neglect, Gray Manor had certainly seen better days. The house itself loomed above acres of untouched fields and overgrown weeds, as imposing as ever.

Spring had blossomed over the rest of the city, but my familiar home was a landscape clinging to winter. Perhaps it hadn't been a prudent decision to fire most of the gardening staff on a whim?

Make that *all* of the gardening staff.

At least the lack of salaries kept the family fortune intact; Mother would certainly thank me for that.

"Have a nice day, miss," the driver encouraged as I slipped from the car.

Even though he'd been under my employ for nearly a month, I had yet to learn his name—though it didn't matter.

I would fire him eventually. Once I got over my fear of driving, that is. I'd fired everyone else.

There was no butler to greet me as I hastened up the front walkway and mounted the topmost step of the front stoop. I had to fish a key from the depths of my handbag and fit it into the lock myself—a fact that would have scandalized my poor parents. To get the solid oak door to budge, I had to basically throw myself against it.

Maybe firing the handyman hadn't been too smart an idea, either?

A minor inconvenience. One couldn't put a price tag on silence—and I had the lion's share as I wandered the deserted foyer. Cold, drafty desolation lingered between the wooden floors and the cavernous ceiling despite the sweltering heat outside.

Home sweet home.

My breath painted the air white, but there was no one around to adjust the heating system, and I didn't know how. Perhaps Georgie—my estranged sister who belonged to a secret society of vampire hunters—did, though it wasn't like I could ask her.

Screaming *Get the hell out!* at everyone around you tended to have that desired effect. They scattered, no arguments. No desperate pleas to stay.

It was like magic, screaming—and I refused to regret the action one damn bit. Why, when I could strip my coat and leave it right there at the foot of the staircase with no one to stare?

No one to judge, or nag, or patronize.

When I crept into my room, there was no maid to snipe about my rumpled bedsheets or to sigh in pity as I crawled onto the mattress and buried my head beneath the covers. There was no one to witness the shiver that ran down my spine as my stomach contracted. There was no doting chef to care that I hadn't eaten a solid meal in nearly two weeks, despite a ravenous hunger that plagued me almost as violently as a near-persistent bout of nausea.

Nothing was wrong with me.

Nothing but the invisible creature ripping my insides apart, contorting my body in agony.

I barely managed to clear my head from the mattress before copious amounts of liquid expelled from my throat and pooled on the floor. Then I turned into the safety of my pillow, but squeezing my eyes shut didn't erase the image of it. Thick. *Red.*

No bother. I already knew the CliffsNotes version of what was transpiring. I was *maybe* dying again. My body was collapsing upon itself, *yada yada yada.* The doctor's diagnosis would soon confirm it, and then I could commence with the drafting of a will and whatnot.

I'd done it all before, so no harm no foul. Only something told me that a mysterious benefactor wouldn't step from the shadows to offer a solution this time. He had every reason to want me dead, after all, considering I owned ten years' worth of his soul…

I was on my own—a fact that didn't make much of a damn difference in the grand scheme.

I was Eleanor Gray. The only thing on Earth I excelled at was being alone.

At least there was one person who wouldn't leave me just because I demanded it. Well, a *creature*, but he's no less valid. Mr. Tinkles, my dearest Siamese rescue cat, served as the second-to-last living creature dwelling within Gray Manor.

The fact that he only had three limbs might have contributed to why he remained behind at all, but that was beside the point.

The moment I opened the door to his suite, he lunged from the shadows, claws drawn in his typical greeting. A bell hanging from his collar—a custom light-blue velvet one with sterling-silver hardware—jiggled manically, tracking his advance. He lunged toward me, his eyes flashing with murderous intent. By sheer luck, the back wheels of his makeshift wheelchair caught on a bump in the carpet, and I jerked out of range unscathed.

Until the room began spinning.

My stomach crawled up my throat as the wallpaper bled into the carpet. White on red, like fresh blood on pale flesh. Gagging, I slumped forward, and I had only enough time to aim opposite the direction of my cat before I ruined a priceless antique carpet with a stream of vomit. Quite the feat, considering I had nothing left in my stomach to bring up. Just more of that unsettling liquid. Red and vibrant, the puddle resisted cleaning no matter how hard I tried to mop up the mess with the end of my skirt.

It wasn't like I needed a maid. I didn't…

Luckily, I didn't need to guard from Tinkles, either. The blatant destruction of his private suite startled the poor darling into ceasing his attack. Eyes wide, he slunk toward his favorite corner. A haughty meow came a heartbeat later, demanding more food instead of my flesh for once. After I'd fulfilled his request, he watched me, swishing his tail through the air. Then he approached.

So much for his brief ceasefire. I tensed, throwing my hands out before me—but he didn't lunge. In fact, his hackles weren't even raised.

The moment he finally reached my side and curled up against my leg—*without* attacking—I knew then and there that something was horribly, terribly wrong.

Fear so raw that it packed a punch rendered me spineless. I sank to my knees, curling up against the invaluable carpet. And my devious, hateful feline didn't hiss at me once. In fact, I swore I felt the silken brush of his fur settling right against my abdomen.

Hours later, I escaped into the bath and made a game out of ignoring the multitude of changes I hadn't reported to the good doctor Goodfellow.

Because they didn't matter.

Like how pale my skin had become: tissue paper over the bluish veins snaking underneath, carrying my newly "healed" blood. Brittle bones stood out like exposed scaffolding, propping up my gaunt features.

One symptom, however, triggered the most alarm. It was a feeling lurking beneath the water's surface and infecting my skin. Itching. In my muscles. In my bones. Food didn't soothe the irritation. Water, either. It felt deeper.

Perhaps the manifestation of some festering tumor?

Oh joy.

Looking on the bright side, I toweled off and hunched beneath a terrycloth robe. Why all the worry? I had no terminal diagnosis.

In fact, I was supposedly cured, thanks to a vampire who gave me his magic necklace. I eyed the jewelry in question, holding it up for inspection. Some women might have cherished the expertly crafted silver cross. If I squinted, I could have called it beautiful.

Or hideous. It didn't suit me, standing out gaudily as I approached the mirror and tried to salvage my appearance.

If my health continued to decline, at least I already looked the part: dead. My frown was the liveliest thing about me. It remained as I ran a brush through my hair and dressed in an old skirt and a sweater. In the end, I put the sweater on backward and only had enough energy to sweep the worst tangles back from my face before my stomach roiled again.

The Eleanor from yesterday would have written the symptom off. *At least it wasn't hemorrhaging to death, no bother.*

But now… The little detail of my vomit seemed harder to ignore. Remnants of it still speckled the corner of my mouth. Red. Salty. When I swiped at a smear with my thumb, the liquid spread, painting my cheek.

Dr. Goodfellow had noticed it too—a fact that suggested I *wasn't* making it up out of paranoia. Perhaps another scenario, other than a psychotic break, could explain the past few weeks?

Like the prospect that, despite his sudden disappearance, Dublin Helos wasn't done with me yet.

Had he stooped to poisoning me again?

Or perhaps a more nefarious ailment to drive me insane for good?

Anything to retrieve the one thing of value I had that might interest him: his contract. He was most likely stalking me from some unseen hiding place, waiting for the chance to pounce. In the meantime, he settled for gloating from afar. *Ignoring* me.

Well, I would give him something to ignore.

Upon returning to my room, I collapsed onto the chair before my desk. Countless brochures littered the surface, and they fell to the floor as I swiped them aside. Some contained the donor lists of city-owned buildings. Others were political donation rosters. Some pertained to the boards of other area hospitals.

I had scoured them all for even a hint of one name. One mysterious benefactor with a fetish for the dramatic.

Again, my fingers caressed the cross hanging from my throat. The moment he'd given it to me replayed in my mind almost daily.

"Wear it," he'd insisted. *"Take it off and you'll die."*

Despite the warning, I had considered doing just that. I'd even *tried* to in the days after he'd left. But something always held me back. Stupidity, most likely. Or maybe pride?

Resisting him was what the pathetic, old Eleanor had done, and look where that had gotten her.

Though look what the opposite had gotten me, current-day Eleanor.

The same damn thing—loneliness.

Dejected, I watched my hand fall onto my lap. Then I wrenched a drawer open and fished out a page of stationery and a pen from inside it. The moment I pressed the nib to the paper, an odd flash of déjà vu made my hand tremble, which made ink splatter onto the page.

I envisioned a painfully handsome man with the face of an angel, his voice cruel as he dished out his trademark proposal.

"Live or die, Eleanor?"

How naïve I'd been back then. After all, there'd never been a choice. Just a game, but this time, I vowed to make my own rules—even if I had to scribble them hastily in black ink.

I never fell for it, you know. I never believed that you could actually want me. I never did…

When I finished writing, I folded the page and attempted to stick it into an envelope. I would never send it, of course.

I had *some* damn sense of modesty. It was the mere thought of it that mattered: shoving all of my pathetic fears regarding him into a small space and sealing it with a flick of a finger.

"Damn!" Faint heat prickled the pad of my thumb and I popped the digit into my mouth, though I barely felt the sting. Just…

Hunger.

My teeth bored down on their own accord, extending the bitter flavor coating my tongue. I must have grazed my hand over something without realizing it. Something that didn't make my stomach rebel in disgust. Instead, it triggered a thought that blotted out all others.

I need more.

I scanned the surface of the desk as I sucked, hunting for whatever substance I might be tasting. Solid oak. Paper. Black ink.

Red droplets on white parchment.

Light flickered over the domed surfaces while my brain finally connected the taste with sight.

Oh god! I wrenched my thumb from my mouth and lurched from the chair. Too fast. My hand flew out, grasping for the edge of the desk, but I missed. Both legs gave way, pitching me onto my knees. My stomach lurched at the pain. Demanding, sharp, pinching cramps…

Food. That would fix it. All I needed was a meal.

I considered bread, or a salad, or whatever might be lurking in the pantry down below, and I'd barely made it onto my hands and knees before my stomach roiled again. There was no hiding from what came up this time. Crimson painted my fingertips, caught beneath the spray, tainting my touch. Still gagging, I snatched the finished letter from my desk, hauled myself upright, and staggered toward the door.

Modesty was for healthy people.

Sane people.

And I was well beyond both states of being.

～

My new driver asked way too many damn questions. *"Did you cut yourself, miss? You know this place is deserted, right? Are you sure this is the right address?"*

To compound my irritation, I didn't even know his name. As he opened the door on my end, I asked him purely out of spite.

"François," he blurted after a moment's pause. His wide-eyed expression probably had something to do with the red liquid drying over the corner of my mouth. And my hands.

Rather than explain myself, I shoved the door open farther and pushed past him to mount the curb. A scorching sun cast the property in an uncharacteristically bright light. Spring was waning and warm weather had rudely invaded. Those who passed by were wearing vibrant sundresses and short-sleeved ensembles in pastel pinks and dreamy hues.

On the other hand, *I* was wearing a thick skirt. And a sweater. And an overcoat.

The layers were in vain—I was shivering anyway.

Perhaps my inner emotions were projecting outside? Though, in that case, I should have felt nothing. Numb was the word *du jour* as I pondered the hollowed-out shell of a building before me.

It had been a bustling cathedral only a few short weeks ago. Now, a sign nailed to the grand entrance claimed it *closed for renovations*. How subtle.

If only its worshippers knew what had taken place within this supposedly holy space, just beyond the beautiful façade of stained-glass windows.

God didn't live here alone—that was for sure. Or at least, that used to be the case. Even now, the back of my neck prickled, but a paranoid glance over my shoulder revealed no one in sight. After a moment's hesitation, I crouched and finally slid my bloodied letter beneath the door.

There. Whether anyone actually read it or not didn't matter. I'd made an attempt to have the last word.

The last laugh.

Nonetheless, I returned to the car knowing that it was a fool's errand—but how else did you reach someone who didn't want to be found?

You shouted into the void, of course.

And only silence answered back.

FORTUNE FAVORS THE GRAY

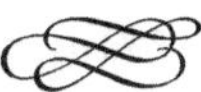

No mysterious visitor appeared to darken my doorstep the next morning. No parcel arrived, stuffed into the mailbox. Either I was losing my touch when it came to dramatic gestures or blood-soaked letters didn't pack the same punch of urgency they used to. Almost as if…

Well, almost as if Dublin Helos *wasn't* lurking in the shadows, watching me.

At least one person did seem interested in my welfare, considering they called almost daily, leaving a message each time.

"Ms. Gray, this is doctor Goodfellow. I am still waiting to hear from some experts in the field about your case. I hope to have an answer soon…"

"Ms. Gray, I've received the results of your last blood test. We should schedule another appointment immediately…"

"Ms. Gray, doctor Goodfellow again. I must ask if you are a government official or in possession of some kind of high-level security clearance, because accessing an opinion on your case at all seems to involve an unusual number of hurdles..."

Dublin Helos had left a void in my life that even one of the best doctors in the country couldn't fill—and he refused to offer any explanation as to why. But I didn't scream, or cry, or fall into hysterics at the possibility of being ignored. Instead, as any uncaring socialite would, I simply wrote him three more letters, each one colder than the last. Four more. What they said didn't matter, just what they symbolized. Nagging. Desperation. Taunting.

I never needed you.

I never wanted you.

I don't dream of you. Every night. I don't imagine slapping you. Punching you. Hating you.

I don't think of you.

Meaningless words. No matter what, he wouldn't have the last say. I would drown him in parchment if I had to. Anything to prove I had already caught on to his little game.

Because I'd come to the conclusion that he was trying to kill me again. How dreadfully uninspired.

I barely had the energy to care. Oh, no, Dublin didn't consume my sole attention. I was much too busy tending my household. There were sheets to change. Puddles to mop. Floors to wear down by pacing circles over them. Most of the time I spent pacing in Mr. Tinkle's room, muttering to him as he watched from his corner.

"It doesn't matter," I insisted, my hands clenched at my sides as I stormed across the Persian carpet. "It doesn't. I mean, even if he is that stupid D.H. donor, I don't care if he ever shows up at all. All he'd want is that stupid book, anyway. Right?"

My cat flicked his tail lazily through the air and blinked.

"Exactly!" Groaning, I paced faster, swaying as my stomach roiled with every erratic movement. "I mean it's not like... It's not like we were a real..." I gritted my teeth rather than hiss the word *couple*. "It was a transaction. I knew that... I *know* that."

My future husband—should the universe decide not to make me a spinster—would be a creature far different from Dublin Helos. Some smug rich aristocrat who would fall hopelessly in love with my wallet. Together, we would suffer a bitter, stiff existence within Gray manor until the day he slipped too many sleeping pills into his nightly brandy.

It was the wholesome, ideal partnership my parents had modeled.

"It wasn't like I even liked him," I added, slowing to a stop. What woman would? Who would consider a man who looked like a pale Adonis attractive? Especially when he ran hot and cold. One minute he claimed to be only interested in money. The next, he had you pinned to a wall, demanding you submit yourself to him fully.

The memory stole into my thoughts, so potent it tore the breath from my lungs. His mouth on mine. His hands, ruthlessly grasping at parts of my body. Him inside me…

Shaking my head, I banished the images. "Who would want that?" I croaked, turning to Tinkles. He extended his tiny forelimbs into a laborious stretch and promptly darted deeper into his corner.

"I wouldn't," I whispered, watching him go. "I don't need anyone. I need… I need to get out of this house."

Every second spent within the ancient dwelling heightened a growing sense of paranoia. That I was being watched, followed and haunted, despite all evidence to the contrary. The walls themselves seemed to be hissing to me, a million admonishments. Secrets and lies.

This was all some elaborate trick, obviously. I wasn't *really* sick. These symptoms were designed to make me seek him out on my own, placing myself right in his trap. Because that's all he really wanted: revenge. Or, more specifically, payback of something more vital than money.

And he would never, ever find it—his precious contract secretly in my possession.

In retaliation, he wanted me panicked and desperate. Paranoia was his goal. Just like before he'd waltz right in with all the answers.

And I would be ready for him.

~

The following day, the phone in the old servant's alcove rang, breaking the monotony. I took my time answering it. Dr. Goodfellow was probably desperate to deliver another vague update as to my health status.

Sighing, I held the receiver to my ear, prepared to humor her. "I hope the test results came back conclusive this time—"

"Hello?" someone replied and I nearly dropped the handset in response. He was… Well, he was *male*. "May I speak to Ms. Gray?"

I held my breath, my fingers tightening over the rim of a nearby table as a single thought set in. *Not him.* I was still sane enough to know that much.

This caller wasn't an ageless figure with a musical baritone and a laugh like the devil. Considering I wasn't the type to get phone calls from strange men, there was only one explanation for this occurrence.

"I'm sorry," I stammered. "Georgie isn't here. However, I could take a message if you'd like." Though only God knew when she might receive it.

"I beg your pardon," the man replied. "But I'm looking for *Eleanor* Gray."

My eyes narrowed. "Why?" Rudeness, aside, it was a valid question. No one ever asked for me. Certainly not by name. Unless, of course, they had souls to buy and sell.

Or money for whoring themselves to an heiress.

"My name is Gabriel Lanic." His suave tone betrayed him as someone used to schmoozing with the upper class. "I'm the chairman of the board of directors at St. Mary's—"

"Oh, y-yes," I croaked, fighting to stamp the suspicion from my tone. "How can I help you?"

"I heard from one of our doctors that you were interested in becoming a core donor?"

Color me impressed; despite such a bold assumption, Mr. Gabriel Lanic managed to sound more charming than money hungry.

"Um, I was," I admitted. "To be honest, I was more interested in learning more about the board members—"

"I'm afraid that I wouldn't be able to divulge much out of respect for privacy."

"Oh, I see—"

"To the typical donor, anyway," he added, before my disappointment could solidify. "Frankly, Ms. Gray, your family name carries a prestige I cannot deny. While I may not be able to divulge much, no one could blame me if a few details managed to slip over dinner. How does eight o'clock sound?"

"D-Dinner?" I gagged at the thought of food, smelling it, seeing it. However, the promise of answers was more than enough to combat the nausea. For now. As long as Mr. Lanic proved my hunch once and for all, he could set a meeting wherever he damn well pleased. "That sounds fine. I mean, y-yes. I mean…"

"I hope you are partial to Italian. The Maria is excellent," he said.

Thick red sauce came to mind and I cringed at the imagery. Still, I managed to choke out, "Wonderful. See you there."

Four hours later, I left the house looking somewhat presentable. For the first time in days, I'd brushed my hair. I even put on a dress, a demure black one my mother had picked out, complete with a modest neckline. When I joined François in the Rolls, I almost felt…at ease?

My stomach was in knots during the quick trip into the city, but for an entirely different reason than usual. Excitement? Hope? Who knew. The only thing I was sure of, as the car pulled up before an exclusive restaurant downtown, was that if Mr. Lanic could give me the answer I wanted, then he could slap his name on Gray Manor for all I cared.

Two words. That's all he had to say. A name. Validation of my paranoid delusion. Evidence to out the man so proud of his own damn mystery that he'd never see me coming.

My blood hummed as I stepped from the car and approached the restaurant's gleaming front. A tendril of unease raced down my spine though I couldn't explain why. It was beyond breathtaking as far as venues went. Glass doors revealed a posh interior, but a man appeared to block my path before I could even make it inside. A professional black suit and tie separated him from the wealthy patrons mingling within the establishment behind him. Given how he cocked his head toward the earpiece tucked inconspicuously behind his ear, I suspected he had been sent to escort me personally.

"Ms. Gray, I presume?" he asked, proving my suspicion correct. "Your companion is waiting. May I show you to your table?"

I nodded, following him inside. A spacious lobby opened onto an intimate space beyond the main dining room with bold burgundy walls and polished floors. Such an obscene display of wealth. My mother would faint at the sight.

Mr. Lanic had gone all out in the hopes of impressing his prey—only one table had been set, strategically placed in the center of the room. No other patrons were dining nearby.

We were alone.

My chest tightened as I spotted the lone creature waiting for me in the center of the room. His back was to me, his build impressive. His hair…black? Not golden.

Disappointment fluttered through my chest as his voice reached back to me.

"Ms. Gray." He turned in a display of poise, flashing a gallant smile no vampire would ever be able to imitate. "I am Gabriel Lanic. Pleasure to meet you."

"Likewise," I croaked, regaining control of my senses.

So, he wasn't Dublin Helos, mysterious benefactor extraordinaire, though he rivaled him in charm. A warm smile offset his handsome Roman features. Dressed to the nines in a tailored gray suit, he didn't seem like the type who'd sold his soul for money and prestige, either. I sensed no air of ice, and the hand he extended for me to shake was warm.

As far as my past year was concerned, he was a rare entity— a handsome, rich *human*.

"Care to join me?" He nodded toward the table.

Silently, I took the seat across from him, and he offered me a business card laden with his personal information.

"Shall we begin?" He'd come prepared, apparently, armed with enough history on the hospital and its various charity enterprises to charm a room full of donors into emptying their pockets. Never once did he mention trading in souls or the like. Instead, he listed target figures and waxed ad nauseam as to the reputation of my family.

So generous we were.

So honorable.

Lies, but delivered so expertly I almost believed them.

"I would be more than honored to receive your investment, Ms. Gray," he concluded. "I would hate to seem forward, but have I managed to woo you?"

He winked, and like a good wealthy checkbook, I reached into my purse on command. It was only as my fingers ran over a brittle piece of parchment that I remembered the question that had brought me here in the first place.

"Your donor list," I blurted, brandishing my brochure opened to the right page. "There's one figure listed by only his initials. Can you tell me his name?"

He leaned forward and brushed his hand over mine while he read. "Why, I believe that is Donald Hildrand," he said with a pleasant laugh, sitting back. "He tends to be too mysterious for his own good. I could arrange for you to meet him if that would put you at ease, though I would be loath to share your company—"

"No." I shook my head and swallowed down the lump that had risen in my throat. "That's not necessary."

Somehow, I had known, even before he'd delivered his answer, that it wouldn't be what I wanted to hear. No, perhaps wanted was too strong a word. What I *needed* to hear. That was how paranoid delusions tended to work out, didn't they?

One healthy dose of reality could make it all fall apart.

"Have I disappointed you, Ms. Gray?" Mr. Lanic wondered. He reached out, his fingertips sweeping upward to bat a loose strand of hair from my face. He must have misjudged the distance, because the tip of his thumb grazed my throat instead.

I flinched back, shaking my head. "No. In fact—" I withdrew my checkbook and scribbled a one in the farthest corner of the amount line. Meeting Mr. Lanic's inquiring gaze, I pushed the check toward him. "Forget I asked. All that matters now is…how many zeros should I add onto this figure?"

Once the poor man returned his eyes back to his skull, I wrote the amount he requested without a second thought. After all, if I were dying, at least my family's name might grace some bench or fountain at St. Mary's to commemorate our benevolent nature. I choked out a laugh, picturing it. It was the only legacy my family could hope I'd pass on. No children or heirs to carry on the name, but an inscription: *From the gracious Gray Family to the whole of the city…*

"Ms. Gray? Are you all right?"

"Huh?" I looked up to find Mr. Lanic staring at the pristine tablecloth in front of me.

Or, at least it *had* been pristine. Three ruby drops now decorated the space beside my plate.

"I'm f-fine." I scrambled to my feet, snatching my checkbook from the table. "I should go—"

"What on Earth?" Lanic frowned, his gaze on something behind me. "I apologize. I insisted upon privacy."

"What?" I turned, catching a glimpse of an intruder, who was already storming out through the doorway, their posture more confident than the average server. Bolder. Not to mention that they allowed the door to slam in their wake, which rattled the wooden frame. Perhaps the restaurant owner coming to bill me for the damage?

No. What little of his features I saw were too impressive for the average man. A luxury suit. Golden hair. Skin like ivory. And a spicy, wintry scent that lingered in the air, tainting my every breath. Either tall, blond men in Armani were becoming a regular occurrence or…

God, it was too dangerous a word to process at the moment. *Or.*

"I was assured this was a premier venue," Lanic groused. "I can have the manager move us to a more private—"

"I-I have to go." I lunged for the door, aware of movement behind me.

"Ms. Gray?" From the corner of my eye, I saw Gabriel start to stand. "Wait!"

I was already in the lobby within seconds, gasping for air. My rib cage had a vise grip on my lungs. My legs were jelly. I almost turned back in search of a chair before I made a fool of myself and fainted.

Obviously, I'd hallucinated.

As if to challenge that thought, the sound of a slamming car door brought my attention to the valet out front. A man was climbing into a car: black, sleek, imported, and most definitely expensive. I couldn't see the owner's face through the tinted windows as I staggered from The Maria's entrance. He drove off, and I had only enough sense to race toward my own vehicle, parked paces away.

"Ms. Gray?" François gaped as I clambered into the front seat.

Then I spit out the most words I'd spoken to him since the day he'd been hired. "Follow that damn car or I will drive this thing myself!"

Already, our quarry had pulled off and woven through traffic nearly a block ahead.

"Okay." François wrenched on the wheel, launching into a pursuit. For all his politeness, my new driver must have driven more than spoiled heiresses in his day. People who valued reckless speed. He tore through alleys and side streets, easily narrowing the distance between us and our prey.

But even he wasn't fast enough.

"Damn!" He slapped the wheel as the other car sped off through an intersection before we could follow. "I'm sorry, miss. Let me try to—"

"Let me out." I tugged on the door handle only to find it locked. "Let me out!"

I slapped the window until he finally unlocked the doors. Even as my heart raced, my strength failed me. It took everything I had to shoulder the door open and climb out. While I staggered down the deserted block, François resisted the flow of traffic to keep pace.

"Where are you going?" he asked.

"I'm fine," I called back, putting all my focus into walking. Moving. *You can do this, Ellie. You've come too far, now.* "Go—please! I'll…I'll find my own way back."

I didn't look to see if he obeyed my instructions. I simply urged my body forward through sheer force of will. Step by step. Sidewalk square by sidewalk square.

How ironic. I knew this part of the city—a rarity for me, despite having lived here my whole life. For instance, this road was one of the few I'd driven on myself. I knew the darkened park to my left. And I especially knew the cathedral looming above.

In the darkness, it watched my approach like a disapproving remnant from a past life. The life of a girl who consorted with vampires. Who'd sold her virginity to one. Who'd let herself be poisoned, tricked, and humiliated by one.

The stupid, foolish woman who might have even trusted one.

I shook off the thought as blurriness disrupted my vision and the gothic structure split into two. With every step, my body swayed, tossing my shadow over the path beside me. My breaths grated on the air, noisy and useless. I was weightless. My trembling hands grasped at my sides, desperate for stability.

By the time I reached the cathedral proper, the grounds were deserted. A lone streetlamp cast the only light to see by as I approached the mouth of the structure. The door remained closed, the sign still nailed to it. When I traced my fingers over its surface, they came away gritty with dust.

Well, you were wrong, a part of me hissed as I slumped forward, pressing my sweaty forehead against the wood. *You chased a shadow.*

But the funny thing about shadows was that they couldn't be stopped by something as mundane as a wooden door. A door that budged the slightest inch beneath my weight…

The wind picked up, tossing my hair around as if in warning, before I even palmed the wrought-iron handle. I pushed once, expecting to find resistance.

It opened easily, issuing a weary creak as if mourning its failure.

One peek over the threshold revealed an empty, cavernous interior with abandoned pews. Some entity took care to preserve the space, however. When I placed my foot on the wooden floor, my shoe didn't slide over a coating of dust.

Someone had been here.

Yet every ounce of sanity I still possessed warned me to turn back. To *not* push the door open wider or inch my way inside.

To run.

Because I had nothing to prove. And even more harrowing to admit—I had nothing to gain. Just more questions with no fitting answers. Like, if Dublin Helos was lurking within the city, then why wait so long to come collecting?

I owned part of his life, after all. Ten whole years. The devil himself shouldn't have been playing hide-and-seek while waiting for me to find him.

He should have been barging into Gray Manor like he owned the place, demanding I give him what I now owned.

His goddamn soul.

Shaking the thoughts away, I took another step. Thickened air irritated my nostrils and set off the reaction instinct could not—I recoiled. Harsh, rattling coughs forced me to cling to the door. Another set robbed me of balance altogether.

Light. Dark. The conflicting shades speckled my vision as everything spun and dissipated. Twisted. Faded.

And all I saw before the world went black was vibrant, terrible gold.

A BED OF ROSARY

François must have brought me home. Considering he had never been *inside* the house, it made sense that he wouldn't know where my room was. The gesture was enough to earn him a raise, though— even if I still slightly hated him.

He'd chosen a decent bed at least. The mattress conformed to my limbs, far too decadent to have been purchased by my mother. Perhaps it was one Georgie had snuck in as an act of rebellion? My nostrils flared, seeking out her scent in the silky fabric, but I wound up inhaling something spicier than her rosy perfume. Something…unnatural. Familiar. Like winter in physical form.

A part of me stirred in alarm, but logic quashed any suspicions before they could form.

You're dreaming, Ellie. Go back to bed. I rolled onto my side, fighting to return to the dreamless sleep I'd left behind. Just as my body began to relax, the bed frame jolted beneath me.

I lurched upright, my eyes flying open to a darkened room. Before I could write off the disturbance as a figment of my imagination, my straining ears picked up another alarming sign. Creaking wood. Footsteps? Heavy ones. They advanced in my direction, far too bold to be a burglar.

A list of potential visitors marched across my brain. Like my sister returning on her own for once? The grim reaper?

After licking my lips, I tested one theory by calling out, "F-François?"

Through the shadows, I sensed a doorknob rattle without a word of warning from the person on the other end. That ruled him out. Unease danced down my spine as I wrestled with the prospect of real danger. Perhaps terminating my entire security team hadn't been the best idea in retrospect? I couldn't regret it now.

Instead, I grasped at my surroundings for a weapon, finding only a pillow. I brandished it as the door opened and moonlight spilled in from a nearby window to illuminate the intruding figure.

A gasp caught in my throat. It wasn't a murderer or a robber —certainly not the lanky François.

He was a far worse entity.

Not real, I deduced. This apparition was just another phase in an all-too-vivid dream. But pinching my wrist didn't jolt me awake.

The Devil stubbornly remained, dressed in his usual soul-collecting attire—a flawless ebony suit crowned with a blood-colored tie. Pale skin contrasted harshly with the shadow surrounding him as did his hair—a gleaming shade of gold the sun couldn't outshine.

With this man's chiseled jaw jutting in the air, not even God himself would dare challenge him.

Let alone me.

Without invitation, he entered the room, and my heart stuttered as anticipation grew with every inch he gained. Admittedly, this was far from the meticulous, sly return someone like him was capable of performing. Almost as if I wasn't worth even a fraction of the effort. Still, I'd imagined this moment so many times, assuming what he'd say down to the last word. The general gist, at least. *Do be a good girl, Eleanor, and give me my contract book back, please and thank you.*

So a rebuttal was on the tip of my tongue before he even opened his perfect mouth. "You're slacking Dublin. That was far from a dramatic entrance befitting the big bad contractor—"

"You look like hell." He advanced another step, sweeping his gaze over me. "No wonder your doctor has been consulting experts the world over concerning your case."

"M-My what?" I blinked, confused. Weeks of fantasizing about this moment, and yet never did I imagine his first words would refer to my medical records.

"Here." One of his arms tensed, revealing something in his grasp. A knife? He threw whatever it was in my direction and I flinched, covering my head with my hands. Coolness brushed my calf, but no pain followed. Had he missed? I peeked through my splayed fingers, spotting a round object. A water bottle, of all things.

"Drink," he snapped. "I can hear your heart straining from here."

His tone was all wrong—deeper than I remembered, for one. Guttural. When I looked up, his mouth firmly resisted even the hint of that cruel, mocking smile I knew so well. The Devil was clearly vexed. Had I interrupted his self-imposed exile with my bloody excretions?

No matter. Matching his tone, I bit back with, "I thought your magic necklace was supposed to help in that regard?" I clutched at the item in question, straining the slender chain. "Or was that just a lie? A way for you to track me all along? I should have ripped it off the second you left—"

"You didn't." His gaze honed in on my throat. "Have you tried removing it?" He surged forward another step, only to halt paces from the bed. I had flinched without even realizing it. "Do you even know the lengths I went through getting the damn thing on you in the first place?" The slightest tremor disrupted his words. "Then again, maybe you *do* know? I'm sure she didn't specify those little terms all on her own—"

"She?"

"Don't play the fool." He inclined his head, exasperated with me already.

But the way he was glaring at me trapped any rebuttal in my throat. I'd almost forgotten this aspect of his persona— how dangerous he could seem when he wanted to, fitting the term I'd christened him with during one of our first meetings.

Monster.

"Removing the talisman disrupts its effects," he growled, a professor begrudgingly bestowing a lesson upon an ignorant fool. "I warned you—"

"I..." My mind raced to keep up as a million words formed and died on the tip of my tongue. In the end, I managed to voice only one pathetic question. "Why are you here?"

"A better question would be: Why were you *there*? To provoke me? Well, congratulations, you have. Is it my blood that you're after?" He nodded toward my extended wrist. "Or could it be that, once again, you're being manipulated by Raphael? Don't tell me that you didn't realize that was no ordinary restaurant?"

I swallowed hard, envisioning the elegant, rich décor of The Maria. Was he correct in insinuating an ominous reason for the splendor? That it was owned by the vampire Raphael...

Shaking my head, I tried to refocus. "I...I didn't. I didn't know you'd be there." Wait. Why was I on the defensive, explaining myself to *him*? I shook my head again. *Deep breaths, Eleanor.*

Obviously, this tactic was one of his many mind games. Mention my sister. Then pretend to care, and even throw in dear Dr. Goodfellow for good measure. How sweet.

I could admire his tact for not launching into demanding his contract back first thing. But what did one say to a creature who'd abandoned them without so much as a second thought, anyway?

Apparently, they said, "You know what? You don't have the right to ask me about a damn—" *Thing,* I meant to add before a violent cough racked my spine. I hunched over, grasping the sheets around me for balance. Sheets way too fine to ever be mine.

Wait... I blinked, finally noticing the rest of the room. One far too narrow to belong in Gray Manor. Even in the near darkness, I could tell that the walls weren't lilac, but made of stone. The bed beneath me was way too wide, the floors wooden. And Dublin...

Well, he looked way too at home in the center of the shadowed interior. Another step brought him closer still and I cringed against a wall of pillows.

"Where am I?"

"Your cough," he started as though I'd never spoken. "How long have you—"

"Where am I?" I forced myself to sit upright and ignored him in my quest to deduce my surroundings. Beyond the doorway, I noted a clue that answered my own question—a wall of breathtakingly beautiful stained glass could only belong in one type of venue. "So, you were lurking here, after all? How nice of you to finally answer the door." A full five days later. "It must have been hard to rearrange your very busy schedule."

His silence gave me my answer—*yes*.

"Well, in any case, it's a good thing you ignored me," I said, shrugging. "Otherwise, I might have struggled to fit you into my schedule. What with *time* being such a precious commodity these days."

The old Dublin I'd known would have scoffed at the bait and seen it for what it was—a deliberate reference to his contract book.

"Oh, I know," he countered, deploying an unexpected change in tactic. "You're a busy woman, it seems." His gaze settled along the neckline of my dress as he nodded. "Why, it is a miracle that I managed to catch you alone at all."

"So, you *were* watching me." I pointed an accusing finger at him. *Checkmate.* "You were spying on me—"

"And why would I do that?" He turned away, disarming me like one would a screaming child. "Pardon me, Eleanor, but I'm already behind schedule thanks to your little visit. What do you want?"

"I…" Bit my tongue. As always, his motives were as elusive as he was. Why would he stalk me? Despite all my suspicions, I still drew a blank. So I improvised. "You and I both know why I'm here."

"Oh?" His tone deepened further. "Do tell."

"You can threaten me all you want." I lifted my arms in a careless gesture. "Just drop the aloof act. Go on… Come out and ask me for it! I'd rather die than tell you, so prepare your poetic warnings—"

"What the hell are you talking about?" His eyes found me from over his shoulder, gleaming like hellfire. "Perhaps you hit your head when you fell?"

He sounded too damn serious.

"I…" My mind went blank. Could this be a trap? A trick?

Then a realization hit me with all the subtlety of a ton of bricks—he didn't know. Or he was a damn good liar. *Or…* Raphael was a far more cunning game master than I'd given him credit for.

As the seconds passed, his expression remained guarded, impossible to read. Left with no other option, I tore a page from my mother's playbook whenever someone had presented her with an uncomfortable truth.

I closed my eyes and willed it away.

"On second thought, it's nothing." I stood, shooing him with a wave of my hand. "I should really get back to Gabriel anyway." By some miracle, I managed to take a step toward the door without making a fool of myself by falling. I *limped* instead, bracing one hand against the nearest wall for balance.

Just as I reached the doorway, Dublin called out, "Your *letters*—"

I didn't miss how he'd stressed that word. So, my blood had made an impact after all.

"I haven't read them," he added, shattering my suspicion. "In fact, I only arrived back in the country hours ago. Though I'm sure you've been far too busy to notice my absence."

I bit my lip, tasting salt. So he claimed to have been gone all this time? It fit. The great and terrible Dublin Helos hadn't disappeared out of shame for what he'd done to me or to plot on how to retrieve his contract book. He merely went on vacation.

"Did they convey anything important?" he wondered.

"I… They're nothing. You can give them back."

I held my hand out and jerked it away once I spotted the red liquid smeared over the palm. But I was too late.

He seized my wrist in a grip so strong that it yanked me toward him. Flashing, his eyes fixated on mine. "How long have you—"

"Well, I'm leaving," I insisted, more than satisfied with this little reunion. Apparently, he hadn't poisoned me, a fact I couldn't dissect at the moment. So I snatched my hand back and continued to make my way to the door with my head held high and an air of indifference on full display. Things like "logic" and "reason" would only matter once he left me alone.

Which, of course, he took his sweet time doing. I could see him within my peripheral vision, standing rigid, his eyes on me.

"You need to see a doctor."

"I have a doctor."

"A *qualified* doctor—"

"Says who? I'll have you know, I've been *perfect* in fact, without your meddling, thank you."

"I'm sure you have," he countered. "Your friend Gabriel certainly seemed to be of the same mind. He looked liable to do more than take your *money*. Bravo, Eleanor. No one would guess that you were a virgin only a couple months ago. I'm sure that, in my absence, you've added a few more conquests to your ever-growing list."

I stumbled to a halt as my eyes went so wide that I figured he could see them dancing in my skull from his position.

"Don't tell me I've insulted you," he added.

"You…" I sucked in a breath, blinking rapidly. *No.* I refused to let him unnerve me. I needed to counter, regain my composure. Something cruel should have been on the tip of my tongue. Anything but, "You don't get to act like this. Not after everything you put me through—"

"Oh?" He came up behind me, casting a shadow that swallowed the pool of light I was standing in. "And what have I put you through?"

I gasped as his hand captured my chin, tilting my head toward him. With his height, only a sliver of his jaw was visible from this angle. And his eyes. They were silver, spitting fury like lightning.

"Do be a polite girl and enlighten me. You can start with the part where I saved your life."

"You left," I blurted, obeying his instruction like a good, pathetic contractee. "You left without even an evil speech by way of goodbye I might add—"

"You don't know, do you?"

A hitch caught in my throat. He sounded so furious at that fact. I came to him, crawling his way like a pathetic victim eager for more—and I didn't even have the sense to know *why* that fact irritated him so.

"Get off of me," I spat, slapping his hand away. "I'll tell you what I *do* know, though—I can press charges."

"On yourself for trespassing?" He moved his grip to my throat, barely applying pressure with flexing fingers. "Do try it, Eleanor. Or have you forgotten? You came to me."

I blinked. Something in his tone made my heart race, hammer a silent warning. "You came to me first," I pointed out, even more perplexed than ever at the image of him lurking in the dining room. "You *stalked* me.

Badly, I might add. You should try a disguise next time—"

"I can smell him on you, you do realize? Here." An icy gust fanned the exposed hollow at the base of my neck, his finger, drawing an accusatory line over the flesh. "You could have showered before coming here, at least. It would have made a more desperate impression. I'm sure you and your sister have some demand to make of me, especially after this little ruse. With her resources, don't pretend like you weren't alerted the second I returned, and I know for a fact that she has been keeping out of the spotlight. What is she planning? Let's not waste any more time. Say it."

"The man I met was helping me," I stammered, choosing to overlook his mention of Georgie—for now. If dealing with him had taught me one lesson, it was to stay focused. Ignore all bait. "I was—"

"Don't play naïve," he warned, applying more pressure to my throat. "You and I both know that he wanted more from you, Eleanor. *More* than your money. Perhaps a desire to corrupt the innocent heiress? It doesn't matter." His fingers flexed, with just enough tension to make me suck in a breath. "You forgot that you've already sold your body. Your soul. To me."

The way he'd said those two words… My brain melted. Disintegrated. Poor Dr. Goodfellow had every right to be concerned, because this was true terminal danger. I gasped like a drowning victim, flailing for a lifeline. In my hazy, scattered thoughts, I found one.

"Is this your trick?" I murmured despite the fragile cage of his hand. "Distract me? Pretend and then gloat—"

"Still the same old Eleanor Gray, as stoic as ever." He forced me to face him and my eyelids fluttered as I tried to withstand the intensity of his gaze. It was no use—I failed. "I did research into your dear Mr. Lanic. Why am I not surprised that you have a preference for dangerous, elusive men?"

A muscle in his jaw lurched, betraying the unbelievable. Hours back and he'd already inserted himself into my life, hunting down an acquaintance I barely knew.

But why?

"I…I thought you just returned to the country?"

"Your heart is racing, Eleanor," he snarled over me. "Perhaps you should see that doctor? I'm running out of contracts to extend where your life is concerned."

"Who says I need your help?" I pictured Goodfellow and her faked concern, but it was getting harder and harder to remember the weakness that had plagued me for weeks. The dizziness, or the coughing fits. Dublin Helos was the cruelest antidote to physical pain.

Around him, my thoughts were in more than enough turmoil.

"Where were you?" Dear God. The question slipped out, too puzzling to remain in my head, a weakness I'd mourn later. For some reason, an answer mattered more to me than shame. "Tell me. Or let me guess? Collecting more souls to add to your bounty?"

"My bounty? I was upholding *my* end of the bargain. I'm sure you know all about it." He waited smugly for a reaction I apparently failed to deliver. His frown transformed into a grimace. "Unless she really didn't tell you…"

I cocked my head. "Who didn't tell me—"

"Of course she didn't." He released me, raking his hand through his hair as if finally hearing the butt of a ridiculous joke; surprise, surprise, he wasn't amused. "When have you ever exercised self-preservation?"

Exasperated, I tried to retort, "You—"

"*You* broke the bargain." His grip returned to the nape of my neck. Using the contact like a leash, he yanked me closer. "Why? Did you fall into league with *him*, aiming to see just how far you can push me? You even smell different." His nose lingered near the crook of my shoulder. Drawing back, he shook his head and refocused his gaze on my mouth. In my quivering lips, he seemed to find an answer to the question he never voiced.

One too terrifying to ponder.

"You're too pale as well." He traced my pulse point with the tip of his thumb and my breath stuttered in response. "If you didn't remove the necklace…"

"I'm leaving." I tried to step past him, but he shifted, easily blocking my path. "Get out of my way," I demanded, trying to shove him back. I might as well have tried shoving the wall.

"No." He stepped into me, forcing me to take a hasty step back. Only for him to take another. Another. Before I could jerk farther out of his reach, his lips grazed my earlobe poised to deliver another insult. "You came to me first." Once more, he seemed to be speaking only to himself—but his hand crept into my hair, too firm to shake off. "Therefore, *you* voided the contract. I'm sure she's on her way, but it doesn't matter. I kept my end—"

"Stop!" It was my turn to utter, "What the hell are you talking about?"

"You let him touch you." He made it sound like the vilest of crimes. "I can forgive that. But not the innocent, childish games."

He tugged me closer. Too close. I tried to recoil, but his other hand latched onto the back of my scalp, trapping me in place.

"D-Dublin—"

"I will even pretend you didn't know about your sister's bargain," he hissed against my ear. "If that will embolden you to drop the act. Was he your plan for drawing me out sooner? Let me guess—Georgiana is waiting in the wings, ready to resurface?"

"G-Georgie?" I flinched at the third mention of her. Beautiful Georgiana consorting with Dublin about a bargain. A contract. "What did you—"

"I can forgive everything else. Even the flagrant disregard for your own welfare. Everything but this…" He eyed my throat as his upper lip pulled back from his teeth. The slightest hint of fangs teased the air, sending every nerve within my skin on red alert. "I gave you your life, Eleanor. I could concede that much. But your body? I don't remember relinquishing my hold over it."

"Stop!" I inhaled, once again fighting for clarity. "You're not making sense."

"Or you're too much of a prude to admit it." His mouth snapped shut, firm and brooding once more. "I'm starting to think I've misinterpreted your little evening. God forbid, I'd almost thought that you were foolish enough to challenge me. But lo and behold, you don't even have enough damn sense to realize—"

"Or you're too much of a pompous ass to quit playing games and just tell me what you want!"

The words had barely left my throat when he pulled me in, surging forward in the same swift motion. Our lips met and my body went haywire as his tongue eased my lips apart with a searching swipe that shattered my senses. Pushing him off was my sole aim for grabbing him in return, curling my fingers around his forearms.

But I'd forgotten…

What it felt like to be at his mercy. To have his mouth on mine. To feel his body—living stone impervious to my touch, resistant to my pathetic attempts to tame him.

He easily overpowered me, despite my grip on his arms. Two advancing steps of his herded me back. Back...until my knees struck the mattress and I fell onto the sheets.

He stepped between my splayed legs, robbing me of the chance to regain my bearings. Ruthless, his hand plunged beneath my dress, cupping me with no warning. No growled demands. Just vicious friction.

And it was as if my body ceased being *mine.*

Nerves unraveled, enslaved by his touch. The memory of him. Months alone and I'd never even tried to replicate the things he had done to me. I couldn't. Nothing compared to the stomach-churning sensation he sowed with every stroke of his thumb—ice over burning flesh. My teeth caught my lower lip as he rubbed, testing the thin lace of my panties, grinding the fabric into my skin. Helpless, my head reared back against my shoulders, a cry trapped behind my lips.

I couldn't resist the fire hissing to life within me, feeding on the motions of his fingers. Rough. Cruel. Relentless.

At the back of my mind, I knew I was hallucinating. This wasn't happening.

Dublin Helos wasn't groaning as he urged my legs farther apart, eyeing me the way Lanic had ogled my checkbook. Like I was millions for the taking, his alone to claim.

"I should have killed you," he whispered. One of his hands still raked through his hair, destroying his suave poise. Gone was the calm, collected contractor. In his place was a creature more beast than man. "I should want to kill you," he added, flicking his gaze up to mine. "The trouble you've caused me. The years. The chaos. The sacrifice. I swore to myself I'd never believe him, not for a goddamn second. But you…"

"I what?" I tensed. Was he finally referring to his contract?

"You *persist*. Weeks spent trying to prove that you were nothing." He chuckled at the absurdity of it, prowling forward, bracing his hands on my knees. "And I return to find you on my doorstep, ready for more." He shoved my dress over my hips and something rare splintered his anger, tugging on the corner of his mouth as he swept his gaze over me.

My legs twitched, ached to clamp together. Hide from him. As if sensing the thought, he traced a path down my inner thigh, observing every twitch of my spine.

"There is something wrong with you," he grated. "Something broken. It's like you truly are cursed. Corrupt. Like he planned you for me after all. He made you for me."

"Who?" My mind reeled. He was talking too fast. Hatred for him was becoming harder and harder to hold on to. And, God, I needed it. My fingers grasped the sheets as if I could find the emotion among them. "Raphael?"

"Why should I fight it?" he demanded, stroking his thumb up over my belly. My heaving breast. My throat. I trembled with every inch gained; drawn nails added a predatory fervor to each, pointed caress. "You are tailor-made to resist me every step of the way, aren't you?"

He lowered his head. A brush of ice against the flesh of my throat was my only warning before…pain. His teeth, I realized belatedly as his jaw nudged mine, urging me to arch, exposing more.

"You are mine, Eleanor Gray," he declared. "Body *and* soul."

Then…

He bit.

And everything went red.

Vibrant, beautiful scarlet rich enough to erase the gray my life had become.

I was too far gone to even care that I was drowning in blood.

DIAGNOSIS

A symphony of beeping machinery lured me into consciousness. Just from the way my nostrils twitched, I knew where I was before my eyes even opened.

A hospital.

Over the past year, I'd been in enough of them to envision the layout of this room entirely from assumption. A spacious one, judging from the echo. Private, most likely.

I wasn't alone, either—that had to be a first. Someone nearby was speaking in a hushed voice. My doctor?

Or perhaps *devil* would be a more fitting term.

"I didn't know who else to call," the man said, his voice easily placed. Dublin. My eyes were too heavy to open, but I could picture him paces away, scowling to match the gruffness of his baritone. "She trusts you, at least. Perhaps you can discover who the…cause of this may be."

"Cause? I should have never let you order me to stay away from her," a woman replied, her lilting accent distinct.

I knew her as well. My brain struggled to recall a name, but forming a solid thought at all felt like grasping at tendrils of smoke. All I could do was listen.

"Though it seems you haven't kept to that stupid 'bargain,' either," she said accusingly. "I thought you weren't planning on returning for at least a few years—"

"There was a complication," Dublin interjected. "A minor one. Once it is resolved, I don't plan on staying long."

"You mean a complication concerning Eleanor," the woman surmised. "I thought you might have been watching her—and you have, haven't you?"

"Only enough to know that she consulted a doctor who began contacting outside experts regarding her case. I decided to intervene before the chatter could catch Raphael's attention."

"Something you could order any one of your associates to do," the woman pointed out. "You could have asked me as well. Though, I should have visited her anyway, with or without your permission. Maybe I could have prevented her from… To be honest, I thought you were joking at first. I mean, Eleanor isn't exactly the type of woman one would expect to wind up in this condition."

"Are you implying that I'm incompetent? I ran the tests more than once," Dublin snapped. "I had them corroborated with several other professionals—"

"Leaving out one obvious reason why this doesn't make any sense, I am sure. Unless… You don't really think she's been with someone else since you've—"

"Are you insinuating another possibility?" Dublin wondered, and a part of me chafed at the grit in his voice. He sounded too calm—and in my experience, that was when he had the most potential for cruelty. "Don't be naïve, Yulia. There is only one logical conclusion."

"Dublin, I was only—"

"And don't insult my intelligence by pretending that you don't know the rumors spreading concerning her, either. Concerning my interest in her. That I lust after the weak little mortal like a wolf would a lamb. Is that what you think as well? I know Raphael in particular rather enjoys that theory—"

"Of course not!"

"My interest in Eleanor Gray extends purely to her bloodline," Dublin insisted. "Raphael attacked her for a reason. Her body reacted to him so violently *for a reason*. I intend to discover why before he can use whatever information he knows against me. Nothing more."

"Fine," Yulia conceded. "So, did you find what you were looking for?"

"The question isn't whether I did," Dublin snapped. "It's whether or not I believe the superstitious drivel in the first place. Don't tell me you do? Is that the real reason you fought so hard to make me notice Eleanor in the first place?

Not that it matters. It seems she hasn't lacked for male company."

"Dublin, I'm on your side," Yulia insisted. "I'm simply trying to understand. This isn't like you. Since when have you cared about what Raphael might think? And how would I know anything about the 'rumors' when you barely even talk about your past—"

"And I'm not willing to start now," Dublin growled. "Once I finish cleaning up this mess, I will leave. Tonight."

"On another wild goose chase?"

"No," he replied, but his tone had hardened. "I intend to take a more direct route, this time. Even if it means going to a monster we both despise..."

"Ah, so that's why you really asked me here?" Yulia's tone turned cutting. Hostile. "You don't give a damn about Eleanor now that she's moved on. You only want my permission to talk to *him*. The very monster *you* saved me from."

A deliberate pause left her statement hanging in the air. Finally, Dublin admitted, "Your permission? No. Your understanding? Yes. You and I both know that Dmitri possesses more knowledge in his twisted skull than anyone."

"Yes," the woman agreed. "Knowledge that he would barter for your soul—or, worse. Whatever answers he could give you wouldn't be worth the price you'd have to pay, trust me on that—"

"It's not merely answers I'm after."

Some internal part of me squirmed, alarmed by the emotion bared in his words. Concern? Or fear.

"You claim to be concerned for Eleanor? Well, the necklace should have preserved her life, but it hasn't. I could smell the sickness in her. If her health remains in such a perilous state, this could kill her. By merely attempting to feed from her, I almost did."

"I know," the woman whispered. "But you weren't yourself. We both know how hunger can affect you. I should have talked you out of ever giving up that stupid amulet in the first place—"

"So, she could die sooner?" Dublin countered.

"No, of course not! Although—"

"Although, *if you had, we wouldn't be in this dilemma.*" Dublin paused before continuing. "Don't look at me like that, Yulia, I know what you're thinking. We both know it to be true." An air of regret laced his words and it twisted my insides like a knife. "Alive or dead, Eleanor Gray seems destined to thwart all logic where safety is concerned."

"That's not what I mean! Look, I won't pretend like I have any other options, but anyone is better than that son of a bitch. Just wait a few more days and I'll try to find something myself. Even Saskia might—"

"Or Raphael?"

"No!" The woman choked out a tortured laugh. "I...I suppose going to him would be even worse than Dmitri. But just listen to me. If you can hold off for a few days, I will help you in any way I can, but I can't... If you do decide to seek out Dmitri, then please don't count on me to accompany you. Give me a week. I'm sure we can find the answers on our own. Please."

"...A week," Dublin conceded after a moment's silence.

"Good," Yulia agreed. "And as far as Eleanor is concerned, I'll do what I can to help her. Let me know when she wakes up, and I'll bring some things for her. God, I can't imagine how scared she must be—"

"I'm not sure if she even knows." Dublin sounded cold again. My tired brain tried desperately to piece together what he referred to. Something concerning me...

Something awful.

"W-What?" Yulia exclaimed. Seconds passed before she regained her composure enough to ask, "And, if she doesn't you will tell her *gently,* won't you? Without making her feel any worse? I mean, it—"

"I found her with someone last night. Perhaps I interrupted a congratulatory dinner?" A laugh undercut Dublin's chilling baritone. "I think we have both learned by now that Eleanor Gray deserves anything but pity."

"Don't be like that. You've hurt her once—you and I both know it. I doubt even someone of your fortitude has the willpower to do it twice. Especially about this. Just tread carefully."

A weighty silence didn't reveal his answer either way.

Finally, Yulia sighed. "I'm just asking you to think this through. Your decisions may have far greater consequences than even you could bear. Now, I need to get back to the club. That bitch Saskia will get suspicious if I stay away for too long. As far as your concerns go, give us a week to find our own answers before you go off again. A *week*. Promise me…"

~

I must have drifted in and out of consciousness, because when I finally blinked my eyes open, a figure loomed near the end of my bed, emanating a chill that resonated in my bones.

"Don't move," he warned.

One flex of my limbs and I understood why. Pain flooded my system, drawing a gasp from my lips. "Jesus Christ." I exhaled a shaky breath as the world gradually came into focus. "I feel like I've been hit by a truck."

"You're still healing," the speaker continued, his face a blobby blur. "You've lost a lot of blood. In your condition, you're lucky to not have suffered a worse fate."

Still healing? I turned, driven by an instinctive dread. And for good reason—more blinking brought an object lurking just beyond me into clearer focus. A long metal pole. Dangling from the very top was a bag of red fluid.

"A blood transfusion?" I deduced, horrified.

"Four pints lost," Dublin declared, stepping closer. The waning daylight was just enough for me to make out his expression—surly eyes and stiffened lips.

Dread unfurled in my belly. I knew that look. He was in a brooding mood.

"Count your blessings that you're even able to move."

"Get. It…" I had to suck in air to form each word. My fingers twitched on command but lacked the strength to rip out the IV. "Out. Get it out of me—"

"Do you understand what I just said? You hemorrhaged. You're weak." He wasn't using his clinical, doctorly voice anymore. "You've been out for nearly two days. There are corpses that portray more vitality than you."

And if I didn't know any better, I might suspect the devil was…exhausted?

His face revealed nothing discernible. As stoic as ever, he stood near a wide bay window overlooking an unfamiliar view of the city. From the bed, I caught snippets of the landscape beyond him: skyscrapers, bright lights. It was an area far from the reclusive hillside domain of Gray Manor—that was for sure.

And far from his cathedral where my last, hazy memories centered upon.

Mainly one image that chilled me to the bone.

"I bled," I whispered, hating how hoarse my voice sounded, "because you bit me."

"I did," he admitted, training his gaze on the view. "I shouldn't have fed from you, but the venom merely exacerbated your underlying condition. It didn't cause it—"

"Condition? Oh, don't tell me." I shifted to observe him fully. "You figured out my mysterious illness? What is it this time? Another blood disease?"

Despite my bravado, my voice broke. The world was spinning around me. Oddly enough, *he* was the stubborn anchor, as unmoving and rigid as the day we'd met. One of his hands fiddled with something hanging from his throat —shining, small, silver…

No, it couldn't be. I felt along my own neck, finding it bare —but too many thoughts battled for attention to care.

The man was an Indian Giver. So what?

So what if some of my last memories were of him scolding me as to the importance of that very necklace?

So what.

"Congratulations." I forced my hands together in a pathetic imitation of applause though it took nearly all of my strength. One pathetic clap was all I could accomplish. "What will I have to sell to you this time in exchange for the cure?"

"Cure?" he wondered in a dangerously soft tone. His shoulders were so rigid that I bit my lip. Odd. He should have been gloating. Not tense, his head bowed in contemplation. "If you want to take that route, then I need to ask you something," he warned.

"Why?" I tried to shrug off his caution. "Are you pretending to be my doctor again? I'm sorry to be the bearer of bad news, but I have a new doctor. A *real* one, who isn't inclined to drink blood in her spare time."

"You don't have any idea, do you?" He looked up, and nothing could prepare me for the ice in his expression. Dublin wasn't just brooding—it was so much worse.

He was *furious*.

"J-Just…" I stammered, wringing my fingers until a coherent reply finally formed on my tongue. "Just tell me, oh wise one. What's wrong with me now?"

His gaze cut away from me as he started to pace. "I don't know how else to ask this other than bluntly. Who have you been with, excluding me?"

Been with…

Fire heated my cheeks. His tone said it all. *How big of a harlot are you Eleanor, now that your virginity is a moot point?*

Needles of shame stabbed through my chest though I bit my lip to disguise my reaction. The only way to counter him was with a forced smile and more faked bravado.

"Other than you?" I coyly raised my hand and ticked each finger off one by one. "Why, Gabriel Lanic. My driver. My maids, before I fired them. My gardener. My security guards—"

"Enough!"

Shock rendered me senseless, and memories that shouldn't have been there popped into my head. Him, on top of me, his hands beneath my dress. More recently, him delivering a tortured observation in a callous whisper. *There is something wrong with you...*

I swallowed hard. This wasn't happening. I wasn't on my figurative deathbed while a vampire taunted me about intercourse.

"Leave me alone—"

"Answer the question," he snarled in a tone so hard I jumped.

"No one," I managed to rasp.

Rather than sneer at the admission, he...frowned. "Your modesty means nothing at this point, so I'd prefer if you didn't lie. Just give me a name."

"No. One," I insisted, clearly enough for him to absorb every single word. My cheeks were aflame, and I had to resist the urge to cackle hysterically. This was some mind game on his part, of course. Accuse me of being a moral-less harlot, right before coming in for the kill: I'd already given him my virginity, why not give him his precious contract as well?

"If there is a point to this," I added harshly, "then I suggest you get to it."

His brow furrowed and then his expression went blank. It was as if someone had flicked a switch, cutting off all emotion the bastard might deign to feel. Even rage. "I've arranged for you to see a doctor."

Something in his tone made me huddle beneath my blankets before I realized.

"What doctor?"

He had already turned on his heel and stormed from the room. Seconds later, a woman appeared in his wake. Slim and tall, her modest features and stern, wire glasses projected a knowledgeable aura even someone like Dublin Helos would defer to.

"Hello Eleanor," she said softly. "I'm Dr. Martin."

Minutes into a brief assessment, I had to admit that she seemed capable enough. She asked pertinent questions and thankfully wasn't as cheerful as Dr. Goodfellow. Hell, I almost felt as insignificant as a lab rat by the time she finished drawing vials of blood and left the room. But then, minutes later, she returned, lugging a sleek, square-shaped machine behind her.

"Ms. Gray," she began in a crisp, efficient tone, "I would like to get an abdominal ultrasound, if that is alright with you."

"An ultrasound?" It was a terrifying term, especially when paired with the high-tech machinery she expertly began to program. "W-why?" I asked, even as a part of me suspected what the answer may be.

Something far worse than a mere cough ailed me. A *tumor?* Rather than voice that suspicion herself, Dr. Martin took advantage of my silence to plug the machine into the wall.

"Ready?" The woman must have mistaken my panicked expression for permission, because she proceeded to turn the machine on.

And I squeezed my eyes shut.

I couldn't stop my hands from childishly flying up to cover my ears as well. But that didn't mean I couldn't feel. My hospital gown withdrew, allowing cold hands to feel my flesh underneath. An even colder substance greeted my belly a second later, biting through my numb skin. And then I sensed pressure, pressing up, down, around. Searching. Hunting. What for? A blockage, a tumor...or something worse?

I didn't know.

There was no cry of triumph, in the end, when Dr. Martin settled the probe near my pelvic bone. No mechanical beeping to alert those nearby of the machine's findings. Just a low, terrifying hum I heard even through my fingers. I was forced to press harder, shutting out everything but the steady, fast thrum of a heartbeat. My heartbeat?

My condition was more dire than expected if my heart was working so feverishly.

Seconds later, the pressure abated without fanfare. As if from miles away, I heard Dr. Martin murmur something to another presence who entered the room, their scent alone broadcasting their identity. Icy. Chilled. Winter. Whatever she said, it was succinct. Conclusive. As the material of my gown lowered, a soft touch ghosted my cheek and I let my hands fall.

"We're done, Eleanor."

"So…what now?" My eyes reluctantly opened to the white ceiling, blinded by the artificial light. I blinked to get my bearings, only to find Dr. Martin slipping through the doorway without so much as a word. But someone new stood in her place. My, what a difference a few minutes and tests had made. Silver eyes honed in on me with a chilling intensity that made me shiver.

"W-what?" Somehow, I managed to choke out a weak laugh. "What is it? How many months do I have to live this time?"

I was only half joking. From his expression, I discerned my condition wasn't too serious. Even he would show some ounce of sympathy. Right?

"What is it?" My voice ricocheted off the ceiling, high-pitched and breathless.

Finally, Dublin cocked his head. "There's fluid in your lungs," he said, sounding remarkably unconcerned by that fact. "You'll require treatment for it. You're malnourished. Your bloodwork is a case study in critical values. And—" He hesitated, turning the full power of his gaze on me once again. Just when I thought I might shrivel beneath the scrutiny, he added, "You're also pregnant, a little over eight weeks along. Congratulations."

I focused on how he said that word first. *Congratulations.* No one in the history of the world had ever sounded less sincere. Then, piece by piece, I dissected the rest...

Eight weeks.

"V-Very funny." I started to sit upright, coughing with the effort. I covered my mouth with my palm and flinched as warm liquid splattered it with every hacking breath. "I hope you got your laugh, at least—"

"Lie down." Only then did I realize he wasn't laughing. Or smiling. "I'm not lying," he continued. "Dr. Martin confirmed it. She is *never* wrong. Shall I phrase it differently? Your body is manifesting a growth of unconfirmed origin."

Despite the insanity leaving his mouth, he looked clinical. He looked detached. He looked every bit like the calloused doctor who'd intruded into my life all those months ago and left chaos behind.

"W-What...what does that even mean? Is that your way of saying I have cancer? Some kind of tumor?"

Anything but *pregnancy.* In this case, the term probably served as a stand-in for yet another made-up illness. Perhaps a blood disease lacked enough dramatic flair, so Dublin Helos had developed a new destructive narrative in his quest for more souls.

"What will it take to 'fix' me this time?" I wondered, switching tact to cut right to the chase. My gaze fell over his hands, waiting for the moment he'd withdraw some magical vial from his pocket. "I'll have you know that I much preferred the 'degenerative blood disease' narrative, by the way—"

"You do realize what I've said," Dublin interjected, still utterly emotionless. "Do I need to explain it to you?"

God, he sounded too serious. Too real. *Pregnancy, Eleanor. Reproduction. Spawn. Should I draw a diagram?*

"I..." A million words welled up behind my tongue. Oddly enough I could only croak out two at a time. "You're lying. You're wrong."

Which was worse? That someone could be so cruel? Or that someone could be so...stupid?

"You've made a mistake," I insisted, settling on the latter. Felt through the thin hospital gown, my stomach curved inward, mockingly concave. Empty... As my fingers drifted lower, they struck protruding hip bones.

"Mistake, no," Dublin said, running his fingers along the collar of his suit jacket as if flicking all implications of failure away. "I will say that the results didn't show up in the normal range. However, I had your blood sample tested. Of course, we'll do more conclusive tests, but the results strongly indicate… Well, I suggest you continue this discussion with the father. That might give you a bit more insight. I could bring him here, if you wish." His eyes cut to mine, devoid of anything remotely compassionate. "Just give me a name."

All at once, I fell back, striking my head off the edge of a pillow. The pain barely registered above a sudden need for clarity. "T-the what?"

"The father, Eleanor," he said, enunciating each and every word.

Father. As in, someone other than him.

And suddenly his previous line of questioning made horrible, perfect sense. *Who have you been with, excluding me?*

"You…you're serious?" As dizzy as I was, I felt the need to haul myself upright as I spoke. That question could only be delivered when I could look him dead in the eye. Piercing, fathomless eyes glared back. Blank eyes. The Devil's eyes. "Are you that inept of how biology works, in your advanced age, or are you just that damn cruel?" That was what I said in my head. The only sound to register against my ears, however, was a moan.

"Enlighten me, Eleanor," Dublin demanded, but his voice… An emotion I couldn't name stripped it down to grated words and harsh syllables—a dangerous baritone I knew all too well.

"Enlighten you?" I echoed, still struggling to understand the challenge. "Perhaps you should enlighten *me*?" I coughed again but the need for answers trumped all concern. My lungs were collapsing. My throat caved in on itself, capable only of spitting words out rather than letting any air in. "How. Could. This. Happen?"

"Sex with a man, obviously," he countered. But even though I only had weeks of knowledge to draw from, I knew him too well: that wasn't honesty. It was a rebuttal. An accusation.

Sex with a *human* man.

Because that is the only way you could possibly become pregnant.

I swayed as the world shifted. Suddenly, he was everywhere, blocking my path.

"You need to lie down."

His nearness alone stirred my body's instinctive flight or fight response. My heart screamed 'flight' but my pride, what little remained of it, wouldn't cow to his accusation. I needed answers. Any answer, and he needed to be the one to give it.

"Do the math," I panted against my palm. I knew he heard me, already piecing the timeframe together on his own.

In simple arithmetic, eight weeks ago resulted in a period roughly around the instance when I barged in on his suite, bleeding and half dead. When he cut me. When he kissed me. When he made me feel, for a second, that perhaps it all hadn't been a complete lie…

No! I pushed back my blankets and tried to stand. Trembling legs collapsed beneath me, and I would have fallen if a hand didn't cinch my arm at the last moment.

As if in a parallel universe, a woman walked by the doorway carrying a clipboard. She startled and looked up, only to turn away again. This moment was insignificant in her life. A chance meeting. A passing glance. Had she anything worthwhile to offer, how different a meeting might it have gone between her and the man behind me?

"Watch yourself!" Dublin's grip locked me in place, hard and punishing.

Through his flexing fingertips, I could sense everything he didn't dare say. Anger. Resentment. Fury?

"Get off—"

"Give me a name," he countered. "Or can you even remember? You had me fooled, I will admit. Oh, that innocent little virgin act was a stroke of genius, but in the end, it seems your hunger needed to be sated by someone."

"Stop!"

"No," he grated against my ear as I resisted his vice-like grip. It was as if the curtain had been pulled back and his poised, suave act splintered, revealing the true beast lurking underneath, demanding answers of his own.

"Tell me. Who was he?"

I laughed. I couldn't help it.

"Who?" His voice had devolved to a growl, lacking any semblance of polish though I couldn't understand why. Certainly not…jealousy?

No. Self-pity instead. Poor Dublin Helos. How had the devious Ellie Gray managed to trick him this time? First by tangling him within his own web?

And now this?

Another sound tore from my throat at the thought of it, though this time I wasn't sure if it was a cackle or a sigh.

"I may have sold you my virginity," I tossed back to him. "But pardon me, Dublin, if I still have morals." That was all I needed to say. Nothing else. Nothing bitter. Nothing real. Too late. More words spilled out. "You were the only one—"

My throat hitched and I grasped for the end of the mattress, leaning away from him. My chest heaved. It ached. God, I couldn't catch my breath. I couldn't catch anything. My senses. My sanity.

"What are you saying?" His voice reached me as if from miles away. I finally looked back.

He no longer glared, his jaw clenched.

A multitude of words sprung to my lips but just a handful escaped. "If I'm… If… You do realize that it would be because of *you*?"

The look on his face. I would never forget it. Like I just told the most beautiful lie. Like I had crushed his soul and self-worth in one fell swoop.

Like I had hurt him this time.

And God, I would have been lying if I claimed I took pride in it.

"Well? Say something!"

Instead, his eyes cut down to my chest, settling over my throat.

But anger and shame had control of my body and my mouth opened for one last petty blow. "Is this your way of payback?" I croaked. "For what Raphael did to you?"

Namely, what his adversary had given to me. A life for a life?

And still, he said nothing. So cold. So…frozen.

So, I did the only thing one could in my situation.

I lashed out, intending to slap him, only to grapple for his lapel as my stomach roiled.

And I vomited blood all over his white shirt.

~

I was in a nightmare, but it didn't end as I opened my eyes.

I must have fainted. Dublin paced before my narrow bed, his back to me. We were still in that clinical, clean room with the door flung open to allow in the hustle and bustle of the rest of the hospital. The faint noises seemed miles away—another universe—mocking me as my reality crumbled to pieces.

"Raphael. He did this," Dublin growled, but the tirade wasn't directed at me for once. He glared instead, his gaze turned inward. "He knew. He...damn him. Damn." He tore his hands through his hair and I swallowed, too stunned to speak. He—the pompous, callous contractor—didn't act like this. Frantic. Unpolished.

Afraid?

Air wheezed from my chest, forming a strangled cough I couldn't suppress.

"Eleanor..." Dublin ceased his hurried pace and turned to me. "Let's assume you aren't lying," he said coldly. "And let's not waste time on petty indignation, either. This is important. What have you been eating?"

I stared at him, still convinced I was dreaming. None of this was real. It wasn't...

"What have you eaten?"

"Food," I croaked in response to the authority in his tone. "But even the thought of it makes me..."

My gag reflex triggered, though my body was too exhausted to follow through. I just choked on empty air. At least there was no blood.

Yet Dublin eyed me more intently than before. His gaze swept downward as if hunting for a certain reaction. "Think," he warned. "What have you tried drinking?"

"Water," I hissed, the obvious response. "And…"

A memory unfolded, too vivid to describe in words.

"What is it?"

His gaze was too severe to ignore. Almost as if he already knew just what images flashed within my mind. *My thumb sliced open. Blood. The taste of it…*

Gritting my teeth, I blurted out, "I pricked my finger the other day." The hand in question rested weakly by my side, my thumb still an angry, bitten red. "It bled and I…"

The knowledge that I was in a nightmare stripped everything of the dire urgency he seemed to feel—at least in my case. I sounded so bored, in a sense. I'd just professed a slight craving for blood. How blasé.

Evidently, Dublin wasn't of the same opinion. He turned on his heel and strolled for the door.

"W-Wait!" I struggled to lift my head from my pillow.

His footsteps continued down the hallway regardless.

There was nothing left to do but count my own surging heartbeat. One. Ten. Fifty. Too sluggish. Too fast. My lungs burned, shriveling beneath each breath I sucked in.

Focus, Ellie. Again, I tried to move a limb. A leg. An arm. Anything? Dripping sweat, I finally managed to raise the hand attached to the IV. First things first, I felt along my throat again, this time searching for bite marks. I found nothing apart from clammy skin. *Damn him.*

Dublin Helos wouldn't be able to swoop in and bestow another "cure" just in time to save the day. My attention reverted to the hanging IV, and I was about ready to rip the damn tubing out with my teeth by the time he reentered the room.

"Look at me," he commanded.

As I did, any argument I could have leveled died in my throat. A clinical, detached posture transformed him—now, he was a cold doctor with a theory to test. In one hand, he held a white Styrofoam cup with a lid and a straw sticking out of the top. In the other was a prepackaged plate of chocolate cake, like the kind one might find in a café.

"I told you I can't keep anything down." As I spoke, the heavenly scent of cocoa reached my nose as if to spite me.

"Sit up." He approached a bedside tray and pulled it closer. Then he offered the cup to me directly. "Drink."

I had a hunch that there wasn't water in that cup. My fingers twitched, unwilling to accept it. I wanted him to leave again. I needed to hate him again. That and silence were all I had left.

"Get out."

"Listen to me—"

"Why?" I scoffed, but he didn't budge.

His hand was unmoving, his gaze drifting from my throat to my wrists, sensing the frailty I couldn't even try to hide.

"You're dying," he warned. "Drink."

Before I could argue, a rare emotion flickered across his gray irises and I flinched. That look compelled me in a way even his surliest of growls could not.

I reached for the cup, wrapping my fingers around the smooth surface, intending to throw it. Before I made my move, he tipped his hand, guiding the straw to my dry, cracked lips. I tried to clench my teeth in defiance.

No!

This is insane.

"Eleanor, drink."

My mouth opened. Dublin didn't beg. Ever. It was a trick, obviously. Too drained to play his game, I relented. One sip. Purely for experimental reasons—the main one being so that I could spit whatever it was out in his face.

But the moment the warm, mystery liquid hit my tongue…

My throat contracted. More. Another sip. More. Long, desperate pulls. *More. More. More.* The desperate mantra drowned out everything else. Like shame, as I remembered how to make my limbs move and snatched the cup with both hands.

God, the satiation was indescribable. Terrifying. As if I had been dying of thirst only to stumble upon an oasis. A salty, bitter oasis flooded with sustenance that I knew instinctively hadn't come from him.

In the literal sense.

Stop! Agony tore through my skin as my conscience overrode hunger. I pulled back, gasping at enough air to spit out a single question he already had the answer to.

"No one was harmed."

Such a carefully worded statement, but it was enough. The straw slipped between my teeth again and I inhaled every last drop, heedless of the horror building at the back of my skull. It could wait. I could hate myself later. For now, my eyes slid shut, my stomach finally contented, and I blinded myself to all other thoughts and sensations—everything but this elusive sense of fullness. It was heaven, cushioning the blow when I finally resurfaced, as he snatched the cup from my hand.

"Eat."

He wheeled the bedside tray closer and unwrapped the slice of cake, which he shoved in my direction, along with a fork.

"I told you that I can't," I insisted. But something had changed. Once I inhaled the aroma in full, my stomach didn't rebel. I didn't need his assistance to sit up, either.

With the tip of the fork, I sliced off a sliver of dessert and settled the morsel onto my tongue. I'd barely convinced myself that projectile vomit onto the man across from me would be a satisfying reaction by the time I finally swallowed.

Rather than rebel, my stomach growled for more. One bite became another. Then a chunk. Then a piece ripped off with my bare fingers when the fork wouldn't suffice to gather up the crumbs fast enough.

Words couldn't describe what it felt like to taste an actual, solid meal after so long.

Words also couldn't describe the look on Dublin's face; it lingered for barely a second, but it was no less intense than his blank stare. Narrowed eyes containing the briefest hint of emotion. Revulsion?

Or fear.

Of *me*.

"What did you do to me?" Chocolate sprayed from my lips.

Quietly, he gathered the empty cup and the plate, tossing them both into the trash. His eyes met mine once again, the longest he'd held my gaze since I'd woken up. Like pools of ice, they reflected my hollow expression back to me. Wide eyes. Open mouth. Flushed, hollow cheeks.

In silence, he left.

And I closed my eyes, determined to wake up.

lack hair.

Frail skin.

Haunting black eyes.

"I will make you a wager, Eleanor," he told me, his name every bit as beautiful as his youthful appearance. Raphael. "I will tell you what Dublin bartered for you—in fact, I will give it to you. As long as you help me discover something that he might value more..."

I should have run. I tried to. Red walls enveloped me, forming an elegant dining room, crowded by watchful figures with hooded eyes. I took a step and the scenery expanded around me, stretching forever. No matter where I turned, black eyes held me captive, boring deep to scrape my soul.

His hand captured mine, as quickly as a striking cobra. "I already have my suspicions."

He was so cold—shockingly, abnormally so. It felt as if death itself had taken hold of me.

"All you would be required to do is help me prove it to be true or false. Then I shall uphold my end of our bargain. Simple enough?"

A frigid thumb traced the back of my hand. As if drawn by an invisible force, my gaze drifted to his throat, where a serpent pendant hung. Its red eyes kept me in place as Raphael placed his hand over my stomach, imparting his chill into the flesh underneath.

"A simple suspicion," he repeated in a burst of breath so cold that I half expected frost to crystallize right there on my skin.

Then he lowered his head and bared his fangs…

I startled awake to a familiar scene—an empty room. Warm daylight streamed in through the massive window, unabated by the curtain someone had partially drawn over the view. My panic subsided as the fragments of my nightmare faded.

But I wasn't at Gray Manor. Noisy machines still monitored my body through various wires and devices—still in the hospital room, then. At least the IV was gone, as was the mysterious bag of blood.

I could recall those details, though my brain seemed determined to avoid remembering anything else. Thinking took a back seat to the desperate ache unfurling in my belly anyway. I sniffed and realized why. The bedside tray had been drawn up close to the bed and on it was a steaming plate of eggs, along with a Styrofoam cup. My selective memory gave me an inkling as to what might be inside it.

Something red that tasted like copper.

Not exactly the most charming of breakfast invitations. My "doctor" was exerting his presence into my life with little effort.

At least he wasn't here. I had no one to prove anything to. No one to judge. Just my own terrified thoughts playing a morbid commentary as I eyed the straw and pictured the liquid within.

This is insane, Eleanor.

You're hungry, Eleanor.

You're starving, Eleanor.

This is insane.

I clung to that last voice, the pathetic whisper of the person I had spent twenty-six years living as. Calm, reserved Eleanor Gray. The woman content to be a spinster. The heiress who needed no one. That girl wouldn't drink whatever was in that cup. She would cross her arms in stubborn pride and suffer.

Don't be so childish.

That newer voice was unwelcome, suspiciously masculine. To silence it, I sank back against the pillows and pulled the thin sheet over my head, smothering as much noise as the cheap cotton could. Almost as if to mock me...I felt.

Movement. Something. Deep down inside me, like the flexing of a muscle I didn't even know existed. It throbbed, demanding attention. Acknowledgment.

The longer I attempted to ignore it, the sharper the pain became. Insistent.

Drink.

I hauled myself into a sitting position. My hands trembled, outstretched before me, but it felt like ages before I gathered up the nerve to reach for the cup. I cringed with the first sip of lukewarm liquid. Before disgust could fully register, I was already swallowing the second. Third. An endless stream that didn't cease until the final few drops noisy crawled up the straw. My hands still shook as I set it aside and pulled the tray closer. The eggs were lukewarm, but I managed to redeem myself by devouring them slowly.

That hollow feeling in my stomach felt sated once I'd cleared the plate, but it still demanded…*more.*

"Eleanor?"

I looked over at the doorway and found a woman standing there. Her dark eyes softened as recognition seared through my chest.

A much more welcome sight than Dublin.

"Yulia?"

"Who else?" Her mouth cracked into the most beautiful smile. With her black hair slicked back against her head and her slender body clad in an ebony pantsuit, she looked as witchy as ever. "I've brought you something to wear other than those hideous gowns." She lifted her arms, each one displaying a dress on a hanger. "Which one do you prefer?"

Amid the chaos and turmoil I desperately fought to ignore, fashion was an abrupt, though preferable, change in subject.

One selection she held was a rich, modest black, made of silk. The other was a similar design but made of white lace.

"I'm partial to one in particular," Yulia admitted, fingering the white dress. "But I'm curious what you think." Her accent gave the words a lilting edge and I relished every note. I'd forgotten how lovely someone's voice could sound when they weren't growling threats or shouting insults.

Or peddling vicious lies.

"The white one," I blurted, pointing toward my selection.

"Of course. I see you still have your good taste." She gently set the chosen dress over the foot of the bed. Slung from her shoulder was a black duffel bag, which she set down at her feet. "Dublin asked me to design a few things for you," she explained while folding the black dress and tucking it inside the duffel. "Luckily I'd just finished some new designs that I managed to tailor in a pinch. Though I probably should get your measurements again…"

I'd been in the process of sitting up while she spoke, and her eyes settled over my concave stomach.

Memories gnawed at the edges of my skull. Snippets of a hushed conversation too terrifying to interpret—*poor Eleanor...*

"You should try it on," she said, gently dragging me back to the present. "Though I should warn you that Dublin made some...specifications."

"Like what?" I ran my hand over the surface of the white dress. It felt silky smooth—not laced with broken glass or any other devious tricks I could discern.

"Things he promised were utterly necessary." Her upper lip contorted in a grimace. "I'm sure you'll discover that soon enough. Here, let me help you."

She eased my gown over my head and guided me into a bathroom suite attached to the room. Facing my reflection in the mirror, I cringed. For a woman who'd needed a blood transfusion, I didn't have much to show for it. There were no bruises. No cuts. No broken bones to explain away my slow, sluggish movements.

But I was still rail thin. Too thin.

"I will definitely have to measure you again," Yulia deduced, observing me with a frown. "You're skin and bones—"

"It's nothing," I blurted, letting myself ignore my hazy memories of Dublin's diagnosis for a split-second. Something about a growth. Utterly trivial. "I'm sure anything you make will fit just fine."

"Oh." Yulia swallowed hard. Her eyes scanned my face, and her lips twitched, resisting a frown. "Did Dublin talk to you?—"

"More or less." I shrugged and turned my attention to the shower. As the water warmed, I tested the temperature with my fingers. Then I stepped beneath the spray, allowing the sound of rushing water to obscure the awkward silence.

Dublin deserved some credit. Pregnancy was an intriguing diagnosis, but no different from hemohemorrahgia—a complex lie designed to extort something at my expense.

That was *all* it was.

"It's good to see you again," Yulia called to me, her voice muffled by the shower spray. I snuck a glance at her while lathering my hair with the bottle of shampoo. "I should have visited you sooner. But..." She shook her head, her smile strained. "Do you need help? I'm dying to get my hands on those curls again."

I let her assist me—and I needed the help. For the first time in ages, water felt hot. My skin seared, painfully raw. There was no residual numbness radiating through my bones to shield from sensation.

But...

I froze, half dressed, transfixed on my reflection in a mirror hanging above the sink. A stranger stared back at me. I scanned her eyes, searching for the hint of a monster dwelling within her fragile frame.

A salty taste still lingered on my tongue, impossible to choke down.

"Eleanor?" A warm touch on my shoulder drew my attention to the woman beside me. "What do you think?" she asked while helping me into the white dress.

"It's perfect." The praise wasn't an understatement. Softer than gossamer, the material fit just as comfortably as any previous item of clothing she'd designed for me.

"I think so too. But damn." Frowning, she glanced at a watch on her wrist. "I wish I could stay longer, but Dublin will kill me if I don't finish at least a good bit of your clothing as soon as possible. In the meantime, I left a few things to tide you over." She winked and headed back into the hallway. "You should get some rest. I will check on you later."

By the time I had the sense to whisper, "Goodbye," she was already gone.

~

Semi-darkness greeted me as I opened my eyes. The ceiling was a swath of flickering shadow, and a lone fluorescent bulb illuminated the room, throwing the man standing at the foot of my bed in stark contrast.

Once again, he'd come armed with a cup of mysterious liquid and a bowl of food. Soup, it smelled like. Along with a thick slice of bread and another piece of cake.

"Eat," he prompted, placing the meal down before me.

Drowsiness rendered me compliant enough to accept the cup without complaint. It was already in my hand as I closed my eyes. Drank.

The moment I downed the last drop, he was there to ease it from my grasp. I opened my eyes and found him eyeing me from head to toe. I squirmed as he lingered over my face.

The rage was gone from his expression, but in its wake remained something far too close to concern.

"How are you feeling?"

"Fine," I croaked. "For someone who has cancer, anyway."

"Cancer?" So much for concerned. He went rigid, his eyes narrowed.

I nodded. "A tumor. That's what you implied, isn't it? I must have vampire cancer. Either that, or I am a harlot with no morals—"

"Eleanor…" His teeth clattered, but he snatched up the spoon rather than arguing. "Here."

Accepting it, I twisted the metal between my fingers. The polished surface displayed my reflection, but I barely recognized it. Wide, green eyes and a pursed, pensive expression. Turning away, I fished for any distraction. My scattered thoughts provided one. "Yulia brought me clothing." I gestured to the duffel on the floor. "But she said you requested an alteration. What?"

"How are you feeling?" he repeated without acknowledging my question. "I've asked Dr. Martin to reexamine you—"

"I have my *own* doctor." I fought to put some indignation into my tone and failed. My voice shook. I spent more time eyeing his suit than meeting his gaze directly. He hadn't changed, and the color scheme made him seem even paler than usual—a statue formed of ivory.

"Your so-called doctor, one Elodie Goodfellow," Dublin said.

Was I surprised? Perhaps. Frankly, I couldn't tell fury from shock.

"A medical doctor with more than a few mysterious donations in her bank account from undisclosed benefactors. I've taken the liberty of severing ties with her on your behalf and canceling your donation to St. Mary's. The fewer who have access to your medical records, the better."

My brain blanked at his audacity. One detail stuck out, however. "So, that wasn't you. The D.H. donor?"

He raised an eyebrow.

"D.H.," I explained. "One of the board members of St. Mary's hospital. A donor, I might add, who only appeared after Dr. Wallis vanished. Literally overnight."

I had two different brochures in my stash at home to prove it. One printed only a week after he'd supposedly left the country.

"That's why you went to see Gabriel Lanic?" He asked. "If I were to stalk you from afar, Eleanor, don't you believe I'd hide behind an identity more obscure than my initials?"

He had a point.

"I… Like hell I'll go to your doctor." With one hand, I shoved the blankets back and sat upright, facing the window. "You have no right to—"

"Do not fight me on this." His tone. I had never heard it quite so hard. As if maintaining this conversation alone had stretched his tolerance paper thin.

I twisted around to face him. "And why shouldn't I?"

He laughed, but his eyes were wide, his mouth partially open—a chilling display of ivory fangs. "You have a rare form of *cancer*," he growled. "And you think that just any doctor in the world can help you?"

"Like you care," I hissed. "According to you, I'm a harlot who should consult another man for assistance in this matter. Right?"

He didn't even look insulted. Or guilty. Or contrite.

He met my gaze unflinchingly and said, "You should pray that you accidentally wandered into another man's bed and developed your cancer. Otherwise…"

My stunned silence seemed to satisfy him enough that he left that statement hanging in the air. He tugged on the hem of his jacket, smoothing the edges, his poised, calculating self once more—but there were cracks. For one, he was still wearing that gray suit from the other day, but it wasn't so neat anymore. Dark splotches stained the suit jacket, rivaling the deep crimson of his tie. Strangest of all, my cross shone against his chest as if he'd never removed it.

Too much. Closing my eyes brought me seconds to regain control of my thoughts. *Focus, Ellie.*

He was something to focus on. My rage. My fear. This impending panic surging through my veins. Grasping for stability, I honed it all like a laser, pointed it directly at Dublin Helos.

"I'm sorry if you didn't realize this," I croaked. "But you don't own me. Not anymore. So take your insults and get the hell out!"

It was the last part of that statement that did it. *It,* as in made his jaw clench and his irises shrink around fathomless pupils.

"Your body is practically decomposing around you." His eyes lowered to my throat. "And you think this is the time to flaunt something as trivial ownership? If I didn't bring you here when I did, you would have died."

Died. He made that word sound too final. Not a joke.

"What are you talking about?" I asked.

His back stiffened as he turned away. "The talisman I'd given you…"

"What?" I demanded. "What did it do?"

When his gaze returned to mine, I barely recognized it. "Let's just say there was a complication I hadn't foreseen."

"So, that's why you took it back?" I watched it swing from his neck as my fingers brushed my bare throat.

"I brought you here," he said without confirming it. "I ran the tests. Trust me when I say that *cancer* is the last conclusion I would come to. So take this at face value. Or as a warning. Until this is resolved, I'm not letting you out of my sight."

Alarm bells went off in my head, but I remained silent.

"I don't intend to spend all of my time fighting with you, either." A deliberate pause punctuated the air before he asked, "Your sister—have you heard from her?"

Don't fall for it, Ellie, my inner voice warned. I didn't like how carefully he had phrased the question. Soft. Almost nonchalant, like a normal change of subject.

Funny, because it was my turn to laugh.

"I told her to leave," I found myself confessing without understanding why. "And she did. I told her I never wanted to see her again. And I haven't. So, no, I haven't heard from her."

"Not even a phone call?" His tone conveyed the suspicion he didn't voice—*I don't believe you.*

"No." I shrugged, eyeing my trembling hands. "Not even a phone call."

I had mulled over the various reasons for the silence. Maybe she hated me for not being the special, chosen one? Maybe I hated her. For leaving me when I needed her, and then coming back…

But only to clean up a mess she'd made.

Dublin would have never poisoned me without darling Georgiana. Despite everything, I thought I could ignore the deception—but betrayal was a strange animal. One day, all might seem well again. Those fresh wounds might even start to heal, scabbed over with assurances of love and heartfelt promises.

But a promise couldn't soothe the underlying infection for very long. Georgie, despite her apologies, had been unwilling to enlighten me on any aspect of her life. She didn't possess Dublin's penchant for brutal honesty, either, and every day that I saw her there, wandering the halls of Gray Manor as if nothing had changed…

The house *was* mine, technically, as was the fortune.

I just never expected her to forfeit it all so easily.

"You haven't tried to contact her?" Dublin pressed, his suspicion palpable.

"And what could I say?" I blinked and moisture spilled down my cheeks. In vain, I tried to banish the tears with a swipe of my hand. "Hello, Georgie. I'm… I have vampire cancer?"

It all had the makings of some sordid, morbid drama my mother would read when she thought no one was looking. I had *some* self-respect.

Enough to realize when another subject change was in order.

"How could this happen?" I directed the question his way, expecting a clear, succinct answer.

It's a tumor, Eleanor, honestly.

Anything but, "I don't know."

"Sorry?" I blinked, convinced I'd heard him wrong. I even patted my ears in case they'd become clogged.

"You heard me." His gaze shot to mine and nothing had ever terrified me more than his expression. Not the nightmares. Not the hunger. The hue of his irises flickered a burnished silver and in them I saw the truth before he uttered it out loud. "I don't know."

A sound trickled out of me that might have been another laugh. It definitely wasn't a sob. I hadn't fallen that far. Not yet. More tears weren't what spilled out of my eyes to paint my cheeks. Just sweat.

"What do you mean, you don't know—"

"Eat." He nudged the side table, jarring it closer to me. The bowl of soup wobbled, precariously close to the edge. "I can hear your stomach growling from here."

"No." I shoved the bowl away. "I don't want the damn soup. I want *answers*—"

"I don't know!" Thunderous, his rich baritone rang out, stinging my ears in its wake. He had shouted. *Was* shouting. "You want answers? Well, so do I. Do you think this is a common occurrence? Well it isn't. Neither is a woman who willingly sells her soul and can't seem to stay out of danger no matter the risk—"

"Sir?" Footsteps raced down the hallway and a woman in a white uniform peeked out from behind the door. A nurse. "Is everything okay?"

I almost envied her. She felt something. Fear, most likely. My physical senses might have returned, but my emotional nerves lacked reception. I still felt…hollow, even as a vampire raged a few paces away.

"It's getting late," I began while lurching to my feet. The nurse rushed forward to assist, but Dublin beat her to it.

His hand caught my arm reflexively, but I wrenched out of his reach, forced to grip the bed frame to steady myself.

"I'm fine," I insisted. "In fact, I should be leaving." I staggered for the door, pushing past him.

"Where are you going?"

"What does it matter?" I tossed back, limping over the threshold. "You can leave without a word, but I can't?"

It had to be late. The main lights were dimmed in the hall, leaving just a faint glow to see by. Up ahead, I spied an adjacent corridor that must have led to the central ward. Rather than head for it, I turned and advanced farther down the hallway. I needed silence. Darkness. Escape.

"I asked: Where are you going?"

Damn. A shiver racked my spine, instilled by the grit in the voice haunting me.

But I didn't give in. Left. Right. My feet moved dutifully, driving me forward even as my newfound strength began to wane again. Pride warred with basic human instinct. I needed to sit down. I needed—

"Stop." A pale hand slammed against the wall inches from my face and I had no choice but to stop. "I'm begging you. Begging that, for once in your life, you exercise *caution*." Though his tone was level, anger bubbled up beneath the surface of his polished persona. Like heat, I felt it sear my skin.

"So, now you care? Funny, considering that you left. Without a word. Without so much as a calling card. After you told me that the only reason you even bothered to tolerate me was to, and I quote, *'Get to the only Gray who mattered.'*"

"Should I tell you where I was?" He shifted to face me, and I took an involuntary step back. He towered above, his features in shadow. "I was trying to save your life, yet again. A task it appears that I take far more seriously than you do."

I swallowed. *Ah.* "What a convincing lie."

"A lie…" His eyes widened and then narrowed into slits. Against the wall, his fingers flexed, and a hairline crack appeared in the plaster. "You think you have the right to pout like a petulant child? When it was your sister who—"

"My sister who what?"

He seemed to hesitate before confessing, "Your sister who signed a contract of her own."

"Oh?" My heart throbbed, suddenly heavy, and I turned away. "Don't tell me you've been with her all this time? How lucky for you. You managed to score not just one Gray sister, but both—"

"No."

I cringed. His tone was far too soft.

"I didn't force *her* into a contract, Eleanor."

He let the silence linger, almost daring me to ask him to continue.

I didn't.

I couldn't.

So, his upper lip curled back from his teeth as he said, "She refused to let me near you—as you lay dying, I might add —unless I agreed to her terms."

Heat prickled up and down my spine as a burning sting stabbed at my eyes. "What terms?"

"I agreed to leave the city immediately," he said. "Cease all contact with you. If I refused, she would stand by and let us *both* watch you die."

"No." I blinked more rapidly, shaking my head. "You're lying."

He wasn't. We both knew it. Still, it helped somewhat to say as much. I could give Georgiana the benefit of the doubt she never extended toward me. I could pretend she actually loved me.

As long as I ignored the truth.

"Do you think I wanted to tell you like this?" he countered. "Trust me when I say this, but I don't enjoy playing the role of your monster."

"So, why come back at all?" I bit back. My heart raced as rage overrode logic. He wasn't the only one with secrets to tell. "No, don't tell me. We both know the answer—for your contract. Is that it? You want it back?"

Of course. His face would reveal as much. I smirked, ready to witness the truth in full view—his gaze widened, horrified. His jaw clenched, made of stone.

He wasn't gloating.

"You knew," I deduced, closing my eyes in defiance of everything his shocked expression conveyed. Yes, he had to know. "You want it that badly? Fine. Just admit it now. I'll shove the damn thing down your throat if you do."

But he said nothing. No quip. No insult.

"I-If we are done here, I'll just be leaving," I stammered weakly. One step was as far as I made it before I found myself shoved against the wall.

Gently. Cool fingers gripped my shoulders, trembling with the restraint needed to keep from bruising—his expression contained no such care, however. Even the suit couldn't save him—man became monster.

Rather than berate me, he reached into his jacket pocket. I hadn't noticed the bulge against his side before, which concealed something thin, made of silver. Two circular bits of metal capped off each end of it, and recognition hit me like a slap. Manacles.

"Are…are you insane?" I exhaled the question.

"I'm exasperated." He caught my wrists in his fist and casually tugged. Two involuntary steps brought me closer to him. In a low voice, he warned, "We can walk back to your room together. Or"—he hefted one end of the handcuff so that the metal caught the light—"I can drag you there."

I fought to keep my head held high, my chin jutting defiantly into the air. "You can't do this—"

In a blur of motion, he lunged. One sweep of his hand robbed me of balance, but before I could sway, I was in his arms. He surged forward, *carrying* me down the hall.

Heedless of any poor soul who might have been sleeping, I screamed. I kicked. I flailed.

"You can't do this!" I attempted to grab at the doorway as he turned into my room.

With little effort, he broke my grip and headed toward the bed. One shrug of his shoulders and I landed in an unceremonious heap over the crumpled blankets.

He snapped one of the cuffs onto my wrist while I was still stunned and secured it to the frame of the bed. I didn't even have a chance to resist. To fight. So I settled for lashing out like a child and kicked him.

If he felt the pain in his right knee, his face revealed nothing.

"You don't want to eat?" he echoed. "Fine." One swipe of his hand sent the tray of food crashing into the wall. Yellow broth slashed the white backdrop like paint and the cake went flying into a far corner. "You don't want to talk about this with some damn rationality, have it your way. Scream, Eleanor. Fight. You'll just give me a reason to gag you."

Shock deflated me. I cringed against the headboard as he stormed toward the doorway. A nurse was already there, gaping in shock.

"Get Ms. Gray something to calm her down," Dublin ordered as he pushed past her. He spared one last searing glance in my direction and snarled, "She's a danger to herself."

With what seemed to be an apologetic frown, the woman nodded and rushed off. Oddly enough, when she returned sporting a syringe, I didn't resist, allowing her to pierce my vein with little fanfare.

Like a good captive, I lay there, one hand chained to the bed, the other resting somewhere over my heart. It was racing. Pounding. Surging.

From unease or rage?

Who the hell knew?

Eventually, the wave of medication kicked in. My pulse slowed and my eyelids became heavy. When sleep came for me, I surrendered to it.

He might have won this round, but he'd already lost another.

When one was locked within a game of wits against a vampire, I'd learned that there was only one way to break a stalemate.

Someone had to bleed.

And I was already wounded.

~

The drug wore off in slow, ebbing waves. When my thoughts finally seemed coherent again, I peeled my eyes open, expecting to find myself strapped to the bed. Instead, both hands moved freely.

That wasn't all. The beside tray had been righted, the mess cleared from the floor. Fresh food had replaced my ruined meal—another nondescript cup and a plate of bacon, eggs, and sausage. Draped over the foot of my bed was the black dress Yulia had brought along with a pair of my sensible flats and a black coat, also mine.

Unease goaded my heart into racing, but I choked the fear back.

Instead, I ignored the food in favor of getting dressed. My body felt stiff, each movement awkward and slow. By the time I fastened the last button on my coat, someone had entered the room to join me.

He was wearing black, I saw when I finally gathered up the nerve to look. A black suit. A blacker tie. His eyes glowed in harsh contrast, taking me in with one callous sweep. But he wasn't angry.

Even worse, he was unreadable.

"I suggest we change tack." He sat on a nearby chair and gestured toward the bed. "I'll open with a threat, since you seem inclined to play the role of prisoner. How much do you value your cat?"

"T-Tinkles?" Panic clenched my lungs, making each breath a struggle. "Where is he?"

"Safe," Dublin replied before I could assume the worst. "I will return him to you, of course. *After* we finish our discussion."

"Or?" Despite my feelings toward him, there were some lines even I had never envisioned him crossing. Then again, I'd never owned a piece of his soul before.

"Or I'll keep him," he warned. "We both know he won't mourn your company."

I bit my lip in anguish. In some ways, it was a far worse bluff than threatening his life. I would be the only one disenfranchised in this equation.

"What do you want?"

"I suggest we revert to our usual method of communication." He placed something onto the bedside table, beside the food: a rectangular, leather-bound book flipped open to a blank page. When my gaze returned to Dublin, he crossed his arms, transforming into his businessman persona. "We negotiate."

"Via a contract?" I backed away near the wall, keeping him in full view.

"Yes. I will apologize for last night if that's what you want."

"And what do *you* want?" I whispered.

He cocked his head and shrugged, smoothing his hands along the front of his suit. "I think it's best if you stay with me."

I didn't miss the marked shift in his tone. Cautious. As though I were a simpleton best communicated with via slow, careful wording.

"For your protection," he said. "You need proper medical care. I will make all the arrangements—"

"Don't pretend like you care," I warned. His words still hurt, smarting on my psyche like invisible scratches. "Just cut to the chase and tell me what you *really* want."

His eyes narrowed. "Should I come out and say it, then? I want my contract, of course."

Ah. It was a game of hide-and-seek I'd planned over two months ago. Back when bitterness had driven me to hide the leather book *where no one would ever find it,* or so the childish part of me had claimed.

Knowing Dublin, everything I had was probably in the gloved hands of one of his agents, being ruthlessly inspected as we spoke. Or he'd searched for it himself. Hell, maybe that was the reason his hair was slicked, damp in a way that eerily coincided with the rain lashing at the window beyond him.

But one obvious fact diminished my glee at the prospect.

"You didn't know I had it. Did you?" Suddenly drained, I crept forward and sat on the edge of the mattress, as far from him as possible.

"No." He glared through the window. "Raphael doesn't part with his trophies easily."

"So, what happens if I tell you? I wind up shackled to another bed? Or is this the part where you threaten me for real?" I squared my chin, fighting to sound brave. Even before I saw his jaw clench, I knew I'd failed.

"To kill you? How about we bargain instead, like I suggested? You want to stay at Gray Manor? Fine. You want to live in denial? Fine. As long as you remain under my protection, you can set whatever terms you wish."

"And as long as I return your contract," I added.

He nodded after a second's pause. "That as well."

I bit my lip. To relinquish the one morsel of power I held over him or not? *Knowledge is king*, my father used to say, during one of the rare moments when he wasn't heralding the importance of money. *Never surrender it willingly.*

"I'd like to know it's secure," Dublin insisted. "However, telling me its location won't invalidate your ownership."

I noted how reluctantly he added that last tidbit of information.

"Even if I tell you, it will change nothing," I felt compelled to say. "I still don't forgive you for insulting me—"

"And I don't expect you to. As for our agreement, shall we put it in writing?" he asked. "You agree to stay with me as well as reveal the location of my contract. In return, you set your own terms."

I attempted to meet his gaze and found no hostility in it. No real emotion, either. Just endless burnished silver. "Fine. I want… François gets to remain as my driver."

He raised an eyebrow as he reached for the pen. "François?"

"I hired him a few weeks ago. He's very…r-reliable," I stammered. Honestly, it was the principle of the matter.

François, though slightly hated, was still someone I'd hired on my own. Dublin could lock me away in a tower if he wanted, just as long as he let me keep what little of my life I'd managed to rebuild.

"Fine." He jotted down a line on a fresh page in the contract book. "What else?"

"And…" I swallowed hard, flexing my fingers against the mattress. "You apologize for what you said about me."

He raised an eyebrow. "If that is what you wish…"

"And," I added. "I want you to be honest with me. If I ask you something, anything, you tell me the truth. No secrets. No games. No lies."

"Agreed." With a stroke of his pen, he added another line. As he finished, his eyes cut to mine. "But I would like to second that request. You keep nothing from me. Nothing."

He held the pen out and shoved the book across the table.

I sighed, biting any more questions back. We were on a dangerous precipice, mere inches from falling off. Only God knew what waited down below, and I wasn't that inclined to find out for myself.

With a single stroke, I signed my name and watched him do the same.

And the sight alone shouldn't have imparted the most stability I'd felt since…

Well, since he'd left.

"So, what now?"

"Now?" He tucked the contract book into his pocket and stood. "You uphold your end—you come with me, no dramatics."

"And," I added with a sigh, "I show you where your contract is?"

He nodded. "Where is it?"

"Where else?" I countered. It was obvious in a sense—what imposing shelter would make for the perfect hiding place for a vampire's soul? "Home."

Gray Manor rose upon the hill like the disapproving relative most people complained about. The one bastion of my life that I could never seem to escape.

My only comfort was that Dublin didn't seem particularly fond of it, either. Stone-faced, he guided his car onto the property, following what little commands I gave. *Follow the main path. Then go beyond the house, beyond the gardens, farther…*

"Here," I croaked once we'd reached the very end of the property.

Looming before us stood what my mother had lovingly referred to as the Crowning Jewel of both heritage and home. Our family crypt. Even now, the structure held the same morbid fascination for me that it had during my childhood.

Made entirely of stone and almost simple in appearance, the structure contained Gray bodies spanning at least three centuries, back from the time of my great-grandfather many times over, James. Given what a diverse and interesting bunch we were, I almost pitied it.

"You hid it here?" Dublin wondered. He had leaned toward my side without me realizing and I flinched as his chill raised goosebumps over the back of my neck. A part of me wanted to hate him still—hate the fact that he could sit so close to me as though nothing had changed.

I snuck a glance at his face, alarmed by how neutral his expression seemed.

Apparently, we were both in denial of recent events.

"Georgie and I used to play here as children," I found myself muttering. Compelled by some need to explain the safety of my hiding place perhaps? Or maybe his skeptical frown amused me. "We used to sneak notes back and forth by stuffing them into this empty urn kept on a shelf for decoration." An ironic fixture, given my mother's general loathing of any frivolous displays. "Sometimes, I used to come here to think."

"You...*played* in a crypt?"

As his expression shifted, I wasn't sure what might appear. A wry twist of his mouth wasn't my first suspicion. God, it couldn't be a smile.

"Why am I not surprised?"

I turned away. I would take that as an insult rather than a harmless quip. Only he could make the cold boundaries I'd grown up obeying seem more trite than tradition.

In fact, he made everything about my past life seem trivial.

Like the days when I could sit beside someone and not recall what their touch felt like, rough with possession. I tried to suppress the thought, but my breath quickened anyway, signaling my unease like blood in shark-infested waters.

Thankfully, he parked the next second, choosing a spot near the shade of a weeping willow, and I used the task of unfurling myself from my seat belt to fill the awkward silence. When I finally pushed the door to my side open, Dublin was already there.

He warily extended his hand, as if expecting me to bite it rather than accept it. When I did the latter, he helped me to my feet. Together, we faced my childhood playground and I pretended like I wasn't affected by his scrutiny.

Neglect reduced the landscape to a wilderness of overrun grasses and weeds. Without its typical manicured appearance, the area resembled something right out of a horror film. The crypt itself was by far the most unsettling fixture. Square-shaped and framed by Romanesque pillars supporting a sharply pitched roof, it was an anomaly compared to the Gothic style of the main manor.

"You used to play here as a child," Dublin reiterated. "For enjoyment?"

I could sense the typical mixture of scorn and pity he usually showed whenever I mentioned personal anecdotes. This day, however, I decided to inhale the damp, humid air of the overcast day and give in to nostalgia.

He wasn't forgiven—but I could pause my ire for history's sake.

"Shall I give you the grand tour?"

The door wasn't locked. Ironic considering that most of the people buried here had spent their entire lives keeping their secrets under lock and key. Inside was a small entryway formed of gray marble floors and dark walls. A lone statue lorded over a spiral staircase built into the earth, leading deeper into the crypt.

"Is something wrong?" I looked back and found Dublin lingering beyond the doorway, his frown more pronounced than usual. "Don't tell me *you* have an aversion to death?"

"It's not that," he said gruffly. I waited, but he didn't elaborate further.

Sighing, I started forward without him. "I can bring it to you—"

"I would have thought you Grays had some elaborate protocol regarding your sacred structures."

I faltered and braced my hand against the wall for stability. Was that another joke?

"Do come in," I snapped rather than decide. "Welcome to the glorious Gray family tomb."

Without so much as a retort, he finally entered the entryway, and memories stirred as I led the way with him on my heels.

"My parents brought us here often," I admitted, brushing my fingers along the stone walls as my voice echoed. Dust coated my fingertips, depressingly thick. "It was the one thing I ever saw my father take pride in, apart from the fortune. He called it our 'enduring legacy.'"

At the foot of the stairs was a light that, once flipped, revealed the cavernous interior containing five chambers that branched from the central room. In the center stood another statue, one of a crying angel, her eyes downcast in sorrow.

"That's been here for generations," I remarked.

Slipping past her, I wandered the circular space and tried to see it as someone on the outside might. Like a vampire perhaps. In death, we Grays were every bit as interesting as we were in life. Our tastes in minimal design had changed little over the centuries. Such as a fondness for our namesake color.

I crept into the alcove designated for the most recent generation, aware of Dublin's gaze on the back of my neck.

"Is this the urn you and your sister used?" he wondered.

I peered over my shoulder and found him staring up at the old marble container on the shelf across from the somber angel. "Yes. It was one of the most reliable ways to reach Georgie back in the old days, if you can imagine that. I should look inside it." I started toward him, hope bubbling in my throat.

Maybe after weeks of silence, she would decide to reach out by recalling an obscure tradition from our childhood?

I changed course only when I noticed Dublin watching me. How pathetic would that seem?

Somewhere around very and depressing, I decided.

I turned instead and approached the wall where my parents were interred. Joined in eternal rest, they dominated the top two places. The layout resembled that of a vertical grid with each tomb marked by a stone placard engraved with the occupant's name. Per chamber, each wall could hold up to eight corpses in rows of two.

And, like any doting parents, mine had ensured that Georgie and I already had plots picked out beneath them. While we'd barely spent quality time together in life, we would spend the rest of our miserable eternity in close proximity.

How charming.

I trailed my fingers over my mother's engraved name, and I swore I could hear her scolding from beyond the grave. *My God, Eleanor, what have you done now? You were always such a dutiful child.*

"Sorry," I told her out loud, as contritely as one could while talking to herself.

Sinking into a crouch, I felt along the edge of the placeholder for my tomb. A sharp tug pried it loose enough to slip my hand into the space beyond. Tucked just within reach was a leather-bound book—and something else. I'd almost forgotten hiding it as well—a small plastic ring with a chipped blue bead in the center.

"Don't tell me you're too enthralled by nostalgia to remember why we're here?" Dublin remarked behind me.

Clutching the book to my chest, I stood. "I've got it." I turned and found him mere steps away. Extending the contract book with one hand, I quietly concealed the ring in my other. "My end of our bargain."

His face unreadable, Dublin took the contract from me and tucked it into the breast pocket of his suit.

Even though he'd mentioned as much earlier, I still felt tempted to ask, "So what does this mean?"

"The book is merely a symbolic token," he explained. "Your name is on it. Regardless, I find that it's best to keep these things close."

"Ah." I nodded along as if I knew the first thing about soul collecting. "Well, now you have it."

An uncomfortable silence stretched on for endless seconds. The longer we lingered, the colder the atmosphere felt. My teeth chattered as the monotonous scenery made me picture…well, decay.

"Yours?" Dublin nodded toward my earmarked tomb. "I suspect this isn't a new purchase."

"Oh, no." I followed his gaze and brushed my thumb over the etched letters of my name. "It was a Christmas gift. My parents presented them to Georgie and me when I was eight."

"A gift?"

"Of course." I chafed at his tone. As if such a thing weren't normal. "At least they had enough sense to realize that I didn't need any space beneath mine. I should have it engraved now: Eleanor Gray, forever alone."

Oh, the poetic justice of it all. One of the last Grays doomed to die a spinster.

"You believe that?" Dublin questioned in a tone that made me bite my lip. It was too stern. Too soft.

"Why shouldn't I?"

"You never envisioned yourself marrying someone? Anyone? You've never wanted children—"

"I'm tired." Sighing, I turned to him, swiping my dust-covered fingers on my skirt. "Now that you have your precious…"

He was looking at me so strangely that I lost my train of thought. It was different from his usual scowl—eyes narrowed, mouth in a firm, odd line. Something flickered across his gaze, too elusive to name. Before I could, he marched toward the central chamber, beckoning with a wave of his hand. "Let's go."

Perhaps talk of tombs was too morbid, even for the undead? I tucked my ring into my purse and then followed him, uneasy. As he mounted the stairs, I couldn't resist slipping my hand into the urn on my way past. Unsurprisingly, I found nothing but dust.

Georgie was probably galivanting on a beach somewhere with a new lover, her pathetic sister forgotten.

"I'd rather not spend the rest of the day among your deceased family members, if you don't mind," Dublin called from above.

When I finally rejoined him, he was waiting for me outside the building and I steeled myself for a plot-twist-style reveal. *Ha!* He had been lying all along. This was the part when he'd entrap my soul for eternity. I could only hope he didn't drug me first before spiriting me away.

"Get in," was all he said, wrenching the car door open for me.

Confined again, I had no escape from the thoughts that months alone had kept at bay. Things like memories of him I wished to smother. His touch. His taste.

The night he returned...

My lips burned and I brushed my fingers along them, tracing the remnants of him. Had that kiss been another twisted game?

A way for him to lower my guard.

Again…

Stop, Ellie.

Rolling my window down and inhaling fresh air helped somewhat. Or at least the biting chill put everything back into perspective. Once again, I'd signed a portion of my life away, though I wasn't quite sure what I'd bargained for in return. In all honesty, I didn't need his protection. A squadron of security guards on my family's payroll would have sufficed—though, admittedly, not as effective as a vampire.

But sufficient.

I didn't need him.

"Where are we?" I asked as the car finally slowed before a building in the heart of the city. A secluded high-rise accessible only through a security gate and a garage activated by a keypad.

"Somewhere safe," Dublin replied before exiting the vehicle. He circled to my end and offered his hand to help me stand.

Wary, I followed him into the building, observing everything as objectively as I could. "You certainly haven't changed," I blurted. "My house would have been just fine, you do realize?"

It was a lie.

"Your house looks like it should be condemned," Dublin replied, tugging me along.

I tried to regain my anger, but I was too busy gaping at our surroundings to remember to be insulted. Dublin had always had a flair for elegance, but this…

Black walls and marble flooring created a hushed world of darkness. Elevators lined in gold led to the upper floors. There was no lobby. No grinning receptionist. Just a silent trip up to the tenth floor, where we exited into a darkened hallway. At the end awaited a black door that opened the moment Dublin approached.

A woman stood behind it, her smile warm. "Good evening, sir," she greeted while stepping aside, allowing Dublin and me to enter what appeared to be a private suite.

I glanced at her from the corner of my eye, hating how my stomach tightened with every detail observed. Blond hair formed a neat bun at the nape of her neck, displaying beautiful features subtly enhanced with makeup. Her modest black dress did little to disguise her curves. A strange sense of déjà vu warned that I knew her.

From where?

It was only when she gestured for my coat that I remembered. *Katherine.* That was her name. The woman whose contract he managed. He'd saved her from Saskia and her henchman if I remembered correctly.

And now she was apparently at his personal beck and call.

"Thank you. That will be all, Kate," Dublin told her, sending her scurrying off across the spacious entryway.

Kate. The nickname echoed inside my skull. The same man refused to call me Ellie, professing a hatred of "unprofessional" monikers. And yet, this woman was *Kate.*

"Nice to see you've had company." The statement slipped out, but I didn't know how I intended it to land. As an insult? A jab? Something innocent, I decided when Dublin trained his gaze on me. Merely a harmless question. "Last I remembered, you lived alone."

Whether out of an unwillingness to fight or simple disinterest, he gritted his teeth against a reply and stalked forward to throw open two double doors directly across from us.

Beyond them was a sight so unexpected that my mouth dropped open, all else forgotten.

A room formed the center of the suite, one almost entirely encased in glass, each massive window displaying a harrowing scene of the city. Multicolored swaths of skyscrapers bathed in nightfall created a fantastical landscape of neon and navy.

"Does this meet your expectations?" Dublin wondered, his tone as smug as ever.

Perhaps for good reason, considering I had to physically nudge my mouth closed with the tip of my finger.

"It's fine." As I spoke, I crossed the room, wandering as close to the glass as I dared. Awe turned out to be no match for pride, however. "It's *beautiful…*"

"There is no family crypt," he added. "But hopefully it will suffice."

Was that yet another joke?

"Luckily, my pre-chosen tombstone isn't going anywhere," I said. "Who knows, by the end of the month, I may be enjoying it the way my parents always intended." A smile shaped my mouth. "I should pick out my coffin tomorrow, I suppose. A nice, sensible, boring one fit for a spinster."

I was breaking my resolve to stay angry again. Perhaps hating him took too much effort? Still grinning, I looked over—but Dublin wasn't laughing. Instead, his eyes cut to mine, imparting a chill that made me shiver.

"We need to talk."

"Oh?" I returned my attention to the view and braced my fingers over the glass. "About what?"

His scoff warned that he wasn't playing along this time— but anger I could stomach. His low tone alarmed me far more. "I think you know what."

Did I? *No,* I decided, shaking my head. "I'm tired." I turned toward a random direction. "Is the bedroom this way?"

"Eleanor."

Before I could take a step, his hand fell over my shoulder pinning me in place.

"I've played along until now," he admitted. "But I lack the energy to pretend anymore."

"Pretend?" I asked innocently.

"Yes, pretend—as though you don't know what really ails you. It isn't cancer."

A part of me felt relieved that I couldn't see his face from this angle—and that he couldn't see mine.

"My contract was one aspect requiring clarity, but now we need to discuss—"

"I don't want to talk about this now," I said. "Frankly, I'm not in the mood for more personal attacks on my character, either—"

"Can you blame me?" His strained tone turned cutting. "Put your pride aside for a second. This isn't a little game, or a fantasy, or a contract that you can confront by stripping naked and turning the tables. This is your life. For whatever reason, I'd rather not see you squander it in denial."

"As if you care." Because he didn't obviously. At least, not beyond some ulterior motives he had yet to reveal. Sighing, I tossed out potential answers, saving him the trouble. "Allow me to guess why. Raphael has put a bounty on my head? Or maybe your aim is more selfish than that? You get your precious years back as long as you—"

"I'm trying to talk to you reasonably. You decide to provoke." His grip tightened, straining the fabric of my dress. I could feel the ridge of every finger and memories triggered. Sensations I didn't want to recall. Emotions I didn't need. All of them descended at once, constricting my chest in a vice. "Look at me." He spun me to face him. "You demanded an apology. Fine. You have one."

God, I trembled at what I saw in his gaze, lurking beneath the gray irises, so faint that it could have been a figment of my imagination. Hate?

Or something far worse. *Guilt.*

"But I won't humor you anymore. I refuse to let you mock me as well." His tone deepened and I understood the true source of his irritation. I had the nerve to taunt the great and terrible contractor with two concepts that seemed to affect him more than any other. Life and death. "According to Dr. Martin, your condition is not fatal. And yet you still choose to refer to your mortality as casually as the weather? Fine. But first, face the fact that you *may* have a tumor. Or—"

"Stop." I had to clench my hands into fists to keep from slapping them over my ears as he snarled his next words.

"*Or* something far different. If I can acknowledge as much, why can't you? Say it."

"Fine. Something *unnatural.*" I blinked, surprised as moisture slid down my cheeks. "So unnatural that you accused me of having loose morals rather than believe it. Is that what you want me to say? I would rather have a tumor—"

"I had every reason in the world to deny it," he pointed out. "Or at least deny that I had any part in it. Can you admit that?"

Maybe I could… If life and death weren't the very tools of his trade.

"So, why believe it now?"

He laughed, spitting out each chuckle through clenched teeth. "Perhaps because I've ceased being surprised by anything where you are concerned? And I don't want to fight with you, but I won't watch you lie to yourself, either."

More tears spilled from my eyes though I wasn't sure why. "Why not? Tormenting me is what you do best, after all."

"Stop trying to bait me into a fight." He reached out, tucking a stray curl behind my ear.

I went rigid—there was no gentleness in the act. He lingered as if daring me to recoil, so I dug my heels in just to ensure I didn't.

But then he remained, taunting me with seconds of contact. So, I gave in and tried to swat his fingers away. "I'm not the one who attacked your character—"

"You are now," he said.

"Oh really?" I laughed. "How?"

"By pretending like you don't see it." He stepped in closer, and I had to crane my neck to hold his gaze. "Forget the rest. You ask why I care? Don't you dare act as though you don't know—"

"What?" I demanded.

"Why I returned despite intending to spend at least a full damn decade abroad." He lowered his mouth to my ear. "What Yulia knows. Saskia. Raphael. They all see it. Mocked me for it. I even told you once, my intentions toward you, didn't I?"

That he had.

"I want you, Eleanor Gray..."

Lies. I swallowed hard, resisting the memory. "Told me what? That you have a fetish for innocence? That I'm the one who toys with you? Who kisses *you* out of nowhere and leaves on a whim—"

"No." He withdrew, his eyes flashing. "That I have an irritating impulse to *not* watch you die. Even if you aggravate me every damn step of the way. Even if it's a goddamn struggle just to keep my sanity around you. It's like you want me to—" He broke off and let me go. "Fine. Run. Play the only role you seem willing to play."

"Wonderful." I turned on my heel, gritting my teeth. "But don't pretend like this is my fault. I didn't leave you. I didn't accuse you of—"

"Damn you." His grip clamped down like a vise on my forearm, dragging me back. The second I winced, he released me only to shift his weight to physically block my path. "You enjoy this, don't you? Pushing me to the goddamn brink. The harder I try to keep my composure, the more you chip away at it. Is this what you want?" He fingered the neckline of my dress, seizing the fabric. "Fine. Perhaps I had every right to question your integrity? I'll offer you another ultimatum—drop the naïve act or we will both discover just how innocent you really are. You named a whole list of others you've supposedly been with—but how many were lies?"

My hand lashed out, colliding with his cheek. *Thwack!* He didn't even flinch—but I did as his thumb toyed with a delicate strip of lace.

"Let go," I whispered. My hand stung as if to warn me away from slapping him again. "Get off!"

"No." He wound the material more tightly around his finger, forcing me on tiptoe to keep it from ripping. "Admit it out loud, your true condition—"

"Or?" I rasped, hating how my voice broke.

He twisted the lace again. "Or I'll lose my patience."

"Stop!"

"Fair enough." His expression blank, he tugged.

Fabric unraveled like wisps of smoke as my dress slipped from my shoulders. Before my eyes, Yulia's creation fluttered in pieces to my feet. Even in shock, I knew he was the cause of the malfunction.

"What are you doing?" I rushed to cover my breasts with my hands, but Dublin didn't even give the appearance of shame.

His gaze raked over me, lingering on the flesh my fingers struggled to shield. Disgust, I could stomach, even if it stung.

While a part of me may have cringed from it, my pride would remain intact.

But his lips parted instead, and my breathing hitched. Alarm bells sounded within my skull, warning me away as he angled his body toward me. Pinprick pupils made his eyes seem even brighter. Burning. Impossible to meet head-on.

It was a dangerous expression. One that triggered a million terrifying sensations I shied from acknowledging. Heat. Heaviness in my limbs that made it harder to stand.

And an ache in my chest that grew more painful by the second.

"*Finally*, you have the sense to be afraid. Or not." His nostrils flared, and he scoffed. "I should have known. As always, this excites you more than anything else. You *enjoy* what you do to me."

Enjoyment? Was that the name for how my heart lurched in time with his callous laugh?

He took another step. I jolted back until my spine went rigid against the unyielding wall of glass behind me.

"Get away from me," I croaked.

He laughed again. Then he lunged, slamming his hands against the glass on either side of my head. In the same motion, his knee nudged my thighs, forcing them apart. Slowly. The fabric of his pants teased snatches of my skin, making me jump with every deliberate nudge.

"You put on a good enough act." He brushed his thumb along the trembling corner of my mouth, tracing my frown. "But your heart betrays you always. It rarely hammers in fear. Instead, your pulse dances with excitement."

My head spun as I desperately tried to regain clarity. Sanity. Anything. "Stop—"

"Then face what you really fear. Do you enjoy mocking me? Parading me through a crypt and spewing poetic notions of death? This truly is a game to you."

He swiped his hand over my belly and I cringed, resisting his touch. But then his fingers drifted lower. Lower, plunging between my legs.

And I forgot how to move. How to breathe. Paralyzed, I was a slave to his reaction.

A hiss caught between his teeth. "Damn you." Eyes glowing, he looked down at his fingers. "Of course you're wet already. Of course you crave this."

A deeper groan resonated in his chest as he flexed his wrist, caressing the part of me only he had ever claimed. I closed my eyes, my lips bitten and raw. Noises escaped my throat regardless.

He was ruthless, utilizing sinful, featherlight passes of his thumb. My head reared back against the frigid glass, a groan ripped from my lips.

"Look at me." His forehead nudged mine until I met his gaze. Both eyes were wide. Unfocused. Less devil now, merely an angel fallen from his perch, hell-bent on dragging me down with him. "I'll destroy you before you destroy me. I will. So stop daring me to. Death is a fucking game to you, but life? *That* makes you run scared. So say it." His mouth found my earlobe, grazing the tip in a silent plea. "Put a name to your *tumor* or forfeit your body if you're so determined to die anyway. Say it or you're mine."

"Why are you doing this?" My eyes were overflowing. All I could see were shadows—dark and light, swirling around us. "Stop."

"Then say it."

My lips parted. I croaked, "C-Cancer."

"Fair enough."

A zipper hummed, sounding miles away, and real panic descended.

"Let me go," I said breathlessly.

He didn't, placing his hands on my hips with a gentleness that contradicted the hate radiating off him in waves.

I should have been screaming. Clenching my legs together.

But when he flicked his thumb along my inner thigh, they spread for him with no resistance. It was as if my body rebelled against my brain, welcoming the pressure inching inside me with no restraint. His hips slammed against mine and my spine arched, driving him deeper.

He stiffened as if waiting for me to shove him off. Scream. Fight. My mouth found the crook of his shoulder instead, stealing his scent in ragged gulps. He raged inside me, so rigid, forcing my numbed flesh to conform. Burn.

And it was an agony some sick part of me relished. Raw friction. Communication he couldn't fake or deceive through.

His body stripped him bare and only like this were we ever matched.

Two desperate, pathetic souls.

Groaning, he rocked his hips and my breathing faltered. He was too deep. Too consuming. My nails dug into his shoulders, my face hidden against his skin—but he wrenched on my skull, forcing me to face him.

"Two months," he declared against my parted lips, his eyes heavy-lidded. "Weeks of torment. Being haunted by this." He growled in time with another slow, searing thrust. "Your skin. The feel of you. The sound of you…"

Lies. I fought the wave of pleasure, my eyelids fluttering—but then he jerked, slamming into me. Mind-numbing fire ripped down my spine, feeding on my blood like gasoline, and I went limp.

"I should have killed you the first time," he said. "It's what you wanted, wasn't it?"

The words he said didn't matter. Each gritted note in his voice set off a chain reaction. Nerves crackled. Short-circuited. I whimpered, grasping him tighter. My hips shifted, urging him deeper. Harder. More.

He hissed, rearing back. Then he lurched into me. "Restraint. You take it from me. Always. And you think you can hide from me? From this." Harder. Sharper thrusts made every fear and doubt dissolve into nothing. "But I own you, always. Body and soul."

His thumb invaded between my legs, and I saw white with each stroke he delivered. Every muscle contracted, contorting me like a puppet on violent strings.

All the while, his thrusts quickened. Faster. Too fast.

My head fell back against my shoulders, my eyes on the ceiling as pleasure built.

"I've had centuries to prepare for you," he growled as I convulsed, mindless. "Years beyond your understanding. Do you think this means anything? No." He stiffened, grunting against the base of my throat. "You mean nothing."

His arms caught me as my thoughts drifted. As if from far away, I could hear him talking still. To me? Or himself?

"I won't let *you* be the end of me. I won't…even if it means I have to ruin you first."

MEMENTO MORI

I came to in frozen arms. Dublin's. For what felt like ages, he carried me, but I lacked the strength to even open my eyes. When his body finally withdrew from mine, a cloud of silken sheets provided a clue as to our destination. Forcing my eyes open confirmed it—a bedroom, darker than the main space. A sliver of moonlight served as the sole illumination, giving his limbs ethereal definition as he stood back.

My heart lurched in my chest. God, he resembled an angel more than ever as his eyes swept over me, his jaw tight. But his grated, hollow voice was pure hell.

"You should be fine," he said, almost to himself. "I cleared it with the doctor. Your labs had improved, and she didn't recommend against it."

Sex, I realized in the depths of my addled brain. He had gone through the trouble of discussing sex with his mysterious doctor. An image of my dress came to mind, how easily he'd removed it…

I didn't want to jump to the obvious conclusion. It was too insane. I wanted to sleep. Forget.

But some cruel sense of curiosity wouldn't let me. Struggling for breath, I croaked, "Yulia—"

"I lied to her," he admitted, easily catching onto my train of thought—the lace had been one of her mysterious alterations.

But the fact that *he* had requested such a detail presented a scenario I couldn't fathom at the moment. I closed my eyes instead, desperate to reconnect with my limbs. They were jelly, disobeying any command I issued. I could only lie at his mercy, blind to his expression. Eventually, he left anyway, his steps resonating through the silence.

Only to return minutes later.

I jumped as warm liquid dripped against my inner thigh. My eyes flew open to watch him kneel over the mattress, a rag in hand. He ran it between my legs as reverently as a worshipper cleaning off a cherished altar, and the insanity of it…

I trembled, but he didn't look up, intent on his task. But something in my silence made his jaw tighten and his fingers stall.

Finally, he grated out a single request. "Say something."

"I'm dreaming," I whispered, clinging to that thin possibility. Otherwise, my brain throbbed with too many thoughts to process. His touch. His words. His rage…

"I won't let you destroy me."

But then he stood, tossing the rag aside, and turned toward the door. Guilt didn't belong in this specter—it made him feel far too real.

"Wait," I croaked.

He froze near the threshold of the hall. Within a heartbeat, tension transformed him into a creature of muscle and bone. An unrivaled statue of perfection.

But his gaze revealed a crack. Something elusive that made my thoughts twist into knots when I tried to decipher it.

So I didn't.

I closed my eyes and willed everything away. Everything but the childish ache worming through my chest where my heart might have been.

In the end, all I could muster up the strength to voice was, "Why? Why leave?" I added, choking every word out. "Then come back. Then kiss me. Then…" My body hummed, riding the wave of lust even as my mind raged in turmoil. "Why?"

I waited.

But footsteps broke the silence rather than words.

He left.

And, alone, I squeezed my eyes shut tighter and fell into the darkness eager to consume me.

~

I awoke in a decadently furnished room accented in shades of ebony and emerald. Solid oak furniture clashed with the modern-style windows and light fixtures—much like I did, in a sense. An old-fashioned creature in a world far ahead of its time.

A heavy emerald canopy loomed overhead, fanning around a bed adorned with silken sheets and lush pillows. A window to my right overlooked a view of the city no less stunning than the one visible in the main room. Overcast daylight streamed in, illuminating a wooden wardrobe in the corner and a door partially opened, which I assumed led to the hall.

That shadowy doorway presented a reality too terrifying to face. Not now. I contemplated staying here forever, unmoving, ignoring reality for as long as I could—though it wasn't as if my body shielded my ignorance for very long. Only a strip of silk covered my naked limbs, and an ache throbbed between my legs. The images of last night loomed, inescapable.

Sitting upright was the only way to banish them. Groaning with the effort, I stood as well and found a robe draped over the end of the bed. I drew it around myself and crept from the room. It was a short distance to the center of the suite, but I didn't find Dublin lurking there.

Instead, a glass table near the edge of the room had been set for one, containing a plate of sandwiches and a lidded cup. I devoured the food without stopping to savor it. Then I paced to keep any wayward thoughts at bay.

Eventually, I wound up wandering throughout the rest of the spacious suite in search of a distraction. He hadn't spared any expense, though that said little given his wealth. There were plenty of rooms lurking behind closed doors. A kitchen. A wide parlor with a billiard table and a piano.

None of it felt like him though—unlike a makeshift apartment hidden within a church.

This place resembled…

Well, a neat, clinical *cage*.

A sudden thud pierced the silence, and I spun around to find an ivory shadow lurking beyond the doorway, dressed from head to toe in steel gray. His closed-off expression was far too dangerous. Cautious. The man might as well have been on tiptoe.

But sleepless hours spent tossing and turning on an unfamiliar bed could put a lot of things into perspective. Like the stark, cruel state of my current reality. And how much better it felt to ignore it.

All of it.

"I'm going to pretend that last night never happened," I blurted. For some reason, my voice sounded raspier than it should have, but it got the point across. "Whatever you said. Whatever we did—it doesn't matter. It never happened."

There. Like magic, I'd willed all the tension away. Sighing, I tilted my head to observe a painting hanging on the wall. A naked angel standing as the sole survivor on a ruined battlefield. How lovely.

"Eleanor..." Dublin fixed me with a strange look. Suspicion? Well, he had no reason to be.

"My cat," I croaked, switching to more important matters. "Where is he?"

I could have kicked myself for forgetting about him yet again in the tumult of events.

Dublin stood there for so long that I started to wonder if he'd turned into stone. Finally, he sighed. "He's in the room beside yours."

"Really?" I raced down the hallway in a direction I'd missed during my first exploration.

Sure enough, a peek into the room beside mine revealed another suite, and curled up on the floor was Tinkles. My beautiful darling looked healthy, whole, and as surly as ever. He blinked at me, flexing his claws. Approaching him directly was a reckless act, but after days away, I couldn't resist.

"Darling!" I sank to my knees and threw my arms around him—but my skin wasn't immediately skewered by his claws.

In fact, something wet and warm stroked my cheek, so unexpected that I flinched back. His tongue, still protruded from his mouth, the culprit of the odd sensation. I had no clue how long I sat there before a familiar shadow appeared in the doorway.

"What did you do to him?" I demanded.

"Come and eat," Dublin said, ignoring the question. Without another word, he left.

After I made sure Tinkles had adequate lodgings—irritatingly, his room was even larger than the one he had in Gray Manor—I returned to the main room and found the table set with another cup and a plate of steaming vegetables and fish.

Dublin retreated to a far corner, his arms crossed while I sat and downed both offerings without complaint. He wanted to say something, I sensed, so I avoided his questioning stare. Presenting me with food at all was no doubt his attempt at getting a rise from me, allowing him to ruin our fragile truce. So I scraped my fork against my plate for emphasis. *See?* I wanted to gloat. Everything was nice and cordial. No need for any horrible reminders of events that didn't matter.

Because they had never happened.

"There is something we need to discuss," he began as I choked down the last morsel of food.

Damn. Fighting to keep my face neutral, I set my fork aside. "Like what?"

"You claimed you wanted answers… Well, do you?"

Answers. That wouldn't break my rule, per se. It would be harmless information I could choose whether or not to believe.

"Y-Yes."

"Good." He rummaged through a nearby sideboard. After withdrawing something from a drawer, he faced me again, revealing the object settled on his palm—a leather-bound book, dark with age. "You can start with this."

He dropped the book onto the table, and I eyed it as one might a bomb.

"What is it about?" I scanned the cover, more puzzled than ever. "There's no title."

"Consider it part of a private collection," Dublin explained, flipping it open to a yellowed page. "A ledger of sorts."

He was right. At a glance, I could tell that it wasn't a normal tome. It was handwritten for one—a series of lines penned in shockingly familiar script. Names and dates. Reading them, I felt my brow furrow.

"James, Agatha…Mary…Edward." I met Dublin's gaze, an eyebrow raised. "These are my ancestors' names."

"Yes." The firm line of his mouth revealed not even a hint of his intentions. Good or bad. "Every last Gray for over three centuries. Dead, alive, or otherwise."

"Ah…" I nearly choked. No wonder he knew so much about my heritage—he'd studied it. Though a better question was: Why? "So what am I, the tenth Gray to fall under your spell? What, do you keep a list of your conquests to reminisce over?"

As much as the thought irritated me to indulge, I couldn't help but wonder if Georgie was written in his little book as well.

He raised an eyebrow. "You still don't realize the gravity of what you've done, do you? Allow me to enlighten you, Eleanor, but most people—spinster or otherwise—do not sell their soul on a whim."

"You sold yours to Raphael," I pointed out, though I didn't intend it as an insult. Going off his stiffening jaw, I suspected he took it as one anyway. "I just want to understand. Why?"

He made me sound so horrible for forging a contract—but what might tempt the infamous Dublin Helos to embrace virtual servitude?

"It wasn't a decision I made out of boredom, I can tell you that," he said coldly. I looked at his face and braced myself for one of his glares, but he wasn't staring in my direction anymore. "And it certainly wasn't one I took lightly, even now."

"It's not like I had a choice," I said, eyeing my hands. They were shaking. "Not the first time, at least…"

Signing his contract had been a life or death decision then —mainly because, unbeknownst to me, he had poisoned me to the brink of death.

"I believe your lineage may provide answers as to this… situation," he said, changing the subject. "See if you can recall any forebearer with an unusual legacy."

"How would I know?" I asked.

He looked back at me. "I'm sure your parents, who gifted you a gravesite as a child, regaled you with plenty of tales of your ancestors. Do you deny it?"

My silence gave him my answer. He was right. In lieu of normal childhood games, Georgie and I had recited the names of our forebearers as reverently as schoolyard rhymes.

"Read," Dublin commanded. "Scour your memories for any relatives that stand out."

"You think this…" I swallowed hard, choking down the word *cancer.* "This condition has something to do with my bloodline?" I could have laughed. It sounded *that* sordid. Until I remembered my sister's secret life, that is. I grimaced as the true depth of my ignorance resonated like a slap. *You're so pathetic, Ellie.* "How?"

"I'm not sure." He eyed me for so long that I felt numb when he finally turned away.

"You're lying." I wasn't sure exactly why, which was the confusing part. But Dublin rarely backed down from a fight —unless he had more to lose by playing his hand. "I

remember when you taunted me about knowing James, n
ancestor, personally. But now I find out that you have
literal book on my family, and you're acting like it's just
normal way vampires pass the time."

By tracking centuries of genealogy. For the fun of it.

"What aren't you telling me?"

"I have my own avenues to hunt," he confessed witho
turning around.

"Like?" I sat forward as he crossed the room.

Staring broodingly from the windows, he looked more t
stereotypical vampire archetype than ever. Eterna
tormented. A snippet of a past conversation crossed 1
mind, uttered in a woman's voice. *"If you do decide to s*
him out, don't count on me to help you."

Just who was he trying to avoid?

"Don't I have a right to know?" I pressed.

"Rumors," he replied. "Even I have enough pity not to b
you with them."

But there was more, I suspected. So much more. Not o
was he lying, but he was hiding something.

"What kind of rumors—"

"Sir?"

We both spun in the direction of the foyer, where the s
feminine voice had come from. The blond from last ni

stood there, framed in shadow, dressed ironically in a light-pink dress. My eye twitched. Dublin would have a conniption if I were to wear such a color.

But in this instance? He inclined his head, his expression neutral. "What is it, Kate?"

There was no scorn lacing the single syllable. No derision. No hate.

Kate.

"Your appointment is here," she said while folding her hands primly before her. "Should I show them in?"

"No." Dublin's eyes flickered in my direction as he spoke. "No... I'll meet them personally. Thank you, Kate."

She nodded and left the suite.

"I guess you won't be joining in on the Gray family history book club," I deduced, trying and failing to sound civil.

"I didn't think you'd be so amicable." The bastard had the nerve to sound surly that I had the gall to thwart his expectations at all. "I will be gone for a few hours." He seemed to hesitate before moving toward the front door. "Read the book."

His true command was easy to interpret: *Stay here. Stay out of trouble.*

Be a good little captive.

"If I have to immerse myself in centuries of dreary family history, it's only fitting that I commence such torture in Gray Manor," I pointed out.

Somewhere familiar, far from his beautiful, luxurious high-rise where a stunning blond could enter and exit as she pleased.

Somewhere I could remember my life's destiny as a grouchy spinster.

"You will stay here," Dublin said without turning around.

I swallowed, tapping my fingers over the surface of the table. "A short trip wouldn't be a bother to you. I could call François?"

He gripped the handle of the front door. "That we will discuss when I return."

I swallowed again, tapping my nails more frantically. So much for remaining cordial; my attempts were straining at the seams.

Desperate, I tried a new line of attack. "We did agree that he would remain as my driver."

"We will discuss it later."

Before I could argue, he stormed from the suite, slamming the door in his wake.

So much for cordiality.

Rather than pout, I flipped the book to a fresh page and started to read. It was a surprisingly enthralling task. Who knew that one could find morbid comfort in scanning the many variations of Margaret, Eleanor, and Mary passed down throughout the years?

I wondered if Dublin had stalked any of them. Drained their blood or taken their virginity? The thought became less amusing once my eyes settled over one of the last names in the book.

Georgiana Gray.

Tears pricked my eyes before I understood why. Did I miss her? My thoughts were so scattered that I couldn't tell. Hell, I wouldn't even know what to say to her.

Perhaps I could only write it down.

Upon rising to my feet, I approached the sideboard Dublin had fished the book from and found a silver pen nestled in a drawer. I ripped a blank page from the journal and filled it with line after line of text. Moisture spilled down my cheeks, obscuring the words, and I didn't even try to make sense of them. In a twisted way, I felt the same impulse that had driven me to write Dublin.

Desperation?

Folding the page, I returned to the room I'd awoken in and scoured it until I found my shoes and my purse on a chair in the corner. Yulia's clothing conveniently stocked the wooden wardrobe, and I chose a garment at random. As I dressed, I did my best to squash any guilt. *He* was the one who'd suggested we bargain, after all. I had upheld my end so far.

Proving I wasn't a prisoner was the least he could do to uphold his.

Regardless, I didn't call François as I slipped from the suite and crept into an elevator. Even I knew where to draw the line.

Apparently, so did Dublin—no one rushed from the shadows to stop me. The first floor was as deserted as when we entered, but the door wasn't locked when I tested the handle. Escaping the garage and locked gate was surprisingly easy as well; none of them required a code to exit from. On the main street, I managed to flag down a cab on my own—only to realize as the man dropped me before Gray Manor that I didn't have any cash.

After shoving a check into his hands, I escaped the vehicle without gauging his reaction. His muttered curse gave me a clue. Still, I tried to banish all guilt as I skirted the manor proper. Waning daylight bathed the grounds in a bluish, eerie twilight, and a screen of mist obscured the mausoleum, thinning the closer I came. A storm must have been brewing.

Once inside, I approached the urn and dropped my missive inside it.

Then…

I lingered, wringing my fingers at the prospect of returning to Dublin's alone. Was he still with his "appointment?"

Or Kate?

Shrugging the concerns away, I craned my neck to appreciate the subtle detail of the mausoleum's interior. Delicate reliefs of angels and demons decorated the crown molding, shaping the stone. Within minutes, I found myself inching from room to room, mentally pairing the names I passed with the ones scribbled in Dublin's ledger. *Agatha. Mary. James II and III and IV…*

Dublin had tracked them all with an alarming level of detail, birth years and death dates included. On closer reflection, the fact that he had studied my bloodline at all definitely deserved more scrutiny.

Perhaps the journal was his subtle attempt at irony. A reminder solely directed at me—I wasn't the only Gray to catch his interest. Therefore, I wasn't important. In the grand scheme of Dublin Helos and his devious intentions, Eleanor Gray was nothing more than a single scribbled anecdote among pages of them.

But this name *wasn't.*

I frowned as my fingers traced the unfamiliar series of letters engraved in stone. Not a name at all, it appeared as I strained my eyes to read it, but a phrase.

Memento Mori.

Latin? I couldn't recall its meaning off the top of my head. Carved within plain sight, it dominated the space placed between my Great-Great-Aunt Maria and Uncle George in a section of the chamber where the light struggled to reach.

A slight roughness in texture differentiated it from the smooth graves nearby. The stone here felt older, more tattered than George's tomb and he'd been dead for at least two centuries.

Driven by an impulse I couldn't explain, I felt along the edges of the epitaph, tracing every divot in the worn stone. At the slightest bit of pressure, something shifted in a way it shouldn't have.

Unease prickled at the back of my mind, warning me away. Secrets, once uncovered, rarely revealed useful information as far as I was concerned. Just more deception. More lies. I tried to move—forsaking the intrigue—but my feet remained stubbornly rooted in place. It was the damn chamber, its mystery feeding a question I couldn't shake.

What would a Gray deem important enough to hide within the family tomb?

Eventually, the curiosity became too much to resist.

I rolled my sleeves up and tugged again, bracing my feet against the floor. The placard budged another inch. Another. Sweat dripped down my neck as I applied even more pressure, straining the muscles in my shoulders. More. More...

Until, with a thud, the lid of the tomb came away altogether. I jumped back, fearful of the prospect of a coffin lurking beyond. A cloud of dust obscured any contents, triggering a furious coughing fit. Hunched over, with my hand pressed over my nose, I peered through the darkness.

The dust cleared gradually, revealing a cavernous space in lieu of some ancient deceased Gray. I pulled back, prepared to write it off as empty, but a glint of silver caught my eye before I could.

Intrigued, I sank into a crouch, squinting to make out the object. Whatever it was had been tucked too far back to observe from my position.

I had no choice but to reach inside.

My heart raced as I cautiously inched my fingers deeper within the tomb, feeling along the marble bottom. My arm was in nearly up to my shoulder by the time I finally brushed something cold. Slender. Familiar?

I withdrew it, holding it up to the light, and a gasp tore from my lips as I identified just what it was—a cross. Dangling from a thin chain, it looked identical to Dublin's. It could have been the exact same one.

But the shape differed upon closer inspection. The tips were pointed instead of squared, and a series of letters had been etched into the metal. A name? I couldn't read it, but as the talisman's weight settled over my palm, it was impossible to shake the sense that it was so much more than a casual piece of jewelry. Dublin guarded his more fervently than his own contract. Perhaps, in his obsessive need for control, he'd hidden a spare here?

Among the decaying bodies of a hundred Grays.

I mulled over the potential answers, none of them comforting. So lost in thought, I almost missed the slight noise at first. It shattered the quiet, reverberating from the upper level. A hiss. A thud.

Footsteps.

I bit my lip, assuming the intruder's identity. Dublin Helos himself, arriving just in time to smack my hands for disobeying? I tucked the cross into my fist and turned toward the central chamber, fully prepared to face my scolding.

Do I need to get the manacles, Eleanor?

"You saw her come in here?" a man whispered—but his voice was too soft. Not Dublin's.

Panic froze me in place as his steps continued their hurried descent.

"The lights are on," another man pointed out. "And keep your voice down. We don't want to scare her."

"Ms. Gray?" the first man called out, his raised voice echoing to the farthest reaches of the crypt. "We're…friends of your sister's."

Georgie. But something in his tone made me creep back toward the empty tomb and I traced the rim with trembling fingers.

"I don't think she's here," the second man deduced. Both sets of footsteps sounded like they'd settled near the base of the stairs. Mere paces away from my corridor.

"Let's fan out just to be sure."

My pulse surged, hammering against my eardrums. As footsteps approached my section of the chamber, I crouched, inching into the open space in the wall. Dust and grime clung to my skin. It took everything I had to shuffle back, peering through the opening of the tomb.

"Anyone down here?" A shadow darkened the doorway, his silhouette large, betraying a muscular frame. Seconds later, a slender figure appeared beside him. "I don't think she's here," he said. "Let's check the house again. The kid said someone came onto the property. If she managed to escape, it's only a matter of time before they track her down."

"You think she escaped?" the larger man replied.

"Of course. He isn't stupid enough to let her wander around alone. At least if she is in here, he won't be able to track her anyway. We can keep watch."

He. *Dublin?*

"I'm surprised he hasn't killed her already. Or sold her." Their shapes retreated from the doorway and I heard their footsteps as they crossed the central chamber. "But it's only a matter of time. He's already summoned the *other* one. I hear the bastard is on his way now. Helos must know she's gone."

"Doesn't this feel strange to you though? Looking...well, hunting down a Gray? Especially since no one's seen Georgiana since—"

"We don't question," the smaller man hissed. "And whatever reason there is for it, I don't really want to know. After what she's been through, she might be better off... Come on."

Their steps faded to silence. In their wake, my thoughts spun. Too much information clamored to be reconciled all at once. Georgie. Her "friends." Their intent—hunting me down.

For what?

And Dublin...

A dull pain seared through my palm, so I loosened my grip on the cross, wincing as warm liquid dribbled down my fingers. I'd gripped the necklace so hard that it had broken the skin. The coppery scent of blood tainted the air, as vibrant as an SOS beacon. I imagined Dublin tracking the smell, using it like a map to find me.

Or not. Deep down, I knew that the fact I'd left his property at all was a miracle within itself. Perhaps he didn't *care* enough to come looking.

Enough! I shook my head to clear it and inched forward on my hands and knees. My entire body trembled as I climbed from the tomb and approached the central chamber, clinging to the wall for balance.

A glance revealed that the space was empty. Taking a chance, I lurched to the stairs, straining my ears for any hint of noise. The upper level was deserted as well, but the heavy door had been left open, allowing a draft to blow loose branches and leaves across the floor. Each sound echoed like whispered admonishments. *Run, Eleanor!*

But to where? Darkness loomed beyond the doorway, impenetrable this deep within the property. I couldn't even see the silhouette of the house.

Or anything for that matter.

I hesitated, racked with uncertainty. A part of me considered taking my chances and crossing the property anyway. Logic warned against it. I should hide instead. Wait for Dublin.

No. The second intrusion of him into my thoughts made me grit my teeth. No longer would I sit around playing the perfect victim, always awaiting his rescue.

I started forward, my muscles tensing to run. I didn't even see the hand rushing from the shadows to grab me until it was too late.

"There you are!" Harsh fingers clenched my forearm, wrenching me forward, but my assailant loomed beyond my sight, too strong to resist.

I lurched, ripped off-balance, and landed on my knees. Instinct took over. I lowered my mouth to the unfamiliar grip, bared my teeth, and bit. The figure hissed in response, shoving me aside, and I spun, failing to regain my balance. *Wham!* Stars exploded across my vision as ringing bells banged a symphony in my ears. Pain came in slow, nauseating waves, each one stronger than the last.

"Damn! Are you all right?" A face appeared before me—tanned and handsome, balanced among a cloud of dark, curly hair. "Ms. Gray? Can you hear me?" Concern constricted his features as he flickered in and out of focus. So real one second. A ghost the next.

Until the world vanished altogether.

And I was alone.

"Ms. Gray? Can you hear me?"

I groaned, blinking my eyes open to a shadowy space lit only by a circle of orange light cast by a bulb hanging from a grayish ceiling. Damp, dank air alluded to an enclosed space with little ventilation. Somewhere underground? The crypt?

"Please, say something."

I stiffened as my gaze settled upon the figure crouched beside me, his face half bathed in shadow.

"Thank God! You're awake," he breathed as our gazes connected. "How do you feel—"

"Where am I?" Panic shook my voice, but I was beyond feigning bravery.

As I struggled to regain my bearings, my gaze darted around the room. It was small, formed of water-stained walls that resembled concrete. A floor composed of the same material sported a rusted drain a few feet away from me. Otherwise, there was nothing else in sight but a wooden door in a far corner.

"Safe," François said. "Try not to move. You hit your head pretty hard."

My head. I attempted to lift it to no avail. My entire body felt heavy, weighted down as if by stones. It took three tries before I could move my arm more than a fraction. When I finally brought a trembling finger to my forehead, warm liquid coated the tip.

"You're bleeding," François admitted, grimacing. "A little pressure and it will stop in no time though." His wide-eyed expression contradicted the confident tone. He was a good liar as well as an expert driver, it seemed.

But hemorrhaging to death was the least of my problems.

Dublin was going to kill me anyway—if he weren't already resigned to my death. Stone walls and distance weren't enough to slow him down. This long without his sudden intrusion could only mean one thing.

What if he wasn't coming at all?

"Please don't move!" François reached for my arm as I tried again to sit upright.

I cringed from him, able to control my limbs with more accuracy. "Stay away!"

But he was the least dangerous of threats to my life.

The world pitched wildly beneath me, and I almost laid back down. My stomach roiled in time with my throbbing skull—a constant melody of pain. Making any solid observation was a struggle.

But I noticed François' hands just fine—namely the weapon glinting in one.

"Are you going to kill me?" I wondered, surprised by how calm I sounded. My heart lurched and I almost couldn't resist the urge to panic. Scream. Fight. Something in his gaze kept me still, however.

"No! Of course not." He eyed the knife in his grip and gulped. Then he shoved it hastily into his pocket without taking care with the blade. The way he flinched led me to suspect he'd cut himself. "I came to help you."

But those men had revealed one bitter truth during their banter. *"The kid said…"*

"Do you work for my sister?" Posing the question at all hurt.

But his contrite frown stung more. "I work *with* her," he admitted. "But she isn't why I'm here now." He glanced over his shoulder, his brow furrowing. "In fact, I need to move you—"

"Don't touch me!" I scrambled back, desperate for a weapon. I might have had one already. The firmness within my grasp alerted me to the fact that I was still holding the cross. Odd. After everything in the crypt, I should have dropped it. Upon closer inspection, I noted its odd shape.

The long, thin arms of the cross seemed designed to conform to my fingers regardless if they formed a fist around it or not. Readjusting my grip, I brandished one of the pointed ends. "Take me home now," I rasped. "And I will forget this ever happened."

"Home?" François cocked his head, his eyes wide. "You don't have any idea what's going on, do you?" He chuckled helplessly, raking his fingers through his hair. He was still wearing his nondescript driver's uniform—a plain black suit and white undershirt—yet he was sporting one glaring violation of the manor's dress code.

Blood speckled the collar, painting it red.

"Ms. Gray." When he met my gaze again, his eyes reflected something far worse than betrayal: pity. "I don't want to scare you, but by getting to you first, I may have just saved your life."

No. I ignored the confession. It was too horrifying to think about just yet.

"Tell me," I blurted, changing the subject. "Have you always been a member of Georgie's...club? Where is she by the way?"

"The Grayne?" He shot me an odd look. "To be honest, I thought you knew. Your sister tasked me to look after you while she went away. A damn good job I've done of that." He eyed me from head to toe, frowning at the blood drying on my hands. "I need to get you to a doctor—"

"Why?" I demanded. "If Georgie had you watch over me, then why are those people looking for me? Friends of yours?"

He looked away, his frown even more pronounced. "It's complicated, Ms. Gray."

"Complicated." I laughed, thinking over all of the drastic, terrifying, horrifying events I'd been through in the past few days—Dublin's return notwithstanding. "Complicated doesn't cut it. Explain. Now!"

"Okay! Okay!" He held his hands out before him in a placating gesture and sighed. "All I know is that I was ordered to protect you. Your sister asked me personally. Then you went missing that day, by the church…" He waited as if expecting an explanation.

One I never gave.

Sighing again, he soldiered on. "After that, I was contacted by a member, but it wasn't your sister." His eyes narrowed as though he were still processing the information himself. "She hasn't contacted me in a while, mind you. But that day, my directive changed. If you returned to the house, I was to inform another member immediately. *Not* your sister. In addition, they said I would be removed from your direct detail. No one could tell me why. It didn't feel right, so I kept an ear to the ground. At the same time, I learned that a certain powerful figure had returned to the city. Someone with a rather gruesome reputation and a connection to you. Let's just say I put two and two together."

That mysterious, dangerous figure needed no introduction —Dublin Helos.

"Who were those men?" I asked. "What do they want with me?"

"Let's just say the kind of people who don't get assigned to babysitting detail," François admitted. "I'm just glad I could get to you first."

"Why?"

He grinned sheepishly and shrugged. "You were different than what the rumors made it seem. Not some naïve, insane lady who fell prey to vampires—" He broke off, coughing into his fist. "I mean...I know your sister wouldn't want this. Until I hear from her, I'll do as she asked. That's all that matters."

"Where is she?" Her avoidance of me was one thing. But if even François hadn't heard from her...

"I don't know," he admitted. "But trust me, she can handle herself. If you don't mind me saying this, miss, you should focus on yourself."

I blinked, my eyes burning. From guilt? Or maybe pain. When liquid began to dribble down my cheeks, I knew from the consistency that it wasn't tears.

"I...I need more than a doctor," I whispered. The nearest wall was my only stability as the world seesawed beneath me and I clung to it, my knuckles whitening. "It won't stop."

François hissed and shrugged his jacket off, wadding up a sleeve. "Here. Try this."

He pressed the fabric near my left temple, but the bleeding didn't slow. If anything, the pressure seemed to encourage more to drain. With every passing second, I felt dizzier. Thinking took deliberate effort and any coherent thought lacked the urgency I needed to possess. They floated within my skull, increasingly silly. For instance, *If I were a surly vampire, where would I be?*

The cathedral? The manor? In Hell?

Somewhere far from here because he doesn't give a damn about me.

"We can try a hospital," François suggested. "I know one beyond the network."

"I need more than a hospital." I shut my eyes in defeat.

There was no use in denying it. I finally let myself face one fact that had been gnawing at the edges of my psyche all this time. Dublin Helos, for whatever reason, hadn't come breaking down the door. Had he finally washed his hands of me for good?

Or were my circumstances even more dire than I could comprehend?

"No one can find you here," François said as if reading my mind. "Not even *him*. This place is protected. So was the crypt. Vampires can't enter without permission."

"How?" Perhaps Dublin's loathing of my childhood playground had been based on more than annoyance? I shifted, attempting to sit unassisted. "It doesn't matter. I need to find—"

"Honestly, Ms. Gray I shouldn't take you anywhere. Or at least somewhere that isn't safe." His gaze darted toward the door again, and his hand brushed over the stashed knife.

"I'll die," I said, sounding eerily calm at the prospect. "Without Dublin, I'll keep bleeding." More liquid ran rivulets down my cheeks as if in emphasis. "Please."

"Damn it!" His jaw clenched, François stood and lifted me into his arms without warning.

Despite his lanky frame, I felt secure. Enough that I went limp, conserving what little energy I had left.

"Close your eyes," he demanded. "I've already broken one too damn many rules anyway. Just hold on to me."

I complied, gritting my teeth as he raced forward, jostling my body in the haste. I could hear doors opening and closing, and eventually, the still atmosphere gave way to fresh night air.

"I hope you don't mind if I've been using your car," he muttered before he released me onto a surface that felt like the leather back seat of the Rolls.

I opened my eyes, noting the familiar interior, as François rushed into the driver's seat. The car jolted into motion just as I realized one key fact. "I don't know where—"

"I know," François said without elaborating. "*Everyone* knows where he is."

Stunned, I could only watch the scenery change beyond the window, becoming brighter as the lights of the city replaced the manor's overgrown grounds. Too bright.

You're hallucinating, my inner voice warned as stars danced across my vision. *Stay awake, Ellie...*

When the car finally came to an abrupt stop, I knew I was dangerously close to fainting. Keeping my eyes open at all was a struggle, and I lacked the strength to open the door on my end.

I reached for the handle in vain. But then the entire structure vanished like magic. Or through violence—a monstrous sound resonated with the power of a bomb exploding. Crunching metal. Shattering glass. François' startled shout.

But each terrifying noise faded the second I looked up into a pair of silver eyes glaring from the face of a monster. The sight of bared teeth and protruding fangs set every nerve in my body on end—but in a way more terrifying than fear. *Relief.*

"Dublin..." I didn't even see the moment he reached for me.

I only knew that I was in his arms within the space of a heartbeat, trapped in a stony embrace.

We were near a deserted road. From beyond the cage of his arms, I saw a car door resting on its side, its window shattered. The rest of the car, however, remained whole. Alarmingly pale, François gaped from the wreckage, still buckled into the driver's seat. Beyond him, I expected to find the looming façade of the high-rise—but this building was made of brick. Square. A warehouse of some kind?

Dublin offered no explanation. He moved so fast that I barely processed the layout of the building at all before I found myself thrown onto a soft surface.

"Look at me." He gripped my chin, his eyes narrowing over my forehead. "Damn."

Hissing, he withdrew something from his pants—a switchblade that expanded into a gleaming knife. With no hesitation, he drew the blade across his wrist and pressed the wound to my lips.

"I don't even know if… Just drink."

I flinched at his harsh tone—frozen with fury. Regardless, my lips parted on command.

And all thought faded as the taste of him hijacked my dulled senses.

I floated, suspended on a wave of ecstasy only his blood could bring. Magical, bubbling ecstasy. Comforting. Suffocating, like the world had been boiled down to a single essence, mine alone.

But eventually, I had to resurface.

And reality held no such joy.

Dublin was already jerking his arm away as if my skin were poison. In the same motion, he rebuttoned his cuff link and slipped his suit jacket on. Armor, I suspected. Strong enough to cage in the emotion spilling from his eyes like fire—rage.

His mouth opened and closed with a sharp snap. Then he turned away, tearing his fingers through his coifed hair. Beyond him, an unfamiliar room unfolded, composed of dark walls and wooden floors polished to gleam.

At least it seemed unfamiliar at first glance.

The light fixtures caught my attention within seconds—silver, shaped like snarling serpents coiled around bulbs that cast pale light. A certain venue came to mind, one I had tried to visit mere weeks ago while searching for Dublin, only to find that it'd vanished.

The Den.

"Look at me."

My savior stood at the foot of the surface I was resting on—a large bed shrouded in black. The sole piece of furniture, it dominated a relatively bare, but no less elegant, room. Ebony walls displayed little decoration, devoid of any windows. Almost as if to make up for it, an eye-catching chandelier dangled from above. Matching the style of the other lamps, it consisted of an array of coiled, silver snakes.

Memories stirred on the periphery of my psyche, each one more dangerous than the last. The only way to vanish them was to focus my attention on the man eyeing me as though he wished more than anything to take every drop of his blood back.

"Are you that determined to die?" His hair hung loosely, framing his thunderous expression. Dressed in a mixture of black and scarlet, he resembled the Devil more than ever. Hungry for my soul. "If so, admit it now and I'll do it myself."

"N-No." I swallowed as my gaze lowered to the knife still brandished in his grip. "I…I'm sorry—"

"Sorry?" He snatched my hand and only then did we both realize I still had something clasped within it.

The necklace. It slipped from my fingers and landed on the bed, caked in fresh blood. Even so, I could finally make out the four letters scratched into its surface—MERO.

I started to reach for it, but Dublin snatched it first. His hand shook, his eyes wide and unfocused. It wasn't a spare, I suspected. He eyed it the way one might a ghost. A remnant from his past he hoped to never see again.

"Dublin!"

I jumped as a door in the far wall flew open, revealing a panting woman who raced inside. Yulia, barely recognizable in a red dress that hugged her slender shoulders. Her dark hair rested atop her head, coiled in an elegant coif—a night-and-day contrast to her usual style.

Stopping short, she noticed me and sighed in relief. "Oh, thank God! You found her. Is she all right?"

"She's fine." Dublin didn't even look at her. He glowered, holding my gaze in a way that nothing—not even fearing for my life—had ever made me feel. Miniscule. With a subtle flick of his wrist, he tucked the necklace into his suit pocket.

"I'm so relieved." Yulia braced a hand against her chest. Then she stiffened and her gaze darted to the doorway. "But you need to get her out of here. *Now*, before he—"

"Oh, I don't think you'll be leaving any time soon, Dublin." Another woman entered the room, letting out a chilling, girlish laugh that set every nerve in my body on end. Loose curls spilled down her shoulders like fire, enhancing the less vibrant scarlet of her dress.

Her name easily came to mind. *Saskia*, Dublin's main adversary in the inner workings of the club he had once traded my soul to. Anemia.

"Oh, you've thoroughly done it now." She cocked her head in my direction as a smile played over her ruby-colored lips. "In fact, I do believe you'll both be joining us for this evening's activities. You *and* Eleanor."

"No." Dublin lunged toward me and grabbed my arm, yanking me upright.

Still dizzy, I staggered after him, fighting to keep my balance. Luckily, his blood was already replenishing my weakened muscles. I remained standing at least as he started for the door, dragging me in his wake.

"We're leaving—"

"He's already on his way," Saskia crooned. "After all, you *did* call him." She tapped her chin with the tip of a manicured finger. "Or should I say you barged into my establishment, threatened my Mikhail with bodily harm, and demanded I summon him for you or—and I'm paraphrasing—you'd *kill me with your bare hands?*" She smiled, but her eyes blazed with barely concealed fury.

Sure enough, a man was lurking in the doorway, just beyond the reach of the lights. Handsome and pale, his name came to me instantly. *Mikhail.* His mouth lacked the smug sneer I remembered, however. Scarlet smears painted his face and his neck in a startling contrast to his dark suit and his ivory shirt. Blood, I suspected. From a wound that had already healed.

"So yes, you will stay," Saskia said sweetly. "And *he* should be arriving within minutes. Actually, he's even called ahead to request your presence *personally.*"

Dublin stopped short, and I had to dig my heels in to prevent myself from colliding with him.

"I said get out of my way." He swiveled his gaze in Saskia's direction and her smug grin wavered a fraction.

Only to reform a heartbeat later, more beautiful than ever.

"What on Earth shall we dress little Eleanor in?" she wondered, turning her attention to me. Wincing in disgust, she scanned my rumpled dress, splattered with blood. "She looks well enough, considering the fuss you made. Still so plain, though I'm sure I can do something with her." She rubbed her hands, and I recalled an unsettling piece of advice Dublin had given me once.

"Saskia is a succubus. She cannot actually read minds—merely the subconscious fears and desires of those around her."

"Come here, my dear—"

"No. *I'll* dress her." Yulia stepped forward and took my hand. She tried to pull me out of Saskia's reach—but an iron grip on my opposite arm kept me rooted in place. "Dublin," she said softly. "I'll watch out for her." She brushed her fingers along my arm in brief reassurance. "I promise."

He let me go. Before I could look back, Yulia was dragging me through the doorway, past a scowling Mikhail.

"Darling Yulia to the rescue," Saskia remarked, sighing like a child denied a treat. "But will her magic work this time? After all, you brought her *here,* Dublin." The way she stressed the word implied a nefarious connotation. Something that made her haughty tone shake with more than just anger. Fear? "*You* called Raphael from his rest, all the way here. And for what? Though it is no matter. You may be the all-powerful Cael, but within these walls, even you are just like the rest of us. Under his rule."

"Come." Yulia steered me forward.

I looked over my shoulder, catching a mere glimpse of the room. Dublin was framed by the doorway, as rigid as a statue. His eyes flickered to mine and my entire body went cold at what I found in them.

Nothing. Not even anger.

Not hate.

Not even concern.

He was beyond feeling anything at all.

AMUSEMENT

"**D**amn, damn, damn!" Yulia raced around a wide room, snatching items from various racks of clothing.

The space we were in resembled a dressing room, so similar to the one in the original club where we'd met. Red walls and floors a dark shade of wood served to enhance the allure befitting the club's mysterious name. At least the moniker I remembered it as—*Anemia*.

In the prime position to display my reaction, a large, golden mirror hung across from us, above a marble vanity.

"I hope you're all right?" Yulia inquired mid-lunge. Her chosen prey was a garment from an overflowing closet. Frowning, she held it up for inspection and then tossed it aside. Then she rummaged for something different, her eyebrow furrowed in concentration.

"I'm fine," I lied. The mirror provided enough evidence to contradict me—my bloodshot eyes stared blankly, my hair matted and damp. Scarlet streaks painted my cheeks and my neck, staining the bodice of my dress.

"Thank God," she muttered. "Finally!" On what had to be her fourth trip around the room, she found a garment that made her nod in approval. Pivoting on her feet, she returned to me and lifted my chin. "Oh, Ellie."

Her irises contracted with pity as she unfurled her selection and held it before me—a long dress made of black silk. While conservative in some aspects, it had a dangerously low neckline that reinforced its purpose in a club like this— a place where souls were bartered and sold on a whim.

Even Dublin's.

"It will have to do." Without waiting for my opinion, Yulia started to tug off my soiled clothing—a task made easier once she found a strip of lace along the neckline and pulled.

There was no other way to describe how the fabric came apart other than like magic. Or expert tailoring.

"Here." She helped tug the new dress over my head, and before the silky material had even settled at my waist, she already had a wet rag in her hand and was dabbing at my shoulders. "Dublin will be angry," she warned in a level tone. "I'm glad you're okay, but you need to realize what is at stake now. The fact that he even came here is—" She bit off the rest of her words, her mouth wrinkled. "Where were you? We thought..." For the first time, she seemed to realize just what substance she was dutifully cleaning off me. Her mouth dropped open in horror and the rag slipped from her fingers. "Are you all right?" She felt along my forehead, inspecting the flesh. "Were you hurt? Dublin didn't seem alarmed, so I thought—"

"I fell," I croaked. "He…he gave me his blood. I'm better now."

"Oh." She drew her hand away and stooped for the rag.

Cautiously, she continued her ruthless cleansing, but her expression wavered, more strained than before. Her lips twitched as if fighting to contain any more questions. Then she left the room in silence and returned with a basin of warm water and a fresh set of rags.

The water, she used to wash the blood from my hair, before forming the semblance of a bun that my short locks would allow. After securing it to the nape of my neck with pins, she stood back and sighed. "I guess you're ready."

But I stiffened, unwilling to move.

"What's happening?" I asked. Something terrible, judging from her grimace. Something involving a man I would have given the Gray fortune never to see again—and the figure Saskia implied would be arriving soon.

Raphael.

"You were gone for hours." Yulia's anguished expression only strengthened the guilt lancing through my chest. "I've never seen Dublin like that. Ever. He thought those radical fools had taken you, perhaps."

Radical fools? The Grayne?

"I don't think he was being rational," she continued in a rush. "Maybe he assumed coming to *him* was his only choice?" She turned away, cradling her chin in her hand. "At least he found you first, before it was too late. I tried to stop him. He *promised* me he wouldn't ever sell more of his time—"

"Let's go."

I turned and found Dublin in the doorway, his face expressionless. His gaze flicked over me once, conveying no disgust. He didn't even bother to utter a mocking quip. He merely beckoned with a nod before advancing down the hall.

"Go," Yulia whispered while tucking a curl behind my ear. She squeezed my arm reassuringly and urged me forward. "It will be okay."

My stomach churned as I staggered a few reluctant steps, leaving her behind. Up ahead, Dublin continued without waiting for me, already halfway down the narrow hall.

His taste lingered on my tongue as my body thrummed with his blood. Every drop prickled beneath my skin, so potent that it burned. In a sense, drinking from him had always been painful. Overwhelming. In fact...

I usually fainted.

I swayed on my feet as I tried to reconcile why I hadn't. A swallow racked my throat as I looked down, surprised to find my hand against my abdomen, the fingers trembling. I wrenched it away, forming a fist, and when I looked up,

Dublin was watching me. The moment our gazes connected, he turned and continued forward.

I crept after him, and far too soon, we entered a spacious room decorated in shades of black. Like a lecture hall, leather seats framed a makeshift stage—a circle of light illuminating the very center of the marble floor. It was a chillingly familiar setup. Much like a showroom, perfect for various wares to be displayed for purchase.

Human wares.

"Stay close."

I jumped as Dublin grabbed my hand, dragging me to his side.

"Say nothing," he told me.

Across from our position, a contingent of people was already flooding in from a different entrance.

Leading the mass of beautiful, elegantly dressed specters was a man almost too perfect to be real. Stunningly pale, his face was that of an angel's, frozen in time. An angel who had been barred from Heaven for too damn long.

Instead of wings, an ebony cloak shrouded most of his slight body, blending in with the long, black hair falling down his shoulders. With a flick of his lips, he greeted me with a nod.

"Eleanor Gray."

I shuddered beneath his scrutiny. Centuries of life had stripped his dark eyes of any expression. Only a chilling aura set him apart from those in his retinue, Saskia and Mikhail among them.

The closer he came, the tighter Dublin clenched my hand until I had to grit my teeth to keep from crying out.

"Raphael," he said coldly.

"Dublin," the other man replied. His voice was so soft, yet it resonated clearly over the hushed murmurs of those around him. "How lovely of you to join us. And with dear Eleanor." He extended his hand to me. "I wasn't sure when we would meet again."

I eyed his slim fingers as the memory of our first meeting flashed across my skull. He'd felt so cold. Like death.

A pointed nudge to my side jarred me back to the present. Glancing at Dublin, I saw him jerk his chin in a silent command. *Do it.* Left with no choice, I placed my hand over the ancient vampire's and winced. He grasped my fingers without warning, bringing them to his lips.

"I'm curious as to the nature of this visit," he murmured, lifting his head. But he didn't release my hand. Instead, he drifted toward another corner of the room, forcing me to follow.

I sensed Dublin right on my heels, silent, my other hand still in his.

"Not to be blunt, but I was under the impression that Dublin had ceded all interest in you," Raphael added. "He claimed to have cut off all communication. Leveraged his contacts so that poor Saskia had no choice but to move from our previous location. The last I'd heard, our dear friend had left this marvelous country entirely. I must confess I understood his aversion. Your bloodline has always been mired in needless superstition." He sighed. "So, imagine my surprise that the first time he deigned to contact me in weeks happened to concern *you*."

I glanced at the man in question, but he wasn't even looking in my direction. His eyes were fixated on the center of the room, his jaw slack with disinterest—even as he kept time with my every step.

"In fact..." Raphael paused before a leather chaise and lowered himself onto it, gesturing for me to follow. When I did, he took my hand again, stroking the palm of it with his thumb. "For Dublin to call me here, this hour of the night, I would have thought you were in danger." His empty eyes cut to my face, scanning it with reptilian curiosity. Without revealing whether he discovered anything of interest, he shifted his attention to Dublin. "Did I assume wrong?"

"No," Dublin replied. He remained standing paces away, angled slightly toward the center of the room. "It was...a misunderstanding. Nothing more."

"Ah." Raphael nodded and patted the back of my hand. The seemingly playful gesture contrasted with his chilling, frozen smile. "*Nothing.* How wonderful. Then, Eleanor, my dear, you must have entered here of your own free will, under no claim to speak of."

Claim. Dublin stiffened at the word. By the time I'd blinked, he had returned to my side. Startled, I took the hand he was offering, allowing him to pull me to my feet. Raphael released me, but each pad of his fingers glided over my flesh like a serpent in retreat.

"She was just leaving," Dublin said, maneuvering me to stand behind him.

"Leaving?" Raphael uttered a sound too cutting to be a laugh. "Oh, no. The entertainment has just arrived. Do stay. Both of you."

Dublin stiffened. "I—"

"I insist," Raphael added, flicking his hand in a dismissive gesture. "Why, look! The show is just beginning."

As if his acknowledgment were the cue, a woman entered, pale and slender. Dressed in a sheer, white slip that barely reached her knees, she was a stark contrast from how I remembered the women on auction dressing. Not overtly sexual, to put it bluntly. Though her purpose was painfully reinforced by the sheer fabric of her dress—pale skin and flushes of pink peeked, fully visible beneath. Her large, green eyes stared out blankly, framed by curly, dark hair. The style chafed my nerves, uncomfortably familiar. *Too* familiar.

"A lovely creature," Raphael remarked, his lips quirked in another mirthless smile. "Don't you agree, Dublin?"

Without warning, Dublin released my hand. Suddenly, the space between us widened as he stepped aside, and my heart surged. A few feet yawned like an ocean to separate us. I tried to meet his gaze—anything but reach out directly.

He ignored me.

"Ah, yes," Raphael continued as though he'd received a response. "The last auction you participated in was such a success that I've had Saskia replicate your ethereal aesthetic. I hope you don't mind." Only when his eyes flickered in my direction did I realize he was speaking to me.

My stomach churned as I faced the girl again. One word could summarize her "aesthetic." *Me.* Everything from her chin-length curls to her slender frame resembled mine. Specifically, how Yulia had dressed me the night Dublin had bartered for my contract.

"I am curious what you think, Dublin," Raphael wondered. "I must say, this style has been a boon for the club. So many seem so curious as to the appeal. What with your discerning tastes, anything you desire must be remarkable."

Murmurs of agreement rose up from those seated nearby.

"You see?" Raphael gestured with a wave of his hand. "I believe the consensus is unanimous. Shall we begin? Saskia, my dear."

"Yes, my lord." Grinning, Saskia stepped forward, advancing on the girl. Once close enough, she brushed her hand along the girl's cheek, tilting it to reveal the side of her throat.

I was reminded of an auctioneer displaying a piece of jewelry for a buyer's discretion.

Circling around to stand behind the woman, Saskia ran her fingers along the flimsy neckline of her shift next. As if waiting until just the right moment, she tugged, allowing the sleeves to fall down the girl's shoulders.

My cheeks heated as I looked away. But Dublin didn't. He stared along with the rest of the room, his eyes conveying nothing. A dangerous thought crept into my brain, impossible to silence—was he inspecting her as well?

"Exquisite," Raphael murmured in a way that made my throat tighten. "But I sense that Dublin doesn't approve? Too short?" he wondered. "Or too thin? No matter. I do believe Saskia has cultivated an entire selection to match these *specific* tastes." He clapped his hands together and four more women drifted into the room, each one more waiflike than the last.

Only slight variations in their height and their size set them apart. Overall, they all were thin with large eyes, short dark curls, and delicate white dresses. It was like looking at a distorted mirror, reflecting variations of me from a million different angles.

All of them slightly prettier.

Slightly thinner.

Slightly more appealing.

"Pick one," Raphael suggested, still speaking to Dublin. "Any one you'd like. Her contract is yours. My gift to you. My only request is that, in return, whatever time you spend with your new acquaintance is time that I would get to spend with dear Eleanor. Alone."

Crackling tension electrified the air. Even Saskia stiffened, her throat contracting around a swallow. Though, no matter what, her sly grin remained firmly in place.

"Well? What say you, Dublin?"

"To your offer?" Dublin faced him, his eyes a burnished, cool silver. Given his lack of emotion at all, one might have thought Raphael had presented him with a blank piece of paper. Not a woman. "No. I'm afraid we have a previous engagement to attend to." He reached for my hand, yanking me forward to close the distance between us. "We'll take our leave."

"An engagement," Raphael echoed. "Perhaps one having something to do with why you demanded my presence here, only to bring Mero's rats to my doorstep?"

It was as though a switch had been flicked. In an instant, the atmosphere thickened further and the entire room seemed to shrink back, scurrying within the shadows.

Only the two men withstood the unbearable tension. Dublin stared unfazed, while Raphael casually sat back against the leather chaise, folding his hands on his lap.

"We've been together long enough for you to know that there are few things I cannot tolerate, Dublin. Having my time wasted is one, though I know that the respect between us is far too great for such an insult." His endless eyes flickered in my direction, flashing with rare interest. "But the second is secrets. Especially when they concern a mutual old friend of ours. Don't tell me you've forgotten him already. Mero."

Silence fell. In a room of strange, undead creatures, something warned that I wasn't the only one holding my breath.

"Even as he waged his little war against both of us, utilizing his human pawns, I have remained a loyal and neutral party," Raphael insisted. "I have even toed your boundaries, haven't I? After all this time? The Grays were but mere mosquitoes buzzing on the periphery, until one of them decided to bite my flesh. I had every right to retaliate, then. Didn't I?"

A second passed without a reply.

And his eyes narrowed. "Answer me."

"Yes," Dublin hissed.

"Good. So, is it too much trouble that I wish to enjoy a few mere moments with an old friend? Even if he apparently has no further use for my services?"

This time, when his gaze slithered in my direction, he lingered, tracing a path up and down my body. There was no lust in the dark pupils. Just calculating, detached observation.

"I even came when you requested, prepared to assist you in any way that I could. All for the sake of dear Eleanor." He tilted his head thoughtfully. "I let you have her when you asked despite the risk. You knew the second you bid for her that you would be breaking *his* precious rules. The Gray family was to remain untouched, always. Do you remember?"

He waited until Dublin made a growled sound of acknowledgment in the base of his throat.

"Yes. As long as you did, he would remain in the shadows. I know you wrote off his threat as mere superstition, but I never did. I even warned you, didn't I? I even offered you others. You refused. So please"—he smiled again, all traces of hostility erased—"allow me to learn your tastes so that I may replicate them more accurately. Choose."

"I…" Dublin's grip loosened over my hand only to bear down more tightly than ever. "I'm afraid that none of your offerings interest me," he said so dismissively that I flinched. "Perhaps I'm just not in the mood for distraction, or perhaps your curator hasn't done her job well enough."

"Is that so?" Saskia hissed through her teeth. "Then why not enlighten us all?" She waved her arm toward the guests. "What exactly excites you, Dublin? Do tell. Is it the pale, bony exterior? The childlike demeanor?" She sneered in my direction and laughed. "Please don't tell me it's her stunning beauty."

"It's simple," Dublin replied with a shrug of his shoulder. "It's the one thing you can't cobble together or clumsily recreate: a pure, pedigree bloodline."

Saskia glared at him, her upper lip curled back from her teeth.

"He is right." Raphael sighed in defeat. "Alas, we always did share a fondness for such…" He traced his mouth with the tips of his fingers as if reliving events too horrifying to picture. But then his small smile faded. "There is another," he added.

Dublin went rigid once more, crushing my fingers.

"The other Gray girl. The one *I* wanted procured. The one you claimed I could not have." If a man like him could pout, I'd name the downturned tilt to his mouth as such. Rather than petulant, he looked more serpentine than ever. A predator denied a satisfying meal. "You did not flaunt your boundary for her—"

"Because she was not foolish enough to sell herself to me," Dublin snapped. He eyed me pointedly and sighed. "I must beg your pardon. She's weak." His apparent explanation for my trembling legs. "I've fed from her too much. She lacks stamina. We should go."

"You'll leave soon enough," Raphael insisted. "*After* the entertainment. Saskia."

"As you wish." She returned to the naked woman and positioned her to better face the crowd. "Offers for this one? I will accept payment only in years—"

"Years?" Dublin interjected, his tone hard.

"Yes." Raphael stroked his chin and nodded. "A peculiar arrangement, but again, you have inspired us to try new methods of business. Our new policy is, rather than bartering for a few wasted nights, we trade our beautiful specimens for years of service. One year of the buyer's for a year of hers. It is only fair."

I nearly choked in recognition. Trade in years—a cruel variation of the bargain Dublin made for me. But something told me it was more than that. So much more.

One of the shadowy guests raised his hand.

"Two years," he declared as casually as if bargaining with play money. Not time.

"A fair start. Any other takers?" Saskia wondered.

Another man raised his hand. "Ten," he said. "For this one and that one." He pointed to another girl. "Each."

"Ah!" Beaming, Saskia clasped her hands together, her demeanor shifting into that of an expert saleswoman. "And what about this charming girl. I must admit I'm not too fond of this 'aesthetic,' but she is lovely, isn't she? Do I hear an offer?"

With every second I watched the twisted event unfold, the more numb I felt. My eyes were fixated on the women, refusing to leave them for an instant. Did they even care that years of their lives were being bought and sold around them?

Apparently not. Each one faced the room with little expression. None flinched. Squirmed. Whimpered. Not even as one of the "guests" stepped forward to claim his prize. He was tall, unnervingly handsome, with eyes so amber that they bordered on ruby.

"Congratulations." Saskia crooned. "She's all yours, though, as per custom, you are allowed a taste before finalizing. Here." She snatched the girl's wrist, extending it.

In response, the man bared his fangs before lowering his head. As the ivory tips sank into her flesh, the girl gasped. But not in pleasure.

She wrenched her arm away, coming to life with another hollow cry. "N-No!" Her eyes blinked rapidly as if she were waking up from a dream. Whatever she saw made her face pale and her eyes widen with horror. "No! No! Let me go! Let me go!"

The man withdrew, his gaze questioning.

Saskia merely sighed and snapped her fingers. As if from nowhere, two men swooped from the shadows and grabbed the girl on either side. Within seconds, she had vanished, though her cries were still audible, echoing off the walls.

"Let me go! Where am I? Let me go!"

"Our new policy requires that we recruit a different breed," Saskia admitted. She flicked the hair of another woman, who remained unmoving despite the commotion.

And their blank expressions took on a more sinister meaning.

"These girls are a bit more skittish and might require a… softer touch. But they are yours alone to break. Do I hear another offer?"

I turned, moving blindly, my stomach heaving. Logic and self-preservation vanished. I could only cover my mouth, solely focused on finding somewhere—anywhere else.

"Don't," Raphael snapped, his voice ringing with authority. "Saskia will attend to her. You and I have a private matter to discuss. Did you truly think I wouldn't realize who you were looking for? The witch. Even though you've pretended not to all this time, you've believed in his curse. Haven't you? I assume that is the reason you ran, the moment I tested that so-called superstition…"

I should have gone back—but a gag ripped from my chest and I raced down the hall until I found an empty room. The next second I was on my hands and knees, vomiting onto polished wood. The gleaming surface displayed my reflection in mocking relief—wide-eyed, frantic. Pathetic. Guilty.

Even now, faint cries echoed off the walls, and I hunched over in shame. That poor girl.

All of them.

They were here because of me.

"Oh, do get a hold of yourself, darling."

Stiletto heels stabbed the floor in tandem as someone advanced on my position. Cloying perfume flooded my nostrils even before a pair of pale legs appeared within my line of sight.

"We all know that Dublin is besotted by the innocent-little-girl act," Saskia harrumphed. "But my God is it tiring! Though I must thank you. Even with that goddamn necklace, he's easier to read now than ever. Shall I share?" She giggled maniacally. "He was always surly before, but now? His thoughts are so devious that deciphering them is child's play. Hungry. Lustful. All those things he acted so *above* feeling before. All because of you."

She crouched down and tapped my chin with the tip of a pointed fingernail.

"He thinks about fucking you," she explained, her lips quirked. "And not in any romantic, poetic sense. You're but a trophy to him. He relives corrupting you over and over. How you felt. Your delicate little body shuddering beneath his. How you squirmed and flinched with every thrust. He felt so powerful then. It's rather hilarious."

My cheeks burned at the picture she'd painted. Nothing in the world felt more violating than having those words flung in my face.

"Or pathetic, actually. He hates you. Despises you. Craves you. Obsesses. It's madness, really. One might think the man had never been laid before." She sighed and pulled her hand away. "But you know what really gets his cold heart pumping?"

She waited as if expecting an answer. Then she chuckled.

"Your *sister.* The pretty one. He thinks of her often, though he guards those thoughts a bit more securely than the ones of you. Perhaps he's fucked her as well? Don't tell me you didn't know… You didn't! Oh, to see the look on your poor face." She licked her lips in glee. "But now it's time to go crawling back. The show must go on, my dear." She snatched at my arm and stood, yanking me upright. "Don't resist. I mean, honestly—"

She broke off, wrenching her hand from me as if burned. A series of unsteady steps propelled her back so suddenly that she struck the wall. Just as quickly, she recovered, and before I could even react, she grabbed me again, sliding her grip down to my wrist. Her thumb pressed against my pulse point as her eyebrows furrowed. When she met my gaze, I didn't know how to read her expression. Something made her bite her lower lip as she finally let go.

"Clean yourself up." She turned on her heel and retreated to a far corner. We were in that dressing room, but Yulia was nowhere in sight. "Here."

I flinched as Saskia shoved something beneath my nose: a white handkerchief.

I took it and warily dabbed at my mouth. Then I gagged as the image of that girl replayed. Over and over and over…

Desperate, I scanned the room, my stomach heaving.

"Do it in this, at least!" Saskia shoved a round basin into my hands.

A wastebasket that held crumpled napkins and a fresh wave of vomit. I recognized chunks of my meals from earlier and cringed, disgusted but partly relieved.

At least it wasn't blood.

"Come." Saskia beckoned with a crooked finger and started toward the main chamber. "He won't tolerate our absence for long," she warned as I lingered.

So, I followed, my heart pounding with every step. I didn't dare look up from the floor in front of me. I couldn't see those women. Their faces.

But I could hear. Frantic breathing. A smothered whimper.

And then Saskia's pleased giggle as she donned her ringmaster role once more. "A beautiful girl to be sure," she called to a man eyeing one of the women. "And I can tell you enjoy her taste. How does five years sound?"

"Keep your head down." The warning entered my ear as a familiar hand cinched my wrist, tethering me to a body chiseled from stone.

"Until next time," a voice called out, dripping with false politeness. Raphael.

"Next time," a woman seconded, Saskia. "Oh, and, Dublin? To new beginnings. For both you *and* Eleanor."

Veering away from them, Dublin steered me through the club until we finally reached the exit.

I barely had the chance to inhale the fresh air before he shoved me into a waiting car and appeared in the driver's seat. As the door slammed behind him, I had enough sense to keep my mouth shut. To keep my expression blank and choke down my horror. I blinked back any tears, but I knew my heartbeat betrayed me, thrumming with shock and terror.

Dublin drove recklessly, cutting into the paths of other vehicles without a damn given for etiquette. He glowered at the road, his body rigid, his knuckles stark white over the steering wheel. The areas where he was gripping it bulged inward, and I feared the damn thing might snap in half as the car finally came to a stop.

Before I could reach for my seat belt, he opened my door—the right way this time—and I was in his arms. Rigid with tension, he carried me into a building I vaguely recognized: his high-rise. The ascent to the suite lasted seconds as he took the stairs in lieu of the elevator. When he finally hauled me into the foyer, Kate was nowhere to be found.

I was alone with him, a fact that he cemented by locking the door as he set me down, leaving me to sway with fragile balance.

"Where did you go?"

I bit my lip, hating the display of weakness. I should have been haughty and defiant, jutting my chin into the air. As it was, I could barely breathe without gasping. Panting. Whenever I closed my eyes, I saw them. Whatever horror they were currently facing was my fault.

All my fault.

"Look at me!" He gripped my chin, wrenching me around to face him, but what he saw in my eyes made him frown and release me. "Were you aware of him all along? 'Protecting' you?" he wondered, sneering the word. Turning his back to me, he started to pace. "Perhaps he's the one you've really been fucking. Is it his?"

Hurt mingled with shame, searing my cheeks. "Who?" I croaked before an answer came as if whispered in my ear. "François."

"Yes, *François*," Dublin snarled, his voice booming.

I had never seen him like this. Smiling. Glaring. Vicious. Cold and blazing in one terrifying display.

"His kind don't risk themselves lightly. And certainly not for a vampire-fucking whore as they would call you."

I winced as the insult landed as intended. But I couldn't even muster up the energy to feel insulted. "Where is he?" I despaired at my driver's most likely fate. Still, I clung to a fragile hope even as I gritted my teeth to steel myself against the answer.

It came, uttered in a tone as cutting as a blade. "Dead. Or at least he *will* be once I'm through with him."

"Please don't." I stepped forward without thinking, reaching for his hand. "It's my fault. He didn't mean—"

"He didn't mean what?" Dublin growled, snatching his hand away. "To lie in wait to ambush you? To carry out his orders like a willing little pawn? You're lucky he didn't run a stake through your chest—his kind are foolish enough to believe in that myth."

"He helped me," I insisted, fighting to keep my voice level. "And I'm sorry—"

"Sorry?" He threw his head back and laughed more deeply than before. "*You*, the innocent, naïve, selfish Eleanor Gray, are sorry. Tell that to those women who will be sucked and fucked because Raphael likes toying with me! Isn't this the part where you cringe in haughty indignation and call me a monster for allowing them to be sold in the first place?" He paused as if waiting for that very argument.

It stung to realize that, in another world, I might have lived up to that expectation. I would have blamed *him*.

"No? Well, I couldn't do a damn thing without presenting you to him on a silver goddamn platter anyway. So, congratulations. Once again, you've made me look weak before that creature. Once again, I've gone against my better judgment to save your life. And all you can say is you're sorry?"

My lips parted, but instead of another apology, a cry escaped. And I broke. Tears spilled from my eyes as sobs ripped from my chest. I swayed, bracing my hands against the wall in a fight to stay upright, but my knees buckled, depositing me onto the floor.

"I'm sorry," I whispered, though he could have been gone for all I knew. Still, it had to be said, if only to cement my own horrid sense of guilt. "It's my fault. I'm sorry. I'm sorry. I'm so, so sorry—"

"Don't cry for them." Dublin grabbed my arm, hauling me to my feet. Without allowing me to find my own balance, he pressed me against the wall, trapping me there with one hand on either shoulder. His eyes a burnished silver, he resembled the "old friend" Raphael referred to more than ever. Someone utterly devoid of humanity.

But then he frowned, brushing his thumb along my cheek. Yulia must have missed a spot, somewhere hidden behind my ear, because his finger came away red with blood that should have been dried by now. He eyed it like it was the most alluring and repulsive thing in existence.

"You should be crying for yourself," he hissed while swiping his hand along the side of his suit jacket. "Those women will suffer their pain. They'll reconcile their choices with whatever price they bargained their souls for. In the end, they'll convince themselves it was worth it. But you?" He caressed my throat with a single finger, tracing my surging pulse. "You sold yourself for nothing. You sold yourself to *me*—and I am not like those other fools who take their orders from Raphael. Do you think you're any different from them? Those women?" He cradled my windpipe, forcing my head back until I met his gaze. "Do you think I wouldn't take any single one of them over you? I would." He stepped into me, lowering his head until our foreheads touched. "I would."

The fabric of my dress bunched at the waist, captured in his fist. I shivered as he tugged. With a violent rip, the material gave way altogether.

And with every bared inch of me, Dublin stiffened further, tracking the gown's descent until it reached the floor.

"Your body affects me no differently than theirs," he growled, his voice thicker. "You don't appeal to me more. This pale, thin, shapeless body doesn't fucking haunt me." He found my nipple, grazing it with the tip of a fingernail until I jerked as if yanked on a string. "You mean *nothing* to me."

His mouth brushed mine and my lips parted. Ruthlessly, his tongue swept inside, harsh and punishing. I could feel the prickling tease of his fangs even as they protruded, catching the edge of my tongue. All the while, his body caged me in, rough through the fabric of his suit. Repelling me even while providing strength. When my knees buckled, holding on to him was the only way I managed to stay upright.

The harder he kissed me, the more my thoughts spun, senseless. There was no seductive method to this madness. Just him gripping my waist, pulling me into him, grinding his body against whatever part of me he could reach.

Until he stopped, leaving me balanced on a precipice.

"This is the part where you agree, Eleanor," he hissed, drawing me into his arms.

The interior of the suite blurred and distorted until I found myself shoved onto the bed in that emerald room, bathed in the multicolored glow of the city lights.

"This is the part where you reinforce that I couldn't possibly have any interest in fucking you." As he spoke, he tugged my legs apart, easily slipping between them.

Fabric swished and fluttered through the air, so quickly I barely registered it. His jacket. His shirt. His pants. All shed within seconds.

My eyes were still on the crumpled pieces of fabric when he slid his hand between my legs, easing the tip of a finger inside me.

"And this is the part where I pretend like you're wet for me alone," he continued as I gasped at the intrusion. "That deep down you relish what I do to your body. That you crave it. That the naïve, prudish innocence is just an act." He ventured deeper, and my nails caught at the silk beneath me, scrambling for purchase. "I convince myself every goddamn time." He groaned as my body quaked, gripping him in trembling waves. "I make myself believe it, even though I know it's a lie."

Another finger. Too much—but the pressure was nothing compared to his expression. Eyes narrowed with hatred even while I writhed, full to the brim with him.

"Women like you are more evil than I even would ever claim to be. It's why you hide through life pretending that you have no appeal. It's why creatures like Raphael try to replicate you. It's why five hundred years of fucking life hasn't tormented me like you do." He drew his hand away, slamming his full length into me instead.

I moaned, my back arching, eyes closing as every nerve came alive with awareness of him.

"The way you feel is sin," he hissed, rearing back for another sharp, punishing thrust. "It's hell. And he made you, didn't he?" He captured the back of my throat as if to coax the answer from it, but I was too far gone to speak. "He made you. To tempt me. To make me crave you. To the point of madness, I crave you…"

God, I didn't even know if he was referring to Raphael or some other creature. I was beyond coherent thought. Fire built within my blood with every burning bit of friction— and his words were gasoline. My spine lit the match, curling and driving me into each pass of his hips.

And then ignition.

Any sound I made was swallowed by his lips parting over mine, taking every strangled cry. It went on for an eternity…

Pleasure bordering on ecstasy. Sensation rivaling pain. Too much. All at once.

And then everything shattered. I fell apart, reassembling over twisted, sweat-soaked silk. When I regained my senses, his mouth was in my hair, his arm over my waist.

And he spoke to me, murmuring words too softly to hear.

But then I made the mistake of relaxing into his embrace, brushing my fingers along his arm. Abruptly, he sat up, pulling away. In a daze, I watched him lunge through the dark, dressing so quickly that he was already in the hall by the time I registered him lifting his shirt.

Gone in an instant.

I lay there in a daze for so long that I couldn't tell if it was still night or day when I finally heard a voice drift from down the hall. Dublin's low rasp, resonating with authority.

"...the plane ready. I want to be airborne within the hour. No delays..."

Then minutes passed, and I sensed he'd started a far different conversation.

"I'm sorry," he growled, sounding fainter than before. His tone had softened, containing a mixture of emotions—some easily recognizable, others more obscure. Guilt? *And* defiance. "I don't have a week! I know Saskia suspects. It's only a matter of time before she starts whispering into Raphael's ear. With this, he'll have enough leverage to tack another six hundred years onto my debt—if only to keep him from turning her into his pet. Is that what you want?"

He paused, allowing someone to answer. Through a phone, I suspected, because I didn't hear another voice nearby.

Finally, Dublin sighed. "It's either Dmitri or Raphael—" The other speaker must have interrupted, because he swore so darkly that I trembled. "I will never sit back and watch him parade her like some sick conquest. Hate me if you'd like. But Dmitri was there at the beginning. If anyone would know what this means, it's him—"

Another interruption drew a hiss of disgust from his throat.

"You think I don't care? Don't you *ever* question that again, Yulia. You and I both know what this has cost me. So, fine. Cast your lot in with Raphael if you'd prefer him as your protector. Just know that I have never forsaken you, and I never will."

He went silent again, for long enough that I suspected the conversation had ended. Heavy, slow footsteps alluded to him pacing. A picture came to mind—him glowering while raking his hands through his hair, furious because of me. I'd made him do something that had even Yulia against him.

But what?

No answer came by the time his footsteps advanced toward my room. Just beyond the doorway, they stopped.

"Get dressed."

His tone stiffened my spine—so cold that it rivaled the chill in the room itself. Cautiously, I sat upright as he retreated, and I had to reconcile the million things I wished to ignore.

The inside of my legs felt wet. My knees were jelly, wobbling as I attempted to stand. I had to cling to the bed frame just to keep from falling.

I made my way to the wardrobe and fished out one of Yulia's dresses. Then I felt along the wall until I nearly tripped over my shoes discarded on the floor. After pulling them on, I entered the hallway, where Dublin loomed in the center room, his back to me. Wordless, he gestured to an open doorway—a bathroom, I realized as I crept closer.

Inside, I quickly washed and ran my wet fingers through my knotted hair. I'd barely stepped over the threshold when I found him in the foyer, wrenching the door to the suite open.

A curt jerk of his chin was my sole cue to follow. Together, we traipsed down the steps and exited the building to darkness. It was either late at night or early in the morning. Bathed in moonlight, his car idled up ahead, but this time, a driver sat before the steering wheel. Dublin ushered me into the back only to slam the door behind me and claim the passenger's seat for himself.

As the car took off, I wrung my fingers over my lap, desperate to find a distraction from the tension thickening the air. I looked down, eyeing myself critically. My dress was a gray one, relatively shapeless, though no less elegant than any of Yulia's other creations. In a way, it fit the somber atmosphere so well that it could have been curated for this moment. My trademark costume as Dublin's dowdy archnemesis, destined to torment him to no end.

Minutes of driving became hours. Eventually, our journey extended beyond the city, but Dublin never revealed our destination and I lacked the courage to ask. Instead, I consoled myself by staring from the window as dawn painted the horizon in brightening shades of lavender and pink. Gradually, the trees of the countryside gave way to neatly trimmed fields designed for a sole purpose.

One that became clear as the driver entered a maze of wide, rectangular buildings and finally pulled up before, of all things, one item even my family didn't possess: a plane, slim, white, and most definitely private.

"Ready for takeoff, sir," the driver remarked as Dublin climbed out and approached my door.

He wrenched on the handle and offered his hand—but his mood hadn't softened during the ride. If anything, the rage had solidified in his very bones, rendering them rigid against me.

"And the arrangements?" he asked the driver while approaching the plane, tugging me along.

The door to the cabin hung open, a set of stairs leading to it. From this angle. I noticed a smiling woman in a crisp black uniform waiting at the top, her hands folded before her.

"Everything has been taken care of," the driver assured. "Have a safe trip, sir."

Dublin maneuvered me to stand before him, ensuring that I had to climb the stairs and enter the plane first. An elegant interior greeted me, well beyond the luxury of the few first-class cabins I'd been in throughout the years. The space resembled a lounge rather than a vehicle designed for transport. A plush, dark carpet accented gunmetal-gray walls, and instead of rows of uniform seats, a black leather couch hugged one wall across from a flat-screen television. Parallel to it, on either end of the room were matching recliners. A doorway straight ahead alluded to additional compartments.

The aircraft even possessed its own attendant, it seemed.

"Welcome, miss," the smiling woman greeted warmly. "Welcome, Mr. Helos. Can I offer you wine or—"

"That will be all," Dublin said, and she promptly scurried off to some unseen hiding place.

Pushing past me, Dublin claimed the couch for himself, leaving one of the recliners for me. Conveniently, both faced away from him, as distant from his position as the space would allow.

My face heated as I marched toward my imposed exile. Memories of last night flooded my thoughts, each hazy image more confusing than the last. Paired with his stony reception today, I suspected that it all was some new, twisted mind game.

Congratulations, he was already winning. I had no idea how to combat him this time. My usual defense—stripping naked and daring him to consign me to Hell—didn't appear to be an option this time.

"Sit," he snapped, fastening a seat belt over his waist. Purely for show, I suspected. "We're about to take off."

I scrambled onto the recliner and buckled myself in. Minutes later, we were hurtling down the tarmac and then airborne.

And it seemed as though the farther we left the Earth behind, the more frantic my thoughts became. Saskia's taunts echoed viciously inside my skull, outlasting the hum of the plane's engine.

"He relives it. Over and over... But you know what really gets his cold heart pumping? Your sister."

"Can I get you anything to drink, miss?" The female attendant asked, suddenly appearing by my side. Balanced on her hand was a silver tray containing a variety of beverages.

I started to shake my head. "No, thank you—" But I broke off as movement caught my eye.

Dublin. He cut his gaze toward the tray, fixated on a beverage in particular. Without thinking, I grabbed the item consuming his interest—a bottle of water. With a few swift pulls, I drained it, aware of him watching.

By the time I returned the empty bottle to the tray, however, he was already back to ignoring me.

When the attendant retreated out of view, I finally gathered the nerve to face him. He eyed the world visible beyond the windows, his arms crossed. At a glance, one might name his posture petulant—but it was so much more than that. Callous. Disinterested.

Cold.

One would never guess that last night he'd sworn that I'd tempted him to madness.

Lost in thought, I rummaged through my purse. Within seconds, my fingers cradled a small object between them: a cheap ring of plastic gold sporting a cracked turquoise bead. I slipped it onto my finger as I refocused my gaze on the creature sitting across from me.

"Saskia told me something," I croaked, breaking the silence. "Several somethings. Confusing things."

"And you believed her?" He didn't even bother to utter his customary scoff; I wasn't worth the effort. "Do I need to remind you that she thrives on deception?"

"No," I admitted. "B-But…"

For the first time, I closed my eyes and allowed myself to relive the images I'd been suppressing. His kiss. His touch. The way he'd held me like I was something he wanted to break and cherish in one twisted breath. Like he craved me as he claimed.

Such a startling contrast to the way he was acting toward me now—like I was something repulsive. A burden he felt compelled to suffer.

Which one was the truth?

For some reason, he assumed I knew.

"Don't bother yourself worrying about Saskia and her lies." Leather hissed as he shifted, presumably starting to stand. "Now, if you're finished, I need to speak to the pilot—"

"She told me you think of me," I blurted out. My eyes were still closed, but in some ways, the blindness enhanced my ability to perceive his reaction.

His harsh intake of a breath he didn't need. The tension crackling in his muscles, his joints stiffening. The man could convey a symphony of emotion when he wanted to. Namely rage.

"That you think of sleeping with me," I added before he could deliver the cruel retort that I knew was poised on the tip of his tongue. "Is that true? Is it?"

His silence became unbearable. So I opened my eyes, hating how they burned. "I could stomach the sex if that were all you wanted," I confessed—and it was the truth. Bartering myself to him had been a mere transaction, nothing more.

Or so I'd tried to claim. Over and over, I had fed on that lie.

"If wanting me was as simple as desiring a pawn in a game, then fine. If my virginity were a token prize to you, I could understand. I could even understand if you had a fetish for innocent little virgins like Saskia sniped. But…" I racked my brain for the right words. Something far more dignified than what wound up spilling out instead. "But stop teasing me. Please."

He stared expressionlessly, so intent. So silent.

Ah. So this *was* another game. A part of me sighed—partially frantic, partially relieved. If only he would admit as much, then all of the confusion could cease. The memories. The ache in my throat as I remembered his touch. The throbbing pulse between my legs when he crept into my thoughts at night. All of it would stop as soon as he said the magic words.

You think I'd lust after you? Think again. Your money is all that is appealing about you. It's your sister I truly want. It's always been her.

When his jaw twitched, I held my breath in anticipation. Finally…

"Why does it terrify you?" he wondered as if truly curious. "The thought that I might want you."

"Why?" I gestured between us with a wave of my hand. "Because I'm *me*. And you're you."

"A monster?" Heavy-lidded, his gaze became more unreadable than before.

"No!" I stammered, too confused to convey what I meant. My only salvation turned out to be the bluntest of terms. "You could have anyone you ever wanted. Beautiful, perfect women." And God, it stung to admit that. More than it should have. "Anyone. Like…Georgiana. Don't tell me you haven't considered her."

Saskia herself had hinted at as much.

"Just tell me and I could understand."

Rather than go slack with relief, his jaw tightened further, his eyes narrowing. Not in anger. More thoughtfully, as if the answer to a puzzling conundrum had just presented itself. One so obvious that he was openly skeptical of it.

"You truly believe this?" His tone conveyed more than he said out loud. *That's why you've been ignoring reality? Living in denial?*

"Of course!" I had to laugh, choking out the pathetic sound. "I have eyes, Dublin." *So just admit it,* was the part I held back. *Please admit it.* "If sex is all you want, fine. But don't pretend like you want something more beyond that."

"Like?"

I wrung my fingers in exasperation. "Like something requiring the serious discussions of *tumors* and what they might mean. I can't... I refuse to play that kind of game with you. You accused me of being in denial, but maybe I'm being realistic? I am not ready to handle something like this." It stung to say it, but at least I could. "And neither are you. The sooner we agree upon that point, the easier this will be."

There. I broke off, panting and satisfied with the extent of my confession.

Now, it was his turn.

"Come here," he commanded, beckoning with a crooked finger.

I lurched, fumbling with my seat belt. Once freed, I crossed over to him, maintaining my balance with the gentle motions of the plane. He shifted, leaving enough space beside him for me to sit, and I did, sighing.

Finally, he would say it. But rather than speak, he took my hand and unfurled every finger. Then he placed it on his lap, right between his thighs.

My palm seared, instantly registering what lay beneath it. Firmness. Hardness. Evidence of something that made my stomach clench and my teeth snap together. In shock, I tried to pull away—he gripped me even tighter.

"Perhaps I've humored your naivety for too long," he mused, sounding eerily calm despite the part of his anatomy proclaiming anything but control. "Do you truly believe that I intended to announce my return at all? Let alone to you?"

I squirmed, uneasy. It sounded so obvious when stated out loud. His abrupt resurfacing hadn't been a trick, or a mind game like I'd assumed, but...

Impulsive?

"How did you even know?" I asked, playing along. "Where I was?"

"Believe it or not, finding *you* was not my priority." A low sound trickled from his throat, too terrifying to be mistaken for a laugh. "My sole intention for returning at all was to convince Goodfellow in person to relinquish your case. My efforts to block her attempts from afar had proven ineffective and she is no fool. When she began consulting experts in the *occult*, I decided to intervene."

I swallowed hard at the dangerous shift in his tone. "She was just trying to help me."

Judging from the stern tilt of his mouth, he did not agree.

"She risked drawing attention to you. Good intentioned or not, she put your life in danger. As long as you wore the talisman, I could sense your location, so I knew you were in no immediate harm at least." He fingered the necklace in question. "But when you suddenly wound up in an area of the city where I know Raphael exerts his influence, I followed. Only to discover your meeting with Gabriel Lanic and..." His grip on me tightened, applying even more pressure against my hand. "I refuse to let you pretend like you don't see what the whole damn world has. What it's mocked me for," he warned. "That you haven't felt every inch of it slammed inside you. If anyone is playing a game here, it isn't me. Goddamn, a part of me wonders if you somehow planned it, if only to make me out to be a fool..." He flicked his wrist, forcing me to feel more of him. All of him, swelling against my hand. "So, no, Eleanor, I'm afraid your supposed innocence isn't a fair enough excuse." He released me, shrugging my presence aside as he started to stand again. "Now that we've gotten that established—"

"Then why leave in the first place?" I demanded, eyeing my hand. It burned and the fingers were trembling, impossible to control. "If you want me so damn much then why leave at all? And don't use Georgiana as your excuse. You don't take orders from anyone."

The fact that he would return merely to exert his control over my life in something as trivial as medical records proved that fact.

"Why?" He paused and his eyes flashed as if the question required serious contemplation. "Perhaps I don't enjoy being at the mercy of a woman who would sooner spend eternity with her cat as a companion than admit her attraction to me?"

"Attraction?" I whispered hoarsely.

He chuckled and began to rise to his feet. "We once established that you've learned more than a few tidbits on sexuality from romance novels. Use that knowledge to draw upon what might cause a woman to become wet—"

"S-Stop." Plush carpet cradled my knees as I sank to the floor, all modesty forgotten. If he wanted to play tricks, then I'd sink to his level. Prove it once and for all—he was lying.

"You use sex like it's a game," I blurted. "Like the whole damn world knows the rules when only you do. You kiss me when you want to. Leave me when you want to. But I'm the one at fault? Even now… You're trying to confuse me for a reason," I decided, shaking my head. "You always throw sex in my face just to manipulate me. You did it at the auction, and in the cathedral, and when you came back."

Each time he had taunted me with a taste of desire.

Only to yank it back the second it suited him.

Even now.

"You're saying these things because you know you can turn the tables," I said.

He didn't move, his gaze impossible to read. "So what will you do now, Eleanor? Run away. Make me hunt you down. Pretend I was always the monster?"

"No." My hands fell over his thighs and hesitation paralyzed me for a heartbeat. Until he tensed beneath me, still seated. God, I could almost hear him hissing a dare. *Do something, Eleanor. But don't fool yourself. You lack the nerve.*

"I want to prove it to myself once and for all. You're lying and I'm not afraid to face the truth this time." Biting my lip, I tugged at the fastenings of his pants to no avail. My hands shook too badly to undo them, but he didn't laugh and shrug me off. He tugged the zipper down himself, his eyes slits, conveying confusion and a warning.

You're playing with fire.

But I was too tired to heed it. I lowered my mouth instead, flinching as his fingers latched onto my scalp. He started to tug, but his grip went slack the second my tongue connected with the silken flesh beneath the cotton of his pants.

Such a vulgar act. I had only ever performed it once before in my entire life.

Only ever with him.

Yet nothing could compare to the feel of it. Having him at my mercy. Exploring his body far beyond physical touch. I could taste him, spice and winter. I could feel him, hard and unmoving. Thickening. Thicker.

And I knew in an instant that I had made a horrible miscalculation.

He didn't shrug me off the way some prudish part of me insisted he would. The smug, confident Dublin Helos would *never* surrender an argument due to such a base impulse.

And yet, I could hear him growling with every tentative flick of my tongue. Soon, he began to buck into every taste, betraying a lack of restraint that made my breathing hitch in anticipation. When his fingers cinched a fistful of my hair, I nearly sighed in relief. I'd won. His rejection would prove it. I all but hissed in triumph as his opposite hand latched onto the nape of my neck—but the touch wasn't resisting. His fingers clamped down, *restraining*, as if to prevent me from pulling away.

And for whatever reason, I didn't…

My eyelids fluttered as my tongue lapped along the crown of him. His blood was addicting, but this was an even more potent drug. *Power*, however briefly it lasted. There was something terrible in his taste. A flavor that made a groan catch in my throat and my stomach clench. Something too elusive to name—I could only chase it, gradually taking more and more of him into my mouth.

All I could.

Dazed, I made the mistake of looking up, seeing him stare down on me, his eyes slits, his jaw so tight that it could have been chiseled from stone.

It was like that very first night. Something shot between us, hot like fire. Electric. Suddenly, he flexed his grip, wrenching me upright. Up, onto his lap. Cupping my knee in his opposite hand, he spread my legs apart, forcing me to straddle him completely. There was no mistaking what pressed against my inner thighs now, pulsing against the fabric of my dress.

No pretending that I wasn't the cause of every inch.

And that knowledge confounded everything I knew about myself—everything I knew I wanted. His nearness made me yearn in ways I barely understood. For his taste. His rage. His need.

Everything.

I shivered as he batted the skirt aside, sliding a thumb beneath my panties. The gusset was no match as he yanked, ripping the thin material right down the middle. Slowly, his thumb burrowed between my folds in its place.

As he applied the slightest hint of pressure, the world ceased to spin.

"*This* is what you do to me." He lingered and my entire body trembled, balanced on the pad of his finger. I sucked in a breath, my eyelids fluttering. If revenge was his aim, well he had won. I was unbearably cruel for making him feel even a fraction of this.

A single, lazy flick of his wrist fed tendrils of fire ripping through me like drops of gasoline. There was only one word for it, and groaning, he murmured it, "Insanity…"

Still vengeful, he stroked me again. Slower. Harder.

"Madness." A grunt edged his words and a part of me knew why. With every caress of his thumb, my breathing quickened. My hips twitched, chasing the pressure and he felt…

Harder. Thicker. Firmer.

Because of me. My body was reacting to him in a way those romance novels he once taunted me for reading referenced. I looked down, observing the confident way he manipulated my body. He pulled his hand back slightly, taunting me with the evidence that I wanted him just as badly.

Needed him.

Craved.

As if aware of the thoughts, he encircled my throat in his entire fist, forcing me to meet his gaze. I swallowed hard, riveted by the sensation of his fingers. Still stroking. Thrusting.

Like I was an instrument at his mercy, one only he could ever tune.

My back arched at the intrusion, but he held me against him as if daring me to watch. How his pupils constricted when I moaned. How his tongue flicked along his lower lip as if to capture the sound. The way he groaned—truly groaned. As if in pain every time I rocked my hips, chasing the firmness just beyond reach.

Our eyes met again. Then foreheads. Mouths. Frantic, I inhaled him, letting his tongue battle mine even as insecurity threatened to shatter the numbing haze of lust.

This isn't real.

It isn't you he wants, Eleanor.

He doesn't want you.

"I won't let you play the innocent this time." Baring his teeth, he positioned me above him, stopping short of lowering me onto him directly. He grasped my hand and lowered it to the tip of his cock. "Take what you want from me. Admit it."

My fingers curled and I marveled at the feel of him. I flexed my fingers and he hissed. Curled them and he nearly came off the couch. I guided him against me and he bucked upward at the same time. He entered me in one slow, tenuous motion and it was sin. Him inside me was pure, hellish sin. The world slowed. The noise of the plane quieted and the rest of the universe ceased to matter.

Just this.

My hands fell over his shoulders, straining for leverage as he cradled my spine, guiding my movements. Slow. Harder. Deeper. So deep…

I stopped caring if the lust barreling into me was real. I only needed to feel it. My moans were broken. Loud. Shameless. In the back of my mind, I knew his pretty attendant could hear me. The whole damn plane could.

But they could also hear *him.*

He grunted with every thrust, his hands scrambling for purchase over my waist, gripping me tighter. Tighter…

I gasped as he stood, lifting me in his arms. Pivoting on his heel, he spun me around and then pinned me down so that I was facing him. My back arched against the leather of the chaise as he rocked his hips, thrusting in from a newer angle. One too intimate. Too close.

He nipped my lips as if to steal away any doubt before it could form. In its absence, fire seared through my veins, building until…

Explosion. My body bore down, gripping him so tight that I saw stars. Nails drawn, I clung to him, my fingers laced through his hair as wave after wave of pleasure ripped me apart.

In the aftermath, he went limp, his arms around me. Skimming along my jaw, his mouth found the crook of my shoulder next, his fangs delivering the barest tease of pressure.

Then he stiffened.

"Sir?" a soft voice sweetly called. "We will be experiencing some turbulence. The pilot requests that you buckle up for safety."

He shrugged me off him, maneuvering me onto my side. A strap of leather fell across my waist, easily secured by his quick fingers. Before I could even register the loss of his touch, he resettled beside me, so close that my face rested against his chest.

As reality reasserted its presence, it became almost impossible to swallow down an irrational panic. Prudish shame nibbled at the flesh of my cheeks, reddening them. Moisture slicked my inner thighs. I could still feel traces of him lingering inside me, and my poor, addled brain struggled to process it all without reverting to the instinct that only now I could admit was a defense mechanism —*denial.*

Dublin's hand tensed over my lower back as if waiting for just that reaction. God, it was as though he could truly read my mind, anticipate every action.

So I bit my lip and then blurted out the only question I could. "Should I be worried that your attendant doesn't seem to mind when you have sex in your private airplane?"

He went still. Then he shrugged. "She's seen worse. Trust me when I say that this may be a welcome change of pace for her."

Something told me he wasn't referring to sex.

And my desperation for any random—*safe*—topic grew. "Where… Where were you born?"

He stiffened further, but his hand remained, bracing me to his side as the cabin shuddered, buffeted by a sudden tempest.

"Eireann," he finally said once the motion settled. "Or Ireland—some called it that, even back then."

A rather obvious realization dawned on me. "Is that why you go by Dublin?"

He shrugged, his fingers fanning out along my spine. "A bit cliché, but it gets the point across."

I had to admit that it did. But there was more to it. The truth lurking within his name that I'd discovered on a whim what felt like a lifetime ago. How, when unscrambled, the letters composing Dublin Helos formed a morbid phrase —*is hell bound.*

"Why don't you live there?"

"Let's just say…" He trailed off, deep in thought, and a part of me tensed. I'd accidentally triggered something delicate. I held my breath as he withdrew his hand, but a heartbeat later, his fingers brushed my shoulder, teasing the edges of my hair. "I haven't earned the right to return."

In my right mind, I might have never pressed him for more. But as the plane jolted again, his arm went around my shoulders, keeping me secured despite the fact that he hadn't bothered to fasten himself in.

"How long has it been?" I asked if only to distract from his nearness.

"In years?" He tilted his head as if he had never thought back to count the time before. "Centuries?"

"Oh." I swallowed. Spending even a full year away from Gray Manor seemed too long to fathom. Not out of fondness perhaps—but duty. It was my legacy, the one thing in existence resolutely mine.

I tried to picture how it might look after centuries of absence. Of one day returning to find my family home a husk of its former self. Would I mourn it? Probably.

And the thought made me realize that anything Dublin might have cherished in his homeland was now most certainly dust. He grabbed my hand and I realized I'd been toying with the object on my middle finger—a cheap, plastic ring.

He eyed it wordlessly, raking his thumb across the bead's dull surface. As he released me, he shifted, pulling me more firmly to his side. The belt fastened around me offered enough slack that I could draw my knees up and rest my head against his shoulder.

"Why did you leave?" he asked, his gaze still on my ring. "When you went to the manor? Let me voice my crude assumption now. François is your lover and you were planning to escape to France and live out your eternity in marital bliss."

I nearly choked. "That's a very…specific suspicion."

"That isn't a denial," he pointed out. A muscle in his jaw flexed, stiff with tension.

"Well, you were meeting with *Kate*," I pointed out. "I remember her, you do realize? The woman whose contract you managed for Raphael. You must have thoroughly enjoyed her 'services' in order to invite her to live with you."

I loathed the raw emotion that leeched into my tone.

My cheeks flamed as his eyes cut down to mine. "You're jealous of her." He phrased it like some momentous revelation.

"And you're jealous of François," I countered—though I didn't truly believe it, even as the words left my mouth.

Not until I saw his face. His mouth flattened as if he had hoarded all emotion behind a mask. It was an expression he only deployed in the rarest of circumstances.

When I'd caught him off guard.

I swallowed hard as he became stone against me. "Do I have reason to be?" he wondered in a dangerous tone.

"No, but do I? If I happened to care that you had a beautiful woman indentured to you for all eternity in your luxurious penthouse—"

"Raphael used her like a pawn, the same way he utilized the others."

I cringed and my indignation diminished somewhat. *Others.* Those poor women made to look like me and paraded before him. Why? As part of some sick, twisted game?

Or perhaps something far more sinister…

"By keeping her close, I could negate his attempts to control her," Dublin explained. "Nothing more."

"And François is my driver," I said thickly. "Nothing more."

He shifted slightly and I wound up leaning against him even more. "So how did you wind up bleeding in his care?"

I sighed too drained to argue. There was no point in lying now. "I was trying to send a message to my sister."

Did he believe me? I couldn't tell. His face revealed nothing.

Cautiously, I continued. "I took a cab and slipped a letter in that stupid urn in the simplest chance she might remember she has a sister and come looking for me. I didn't want her to worry."

How pathetic, all things considered.

"I was in the crypt when two men came in. Something about them felt off so I hid. When they left, I tried to leave and François found me."

"Did he hurt you?" I flinched. His voice was too soft. Too low.

"No," I fervently insisted. "I fell. He helped me. And when I asked, he brought me to you."

"How long have you known him?" Again, he used that alarmingly soft tone and I wondered just how naïve I'd been all this time not to realize my "driver's" identity on my own.

"Just a few weeks. I didn't know he was working for my sister. I swear I didn't."

But he had known. He nodded once as if confirming his own dark suspicions. Which of course he didn't bother to convey out loud.

"Is he dead?" My voice broke in anticipation of the answer.

"No."

"Good." I squeezed my eyes shut, too relieved to watch his reaction as I added, "Please don't hurt him."

He said nothing for so long that I feared I'd done it—broken this fragile moment. My heart ached at the thought. This time had felt so different from our other brief truces. I could still remember the way he'd looked at me, his eyes burning, his lips hollowed around a groan.

"And the necklace?" he said before true panic could set in. "Where did you get it?"

My belly tightened. His tone was more cautious than ever, laced with something so rare that I marveled at the sound. The same cold, detached note he utilized only around Raphael.

"It was in a tomb," I confessed. "An empty one. It didn't have a name on it, just a phrase. Latin, I think."

"Latin?" Dublin echoed hoarsely. He sat forward, dislodging me from his side. "What did it say?"

"Yes. Um… *Memento mori*. That was it. Do you know what it means?"

I watched him, startled by his reaction. He was staring off as if seeing something far beyond this space. Far beyond this reality. A wistful tilt to his mouth betrayed his true nature more than ever: a creature unmoored by the constraints of time.

"Remember death," he declared, uttering the phrase with a chilling sense of finality. Slowly, he sat back and his hand hooked around my waist, drawing me against him once more. "It means remember death."

"That sounds like something a Gray would want on a tombstone," I admitted, trying to picture the mysterious culprit. "Perhaps they got their necklace at the same sale you got yours?"

A lie of course. The way he fingered the thin chain—always without seeming to realize it—revealed its personal nature. He hadn't bought it at some thrift shop. No. It held far too much sentiment. A gift?

Though that presented more mystery as to why its twin just so happened to have been hiding within my childhood haunt and family mausoleum. For *years*, judging from the dust surrounding it, if not decades. Centuries?

"Unless of course," I added, shrugging away the morbid connotations, "you gave it to some poor ancient Gray woman you seduced." Though most likely not within an airplane traveling to only God knew where. I could claim that scorecard, at least. "She stole it, because we Grays are nothing if not spiteful, and left it somewhere only one of her poor, bumbling descendants would be able to find it. Was it Agatha?" I wondered, naming one of the members of his thorough list. "You did write her name rather peculiarly—"

"You are a singular creature." He gripped my chin, tilting it so that I faced him. Lips pursed, a ruthless sweep of his gaze was all he required to decipher me. "To be honest, if there were more than one of you with your abject lack of self-preservation, I'm sure your bloodline wouldn't have lasted this long. Poor Agatha would have already wandered off a cliff on a whim."

"Or an evil vampire would have goaded her off," I croaked. Because he had the gall to profess that he had an interest in her that extended beyond her plain looks and massive fortune. "Poor Agatha—"

"*Agatha* would have written me a check during our first meeting," he countered, suddenly serious. "*You* insisted upon your own terms, no matter how reckless and inane they might be. The first time I offered you an out, you stripped naked and demanded you have your way." He pulled me closer and his thumb swiped my lower lip as if in punishment. "I told you to make yourself unappealing at the club. So you decided to dance in a way that made me offer up more time to that bastard Raphael just to keep you out of his reach. I turned you away for your own good, yet you came marching back with your chin in the air, daring me to have you again."

He sighed, such a hollow, tortured sound. "Then I leave the country to try to regain my sanity, only to return and find you on my doorstep. And again, when I try to *finally* let you go, you get on your knees and suck my cock." Awe painted his voice, as did anger, and hopelessness, and eternal frustration. "At every turn, you confound me. At every attempt to ignore your albeit lacking charms, you find a way to hook your claws into me. You called me the monster, but frankly, I must admit that I am at a loss when it comes to you. A part of me suspects that if I *did* kill you, you'd merely come back to life, giggling with glee that you'd finally managed to break my resolve." His other hand came to cradle the side of my face, brushing the stray curls back. "I'm confounded by you," he reiterated. "So I have decided that the only way to survive you with my sanity intact is to utilize you. As I see fit."

My breath caught at the raw lust his tone revealed. As if chasing the reaction, he worked the tip of his thumb between my lips, seeking out my tongue.

"And how is that?" I managed to ask.

He seemed to mull it over. "I will no longer resist your impulsive inclinations. I'll merely combat them. The next time you question my supposed lack of attraction to you, I will take it as an invitation over an insult."

I drew my thighs together, aggravating the slight ache between them. "Oh?"

"I'll strip you naked," he mused. "For a start, at least. There is no use in humoring you like one would a sane woman. You thrive on this—corruption. I think it's what you've wanted all along."

I thought back to our very first meeting, when he'd barged into my bedroom and presented a choice: life or death?

"Stripping naked or dropping to my knees does seem to be an effective way to render you speechless," I admitted. Then my teeth skewered my lip. "As is presenting a, let's say *unlikely*, challenge to your understanding of vampire biology."

He remained silent for so long. I flinched when he finally moved and settled his hand along my hip. Outstretched, his fingers grazed the flat of my belly. The sight triggered a flurry of emotions too complex to name. They thickened my throat and obstructed my breathing—overwhelming in every aspect.

"Regardless of what happens between us… I don't want to face this alone," I admitted, my voice hoarse.

"You won't. It is true that this 'challenge' is unexpected," he finally confessed. "Though, I would ask that you not make a habit of deconstructing my concept of reality."

"What did Raphael mean?" I asked. "When he said that my bloodline is cursed. That you knew someone who—"

"It doesn't matter." He brushed his mouth along my jaw, taking his time in the advance toward his true destination. I inhaled raggedly, my lips parting even before his finally settled over mine. This kiss was slower than the others. Deeper. Savoring instead of frantic. His flavor lingered on my tongue, and I took my time deciphering every subtle nuance of it. He was a creature born to be deciphered.

He could taste as unyielding and relentless as ice in some aspects one moment. Then hot like winter spice the next. Sweet like wine, all the while laced with a bitter, dangerous hint that made my stomach constrict and heat spread through my belly.

When he started to pull back, I followed, craving more. His blood was an addictive substance, but even it was unmatched compared to him.

"I really do need to speak to the pilot." The raw regret in his tone soothed any sting of rejection I might have felt. He looked tormented as he pulled away and stood. Surprising me, he reached for my seat belt and unfastened it before helping me to my feet as well.

Instead of toward the cockpit, he led me down the length of the cabin and into a space dominated by a bed. Something I suspected a vampire's private jet might otherwise not contain.

"You need sleep," he said, urging me onto the mattress. "The bathroom is there." He nodded to a small door just beyond the bedroom. "I shouldn't be long."

I watched him go. Even disheveled in his polished suit, the man remained unmatched in poise. Doubt, that terrible fucking thing, was harder to quash without his mouth to silence it, however. That vicious voice returned, slightly louder than before.

You think he truly wants you? It's all lies, Eleanor.

The only way to banish the thoughts was to enter the bathroom—unusually spacious with a wide sink and enough space to wash myself in comfortably—strip my soiled dress, and attack my body with a warm, wet cloth. I washed slowly, swaying in time with the plane's various jolts and tremors.

I was doubtfully eyeing my dress, considering whether to wear it at all or just leave the bathroom naked, when someone knocked softly on the door.

"Miss? Mr. Helos requested that I bring you some of your belongings so that you can make yourself as comfortable as possible. We have about eight hours until landing." The attendant opened the door and offered an array of items balanced on a tray. A length of black material that resembled a robe. A fresh dress. Slippers and various toiletries.

I accepted them all gratefully and dressed in the modest black shift and the silken robe. When I reentered the bedroom, Dublin still hadn't returned. I climbed onto the mattress, gasping at the quality—divine. Before I knew it, I was groggily stirring to awareness and finding a presence looming over the bed.

"The plane won't crash, I hope," I murmured as another bout of turbulence rattled the cabin—though honestly the mattress was so luxurious that I barely even felt the disturbance at all. "Is everything okay with the pilot?"

Dublin said nothing, his face expressionless. Closed-off.

Unease made me swallow as I scrambled upright. "What's wrong?"

"What exactly did you tell your sister? Perhaps you've had a line of communication to her all along? I had my men check for your little note. It's gone." His voice was so cutting that I ran my fingers along my throat just to make sure he hadn't drawn blood. "Tell me now. Did you mention the contract? Gloat over the fact that you own me like a dog on a leash?"

I shook my head. "What are you talking about? What's wrong?"

"We're being followed." He eyed me pointedly, as if waiting for a confession.

When all I could do was sputter wordlessly, he turned on his heel and stormed into the main cabin.

"Wait!" I started to follow but he stopped short, his voice like a whip.

"Don't. Stay in here. Get your *rest* while I try to ensure we both don't end up killed."

I stared after him, my mouth agape. He crossed the central cabin, disappearing through a doorway at the other end.

I crept toward the threshold, his rage an invisible line that kept me from stepping over it. Doubt became full-blown paranoia. And then dread.

My heart felt a bit like that goddamn Gray family crypt. Dusty and chambered, filled with a million dark, shadowy spaces. And every time I let him in, he slammed the door on his way out.

COLD

It seemed that we landed hours later. An eternity perhaps, suspended in time and space—the perfect environment for Dublin's anger to fester into full-blown apathy when he finally appeared outside my unofficial prison cell.

"Come," he said. Dressed in a fresh suit entirely composed of black, he didn't even resemble the man I'd clung to just a few short hours earlier. He was a stranger who dabbled in the trade of souls—but mine was already far beyond his reach. "We need to move quickly." Suspicion lanced from him, honed like a blade.

So I parried in the only way I knew how: with equal vitriol.

"I'll move," I snarled, my hands on my hips, "just as soon as you tell me where the hell we are."

He lunged, snatching my wrist, and yanked me across the main cabin.

"Get off of me!" By the time I'd managed to wrench out of his grip, we were already descending the steps onto a secluded tarmac, seemingly in the middle of nowhere.

A car waited nearby, another stern-faced driver standing at the ready. But Dublin's silence couldn't obscure everything. Evening painted the sky a stunning ochre shade, for one. Like fire, smoldering down to ebony embers speckled with starlight. Given that we'd left the city only early in the morning, it shouldn't have been this dark yet.

"Where are we?" I demanded as I continued down the steps.

Dublin said nothing, but the moment I reached solid ground, he grabbed my arm, all but hauling me to the car. I sputtered as he shoved me into the back seat—but this time, he followed, slamming the door after us.

I scrambled as far away from him as I could, squeezing myself against the opposite door. He didn't even spare a glance in my direction.

His attention on the driver, he commanded, "Go."

"Where are we?" I demanded. Somewhere far, far from my home I suspected.

Foreign air lingered in my nostrils, far crisper than the stench of the city. Twisted trees lined the road and loomed above, easily displacing any view of the sky. In some ways, it felt like a parallel universe, one frozen in time.

"I'll keep our location to myself for now," Dublin said in a tone that made me grit my teeth. "Just in case you decide to write more letters to your sister. And here I was, assuming she might be in danger. I actually considered offering my services to assist you in finding—"

"Something happened," I deduced. "Just tell me. If I did something wrong—"

"*You?* Make a mistake?" His eyebrows furrowed in mock shock. "The woman who's gotten more people killed in her wake in a month than most will in a lifetime?"

Pain ripped through my chest, so potent that I pressed my hand against it as if that might lessen the blow. It didn't. Once again, my defensive mechanism threatened to deploy. I wanted to say something equally harsh, enough to combat the way my eyes burned. But as I observed my hand in the waning daylight, something displaced even my anger.

"My ring." Panicked, I felt around my seat, finding nothing. "It's gone. Go back! I must have left it in the—"

"Did you not hear me when I said we were being followed? Yet you suggest we go back for a worthless trinket. And you still claim you don't have an ulterior motive?"

I bit down on my tongue so hard that I tasted copper. Aching, I brushed my naked finger with my thumb as I tried to reconcile why a *worthless trinket's* loss was troubling me so much. Especially when the man who'd given it to me didn't seem to give a damn either way.

"You're right," I admitted, turning away from him. "It's worthless trash. I truly hate you, and I spilled all of your secrets to a sister who abandoned me without a word. *And* I hope her spies blow us both up because, obviously, I have a death wish. Hopefully my *cancer* will speed along that outcome, at least. So tell your driver to hurry up to wherever we're going. I'm bored."

He said nothing, but I cut myself off from any senses that might decipher him. Instead, I did what I should have done all along—trusted my suspicious, doubtful instincts. Oh, how right they were.

But admitting as much hurt more than it should have. I hunched beneath the pain of it, wrapping my arms around my chest in a vain effort to mitigate the ceaseless throbbing.

But it didn't.

All I could do was whisper out loud the confused, pathetic questions circling my brain in an effort to weakly combat the self-loathing.

"You want me to trust you, but how can I when every time I try you push me away, or insult me, or disappear?" Oh God. My voice was trembling, breaking openly. Tears stung my eyes, impossible to blink back. Oh well. He'd accuse me of lying regardless. I had nothing left to lose. "I confessed to you that night in the cathedral how you made me feel. You left days later, and I'm the cruel one? But now you return and I'm not only supposed to believe that you might give a damn, but that I might be—" No. I bit off any more. That was too pathetic. "I think it's best if from now on we just…"

Exist in a silence so heavy that I didn't have to finish defining it. We fell into our roles far too well, retreating to opposite ends of the car, glaring from our respective windows.

He never offered a word in his defense or otherwise.

And I was too tired to demand one.

~

Our eventual destination awaited at the end of a paved driveway lined in trees and illuminated with orange lanterns. When my gaze fell over the structure, I gasped aloud as the driver finally came to a stop.

Poor Gray Manor would blush in shame.

Composed of stone, a sprawling mansion gleamed in the moonlight as if crafted from a fairytale. Light spilled from every window, painting neatly manicured lawns, complete with bubbling twin fountains placed on either side of the cobblestone driveway.

I still gaped as Dublin exited the car without a word. His hand appeared seconds later. Warily, I took it. Had he decided to apologize? I eyed his expression, hunting for any softness as he guided me up the path to the front door. There, a man wearing a stark black uniform ushered us inside.

"Show Ms. Gray to her room," Dublin commanded him, releasing me. He turned on his heel and stormed out the way we'd come.

I watched, flinching as the door slammed behind him.

"This way, miss."

I turned to the butler and tried to shift my attention to my surroundings, letting their beauty negate any pain.

Breathtaking was the operative word. I'd thought his beautiful penthouse suite was impressive, but this was luxury on an entirely different scale. My mother would approve of the plain-but-quality oak-paneled walls and polished floors. The golden light fixtures illuminating wide, open hallways with high ceilings and furniture in shades of emerald and ebony, however?

She'd scoff in disgust at those.

My room, unsurprisingly, was no less elegant. For all his moods where I was concerned, I couldn't accuse Dublin of compromising my comfort out of spite. The bed looked heavenly—solid wood, carved with extravagant reliefs of roses and vines, draped in a ruby canopy. A wide window displayed a view of yet another garden, its details obscured in the darkness.

"Goodnight, miss," the butler called before leaving the room and closing the door.

I swallowed hard, blinking as my eyes started to prickle. It was funny how silence could bring everything into painfully clear focus. Like the fact that I was alone again.

That my lips were still swollen—again.

That the inside of my thighs ached and I couldn't tell if it was from pain or just the shame of rejection.

I wanted to be angry. Or bitter, or hateful. I wanted to storm about the room and declare just how unaffected I was by Dublin Helos and his switchblade rage. I wanted to do anything but crawl onto the mattress and huddle beneath silken sheets as moisture spilled down my cheeks once more.

Morning came with the intensity of a punch —literally. Ruthlessly aimed, it slammed against my abdomen and the pain jolted me from a fitful sleep. Gasping, I rolled onto my side, clutching my stomach. Every breath hurt. It was as though my lungs were in a vise grip. An invisible fist squeezed only to release. Again. Each vicious cramping wave left me writhing over the sheets.

"What's wrong?" The door flew open and Dublin rushed in. Pale dawn light painted him in shades of gold, making him seem more angel than Devil. He wore a fresh gray suit, his hair slicked back, his overall appearance perfection.

Gritting my teeth, I sat upright and placed my feet on the floor, my back to him. "Nothing," I said even as another wave of pain stole my breath away. My eyelids fluttered as I inhaled through my nose, gripping the sheets so tightly that my nails pierced the fabric. Eventually, the tension subsided, and I attempted to disguise my rigid posture with a shrug. "I'm fine."

He didn't move—and his concern irritated me far more than it should have. *Now* he wanted to care after accusing me of being a suicidal traitor. Yesterday's Eleanor might have forgiven him, swayed by the display.

Not me.

"I'm fine," I hissed, biting the words out. "And I'd rather be alone now, if you please. How else will I contact my sister via telepathic Morse code and give our location away?"

He moved—a series of slow, heavy footsteps that paused near the threshold. "I'll be gone for the day," he told me, his tone devoid of warmth once more. "When I return tonight, be ready. There is clothing in the wardrobe—"

"Fine," I snapped, deliberately avoiding asking him where he planned on taking me.

"And…"

I could almost taste his hesitation, cracking his callous façade.

"If you need me, ask for me."

"I won't." I eyed my fingers lazily, inspecting the nails. They were trembling and I balled them into fists to hide it— though the act was in vain.

He was already gone, marching down the hall and then the staircase.

Alone, I crawled onto the center of the mattress, tense in anticipation of another bout of pain. I'd never felt anything like it before. Was this a new phase of the cancer I'd deliberately avoided thinking about until now?

Fear goaded my pulse into a frantic thrum. I tossed and turned, wavering on calling for Dublin after all. My lips parted. Closed. Parted again…

If I did call for him, it wouldn't be out of weakness. Just in case I truly was dying, he deserved to be told what an ass he was to his face. That was all.

When footsteps approached my room, I sat upright, wondering if my thoughts alone had conjured him. But no. A smiling woman wearing a plain gray dress approached the foot of my bed, holding a tray. On it was a simple breakfast and a nondescript black cup containing a suspicious-looking liquid.

Once she left, I ate quickly, tasting nothing. The food helped. After a few minutes passed devoid of any cramping, I paced before venturing from my room to examine the manor proper.

Something told me that Dublin hadn't bought this property on a whim. There was too much of his personal style embedded within everything from the subtle silver accents to the almost cathedral-like architecture. I suspected he had owned the place for a while, a fact that intrigued me more than I wanted to admit. It was easy to forget just how old he was. And how wealthy. How powerful.

The man possessed a string of unknown credentials—being a doctor included. I'd witnessed firsthand his procurement of an orphanage, and he seemed to own countless buildings and enterprises. A collector, in a sense. If I wanted to be morbid, his interest in me made perfect sense—a man so wealthy and bored that he collected properties and money like candy. What else was Gray Manor but a token to add to his list?

And what was I other than a fun diversion?

Stop, Ellie. I rubbed my arms, shivering. A chill lingered over the lower level as if no one had thought to heat it. Considering that a vampire owned the place, who would?

Seeking warmth, I returned to my room, and there I lingered, no better than a bird in a cage.

~

*I*n my quest to prove as a fitting antagonist to Dublin, I did my best to appear only *somewhat* presentable before he came for me. The resulting look required one of Yulia's dresses—mysteriously found within the room's only wardrobe. Floor-length and composed of black lace, it sported a modest though no less elegant neckline. After a halfhearted bit of styling with my wet fingers, my curls no longer stuck out in all directions, so that was a plus—and about where my efforts extended.

If he expected more, that was his problem.

As night fell, I finally descended to the foyer. Only to find Dublin already there waiting. One look at him reinforced just how futile my pathetic attempts had been.

The air left my lungs, driven out by the formidable silhouette he cut. His suit was black, crowned by a silver tie that made his eyes nearly unbearable to meet head-on. So I stared at his chest instead, noticing a ruby-red corner pocket.

"How are you feeling?" he asked as I descended the final step.

A quick, disinterested glance in his direction was the only response he received. In silence, he extended his arm for me anyway. As we exited through the manor's main door, flecks of rain fell from an indigo sky and I shuddered.

It was colder here than in the city. My teeth were chattering within seconds, lending an eerie backdrop to the howling wind playing through swaying trees. Where exactly were we?

Dublin provided no explanation. Using my grip on his arm, he guided me down a paved stone path toward a circular driveway where a car waited. A new driver stood at the ready, and I felt more disoriented than ever.

"Where are we?" I finally asked.

While I couldn't see Dublin's face from this angle, I recognized the subtle clenching to his jaw just fine. I wasn't the only one capable of giving the silent treatment. Fine.

Biting my lip, I withheld any further questions as he guided me into the back seat of the car and climbed in beside me.

He leaned forward to mutter something to the driver and the man nodded, flicking a dial on the console. Then he sat back, staring in any direction but mine. It wasn't long into the drive that I realized we weren't far from civilization after all.

Though one very different from the world I'd grown up in. Judging from the few street signs we passed—all written in the same obscure language—I seriously doubted that we were still in the country. Beautiful renaissance-style architecture cemented that suspicion. Buildings framed in Romanesque columns, and ruby tiled roofs cast a surreal atmosphere, almost as though we'd stepped back in time.

"Can I ask where we are now?" Awe colored my voice, but I struggled to swallow my irritation as Dublin remained silent. The hostility between us felt as palpable as the heat flooding the car's interior from the vents.

Later, I'd let myself mull over the fact that he must have requested as much for my benefit—it wasn't like he was the one shivering. At the moment, I didn't even bother to thank him but stoically faced ahead.

Until the driver finally pulled up before a grand building made of tan stone, built in a stunning mixture of classic and renaissance architecture. My mouth fell open. As Dublin circled around to my side of the car and helped me out, I still gaped.

"I plan on meeting someone here." He finally spoke, lowering his mouth to my ear as we joined a throng of beautifully dressed patrons queuing up to enter the building. "Stay close to me."

The venue was a theater—a fact that became obvious the moment we passed through the grand entrance and entered a lobby draped in hues of red and gold. It was a luxurious sight far beyond that of even the vaulted theaters my family frequented.

Without bothering to stop near the box office, Dublin led me up a set of stairs, draped in scarlet runners, that deposited us within a secluded hallway. Gilded doorways lined it, shrouded by hanging ruby curtains. Near the very end of the corridor, Dublin pulled me through one, revealing a small, enclosed space with a breathtaking view of a circular stage below.

It was a private box. Four red velvet chairs lined in gold were positioned near the balcony. Placed on each cushion was a cream-colored program revealing the details of tonight's show—written in the unknown language.

"Have a seat," Dublin commanded, pulling out the nearest chair for me. "He should be here soon."

He didn't look very excited for this meeting. I wasn't the sole reason for his thunderous expression, apparently. Though before I dared to ask, his clenched jaw warned that he wouldn't divulge any details of our mysterious guest. Rather than press him for any, I busied myself with perusing a program I couldn't even read.

Eventually, Dublin settled onto the chair beside mine, and beyond us, the theater began to fill. One by one, nearly every seat became occupied with a beautifully dressed patron—all but the two empty ones beside us. By the time the curtained entrance to our box finally shifted, the main lights had already begun to dim.

The man who entered—with a chilling smile and blood-red hair—was a vampire. I knew even before his grin widened to reveal sharpened fangs. A poisonous chill proceeded him, setting every nerve in my body on edge. In his wake stood a tall, blond woman wearing a floor-length navy gown. A thick strip of black velvet obscured her throat, forming a fashionable choker, and a matching headband held the curls back from her face. But the style only enhanced her lifeless, glassy eyes as they drifted aimlessly around the room.

"Dmitri," Dublin said gruffly. He stood and shook the hand the man had extended in his direction—but his shoulder flexed as if he were applying far more strength to the gesture than protocol called for.

"Dearest Dublin! I was surprised to receive your invite." Surprisingly lilting, the other man's voice betrayed a distinct accent. Russian? "And I must say that I'm even more intrigued to find you have your own guest. I was intending to share." He gestured absently toward the blond.

She staggered, giggling at nothing.

"There's no need to share tonight," Dublin said, but even I didn't miss the subtle warning in his tone. He extended his hand to me and I took it—but even I had enough sense to realize that it wasn't a loving gesture, but a possessive one.

"Relax, Dublin," Dmitri urged with another hearty chuckle. "Do sit. We have so much to discuss. You as well." He gestured to an empty chair and snapped his fingers before his companion's nose.

The dazed blond stumbled forward and obediently claimed the seat beside him. At the same time, a hum from the orchestra warned that the show was starting.

The four of us watched in unnatural silence as the curtains lifted and the actors took their places. It was an opera. One performed by singers who bared their souls upon the stage —but it wasn't the typical tragedy.

A young girl lamented her fate—doomed to love a man she could not have. Her anguish easily translated the language barrier, and I could follow the plot as easily as if someone were whispering it to me in my ear.

Her lover belonged to a faction far beyond her station. Their love was all but impossible, yet he had been willing to forsake it all.

For her.

Together, they escaped and were even blessed with a child along the way.

But ultimately, their romance was doomed.

A man her lover cherished like a brother tracked them down. Unwilling to accept their union, he slaughtered the woman and her unborn child, leaving her lover to mourn them alone.

And plot his revenge…

By the time the final scene before intermission drew to a close, I felt chilled to the bone, my throat dry. Even Dublin sat unusually stiffly, his gaze fixed on the stage. Something told me that this particular production had been chosen specifically.

For him.

"Marvelous! Marvelous!" Dmitri exclaimed, clapping his surprisingly slender hands. "They were going to perform a ballet," he added as the lights returned to full brilliance and the curtains drifted shut. "Something about a swan. I casually slipped the director some inspiration, however." He laughed, his teeth glinting like ivory in the orange glow of a hanging chandelier. "Dublin has always nursed a fondness for the arts," he told me with a wink. "Theater. Music. What was that phrase you used to spout? *'Music is the only damn thing humanity possesses worth saving.'* He was a different man back then though, called by another name."

I shuddered in remembrance of it. *Cael.* A creature even Saskia had feared.

"I hope I've impressed you both," Dmitri added, fingering the collar of his scarlet suit.

"It's entertaining. That's for damn sure," Dublin replied. His tone was anything but impressed. He sounded uneasy.

Feeding off the grim emotion, I shifted, uncrossing my legs. Re-crossing them. I couldn't keep still. Dread formed a physical pressure, crushing my stomach. More cramping? I brushed one of my hands against my belly, just for a second —but even as I drew it away, Dublin had already snatched my wrist.

Casually, he settled my hand against his lap instead.

"So, what has brought you here?" Dmitri wondered, eyeing us, a smile playing on his red lips. "All the way to *Italia*. I know you prefer the States—"

"Remember that favor you owe me?" Dublin interjected.

"Ah…" He nodded. "And how is the dearest Yuliana?"

"Consider this a collection call," Dublin hissed, ignoring the question. "You want to remain in hiding? Well, my friend here has a morbid fascination with vampires. In fact, she's too curious for her own good. You know more about our kind than anyone. So, *humor* her."

"Lies," Dmitri scolded with another hearty laugh. His eyes glinted, a mysterious mixture of brown and green. "I'm surprised it's taken you so long to try and weasel out my many secrets, old friend. But you've never expressed an interest before. Especially not after my 'exile.'"

"*I* have no interest," Dublin insisted. "However, my companion has a rather naïve outlook on our condition. Her innocence amuses me, but I've grown tired of having to humor her questions. Enlighten her."

It was a dare. One Dmitri seemed more than willing to accept.

He shifted in his seat to offer me his hand directly. As pale as snow, his palm glowed in the soft lighting. I eyed it, motionless, until I sensed Dublin's gaze on my throat, issuing a silent command. *It's okay.* But when I finally placed my fingers within Dmitri's, his clamped over them in a vise grip.

"Such a sweet girl," he murmured, his smile widening. "Where on Earth did you find her?"

"Don't talk to me," Dublin snapped. "You answer her."

"V-Vampires seem…n-nice," I managed to croak in the silence following their banter. Mentally, I berated myself for sounding so damn naïve—but then I felt Dublin nudge my shoulder. *Keep going.* "D-Do you get married?"

"Marriage? Oh, she is darling!" Dmitri chuckled in amusement. With deft grace, his fingers skimmed my palm and I shivered.

He felt even colder than Dublin.

"Marriage is a very human concept, my dear," he explained in an almost fatherly tone. "When you've lived as long as we have, something as trivial as a ring ceases to hold any true value. There is much more stock placed in loyalty. Obedience. Isn't that right, my darling?" He glanced at the blond, but I doubted she'd even heard him. Had she been drugged? If so, something told me that the poison in her veins wasn't what most women used to chase a high.

Her dreamy smile concealed the taste of something a bit more…organic.

"What about children?" Dublin wondered offhandedly. His expert skills of manipulation were on display, steering the conversation while he still feigned disinterest. "She's mused on that before."

"Has she?" Dmitri's eyes snapped in my direction so quickly that I recoiled. "What a strange question, my dear." As he spoke, his frigid fingertips continued to stroke my hand, and it took everything I had in me not to yank it back.

"I… It's just something I saw in a movie once," I stammered. Not a total lie. In the early days of my self-imposed loneliness, I might have decided to torture myself by renting every vampire-based movie known to man. All of them. "Can vampires—and humans—have children—"

"Of course not." He released his grip, allowing my hand to fall. "At least nothing that I could dare call a 'child.'"

A cold, icy feeling resonated through my stomach. "How…how so?"

"It would be an abomination, my darling." He flicked his fingers to dismiss the mere idea. "A nonviable creature. There have been stories, terrible things." His eyes sought mine, gleaming with callous amusement. "Thankfully, such creatures are rumored to have mercifully died within the womb. And there is almost always a curse within play, those nasty things. Why, any of my kind foolish enough to even *attempt* to sire a living child would most surely forsake his eternity."

"Forsake?" I asked in a whisper.

Beside me, Dublin was stone. Had he known any of these rumors? I couldn't tell from his expression—hard and unreadable, stone once more.

In a sense, I probably resembled him. I couldn't breathe.

"He'd become forever damned." Dmitri shrugged. "A creature doomed to never die, no matter how the world may decay around him. A terrible bargain, I'm sure. Especially in exchange for such a twisted parody of nature. Oh, I wouldn't trouble your pretty little mind with such horrors." He mimed shooing away an invisible fly. "Best to not even think of such things."

"Oh." It was all I could say—just a gasp disguised as something intelligible. Twisted images filled my head before I could block them out, giving vivid life to his brutal imagery.

Death. Dying. Deformed.

"Though Dublin would know better than I," he added, chuckling. He inclined his head at the man beside me. "Right, old friend? After all, I believe that Mero was the first to—"

"Don't," Dublin warned, sitting forward. "Do not mention him."

"Ah." Dmitri rubbed his hands together with barely concealed glee. "We still aren't allowed to say his name, I see. Not even his given one? Oh, well. His little friends certainly seem emboldened these days. I hear even the bothersome Gray girl has taken a side for once. Either that or vanished. The *other* one, of course." He eyed me pointedly, his lips quirked. "Georgiana, I believe her name is?"

"Side?" I croaked. Something in how he'd emphasized that word…

It terrified me to my core.

"Well, I'd consider it more like a lack of objection, one might say. Though it could be as the rumors claim and the poor girl has simply disappeared, gone without a trace—"

"Enough," Dublin bellowed. "This isn't the time for your mind games."

"Mind games? I'm sure *you* learned the truth well before I did, what with your network of little spies. *Mine* told me that you were on your way the second your plane landed. And while you didn't bother to introduce your guest, I know *her* name well enough." His head swiveled in my direction. "Eleanor Louise Gray, the second-to-last living heir in the entire Gray line, barring her uncle of course. My my, Dublin, you didn't think to tell her that her own sister has signed her death warrant? That is rather cruel, even for you."

"What?" The room bled into formless color around me. Only Dublin's face held any real definition—his mouth strained, his eyes turned away.

"I said *enough*," he growled.

"Pity. I could tell her so much more." Dmitri lifted his hand to my cheek. "Such a pretty little thing—"

"You touch her and I'll kill you." Dublin didn't even look like himself anymore. Hunched forward, he radiated an ageless power, every bit as commanding as Raphael.

Dmitri's smirk never wavered, but he shrank back, contritely bowing his head. "I meant nothing by it, Dublin," he simpered. "The rumors have buzzed with how much of a liking you've taken to her. I wouldn't *dream* of harming her—though I do wonder how long it will be before…"

"Before what?" Dublin hissed.

"Before the owner of her bloodline comes searching for his little toy. They've followed you here, though I'm sure you know that. I don't think they even know why they need her dead. Mere soldiers following orders. *His* orders. How ironic that her sister may have volunteered to carry them out—"

The room spun as their conversation divulged into distorted noises and hushed voices. Nothing mattered but a single thought I couldn't suppress. Georgiana wanted me dead?

Or…she was missing.

"…must ask why you care about this one anyway?" Dmitri added, his voice regaining clarity. "Everyone knows that you kept an unusual interest in the other one. Such a beauty. If I had to place money on which woman you might desire, it would be—"

"Eleanor!" Dublin reached for me as I knocked the chair over in my rush to stand, hitting the floor on my hands and knees.

Air clawed its way into my lungs as I hauled myself upright using the wall for balance and threw myself between the gap in the curtains shielding our box.

The hallway beyond was deserted. Spinning and distorted. No matter where I looked, all I could see was endless red. It dripped from the walls and coated the floor. Drowning me…

Fabric snatched at my hands as I ran, feeling along the wall, desperate for a door, an exit. Anything. In the end, I staggered into an empty box and spotted a vase of roses. I ripped out the flowers by their stems, lowered my mouth over the neck of the vase, and—

Watery liquid erupted from my throat. The force of each wretch brought me to my knees, and it was all I could do to clutch the vase to my chest and heave.

I cringed into the shadows as heavy footsteps approached my corner and someone drew the curtain back.

A lingering chill lowered the atmosphere, identifying the intruder as clearly as if he'd shouted his name. But he said nothing, advancing toward my corner with broad strides. He crouched instead, sweeping my hair back as another wave of vomit spilled into the vase. When my stomach finally had nothing left, he took the vase away.

"Don't," I pleaded when his hand brushed my shoulder. I scurried out of reach as if burned. My face found the safety of my palms and I hunched into myself, too tired to keep the tears at bay. "Don't touch me—"

"Eleanor, look at me." He sounded too soft. Too gentle. "Look at me—"

"I can't take this." My voice bordered on shrill, alarmingly high-pitched. Broken. I couldn't get enough air. My lungs were deflated, impossible to fill. God, I needed him to leave—only then could I break. "Get out! Just leave. Get away!"

"You're hyperventilating. Breathe!"

"Stop!" My hands muffled the plea, but I couldn't look at him. "Just leave me alone. Please. Leave me alone. I can't… I can't take it anymore—"

"You can't? I knew that very first day," he gruffly admitted. "That first day when you met my gaze, completely unafraid. I knew." Heedless of my plea, he remained, still restraining my curls. "I knew you'd torment me to no end. I knew that you would thwart even my most well laid plans. I knew then and there that one encounter with you would never be enough."

His voice was deeper than ever. Gone were the harsh bravado or bitter anger. This was Dublin Helos in a way I'd rarely experienced him.

Open and honest.

Yet I wanted to scream loud enough to drown him out.

"Please, go—"

"I'd met your sister before you," he continued. Even level, I could never overpower the gritted cadence of his voice. "A beautiful creature. If there were any Gray doomed to tempt me, it would be her..." He trailed off, and nausea constricted my throat as I imagined everything he'd held back.

Him with Georgie, laughing at my naivety. Stinging tears fell without restraint, but in a sick, twisted way, there was peace in the agony. Finally—*finally*—he was telling me what I'd wanted to hear all along.

The full truth.

"I've avoided your kind throughout the centuries for a reason, the Grays, but...something made me confront her directly when she grew bold enough to challenge Raphael," he continued, unconcerned as I shook my head in a silent plea. "I expected... She was beautiful, yes, but she aroused me no more than any other beautiful, talented soul I'd traded for centuries. In a way, I pitied her—the most interesting creature to spring from your bloodline since James and I was immune to even her charms. Still, I decided that selling her to Raphael would be a waste, so I intervened. Her dowdy, plain sister would make a useful pawn, but it would be for her benefit in the end. In one fell swoop, they'd both be spared, and I would have the last laugh over a creature I'd grown bored of serving. My plan was infallible—until I saw *you*."

His voice lowered to a hiss. Me, Eleanor Gray, the bane of his existence. So infuriating that he couldn't even refer to me without rage constricting his voice. He grabbed my wrists, wrenching me upright, tearing my shield away.

I closed my eyes instead. Facing rejection was easier this way. If only he would just get it over with. Stop twisting the knife.

"I get it," I insisted. "I've always gotten it—"

"Do you?" His voice dripped directly into my ear, preceding the sensation of ice brushing my earlobe. His mouth? "I saw you and I experienced an irritation unlike anything I'd ever felt. This pathetic mortal woman had the nerve to spite my plans through sheer stubborn denial. Rather than come to me begging for life, you shrugged me off. Turned away. *You* looked me in the eye and merely scoffed at what I was— even your sister hadn't done that." He sounded more incredulous than impressed. "No...you were determined to spite me, even then, and I knew... No one could imagine such a doom."

The coldness of his finger swiped at my cheek, brushing away a fresh wave of tears.

"And even now you'll still deny it. I all but tell you out loud and it's as though you slam your hands over your ears, childishly refusing to hear it. Then I push you away and you react as though you're the one who has been wounded. Regardless, I am a fool."

The stark admission startled me into opening my eyes. He looked so hollow, Dublin. A frown replaced his polished persona, his eyes narrowed. Gingerly, he brought his hand to the side of my face, tilting my jaw for his inspection.

"I am...sorry," he confessed, but the words lacked true sympathy. It was almost as if he wasn't used to saying them. In real time, he was relearning how to feel something as simple as empathy. "For doubting you. For hurting you—"

"You didn't!" I scoffed. "You're trying to get inside my head —you're always inside my head!"

And I wanted to rip my hair out in frustration. My fingers curled, nails drawn, and I started to raise them, but he renewed his grip, stepping forward in the same smooth motion.

"Let me go," I hissed.

His eyes flashed, and I waited for a cruel retort. He lowered his head instead, brushing his mouth against my forehead. Shock paralyzed me—his end goal.

"You're in no state to be alone," he murmured against my flesh, but his tone made me recoil. Soft again. Deceptive again. He sounded too much like he cared. "That's why you are this way."

"I'm always alone," I pointed out, my voice hollow. "Always. Even my sister…" I couldn't even say it. "And I'm dying, and I'm scared, and I'm alone. I'll always be alone—"

His mouth found my lips, sealing them with a single motion. I faltered, flicking my tongue against his. It wasn't fair. His taste teased my senses, a tempting drug, potent enough to take the pain away.

It hurt. My heart. My head. I couldn't focus on everything Dmitri had said all at once or I'd go insane. I *was* going insane.

"Look at me." He gripped my chin, tilting my head back, and met my gaze. His tongue traced his lower lip, reminding me of a predator wondering where to strike first on vulnerable prey. "You asked me once, why someone like me might be attracted to someone like *you*." He brushed his thumb against my mouth but nothing more.

I inhaled raggedly, wanting…needing. Something. Anything.

As if aware of that, he angled himself even farther away from me. "I suppose that's part of your appeal. Your innocence. You don't even know what you do to me, do you?"

I bit my lip as our gazes connected. His burned, impossibly bright.

"Your smell. Your taste. You pretend that I bought you from Raphael to rescue your delicate soul from any other, but deep down, you know the truth: I wanted you for myself."

"Lies," I croaked. It was all I could say.

And he laughed. "What did I promise I'd do the next time you countered me?" He pretended to mull it over, stroking his chin, even as he advanced.

I held my breath.

With deliberate slowness, he fingered the delicate silk over my shoulder. Then he tugged, easing the fabric down until my breasts threatened to slip free. "I said I would strip you naked."

I watched in slow motion as my dress continued its guided descent. I didn't recognize my body anymore. Flushed pink with arousal as if coming to life for him alone. Even as my mind was in turmoil.

Even as the world shattered beneath my feet, I belonged to him.

"And you questioned..." He shook his head, eyeing me the way one would a feast. Someone starving—but there was a flaw with his meal. Frowning, he grazed my cheek with his thumb, smearing the tears still streaming down it. I could see his thoughts shift—lust becoming pity. The contrast made my head hurt.

So I lunged forward, risking my balance to reach for the fastenings of his pants. "I don't want to think," I confessed as he stiffened. "Please. I don't need coddling or sympathy. I just want..."

Sensation. His mouth on mine, his hands between my legs, delivering a dose of pleasure so potent that I'd shudder, arching wantonly into his touch.

Grays did not perform or require physical acts of comfort. We endured. "A strong inheritance is the only embrace you ever need," my mother used to say.

So he didn't hug me. He merely held me close instead. Close enough for me to cling to the front of his suit as though I were drowning. Close enough to bury my face against his chest and smother whatever sounds I made. I was shaking—that's why his arms tightened around me, keeping me there, keeping me from completely breaking apart.

His hand caught my throat, but there was no violence in the gesture. Guiding me to face him, he met my lips with his. Chilling. Frozen. Distracting. My arms went around his neck, drawing me further into the kiss. Sloppy, bruising, skin against teeth.

I needed more. Only this could make the harsh interior of the theater and the agony in my chest disappear. Only he could make it stop. With more pain—his teeth grazing my tongue. His hand plunging between my legs.

More. More. More.

I rocked my hips into every touch, not giving a damn for anyone around to hear the groan that tore from my lips. It clashed with the opening lines of the orchestra. The opera was continuing, somewhere in another realm that felt eons away.

In my world, there was only him. Ice and fire. Skin and silk, twisting, rubbing, claiming.

Dublin.

"Please," I croaked as he withdrew. My fingers shamelessly reached for him, clinging to whatever they could. "Please, I need you—"

He stood and snagged my wrist to haul me upright after him. One shift of his weight shoved me against a wooden sideboard pressed against the wall. It held only a vase of roses, which he easily batted aside. Then his hands gripped my hips, hauling me onto the smooth surface while he forced his bulk between my legs.

I spread them easily, allowing him to peel back the sleeves of my dress. My body spilled out from the silk, eager for his touch, and he devoured me with ravenous, groping hands.

My nipples stiffened for him, roughened by the merciless sensation of his chest against mine. Our mouths reconnected. Devoured. Fabric tore. Cool air assaulted my skin, preparing me for ice as he undid the fastenings of his pants. The flat of his hand caught my lower back, dragging me closer as he lunged, entering me in one thrust. Hard. Brutal. No mercy.

No care.

Just need that outlasted the soreness from the last time he'd taken me like this.

A scream caught in my throat, smothered by his palm. My head fell back. All I knew was pleasure and pain as I let my eyes close and rode every deep, punishing thrust.

With every one, I clawed at him, demanding more, more, more. Everything.

Only he had the power to erase my mind.

All I had to do was feel.

All I had to do was fall.

But even the Devil couldn't extend the violent descent from Heaven.

Eventually, we both crashed, breathless and senseless. His mouth was on my neck. My hands were clutching fistfuls of his suit jacket, but even buried inside me, crushing me with his weight, he wasn't close enough. His presence couldn't snuff out the fear. The guilt. The doubt.

"Look at me." He caught my chin in his palm, forcing me to meet his gaze.

I saw nothing there but silver. It blinded me just long enough for him to shrug his suit jacket from his shoulders and draw it around me. There was no one in the hallway beyond the private box as he helped me from the sideboard and pulled me out after him.

Any usher we passed said nothing but a cheerful greeting, and the rest of our surroundings blurred as he led me through winding corridors, then out into fresh air. Eventually, we entered his car.

The driver pulled off without a word, returning us to that secluded manor in the hills. I wondered if he owned it. I wanted to ask. Something trivial. Something mindless that might devolve into pointless small talk. My lips sprang apart, but by then, he was already hauling me out onto the curb and up the front walkway.

The door opened automatically, held by an unseen figure. I could only make out a blur of formless features before I found myself being dragged up the stairs. Into my bedroom.

There, in the darkness, he shoved the jacket from my shoulders, leaving my body bare. One bruising kiss robbed me of my senses. Then the mattress struck the back of my legs before he shoved me onto it fully.

Another kiss stopped time, kept eternity at bay.

I moaned, arching into every touch, every stroke, extending the barrier between reality.

Silk and ice became my world.

The only thing that mattered was feeling.

As long as he stayed.

Sleep was the one realm Dublin couldn't follow me into, and alone, I traversed a hellscape of memories with nothing to shield myself from the pain.

Shadowed specters watched me, peeking from beyond a darkened veil. Only snippets of their faces were ever visible, but I knew their identities well enough.

Georgie. My parents. Death.

They all taunted from the abyss, cackling at my attempts to chase them away. But sprinkled in between their insults was a cruel truth that never ceased to echo.

Deformed.

Abomination.

Unnatural.

I startled awake, but reality was just as unwelcoming: a labyrinth of twisted sheets threatening to suffocate me. My fingers fanned out desperately, finding only empty, frozen space. Alone, I writhed, screaming my throat raw—but no real sound came out. Just gasping, broken whimpers. Sobs. Cries.

Despair weighed on my chest, crushing every ounce of air from my lungs.

I couldn't breathe.

"I'm here." Cold fingers caressed my spine, banishing the terror. Their owner rested beside me, and his mere presence was enough to keep the darkness at bay.

Tension drained from my limbs as gulps of air entered my chest. Drifting from my back, his hands cradled my hips, pulling me against the firmness of his body.

But the contact wasn't enough. I squirmed until his grip tightened and comfort became possession. Grasping fingertips. Scratching nails. I was a slave to whatever he could make me feel.

Pain. Misery. Mercy.

Anything.

I craved it all.

And much like the doctor he pretended to be, he delivered each necessary dose. In his arms, hours unfolded like seconds. I endured them in a daze, aware of him leaving only long enough to let me catch snatches of sleep or to shove food into my mouth.

Eventually, I started to refuse even that much.

But my Devil persisted, unwilling to see me in Hell just yet.

"Eat."

I cringed as he pressed something to my lips despite how hard I pursed them shut. Then I rolled onto my side to escape him, but he merely circled the bed, remaining in my line of sight. Balanced on his hand was a steaming plate, but I felt nothing even as the smell tickled my nose.

"Eleanor, eat."

I shook my head, eyeing the ceiling in lieu of his darkening expression. "I'm not hungry."

"You're starving." He matched my apathy with aggression, his tone bordering on a growl.

But I couldn't muster up the fear to heed him.

Numb, I buried my face against a pillow. Exhaustion preyed on my psyche, warning that sleep would come for me again. I didn't even have the strength to fight it.

"Look at me." He fisted his fingers through my hair, forcing me to face him.

For the first time, I noted how these hours had changed him. His eyes glowed, his fangs hanging freely.

Yet he still played pretend, trying once again to tempt me with a morsel stabbed on the end of a fork. "Eat."

"Why?"

His throat jerked, but his lips trapped the answer. *Because you'll die.*

"I'm fine."

"Look at me." He reached for my arm, but I didn't mean to swat his hand away. The plate fell from his grip anyway, smashing into pieces at his feet.

"I'm sorry," I whispered, closing my eyes against the mess I'd made. Guilt slipped through my numb armor regardless, heralding dangerous, whispered thoughts. Desperate, I tried to banish them, gritting my teeth in concentration. *Don't think. Don't.*

Nonetheless, Dmitri's words echoed in my skull anyway. *Deformed. Dying. Horror.*

I hunched away from them, clinging to the sheets, craving oblivion again. But already, Dublin wanted nothing to do with me.

He stood, crossing the room to snatch up the broken pieces of a porcelain plate. The sight of his back was a familiar one, all things considered. But God…not now.

My voice broke. "Don't leave me—"

"I'm not," he hissed even as he approached the door and wrenched it open. His gaze met mine as he crossed the threshold, honed like a knife's edge. "But you *will* eat."

The door slammed in his wake, but my boneless limbs kept me from chasing after him. I crawled to the edge of the mattress anyway. I was that pathetic. I'd fallen *that* far. His nearness alone could keep the thoughts at bay. The fear.

I would have done anything to extend it. Anything.

The sound of his returning footsteps made me tremble with relief. When I looked up, I found that he held more food. This time, a platter of apple slices, cheese, and fresh fruit.

"Eat," he commanded, stopping short just beyond my reach.

I squeezed my eyes shut. In vain, beads of moisture escaped, clawing down my cheek. "I can't…"

"Look at me."

The gritted cadence of his tone held sway. I obeyed just in time to find him brandishing a knife in his other hand. Naked, his skin gleamed like marble, and it seemed laughable that anything could hurt him. Even the blade he dragged across his collar bone.

Crimson bubbled up in a single line, painting him in gore like a true predator. After stalking closer to the bed, he set the tray at one end of the mattress and then lifted an apple slice.

He brought the red end of the fruit to his wound, letting his blood taint the apple's ivory flesh. Then he lowered the offering to my lips, ignoring how they twitched in defiance. "Open."

It wasn't fair. My body craved pleasure—distraction—but my mind only wanted an escape. Oblivion. A drop of his blood could serve both purposes.

Aware of that power, he taunted me, pressing the fruit more firmly against my mouth. "Eat."

A drop of moisture grazed my lip. Burning. Tempting. Sweet.

My tongue darted for it, rebelling against my pride. When he threatened to draw the apple away, I finally pried my jaws apart.

"Good," he murmured as one reluctant bite became two.

I licked my lips, ready for more. Even the hint of his blood was...

Explosive.

Warmth blossomed in my veins, battling the chill persisting in my heavy bones. With a burst of renewed energy, I drew my knees up to my chest and sat upright as my thoughts clouded, deliciously dizzy. But nowhere near high enough.

Thankfully, he already had another apple slice in hand. Fresh blood painted its milky interior, and I didn't require coaxing this time.

"Good."

The guttural praise resonated in my skin as his free hand cradled my cheek. He used the contact to tilt my head back and fed me another slice. Then another. With every tentative swallow, his thumb stroked my jaw in a rewarding caress.

I wasn't sure how much I ate before I finally refused the next morsel, legitimately full. In silence, Dublin removed the platter from the bed and set it down in some distant corner of the room.

I watched him, uneasy again. I should have been high on cloud nine, giddy and detached from the world. But I wasn't. Reality remained way too close. Even his blood couldn't push it away for very long.

"Lie back," he commanded as if reading my mind. "Trust me."

Confused, I fell against a pillow, eyeing the ceiling. The slow thud of his footsteps matched my pulse, quickened by the second. Only it ceased amid a growl as his hand caught my thigh so he could drag me to the edge of the bed with no warning.

Panicked, I grabbed at the sheets, nails drawn. "W-What are you doing?" I tried to sit up, only to be rewarded with a sharp pain that flared along my knee. His fingers, pinching ruthlessly in warning.

"Lie back."

In my weakened state, I had no hope of denying him again. My spine went limp, forcing me to crane my neck down just to see him. Like a true predator, he crouched at the end of the mattress, his head lowered as his hands pinned me in place, pressing down on either thigh. Aware of me watching, he hovered there as if tracking my pulse through feel alone.

A jealous creature, he hoarded my every reaction to him— every breath to scrape from my throat. The twitch of anticipation racking my spine, impossible to suppress.

The soft moan that escaped as his fingers bit down, melding his touch with the slightest hint of pain.

His eyes flicked up to mine once, conveying a silent warning: *Surrender.* Then he lunged so quickly that I could only *feel* him driving between my legs. My eyelids fluttered at the alarming mixture of sensations—not his hands. Not the part of him I'd barely grown accustomed to feeling inside me, either.

This newer, deadly heat came like a lightning strike. So sharp. So potent. My brain struggled to match sight with feel… Only as I saw his head rock in time with the relentless pressure could I finally give his weapon of choice a name.

His *tongue.*

Thoughts scattered. Fears vanished. As if injected with a lifespan's worth of his blood, I transformed, a greedy, broken creature. Senseless, I could only watch. Gape. From a handful of romance novels, I knew what he was doing. Something every bit as vulgar as the act I'd performed on his plane.

But he didn't lick, too coy to avoid naming the act in his head. His tongue battered me open, sowing friction with every taste. Fire. Lying still was impossible—I writhed as if my spine were a string.

And he ruthlessly tugged with every stroke. Nothing was sacred to him, no place beyond his reach. My Devil dove into my soul, taking whatever he could claim and sowing discord in his wake.

He was sin.

And I was a corrupt, lost soul desperate for damnation.

My fingers curled, clutching the sheets to their breaking point, until the sensation changed. Deepening. Thickening. His finger? His *thumb*. Pressing, pushing, swirling.

A slave to every motion, my back bowed urging him closer. Closer. Closer. Too senseless to beg, I tried to demand more, lurching forward to grasp at his hair. Impervious to pain, he shrugged my attempts off and continued his exploration at his own leisurely pace.

My pleasure was at *his* discretion—not mine. As if to prove as much, he captured an aching bit of flesh between his teeth, threatening to bite. I jerked, my back bowed so violently that the top of my head was all that remained on the mattress.

Lost in his hell, he refused to allow me to come down, pushing me higher and higher with every sharp, pinching nip—but I wasn't the only one lost in the onslaught. His savoring groan reverberated through my flesh, and I shattered.

Stars prickled behind my eyes, punctuating explosions of pleasure as they ripped through every muscle and nerve.

Drugged with the million different reactions, I faintly heard him mutter, "Refuse to eat again and I'll never…"

He didn't say what. Nonetheless, the threat resonated, paired with the violent, dangerous note in his voice. So I ignored it all and focused on feeling. On breaking. On flying.

He coaxed me so, so, so high.

Then let me fall and watched my descent with glowing eyes.

Even panting and breathless, I knew when he pulled back from me. My body ached, desperate for more. I *needed* more.

The mattress dipped beneath his weight before I could mourn his absence in full. One of his hands cupped my waist, drawing me into him, as the other caught my skull. While he pinned me in place, he made me suffer a different form of contact. Another first.

Intimacy.

But sex I could stomach. I could pretend, once I woke up, that none of it had meant a damn thing.

Not this. Nestling my face into his chest, still panting, felt ten times more addicting. More dangerous.

Not even the headiest drug could compare to the haven of his embrace. He could desolate me with *this*.

But I was too weak to resist the destruction.

And he was cruel enough to know as much.

~

Cold. That was how I awoke. Cold and sore. Hungry and lonely. It was like being transported to only a few days ago and nothing in the world terrified me more than having to relive that reality. Solitude. There was only one cure and my fingers scoured the sheets in search of it.

Dublin.

I found nothing, not even when I peeled my eyes open to an empty room bathed in the gray glow of dawn.

Fear unlike anything else shredded me to my core. A sick part of me welcomed it. Misery was what I really craved. What I needed to feel. I could chase a reprieve all I wanted, but this…*this* was my fate.

Abandoned once again.

Perhaps this time he'd left a note behind? I scanned the room, finding only a gray robe slung over the end of the bed. When I climbed off the mattress and pulled it on, I realized the door to my room was ajar as well. Once in the hallway, I made out the faintest notes of music and hope guided my motions, a pathetic lifeline.

I followed the sound, creeping down the stairs and through a maze of rooms until I reached one at the very back of the house. Contained within was a lone piano placed before a row of bay windows. Devoid of curtains, they displayed an unobstructed view of a small garden overrun with sprouting roses.

Hunched on the bench was a figure wearing only a pair of wrinkled black pants. I'd never seen him so disheveled. So...tired. His bare torso caught the light, displaying the numerous silvery lines speckling his skin. Scars was too ugly a word to call them. Merely...decoration, deliberately chiseled there by whatever artist crafted this stunning creature.

The moment I stepped foot within his domain, the music ceased on a single plaintive note.

"You were sleeping," he said without turning around. The emphasis he placed on that word betrayed another meaning —*sleeping* free from nightmares, for once.

A part of me recognized the words as his reason for leaving. Which felt...odd. Even odder was that some of the irrational fear eating through my chest abated.

There was a word for women like the one I was becoming. Clingy. *Needy.* My mother used to gossip about a socialite she'd known once, who'd actually had the gall to take offense when her husband's work hours grew from days into weeks. *She has his estate. Why should she care?*

Perhaps because poor Mrs. Perriweather suffered from the same irrational darkness that plagued me? The fears lurking within the shadows of her psyche, threatening to swallow her whole if someone—anyone—wasn't there to keep them at bay. All they had to do was stay, just long enough for her to find herself again.

However long that might take.

This feeling was temporary, I was sure of it. So why couldn't I cross the threshold until he beckoned me closer?

My hesitant footsteps were quickly swallowed by the notes of music that rose to a crescendo as he continued to play. I'd misjudged his skills as simply *good* before. Talented. Only now could I appreciate the full wealth of emotion he layered into every single note. He didn't look down at the keys once as he sat with his posture erect and his eyes on the window. He didn't merely play. He *bled*.

He never stopped, even as I perched myself on the end of the bench. I wasn't sure who closed the distance first. Which body shifted to bridge the gap. All that mattered was that my head was on his shoulder and I huddled into the contact while his fingers still flexed to stroke the keys.

"What song?" I asked as softly as I dared.

"Something Puccini," he explained. "*Vissi d'arte,* I believe. A bit dramatic for my tastes, but it gets the point across."

"The point?"

"Here." He grabbed my hand, manipulating my fingers where he wanted. With quiet motions, he guided me to strike the keys in tandem, and the melody continued.

I suspected that a million answers to my question lurked within the tune spilling out around us. Including what Dmitri himself had hinted: *Music is the only damn thing humanity possesses worth saving.*

Closing my eyes, I tried to listen—but nothing rivaled his voice and I was too greedy to deny myself it. "What does the title mean?"

He hesitated, the music faltering slightly. "'I lived for art.'"

"What is it about?" The mixture of sharp and low notes conveyed longing. Pain.

"In short?" He inclined his head and ceased playing altogether. "*Nell'ora del dolore.*" His mouth grazed my throat, allowing his voice to enter my ear, lowered for me alone. "*Signore, perché me ne rimuneri così?*"

He sat back, continuing the melody unassisted. Something warned me against pressing him for clarity. Not yet. I listened instead, somehow sensing the meaning in every strained tone before he translated, his gruff baritone melding with the music.

"In this hour of grief... Lord, why do you reward me thus?"

His tone barely wavered, yet he conveyed the passionate plea effortlessly. The pain. The desperation. Did he truly feel that way? Or was he merely interpreting the agony written into the music?

I watched his fingers fly across the keys. My teeth tore at my bottom lip, but I barely felt the pain. Sighing, I leaned against him, sensing him shift to support me.

"I'm afraid." My voice fell to a whisper, nearly swallowed as the music swelled. "I'm so afraid. I don't want to die."

He had been wrong about my supposed death wish.

I wasn't ready.

The music slowed, becoming an array of scattered notes, seconds apart.

"You will."

I flinched at his tone, but his fingers drifted through my hair before I could interpret it as an insult.

"Sadly, I'll be there to witness it, I suppose. When the time eventually comes. In fact, I imagine it to be a rather boring affair, given your track record." He cocked his head as if picturing the moment and sighed in disappointment. "Oh yes. You shriveled in old age, laid out in your precious little manor, irritating me until your last breath. Predictable until the very end."

My lips twitched into a painful expression. A smile? "Who said I'd even let you in through the front door?" I croaked. "I *do* have standards, you know. I'd prefer my mourners sniffling and tearful if you please. Not smug and irritating."

"Tearful?" He nudged my jaw with the pad of his thumb, eyeing me with an eyebrow raised. "Hopefully not from boredom. Did you not hear my first request?"

A sound ripped from my chest that I recognized only as he started to play again. A laugh, hollow and broken. But real nonetheless.

And it chilled me to the bone that he had the power to conjure such a reaction from me at all.

A SMALL FAVOR

I startled awake at the exact moment the melody died in a jarring array of clashing notes. Beside me, Dublin lurched to his feet as footsteps raced in our direction.

"What is it?" he demanded.

I turned, following his gaze. An unfamiliar man stood in the doorway. Dressed in nondescript black, he conveyed the readiness of a soldier.

"There's someone at the..." A thick accent made it impossible for me to discern the rest of what he said, but Dublin hissed through his teeth.

Before my eyes, he transformed—a monster again. "Are you sure?"

The man nodded.

"Eleanor." Dublin didn't even look in my direction. "Get upstairs. Now."

Standing, I drew my robe around me with one hand. Dublin headed through the doorway and I followed in his wake, moving straight for the staircase.

I nearly missed the figure strolling boldly across the foyer to meet us. Blood-red hair would have rendered him striking —even without the vibrant emerald-green suit complementing the color of his eyes.

The vampire from the opera house. Dmitri.

"I suggest you let her stay, Dublin," he said, his upper lip quirked. "Considering that what I have to say concerns *her* more than it does you."

"Move." Dublin lunged, all but dragging me up the remaining few steps. "Get to your room—"

"I know it was rude to intrude," Dmitri continued, unaffected by our retreat. "Especially considering how much effort you put into your protection. It might amuse you to know that you weren't *quite* as discreet as you thought. As always, the rumors precede you."

Icy hands met my shoulders, pushing me down the hall. He didn't even waste energy on words this time. The command was clear. *Go!*

"But never in a million years—and I think you'll appreciate the joke—would I have expected this. Did you really think I wouldn't notice?" Dmitri wondered, sounding legitimately amused. "That thing growing in her stomach?"

The world shifted underneath me, and I staggered to a stop, clinging to the wall for balance. Behind me, Dublin went rigid, his grip a vise on my forearm.

"I'm surprised you risked bringing her to me directly," the man below added, raising his voice for our benefit. "Then again, I do remember your rather possessive nature. Regardless, I knew the moment I saw her just *why* you'd sought me out after all this time. It certainly wasn't to humor her with trivial stories."

"Get out."

I risked looking over my shoulder again as Dublin released me and advanced toward the mouth of the staircase. I only caught a glimpse of his expression from my position, but I recoiled at the sight. His eyes practically glowed, a chilling shade of silver.

Soulless.

"I could hear its *heartbeat*, Dublin," Dmitri crooned, his voice trembling. "A marvelous sound if you know what to look for. Steady. Strong. This is all so very interesting that I couldn't resist flaunting your rather elaborate security."

My thoughts swam aimlessly, desperate to process two words. *Steady. Strong?*

"What do you want?" Dublin demanded, snapping me from the confusing turmoil.

"I want…merely to satisfy my own curiosity," Dmitri said. Excitement bubbled from him. He sounded on the verge of laughter. "It's not every day that such a rare case study lands upon one's lap. And it isn't every day that a man who once proclaimed a lack of a soul goes through so much trouble to protect a mortal woman—"

"I would assume that you more than *satisfied* your curiosity already," Dublin interjected. "You chose your words carefully, didn't you? Knowing just which wounds to prod. Did you want to shatter her mind the way you break the rest of your toys?"

Dmitri's reply took seconds to reach me, deceptively demure. "All right, I admit it. Perhaps I was *exaggerating*."

"Exaggerating?" My voice broke as something snapped inside me. Something raw and violent that made even someone like Dublin Helos an insignificant obstacle in my path. "Why do you care?" I was halfway down the staircase before I knew it, stopped only by a single icy grip on my arm. "Why? You said that…that…"

"That you were carrying a deformed, doomed, worthless creature?" He blinked his multicolored eyes just once. "Well, it's simple, my dear. I lied."

Red. That's all I saw. All I could taste. Anger. Rage. Blood.

Now I knew how Dublin could switch from man to devil so easily.

Madness.

It was the only word capable of describing it. Poised, quiet Gray girls didn't give into fits of hysteria. We seldom launched ourselves down a staircase toward a creature who could easily break our necks with the strength in his pinky. We never shouted—and certainly not the tumult of words spilling from my throat. I couldn't even decipher them all, just one plaintive howl that echoed incessantly off the walls.

"What do you *mean* you were lying?"

"Eleanor, stop!" A grip of steel cinched my waist, lifting me from the ground. I resisted senselessly, my legs kicking at nothing. "Stop!"

When I finally felt the floor again, I swayed, unable to keep my balance. All I could do was cling to the nearest source of stability within reach—firm, frozen flesh. He held me, even as the tears spilling down my cheeks painted the flesh of his chest.

"What does he mean he was lying?" I couldn't stop demanding it. Screaming it.

"I won't let him hurt you," Dublin insisted, his entire posture possessive.

But it was far too late for that. *Hurt* was the only way to describe it—being yanked from one extreme to the other within the span of only a few days. From despair, to numbness, to…hope?

Hope was the most bitter of the three to swallow. The most painful. I choked on it as Dmitri's chilling laugh resonated off the walls.

"Look at me." Dublin captured my chin, commanding my attention. "Five minutes. Give me five minutes."

He cut his gaze to my bedroom door and I knew instinctively what he meant. Five minutes to reestablish control. Five minutes of secrecy with the man who seemed to relish in mind games designed to drive me insane.

Five minutes of *trust*.

When I finally stopped shaking enough to stand on my own, he let me go. Watchful, his gaze tracked my every tortured movement as I entered my bedroom and closed the door behind me.

Five minutes.

I could have lingered, straining for every snippet of their conversation like an eavesdropping child. God knew I wasn't above the action. But...

I turned away, observing the room clearly for the first time since returning from the Opera.

Crumpled bedsheets covered the mattress I'd barely left in three days—but telltale signs revealed how someone had done their best to take care of me. There was an empty glass on the nightstand, once containing the water they'd urged me to drink in my stupor. Another pillow rested beside mine, utilized by someone who didn't even need to sleep. He had shared the cold bed with me anyway.

My throat tightened with too many emotions to decipher at once. After everything, the least I owed him was five damn minutes. But then what?

"I lied."

"I lied."

I couldn't focus on what that confession might mean. I decided to shower instead. Hours of despair clung to my skin, more unbearable than any stench.

I found an adjacent bathroom and drew a bath as hot as I could stand it. A groan tore from my lips as I sank beneath the rushing liquid. It felt good. It *felt*. Ignoring my five-minute deadline, I took my time, washing my body with some lavender-scented soap and a washcloth I'd found in a cupboard.

Without observing my reflection, I ran my fingers through my wet hair once finished and then redonned the robe.

By the time I returned to the foyer, it was well past five minutes. Regardless, Dublin waited for me at the bottom step. He was still wearing only the black pants. Nonetheless, he appeared as imposing as ever. His gaze roamed my body in silent scrutiny, tracing the contours of the robe. If he didn't approve of the outfit choice, he didn't say so. When I held my hand out, he took it, drawing me to his side.

As we advanced down the hall, his clenched jaw betrayed a warning. *Be on your guard.*

Dmitri was waiting in a small sitting room, holding court from a leather chair positioned near a curtained window. "Allow me to apologize, my dear," he said to me. The amusement flicking in his eyes contradicted the contriteness of his tone. "I had no intention to startle you."

"You didn't?" I'd never known how disdainful I could sound. Not even Dublin had drawn that snarl out of me. "Then what was your intention?"

His smile widened. "To test a small theory." Uninvited, his gaze cut down to my stomach and I found myself obstructing his view with the flat of my free hand.

"What theory?" How to drive a woman insane with as little effort as possible? Because as much as it confused me to admit it…

I'd gone insane. Only now could I climb out from the chaos of my own thoughts and see the smoldering ruins for myself. Days spent in bed clinging to a vampire for emotional support. I didn't know whether to laugh or cry. Cry perhaps?

Because those three days had been the first time in my life that I'd ever had *anyone* to drain for emotional support. Like a leech, all irony aside.

And more baffling, Dublin had let me take every last drop I'd needed.

Shame flooded my cheeks, setting them on fire as I glanced at him beside me while he glowered as stoically as ever.

"What theory did you want to test?" I finally demanded of Dmitri.

He raised a reddish eyebrow while stroking his hairless chin. "A hunch," he said vaguely. "The truth is that your condition is rarer than you realize. There are only rumors, many of them…disturbing." He smiled. "Though I am now positive that dear Dublin knows better than any of us—"

"Don't," the man beside me warned. "Peddle your lies again and I'll rip your tongue from your mouth."

"As you wish." Dmitri nodded, lifting his arms in a gesture of surrender. "Frankly, I understand your skepticism. Such is the nature of hearsay, you see. More often than not, you'll find it circulates merely to serve a certain advantage. Much like a rumor being murmured about *you,* dear Eleanor."

The line of my mouth tightened in foreboding anticipation. I had enough sense to recognize a dangling carrot when I saw one. No doubt, another "exaggeration" would serve as the punishing stick should I take the bait.

So I said nothing, yet his grin took on a more satisfied tilt.

"Some speculate that you might be in possession of something… Let's just say something *intangible* worth more than you can possibly imagine."

An answer came to my mind instantly. A prize tempting enough to spark the greed even Dmitri's cool grin couldn't disguise. *Ten years.*

"Dmitri…" Dublin's tone deepened well beyond a warning.

"Well, yes. Anyway, while the information is scarce, I've always had a fondness for tracking down the sources of any rumor to catch my ears." He clasped his hands together, balancing them on his knee. "It just so happens that I stumbled across a few tidbits of information that might interest you about your current condition."

"How do I know you're not lying?" A better question might be why my voice broke over the thought of it. Answers, good or bad. Ignoring my "cancer" until now had been a foolish, childish whim. I could see that.

But could I stomach the truth?

Dmitri sighed and reached into the breast pocket of his suit jacket. "Easy," he warned as Dublin stepped between us, shoving me behind him. "I bring gifts, as promised. A bit of light reading."

When Dublin didn't rush to disarm him, I assumed whatever he was holding must have posed some semblance of legitimacy. Skirting the formidable body before me, I observed his offerings.

Two slender leather-bound books. They looked old, more worn than Dublin's mysterious Gray family tome. Yet as the light reflected off their stained covers, I couldn't suppress a shiver.

"You sense it, don't you," Dmitri murmured smugly. "Knowledge that our beloved Raphael wouldn't dare allow to circulate that Den of yours. I am more than willing to share of course." He withdrew the books slightly beyond my reach. "For a price."

"And now you can leave." Dublin placed his hand over my spine. In that simple touch, I sensed a silent promise—*This isn't the end. I'll find another way.*

"So soon?" Dmitri chuckled. "Dare I say I'm not surprised. One could only expect you to be skeptical. Perhaps I can divulge a glimmer of what I've learned? Something tells me that you've already gleaned that small detail involving fresh blood?"

I flinched, betraying the truth, and he nodded. "Ah... There's more, of course," he said, his tone suddenly serious. Narrowed in thought, he flickered his gaze to Dublin. "But first, I have to ask. Very few events could trigger such an occurrence from what I've read. Dear Dublin, tell me that you didn't try breaking your little rule for her, did you? Forget your little hang-up about feeding from a live host, but to go a step further—"

"I warned you once about your lies, did I not?" Dublin said so softly that I shuddered, fingering the edges of my robe.

"Lies, yes," Dmitri admitted. "But this is just a mere question." He took a step forward, honing his gaze on my throat. Whatever he saw made him frown and that simple expression transformed him entirely. Gone was the sly intruder. He resembled a scholar mulling over a puzzling mystery.

And somehow that made him more intimidating than ever.

"You haven't fed from her in a while," he mused aloud. "For all your loathing of the act, you must have feared for her life, I suspect. I'd heard Raphael tried feeding from her. That could… But that wouldn't explain why she didn't die. No. Though if you *did* try to turn her—"

"Enough!" The bellowed command resonated through the manor's foundation, and I found myself bracing my hand against Dublin's shoulder.

"Don't!"

He swiveled his head in my direction, eyeing my fingers coldly, but the tension in his body eased just enough for me to breathe again. For whatever reason, I sensed that the contact had kept him from lunging.

"And I will take my cue to leave." Still smiling, Dmitri bowed. "Such a shame that we couldn't come up with some kind of agreement," he lamented as he headed for the entrance of the room. "What a shame. I had so hoped your child might survive unharmed."

I staggered an involuntary step toward him. "Wait!"

Obediently, Dmitri lingered.

Dublin simmered. "A word?" He took my arm, dragging me into an adjacent room.

The door slammed behind us, rattling in its frame, as I found myself spun around, forced to face him directly.

"Listen to me." Something within his gaze made goosebumps creep over my skin. Unease. Wariness. Those rare few emotions he only displayed in the presence of Raphael. "You do not want to play his game," he warned. "Yulia was right. I should have never even—"

"I need answers." It sounded like such a pathetic contrast to his caution. As if answers could ever change what a part of me already knew deep down.

Some things you couldn't change. Studying the sordid reasoning behind them didn't make the truth any easier to stomach. Yet, at the same time, ignorance could be unbearable torture.

"I need answers." I couldn't disguise the bleating, pleading note in my voice. But the longer I observed Dublin's face, the more I realized that I might not have been the only one desperate for a lifeline. "I will admit that I don't know your history," I added. "But please. This isn't cancer. I…I don't want to pretend anymore. So, you can gut him like a fish with your bare hands when this is over, but I *need* answers."

"Should I be on my way?" Dmitri called from across the room. A glance over my shoulder revealed him standing in the doorway, observing his right hand with dejected interest. "I suppose I must—"

"Wait!" It terrified me, how desperate I felt. Desperate enough to beg. I reached for Dublin's hand, squeezing it so tight that I was sure, despite his superior strength, he still felt the pressure. "*Please.*"

Like always, his blank expression gave me nothing to cling to. I floated in uncertainty for what felt like an eternity. Then…

"What the hell do you want?" He advanced on the other man, using my grip to tether me behind him. "No riddles. No games. Just lay out your terms. Now."

Once more, Dmitri seemed to drop the carefree act. His eyes found me again, sparkling with undisguised interest.

"I merely want to observe," he said. "And conduct my own research. Why should these ancient bastards"—he hefted the journals—"have all the fun, eh? To put it a bit more bluntly, I simply want to come along for the ride."

If anything, that response made Dublin stiffen further. Remnants of winter emanated from his gaze, freezing me down to my core.

Wisely, Dmitri seemed well aware of the delicate line he was toeing. "And I'll even play nice," he insisted. "No mentions of the past—for now. *And* I wasn't even lying when I mentioned that little bounty on her head. I'll even go further and share another tidbit of information—they fully intend to collect on it. Soon."

He let the word hang there, gauging my reaction, which— surprisingly—was more subdued than Dublin's. I simply stared at him as my brain struggled to process the reality. While the man beside me nearly broke my hand.

"Damn." He released me, forming a fist. I swore I heard bone crunch and meld within the span of a second—he had clenched his fingers *that* tightly.

"The funny thing is he is more than aware that his human soldiers can't harm her as long as she's under your protection. Oh, Mero—I mean, *he of whom we will not speak*." Dmitri made finger quotes as Dublin snarled in warning. "You remember how he loved his deception? His games? Though he preferred poison over intrigue. Oh, the things that man could do with poison." He sighed as though reliving a cherished memory. Then he cleared his throat. "So, if he truly wanted her dead, she would be. Therefore, her death isn't his main goal, for now at least. Which means his ultimate plan is a bit more abstract. In fact…the sister is missing, correct? I'm sure he knows the value of that life to her." He nodded toward me. "Oh, come now, don't you see it? He's deliberately trying to provoke you—"

"Enough." Dublin didn't shout that time, but the low, raspy baritone seemed to reach even deeper, clawing open the part of me that recognized the beast he truly was beneath his flawless skin.

"And I'd wondered why," Dmitri mused, completely unperturbed. "I admit that I had to rack my brain for quite a while to come up with the solution. After all, why come out of hiding after so damn long? Raphael is of no interest to him, and we know how much he craved his peace. But then, if I may be so cliché, the answer appeared right in front of me."

He stepped closer, grazing my cheek with an icy finger. "Was that his one condition to end that bitter war between him and your master? Stay away from those under his ownership. But you couldn't resist, could you? No, after years of atonement, you *dared* to defile one of his precious, sacred Grays. Though I'm sure that was his plan all along."

A hand brushed my hip, knocking me off-balance, and I found myself staggering out of Dmitri's reach. Dublin stepped forward, filling the space I'd left behind.

"Touch her again and I'll keep the arm," he promised as casually as most men might comment on the weather. "And the next time I choose to hunt you down to whatever corner of the world you've run to, you'll owe me more than just a favor."

"Fair enough." Dmitri met the cold expression directed his way with a surprisingly chilling one of his own. "But now, down to business." He clapped his hands, all smiles once again. "When do we leave? Dare I request we take my jet? It's climate controlled—"

"Is there a point you're trying to make?" Dublin countered.

Dmitri blinked. "Why yes, I suppose I did forget to mention that particular detail. Those friends of yours... Well, they've decided to launch an attack here, on this very estate you think no one else knows about. Right...*now*."

As if to accent his words, a sudden barrage of noise resonated in the distance. Shouting?

"Go get dressed." Dublin shoved me toward the stairs and I didn't hesitate.

Once in my room, I snatched a dress at random from the closet and pulled it on while staggering down the stairs. I had to have been gone less than a minute, yet Dublin was already dressed, appearing by my side as if from thin air.

"Stay close." He took my arm, tethering me to his side as two armed men came from the shadows to flank our position. His calm demeanor warned me that they worked for him.

Had they been here all this time, lurking out of sight?

"I see you decided to play him at his own game," Dmitri remarked. He grinned, apparently entertained by the air of urgency. "Using your own human pawns. Certainly creative if not necessarily prudent. May I suggest again that we take my jet—"

Dublin pulled me forward, and within seconds, we were exiting from the front door. I didn't know what to expect as I took in the scenery waiting beyond. Weak daylight filtered down through storm clouds, adding a silvery sheen to the breathtaking landscape—but despite Dmitri's warning, there was no one else in sight.

Apart from Dublin's driver standing at the ready.

Not particularly hurried, Dublin guided me into the waiting car and the driver sped off. Every now and again, however, he spared a wary glance at the figure seated beside him.

Somehow, Dmitri had insinuated himself into the passenger's seat. Occasionally, he decided to provide casual commentary. "Again, I must insist we take my jet."

Dublin seemed murderously determined to ignore him, glaring from the window instead. Eventually, we reached a remote area where the hills gave way to grassy lowlands and desolate fields. In the distance, I made out the shape of a building on the horizon. An airport hangar?

No sooner did the thought cross my mind before—

Light. Noise. *Bang!*

A tremor rattled the earth. I screamed as the driver swerved severely to stay on the road. Dublin flung his arm over my hip, pinning me in place until the motion subsided. Just as the driver righted himself, black clouds began to billow over the horizon. Smoke. Soon after, tendrils of orange flame licked at the sky as if alive.

"Well." Dmitri delicately cleared his throat. "I suppose it's a welcome coincidence that I had *my* private jet moved to a lesser known runway not too far from here. Isn't it?"

BLOODY HELL

Dmitri's climate-controlled private jet proved to be surprisingly…cheerful. In a contrast to Dublin's monochromatic color scheme, tanned leather created a cozy backdrop, punctuated by hints of elegance. Like the grinning, glassy-eyed flight attendant already on board, waiting to serve crystal flutes of champagne.

Ignoring her, Dublin marshaled me into a recliner-style seat by a window and claimed the one beside me, effectively serving as a barrier between me and his "old friend."

Dmitri didn't seem to mind. He unfurled himself into a seat near the back of the cabin, grinning like a well-fed cat. Something told me that turning our back to him at all was a risky endeavor.

But Dublin consumed my sole focus, and I couldn't spare an ounce of concern for anything else. Tension radiated from him in waves. I suspected little was due to Dmitri's presence. No…

My heart raced as I brushed my hand along my front, watching the fingers settle against my stomach. Panic danced on the edges of my conscience, urging me to deny. Ignore. Pretend. Facing the truth of my "tumor" terrified me more than anything in the world.

More than Dublin.

More than Raphael.

The mere possibility shattered my safe, cautious mind state. I'd been groomed to spend most of my life alone, sans even human children.

But now?

The thought of another reality terrified me. Almost as much as the threats building against it.

"Who is Mero?" I whispered, still eyeing my splayed fingers.

Dublin flinched, but he'd had long enough of a reprieve from the question.

So had I.

Though perhaps we both were no match for the topic in the end. After all this time, I'd thought I'd witnessed the full spectrum when it came to the emotional range of Dublin Helos.

Anger. Guilt. Rage. Pity.

But the expression contorting his features now was unlike any I'd ever experienced. Pained.

"One might call him the *founder* of the Grayne," he rasped in a tone devoid of emotion.

Not for the first time, I truly understood the vast gap between us forged by more than mere age. Sheer *centuries* of distance. He looked eons older in the space of a heartbeat. Ancient.

"I thought you said my ancestor James was the leader of the Grayne?" I remembered as much from his impromptu history lesson delivered the night before my fateful meeting with Raphael.

Though, to be fair, that was all I knew about this mysterious order that had consumed part of my family. Any attempt to pry a single bit more from Georgie had been met with deflection and stonewalling.

Until we both couldn't take anymore.

"He was," Dublin said. "Mero was…let us just say the catalyst to your predecessor's sudden fervor when it came to hunting my kind. In the grand scheme, Mero knew that his human pawns would be all but useless against a foe like Raphael. You were merely a vehicle."

"You knew him?"

"I did." And that was that. He closed up. Turned to stone. Something told me that even bringing up our contract now wouldn't get him to soften to me again on the subject.

So I changed tack. "How did you know? About the blood," I clarified. It was something that had always bothered me beneath the surface. Perhaps I hadn't admitted it to myself until now. "That I would have to…"

"You were dying," he said simply. "You claimed that food held no appeal. In the name of saving your life, I took a risk and decided to… Let's call it thinking outside of the box."

"And what about *your* blood?" I observed the bluish veins twisting beneath his skin. "You told me it wouldn't work anymore. That it couldn't heal me."

Yet here we were. His blood had already saved my life ten times over since his return.

"And," I added as something else rose to the forefront of my thoughts, "it used to overwhelm me. I would be out for days, but now…"

"There is something I need to tell you." He turned away, staring beyond the luxurious cabin into a world I could never follow.

Biting my lip was the only way to brace myself against whatever he might reveal. But I was no match for his touch; he captured my hand, swiping his thumb across the palm. And just like that, I was disarmed.

"That day Raphael fed from you. His venom hurt you, didn't it?" he asked without meeting my gaze. "More than as just a mild discomfort."

"Yes…" I cringed at the memory. One bite and it had felt as though my insides were melting around me even as my heart struggled to beat. "But yours didn't."

"That's because he killed you."

I looked up in confusion, but he still faced away from me. Purposefully, I realized. Whatever tinged his gaze now, he didn't want me to see.

"I… What do you—"

"Your heart stopped beating," he explained, as detached as though reciting a well-known tale from heart. At the same time, his fingers tightened, holding mine firmly captive. "I heard it. I saw it. You were gone before I could even reach you. And in that moment, I had to make a *choice*." His voice grated over the word, conveying more than the usual definition. *Choice.* Something life changing. Life altering. "You wouldn't understand. There was no time to think. No time for hesitation. For once, I was—" He broke off and released me, but he didn't pull away. His fingers formed an open cage, almost as if he expected me to recoil first.

For whatever reason, I forced myself to stay.

"What choice? What did you do?"

When he didn't respond, I eyed my naked fingers, too numb to process my emotions. Was I horrified by the potential answers? Shocked?

"Let's just say I pushed your body beyond its limits and I nearly killed you in the process. All for nothing, because I failed anyway."

I swallowed hard, too uneasy to even press for answers. Did he overdose me with his blood? Give me too much venom?

"But I'm still alive," I pointed out before swallowing the lump that had risen to my throat.

"Yes." He sighed, deflated of all tension. "You came back. Still breathing. I assumed I'd made a mistake. Perhaps it was the venom? The why didn't matter. I decided to leave in search of answers. In my absence, I ensured the necklace would protect you."

"But what you told me was a lie, wasn't it?"

Its purpose hadn't been solely to keep me alive.

"As long as you wore it, I could find you," he admitted, finally lifting his gaze to mine. "No matter your location."

Deep down, maybe I'd known that. In some ways, it had been easier to let myself pretend my survival could be so simply insured—a magic necklace slipped around my neck just in the nick of time.

But in his world, *nothing* came without a price.

"I didn't realize my miscalculation until I tried feeding from you," he admitted, referring to the night I'd found him at the church. "You reacted violently. Not to mention that you were weak. Malnourished and… When your *cancer* was discovered, in a way, I wasn't surprised. Merely by attempting to change you, I had unknowingly encouraged a new breed of 'life' to take root. Mero always did have a rather ghoulish sense of humor."

I exhaled sharply in a poor excuse for a laugh. It was a morbid joke, even for a vampire.

"I know it was wrong to deceive you." He reached for my hand again, and a part of me scoffed, eager to write him off. But he had never sounded so raw before. *So* open.

And for whatever reason, I couldn't pull away.

"Why didn't you tell me?"

"How could I?" He laughed darkly, shaking his head. "When I didn't even understand myself?" He eyed me warily and reached out with his thumb. When I didn't cringe, he brushed my cheek, lingering against my skin. "I still don't. Years of servitude to that bastard, yet he's never toyed with me. Toyed with *lives* just to test me. Not like this."

And perhaps that fact alone was Raphael's driving motive.

But trying to understand the man at all made my head throb. I cradled my palm against it, rubbing my aching temple.

"I need time to process this," I said softly. "I just… I need time—"

"I understand. But there is one thing you mentioned that I would like to explore in further detail." He cocked his head, his eyes narrowed. "What did Raphael say when he gave you my contract?"

I sucked in a breath. "He said that if I helped him prove something, he'd give me what you bargained for."

"Damn him." Lurching to his feet, Dublin transformed once more into stone. Ruthlessly focused, he scanned the length of the cabin until he eventually found Dmitri.

The other vampire was seated in the same spot, balancing the giggling flight attendant on his lap.

"Do you have an ability to communicate with the ground?" Dublin demanded. "Where?"

"A satellite phone, of course." Dmitri inclined his head toward an alcove at the very back of the cabin.

Without a word, Dublin crossed over to it, leaving a trail of rage like a storm cloud.

"I hope you ring lovely Yuliana," Dmitri called after him, smiling sweetly. "I do so hope to see her." As he turned to me, his grin widened. "There is no use in torturing yourself, dear. Come sit with me." He patted the space beside him.

"No, thank you." I crossed my arms, fighting to keep any of the turmoil ripping through my heart from showing on my face. "I'm fine."

Accepting defeat, Dmitri sighed. "Suit yourself. It's much harder these days to make this old voice carry far, but I suppose I must try. If you want answers, I am willing to trade."

Trade. The way he'd said the word almost reminded me of Dublin—full of mysterious innuendo. And I knew better than to take any bait he might offer.

"I know more than you realize," Dmitri added. "Like the fact that you are hungry. That you've been starving yourself and your child for far too long. That if you continue to be so reckless with your health, the results may be disastrous."

"Helpful advice, considering you claimed it was an abomination," I snapped. But as Dmitri raised an eyebrow, I realized I was shielding my belly with both hands.

"Ah, but that is where you misunderstood the meaning of the word, my darling." He chuckled once and leaned back against the leather cushions of his seat. "*I* am an abomination. As are Dublin and Raphael. Powerful, unfathomable creatures are always glitches in the grand design, or so I choose to believe. I will admit that even I do not understand the nuances of your predicament. Why would you require blood, for instance, when from what I can tell, you are persistently mortal? Perhaps the requirement is meant solely to mock him with what you may never become? Ah, but who could envision such a cruel torment?"

With that, he turned his attention to his giggling flight attendant and nuzzled her throat. Then he wrenched her head to one side and—

I turned to the window and didn't dare take my eyes off the view until Dublin returned. He occupied the seat beside me without a word, resolute in whatever mood had been building in him since the moment Dmitri had arrived.

It all had to do with that name. The figure who had driven us out of the country and was no doubt awaiting our return.

The man who seemed to want me dead, though I didn't even know why.

Mero.

"*E*leanor."

A gentle pressure settled over my shoulder, jarring me awake. Blinking, I gradually pieced together my surroundings. Somewhere small. Darkened. Confined. A car—*his* to be exact. Dublin himself was driving, and a glance at the back seat revealed that Dmitri was nowhere in sight. I was sitting up front, slumped within a leather seat, my head propped against a firm, muscular forearm.

"We're in the States," Dublin explained while manipulating the steering wheel. "Not far from the city. It's been about an hour since we landed. I didn't want to wake you."

Oh? I scrambled upright and peered through the windshield. Dawn painted the horizon in a mixture of pink and orange hues.

Already, I could sense my body protesting the change in time zone. Exhaustion weighed my eyelids down, and my stomach rumbled, voicing its displeasure at having been denied a solid meal in nearly a week. An unwelcome reminder, Dmitri's warning invaded my thoughts.

"If you continue to be so reckless with your health, the results may be disastrous…"

Gritting my teeth, I banished him with a shake of my head. "Where to?" I asked Dublin, steeling myself for another whirlwind journey.

Another high-rise? Another distant country?

"Somewhere safe," was his reply.

He was still wearing the same black suit, his hair only slightly mussed from the journey. I eyed his expression, hunting for a clue to feed on. A frown. A raised eyebrow. Anything.

The man didn't even blink, remarkably closed-off.

"What about the books?" I didn't spy them in the car anywhere. "And answers. And what if—"

"I'm handling it," Dublin gently insisted. "You've been through a lot. At least allow yourself a few days to readjust —in fact, consider it nonnegotiable. I promise arrangements have been made in the meantime."

Yet not even five minutes later, he parked and exited the vehicle without waiting for me. Or a word of explanation. Frozen with shock, I gaped after him, struggling to process our destination.

"Safe?" I hurried from the car, craning my neck to eye the structure before us in disbelief. "Here?"

As though Gray Manor wasn't what loomed up ahead, Dublin leisurely strode to the front door.

"Trust me when I say that I can protect you here as well as I could anywhere else."

But there was a caveat to his statement, I suspected. One betrayed by the subtle clenching of his jaw. This newfound protection had come at a price.

One he refused to reveal as he opened the door and ushered me inside with a wave of his hand.

"You have nothing to fear," he insisted as I hesitated beyond the threshold.

I wasn't sure if the words were meant to be comforting. They weren't, considering that everyone from my sister to her mysterious club apparently wanted me dead. *Plenty* to fear in all respects.

Returning here at all—especially after what had happened in the crypt—felt like slathering myself in butter, ready for the slaughter. I eyed Dublin's neutral expression as doubt strained my worn, battered nerves. My trust felt all but indebted to him after the way he'd cared for me. Yet…

"Trust me." He reached back for me as his eyes met mine again. The stoic grip on his emotions wavered, allowing a hint of softness to ease the stiffened corner of his mouth.

"I've ensured your protection. Not even a spider could enter without my permission."

His confidence soothed my fear just enough for me to mount the front steps after him. Once we crossed the threshold, the house didn't transform into a horrific trap at least. No monsters sprang from the shadows to attack. In fact, the dour interior greeted us with little fanfare, and any fear quickly turned to suspicion.

"You've had people here," I accused.

In my absence, someone had cleaned the drafty foyer and figured out how to restore heat to the house. In honor of the dreary, overcast day, a fire roared in the drawing room, basting my skin with heat as he led me past it.

"I'll have them stay out of sight," Dublin proposed with the air of a kindly benefactor humoring his bothersome charge. "I wouldn't dream of standing in the way of your apparent independence."

I swallowed hard, biting my lip. Just how much of my month in self-imposed isolation had he deduced so far?

"Given how long you've survived without your staff, I'm sure you don't even require a maid anymore," he added.

Ah, *that* was a definite jab.

"You're wrong," I snapped. God help my instinctive impulse to needle him at every turn—though he had asked for it. "I am an *heiress*, after all. Whoever shall bathe me, and clothe me, and put me to bed?" I did my best to channel my mother, who would have pointed out those very dilemmas in horrified indignation. "Why, look." I wiggled all ten of my fingers, pouting. "I have delicate hands."

"Is that so?" He seized my wrists. A ruthless tug brought me closer to him, rendering me at the mercy of his gaze. "One of your defining attributes," he murmured, turning his attention to the prized hands in question. "Worthy of protection. So, from now on, I suppose I will be the one to bathe you, and clothe you, and put you to bed." His serious tone cast doubt on if he truly intended the proposal as a joke.

Laughing, I shrugged as though unaffected. "Via one of your contracted proxies? Kate, perhaps?"

He blinked. "Naturally, only I would ever be permitted to touch you. Such an important heiress couldn't be trusted to the care of just anyone."

My heart seized and I took the tiniest step back. Running away was my first, cowardly instinct. He could have this round. I had no trouble admitting how poorly unmatched I was in this arena. Nothing in my pathetic verbal arsenal could counter the sensual gleam flicking across his gaze.

But then I remembered just how sinful his touch could feel. One dose of those sordid memories banished all logic.

"Well, I do own your contract," I blurted, my face heating. "It's about damn time I put you to work, isn't it?"

"That you do." The grit in his baritone resonated down my spine. I'd barely processed the lust contained within it as he stepped in even closer, forcing me to crane my neck just to maintain eye contact. "Though, frankly, Eleanor, you've been rather lax in exerting such ownership. No commands to do your bidding. No humiliating assaults on my autonomy. I have to wonder…do you even have it in you?"

I shuddered, recognizing both the dare *and* the threat he'd posed in one go. Did I have the gall to command him? Would he really listen if I tried?

And if I didn't take the bait, could I stomach the million terrifying questions still looming overhead? My decision took mere seconds to settle upon.

"I…I'm hungry," I croaked, jutting my chin into the air. "Make me something to eat. *Slave.*"

"As you wish, *mistress.*" He released me and inclined his head. "What would you like?"

"Baklava," I blurted, recalling how the old chef used to despair whenever my mother had requested that particular dish. "From scratch."

He crossed his arms, unimpressed. "What else? Surely you want more than just a dessert."

"Spaghetti, then," I countered. "With meatballs *and* homemade noodles."

"Interesting choice." He nodded in earnest. "What else?"

"Baked Alaska." I was just being ruthless now. "And some fish. I prefer to have it gutted, descaled, and filleted in front of me."

"As you wish. Shall we?"

He grabbed my arm and steered me into the old servant's alcove. While I watched, he made several calls in rapid-fire succession. Each one progressed way too quickly for me to make out much. When he finally hung up, I found myself dragged into the kitchen, where he shoved me onto a stool and then proceeded to hunt for supplies.

Had I been inclined to help him, I honestly wouldn't have known where to begin. He didn't seem to require much assistance as he fished various pots from the cupboards and pulled utensils from drawers. If anything, the bastard seemed a tad too confident in his actions, as though he knew my kitchen far better than he should have.

Not long after, a courier appeared, laden with groceries, and Dublin spread out his bounty over the countertops. After shedding his suit jacket, he set to work. Begrudgingly, I soon realized that my impromptu menu had been ignored. In lieu of pasta and tomato sauce were fresh apples and vegetables, some of which I'd never seen, and a loaf of delicious-smelling bread.

"Should I have you whipped for your insolence?" I wondered as I sat forward, propping my chin on my hands, enthralled by the sight of him.

Who knew the big, bad contractor could make for a capable domestic?

Oblivious to my thoughts, he remained intent on his task. His fingers flew from ingredient to ingredient, sorting them as he went.

"I decided to exert a bit of creative control," he confessed without a hint of guilt. "Your nutrition means more to me than fear of your legendary wrath, oh *mistress*."

I let the taunt slip by unchallenged, unwilling to explore the unfamiliar sensation lancing through my chest. Instead, I peered at the assembled ingredients with a frown. "Well, what *are* you making?"

He reached into a brown paper bag that had yet to be unpacked. From it, he withdrew something wrapped in butcher's paper—a large, completely whole fish. After selecting a knife, he proceeded to slice off the creature's head. As his gaze met mine, something that might have been amusement lifted the corner of his mouth. "You'll see."

I crossed my arms. "Fine."

Damn him. Watching him cook shouldn't have been nearly so fascinating. The man possessed an alarming skill with a knife. With unnatural ease, he chopped veggies, washed herbs, and shifted things from pots and pans. It wasn't long before a delicious aroma filled the entire room and I eagerly sniffed, lightheaded in anticipation.

Though, to disguise my interest, I made sure to sigh loudly at random intervals. "Does your sudden concern for my 'nutrition' mean no evening brandy, then?"

I was just being petty now, but Dublin was prepared for me.

From another paper bag, he fished out a bottle that resembled champagne at first glance. "Sparkling cider," he explained, setting the bottle down. "I wouldn't imagine denying such an esteemed heiress of her customary nightcap."

Touché, Mr. Helos. Resigned, I waited patiently while he finished. As he removed the final boiling pot from the stove, he looked back as if noticing me there for the first time.

"Shouldn't you be getting dressed for dinner, mistress?" he inquired, raising an eyebrow in mock surprise. "I wouldn't dare to presume that you eat in casual clothing like some common riffraff."

Apparently, he too was capable of channeling my mother from beyond the grave.

Throwing my head back, I performed a haughty appraisal of him with a sweep of my gaze. "How could I? My lazy servant hasn't offered to dress me yet."

"Ah, I beg your pardon." He stepped around the counter while wiping his hands on a dishcloth. "How unacceptable."

I stiffened as he advanced on my position step by dangerous step.

"Can you walk up the stairs on your own?" he wondered. "Or are your feet as delicate as your hands?"

A flame jolted to life in the pit of my stomach. As if fed by gasoline, it spread, feeding an inferno only he could ever spark. Nothing else affected me the way he could with a single searching look. Nothing except his touch.

"I…I can walk," I conceded, rising to my feet. I swayed. Finding my balance at all was a feat of sheer willpower on jellied limbs.

"Good." Dublin inclined his head toward the door with a gentlemanly nod. "After you."

I led the way to my bedroom, where I was alarmed to find that not only had someone cleaned it, but the door to my wardrobe was hanging open, mysteriously brimming with new clothing.

"Yulia works fast," I blurted, recognizing her handiwork in the delicate satins and artfully applied lace. A red dress in particular drew my eye. The moment my gaze settled over it fully, Dublin had already yanked it out by its hanger.

"Turn around and raise your arms," he said, manipulating the fabric in his hands.

"Shouldn't I be the one issuing commands?" I couldn't even muster up enough air to sound truly indignant.

"I am simply eager to serve."

A shiver ran down my spine at that chosen word. The hoarseness I thought I'd heard in it was simply my ears playing tricks.

"Arms." Impatient, he took it upon himself to spin me around. Then he tugged the zipper of my dress down.

Gradually, the fabric slid down my hips to pool at my feet. "Step."

Shivering from head to toe, I took two steps forward, freeing my ankles from the discarded fabric.

"Now…" His fingers fanned across my torso, radiating possession. "Hold your breath."

I looked back in confusion. "W-Why?"

He shook his head, but his fingertips flexed against me in silent encouragement. "Do it."

So I inhaled, trapping the air inside my lungs. While I slowly exhaled, he drew his hands up to my shoulders, smoothing the hair from my neck. A tendril of ice grazed the exposed flesh. His mouth? Nuzzling…

Just when the lack of oxygen became uncomfortable, he slid the new dress on over my head. The moment he drew up the zipper, I let my lungs expand.

"Why?" I wondered. The gown fit fine, even as my chest heaved frantically against the fabric. I was breathless—that was why I was panting. Of course that was why.

Rather than some pre-prepared quip, Dublin tugged on the dress, adjusting it. It was only when I turned to face him that he finally relented.

"I wanted to hear your heartbeat." His gaze was on the violet wall behind my head, his jaw clenched.

"And?" I rasped.

"It is…adequate." He met my gaze, holding it for so long that I felt senseless when he finally turned away. "Come and eat."

He made me sit at the dining room table while he returned to the kitchen. Moments later, he reentered with a full-blown meal on one of my mother's prized porcelain plates.

"Does this offering please you, mistress?" he wondered while placing a set of silverware before me.

He'd prepared fish in addition to an array of steamed vegetables and various side dishes too exotic to name.

Scowling, I took a bite, fully intending to lie. Unexpectedly, rich flavor broke my resolve, and I shoved in another forkful before I could stop myself. Another. In the midst of my chewing, Dublin pressed a cup into my hand. Aware of its contents, I did my best to choke down the warm, wet liquid before returning to his meal with vigor.

"Is everything to your liking?" he asked innocently, well aware of his victory.

A helpless moan tore from my throat as my unofficial verdict. It just wasn't fair. The man could cook like the devil.

Once I'd cleared my plate of every last crumb, he made a show of pouring the sparkling cider into one of the crystal flutes that I was fairly certain my mother had sold her soul for.

I took a sip. Made a face for the sake of putting up a front of displeasure. Then I drained the rest.

Barely concealing his triumph, he cleared the table while I stood. From this angle, he resonated a presence my childhood home struggled to contain. In the glow of the chandelier, his chiseled features stood out in harsh relief. Beautiful.

Unattainable.

Who are you kidding, Ellie? a part of me snickered. *As if he could ever want you.*

And maybe that vicious little whisper was right? I was halfway to the doorway when his voice reached me, low with warning.

"Where are you going?"

I lingered over the threshold without looking back. "To bed." My tone fell flat, deliberately stripped of innuendo.

All insecurities aside, sex within these walls was definitely *not* an option anyway.

My mother and father had lorded over this house once. Their prudishness was etched into the wood. Hell, even now, I could feel their judgmental eyes on me, casting shame for the way my heart picked up speed at the low, dangerous tone that reached me next.

"And have me risk another whipping?" He was behind me in an instant. His chill basted the back of my throat and my body reacted. Tightened. Tensed. Craved. "You are to be bathed and put to bed," he reminded, throwing my own words back at me. "Or do you not remember?"

I wanted to back down right then and admit defeat. He would always win when it came to games like this. Dangerous games. He was a man who'd staked his entire livelihood around sex. There was no way in hell I could best him in that arena.

It would be foolish to try.

Sighing, I tried to convey as much. "No matter how many times we…" I trailed off, exasperated. "It's like my brain won't let me believe it."

But he wasn't looking at me—not directly. His eyes traced a path up my hip and settled over the cleavage bared by the low neckline of my dress. My heart lurched against my rib cage as if trying to save itself from the onslaught of sensation that assaulted me. Too late. Heat blossomed in my veins. My throat went dry. Moisture gathered in sensual places.

But one word from him made my belly clench, all thoughts of doubt and propriety forgotten.

"Upstairs."

I turned automatically and staggered toward the staircase. He followed, keeping his distance during the entire long, winding trek to my bedroom.

Once inside it, he continued to advance, backing me toward my bed. His eyes burned too damn brightly. Maintaining contact for long was impossible. I tore my gaze down to his chest, seeking a reprieve. I found one. The contours of his body strained beneath his shirt, hypnotizing me with every shift in fabric as he came closer…

Closer…

An icy finger lifted my chin, forcing me to look up. His expression was guarded again, devoid of even the smugness I'd come to associate with him. When his lips finally parted, all he said was, "Is there anything else I can do for you, *mistress?*"

My answer rode a gasp. "P-Put…put me to bed."

In return, he seized the front of my dress and yanked, ripping the material without the aid of Yulia's tricks. The next second, he had me against the wall, his lips on mine, and there was nothing left to think about or worry over.

He controlled every motion, guiding my lips apart with his own to coax my tongue into submission. Coaxing—that was the only way to describe it. He teased the shame away, reawakening all those strange, unfamiliar sensations. I panted, breathless in the aftermath. Mindless.

Starving in an entirely different way than I'd been earlier.

When he finally did "put me to bed," it was in the literal sense. My back struck the mattress. He followed, settling over me, nudging my legs apart. Like a true subservient, he stripped down entirely for my benefit, watching as my lips parted and my eyes widened at every inch of chiseled muscle revealed.

Then he lunged into my touch, offering up his body to explore as I wished.

The mattress moaned beneath our combined weight, obscuring any sounds smothered into the sheets.

And my poor parents could only watch on in despair from beyond the grave.

MASTER AND PROTECTOR

The next morning, I woke up alone. Ruffled sheets betrayed that someone had shared the bed with me during most of the night, leaving recently enough that the space beside me still resonated with their chill. I sighed, smelling him in the sheets, his scent mingling with mine.

For now, a voice hissed at the back of my skull.

I rolled onto my side to escape it, but doubt nibbled away at the pleasurable ache dissipating from my limbs.

For now… But how long until you drive him away again?

"Stop," I scolded myself out loud, rising to my feet.

After dressing in a plain gray shift, I descended the steps and found Dublin lurking in the foyer. He was wearing black now and my tongue darted along my bottom lip in appreciation. Damn that color. It emphasized his eyes like nothing else.

And as they flickered in my direction, that terrible, doubting voice went silent.

"You there, servant." I pointed at him, my chin in the air. "I'm famished. Make me something to eat."

He inclined his head graciously in mock servitude. "What would you like, *mistress?*"

"I want…" As I descended the remainder of the steps, my hand shot out, demanding assistance.

He stepped forward, cradling my palm against his—but then my act slipped as my stomach growled. I truly was hungry, and even the prospect of spending hours watching him slave over a meal was no match.

"Grilled cheese," I blurted, naming one of the few meals that even I knew didn't require much fuss.

He raised an eyebrow. "In lieu of filet mignon and braised leg of lamb?"

I'd surprised him. Triumph left me beaming as he led me toward the kitchen.

"Yes, and not only that," I added, stroking my chin. Cooking the meal himself would be far too easy. This time, I had another challenge in mind. "I want you to teach *me* how to make it."

"As you wish," he agreed. "I'm sure even someone of your delicate nature can learn how to slice a loaf of bread."

I grinned wickedly; the poor man had no idea how daunting a challenge he'd just undertaken.

~

"*E*ven slices," Dublin instructed.

I chafed at how damn patient he managed to sound—despite the fact that I'd already butchered at least two loaves of bread. Relentlessly gentle, his fingers slid over my spine as he adjusted my grip on the blade with his opposite hand. I tried not to agonize over what served to be my fifth attempt.

"Try again."

"Okay…" I inhaled with determination and lowered the blade. What began as a semi-clean slice quickly resulted in a deformed chunk of mush as the knife slipped and smashed the loaf entirely. "Damn it!" I tossed the blade aside and tore at my hair. "I give up!"

My own challenge be damned.

Ironically, this task had proved to frustrate *me* more than Dublin. And the more aggravated I became, the more insufferably patient he seemed determined to be.

"Try again." He returned the knife to my hand, sealing his grip over mine. Parting, his lips brushed my throat as he warned, "You apply far too much pressure. Now"—he positioned what little bit of bread remained before me—"all you need to do is guide it…"

He flexed our combined grip and the result was a perfectly uniform slice.

"Now, you."

I did my best to copy his easy, effortless motion. Lost in concentration, I closed my eyes midway and reopened them only when the blade hit the cutting board.

"Finally!" I exclaimed in relief. My prize wasn't as neat as his, but at least it was useable.

"Good. And now for the next step." Dublin moved to a different section of the counter and coated the slices in butter. Then he slipped a slice of cheese in between them and fried the creation in a hot pan.

I grinned with unabashed pride as he finally placed the meal on a plate. "Next time, I want you to teach me how to fillet a fish," I joked as I followed him into the dining room.

He had enough sense not to respond.

While I'd been distracted during the bread debacle, he must have conjured up the steaming bowl of tomato soup, which he placed beside me as well. One sniff and I registered the unusually salty undertones to the tomato aroma. It betrayed an ingredient not found in most variations of the dish.

"Where's Dmitri?" I wondered as I lifted a spoon. Given his request to "tag along for the ride," his absence puzzled me more than I wanted to admit. While he was no comparison to Dublin physically, I couldn't deny that the man possessed more than enough skill in manipulation to be a threat nonetheless.

And while my sanity wasn't the healthiest to begin with, I'd never heard voices.

Certainly none so persistent. So insidious. Even as I ate, a cruel taunt echoed on the outskirts of my thoughts. *He doesn't want you...*

Clearing my throat, I pushed the unease aside and refocused on Dublin. "Don't tell me his promise for 'answers' turned out to be yet another lie?"

"He's around," Dublin said coldly. "He'll return soon enough. I won't have him toy with your hopes again. Therefore, I suggested that he ensure his information be *accurate* before sharing it."

"Or?" I risked asking as I fiddled with my sandwich.

His eyes narrowed, glowering beyond me. "Or I'd slice him into pieces thin enough to fit within the pages of his goddamn books."

Ah. A threat far too specific to be a mere boast.

Rather than linger on the topic, I busied myself with sipping from my soup and devouring the surprisingly good sandwich. Perhaps the full belly lulled me into a state silly enough to question, "Have you ever been in love?"

I flicked my gaze across the table, gauging his reaction.

He gave me little to go on. Merely a furrowed brow. "Love?"

"Something beyond mere lust." I waved my fingers through the air. "In your old age, I'm sure you've plied plenty of women with heartfelt poetry and roses." I laughed, but the joke turned out to be at my expense.

Of course, he'd had others. He'd all but alluded to it.

"Roses are a bit cliché," he countered, sounding bored at the prospect. "I'd like to think I have more creativity than that."

I shrugged, turning my attention to my plate. "You sent me one that first day, remember?" Along with a written choice. *Life or death?*

"They make for an effective tool to craft a grand entrance, I will admit." He laughed. "Though I would like to believe I'd profess my love in something a bit more impressive than a rose."

Something he'd never give to you, that doubtful voice hissed. I shook it off like a bothersome fly.

"Like?" I asked Dublin.

He said nothing.

"You know, Georgie's many lovers—the ones she risked sneaking in the manor—would leave roses for her as gifts, smuggled into different rooms," I said. "Sometimes, they'd assume my room was hers—which goes to show that brains weren't high on her list of attractive attributes. Every time I saw a rose on my floor, I knew… It was never for me."

What a melancholic admission. After a sigh, I sipped more soup and then shoved the rest of my bread into my mouth.

"Do you miss her?" Dublin wondered.

His voice was too soft. I could stomach his concern when it came packaged within an elaborate joke—but it was another thing entirely when he didn't bother to disguise it at all.

"Georgie?" I stared down at my hands, blinking rapidly. "I..."

He only cares because he wants her more. And you know it.

"Stop!" I rubbed at my forehead.

Dublin's hand brushed my wrist. "Are you all right?"

"I'm fine." I set my empty plate aside as proof. "I'm just... tired, I think."

"Should I assist you?" He grinned, utilizing his dangerous mixture of charm and smug amusement. With unmatched grace, he stood and approached my chair. "Or are you willing to bruise your delicate feet by walking yourself?"

I choked out something that passed for a laugh. "I wouldn't want to tire out my weak servant so soon. I'm fine. I think it's the time zone change."

He let me mount the stairs alone, but I could sense him watching. Even as I entered my room and closed the door, I knew he was listening down below, waiting for any hint that something was wrong.

So, willing to put him at ease for once, I calmly shed my dress and pulled on a robe. Then I carefully lowered myself onto the bed with a contented sigh for his benefit.

But I didn't dare to close my eyes. I couldn't. Shadows painted my room, swallowing up the violet beneath a sea of impenetrable darkness. My breath tainted the air in puffs of white. And the voices persisted, louder without his presence to smother them.

Silly Eleanor.

Stupid Eleanor.

Fucking you is all he desires. Fucking. Fucking.

You don't matter. You or that thing growing inside you.

Abomination. Abomination.

I tossed and turned, burying my face against my pillow. Air caught between my lungs and my throat, unwilling to move. I was suffocating. Gulping for breath, I inhaled and struggled to regain my bearings. *Breathe, Ellie. You're being ridiculous.*

"Eleanor?"

"I...I'm fine," I blurted even before I found Dublin in the doorway, poised forward as if to lunge. "I promise."

He didn't seem convinced. His grip remained on the doorknob as his gaze scanned the room in a cautious sweep.

"I'm just tired..." I let my eyes drift shut and my head fall back against the pillows.

If my act convinced him, he didn't let on.

As stubborn as a guard dog, he stood there even as I felt myself finally drift off.

But the voices chased me, hissing into the void.

He doesn't care.

He doesn't want you.

He could never love you.

~

Breakfast came in the form of a cup of red liquid shoved beneath my nose the moment I peeled my eyes open. Quite the departure in service from last night —though I wasn't particularly compelled to complain.

Groaning, I sat upright and obediently drank. Watchful eyes chased every single swallow until the last drop danced over my tongue. Then my servant withdrew the cup without warning and left the room.

"Sleep," he commanded from the hall before unease could even take root in his absence. "I have some business to attend to, but I'll be back."

I must have dozed off again. The next thing I knew, my eyelids were fluttering open and the sun painted my room in shades of gold.

But Dublin was still gone.

His promise echoed in my thoughts, becoming a mantra. *He will be back. He will be...*

Or not.

For all I knew, he could have left again. Abandoned me again. His kiss, his touch—it all could have been a trick designed to lower my guard. Because the walls of this manor reinforced the truth more than anything—I was no different from any other Gray, and I held no real appeal beyond this storied fortune.

And Dublin Helos wouldn't want you, a vicious voice seconded from inside my skull. *Stop kidding yourself, Eleanor. It's pathetic. You're pathetic.*

"No!" I stood and paced, tearing my fingers through my hair. I was being irrational. Pathetic. I...

Don't matter.

Something caught my eye, lying on the floor beside my bed, discarded. I stooped to retrieve it, confused as I found myself holding a beautiful white rose glaringly out of place. I brought it to my nose, inhaling the delicate perfume.

And the longer I observed it, the more dread solidified in my bones. It wasn't for me. No. Just like in the old days, it had been left for someone else. Someone beautiful he'd smuggled into my room while I'd been away. *That* was why he stayed. There was always someone else.

"What are you doing?"

Dazed, I looked up, still holding the rose to my chest.

Dublin stood in the doorway, his eyes wide, fixated on the item contained within my hands. *Proof,* a part of me despaired.

"Eleanor." Racked with guilt, his voice shook, unnervingly soft. "Put it down."

"Why?"

When I pressed the rose to my chest, he lurched a step closer. "Don't! Put it down. *Now.*"

"Tell me *why?*" I tightened my grip even more. His reaction only reinforced my suspicions. He was lying to me. Deceiving me.

"Eleanor." His voice deepened imploringly. "Put the knife down!"

Knife? Confused, I eyed my hand and gasped in horror. The leather hilt of a slim dagger trembled within my fist—not a flower. Honed to a lethal point, the tip grazed my throat with every frantic breath I took.

"Oh God!" Panicked, I threw it aside and hunched over, staring down at my hands. "I'm sorry! I think… I think I'm still dreaming. I—"

"It's okay." He knelt before me, easing me into his arms. From over his shoulder, I saw the knife disappear, tucked beyond my reach. "What were you thinking?"

"I…"

He pulled back, forcing me to meet his gaze before I could form a coherent explanation. Yellow sunlight spilled in from the window, almost blinding as it reflected off his features. How could I tell him the truth?

I'm hearing voices, Dublin. Voices in my head, and they won't stop.

They won't stop…

"I'm fine," I croaked. "I…I was cleaning up."

"Cleaning up?" He sounded more cautious than ever.

It wasn't until I followed his gaze down to my chest that I realized why. I was trembling.

"Yes." I staggered to my feet and shook my head to clear it. The paranoia had been the mere remnants of a nightmare. Yes… "I need a bath. That's all," I decided, staggering toward the bathroom. "I expect you'll have lunch waiting for me, slave."

I didn't look back to see his reaction. I raced into the safety of my tub instead, running the water as hot as I could stand. Lavender-scented soap helped erase the unease somewhat.

When I finally reentered my bedroom, I wasn't shaking anymore. Heat kissed my clammy skin, displacing some of the unnatural bitter cold.

And I felt fine.

I was fine…

Liar, that voice cackled from within. *You're going insane, Eleanor.*

You're going insane.

QUIET

The following days passed in stiff, tense stillness. Desperate to put the knife incident behind us, I fell into my role more fervently than ever—the obedient ward under a monster's control. I didn't dare so much as breathe the word "answers" or mention Dmitri.

Yet, with each passing moment, our delicate routine strained at the edges.

For one, Dublin stopped serving me anything requiring silverware, insisting more often than not that I drink my meals. If I asked him why, he evaded giving me a solid answer—and, as if to disguise the concern, he tried distracting me with taunts.

Insults, even.

"If you become any thinner, I won't have anything to hold on to the next time you decide to straddle me while airborne."

But I knew he was worried—and that terrified me more than hallucinating a weapon into a rose. When he looked at me, his expression became hollower than ever. Trying to maintain eye contact was a game of averted, downcast glances. Eventually, the man began to resemble a living statue in my presence more than a protector.

Always on guard. Always watching.

Even worse, I could sense what little glimmer of trust we'd built up slip further away. The quest for answers itself had cemented our unnatural union, yet each day without them felt like another unwelcome shove off a cliff toward an unknown drop.

Maybe the delusions were my body's way of trying to warn me?

You aren't ready for this.

You can't handle this.

You shouldn't prolong this.

"...consider your time up," Dublin snarled. He sounded faint, as if his voice were coming from down below. But, bellowed like thunder, each word reached my ears clearly even as I lay in bed, too drained to eavesdrop. "You have an hour to return with whatever 'answers' you have. I won't even waste my breath on a threat. And if I learn that you've somehow harmed her..."

Murder resonated in his tone and some numb piece of my soul stirred in response. Me. He was afraid for me.

Faked of course, the callous voice in my skull taunted. *Lies.*

"Something is wrong. I talk to her and it's like she doesn't even hear me. I've never seen her like… Do you think I haven't? I've taken the precautions. I've restricted her meals. Any blood I give her has been vetted to Hell and back. But if you are behind this, then know that I won't stop at merely killing you—"

Lies. Lies. Lieslieslieslieslies…

"Eleanor. Look at me."

I flinched; he sounded closer now. From the doorway, I realized as I turned toward it. Without an invitation, he entered my room, consuming the small space with his presence.

"How are you feeling?"

"Fine," I insisted. "Just tired." To prove as much, I shifted, placing a pillow over my head, my eyes squeezed shut. Nonetheless, I sensed him step closer—remaining far away enough to judge me unmolested should I ache to touch him. Far enough away that *he* didn't have to touch *me.* "I'm fine," I repeated hoarsely. "I just need rest."

"You're not sleeping."

I winced at his accusatory tone. Was he angry?

Of course he is.

Alarmed, I lifted the pillow enough to observe him. Stern frown. Blazing eyes. Hell yes, he was angry.

Because he hates you.

"You need to eat."

"Like you care." My words echoed the voice hissing in my head, but I was too tired to ignore them anymore. They were the only truth to be found within these walls lately. The only answers I had to cling to.

His lies. Lies.

"I wouldn't be here if I didn't," he stated bluntly.

But that voice overpowered him. *He's lying. He's…*

"You're lying," I whispered. "Like you really care whether or not I live or die—"

"Oh?" His expression darkened, his eyes flashing with warning. Any other day, I'd rush to heed it. "You don't want to play this game with me. As you recall, our contract specified honesty. I'm demanding my fair share now. Tell me what's wrong."

"Nothing," I insisted. Because saying it out loud would have been far too insane. Too real. If I had to gauge his reaction in real time… I wasn't sure if I could handle the truth I might find.

Because he hates you.

Hates.

Despises.

Obsesses.

And you know it.

"I'll come back later." His voice cut through the chaos for a heartbeat's reprieve—but then he turned for the door and the whispering intensified. I barely heard him growl, "You need to get some rest—"

"No, you know what I really need? I need *answers!*" I sounded so damn tired. So worn. A hundred-year-old woman howling from her deathbed. "I need the truth. And you're hiding it from me, aren't you? You're keeping me here. You're waiting, aren't you? Waiting for me to die—"

"Eleanor." His face was stone, but that of a statue carved in the guise of concern. Eyes too wide, mouth too tense. "Listen to yourself."

"I know why." I wrenched my blankets back and stood, pacing as everything became clear. His motives. His true intentions. "You're just waiting for me to die. You want me to. You don't give a damn about me—"

"Eleanor…" Confusion crept into those hollow eyes, a more terrifying sight than the visions. "I think you need to lie down—"

"No!" I cringed against the wall as he took a step in my direction. "Stay away from me!"

He doesn't care about you, the voice warned, growing louder. Deafening. *He doesn't. It's obvious.*

"You don't care! Get out!"

But he didn't look smug, like a villain called out in his vicious grand plan. He looked at me like I'd grown three heads. Like *I* was the monster.

"Get out!"

"Eleanor—"

"Get out!" I lunged for my bed, grabbed a pillow, and threw it at him.

When he easily sidestepped it, I snatched the vase on my bedside nightstand instead. It smashed against his chest, the broken pieces speckling the floor, as sharp as knives. But he remained, so I hurtled a picture frame at him next. A lamp.

Each weapon betrayed a shifting intention—less to repel him and increasingly to *hurt*.

"Get the hell away from me!"

When I aimed for the doorway again, another pillow in hand, he was already gone. I swayed, my weapon slipping from my fingers. Maybe he'd never been there at all? Maybe...he was already away from the manor, leaving me again.

Abandoning me again.

He didn't give a damn about me. All he wanted was…

No. I tugged at my hair, desperate to clear my thoughts. My memories portrayed someone far different than what the voices painted. Someone who'd held me at my darkest moment. Who'd claimed to crave me. Protect me.

Voice breaking, I called out for him. "Dublin? Dublin!"

No response. My room remained empty—or was it?

No. Something was at the foot of my bed. Moving.

"D-Dublin?"

He didn't come, and the noise strengthened, intensifying. Soft. Sweet.

I crept along my bed frame, drawn forward as if hypnotized. When I finally spotted the creature lying on the floor…

Shock brought me to my knees. I couldn't breathe. I couldn't even scream.

It was a baby. Someone had left her there naked, her tiny limbs perfectly formed—and an emotion unlike anything I'd ever felt drowned me.

She wasn't a grotesque monster. No abomination.

She was beautiful.

Lively. *Alive.*

And as I gaped, her hands grasped at the air for me, her impish grin infectious. But the longer I stared, the more demanding her cries became. Insistent.

She needed me. I needed to hold her.

Cautiously, I drew closer, bringing a trembling hand against her tiny head and the cap of golden curls that shielded it. The strands felt like silk, a hue I'd only seen one other person possess. But her eyes… They were a blazing, burning green.

Like mine.

"Shhhh…" I tried to slip my hand beneath her tiny body. To hold her. To soothe her. Everything would be all right. She was safe. No one would ever hurt her. No one.

But my fingers disobeyed and encircled her throat instead.

"No!" One by one, they clenched no matter how hard I tried to stop. "No! No!"

Tighter I clenched, until her beautiful babble ceased mid-song. That delicate face turned blue, those tiny limbs frantically flailing.

"No!" I tried to pull away, clawing at my frozen wrist, but it wouldn't budge. I tugged harder, scraping with my nails. "No! No! Stop!"

My grip wouldn't loosen, and her tiny body grew limper by the second. Lifeless. With every heartbeat, the color faded from her rosy cheeks.

And I'd lose her forever.

"No! No! No!" I scanned my room, desperate for help. But salvation appeared like magic in my hand—a jagged piece of broken glass, honed like a knife.

And there was no time to hesitate. I slashed, unconcerned as the sharpened edge bit into my wrist. Deep. Deeper. Blood spilled, splattering the floor, but I didn't matter. Only she did. I needed to save her.

But even the violence didn't loosen my grip. The next cut went so deep that the blade scraped bone—but not deep enough. So I slashed again. Again. Still, my fingers wouldn't loosen.

And she wasn't moving anymore. She wasn't moving…

"No!" I wailed, trying harder. Cutting deeper, slicing into any part of my arm I could reach. "No! No—"

"Eleanor!"

A cruel hand stole my weapon, struggling to contain my flailing, kicking limbs.

Teeth bared, I fought like hell, but I was no match. "Let me go! Let go! I can't leave her!"

But when I looked down, she had vanished.

And in her wake: red, red, red. The floor became a sea of it, frothing beneath my feet.

Endless amounts of blood.

"No! I didn't mean to." I choked out the confession, my heart breaking as much as my voice was. "I did it. I didn't mean to. I didn't want to hurt her. I couldn't save her—"

"What's wrong with her? Eleanor! Eleanor, look at me!"

I barely recognized the sound of Dublin's voice—ragged, distorted by a horror I couldn't begin to fathom—but I couldn't see his face. Though his words lashed at my eardrums, I barely heard him. Just darkness and noise. That goddamn noise.

You're pathetic. Pathetic. Pathetic. Pathetic.

Desperate, I tried to claw at my ears, but with my body restrained, I could only scream, "Stop! Make it stop, please!" I didn't know who I was pleading with. Dublin? God? Anyone? "I can't take it. Make it stop. Make it stop! Make it stop—"

"Dmitri!"

"I have it. Shhh, my dear," another voice crooned sweetly into my ear. "A little pinch… There. This will take the pain away, I promise."

I was only vaguely aware of a burning sting along my arm.

And then…peace.

"You are restrained," a man warned as I floated on the cusp of consciousness. His voice served as a steadying anchor, drawing me back when I only wanted to drift.

Dublin? No. Someone sly, their accent thicker.

"Try not to panic," he insisted. "You're wounded, and frankly, I'd rather not have to bandage you *again*. So deep breaths and all of that. Prepare yourself, my dear. It isn't pretty."

I stirred, fighting to remember how to control my limbs. All senses felt cut off from my brain as if locked behind a wall with no key. In vain, I tried to flex my hands. Blink. Anything.

"You were poisoned," the speaker continued as my thoughts spun, still hunting for a name. "With something known as Ergot—best to get that out of the way. It's a rare compound known to inspire all sorts of nasty things in those who ingest too much of it. Paranoia. Hallucinations. Psychosis. It builds up in the blood, you see. Slowly, over time. Months. Years. Though, judging from your recent state, you've managed to receive a full dose in mere weeks. An impressive feat, I must say. Admittedly, I should have guessed from your rather thrilling reaction to my little lie that your mental state may have been exceedingly delicate." He sighed in admiration.

An image formed in my brain of a handsome, angular face. Hair the color of blood. Shifting eyes.

"No bother! I'm not the only one who overlooked your symptoms. Helos may be an arrogant bastard, but I know he tested the blood he gave to you. You're just lucky he caught on before you finished severing your hand. *That* might have made things a tad unpleasant."

I finally managed to open my eyes. Blurred and unfocused, it took them several seconds to clearly interpret the figure before me. But that mocking grin required no introduction. *Dmitri.*

"Where…" My throat ached as I tried to speak. "Where is Dublin?"

"Off getting more bandages in case you reopen your wounds, I suspect," Dmitri replied. He almost resembled a different person without his playful sneer. "You scared the hell out of him. Dare I say, that's quite the feat, given the man's rather fearsome reputation." He didn't even chuckle. Hell, as his eyes took on a wistful gleam, he almost appeared…impressed? "And yes, this is a lot of information at once—I apologize—but this is the fifth iteration of this damn speech I've delivered and I pray, for both our sakes, that you aren't faking your sanity this time."

Faking? I eyed the room beyond him, increasingly uneasy. It wasn't mine. And the rich, golden décor didn't resemble something Dublin would own, either. It boasted of more exotic tastes, far beyond typical elegance. Above me, a vaulted ceiling sported a gruesome fresco—a horde of angels slaughtering an opposing army.

I swallowed hard, tearing my eyes from the chaotic scene. "Where am I?"

"Hell," Dmitri replied. Sitting on a gilded chair near the bed, he snatched a book from a nearby table. With a casual flick of his wrist, he flipped through the pages. "I never thought I'd ever see a day when Dublin would willingly return to the enclave, to be honest." He eyed me with a thoughtful frown before turning yet another page. "Then again, I never thought I would *join* him in said enclave. You, my dear, have provided quite the adventure."

Enclave? I tried to sit up, but my arms resisted any movement. Literally—not for lack of trying. The harder I strained my wrists, the more I felt the weight of resistance. Something encircled each one, rendering them immobile.

"Manacles," Dmitri admitted. "Or at least silken ones. Your Dublin refused to let me use the metal pair after you tried slipping out of them."

I couldn't remember anything he'd mentioned. Panic bubbled out of me on a single word. "W-Why?"

"To keep you from killing yourself, of course." Sighing, he set his book aside and propped his chin on his fist, sitting forward. "Ergot is a powerful poison. It lingers in the blood and renders the mind susceptible to all manner of disturbing hallucinations. For instance, when you had no luck cutting your hand off, you tried clawing out your throat. As you can imagine, it made for quite the mess. You're lucky that I happened to arrive in time," he added smugly. "There is only one antidote for Ergot, and I happen to be among the few in the world skilled enough to make it. Which reminds me..." He tutted with his tongue and stood, smoothing his hands along his suit, a brilliant indigo. On the same small table as the book rested a teacup, which he lifted by the handle and lowered to my lips. "It's time for your next dose, my darling. Do drink up."

I clenched my jaw shut.

He sighed heavily. "Come now, Eleanor. I really don't want to force-feed you your medicine." His eyes flashed a menacing green. "*Again.*"

His words were too much to process all at once as a million realizations washed over me. *Tried to kill yourself. Ergot. Blade. Poison. Dublin. Gone. Gone.*

When he lowered the cup to my mouth again, I squirmed helplessly, resisting my binds. "Get away from me—"

"It's all right."

That voice... I turned toward it, my heart aching—but when I finally spotted Dublin advancing toward me, he looked…

Haggard.

Hollow circles swallowed his eyes, though he didn't require sleep. The unusual color enhanced the planes of his face in gaunt relief. For a horrifying second, he looked every bit his age. Centuries of pain and exhaustion clinging to a human form. Then his eyes met mine and his entire expression softened.

He became my Devil again, wary and distant.

"Drink it," he said, nodding to Dmitri. "It's all right."

A part of me wanted to rail against the commands. It wanted to shriek and scream and demand answers.

Why was my skull on fire? Why was I shivering even beneath mounds of blankets? Why did my throat taste like dirt?

And why, oh why, was my arm throbbing like hell?

My throat provided another dose of agonizing pain. The skin burned with every breath as if rubbed raw. Or, if Dmitri was to be believed, *clawed* at by a madwoman with brittle nails.

"Eleanor," Dublin rasped. "Drink."

For the moment, I chose the safety of his baritone over questioning. As Dmitri returned the rim of the cup to my lips, I obediently pried them apart. The liquid within smelled pungent, as if tinged with a million different spices. With the first sip, I realized where the gritty taste in my mouth had come from.

"It was a very clever method," Dmitri mused as I gulped at the tea. "Slow. Sustained over multiple hosts. He must have started not long after you began supplying her fresh blood." He eyed Dublin, smirking. "I used to muse which one of you two might best the other when you eventually did resume your trite little war games. Believe it or not, Dublin, but I always had my money on you. Mero could be cunning, but he had his boundaries. Even if he *is* using the other Gray girl as a pawn, like I suspect, I doubt he's killed her. Yet. *You*, on the other hand, were ruthless—"

"Enough." The growl lacked any of the intensity I was used to. In its absence, Dublin resembled a mere shadow of his former self. A specter on par with Raphael—a hollow soul, somewhere in between the man and monster. But as he turned his attention to me, some semblance of the Devil I knew returned again. Namely in his eyes as they flickered with an unreadable mixture of emotion. "How do you feel?"

"Tired," I rasped, my voice breaking.

"You should be right as rain in a few more days," Dmitri insisted. "Ergot is resistant but not infallible—"

"I need to speak to her alone." Dublin didn't even look at him, expecting his will be obeyed.

"Fine." Dmitri shrugged and headed for the doorway. "Though perhaps now isn't the best time to mention that you shouldn't trust all you see or hear, Eleanor," he told me with a playful wink. "The Ergot is still in your bloodstream, after all."

His laugh echoed in his wake, but Dublin's voice easily overpowered it.

"Tell me what happened." He sat on the edge of the bed, his back to me, but his hand settled over my hip, palpable even through the heavy blankets. "From the beginning. Everything."

"I was hearing voices," I admitted. My throat felt sore from disuse. Just how long had I been beneath the spell of the drug?

"What did they say?" he prompted.

I hesitated, swiping my tongue along my dry, cracked lips. "That... That you hated me. That you didn't want me." I realized now just how insane it sounded out loud. "I think I knew I was being irrational, but I couldn't help it. It felt so real. I could hear it—"

"Telling you that I couldn't love you?" He didn't meet my gaze. Instead, he eyed the far wall, his jaw clenched. "You screamed that line the most."

I closed my eyes, hating the vicious memories as they teased the edges of my psyche. "How could this happen? Dmitri said—"

"You were poisoned," he said over me. "Right under my nose and I didn't even see it until it was almost too late."

As my eyes reopened, I found him watching me, lingering over my face. "Why?"

"To punish me." He sounded more resigned than vengeful. "I suspect that was his design all along, as far as you were concerned. Punish me."

"Why?"

"Why?" He laughed, shaking his head as if unsure how to even phrase the answer. "He... I loved him like a brother once," he admitted softly. "I trusted him above all others. Always. And you are his vehicle to punish me." The hand he rested over me withdrew, becoming a fist he slammed onto the mattress. "But he's overplayed his hand, and if he tries to hurt you again, I will kill him."

"Dublin..." I'd forgotten how formidable he could sound. How dangerous when confronted. Blazing silver eyes cut me to the bone as he held my gaze. "What about Georgie? Dmitri said she might be—"

"You need to focus on yourself for now," he warned. "Trust me on this."

It was as close to begging as a man like him might ever come—and despite his nearness, I sensed he could drift from me farther than ever if I pushed him away now.

And I wasn't the only one who needed him.

"I saw things too." The words almost hurt to say, conjuring a memory sharp with a pain I'd never ever felt. Longing. Fear. Guilt. "I saw… She was so beautiful…and I killed her." Panicked, I flexed my fingers, grasping at nothing. "I killed her—"

"It was a nightmare," he said, but it wasn't the truth. A nightmare was comparable to what I'd witnessed, but I'd rather burn alive than feel that pain again. "The drug should help you sleep without any more dreams. Get some rest."

I steeled myself for him to leave, but he found my hand, still bound to the bed, and grasped it tightly. He remained like that for only God knew how long.

Long after I surrendered to unconsciousness again.

The vicious specter of doubt chased me through a nightmarish maze. I couldn't escape it, assaulted by its cruel taunts. *You're pathetic, Eleanor. Pathetic…*

I awoke, gasping as panic formed a noose around my throat more restraining than the binds still pinning me in place. Straining my shoulders, I struggled to sit up, blinking my eyes open to the morbidly decorated ceiling above. A twisted sense of relief slowed my frantic heartbeat by a fraction. I was still in that room.

And someone remained beside me, brushing the sweat-soaked curls from my face.

"You're safe."

I turned toward the sound of his voice.

He hadn't moved from his position on the side of my bed, even though I sensed I'd slept for hours at least. "Eleanor?" He sounded worried.

Should he have been? I wasn't sure. I needed to move. I needed to think.

"I…I think I just need to use the restroom…"

The corner of his jaw twitched, betraying his thoughts in a way I'd never been able to interpret before: suspicion. He didn't trust me.

"This isn't the first time you've woken up seemingly lucid," he murmured, more to himself than to me. His eyes narrowed over my hands as they grasped at the sheets, yet he made no attempt to free me. "How do you feel?"

I took my time answering. He was cautious for a reason, and I sensed a need to make my reply as coherent as possible.

"Sore," I admitted finally. "And my arm hurts. And my throat."

Some of the tension constricting his brow eased. "Your wounds need to be healed, but you've been refusing to drink my blood. Dmitri's had to rebandage you at least four times. It's a miracle you haven't bled out. We couldn't even inject you because you fought like hell every time, even while sedated." His mouth softened further.

Was my Devil impressed?

But his words only emphasized what Dmitri himself had hinted at. *This is the fifth iteration of this damn speech I've delivered…*

"I still feel strange," I added hoarsely. "Like my thoughts are scattered and… But I don't want to hurt myself."

His gaze flickered to my right arm, tracing the length of bandage wrapped from wrist to shoulder, but the pathetic note in my voice must have been enough to overcome his concern. For now.

He approached the limb closer to him. With some sleight of hand I couldn't make out, he undid the manacle—a strip of thick, black silk—and placed it on the nearby end table. I flexed my fingers carefully, hissing as blood returned to them. But I kept the rest of my body still, avoiding any sudden movements. Watching me like a hawk, Dublin circled around to my opposite side and did the same.

Freedom hurt. I groaned as I stretched my limbs and attempted to sit upright. Dublin assisted me, utilizing his touch where I lacked the strength. Despite how my muscles were throbbing, it felt good to move. Even while being observed with an intensity most men might reserve for a lab rat.

Unnerved by his concern, I decided that my best option was to utilize it. "Help me up."

I extended my uninjured arm, allowing him to pull me to my feet. From this angle, the rest of the unfamiliar bedroom unfolded before me. With every detail, the unease within my skin grew into an itching dread. It was large, as cavernous as Dublin's cathedral. Dark walls lacked a window, instead sporting exquisite macabre paintings depicting images of war and violence.

Marble floors were adorned with Persian rugs woven with intricate designs composed of gold and ebony threads. A fireplace—black stone carved into the open maw of a serpent—yawned against the far wall and the fire roaring within basted my skin with what little heat I felt.

"Come here." Dublin approached, his hands raised as if to ensure he didn't startle me.

Once satisfied by my reaction, he lifted me into his arms, and within seconds, we were in an adjacent bathroom, the interior of which was no less extravagant than the bedroom. And just as imposing.

A large sunken tub had been cut within the center of the marble floor. Dublin set me down near the edge of it. His touch lingered along my arm as if to gauge whether or not I'd suddenly try attacking myself. Then he withdrew to the corners of the room, fetching various supplies.

Overall, the layout resembled how I figured an ancient Roman bath might. Golden columns accented the space at various intervals, and a large mirror consumed an entire wall alone. Once I saw my reflection on its surface, I failed to muster up the energy to even gasp. My skin lacked definition, my cheeks sunken and hollow.

I looked more dead than alive.

No wonder Dublin seemed unwilling to leave me unattended for very long. He returned to my side and guided me into the basin of the tub. There, he stripped my thin nightgown and ran the water.

The nuances of his expression eluded me once more, so I observed my skin instead. A thick length of bandages covered my right arm from wrist to shoulder. Crimson splotches betrayed signs of fresh bleeding, but I wasn't brave enough to check the wounds underneath. My throat was another matter. I ran my finger over it, sensing uneven, inflamed skin that matched the violent array of scratches my reflection revealed.

"You need blood," Dublin warned as the water lapped up my sides. "You need to eat."

He sounded hesitant and I couldn't help but wonder why. Though maybe I already knew. I'd been so hysterical that he'd had no choice but to bind me just to keep me from hurting myself.

"How was I poisoned?" I asked as he settled behind me.

"Methodically. You were never given blood from the same person twice," he said. "From the outset, I knew to source anything I gave you carefully. Every drop came from donors I considered to be the highest quality and least susceptible to corruption. For you to receive the dose you did, each one of them must have consumed trace levels of the poison long before I drew a drop from their veins."

His gruff tone conveyed just how elaborate a scheme the level of planning revealed. Someone cunning enough to outsmart even his best efforts.

All part of a systematic scheme meant to infect me.

"Anyway, I'm not offering you *human* blood this time." As he spoke, he withdrew something from his pocket. A small, thin blade—small enough, I realized, that should I grab it, I wouldn't be able to do much damage to myself. "Do be a good girl," he said as he slashed the blade across his wrist, drawing a line of blood. "You've bitten *me* with every attempt before now. Admittedly, it wasn't very pleasant."

"I did?" My skull throbbed. "I can't remember."

He stroked my cheek. "Drink."

A million questions bubbled beneath the surface as I eyed the smooth skin of his wrist. Like how did he know if his blood alone would even sustain me? What happened if he was carrying the poison as well? And most importantly, was there some proper etiquette to follow while feeding from a vampire?

In the end, his free hand caught the back of my neck, guiding me forward.

My lips parted, allowing a sliver of liquid between them. The moment his taste registered, I no longer required coaxing. I lunged, gripping his arm to keep it in place as deep, ravenous pulls racked my body. Perhaps the fact that I was starving was the catalyst, but he tasted better than good. Better than sin. I drowned in his flavor, craving more…and more…more…

It was like surfacing from an eternity spent submerged beneath water when I finally came up for air, unbearably full. Regardless, my tongue was already chasing what few drops I hadn't managed to swallow.

Fully prepared, Dublin brought a wet cloth to my chin and dabbed it along my bottom lip. "Already, you look better," he murmured, a rare hint of praise.

I glanced at the mirror, which seconded his claim. Color gradually returned to my skin. The pain lessened. I didn't feel quite as dizzy, and my thoughts felt easier to grasp and decipher.

Like the threat still looming above our heads, for instance.

"What about you?" I eyed him over my shoulder. "What if the poison is in your system—"

"It doesn't affect me, which is why I didn't sense its corruption until it was too late. No matter… From now on, I will take the necessary precautions."

What they might be? He didn't explain, leaving it at that.

By then, the water had reached a comfortable height, and he set about washing me thoroughly from head to toe. My body sang beneath the ministrations, and once again, I wondered just how long I'd been strapped to the bed.

Which brought up an even bigger question.

"Where are we?" I supposed deep down I knew at least part of the answer—nowhere good. Much like the bedroom, a decidedly 'serpentine' theme continued even in here. The water fixture on the bathtub was in the shape of a snake, spitting water in the place of venom through golden fangs.

Dublin ran a cloth across my shoulders, seemingly too intent on his task to respond.

I tried again. "Dmitri said something about an enclave—"

"You're safe," he said, parting my hair with his fingers.

A moan caught in my throat. I arched into his touch before I could help it, relishing the surprisingly pleasurable sensation of his chill on my scalp.

"You no longer seem determined to harm yourself, at least."

I shivered, glancing at my bandaged arm. There was no use in avoiding it any longer. Gritting my teeth, I fingered the end of the strip and began to unwind it as Dublin's hands stilled.

Once the entire length had come undone, pale, untouched flesh was revealed underneath. The properties of Dublin's blood never ceased to leave me speechless. A few sips of it and I was already healing. Yet I had no trouble imagining the carnage that had marred the limb just minutes before. Damage *I* had done. The crumpled bandage conveyed as much, splattered with alarming amounts of scarlet liquid.

"It felt so real," I whispered in horror. "All of it."

"Even the doubts?" He sounded unusually calm as he continued to detangle my matted curls. "That I didn't care about you? That I couldn't love you?"

"Yes." I hunched over myself, drawing my knees to my chest. I eyed the mirror across from us, marveling at the scene it showed. Dublin Helos, crouched in the water behind me, studiously arranging my damp curls. "It doesn't matter. I know that—"

"Should I say it now?" His mouth lingered over my shoulder as he moved his attention to washing my back. "To counter him should he ever steal inside your mind again? At least then you'd have heard it once."

I couldn't breathe—equally alarmed *and* fearful. Even now, doubt festered somewhere inside me, fighting to resurface. Once acknowledged, it gleefully feasted on my unease. *His love would be a lie. A lie...*

"No," I insisted, shaking my head. "I can ignore it."

"I suppose you might require some token to assist in that quest." Lowering the cloth, he lifted my hand from the water, extending the fingers for his inspection.

In confusion, I looked down, frowning as something caught the light. Something small, encircling my finger.

Recognition prickled through my chest.

"My ring..." Only it wasn't. A fact made apparent as I drew it closer for inspection and realized the gold band shone far too brilliantly. Real? A delicately thin band, it encased a stunning blue stone far too beautiful to be formed of cheap plastic.

A replica, but one recreated of materials that I sensed were a million times the worth of the original design.

"Love is an archaic concept, I must admit." Dublin sighed, brushing his lips against my throat as he spoke. "But I suppose we could name it that. What I feel for you. *Love*, in a sense."

As his fingers traced the pulse quickening in my arm, I quaked, too stunned to speak.

"So remember that the next time you dare to slice into this flesh. Every inch belongs to *me*."

My lips parted, a startled laugh escaping them. Only he could turn a romantic confession into a threat. But the reaction made him brace me more firmly, his body molding to mine.

His thumb brushed my jaw, urging me to face him. "Look at me."

His eyes burned, nearly impossible to meet head-on—but in this arena, he offered no reprieve. Our lips met, the kiss slower than any other. Deeper. In it, I sensed more than he could ever convey out loud. Anything. *Everything.*

Enough to silence the remnants of the voices the way sunlight scattered roaches.

"I dearly hate to interrupt…"

I jumped at the intrusion. Before I could cover myself with my hands, Dmitri appeared near the mouth of the bathroom. Not even a heartbeat later, Dublin stood toe-to-toe with him, obscuring any view he might have glimpsed.

"Pardon the interruption," Dmitri simpered as he was promptly herded from the room. "But I figured that you would prefer hearing this from me. *He* requests an audience with you and her." He waved in my direction over Dublin's shoulder. "I take it one of his little spies told him she was up and moving. You knew he wouldn't wait for long. Not when you've come crawling back so conveniently into his control."

"Who?" I croaked, snatching for a nearby towel. Dread thickened my throat as I stood, drawing the material around me. Again, I suspected that a part of me already knew the answer.

"You didn't tell her?" Dmitri remarked, practically *singing* with glee. "Oh my. Well, this will be quite a shock. I'll save you the trouble. Raphael requested your audience, my darling Eleanor. Though I take it you've met our dear, dear mutual friend already?"

That I had.

"He suggested you dress for dinner," Dmitri added as his giddy footsteps retreated. "Oh...and, and Eleanor?" He poised his next statement as if knowing the exact moment I'd flinch in response. "Welcome to the enclave."

LOST

Dublin toweled me off in silence. As if conjured by magic, he pulled a black dress on over my head and guided me into a pair of matching heels. He said nothing, his expression stony—though, to be fair, I wasn't inclined to ask too many questions.

Whatever this "enclave" might be, I suspected that its real purpose lacked any mystery in one context: This place was Raphael's lair. Somewhere beyond the club where the ancient creature held full sway.

And where Dublin did not.

I eyed my ring as he swept my wet hair back from my face to observe his handiwork. Satisfied, he took my hand and steered me from the bathroom. As we crossed the threshold of the bedroom and entered the unknown, he pulled me closer. Enough so that his bulk obscured my view of our surroundings. I could only make out a floor a milky shade of marble and blood-red walls accented in gold.

As blinded as I was, the trip through unseen corridors felt as disorienting as being led through a maze. While blindfolded. In the dark.

Eventually, the corridor must have expanded into a larger, more open space judging from how our every footstep echoed like a gunshot. My ears caught whispered conversations from unseen figures. When Dublin finally drew to a stop, he tugged me to stand beside him.

And when I finally scanned our surroundings unobstructed, my shock transformed my expression, impossible to contain.

We were standing in a throne room. One decorated in swaths of scarlet and gold. More disturbing frescos adorned the walls and high ceilings. Images of angels slaying demons and fiery portrayals of Heaven and Hell.

Like an angel himself, a lone figure was sitting upon a raised dais positioned with the commanding presence of a throne. Raphael. His shoulders draped with a scarlet cloak, he looked every bit as chilling as when I had seen him last. His skin was a thin sheet clinging to bluish veins, enhancing the hollow bones of his eternally beautiful face.

"Eleanor Gray." His faint tenor slithered against my eardrums, conjuring imagery of death and decay. "I am pleased to find you safe and sound...as promised." His dark, lifeless eyes flickered toward Dublin. "You were wise to come to me, as well as to reveal such a miracle. Such... gifts must be guarded at all costs—"

"She is still under *my* protection," Dublin interjected. His hand gripped mine tight, boldly conveying possession. "Barring whatever agreement may be between us."

"And what a marvelous job you've done." It was impossible to discern from Raphael's blank smile whether he meant the phrase as a genuine compliment or an admonishment.

The figures on the outskirts of the room collectively flinched, providing the answer. A *threat*.

"But I do not humor Mero and his toys like you have. Now do you realize the danger he represents? I warned you once when he chose to forsake this life. My Cael, I *warned* you." His voice resonated more strongly. "You should have destroyed him along with his abominations. And yet you let him scurry in the shadows, protecting him even as he taunts you." Something that may have been genuine emotion made his eyes narrow a fraction. "It saddens me to see what you have become, old friend."

"You've always seen time as a commodity," Dublin replied, matching his detached tone. "You command thousands of years' worth of it. A *lifetime* at your disposal, yet that is all you choose to do with it: hoard."

"You mean without *living*?" Raphael issued a chilling, whispery laugh, his disdain for the concept palpable. "As Mero did. Back when you rightly chastised him for forgetting his true nature. Oh, how I wish I had been there. To help you command your senses without this pointless guilt." He shook his head, gazing expressionlessly at events far beyond this room. This century. "While I sit here now, you and I both know whose soul carries a deeper stain upon it. But ever since that day, you've tried to appease him, haven't you? Obeying his inane rules. Until now. Suddenly, you seem determined to consume everything dear Mero cherished. His little pawns. His Grays. Even his old pet... I know you've been trying to find her."

His eyes flickered with renewed interest as Dublin went rigid. "Has it truly come to this, my friend? Hunting a witch in the hopes that what? She could undo the curse she placed at his behest? *Ignorance*," he chided, clasping his pale hands over his lap. "Then again, so was the mere belief that saving dear Eleanor from Mero's curse would be as simple as turning her. Did you think I didn't realize?" A cold sound trickled out of him, a soulless imitation of a laugh. "I knew from the moment you resisted Saskia's attempts to sell her just what she meant to you. Your *prize* in Mero's game. I can only imagine her appeal."

His attention cut to me with the swiftness of a slicing blade, further scattering my thoughts. *Turned?* That word teased the fragile order of my psyche. I trembled, deciding to ignore it. Not now. I couldn't examine it now.

"I admit I was skeptical at first," Raphael continued. "When I heard of his curse. I should have anticipated its power, however. *His* little witch was a rare creature. Such arcane talents she possesses." He sighed, lifting his slender shoulders in defeat. "How I regret not claiming her for myself. You think *you* are the only one hunting for her? Perhaps the next time you come prostrate before me, I'll name her as my price."

"You want to berate me?" Dublin inquired, stepping forward. "Fine. But *none* of your anger concerns Eleanor." He released my arm, his posture stone once more. Only his eyes reflected life, and I suspected that what little humanity remained in them was wasted on the glance he spared in my direction. "She needs rest. Let her go."

"So desperate to shield your true nature from her *still*, Cael?" Raphael's lips twitched in amusement—but in the end, he nodded and raised his hand in a silent command. "*You.* Show Ms. Gray back to her quarters."

A slender figure stepped forward, his head bowed, his red hair gleaming.

"There." Turning to Dublin, Raphael murmured, "I assume this is agreeable with you?"

Dublin said nothing. But he didn't react when Dmitri appeared by my side and reached for my hand, either.

"As you wish," the vampire simpered with mock piety. Even before Raphael, he lost none of his coy amusement.

Dublin on the other hand…

When I looked back, my Devil no longer existed. A stranger was standing in his place—a tormented creature who answered to only one name.

"Well, Cael," Raphael murmured. "What do you have to say for yourself now?"

Dmitri murmured into my ear, "Let us make our escape before the shouting begins, eh?"

Moving quickly, he guided me back to the room I'd woken up in.

"Do have a seat, my dear." He gestured to the bed but remained standing while I perched myself on the end of it.

I was too uneasy to care as he watched me, his eyes gleaming.

"You're shaking." He sounded positively pleased by that fact. "But try not to pout too much, my darling. While the men chat, we can hold a conversation of our own."

"What kind of conversation?" I eyed him sharply, an eyebrow raised.

"Ah, now, that is the question." His eyes glowed an ominous golden hue in the firelight. "You want answers, I presume. More than dear old Dublin has given you, yes? Not that I can blame him, of course," he admitted with a sigh. "This is such a very sore subject for him—"

"What do you want?" Even as I bristled in annoyance, I couldn't deny that he was right.

I wanted answers. But I also wasn't naïve enough to assume he'd give me anything for free. Something warned me that even his assistance during the aftermath of my poisoning had carried a price tag.

"You misunderstand me, my dear one." His smile did nothing to ease my suspicion. "I merely want to wheedle myself into your good graces."

Common sense told me to ignore anything he had to say. To wait for Dublin. To play my hand if I had to. But that same part of me warned that I could maintain my innocence for only so long…

"Who is Mero?" My lips felt dry. I had to drag my tongue along the bottom one.

"Mero?" Dmitri laughed. "That's the wrong question, my dear. The rather boring history between him and Dublin doesn't matter. Not a bit. What you really should be asking is where do *you*, and your child, fit into the grand scheme?"

"M-Me?" But I was well aware of my role—I was a liability to Dublin. A burden he had gone out of his way to bear. His pawn requiring protection.

"Oh, but that's where you are wrong," Dmitri claimed as if reading my mind. "You need to go deeper than that. Right to the beginning. Ask yourself, do you know why only Dublin could feed from you, though I am well aware that is no longer the case? Why is it blood that sustains your current condition, as if to mock his very nature?"

My eyebrow rose. "How did you—"

"Rumors," he said with a dismissive wave of his hand. "Answer the question."

I shrugged; the answer didn't seem to have the makings of a trap. "He said his venom made it so that only he could—"

"*That* is what he told you?" Barking out a harsh bit of laughter, Dmitri slapped his hand against his knee. "You can't fault the man for creativity, though I suppose it is true in some sense. But really, Eleanor, use that critical mind of yours. Go deeper than that. What happened when another vampire fed on you? Someone other than Dublin?"

Someone like Raphael.

My throat went dry. "I…" Even as my voice failed, I knew that my horrified expression revealed the truth. *I died.*

"Dublin has never offered to turn another mortal," Dmitri murmured, his tone suddenly serious. "Never. Not once. Not even in his most…shall we say, his *heyday* as a man who made Raphael quake in his cape." He smirked at the memory. "I think, all along, you've already suspected as much," he added knowingly. "The real catalyst for your pregnancy. The blood you require, though you remain mortal still. Mero, I suspect, had counted on him breaking his one rule all along. For *you*. But it's corrupted you far beyond what poor Dublin intended. While not a vampire, you are…changed."

He eyed my belly. "You just haven't bothered to admit it to yourself. You know there's more to it, and I will tell you what—it is your bloodline. You Grays have been cursed for centuries. Everyone knows it. Especially Dublin. Before you, he has spent years ensuring that none dared feed from any of your kind. Did you know that? It's why the Grayne still exist—he lets them thrive, purely out of courtesy to Mero, the dear friend he betrayed."

"How?" I whispered. "How did he betray him?"

He waved his hand dismissively. "Oh darling, I'm sure you saw my beautiful opera. You are no fool."

I tried to picture the morbid performance and its grisly themes. A man had escaped those in his faction, only to have everything he'd fought for ripped away by someone he trusted.

"Mero was the first to crave another life," Dmitri said as though settling in for a long tale. "A different life from the hell he'd consigned his soul to. I suppose ruling hand in hand with the ruthless Cael took its toll. Rather than trade in lives, he wanted to *live*. And he craved it so badly he found a cunning little witch talented enough to give him and his mortal lover the life he so desired. There were a few caveats, of course."

He lifted his hands in a makeshift scale, raising one while lowering the other. "A terrible price would be paid by both parties involved. I assume they considered it a worthy sacrifice however, in exchange for an abomination in every sense of the word. But then what happened, my dear?" He chuckled darkly when I flinched. "Come on. Continue the tale."

As he had taunted, his opera revealed the answer. The villain of the story had slaughtered a woman and her unborn child in the name of duty.

"Dublin killed her," I choked out in a whisper. "The woman. Didn't he?"

God, I wanted him to laugh, proving I'd been wrong.

"Yes," he said instead, displaying his fangs in full. "And in his grief, Mero founded the Grayne, utilizing your dear ancestor in the process. At his behest, his witch cursed your entire bloodline, though some might say 'protected.'" He scoffed. "Serving within the Grayne was a mere small part of the deal your ancestor made. Mero would protect every Gray to follow, just as long as a few descendants contributed to his lunatic cause. For years, he has maintained that bargain, always watching from the shadows. And in guilt, Dublin has kept even Raphael from destroying them. Though now I have to wonder if perhaps his motive all along was *fear?*"

He searched my face for any reaction. In the end, he sighed. "What better way to punish the man who stole everything you desired than to ensure that he too one day will dare to crave the same simple, honestly boring, wish? *Love.* A family. A reason to endure these wretched, lonely years. And then, were you such a man, you would get to rip it all away."

Pausing his story, Dmitri waited, as if expecting me to realize something. To *feel* something. I just felt numb.

"I see I may have to spell it out for you, dear." He inhaled sharply. "Dublin's always known that one of your kind might set Mero's devious revenge into motion, I suppose. And now..." He gestured toward my stomach. "Have you wondered why he has accepted your condition so easily? It isn't usual—I can tell you that. Or why he hasn't killed you, despite the obvious danger you pose? Why he can't even bear to face the truth by telling you the very things that I am now? Or why the *one* soul you care for more than him perhaps has vanished and he hasn't even offered to help you find her?" He leaned forward, and almost in a whisper, he declared, "You are his doom, Eleanor Gray. Always have been. Always will be."

He stood and stretched his arms over his head in a mock yawn. "I will leave you to your rest," he said before exiting the room. Near the threshold, he paused long enough to add, "Pleasant dreams."

TOKENS

With my thoughts raging in turmoil, I couldn't sleep. I sat hunched over the side of the bed instead, so lost within myself that I barely heard Dublin when he finally returned. Whatever he saw in my expression made him stiffen with one foot poised over the threshold.

"What's wrong?"

God. The sight of his cautious, careful frown banished some of the agonizing tension in my chest. Gone was the stranger from the throne room. He resembled *himself* again, radiating his usual mixture of fury and frustration—but still *Dublin*, the bastard soul collector extraordinaire who'd stolen into my life uninvited.

The man who had corrupted me in more ways than one.

The man who had lied to me.

Tears spilled from my sore, bloodshot eyes, streaming down my cheeks before I could keep them at bay. Despite the roaring fire, my teeth chattered. Tremors racked my hollow frame, yet all I could manage to rasp was, "I'm fine."

"You're not." He spun on his heel, aiming for the door, "I'll get Dmitri—"

"No." I shook my head until he stopped, his back partially to me. "It's not the poison."

Just horror.

Just anger.

The worst part? I didn't know whether to direct it all at him or myself.

"Dmitri," Dublin hissed, this time without concern. Suspicion laced every uttered syllable. "What did he say?"

Anxiety clawed through my blood, sowing bitter regret. How funny that my demand for answers had come back to bite me—after weeks of questions and unintended answers, I doubted I could withstand any more revelations.

"Did… When Raphael bit me…" I closed my eyes as the memory threatened to unfold in painful clarity. "Did you try…t-to turn me?"

"That sly fucking bastard." His voice was a low rasp. "What did he tell you?"

And for some insane reason, I found myself laughing. "That I am destined by blood to destroy you."

"Is that all?"

I bit my lip. His tone was all wrong, suddenly neutral. Confused, I opened my eyes, gaping as he shrugged.

"Frankly, Eleanor, I'd like to think that my doom lies in something a little more formidable than you." He crossed over to my position and stroked his chin, eyeing me with a sweep of his gaze.

"Don't lie to me," I countered. "Is it true?"

He raised an eyebrow. "Is what true?"

"The curse." I ran my fingers through my hair, parting the curls. His reaction didn't fit the morbid, somber tale Dmitri had told. If anything…God, his lack of concern made it all sound so silly when put into perspective.

So silly. So morbid. So very much like Dublin.

"That my family's bloodline was *cursed* by a witch so that one of us would ultimately result in your destruction. Is that ringing a bell?"

"Not particularly?" Dublin frowned as though seriously mulling it over, hunting for that obscure detail among the centuries clouding his ancient brain. "Eleanor, I get damned to Hell on a weekly basis. You can't really expect me to remember *one* witch from—"

"There's more." I stared at my bare toes rather than face him. "That the reason why you could feed from me had nothing to do with venom. No other vampire can. That's why Raphael's bite killed."

"Raphael killed you because he grows more sadistic with every year he's aged." His upper lip curled from his teeth in disgust. "Toying with mortal lives is a game to him. Think of it as a child ripping the wings off a butterfly merely to watch it squirm."

"Then…why are you drawn to me?" I wondered helplessly. Magic would certainly explain it.

"Why?" He raised a golden eyebrow as though I were a simpleton asking why the sky was blue. "Honestly, for the same reason a lion might be drawn to a psychotic, bold, fearless little lamb who acted so peculiarly from the rest of the sheep. I think I'd have to be blind *not* to notice you merrily skipping into danger."

"But…" Doubt returned, planting itself firmly in my chest.

"In fact"—he swiped his finger along the length of one of my curls and then snatched my wrist, inspecting the ring glinting on my finger—"I'd say you are the very opposite of what a curse might conjure to tempt me. I've always despised the color green." He peered into my eyes with a frown. "I also prefer skin that has some definition to it. As well as sun-kissed hair—"

"You mean like Georgie?" I was too stunned to feel offended.

"Yes," he mused, the corner of his mouth lifting. "If some witch designed one of you Grays to 'doom' me, as you put it, it would be *Georgiana* who'd fit the bill. Beautiful, sane, agreeable. A cliched, whirlwind love affair would commence, I suspect."

"Do you know where she is?" My eyes stung. Blinking didn't banish the sensation. His ring threatened to crush my finger. It suddenly felt so heavy. "Have you both just been toying with me this entire—"

"No." He grabbed my chin when I tried to turn away, forcing me to face him.

"I don't know where she is now exactly, but the day I met her, she didn't infuriate me," Dublin went on callously. When I tried to wrench my head away, his grip tightened, holding me captive, forcing me to see. That alarming shift in his gaze—I sensed he *wanted* me to see it. "She doesn't make me question things I have never questioned. She didn't make me sell my soul to Raphael after one ridiculous dance. She didn't arouse me to the point of madness. So if Dmitri meant 'doom' as in 'liable to drive me insane,' then you, Eleanor Gray, fit *that* bill perfectly."

Furious, he swiped at a bead of moisture rolling down my chin, crushing it.

"Come. Raphael doesn't keep his dwelling as well ventilated as I do mine." He tugged on my wrist, yanking me to my feet. "The air in this damn place is making you delirious."

I had no choice but to stagger behind him in a daze, my head spinning as deliriously as he'd claimed. As we entered the hall, he didn't shield me with his body this time. Side by side, we wandered the empty, breathtaking corridors until he shoved me through a doorway and I had to shield my eyes with my hand, blinded.

When my vision gradually cleared, I was convinced we'd entered another realm. One of luxurious sunlight painting a landscape of emerald green, surrounded by stone walls and positively *brimming* with roses. At least thousands, bloomed from vines and shrubs, spanning every shape and color imaginable. The moment I inhaled, I realized it was open to the air. Beautiful, crisp, fresh air. Up above, a blue sky melded with the scenic landscape, and I nearly forgot all of Dmitri's grim tale.

"Is this your apology?" I blurted as Dublin pushed past me.

"Whatever on Earth for?" He shot me a weird look even as he snatched a fresh rose from a nearby bush and held it out for my inspection. "It's merely somewhere we can talk in private." He glanced warily at the structure we exited from —a wall of gray stone. A castle?

"Talk about what?" I asked, struggling to stay focused.

"So, perhaps Dmitri wasn't entirely lying." He stared dead ahead, and I could only guess at how hard it had been for him to admit even that. "There's more to the Grayne's history than I told you. Superstitious drivel, but if you want to hear it…"

"Tell me." I crossed my arms, approached a worn stone bench and sat, still marveling at the wild space. It reminded me of some fairytale castle's crumbling courtyard, abandoned by a monarch who no longer craved the sun. I cradled a nearby bloom between my fingertips, surprised by the petal's softness. As Dublin neared, I whispered, "Tell me about Mero."

After the snippets painted by Dmitri and Raphael, I needed to hear the rest from him.

He came to my side, threading his fingers through my hair while snatching my rose away. "His name was Abrahaim." In a hollow contrast, his voice echoed cold and detached while his fingers casually parted my curls, easing a rose behind my ear. "Descended from Spanish Moors, he worked as a hired missionary in the heart of Andalusia, Spain. The stories he used to tell…" Something pained flitted across his expression too quickly to name. "He used to boast of sneaking into the Alhambra palace, stealing trinkets from the royal apartments. Of charming his quarry with myths of the crusades. A master thief. I met him as nothing more than a wandering vagrant."

He turned on his heel and approached a shrub containing a soft, pink variety of blossoms. He fingered one, manipulating the delicate petals with ruthless intent.

"By then, I had escaped Ireland, stealing away on an English ship. To skirt the British occupation." He shrugged as though referring to a minor inconvenience—not a defining event in a country's history. "I had no plan. No goals. I merely deigned to explore wherever work or curiosity took me. It just so happened that, in Spain, I decided to try my hand as a hired mercenary working for a merchant who traded along the coast. There, he caught wind of a series of vessels returning from some new, mythical land. The Americas.

"Rumors ran rampant of the riches the vessel might contain, ripe for the taking. At his behest, I snuck onto a ship—one whose name you won't find in the history books, mind you—in search of unspeakable treasure." He looked away, gazing into the past. "And I was nearly gutted by Abrahaim, who worked for a rival merchant. After some rather heated back and forth, we decided we were too evenly matched to kill each other within a reasonable amount of time. So we would split the treasure between us, our masters none the wiser." His faint smile fell flat. "Instead, we found a creature far beyond our understanding."

"Raphael," I supplied as he went silent.

He returned, pressing a new conquest against my palm—another rose. "Yes, Raphael," he admitted. "Starved after months at sea, he attacked us both. To this day, I still don't know his true origins. The man is, shall we say, obsessive regarding his past. Even the dates in the history books have been tweaked by him. I suspect your sister must have come close to the truth, for him to grow irritated enough to notice her."

He sighed. "But in those early days, believe it or not, he was but a scared young man tormented by a curse he didn't understand. One he'd inadvertently passed on to Abrahaim and me. But as *we* realized the new limits of our power, his curse became our gift. Our *revelation*. Anything we wanted or desired was ours with nothing more than a flash of fangs. I struggled at first, if you can believe that."

He laughed, fingering his cross. Slow, his steps carried him away from me again, to yet another rose bush. "The constraints of my religion weighed heavily on me. I was a damned, hell-bound creature. But in a way, I grew to accept that doom. I embodied it. Raphael and Abrahaim may have enjoyed their newfound control, but I relished in it. And under my command, we consolidated it, conquering cities from the shadows, building influence through contracts as we discovered creatures more varied than even the creators of the Bible imagined."

Awe painted his tone as he snapped the stem of another rose —a beautiful, creamy white.

"A triumvirate of allies, we were unmatched. If only you knew. Your little history books. Your legends and myths. If only you knew how much of it was a lie." He laughed bitterly, twisting his blossom between his fingers. "But then…the years marched on, unending, taking their toll on each of us in different ways. Raphael grew more reclusive, content to control his reality through proxies on puppet strings. Abrahaim on the other hand, became pensive, racked with more guilt with every additional life ruined. And I…"

He turned to me, but I doubted he even saw me. His eyes were wide, consumed by the past.

"I grew numb. Detached. It was as though I could only ever feel anything through violence. Through sowing fear.

Crushing souls." He formed a fist, crushing the rose into nothing. "Destroying lives. The more they bled, and agonized and screamed, the more intoxicating the power became. There is something terrible and addicting in sowing chaos… But every drug presents the danger of a relapse. When its high breaks and you fall from the glorious height. Increasingly I felt it, that *guilt*. A woman desired money to save her ailing father. In return, I consigned her to years of servitude, whoring herself, no different than hundreds before her. But in those days, I'd see her pain and, for a second, I'd feel it. *Guilt*."

He gritted his teeth against it, and I knew deep down that if he could have purged that emotion from his soul entirely, he would have.

"It became too frequent, too much. In yet another instance, I desired the soul of a succubus, and in the process, her daughter was harmed."

Saskia, I realized.

"As if conjured by heaven's mercy, Abrahaim was there to convince me that there was another way. We could control our impulses, he claimed. Leave that life behind. He made it sound beautiful. I will give him that." His mouth contorted into a painful imitation of a smile. "We took new names to reflect our rebirth—mine a reminder of where my was soul bound, while his was a simple phrase, chanted during the crusades his ancestors fought within. *Memento Mori*. Remember death. From it, he took the name Mero. Then he told me of a witch he knew, powerful enough to create a totem to keep him grounded. Help him remember the humanity we both had so eagerly shed."

"Your necklace," I whispered, eyeing the silver totem hanging from his throat. The one I found in the crypt took on a darker meaning. Not a backup of Dublin's, but something far more meaningful…

"Yes." He bowed his head, stroking his fingers along his cross. "Mero had one as well."

"How?" I whispered. "Doesn't yours…help you somehow?"

He nodded. "It's more than just enchanted by petty magic. It contains my blood. When you wore it, I could sense you even while halfway across the world. And while I wear it, I can control the urge to feed."

I swallowed hard as my thoughts spun, replaying all of the times he'd forsaken the necklace around me. Namely the night he returned when, by his own admission, he nearly killed me.

"We both know how hunger can affect you," Yulia had told him during a hazy conversation I barely remembered. *"I should have talked you out of ever giving up that stupid amulet in the first place…"*

"Mero never relied on his totem the same way," Dublin continued. "He spoke of a future. Of a life beyond this curse we'd been stricken with. The fool even mused of children born mortal. The only price would be his soul. His eternity. While he could never die, his seed would grow, and spread, and prosper. It was his dream. But Raphael was not pleased."

He turned, starting to pace. I doubted he was even speaking to me anymore. No, this tale ripped from his soul unabated was for his benefit alone.

"He considered it a betrayal, and in my selfish, callous addiction, I let myself believe it. Gratitude toward my old friend for showing me the light of redemption became hate. How dare he believe that we could change? How dare he threaten the world we had spent countless years creating?" He demanded the question of no one, his face upturned skyward. "Blinded with rage, I hunted him down, finding him in the Americas. I killed his lover, slitting her throat right before his eyes. He would see reason then—or so I convinced myself. He would surely realize it. Chasing happiness, and mortality and pointless joy was futile. We were Gods among men, how dare he forsake that?

"But I quickly realized that there are no gods. No Heaven. No Hell. Just pain and redemption. And as I watched Mero mourn for a woman whose life was but a speck of dust in the stream of time, I realized that my grip on power was just as futile as his lust for freedom. Neither path would lead to salvation. Just destruction."

He turned to me, running his finger across my throat. "In his grief, my old friend found a mortal to corrupt to his will."

"James," I whispered. My mysterious ancestor.

"Yes. I'm sure Mero spun his aim as some grand crusade against evil, but that was merely a lie. He wanted a bloodline to poison. A fertile bit of soil within which to plant his revenge. Yet I didn't want to fight that war with him. Call me a coward, but I alas, I was tired…"

He bowed his head, his eyes downcast. "So I went to Raphael. I traded my time in exchange for his avoidance of the Grayne. I let Mero plot in obscurity, telling myself that his promises of revenge were nothing more than fantasies. And I still believe that." He turned to me again, an eyebrow raised. "Do you want to know why? Because if my affections were the result of some twisted curse, I imagine I'd be easily wooed by a creature like your sister. I'd succumb with no resistance, hypnotized. But you…"

Step by step, he advanced on me and there was no escape. "I resist you, and you tempt me further. There is no mindless surrender. You claw your way through me like poison. There is no ease with you. I'm tormented. In lust, you torment. In pain, you torment. In happiness even…you torment me."

He trailed his lips across my forehead, lingering there. "I am the soul at your discretion. No curse could inspire that. You claimed Saskia told you I thought of your sister? How could I not? Let's say she is missing. That Mero has her. That he is using her as a pawn to lure you to him, knowing you would never abandon her. Killing her without your knowledge would easily solve the threat she poses to you. And yet…" He sighed and withdrew. "I know you would never forgive me if I took her life. So I haven't. He knows as much. I am sure of it. He knows exactly how to win this game."

My breath caught. I couldn't avoid asking, "Do you know where she is?"

"I suspect she's in hiding," he said. "And not only from me."

"Oh?" Fear gnawed at my stomach. I'd been able to ignore it until now—but as if conjured by his mere mentioning, weeks of pain descended. My sister. God, I wanted to face her. Demand my own answers. See her face.

Did she ever love me?

"Well, you'd think she could send me a letter, or a phone call, or even a goddamn homing pigeon just to let me know that she was still alive."

"Would that change anything if she had?"

"It would certainly make it easier to hate her," I blurted. Only he could do this to me—drag out the truths I wasn't even aware of myself. I eyed the rose in my grasp, ripped a petal from the beautiful mass, and watched it dance in the still air. "As it stands, she can't even bother to send me so much as a postcard."

Something in his silence made me look up, but for once, he didn't seem willing to meet my gaze.

"You wouldn't keep her from me," I insisted. Why did I sound so damn terrified? Georgie's abandoning me was one thing. But if he had purposefully led me to believe...

"Here." He reached into his pocket. "I found this in your crypt. I suspect it had been there for at least a few weeks before then."

I froze as he shoved something into my hand. It was small, soft. A crumpled piece of paper. Written on it was a simple message scrawled in painfully familiar handwriting.

Elles. I wish I could smile in that scrunched-up way I used to back in the days I could easily charm you after stealing one of your biscuits. I understand that this is different. I'm trying to find my own way to answer your questions. But remember what Mother always said—above all, blood remains. Remember that and you will always be able to find me. — Georgie.

God, it was the exact thing she'd say at a time like this. Clueless, mocking, and coy. Heat burned behind my eyes, impossible to fight back.

"Where…" The answer came to me before the words finished leaving my throat. The urn. Telltale signs of dust coated the edges of the paper.

He'd stolen it, perhaps that very day I'd mentioned our hiding place.

Teeth bared, I whirled on him, "I should kill you for this. Were there more?"

"No," he admitted. "But if there were, I would have burned them."

A scream of frustration left me hollow. When that wasn't enough, I found myself pacing in a circle, tearing my hands through my hair. It still wasn't enough. I had to hit him, swiping my nails at his flawless features. "I hate you!"

"You should," he agreed, not flinching so much as an eyebrow in the face of my assault. Without even leaving a mark, my fingers glanced harmlessly off his flesh. "Because if she proves to be a threat to you, I'll do far worse than that."

The veracity of the promise drained me of rage entirely. I just felt numb, watching the hint of a monster lurk beneath his callous façade. "You had no right—"

"I don't?" In a motion so effortless that I felt it rather than saw it, he snatched up my wrist, yanking me so close that my lips met the skin of his throat. Against my scalp, he murmured, "I don't have a right to be concerned when your sister consorts with a band of cultists who want you dead? I don't have a right?"

My skin stung beneath the venom in his tone. I'd never heard him quite this cold—passionless and passionate at the same time.

"Do you have any idea—" Within seconds, he had me backed against the stone wall enclosing the garden. When I dared to meet them, his eyes were midnight, flashing with rage. "Do you have any idea what I've done—what I had to bargain—to even bring you here? *Time*! More than you can ever imagine!"

He was shouting. Smoldering with rage, he alone made the sun seem powerless, and the world became gray with shadow.

"Do you have any idea what I'd do to anyone who threatened you? I won't apologize for any of it. So do not expect me to. And do you want to know why?" His mouth was against my hair, his words a low, mocking hum.

"I should never forgive you for this." I'd felt compelled to say it. To mean it, even as the words broke off in a gasp when his lips met the side of my throat. "Never... Not even if you beg."

"I never beg." The promise taunted me as he sank to his knees. In front of me. Right there in broad daylight. Swift fingers wrenched up the hem of my dress. His head darted beneath it, and then...

Slow, deliberate pulses of his thumb nudged my legs apart and a moan ripped from my throat, echoing on the secluded silence. I squeezed my eyes shut, throwing my head back against the stone. Neither action helped reduce the insanity of what was happening.

"Stop!" I wanted to cling to my anger. I tried to.

But a brush of his touch against my skin disrupted my senses. Perhaps he had been right all along? I was delirious.

"I believe we have concluded this discussion," he murmured against my inner thigh. "I promise to avail myself to your rage at a later time. But now... You were beyond me for days. I believe I am due some kind of recompense."

Recompense?

"But Georgie is your ideal," I hissed even as my body remained rigid, at his mercy. "And it's not like you're my type, either."

As my thoughts scattered, they turned to what my pride considered his worst offense, in addition to lying and scheming. Insulting my apparent appeal.

"*You're* too bold." As if to prove it, what felt like his lips grazed the side of my hip, making my train of thought sputter and nearly derail. "Too cold. Mean. C-Cocky—"

"Those sound like defining attributes to me." As he spoke, he did something with his hands that stole my breath. Soft, dangerous fingertips. Rough, sinful heat.

I found myself gasping for air. "You're too blond," I breathed. "I prefer brunettes—"

"Like that man you dined with?"

I heard the question as if he'd spoken to me through a tube.

"What was his name again?"

"Hmph?" My brain was too busy detaching from my skull to keep up, floating.

"Gabriel something," he recalled. Muscle and nerves melted. The vibrations of his voice dangerously enhanced the slow, steady pressure building between my legs.

I wanted to correct him. But then his lips slid lower, too low, and I panicked, desperate for ammunition.

"Oh, him… He was charming. A gentleman. The usual list of everything you aren't—"

He went too low. My back bowed, nails scraping against the stone on either side of me for any hint of stability. In response, he laughed, really laughed, and it was sin. Evil. Devastating. My spine turned to putty. Rudderless, I had to brace one hand against his skull, fisting my fingers through his hair.

"The man shrouds himself in an unusual amount of mystic," he admitted. "I do suspect he has ties to the mob. Or that he's secretly a crossdresser given his rather feminine aesthetic. I daresay you dodged a bullet."

"You actually stalked him?" Alarm countered pleasure. Mr. Lanic may have been a money-hungry grifter, but mere greed didn't warrant the wrath of Dublin Helos.

"I nearly killed him. Or just maimed, perhaps." His mouth withdrew just enough to make it easier to breathe again. "Alas, a sudden intrusion into my private sanctum by a madwoman made me rethink that plan."

Had I been? A madwoman?

Cool hands brushed my neck before I could decide, seizing the collar of my dress. When my eyes opened, I found Dublin on his feet again. With little care, he tugged on the silk in his grasp, tearing it right down the middle. He was intent on guiding my arms from the sleeves so that the material could fall at my feet. I barely registered then that I was naked in broad daylight. That he was quickly removing my panties as well. That his touch became more possessive by the second.

Hungrier.

But then he entered me in a single thrust and the world fell away. Hate disappeared. All that remained was selfish, desperate, grappling need. I lunged against him, seeking only one thing. He gave it to me. He took it from me—screams, moans, repeated whimpers of his name.

Guided by his corrupting touch, I floated to heaven and crashed to Earth while the sky darkened above me.

DECEPTION

Peace could be more insidious than poison, stealing into a breathless silence with no warning. No escape. I would never be able to erase this moment or deny the emotions sowed with every breath spent lying naked beneath the stars—even if the person holding me in his arms contained a million secrets unwilling to be shared.

I was content.

Though I should have been worried that, any minute, someone might intrude upon our hidden space and find us. Dublin didn't seem concerned by the prospect, either. His only movement was to rake his fingers through my hair and guide me to face him.

"Drink." His bleeding wrist found my mouth before I even had the chance to question.

I obeyed, lapping obediently at my "meal" while my stomach churned for more. When I finally came up for air, he was already on his feet, still brazenly naked. His skin gleamed silver in the moonlight, enhancing the muscles rippling in his back as he retrieved our clothing from near the bench.

After observing the ruined state of my dress, he tossed me his shirt instead. "Put it on."

The soft fabric smelled like him. Like ice. Like winter.

"I still don't forgive you for lying about Georgie." I felt the need to tell him that even as he approached me and crouched to slip my shoes on.

Without a word, he took my hand and led the way into the dark until we exited from the door we'd entered through.

The corridors remained empty, though I swore the shadows flickered, betraying unseen figures lurking in our wake. Spectators, I suspected, spying in silence as the powerful Cael paraded his little mortal prize right past their noses. If Dublin sensed them as well, his expression didn't reveal as much. Serving as my stone-faced guide, he steered me through the hostile elegance. It was only as we entered the chilling interior of the bedroom that he spoke again.

"What would it take, should I be inclined to return to your good graces?" he wondered as I crossed to the bed.

I looked over my shoulder and found him watching me, stroking his chin in serious contemplation. As our gazes met, his tongue flicked between his lips and I choked. Something told me he enjoyed my anger far more than he should have—namely the possibilities that said "redemption" might present to *his* benefit.

It was surprisingly easy to come up with something nonetheless. "You could let me string you up by your toes and heed my every command and even then...I'd only consider it."

"We can add that as leverage," he decided. Suddenly serious, he averted his gaze and withdrew something from his pocket. Whatever it was, he kept it concealed between his fingers. "I propose another bargain—Raphael insists that no mortal knows the location of his precious little sanctum, and I do believe we have overstayed our welcome." He grimaced and opened his hand, revealing the small vial. A dark liquid glinted within as he held it up to the firelight, a deeper scarlet than even his blood. "Getting you out of here without catching his notice will require some drastic measures."

I smoothed my fingers over the front of his borrowed shirt, drawing it tighter around myself. "Like what?"

"Smuggling," Dmitri prompted, uninvited.

I spun around and found him near the door, leaning against the gilded frame. Just for how long had he been there, watching? His smug grin revealed no answer. "Raphael will not willingly allow you to leave. Especially not now." His gaze drifted down to my belly. "Not when you present an untapped well of time belonging to his most favorite of toys. So we must slow your heartbeat, and then act quickly before he and his spies notice the silence." He pointedly tapped his earlobe as if for emphasis. "The drug will help, but it is not infallible. Luckily, *I* mentioned how convenient it might be if we could disguise you beneath enchanted fabric designed to suppress the stench of your charming mortality. Not even Raphael would be able to track us in time."

"Enough games. Is she here?" Dublin demanded, turning to him.

Dmitri shrugged. "I think I heard someone screaming in French near the grand foyer. You must be such a lax master for her to rage so indignantly at being summoned. I, on the other hand, always kept her *disciplined—*"

"And you remember your boundary," Dublin warned in a tone so biting that I flinched. "You so much as look at her. Touch her. Think of her and I swear I will cut you down where you stand."

"Hmph." Dmitri pursed his lips, but the bravado was purely for show. The pointed glance he shot Dublin's fingers revealed just how seriously he took the threat. "I suppose. But we really should be hurrying this mad scheme along. Time is of the essence. Especially if you still plan to hunt down that devious little witch."

"Eleanor," Dublin returned his attention to me and captured my chin in his free hand. "I need you to drink this." He nodded to the vial in his grasp. "It's a mild sedative, but it will render you unconscious. Just long enough for me to get you somewhere safe. It won't harm you," he insisted. "And this way, I can arrange our...*escape* may be too dramatic a word. Let's call it, fashionable departure."

Warily, I took the flask. One inhale of the liquid contained within and I forgot my doubt. It smelled like him—spice, ice and winter. After a hesitant sip revealed nothing alarming, I downed it entirely. Before I'd even finished swallowing the last drop, the flask fell from my grip.

I staggered, too sluggish to catch it. My eyelids were heavy as well, my body weighed down.

And before I knew it, I fell into oblivion.

SHE WHO DARES TO QUESTION...

*R*eality reasserted its presence with the aid of a million unnerving sounds. Wood creaking. Fabric swishing. A man pointedly clearing his throat.

"The drug should have worn off an hour ago," he remarked, sounding somewhere between bored and concerned. "So either you're ignoring my attempts to wake you or you're really in mortal peril and require some lifesaving remedy. Either way, your lover will threaten to kill me if you don't show signs of life soon."

Ice fluttered across my cheek. A finger?

"I can hear your pulse racing," its owner taunted. "Do hurry. I would hate for you to miss the show."

I peeled my eyes open. As I blinked, my vision quickly adjusted, focusing on the beautiful creature watching me from a seated position nearby. Dmitri, his eyes flickering with mischief. Propped on his lap was a newspaper he was pretending to read while the two other occupants of the room argued nearby.

One of them I instantly recognized, his voice a growl. Dublin. He was standing near a wood-paneled wall at the back of a small, modestly decorated sitting room.

"I don't want to fight with you," he warned. Even in anger he seemed to be trying his best to refute the figure standing opposite him without shouting.

"You had no right!" the woman hissed, her musical accent beautiful even while shaking with rage. "How dare you even —" She broke off and flashed a strained but friendly smile in my direction. "Oh, hello, Eleanor. I'm glad you're awake." A heartbeat later, she rounded on Dublin again. "How dare you?" Raw pain sucked away some of the youth conveyed by her features. She looked old, aged overnight in a demure gray dress devoid of her usual flair. Her hair hung loosely around her face, swinging through the air as her hand lashed out and collided with Dublin's jaw. "You had *no* right. And I don't even get the courtesy of a full explanation—"

"I'm trying to explain now," Dublin insisted. "If you would just listen—"

"Listen?" Yulia threw her head back and cackled. "What? Are you going to exert your ownership of me again?" Her tone was ice. "I have always trusted you with my life. You have never given me a reason not to. But if you ever yank me around like this again, you will no longer have a loyal servant to do your bidding. Goodbye, *Eleanor.*" With one last genuine smile in my direction, she stormed off through a nearby doorway.

"What happened?" I struggled to pull myself upright, staring after her.

"I happened," Dmitri mused without looking up from the current page of his paper. "Dearest Yuliana seems to be unwilling to let bygones be bygones. Even if her beloved new master puts his boot to her backside."

"Don't."

I shivered at the warning lacing Dublin's tone and my gaze flickered to him. He was Mr. Contractor once again, reinforcing his ownership over a soul in his possession.

"Remember what I told you?"

"Yes," Dmitri sighed, rustling his paper. His bright-teal suit diminished his attempts at seeming modest, however. As did his ever-present smirk. "No looking. No touching. No thinking—"

"And don't you dare say her name, either—" Dublin broke off, finally seeming to notice me. He took a step toward me, his hand outstretched. "How do you feel?"

"Fine," I croaked, still staring after Yulia. I sensed that her anger had something to do with the snippets of conversation I remembered before I'd drunk the drugged liquid. *Smuggling,* Dmitri had said.

I glanced down, noticing my surroundings for the first time. No longer were we in Raphael's lair. There were windows, for one, revealing a view of emerald trees and blue sky. The décor lacked any serpentine accents, instead consisting of dark, muted colors and simplistic furniture. I lay outstretched on a leather couch matching the style of the chair Dmitri was occupying.

And from here, furious footsteps were audible, storming deeper within the structure.

"Is she all right—"

"She's fine," Dublin snapped.

"She's upset. Is it because you made her help you take me from Raphael's?"

"No," Dublin admitted. "It's a bit more complicated than that."

"Complicated?" Dmitri folded up his paper and flashed a beautiful, chilling smile. "No, my dear. It wasn't making her 'escort' you with her poor, old master. It was *ordering* her to, utilizing the power of her contract. Even if she wanted to— which she very much did—she couldn't resist a direct command. All to ensure that dear Eleanor Gray remained safe and sound. I suppose that's the only reason why she hasn't snuck a curse into your suit jacket yet," he added, stroking the collar of his flamboyant jacket. "Nasty stuff. I know firsthand how devious her little brain can be—"

"Enough." Teeth bared, Dublin shot him a withering glance. "Do I need to remind you again of your boundary?"

Dmitri visibly shrank into his chair. "I will remain on my absolute best behavior." He returned to the depths of his newspaper, but I didn't miss the devious tilt to his mouth.

"She'll be fine," Dublin insisted before changing the subject. "Now. What did you learn?"

Dmitri rolled up his paper and set it aside entirely. "Despite my unwilling accomplice, we were able to make some headway to my connections," he murmured. "You probably don't want to know the details. Something involving a cursed negligee… Regardless, we did discover one kernel of information."

Dublin's eyes flashed and narrowed. With just a few lethal nuances in his expression, he made impatience into an art form. "And?"

"Our quarry lies in Leon, not far from here," Dmitri admitted. "It's a fitting hiding place, the rural wilds of France. Rumor has it she's made her home amongst the witches who still dwell there. Though it could be an elaborate ruse and she could be living under a bridge in some city in the States. You know how she loved her mind games."

My head was spinning. *Witches. Quarry. France.*

"Who are you talking about?"

The two men shared a look.

"Answers, my dear," Dmitri finally said. "As to your… condition." He nodded toward my stomach. "From the very witch who may have set it into motion, so to speak."

Answers. I looked to Dublin and he said nothing. His jaw was clenched, his eyes thoughtful.

Licking my lips, I asked, "How do we find her?"

"Well, we hunt her down," Dmitri said wryly.

Dublin, however, didn't seem convinced. He paced, his eyes focused on a section of the wall. "How accurate is this information?" he demanded of Dmitri.

The vampire shrugged. "You'd have to ask dearest Yuliana of that. I'm sure you won't trust *my* assurances—"

"It's true." Yulia appeared in the doorway of the room, her arms crossed. I'd never seen her so cold, her eyes frozen over, devoid of emotion. "I made sure of it. But I can recognize embellishment as well. There is every possibility we're being misled. After all, to stay undetected for centuries, I'm sure Adara has taken the proper precautions."

Dublin nodded once and met her gaze. "Thank you."

Yulia said nothing, but she didn't storm off again, either.

"So." Dmitri clapped his hands once and rose gallantly to his feet. "When do we leave? An adventure, how exciting—"

"Who said anything about you coming?" Dublin shot him a look that made even his cheerful façade crack a bit.

"Ah, but remember my price, Dublin." He fingered the white pocket square accenting his breast. "My assistance has not come cheaply. Think of it as a loan I expect to be repaid in full. Besides." He shrugged. "You don't even like witches, apart from the person whose name I am forbidden to mention. Especially *her*—"

"Fine," Dublin snapped. "We'll leave in the morning."

Dmitri beamed. "Oh, excellent!"

Yulia crossed her arms, her gaze fixed on the wall—coincidentally avoiding both men in the process. "Am I still under your command, *master*?" she inquired coldly.

"I would like you to stay," Dublin admitted. "As my friend—"

She stormed from the room. Dmitri snickered, fiddling with his paper once more—until a glowering stare from Dublin made him lurch to his feet.

"I suppose I will excuse myself as well," he simpered while exiting the room.

I sat there awkwardly, drawing my knees to my chest. "You've royally pissed her off," I remarked. I racked my brain, but I doubted I'd ever seen her frown, let alone furious.

"For good reason," he admitted. "I've never invoked her contract against her before now." He sighed and drew himself up to his full height, his jaw set in determination. "But she won't stay angry for long."

"What is her past with Dmitri?" I wondered. Though did I really want to know? On the surface, the other vampire seemed more mischievous than vicious. But even I knew that appearances could be deceiving.

In his own way, the vampire seemed more than matched with Dublin in the potential for sowing chaos and pain.

"He owned her," Dublin said, phrasing the words as carefully as he could. "Once. It was not a mutual partnership, if you can't already tell."

I nodded, hunched over my limbs. My shoes were off, and a thin blanket crumpled at the end of the couch made me suspect that someone originally draped me beneath it. "What did he do to her?"

"He abused her skills for his own gain and warped her mind just as viciously as Mero's poison did yours."

I cringed. Even now, that crippling, whispering doubt still snuck into the silence when I least expected it. *You're worthless, Eleanor.* A part of me feared it would never completely cease—and Dmitri seemed more than capable of such manipulation. I could still picture the dazed girl he'd brought to the opera, fully under his sway.

"That's horrible," I rasped.

"Neither of them will ever harm you again," Dublin swore. He was beside me in an instant, brushing his fingers along my hand, including the one sporting his ring.

"Tell me." I curled my fingers around his and marveled at the sight of my slim ones, intertwined with his larger, albeit more graceful appendages. "Tell me what happened between them."

"She was devoted to him," he said. "Wholly. Perhaps he thought she loved him? Either way, he enjoyed testing her, pushing her skills to their very limits. He would have her dress in clothing designed to tempt men and women alike and watch her struggle to ward them off. He would pit her against other witches with her skill and punish her should she fail." He frowned at the memory and I felt my heart lurch. Any cruelty that could arouse even Dublin's pity had to be unimaginable. "One night, he went too far and I intervened."

"And then you offered her a contract?"

He frowned. "Let's say I made Dmitri an offer he couldn't refuse."

"And she's been with you ever since?" I spoke softly, lost in thought as I tried to imagine just how old Yulia might be. She looked no older than I was on the surface, but there was no mistaking the ageless wisdom glinting in her gaze. "All this time and you've kept her away from him, I'm assuming?"

Dublin said nothing, though he didn't have to. I could already guess that part of the tale. *Yes.*

"And she's upset because you made her face him now," I suspected. But no, it was more than that. "You *forced* her to—"

"I had to." He didn't sound even remotely apologetic. Guilty, yes, but his eyes burned as determinedly as ever.

It was a harrowing reminder: He was more than willing to sacrifice even the trust of his few friends in order to get what he wanted. Which, in this case, seemed even more obscure than usual: the location of someone who might or might not be found there anyway.

"But she will forgive me," he said, sounding more than confident of that. "She's strong enough to face him, or I would never allow him in her orbit. I suspect her unpleasant reaction is merely her fear. He controlled her for so long, I wonder if she doubts that she can withstand him, even now?" He inclined his head, mulling over the prospect. "She's known all along that she would have to face him eventually. That he still holds some part of her soul she can never erase. Running from him could stave off the inevitable for only so long."

The wistful, deepening note in his voice warned me that he wasn't solely speaking of Yulia and Dmitri anymore.

"That's remarkably astute," I admitted. "For a man who is keeping the poor, innocent woman in his protection away from her only sister."

He flinched and dismissed the comparison with a shrug of his shoulder. His voice low, he countered, "Dmitri would never pose the risk of *killing* Yulia."

Fair enough. I swallowed hard, tearing my gaze away.

"Why go through all this trouble anyway?" I wondered, returning to our previous, safer, topic.

He sighed. "As Dmitri said, we needed information. A way to reverse—" He broke off, forming a fist with the hand he withdrew from me. "Just trust that my reasons are more than valid."

Rather than press the issue any further, I settled deeper into the leather cushions beneath me and watched the breathtaking scenery from the nearest window. "Where are we?"

Somewhere far more beautiful than the grim interior of a vampire lair, at least. Silvery clouds streaked with violet painted the edges of the navy sky. The sight reminded me of Dublin in a way: dark except for a few barely imperceptible dashes of color. Beautiful. Frightening. Navigable only with courage and ample skill.

"Somewhere safe," he replied, his back to me. "Somewhere safe…in the rural of France."

"Ah," I croaked, somehow not surprised. Apparently, Dublin had a knack for amassing reclusive properties—as well as for transporting an unconscious woman across the globe.

At a glance, this house appeared smaller than the last, yet the plain décor seemed cozier than even his lavish high-rises and manors.

"A tour?" I requested, extending my hand.

He took it, helping me to my feet. Whatever drug he had given me had little aftereffects, thankfully. I felt steady as I fell into step beside him.

The foyer was small, the walls inside reflecting the simplistic design of the sitting room. Hardwood and soft gray cast a neutral elegance. I was instantly endeared.

"Your room is at the top of the stairs," Dublin told me, nodding to a grand oak staircase straight ahead.

"And mine?" Dmitri wondered.

I jumped, turning to find him standing uncomfortably close behind me. His eyes sparkled, his lips quirking as he folded his arms over his chest.

"There's a shed out back," Dublin replied without missing a beat. He continued forward, leaving the foyer to show me the rest of the house.

There was a dining room, a modest kitchen, and a parlor-slash-library. Overall, it was a smaller dwelling, as suspected, but an air of security tainted the atmosphere, impossible to ignore. Something told me that Dublin had more of his shadowy agents already positioned at various stations. Watching.

And waiting.

Yet...

I couldn't name what else was lingering in the air, taunting me as I followed Dublin up the stairs next. An inexplicable unease deepened the shadows stretching across the hallway. For some reason, I found myself holding my breath as he approached a closed door and palmed the doorknob.

"You can sleep in here," he explained, pushing the door open.

Tension crept into my muscles, holding them rigid as I peered into the space beyond, wary of what I might find. Then...

I laughed, my eyes widened in shock. "Interesting color choice, Mr. Helos."

The furniture was white. The bed, the wardrobe, the curtains, the sheets. Even the fur rug spread over the hardwood floors was a pale, delicate shade.

For all their brooding seriousness, apparently some vampires still retained a sense of humor.

"I thought you hated the color?"

"On you," he admitted, but something in his gaze made me doubt that assertion. "I suppose it will do for décor."

I grinned wickedly. "I should redecorate Gray Manor in the color scheme. White lace everywhere."

He grimaced and I nearly clapped my hands in glee.

"Can you imagine?" I asked. "My room will resemble a biblical virgin's paradise. I shall order doilies and I'm sure I could find a cradle that—" I broke off, confused by the careless admission. Cancer had been a pathetic denial to cling to—I could admit that now—but the inverse of that claim terrified me far more. Even acknowledging it to myself was a struggle. God, I couldn't even look at Dublin.

"I'm sure that could be arranged." His finger slipped under my chin, lifting it despite my attempts. He frowned, brushing his thumb across my lower lip. "Though there are other rooms to choose from if this one doesn't satisfy you."

"No." Pushing past him, I approached the bed and ran my fingers over the delicate duvet. "This is perfect. Though"—I bit my lip—"it's just that this bed is so very large…"

"Oh?" His gaze was awaiting mine when I looked over, swallowing me whole, body and soul. "It might cause a bit of inconvenience on my part, but I think I can find a solution to that."

Heat sweltered in my blood. The hand I braced against the bed involuntarily clenched, seizing a fistful of soft fabric. At the same time, he reached for the door handle, shoving it back.

In retrospect, the bed wasn't all that big. His body had to curve around mine just to fit. Neither he nor I were prone to hugs. So the arm he allowed to fall across my hip was merely there by necessity. The cool fingers that brushed my belly were accidental.

The shiver that racked my body was entirely from his chill alone.

Nothing else.

Regardless, I slept, unplagued by nightmares, his taste on my tongue.

And I knew, even as I drifted off, that my mother's iron-grip on Gray Manor's interior would most definitely come to an end.

A COMPANY OF WITCHES

"$\mathcal{O}$h dear." Dmitri's narrowed eyes flickered along the length of my body as I descended the stairs the next morning. "This will simply not do. You are dressed all wrong."

"How so?" I fingered the hem of my skirt. It was a sensible cut, exquisitely detailed though relatively plain. "What's wrong with it?"

"Yes," Yulia pitched in from the doorway, addressing him for the first time. Cold, her gaze slithered over his face as dispassionately as Raphael's. "How so?"

Dmitri scoffed, but I didn't miss the step he took in my direction, widening the space between him and the person he was expressly forbidden from speaking to. There wasn't far for him to go, considering we were in the foyer, marshaled together, a motley crew of four.

"Do either of you understand adventuring attire?" He gestured to his lime-green slacks and his white button-down. On his head, of all things, perched a straw hat. Tutting in exasperation, he turned to the figure waiting for me at the base of the staircase. "Dublin, will you stand for this?"

The vampire in question seemed to be far beyond giving a damn about clothing. Distant eyes flickered between awareness and emptiness. He'd been that way ever since I'd woken up. Locked within himself, venturing from the depths of his psyche only for seconds at a time.

Why?

I wasn't brave enough to question it.

"It's fine," he muttered without looking my way. "Let's get moving before you bring the whole damn village down on us."

He left the drawing room. A second later, the front door slammed against what felt like the inner wall of the foyer.

"Well then." After smoothing his shirt, Dmitri followed him.

I fell into step in his wake, sensing Yulia behind me. Together, we packed into one car driven by Dublin, who said nothing during the terse hours-long trip through fields and forest.

The forested, beautiful landscape felt like a different realm from the city I was used to. Another world entirely. Breathtaking, yes. But also unsettling. Dread came to life in my stomach, twisting. Twinging. I had to flatten my palm beneath my rib cage to ease the discomfort.

Despite all the bargains and deals Dublin had made for my safety, I knew without a doubt that we were far from Raphael's territory. Could the old vampire's influence stretch this far? Something told me it didn't. Close-set foliage grazed the sides of the car as we drove through cramped roads, the sounds echoing almost like whispers.

No one can save you here…

"It will be a long trek," Dmitri promised as we crested the ridge of a hillside cut deep within a dense cluster of trees. "These crones hide themselves well among these hills. Though I'm sure you're prepared for any booby traps." He looked at Dublin, who didn't answer.

Eventually, the car came to a stop, seemingly in the middle of nowhere. As in Dublin didn't park, the engine just stalled, jarring me forward so violently that I had to brace myself against the front seat.

"Stay here." Dublin exited the vehicle, swiftly followed by Yulia and Dmitri.

Apparently, his command only applied to me.

With anxious glances at their surroundings, the trio continued up the road, led by Dublin. Only after two paces forward, they too abruptly stopped. Heart in my throat, I leaned forward and peered through the windshield to see why. At first, I saw nothing. Just swaying branches dripping with shadows and foliage. It was only on my second search that I saw her.

She stood, flanked by two sprawling trees, their gnarled branches twisted in her direction as if shielding her from sight. She was thin and fair. Hair so pale that it rivaled the hue of Dublin's skin fell down her shoulders in wild, unbrushed waves. Given the color, I expected her age to be reflected in her face, but she looked even younger than I was. Just a girl standing alone in the woods, confronted by two vampires.

Dublin said something. His posture was neutral, his stance open. From this angle, I could only see his lips moving, deaf to whatever words were passing between him and the woman.

But I didn't need to hear to notice the marked shift in tone when she shook her head and pointed to the car. To me.

Shivers racked my spine. The scrape of branches against the car's roof became more pronounced. Less like whispers and more like distinct words. *You...*

You. You. You.

The wind picked up, tossing scattered raindrops across the windshield. What little daylight there was dissipated, leaving an eerie glow that drenched the landscape in indigo darkness. Only Dublin had any definition anymore, his hair shining like burnished gold.

All the while, the woman beyond the trees just stared, her finger still pointing.

And that whispering within my skull grew louder, transformed into a faint, childlike murmur. *You. You. You must come alone...*

My hand was on the handle of the door. Before I realized, I'd pushed it open. Wind and rain lashed at my skin, trying in vain to slow my progress. My flats sank into the damp earth as I stepped out onto the path. It was freezing. The thin fabric of my blouse felt glued to my skin in seconds, sliced through by a bone-numbing chill.

The noise caused by the burgeoning storm should have been deafening: swaying trees, echoing thunder. But all I heard was silence broken by a low, distant hum. Thump... thump...thump...

And a woman's voice. "Only she can go any farther."

She stood on an incline and in reality barely came to Dublin's waist in height. Her hair hung down to her waist, mingling with the pale fabric of her thin shift. Grubby, bare toes melded with the earth and underbrush. Her delicate, small features formed no expression as her eyes cut in my direction.

"Just her," she repeated, her thin voice easily overpowering the growled hiss of the man before her. "Only she can come any farther."

"Then we're done here." Dublin's voice slammed into the eerie stillness like a wrecking ball. Anger flashed through his gaze as he snatched for my wrist, pulling me after him.

Hauled to the car, I found myself shoved into the back seat and immediately flanked by Yulia and Dmitri. The door slammed and Dublin appeared behind the wheel a heartbeat later. When he wrenched the car into reverse, it roared to life amid the squeal of skidding tires, jolting down the hillside. I looked back, and through the screen of green and swaying branches, I still saw the woman standing unmoving. Just watching.

Waiting.

You will come alone. The whispered promise haunted me, even as the dense forest gave way to lush, open fields and a gray sky. *Or she will come to you.*

~

The moment we returned to the cottage, Dublin pressed a cell phone against his ear and snarled commands into the receiver. From the general gist, I sensed a narrative along the lines of: *get the goddamn plane ready,* and *leaving as soon as we can.*

"Well, that was disappointing," Dmitri remarked on a sigh. He forlornly removed his straw hat, but even he seemed unusually on edge. "But I agree that a retreat is in our best interests. One never meets alone with witches, or so the saying goes." He cleared his throat, glancing in Yulia's direction. Then he promptly turned away. "Well, Dublin, I shall assist you in making the arrangements. As always, I do believe my jet will suffice perfectly..."

He simpered after Dublin.

"Eleanor," Yulia called to me with a strained smile. "In the meantime, we can catch up."

"Sure." I nodded, lowering my voice as she came to my side. "And then *you* can tell me what's really going on."

She faltered and shot a nervous glance at Dublin. Thankfully, he was too busy issuing rapid-fire commands like a general to notice my attempts at subterfuge.

"As you wish. Come."

I was hot on her heels as she entered the drawing room.

"Sit," she called before disappearing through a doorway that I assumed led into the kitchen.

I sat, wringing my fingers. When she finally returned, she had a tray containing steaming tea in two cups.

"It's a long story," she warned as she settled onto a chair across from me. Her gaze cut to the doorway and she shuffled closer as Dublin's shouting reached glass-shattering decibels.

"I think we have the time," I said.

She nodded. "I do believe you're right. Though perhaps I should apologize? I haven't been the best company as of late."

"I understand," I admitted.

"Do you?" She laughed softly, shaking her head. "Even I don't. It is strange how you can convince yourself for years that you can overcome any obstacle. But the second something unexpected arises…" She snapped her fingers. "You crumble."

"You don't have to talk about this," I said.

"In a way it ties to your own dilemma," she said, tilting her head thoughtfully. "They claim that there once was a witch who fell in love with a vampire, though he loved another. Even so, she was foolish enough, selfish enough, to give him whatever he wished…"

"And what was that?" I croaked, sensing her pause was my cue to ask.

Her gaze turned wistful, "A child with his lover. A *natural* child. It sounds pretty melodramatic," she admitted. "But love and devotion can be poisonous to your senses. While *that* witch perverted nature in her lust, I know of another who tried to kill one of the most powerful vampires in history by enchanting one of his tailored suits. Merely because her master commanded her to…"

Something in her pained tone made me suspect this other witch wasn't some distant figure from her memory.

"You?" I whispered, hazarding a guess.

She nodded and averted her eyes to her teacup.

Which meant that the powerful vampire she tried to kill could only be…

"Dublin?" I asked out loud.

Her lips twisted into a tormented grimace. "Dublin. Looking back, I realize now that he—Dmitri—" She hunched over as if saying his name physically hurt her. "I know now that he was just trying to test me. He'd grown bored of me then, I think. Whether I succeeded or not didn't matter to him. Just the fact that he could manipulate me into trying… I knew it was suicide, but Dublin…" She trailed off, her lips thoughtfully pursed. "Dublin didn't kill me. I can only assume that he knew taking me from Dmitri's control would punish him more. Be careful with him—" She reached out, grasping my hand in hers. "He may seem silly and harmless, but some fear him more than Raphael, or even Dublin. He likes to collect rare, talented creatures you see. Beautiful humans. Talented witches…" Her eyes roved down to where the table obscured the view of my stomach. "Anything or anyone gifted and unique. Don't trust him. Alas, the past is in the past, isn't it?"

She sighed and sipped from her tea. "Back to the topic at hand, the former witch's name was Adara. She was rumored to be remarkably gifted. I never knew her, but we all heard of the twisted magic she worked in the service of Mero. When he took a human bride, she corrupted the very gift he despised to sow a new life: a mortal life."

She stared off, her voice soft in awe. "But in return, she forever denied herself the possibility of death, as did Mero. Damned for eternity, they will never die, and trust me when I tell you that is not a fate anyone would desire. Even Raphael, as far gone in madness as he is, would shy away from such a bargain. The years change you with every passing decade. You become further adrift in a sea of numbness, losing contact with anything that may ground you."

She stirred her tea rapidly, shaking her head. "Such is the price for daring to pervert nature beyond its bounds." Her eyes met mine again, brimming with sadness. "But it is a price some men may pay, even in a reckless impulse, to save another."

While taking a sip of my tea, I nearly choked. Dublin didn't exactly tout the effects of vampirism, but to never die? And to think, the most reckless thing I'd ever done was sell my soul out of spite.

"And?" My throat felt painfully dry. I woodenly sipped more tea, but that only worsened the discomfort, not all of it physical. Shadows lingered on the horizon. An unshakeable chill prickled the back of my neck, patiently insistent. *Don't be so daft, Ellie. You know what she's hinting at. What he's done.*

"It's not that complicated, really." Yulia lowered her gaze to her tea, continuing to stir it. "Dublin wants to find her because he—"

"Tomorrow." Dublin himself appeared at the doorway and shot Yulia a pointed look, thus ending the impromptu teatime. "We'll leave then." This clearly wasn't his ideal choice; he wanted to go now.

Quest for answers aside, I couldn't shake the tense, suffocating pressure building on the air. Like a noose, it cinched my throat, tightening with every inch the remaining daylight retreated beneath the horizon.

While Dublin disappeared again, I retreated to my room and attempted to sleep. Attempted being the keyword. A storm crept in the moment I crawled beneath the sheets. Lightning flashed, illuminating the windows and casting the shadowed furniture into stark relief.

In a way, the chaos felt comforting. I couldn't hear the whispers. Nothing but nature raging…

CHILDISH GAMES

*D*mitri's private, climate-controlled jet felt ten times smaller with Dublin *and* Yulia on board. When we finally landed, I gulped at the fresh air, as relieved as the sole survivor of a grueling war. One fought with verbal jabs and biting sarcasm.

At the tarmac, Yulia went her own way in silence. Not long after, Dmitri retreated as well, slipping into a golden limo conveniently waiting nearby.

Dublin had also come prepared. Parked not far from the plane was a car I recognized as his. He drove silently, and we re-entered the city just as the midafternoon sun reached its peak. Of all places, we passed the park near the cathedral and I couldn't resist.

"Could we take a walk? For a second?" I couldn't suppress the longing in my voice. A walk. In peace. Among the sunlight and fresh air, devoid of shadow and secrets.

Dublin's grip tightened over the steering wheel.

So I pulled out all stops and resorted to one weapon I sensed even the devil was susceptible to—shameless begging. "Please?"

Sighing, he relented and pulled over to the side of the road. "Five minutes."

As we exited the car for the cultivated landscape of the park, I tilted my face into the sun, practically skipping beside him. For five glorious minutes, none of the danger surrounding us mattered. Just this. His presence. The easy silence between us, my hand in his.

I could pretend—for the briefest moment—that I was as carefree as I imagined Georgie used to be. Cherished, and wanted, and reckless in her happiness.

That was the terrifying, unnatural part of it all—I *wanted* happiness.

"The tumor," I began, eyeing a glorious array of flowers dotting the field around us. "If it can't be removed, then… We need to agree upon some course of action."

Dublin stiffened, his jaw clenched as if to bite back a phrase I could guess as clearly as my own thoughts—*Not this again. Please. I thought you were making progress.*

But he didn't mention as much out loud.

Not even as I came to a stop and hesitantly placed my hand against my belly. I felt nothing. Just flesh, and warmth, and skin. I closed my eyes, attempting to acknowledge some deep-down impulse for the first time.

I didn't feel any magical maternal impulse, strong enough to erase days of dread and terror.

But I no longer felt that terror as strongly as before.

"If it was a girl, would that bother you?" I slowly peeled my eyes open to gauge his reaction.

He cocked his chin, his gaze shielded behind an impenetrable stare. "Yes," he grated. "Yes, it would." Gradually, his mouth twitched, lifting at the corner. Softly. Higher. A genuine smile, though cautious in width. "Another Eleanor Gray? The world is not ready for such a creature."

"A boy would just conspire with you," I pointed out smugly. "But a girl? She and I can plot all sorts of mischief and you will be none the wiser."

"As long as it's healthy… As long as *you* are healthy, I would take any specimen imaginable." He looked so tired again. An ageless man, approaching my side, his hand outstretched for me.

I curled my fingers around his, marveling at the sensation of him. No fighting. No hating.

Tilting my head back, I eyed the sky, allowing him to steer me along in peaceful, beautiful silence.

But how reality loved to deny me. Within minutes, our haven was invaded and nothing could reclaim those cherished minutes.

"Eleanor." Dublin tensed, yanking me against him.

I looked around, expecting assassins to lunge from the trees. Instead, I noticed a young girl dancing across the expansive lawn paces away.

Dressed in a flowing white frock, she was prancing with more energy than I ever could, darting around flower beds. Her features were delicate, her dark curls spilling down her shoulders. But her eyes…

They fixated on me as she approached and I shivered. A deep brown, they were as ageless as Raphael's.

"I hear you've been looking for me," she accused, wrinkling her nose at Dublin. Just beyond his reach, she stopped, her hands on her hips. A small strip of blue velvet encircled her throat, supporting a small silver charm that swayed against her pale skin. "Why? Do you think you can kill me, Cael? Torture me until I surrender to your bidding?" She giggled into a hand tipped with hot-pink fingernails. "Have you not learned your lesson after all these years? Maybe you will during the many more you have left to your debt? He's been gloating, you do realize. He will never cease to own you."

"Adara," Dublin said tonelessly. Her name? Clearly, there was no love lost between them. He eyed her coldly, his eyes narrowed in disgust. "A rather unimaginative disguise, I must say."

"You should try it sometime," the girl countered, sticking out her tongue. She fingered the neckline of her dress. The white material formed a tight-fitting bodice that flared out over her waist—though at second glance it was *mostly* white. Three small scarlet drops stained the very center of the bodice. "Young ones are surprisingly nimble. I may keep this form for good—"

"Why show yourself now?" Dublin demanded. "I do admit your stunt in France was impressive."

She giggled. "Those old biddies do love to give a good scare. And I've always loved a good game of hide-and-seek. Don't you?" She twirled in a circle, eyeing the skirt of her dress as it billowed around her. "And you *play* with ruthless intent. So much so that you miss the most obvious moves your opponent may make." Skidding to a stop, she met my gaze and winked. "So wonderful to meet you again, Eleanor. Oh, do you not recognize me?" She raised her arms, indicating her dress. "I do appreciate your very generous *donation* my dear girl." Her voice deepened well beyond the range of a child's. Into a man's, one brimming with suave charm and undeniably familiar…

I recoiled in horror, just as my gaze fell over the small splash of color on her chest once more. The three splotches uncomfortably resembled three droplets of blood. Like the ones I'd bled during my "meeting" with Gabriel Lanic.

"I so do love this as a fashion statement," Adara chirped, sounding young once again.

In the flickering daylight, the nuances of her "dress" stood out to me more clearly. A slight design distorted the surface —one eerily similar to what might adorn the tablecloth of an exclusive restaurant.

"So, before you act upon that devious thought lurking in your brain, Cael, remember that *I already have her blood.*" Her voice transformed again, expanding into the warning hiss of a grown woman. "I could kill her, as the young ones say, six ways from Sunday." She licked her finger and lowered it to the reddish stains.

Darkness. Suddenly, I was lying on my back, blinking up at the sky.

"Eleanor!" Someone was holding me in his arms, cradling my head above the ground. "What did you do to her?"

"She's fine," Adara insisted. "That was merely a warning. Do play nice with me. I don't want to hurt her—"

"So, what do you want?" Dublin demanded. "I'm sure that's the only reason you've chosen to show yourself now."

"What do I want?"

I looked over and found her stroking her chin, her gaze thoughtful.

"Maybe I want to see your face when I finally convey the bitter, cold truth I think you've known all along."

"Your curse," Dublin said coldly. "So tell me, what exactly did it entail?"

"What?" Adara shrugged her tiny shoulders. "You forget that this was never meant to be a punishment. At least not at first..." She smiled, teeth bared ferally. "It was a gift. Everything he wanted—life from death. There was a price to pay, of course. I'm sure you've already figured it out by now."

Dublin said nothing, his expression drawn tight.

"Oh, you *have*," Adara deduced. She cackled with glee, clapping her hands. "That's the whole bit of irony, I suppose —just as Mero intended. You see, the only way the curse would have ever triggered in the first place was if you tried to do something naughty, Dublin. Something, you swore you would never ever do."

My mind spun with her words. Something in her mischievous tone made me recall something Dmitri said the day he barged into the manor in Italy. *For all your loathing of the act, you must have feared for her life, I suspect. I'd heard Raphael tried feeding from her. That could... But that wouldn't explain why she didn't die. No. Though if you did try to turn her...*

"You tried to turn her," Adara said. She lifted her skirt and twirled in a circle while Dublin watched on, as frozen as ever. "I've heard the rumors: Raphael bit her, didn't he? I'm sure the bastard knew about the agreement you forged with Mero. He would stay in the shadows, averting a nasty war with Raphael. As long as you...what? Go on, say it."

When Dublin remained silent, she sighed.

"As long as you stayed away from the Gray bloodline. Why? Perhaps he owed it to his loyal servant, James? Or perhaps he knew all along." She giggled mischievously. "He knew that one day, you wouldn't be able to. That you who so cherished your restraint wouldn't be able to hide behind that silly necklace any longer. You defiled the charming Eleanor Gray—but in doing so, you triggered the so-called curse. A fate that Mero had always intended for himself. That kind of magic requires a price, you see. A blood price. His blood, or in this case yours. As the new life grows, that price must continue to be paid, or both will die."

"Blood," I croaked, the only word I seemed capable of saying at first. My mind grappled with the insanity of her words, piecing the morbid puzzle together. "That's why I could drink…"

"Yes," Adara said, as though it was as trivial a matter as a buzzing fly. "You need blood, but only to sustain the life growing within you—but that is not the true price paid."

"Keep talking in riddles, and I'll reconsider this conversation," Dublin warned.

Adara giggled, but I didn't miss the slight step backward she took. "Careful, darling. I truly won't hesitate to kill her." She fingered the front of her dress again, inching toward the reddish stains. "Alas, the true price is that…well, you've lost. You've forfeited her already, and you did it—here's the funny part—to *save* her. Funneling all that time to Raphael. And the cruel bastard gave up just enough to drive that point home, didn't he? Ten years, was it?" She eyed me, her lips bared in a hellish grin. "Ten years to spend with her. Ten years with your delicate, mortal child. Ten years before Raphael gets to yank your leash and call you to heel. Have you told her? No, you haven't. Because I doubt even you can admit it to yourself."

She stepped forward, her hands folded sweetly before her. "Your precious Dublin tried to circumvent nature when he attempted to turn you. In return, he gave up his mortality, and he doomed you to a life that he will—at best—enjoy ten years of before you age and wither and die. Your beautiful little daughter will only know him as a shadow flickering along the edges of her life before it fades entirely. Raphael may allow you to see her every now and again, but only so that he can use her to milk you for more, and more, and more, and more. So why have you sought me out? To save you? I cannot do that."

"Then we're done here." Dublin grabbed my wrist and pulled me to my feet. Using his body as a shield, he tried his best to shelter me from view.

"No!" Adara admonished, wagging a small finger as she sidestepped his attempts. "I'm not ready to let you go running away just yet, either…" Her grin turned feral. "As a courtesy for my visit, I would like to request a reward."

"What the hell do you want?"

"Eleanor, of course. Now you have to let me play with her!" She lunged forward, snatching my wrist, and took off, pulling me beyond his reach.

The fact that he even released me at all betrayed just how seriously he took her threat. *I don't want to hurt her.*

"Come on, silly girl!" She cackled maniacally, tugging me along. "Keep up!" Halfway across the park, she released me and collapsed, giggling into a heap. From the rumpled cloud of her dress, she eyed me and sighed. "You poor, pathetic little fool. If you at least showed some intelligence, I might be tempted to pity you."

I tensed, somehow knowing not to let the insult slip unchallenged. She reminded me of a cat in a sense, testing with claws drawn, every bit as mercurial as Tinkles. "How am I a fool?"

She fingered her necklace, twisting the tiny charm between her thumb and her forefinger. "Because you cower, and whimper, and *whine*," she spat. "You don't *play* the game. Like a good little pawn, you huddle in silence and let Dublin growl over you like some kind of a wild beast. It's disgusting!" She raised her arms in exasperation and kicked her legs into the air. "The worst part? You know he doesn't truly want you. It's the curse, you see. It's *Mero* who truly owns him. Everything he's done for you has been a mere delusion."

I swallowed. "You're wrong."

Or she was right and it was the truth…

"You don't even sound convincing!" She threw her head back and cackled. "Oh, the look on your face. You know it too, don't you? The little lie you let yourself believe."

That I could have a future. Happiness. Dublin.

A life beyond the grim existence that I spent years telling myself awaited me.

"I should just kill you now," Adara remarked, her tone flat. Bored. "With his life sold to Raphael, ten years of forced, dutiful contact with dear 'Dublin' would be pitiful to endure, even for me—"

"No." I shook my head, gritting my teeth. Those horrible voices lingered, whispering and taunting. This time, I *made* myself banish them for good the only way I could: by countering them out loud. "No! You know what? I'm done! I'm tired of denying myself. Why *shouldn't* I demand my happiness?"

I glared at the sky as if expecting an answer. "Why shouldn't I want to believe that Dublin Helos could want me? He's handsome. He's more beautiful than anyone I could ever dream of. Why can't I want him?" I started to pace as rage built within me. I wasn't just arguing with the voices in my head anymore—but my mother. My family. Old friends. Society. My sister. "Why can't I dream, for once, of a future with someone who loves me? That I deserve that future? No, you are wrong. I do deserve it. I want it, and I'm tired of everyone acting like I can't have it. Who cares if Dublin even wants me or not? I want him!" And I slammed my foot to prove it, as if twenty-six years of suppressed temper tantrums chose that second to explode from me at once. "So sorry, Miss…" My mind buzzed, so incensed that I couldn't remember her name until a heartbeat later. "Call me whatever you want. I refuse to continue to believe that I am worthless anymore."

Adara eyed me with no expression. Then she sighed. "Men." She rolled her eyes, even as her voice betrayed a wistful, almost pained note. "Sometimes they forget that *they* are the true pawns. I mock you when I am the one who loved a man so much that I stained my soul black for him, even though he loved another. And where am I now?" She shrugged. "And where is he…"

Slowly, she stood, dusting off her dress. "You should go back," she said, nodding to the vampire waiting in the distance. "Tell him that I cannot help you. He knows what must be done."

"What?" I croaked. Even though I didn't know Dublin's true reason for seeking her out, a deep-seated impulse made me press for whatever answers I could. "What must be done?"

"He must face his punishment like a good boy and own up to the pain he's caused. He can no longer run from it. He knows as much. I think our dear Cael is merely afraid of what he will learn: the truth." She eyed me with a sigh, and for once, she looked more childlike than anything. Helpless. "No matter how hard he fights, you are destined to die eventually. Such a fate is both his redemption and his doom. Goodbye, Eleanor Gray."

She turned and skipped toward the trees, vanishing beneath them.

And I watched her go, frozen in place until Dublin lifted me in his arms. He hurried to the car, and in his haste, the world blurred, reduced to a smattering of color and shadow.

When viewed in the grim, overcast daylight, Gray Manor felt less like my old childhood home and more like a diving board extended above an unknown depth. Every inch we traversed would merely hasten the inevitable fall.

Yet a part of me knew deep down in my soul that we were bound to it. Even as the danger of the Grayne, and Mero, and Raphael, and only God knew who else loomed overhead…

Somehow, Gray Manor seemed destined to be where it all would end.

Dublin's expression all but cemented that. He silently parked the car, his eyes a tormented silver—but above all, *resigned.* Whatever the witch had told him had sowed an air of surrender so alarming that I squirmed in the face of it.

It was the same expression he had been wearing the day before he'd vanished all those weeks ago.

Hopeless, vengeful, and cold.

Adara's words resonated in my mind, a foreboding declaration. *"He doomed you to a life that he will—at best—enjoy ten years of before you age and wither and die."*

His heavy sigh drew my attention, but he merely exited the car without saying a word. I remained seated as he crossed to my end of the car, but his hand extended before me was my only command to obey him.

I did, entering that drafty, unwelcoming home in his wake. I knew that its dull, dreary walls would never feel the same again.

The old Eleanor would have succumbed to the silence, allowing him to brood, and plot, and drift further from me by the second.

But I couldn't.

"Talk to me," I demanded as he started across the vacant foyer. "Please. Tell me."

"What?" He turned and I sucked in a startled breath. Shadows enhanced the contours of his face, making him appear hollow.

He was before me in an instant, cupping my cheek in his palm. His mouth lacked its usual frown. All things considered, he looked more neutral than upset, but I could sense the tension lurking in his muscles. The dread.

Adara's words had cemented something in him, making his posture rigid with resolve.

I could have danced around the topic, changing the subject to something trivial. Instead, I steeled myself against the discomfort and forced myself to meet it head-on.

"How much time did you barter for me? In exchange for Raphael's protection?"

His narrowed eyes scanned my face with ruthless intent. "I'm not sure you truly want to know the answer to that."

"Please," I whispered. Though he was right.

"How much?" He stepped up to me, lowering his mouth against my ear. "Enough." His hand twitched, hovering between us. Uncharacteristic hesitation kept the fingers suspended until, finally, they settled over my belly, remaining in spite of how I flinched. "Enough to ensure that neither Raphael or Mero—or anyone—will ever harm you."

"Why?"

"What else was I supposed to do?" His lips grazed my jaw in an almost apologetic caress. "I tried to protect you on my own. I failed. Should I just sit back and let him…"

"What if *I* sold myself to Raphael?" I countered thickly. "How would you feel?"

He laughed as if too stunned by the idea to take it seriously. Then his eyes narrowed into slits and I had enough sense to shudder. "I would kill you with my bare hands. Nothing would be worth anything he could offer. *Nothing*."

Letting me go, he started across the foyer.

But I chased after him. "There is something you're not telling me—"

"If I had turned you, would you have hated me?" He waited until I'd reached him and then flicked the curls back from my face, his expression unreadable. Regardless, I sensed he required an answer. The truth. "Would you have despised the creature you would have become? Something your sister had been conditioned to despise?"

"I..." Didn't know. Mainly because that girl felt like a stranger now, someone I barely even understood. Fearful, doubtful, so determined to deny herself happiness that she'd preferred to await death instead. It had been easier that way; I could admit it now. No hope. No fear of the unknown.

No joy of what might come.

"That day after Raphael..." He began. "I knew the second your eyes reopened, still bright with mortality, that something had changed. That, in my impulse, I'd broken some boundary that could never be repaired."

And I sensed he wasn't speaking of me any longer.

He brushed his lips across my forehead, lingering as if to impart his next confession into my very soul. "Your sister knew. She wouldn't even let me do the one thing that I thought might save your life unless I agreed to leave you in exchange."

I flinched, recalling the strange tension that had grown between Georgie and me.

"I tried to find Adara," Dublin continued. "If I had, I could have demanded she fix it. I knew Mero was waiting for me —that he would use any pawn he could to lure me to him. Every waking second, I could hear him hissing in my ear. Reminding me of his goddamn curse. And when I returned, I knew, even as all logic warned me to deny it. He was right.

"How much one could crave what life could offer, beyond this tormented existence. In a way, perhaps I'd always consoled myself with the belief that ultimately...I could always end it. What did I have left to cherish?" He gripped me tighter, pulling me against him.

I remained still, letting him hold me.

"Perhaps I would have surrendered it anyway," he murmured. "Had I known. The ability to die. To follow you..." He pulled back, turning across the foyer. "Get some sleep. I'll make you something to eat. Should I prepare the baklava?"

"Yes," I whispered hoarsely, letting him retreat alone.

Something told me that now was not the time to argue. He needed silence.

And I needed to allow him that reprieve no matter how my heart twisted in agony.

Obediently, I went to my room and crawled beneath my blankets, but sleep wouldn't come. Doubt, that terrible thing, crept into my thoughts, but it felt different than before. Less disembodied and formless.

More desperate: a warning plea that dragged me into the hall and through the rest of the house.

Move…move. Move!

"Dublin?" I called for him to no response as I crept down the staircase in nothing more than a thin nightgown. "Dublin?"

I kept going, exiting the servant's wing on bare feet. My breath escaped me in pants as I raced down the walkway in the moonlight, driven faster. Faster. Eventually, I sprinted more than walked. Then ran. The wind nipped at my hair, turning it into a cape that fanned my shoulders as I wound up breathless before a structure that had never seemed more imposing.

My hand shook as I pushed the door open. Something wouldn't let me turn around. It was as if a hook had caught the center of my rib cage, tugging me forward ruthlessly.

A slave to the impulse, I descended the steps, passing the angel. I shivered, venturing deeper. Deeper still.

Then farther within the mausoleum than I'd ever been, in a section so distant that even Georgie and I had never explored it. Near the final chamber, barely concealed behind another hunched angelic statue lurked a doorway.

I hadn't known it even existed: a wide chamber containing a single stone sarcophagus, cut into the heart of the crypt itself.

A man was lounging outstretched on the stone lid. He glowed as if bathed in moonlight—though I couldn't make out any windows or entrances. Nonetheless, I had no trouble seeing him in excruciating detail.

Rich, dark skin set him apart from the colorless backdrop. Closely cropped black hair enhanced his stern features, no less beautiful than Dublin or Raphael's. In contrast to their formal dress, he was wearing a plain gray shirt and jeans that seemed insulting in comparison to the regal tilt to his chin.

I knew his name instantly, even without an introduction. *Mero.*

"And now," he declared in a voice that reverberated like thunder, "we may begin. Did you really think I'd let you confront me without allowing dear Eleanor to hear the truth as well?"

He was speaking to someone I didn't realize was standing nearby until I turned, spotting him there. Dublin. Confusion mingled with the fear goading my pulse into a surging rhythm. François had claimed the crypt was protected—a vampire could only enter invited.

Though Mero supposedly had invested in the Grays since our humble beginnings. In a sense, this land belonged to him over anyone else.

And he had presented Dublin with an invitation he couldn't refuse.

"And here I am," my Devil said, his arms outstretched. "You lured her here, and why? So that she can see how callously you toy with her family? Go on and reveal your final pawn."

"My pawn? I made it no secret that I held her." The man grinned in a stunning display of white teeth and stood. Gracile movements propelled him upright with the elegance of a dancer. "You merely chose to run and hide rather than face me, Cael. But alas, here you finally are. So, as you wish…" He brushed his hand across the lid of the sarcophagus behind him. The simple gesture seemed incapable of the strength required to knock the stone slab aside in a cloud of dust.

I stiffened in anticipation of a body—and there was one.

A woman lay slumped in the pit of the coffin, visible even from where I was standing. Tangled blond hair shielded her face, but her softly rising chest and the pink hue of her skin revealed that she was alive.

"Georgie?" I cried out, rushing to her. Cold, hard stone scraped my knees as I crouched and plunged my arm into the cavernous space in search of her hand. "Georgie?"

Her eyes were closed, her body unmoving. But her clothing… I swallowed hard, racked by confusion. The faint illumination in the chamber was just enough for me to make out her pink shirt and jeans. It was the same outfit she'd worn the day I screamed at her to leave.

"She is alive," Mero explained. "Despite her slumber, she'll suffer no lasting damage."

"Her letter," I croaked, stroking the hair from her face. I didn't even care that I was speaking to a creature even Dublin seemed to fear. Facing him, I demanded, "She tried to contact me. How?"

He smiled. Unlike with Raphael, emotion shaped his handsome features, giving them life. Definition. And in a way, the subtle nuances in his expression only served to enhance his imposing nature. "I woke her when it suited my needs," he said softly. "But you can rest assured that little she did was under her own will."

Including the bounty on my head? I tried to ask, but Dublin's voice sliced over mine, harsh and biting.

"And now what?" he demanded. "You want me to kill her? Slice her throat in front of her sister to prove once and for all what a damned, selfish creature I am? I know how your mind works."

"Is *that* why you have waited this long to face me?" Mero laughed as he turned to him. "I won't harm the girl. She knows nothing to be a danger to you, regardless. *Nor* will I harm your Eleanor. Why would I?" He raised a hand and slowly curled the fingers into a fist as if trapping my soul within them. "Killing her now would be a mercy to you."

"Don't touch her." Dublin lurched onto the tips of his toes, his teeth bared as Mero shifted his attention to me. But he didn't come closer, not even as the other vampire's hand settled over my scalp in dangerous reassurance.

"No. You would rage and attack me of course—but in the end, you would thank me. I would save you from it, this pain…" He stroked me once and withdrew his hand, placing the outstretched fingers over his heart. "This knowledge that there could have been so much more. No, Cael. I am afraid that what you truly fear will come to pass. I suspect you've already inferred as much."

He inclined his head, but Dublin said nothing.

Silence filled the chamber, unbearable in its all-encompassing weight.

"She *will* die," Mero finally declared. "As will your mortal child. But they will live before that day will come. Live and wither before your eyes to the point that even your blood will cease to have an effect. You can never turn them. Never chase them beyond the void." His voice softened, a lethal hiss as his gaze returned to his old friend's. "You will know what true love, and joy, and peace are, and then you will watch it slip away through your fingers, swallowed by time. And like me, you will not have the mercy or option of death. You know that now, don't you?"

Slowly, he advanced on Dublin's position, but his posture wasn't triumphant or mocking. Everything from the set of his shoulders to the tilt of his jaw conveyed only one emotion above all others.

Pity.

"In the end, you will come to know what true despair is, Cael," he murmured. "True madness. She will never be more beautiful to you than her next breath. You will grow to love her more by the second until you swear your soul can no longer contain it. And you will grow to hate her." He extended his fingers toward me in a fatherly gesture. "For her innocence. Her freedom. Her fragility. I pity you, my friend. Adara's magic turned out to be far crueler than I could have ever imagined."

He drifted toward the doorway and then looked back at me from the threshold, his eyes brimming with unshed tears. "She wasn't supposed to love you in return. That I did not foresee. And now that you have sold yourself to Raphael for more time than she could ever outlive, you will truly suffer."

He slipped from the room, but Dublin didn't follow.

And as if carried on an unseen wind, Mero's voice drifted back to us regardless.

"Know that I will be watching, old friend. Waiting. I will even leave the other Gray girl, for now... But I will return, merely to witness the moment you truly understand. There is no end to this life awaiting us. No end to the pain." A heavy sigh trailed the words as his voice softened, barely a whisper. "This beautiful, innocent creature you cherish will one day be an agonizing memory. And then we shall see in just how many ways I can extend your suffering..."

As if a spell had been broken, Dublin finally lurched into action. He raced through the doorway, a blur of motion. "Stay here," he hissed back to me.

I couldn't move even if I had the strength to.

My hand remained entwined with Georgie's, gripping her fingers though hers remained limp in response.

Despair, that bitter poison, lurked on the edges of my psyche, desperate to invade the second I allowed it to.

But I couldn't. Because if I surrendered to it now, even for a second, I would never rise from its depths again.

Eventually, footsteps approached, clattering over the stone.

"All is well, I hope?" a man called out. His voice sounded distorted, as if he spoke from outside of the structure, though I recognized his dry tone regardless. Dmitri. "If it really is how you say for the other one… My, my, he must have used quite the powerful drug on her delicate soul. Curing it could take some time—"

"It's all right, Eleanor," Dublin warned.

I hadn't even realized I was on my feet, hissing through my teeth as he approached the coffin.

"I can help her," Dublin insisted. But his eyes were averted away from me, his voice cold. In silence, he retreated and the sight of his back lingered even after my vision blurred with tears.

A DANGEROUS GAME

"*You sold your soul to Raphael for more time than she could ever outlive.*"

Mero's return could have been a cruel nightmare, easily banished as I awoke in my bed to brilliant sunlight. The old Eleanor would have certainly taken that lifeline—ignorance.

Denial.

She would have pushed the terror to the back of her mind and merrily embraced her terminal cancer.

But I couldn't. Ten years had never seemed so daunting a timespan. Or so little.

And if Raphael's power could extend over Dublin the way his power had controlled Yulia, I didn't have to try hard to imagine what awaited us both as soon as my pathetic hold on his soul came to an end.

Moving as stiffly as an old woman, I stood, cradling my belly with the flat of my hand. Tears burned behind my eyes, but I refused to let them fall. Instead, I wandered the manor in a daze, finding no one in the upstairs hall.

Though I'd sensed his presence in my room throughout the night, it was as though Dublin were intentionally avoiding me now. My sole company was Dmitri, who was lurking within the main drawing room, reading a book as I wandered past.

"Morning," he groused, biting his lower lip. "Before you panic, your Dublin is nearby. In fact, he politely informed me that my services are no longer needed." He did his best to parrot Dublin's raspy baritone, but even then, his voice wasn't anywhere near deep enough. "Alas, I am waiting for my jet to be refueled…" He trailed off and looked up from his book, eyeing my face with a raised eyebrow. "What is it, my dear?"

"I need a favor." I crossed my arms, too exhausted to put effort to even attempt to intimidate him. So I improvised. "Deny me and I'll tell Dublin you tried to touch me in my sleep."

"Oh?" He set his book aside, his head cocked. "However can I help you?"

"Don't pretend like you don't already have a price in mind. Name it."

He smirked. "You misunderstand me, my dear. I know when exactly my services will be repaid. Everything I've done hasn't been for *you*." He eyed my stomach and reached out, boldly brushing his fingers against my abdomen. Even as I jerked beyond his reach, he kept his hand extended, chuckling. "It's been for *her*. My, what an interesting creature she will be. I would think of myself as her godfather of sorts. I am sure she will repay me more than enough for all of my exertions."

"What makes you think I wouldn't kill you before you could ever touch her?" Both hands shielded my stomach now.

His smile widened further. "Of course, my dear. I have no doubt that you could… Now, what did you want?"

"I need a distraction," I said hoarsely, choosing to overlook his assertion for now. "A very big distraction."

"Ah. You wish to lure the wolf from his lamb." His eyes narrowed, skeptical. "Ah, knowing his current mood, I suspect you plan to deceive him for good reason?"

"Can you do it or not?"

He frowned, betraying genuine unease for once. "There are antics I could perform that would draw him away from you. In fact, they all tend to carry an uncomfortably high risk of my death." He brushed his fingers along his throat.

And I bared mine in response, a dare in my tone. "Well, I suppose that's the risk you'll have to take, isn't it?"

"My my." A slow smile unfurled over his lips and he clapped his hands. "Oh, I do love this side of you! All right, you've convinced me. I can buy you an hour." He stood and approached the foyer. "But I will warn you that you should act quickly. And." He grinned and nodded to his discarded book. "I've already taken the liberty of mapping out your destination should you require it. Call it a hunch."

He wandered out of reach before I could demand an answer.

Not that I needed one.

This all felt like some twisted, unending game in which everyone *but* me had a clear view of the gameboard.

The only way to win was to give in to the one impulse that had never steered me wrong—stubborn childishness.

If I couldn't play on their terms, I would merely have to upend the entire damn table in defiance of it all.

~

I was in my room when I finally heard it: a door slamming below, betraying a figure racing through the manor so quickly that I barely scrambled down the stairs in time to catch him.

"Yulia," he muttered before taking off, an apology lurking in his gaze. "I'll be back as soon as I can."

I watched him go; then I spun on my heel and tore across the manor. Past the servant's quarters, the garage loomed empty, the old family Rolls stationed in its usual spot—

newly repaired, its backseat door fully intact. Banishing all doubt, I snatched the keys from their customary hook and climbed behind the steering wheel before I could talk myself out of the insane plan forming within my brain.

Driving was a terrifying, jerking excursion following Dmitri's scribbled directions, but eventually, I reached my destination unscathed.

A warehouse on the outskirts of the city, its brick façade containing a world of darkness within.

The entrance was unguarded, the door inexplicably unlocked. Perhaps such creatures felt no need to repel potential thieves; after all, they'd simply make for more fodder to sell.

I, for one, was through with having my soul bartered, however.

I barged into the structure with my head held high. A darkened hallway provided little by way of navigation. So I boldly marched from room to room until a furious Saskia appeared within the mouth of a doorway, dressed in a blood-red robe.

"What the hell are you—"

"Summon Raphael," I demanded, cutting her off mid-hiss. "*Now.* I wish to make a bargain."

～

I was afraid the ancient vampire would arrive far past my deadline, giving Dublin plenty of time to track me down—but a chill preceded his arrival before I could panic.

"Eleanor Gray." He stood alone at the back of the chamber Saskia had sequestered me in. Judging from the cavernous space, it was where that impromptu showcase had taken place, though now only two chairs positioned across from each other remained.

Raphael retained his regal aura, even at what I guessed was an unwelcome hour for him. His lifeless eyes honed in on me with interest. Today, in lieu of a cape, he was wearing a simple black suit with an unbuttoned ivory shirt underneath. Visible against the pale skin of his chest hung a silver pendant in the shape of a serpent. As he approached, its red eyes studied me, flickering like hellish flames.

"I was surprised to receive your request, I must admit. To what do I owe this visit?"

"I want to bargain," I confessed, meeting his gaze. "Via contract."

"Oh?" A cold smile twitched over his mouth, quickly suppressed in an instant. "In exchange for Dublin's, I suspect?" His laugh echoed, toneless and hollow. "You hope to trade your time for his. I'm sure I could find a use for you in some capacity."

"No," I admitted, my throat tight. "Not a trade, but a wager. The winner will take everything."

"Everything?" His eyebrow flickered, too frozen to rise fully.

But I had something so powerful and elusive that I knew better to squander it by wasting time: his interest.

"Dublin's time that you have in addition to *mine*. Every year I have left to live. That is what will be on the table."

"Oh?" Another smile twisted his lips, but there was no amusement within the expression. Just hunger. "On what wager?"

"The amount of time doesn't matter," I admitted. "I want us to bet it all on one simple outcome: How will Dublin react when you tell him?"

"With relief, I suspect," Raphael mused, clasping his fingers together. He drifted to the chair across from me and sat. I shivered, subjected to his chill despite the distance. "Pity for you, perhaps, but relief nonetheless. Do you truly think you mean that much to him?" He waited for a second and then sighed as if my silence alone contained my reply. "The man has spent years pining for his time. I am sorry, dear girl, but I believe the answer is too obvious to take advantage of your naivety."

"Even if I claim differently?" In response to the amused tilt of his chin, I lifted a folded slip of paper, previously hidden in my jacket until now. "My guess as to his reaction is on this paper. I'm assuming you'll think he'll leave in gratitude, and if you are correct, then you own us both."

He eyed me in silence. Just when I feared he may never speak, a pink tongue flitted across his lower lip. "And if you win?"

I inhaled raggedly. Even inside my head, the plot seemed insane. Madness.

Something reckless enough to befit the broken little lamb Dublin had described me as.

"If I win, then Dublin is free and you agree to never threaten me or…or our daughter."

"And how do I know that this isn't a planned arrangement?"

Despite everything, I had to laugh, and his eyes narrowed at the hysterical sound.

"Do you really think Dublin would let me meet with you alone, even as part of some harebrained scheme?"

Hence, I was here on a whim, trembling as the seconds ticked past, cutting my brief window of time shorter and shorter.

Raphael cocked his head as if catching a far-off sound. "Of course…" In a dazzling display, his smile widened. "Well, then we have a deal, my dear. And just in time, I suspect."

He turned to the door as a figure appeared there, his eyes blazing silver. They cut to me and he was beside me in an instant, shielding me with his towering frame.

"Eleanor—"

"It's okay," I told Dublin, bracing my hand over his forearm. Coiled muscle lurched beneath my fingertips, readying for battle. "Everything is okay. I've gotten your time back."

"In exchange for her own," Raphael murmured. His eyes danced, portraying something akin to glee. "Every year of her life, sacrificed for you. It is very touching." He brought a pale hand to his chest. "What say you, Dublin? Do you accept this freedom so graciously bestowed upon—"

"No!" In a blur of motion, Dublin whirled on me, his expression agonized. Gripping my shoulders, he yanked me from my chair and shook me so violently that my head jerked back and forth. "Tell me that you didn't—"

"It's too late," I whispered. "It's already done."

"No…" His hands skimmed my shoulders, caressing my throat. Encircling it…

Tightening.

Clenching.

Suffocating.

Gasping, I strained on the tips of my toes. Terror goaded my pulse into a frantic hammering—but whatever I was feeling was nothing compared to what his expression revealed. His eyes glowed, radiating pain and agonized intent. With every ounce of air to escape my lungs, something vital drained from his soul, rendering him hollow.

Lifeless.

Merciless.

And, as if from lightyears away, I heard Raphael...growl.

"Enough."

I broke away, sputtering, clutching my throat. Through watering, burning eyes, I watched Raphael's flicker in my direction. A crumpled piece of paper slipped from his fingers to the floor at his feet.

"Release her," he commanded, though Dublin had already let me go. "Such a foolish game," he hissed.

"But I've won," I declared hoarsely, still rubbing my throat. "Haven't I?"

Raphael said nothing, turning on his heel to leave the room. But his poised frame was trembling. For the first time, he no longer resembled that frozen, emotionless angel. He raged, every bit as vengeful as the serpent hanging from his throat.

Near the threshold of the room, his voice slithered back to reach us, a furious hiss. "You are freed. But trust, Cael, that when you falter. When your pathetic attempts at protection fail. When you require my mercy...I will be waiting. And you will come."

He left, and tension I didn't even know I'd been carrying within me snapped. I fell to the floor on my hands and knees, eyeing my reflection in the polished surface. Who was that wide-eyed woman with the stubborn tilt to her chin? Emotion constricted my chest, more suffocating than the hands that threatened to choke me only seconds earlier.

I wanted to laugh.

I wanted to cry.

I wanted to scream.

"I'm sorry." Dublin stood above me, staring down at his hands, his brow furrowed in agony. "Eleanor, I'm sorry—"

"Don't be." I managed to stand on quivering legs, but rather than comfort him, I crossed to the center of the floor and stooped for the page Raphael had discarded. On it was my scribbled answer. I traced every word as tears escaped down my cheeks, impossible to contain any longer.

Facing Dublin, I held the page out to him.

"I'm just glad that you were honest with me," I whispered. "My bet was that Raphael couldn't guess your reaction, and I was right."

He eyed the paper, scanning the words written on it. A simple phrase in retrospect.

What would Dublin do should I dare to throw my life away on a whim? If I dared to forsake everything he'd sacrificed? If I so much as dreamt of betraying my trust in him?

Nothing short of what I would deserve, I supposed.

He would kill me.

His eyes shot up to mine and I was in his arms within an instant. Our lips met and I tasted salt as my tears flavored the kiss. I was shaking, clinging to him with everything I had as the full weight of what I'd done crashed over me.

In the midst of the turmoil, I almost didn't hear the footsteps approaching. But the slow, callous clapping drew our notice. I stiffened as Dublin's grip shifted into a protective vise.

"Beautiful," Saskia said, her teeth bared in a snarl. Her features seemed grim without the aid of makeup, beneath the harsh, silvery lighting. "So beautiful. So pathetic. So pointless." She laughed, sweeping her gaze from me to Dublin. "I sensed her condition the second I touched her, and yet I didn't tell Raphael. Do you want to know why? No revenge that he nor I could plan would ever match the cruelty of *this*."

She gestured my way with a wave of her hand. "Your Mero is quite the sadistic bastard. She's broken, unable to be turned, but still doomed to die. I could taste her fate like sugar on my tongue." She licked her lips pointedly, her eyes glowing. "And yet you, dearest Cael... You will get to watch her grow old and haggard. You'll get to watch her die, knowing you can't ever slow the relentless march of time. And I will be there to witness every fucking second of it."

She turned on her heel, her laugh echoing throughout the chamber in her absence.

Even as Dublin led me from the warehouse entirely, it echoed.

I couldn't ignore it.

My stunt with Dmitri cost me nearly a full week of freedom. In the chaotic aftermath, Dublin shadowed my every movement. To be fair, it wasn't a particularly unbearable imprisonment.

I was allowed to leave the house at least, if only in the company of my new team of drivers. François had returned from wherever Dublin had held him all this time, looking none too worse for wear—but joining him in the garage was a figure I recognized the moment I spotted him across the foyer one morning.

He stood near the entryway, his hands folded before him, his eyes warily watching my approach. If I'd still felt any anger toward him for deceiving me, all of it faded the instant I saw his face.

"Harper!" I broke decorum—and Gray tradition—by crossing to him and throwing my arms around his shoulders. If I wasn't mistaken he squeezed me in return, just once before withdrawing to a respectful distance and inclining his head.

"At your service, Ms. Gray."

Dublin could be good for something apparently. In addition to Harper's return, he had also ensured that Mr. Tinkles was returned to his private suite and that a majority of the staff was quietly reinstated.

But overall, he was a corrupting presence.

Poor Gray Manor. My childhood home, once the pinnacle of emotionless, joyless living. For so long, the dust-covered walls had witnessed sex in only the most passionless form, as God intended.

But my Devil was so much more creative. By the fourth day, we'd corrupted at least three bedrooms. And the downstairs drawing room. *And* the alcove where the phone was kept in what had begun as a serious attempt to stock the pantry.

After that, Dublin retreated to the kitchen, and I—in an effort to return to normalcy—retreated to my room, ran a brush through my hair, and slipped into a robe.

Down the hall, I peered into a room where Yulia was dutifully keeping vigilance over a figure lying in the bed. "She's still sleeping," she said as I eyed Georgie's gently rising chest. "If she wakes up again, I'll let you know."

Whatever Mero had done to her had drained her body of all energy. Dublin claimed she would recover with time, but consciousness returned in ebbs and flows.

"I promise," Yulia insisted with a nod. She eyed my ensemble and winked. "I'm sure you're hungry, and I can smell something cooking."

When I approached the kitchen, sure enough, the scent of spices and cooking meat had my mouth watering. Even before I drew even with the figure busily at work behind the counter and realized one of two very important things.

The lesser item was that he was doing something incredible with his hands, manipulating a knife through various vegetables at once. The other realization was that he was stark, unashamedly naked.

I should have been appalled, I supposed. Yulia or my sister could intrude at any time, but Dublin was well aware of the limits of my manor and its occupants' positions.

As well as the fact that it was impossible to hear anything occurring in this section of the house from the wing containing my bedroom.

Pale daylight basted his skin, shimmering against the ivory so that he almost appeared silver. Muscle and limbs moved in tandem as he worked. So intent was he that he didn't even look up until I pulled up a stool to the counter and sat.

The moment I did, two gray eyes drifted up to notice me there. Almost instantly, he returned to his task of slicing up raw onions. Then the knife slipped, the blade slicing through the pad of his finger. The wound healed in an instant, even before my cry of shock left my chest.

"You make it hard to focus entirely on your welfare," he told me, his voice a dangerous rasp on the cool air. His eyes found me again, this time leisurely raking over my hastily tied robe.

Yulia, bless her soul, was a goddess. A devious, vengeful one who seemed to relish making Dublin Helos squirm. If only she knew.

"You don't like it?" I innocently fingered an exceptionally crafted collar formed entirely from lace. Ivory lace to be exact. The whole garment in general was composed of delicate lattice-like patterns that extended just above my ankles. Modest in theory, but certainly not in action.

Dublin observed the ensemble with a look that could only be considered aggravated. Carefully, he set the blade aside and wiped his hands on a nearby rag. Then…

His hand shot out, capturing the back of my skull and drawing me in. Cool lips met mine. Briefly. Softly.

Against them, I couldn't help but murmur, "This feels strange…"

Him in my home felt strange. Us interacting in this way felt strange. Strange as in natural. I didn't have to think. It took so much effort to hate him.

"It does," Dublin agreed, drawing back. "You know what else would feel strange?" Suddenly, his mouth was near my ear while one of his hands brushed the collar of my robe, nudging the panels apart. "Me...taking you against the counter, making you clutch it for balance while I..."

Dark scenarios dripped against my earlobe, each one more scandalous than the last.

"I agree," I forced myself to rasp as my cheeks caught fire. "If only I weren't so hungry..." My eyes were on the fangs glinting beneath his upper lip. "Then I might say no."

~

Another presence in my room drew me awake.

Startled, I opened my eyes and fixated on a blurred figure nearby. "Georgie?"

No. Another woman was sitting on the edge of my bed, her skin the shade of caramel, her hair like spun gold coiling down her back. A plain black shirt and jeans disproved her potential as a maid or one of Dublin's henchmen.

I started to sit upright. "Who are—"

"So maybe you aren't entirely boring and worthless," she told me with a sigh while kicking her feet over the floor. "And maybe...you were right. Why can't you take your happiness? Why should *they* have all the fun?" She stood and languidly stretched her arms above her head. "And I must admit you were good to me, even if I *loathed* you at times." Eyeing me from over her shoulder, she stroked something encircling her throat: a light blue strip of velvet with a charm dangling from the center. "It was nothing personal, honestly. Something about that form just makes me despise all affection. As for Dublin, well... I couldn't resist rubbing it in his face, now could I?"

My breath caught. "Mr... Mr. T-Tinkles?"

"I did hate that name though," she hissed, crossing her arms. "Alas, I loved taunting Dublin right beneath his nose more. I can reward you for that. Or perhaps I merely want to pat myself on the back for guessing which sister he'd fall for?" She smirked. "Everyone was sure it would be the other one... But I grow bored of watching him agonize and brood. Besides, it's just not fair if he stays young forever while you age and wither. Eww." She shuddered, twirling to face me.

At a glance, she looked painfully young—younger than I was, even. Though who knew what her true form was, given her affinity for switching sexes as well as species on a whim?

"I've lived far too long for the words of a mortal to have any effect on me, but yours did for whatever reason. You said you deserved your happiness. *So fine.*" She waved toward the hand I had clutching my pillow. "I've enchanted your ring. As long as you wear it, you will never age. Only you have the power to remove it, should you decide that immortality is not to your tastes. And your daughter may have one as well when she comes of age, should you wish. The only caveat is that you cannot tell Dublin—*especially* about my feline form." She fingered her collar-like necklace, still smirking. "Should I need to utilize it again, I would hate for the fun to be ruined so soon. Besides, it will be so much more fun to watch him guess throughout the years. Just imagine ten years from now!" She giggled and skipped to the door. "But enjoy your happiness for however long it may last. And perhaps it's time, I find my own? Goodbye, Eleanor Gray."

I blinked and she had already vanished.

EPILOGUE

At the top of the grand staircase, I directed the movement of various pieces of furniture. It was a parade of everything from couches, to bed frames, to even a brand-new ivory piano imported from somewhere very expensive.

The frivolity would make my poor mother's head spin.

As would the breathtaking beauty of my sole, one-man "army" of movers.

"That goes in the drawing room," I declared, pointing to a pure-white chaise accompanied by matching armchairs. "Do be careful with it, slave. It's worth more than your yearly wages, I'm sure."

"And this?" the rather bold mover inquired, his gray eyes sparkling with mischief. In his arms was an ivory headboard, contrasting sharply with the ebony hue of his tailored suit. "Wherever does this go, mistress?"

My cheeks flamed. "Upstairs," I said with the air of a queen.

He approached me, mounting the first step. Then he paused, his gaze drifting to someone behind me.

I turned as well, spying a pale figure lurking near the end of the hall.

All thoughts of furniture forgotten, I rushed toward her. "Georgie?"

"I'm okay," she insisted, shrugging off the hand I'd placed on her shoulder. "I'll never get my strength back if you keep coddling me." Her mouth was flattened in determination, but the softness in her eyes robbed any resentment from her tone.

Forcing my arms down by my side, I followed her back into her room.

It'd been over a week since being rescued from under Mero's influence and she still slept for most of the day. Our interactions since had been few and far between. In fact, now might have been the first time she'd had enough energy to speak let alone leave the room on her own.

"It looks like things have changed," she whispered, eyeing me from head to toe. "It feels like I was out for years, not days—"

"I'm so sorry."

She dismissed me with a wave of her hand and sat on the edge of her bed, facing me. "I should be the one who is sorry." She bit her bottom lip, turning her gaze to the floor.

"Everything is still fuzzy, but…" She looked up, meeting my gaze with a sigh. "I remember leaving. I remember walking away, convinced that there was no way to save us. I know we were never close but… I shouldn't have lied to you."

"I wasn't exactly the easiest person to talk to," I admitted, inching closer to her. "I don't think I would have been able to understand, not then."

Her lips parted in a faint smile. "Well, apparently there is still much that I don't understand." Her gaze settled on my stomach, and I sensed that Yulia had attempted to catch her up on some events that had transpired in her absence. "I have been in contact with the Grayne though."

I stiffened. As far as Dublin would say, the faction was in chaos. There had been no further sign of Mero. No attacks. Perhaps he truly was lying in wait for my inevitable death.

Though, for now, my ring still sparkled on my finger, its promise elusive. Would I wear it for eternity, accepting Adara's gift?

"As far as I know, the entire cell has gone into hiding," Georgie explained. "I'm not sure why. But even if I decide not to run Dublin through with a stake"—she lifted her hand, scowling at the trembling fingers—"there is still evil being committed. Far beyond anything you realize. I can't sit back and let our family's legacy just…crumble."

"I know," I whispered, taking yet another step toward her. When I was close enough, I brushed my hand against her shoulder. She didn't flinch beyond my reach. "But we could always start our own legacy?"

She took my hand. "So…how are you planning to redecorate exactly?"

I laughed. "Well, I'm starting with a basic color scheme of white."

~

I left her room hours later and reentered the hall to find my "mover" carrying a piece of furniture down the hall. One I did not remember approving during my impulsive redecorating shopping spree.

My throat tightened as I observed the delicate contours making up the relatively simple square-shaped object. Once Dublin spotted my expression, he paused. His jaw clenched, his gaze wary.

"If you're not ready, I can—"

"No." I swallowed hard and approached him, my shoulders back. As I approached, I hesitantly trailed my fingers along the rim of the item, impressed by the quality of the wood. "It's beautiful," I croaked.

He had gone a step further. On top of the wooden frame was a small mattress draped in white.

"I've been thinking of names," I admitted without looking up. "What about Agatha?"

The silence that fell was deafening. My cheeks heated as the seconds passed until I finally mustered the strength to meet his gaze. His eyes were a stormy silver, a blond eyebrow raised.

"Agatha?" he echoed. "Absolutely not. No child of mine would ever be saddled with such a horrid name."

I narrowed my eyes. "Oh really? Then tell me, what name would please the big, bad Dublin Helos?"

He stroked his chin in genuine contemplation. "Something worthy. Like Drucilla. Or Mildred. Or Cornelia—"

"Cornelia?" I sputtered, my hands on my hips. "You think that is prettier than Agatha?"

"Immeasurably." He circled the cradle to stand before me.

Within a heartbeat, I was in his arms, his mouth near mine.

"Though, I suppose I am willing to negotiate," he told me. With every word, his lips brushed my cheek, sowing a million thrilling sensations I would never be able to fully decipher. "For a price…"

Hey there!

Thank you so much for reading! If you enjoyed the story, please leave a review and recommend the book to any friend you think would love this twisted world. You'd have my eternal gratitude. Even a short sentence goes a long way!

Then, come join the rest of us dark romance lovers in my Facebook Group where you can get snippets, sneak peeks of upcoming books and even help vote on aspects of future novels.

Come to the dark side:
https://www.facebook.com/groups/lanasbeautifulmonsters/

WANT MORE STUFF TO READ?
Join my newsletter and get a **free book**! Plus, you get to stay updated with any new releases, random giveaways and exclusive sneak peeks!
https://www.lanaskybooks.com/newsletter

A WORD FROM THE AUTHOR

Other Novels: https://lanaskybooks.com/

DARK, TWISTED ROMANCE

Join my newsletter and get a **free book**! Plus, you get to stay updated with any new releases, random giveaways and exclusive sneak peeks!

https://www.lanaskybooks.com/newsletter

ABOUT THE AUTHOR

Lana Sky is a reclusive writer in the United States who spends most of her time daydreaming about complex male characters and parenting her Cockapoo Joey. She writes dark, twisted romance across several genres. Her titles include everything from mafia romance to vampires.

facebook.com/AuthorLanaSky

twitter.com/lanasky101

amazon.com/author/lanasky

pinterest.com/lanasky101

goodreads.com/lanasky

instagram.com/lanasky101

bookbub.com/authors/lana-sky

ALSO BY LANA SKY

For more titles by Lana Sky, please visit:

https://www.lanaskybooks.com

www.ingramcontent.com/pod-product-compliance
Lightning Source LLC
Chambersburg PA
CBHW070340220726
48292CB00022B/1

9 781956 608267